Mustang Moon

Also by Terri Farley

The Wild One

Mustang Moon

ALADDIN
New York   London   Toronto   Sydney   New Delhi

If you purchased this book without a cover, you should be aware that this book is stolen property. It was reported as "unsold and destroyed" to the publisher, and neither the author nor the publisher has received any payment for this "stripped book."

This book is a work of fiction. Any references to historical events, real people, or real places are used fictitiously. Other names, characters, places, and events are products of the author's imagination, and any resemblance to actual events or places or persons, living or dead, is entirely coincidental.

ALADDIN
An imprint of Simon & Schuster Children's Publishing Division
1230 Avenue of the Americas, New York, New York 10020
This Aladdin paperback edition July 2023
Text copyright © 2002 by Terri Sprenger-Farley
Cover illustration copyright © 2023 by Louise Meijer-Åström
Map on pages vi–vii copyright © 2023 by Francesca Baerald
Also available in an Aladdin hardcover edition.
All rights reserved, including the right of reproduction in whole or in part in any form.
ALADDIN and related logo are registered trademarks of Simon & Schuster, Inc.
For information about special discounts for bulk purchases, please contact Simon & Schuster Special Sales at 1-866-506-1949 or business@simonandschuster.com.
The Simon & Schuster Speakers Bureau can bring authors to your live event. For more information or to book an event contact the Simon & Schuster Speakers Bureau at 1-866-248-3049 or visit our website at www.simonspeakers.com.
Designed by Tiara Iandiorio
The text of this book was set in Adobe Garamond Pro.
Manufactured in the United States of America 0523 OFF
10 9 8 7 6 5 4 3 2 1
CIP data for this book is available from the Library of Congress.
ISBN 9781665916356 (hc)
ISBN 9781665916349 (pbk)
ISBN 9781665916363 (ebook)

To my husband Cory: every writer should be so lucky. A writer himself, Cory does all of the deadline childcare and cooking and encourages me to get back to work by brewing coffee and buying me floppy sweats in emerald green and black, remembering that those were the "stable colors" of fourth-grade me.

Chapter 1

A CRESCENT MOON, THIN AND SILVER AS THE edge of a dime, shone on the lone stallion. With nervous steps, he crossed the river, then picked his way up the bank to the dark and silent River Bend Ranch.

It was midnight. No dogs barked. No coyotes howled, and no night birds called an alarm. The high Nevada desert had lost its daytime heat, and every creature slept. Except Samantha Forster.

For weeks Sam had waited through the night, hoping the silver mustang who'd once been hers would return.

Tonight, after she'd fallen asleep, questioning nickers from the saddle horses had wakened her. Sam had run on tiptoe downstairs to the kitchen. She didn't dare turn on a light or fling open the door to the ranch yard.

Wild as any deer or wolf, the Phantom had good reasons to flee from humans. Just weeks ago, he'd been roped and confined in a corral. Since the night she'd helped to free him, the Phantom hadn't been back.

Standing at the kitchen window, Sam could only watch. What she saw confused her.

The stallion stalking toward the ranch wasn't silver. He wasn't galloping with liquid grace. He wasn't the Phantom, and he wasn't supposed to be here.

Fighting to see through the darkness, Sam opened her eyes so wide they burned. She pressed so close, her nose touched the windowpane.

Her breath fogged the glass as she whispered, "Who are you?"

As if he'd heard, the horse stopped. His tail switched over thick haunches. He shook his shaggy mane before lifting a head that seemed too big for his sturdy neck.

He studied the empty round pen in front of him and then glanced at the white house with green shutters on his right. His ears aimed down the gravel road, toward the barn and small pen, but he didn't seem to notice the white-faced Hereford calf staring back.

The stallion turned toward the big pasture and paraded along the fence. A dozen tame horses edged closer, heads bobbing as they watched. Sam couldn't hear their snorts and nickers, but she knew the horses were talking.

Frustrated, Sam brushed overgrown bangs back from her eyes. No, the stallion didn't look like the Phantom, but what were the chances another wild horse would just trot across the river and down the Forsters' driveway?

Zero, that's what.

The Phantom had been born on River Bend Ranch. Sam had hand-raised him from a wobbly legged foal to a swift two-year-old. Only a terrible accident had parted them. But the Phantom had remembered her, and he'd come back.

This horse didn't move like the Phantom, but Sam

needed a closer look. She turned the knob, opened the door a few inches, sucked in her stomach, and almost slipped through.

When her nightgown snagged on the wooden doorframe, Sam gave it a tug. It came loose with a soft rip.

The heavy-headed stallion wheeled just long enough to see who'd launched this ambush. He wasn't white, but a sifting of pale hair flickered in the weak moonlight as the stallion headed toward the river. River Bend's tame horses neighed in excitement as the wild one galloped along the fence.

When the horse abandoned his noiseless moves, Sam blinked. It wasn't his suddenly thunderous running that surprised her. It was his sudden stop.

The stallion glared over his shoulder directly at Sam. Then he struck the fence with a deliberate kick. Amazed, Sam wondered how the collision of hooves on wood could sound just like a dare.

"'Catch me if you can.' That's what he seemed to say." Sam waited for her friend Jake Ely to laugh out loud.

Being Jake, he didn't laugh.

He smacked his dusty Stetson against his jeans and leaned against the rails of the round pen. With glossy black hair tied back from browned cheekbones, Jake looked a lot like his Shoshone father. He did, at least, until he squinted against the sun and gave Sam the world's smallest smile. Then Jake looked like a lazy tomcat.

"Now you've got two horses talkin' to you, huh, Brat?"

Jake was sixteen, just over two years older. He and Sam had been friendly enemies forever. During summer and after school, Jake worked on River Bend Ranch as a cowboy, but he'd never stopped teasing her like a big brother.

"Three," Sam said, jerking her thumb toward the big pasture. "You forgot Ace."

Hearing his name, the bay mustang with the perfect Arab-shaped face trotted toward the fence of the ten-acre pasture. He tossed his head, his black forelock flipping to show his white star, as he came toward Sam. He didn't get very far.

Strawberry, a big roan mare, darted forward, ears flattened. Ace stopped.

The gelding lowered his head and backed away a few steps, but not before Banjo, Dad's bald-faced bay, joined in. He flashed Ace a devilish look and launched a quick kick.

"Knock it off!" Sam jogged toward the fence, waving her hands.

Banjo's kick didn't connect. He and Strawberry didn't let Sam's shout hurt their feelings either. Both swished their tails and moved farther into the pasture.

"Ace, come here, boy." Sam extended her hand over the fence, but Ace stayed back. He looked so forlorn, Sam took his loneliness to heart.

"I wish Ace could tell us why the other horses pick on him," Sam told Jake. "They're just evil."

"They're not evil." Jake gave her shoulder a shake. "Animals have a pecking order. Somebody's the boss, and somebody's at the bottom. With these guys"—Jake nodded toward the horses—"Ace is the outsider."

Sam watched Jake. The youngest of six brothers,

he'd inherited all the most boring chores at home on the Three Ponies Ranch. When he'd started working at River Bend, Dad had quickly recognized Jake's intuitive handling of horses.

Sam sighed. It had been Jake who'd taught her Shoshone taming techniques to gentle her own colt.

"Ace looks like he might have lost a little flesh," Jake said. "Beyond the normal cuts and kicks, he's showing ribs. That means they're not letting him eat. I think we'd better talk to your dad."

"Don't have to." Dad's voice came from behind them. "I've been watching Ace myself."

Sam could've sworn Dad had already ridden out for the day. As he moved between her and Jake, Dad's shirt smelled of wind and summer sagebrush, so he must have just returned. Dad worked hard for the bare living the ranch brought in.

Wyatt Forster shifted his weight on one leg, moving with a stiffness that had nothing to do with his boots. Tall, with a face tanned the color of saddle leather, he looked like what he was—a man who'd been a cowboy all his life. As usual, Dad's jaw was set in a stubborn expression Sam had no problem recognizing.

Gram always told Sam that she looked like Mom had when she'd been a teenager. But Sam knew different. She might share Mom's auburn hair, brown eyes, and way with animals, but each time Sam looked in the mirror, especially when she was mad, it was Dad's hard-set expression that stared back at her.

"We'll move Ace into the barn pen and try Buddy in here," Dad said.

Sam pictured her orphan calf, Buddy, out with the horses. Buddy wasn't much taller than a big dog. For short distances, though, she might be the speediest animal on River Bend Ranch.

Buddy would be fine, but Ace would be lonely.

"We'll put another horse with him, of course." Jake glanced toward Sam.

"Of course," Sam echoed, and she felt her shoulders loosen in relief.

Though she'd been born on the ranch, Sam had just

returned home a couple of months ago. After a serious accident, she'd had to spend two years in San Francisco with her aunt. When Jake clued her in about details like this, she was usually grateful.

"He's your horse, Sam," Dad said. "Who should he be penned with?"

She held out her hand and wiggled her fingers toward Ace. Before Dad had given Ace to her at the beginning of summer, the gelding had never been babied. Now he understood an open hand could mean affection as well as food. Even though he could see her empty palm, Ace sidled along the fence toward her.

"C'mon, boy," Sam crooned.

She ignored Jake's groan. He thought she pampered Ace too much. But Ace was a mustang, used to the security of a herd, even if the only other member of that herd was Sam.

Sam considered the horses in the pasture.

Although cattle paid the bills, horses were the pride of River Bend Ranch. In this pasture alone, there were three purebred Quarter Horses, a lean buckskin with

Thoroughbred blood, several mixed-breed cow ponies, and some young stock Jake and Dad were schooling for resale. And Ace.

Which of the horses wouldn't bully Ace in the small pen? While Sam tried to decide, the screen door slammed.

"Oh shoot," Sam muttered.

Gram walked toward her, jingling the keys for her huge boat of a car. In khaki pants and a pink polo shirt, with her gray hair coiled into a knot, Gram looked downright stylish. And ready to go.

She and Gram were driving into Darton to shop for a backpack and school clothes. Gram had said Sam had time to feed Buddy her bottle if she hurried. Sam *had* hurried, but then she'd started talking to Jake and one conversation led to another.

Before she had time to explain that she was choosing a roommate for Ace, there was a snort, a grunting neigh, the sound of hooves. Then pain.

"Ow!" Sam shouted.

As Ace had sprinted away from Strawberry and

Banjo, he'd brushed Sam's hand. With a pop, her fingers had bent at a weird angle.

"I'm fine," Sam insisted, but Gram paced toward her at double time, wearing a frown.

Sam's ring and little fingers had already started to swell, but she knew they weren't broken. Biting her lip and keeping the squeal of pain inside, Sam made a fist and showed Gram.

"Just fine, see?"

Gram was too busy glaring at Dad to see.

"You know I love everything that breathes on this ranch—with the exception of that rattlesnake I saw by the woodpile, and even he's keeping rats out of the house—but, Wyatt," Gram lectured, "I do *not* and never will think a mustang makes a good mount for your daughter."

Gram did love every living thing. Just yesterday, Sam had come upon her fretting over a butterfly in a spider's web.

"Heavens, Samantha," Gram had said. "To free that butterfly means to starve that spider."

Gram had stood watching for ten minutes before a hot August wind blew both predator and prey into the air.

Now, though, Gram was talking about Ace. And the Phantom. Sam couldn't bear to lose either of them.

"I guess Strawberry and Banjo are out as stablemates." Sam tried to change the subject.

"I don't know what I was thinking," Dad said. He rubbed the back of his neck.

"About what?" Sam looked between Dad and Gram. "I guess I'll get used to being ignored." Sam tried to make it sound like a joke, but something in Dad's expression told her what he was thinking.

He and Gram were picturing that night three weeks ago when she'd clung to Ace on a wild ride away from the Bureau of Land Management corrals. In a rare decision, the BLM, the government agency charged with overseeing the country's wild horses, had agreed the Phantom was better off free and wild. So Sam had ridden Ace, charging down a steep rock-strewn hillside, galloping beside the Phantom, leading the terrified stallion to safety.

Dad drew a deep breath. Then far more than his usual few words came streaming out. "You could've broken bones. You could've fallen and knocked out your teeth or hit your head like you did last time." Dad gave her a hard stare, then closed his eyes.

Sam might have asked what all this had to do with picking a roommate for Ace if she hadn't heard what Dad didn't say: *You might have been killed.*

"I'm mad at myself, not you," Dad said. "I shouldn't have let you do it."

"That's the truth," Gram said.

As Gram's voice faded, Sam imagined Ace and the Phantom running across the desert together. Ace might be bullied by the saddle horses, but he had a powerful friend in the Phantom. He trusted Ace. The two horses had matched strides all the way down the hillside.

They shared a wild spirit. If only things could work out like they did in the movies, Ace would be the nerdy sidekick to the superhero Phantom Stallion.

"That stallion hasn't been around since the BLM caught him, right?" Dad asked.

"No, and it's not like I rode him, even when he did come around," Sam said.

"That's not saying you wouldn't do it if you thought you could." Dad's eyes locked onto Sam's, and he waited.

Dad hadn't asked her a question, exactly, so Sam stayed silent. She'd never been able to lie, even about snatching an extra cookie. When Gram interrupted, Sam relaxed, until the words sank in.

"Samantha," Gram said, "you'd better stay in the house at night."

"I can't—"

"Yes, you can. You'll have homework to keep you busy soon."

"But I'm a good student. I get my homework finished fast, and—"

"You'll need a full night's sleep to keep up." Dad glanced at Jake, then saw he wouldn't get any backup there. "You're probably thinking Darton High is a little hick school, way behind your San Francisco classes, but you might be surprised."

Sam pretended to study the horses in the pasture. She was really replaying Gram's and Dad's words.

You'd better stay in the house. . . .

You'll need a full night's sleep to keep up. . . .

So far they hadn't forbidden her to go out. She needed to distract them before she was forced to make a promise she'd surely break.

"Sweetheart!" Sam pointed at the corral.

Everyone turned to look at the long-legged pinto. Sweetheart was solid black, except for a heart-shaped white patch on one hip. Sweetheart had been Gram's saddle horse for as long as Sam could remember.

"Sweetheart would be perfect to put in with Ace," Sam said hurriedly, although the way Gram's lips tightened, Sam knew she wasn't fooled one bit. "She's never bitten or kicked him. Have you seen her do it, Jake?"

"Nope."

"In fact, I haven't seen her lash out at any of the horses," Sam said, "ever."

"Wyatt schooled that horse to have perfect manners, especially in company," Gram said, looking a little dreamy. "He gave Sweetheart to me right after he and your mother were married."

A bit of the silence was filled by the sound of a crow cawing from a fence post. Buddy slurping clumsily from a water trough took up a little bit more of the quiet. Still, Sam heard the same throat-tightening hush that fell each time Gram talked about Mom.

"I don't have time to stand around and gossip. Sam, you move those horses when you get back." Dad jerked the brim of his hat down to cover his eyes. "There's work to be done, Jake, unless you're scooting off to town with these girls."

"No, sir," Jake said, and Sam wondered if he knew he'd tugged at his hat brim just like Dad.

As Gram's Buick bumped across the bridge over the river that had given the ranch its name, Sam sighed.

With a quick sidelong glance, Sam checked out Gram. She showed no sign of anger, no sign she was ready to lay down the law.

Sam watched the high desert hills swing up into real

mountains to the north. Thick sagebrush made them appear carpeted with green, but Sam knew better. Rough terrain led to the Calico Mountains. Up there, somewhere, lay the secret valley where the Phantom hid his herd.

She and Gram headed the other way.

The two-lane asphalt road ran straight at the horizon, toward Alkali. Too small to be called a town, Alkali had a coffee shop and a gas station. On Tuesdays, the county bookmobile—a library on wheels—stopped there. Sam had convinced Dad to let Jake borrow the truck and drive her there, twice.

Today Gram drove right on through Alkali.

"I thought about stopping for a soda," Gram said, nodding at the diner, "but we'll get lunch at the mall."

"Great," Sam said, then turned on the car radio. One thing you could say for Gram's old Buick: its antenna picked up every radio station for hundreds of miles around.

Sam found herself humming along with the oldies station Gram favored. Even if funds were short, and they were, Sam liked shopping. She'd been in sixth grade the last time she'd gone to the mall in Darton. From what she'd heard, it had grown.

"Samantha?"

Sam turned. When Gram kept her eyes on the road, Sam knew it was a bad sign.

"I won't lock you in your room at night, but I'm serious about staying away from that stallion. If I catch you sneaking out, you'll be grounded." Gram looked at her then. "I mean that literally. There'll be no riding until you've learned your lesson."

What could she do? Sam looked down and saw her hands shaking in her lap. She put them out of sight, tucking her fingers between her thighs and the car upholstery.

Gram was making her choose between Ace and the Phantom. It wasn't fair. She couldn't stand even the idea of giving up her long daily rides on Ace, but it would break her heart if she never saw the Phantom again.

Chapter 2

CRANE CROSSING WAS A FINE MALL. IT WASN'T San Francisco, but Sam had never adored side-street specialty shops the way Aunt Sue did. Crane Crossing was more her style. It had a big department store, where Sam got a backpack, jeans, socks, Darton High's green-and-gold gym clothes, and a skirt Gram insisted on buying. The mall's three casual-wear stores were hard to tell apart, but Sam bought two shirts in one and a blouse to match the skirt in another.

The worst part had been seeing her goofy hair in the

bright fluorescent lighting that spotlighted the dressing-room mirrors. Sam decided she could plead temporary insanity for cutting it. She'd thought short hair would make her look older when she returned to the ranch, but it was growing out weird. She needed professional help, but she couldn't ask Gram to pay for a haircut when it was a stretch to afford clothes.

The best feature of the mall was a Western wear and tack store called Tully's. There, Sam saw a split-ear headstall that was a work of art. With delicate care, Sam touched a flurry of feathers hand-tooled on smooth, mushroom-colored leather. How beautiful it would look on Jake's black mare, Witch.

If a good fairy flew down and sprinkled her with silver dollars, she'd buy it. Jake's birthday was October 1.

Gram came up behind her.

"Gracious, that's more than we spend on groceries in a month," Gram tsked.

Sam almost snapped that not *everything* was about money. She was glad she hadn't when Gram added, "Wouldn't Ace step proud wearing that on his pretty head?"

Sam guessed it would take a while to get used to Gram, Dad, and Jake again. Right now she could not guess what Gram would do or say next. Frustration made Sam decide that adults—Dad and Gram included—were more unpredictable than horses.

At a table in the mall's food court, Gram chowed down on a huge plate of Chinese food but didn't show a flicker of excitement when Sam pointed out Crane Crossing's multiplex theater and suggested they go to a movie.

"Maybe next time," Gram said as they loaded their purchases into the Buick's back seat, but Sam didn't have high hopes.

The television in the ranch house living room was ten years old. Dad and Gram had no interest in updating their entertainment system. They watched the news every night, but rarely anything else. Sure, Dad did tiring physical labor each day, but Sam couldn't imagine going up to bed at eight o'clock if you weren't sick. And all Gram did after dinner was read novels and piece together quilts.

They were driving back toward the ranch, when Sam shivered. Something told her the Phantom was nearby. Sam studied every bush moving in the breeze and every dark rock in the distance.

But it was Gram who spotted the Phantom first.

War Drum Flats spread out like a beige tablecloth below them. From the road, Sam saw a basin scooped from the sagebrush and piñon landscape. Gram glanced at where the brush faded to dusty green and gave way to a sandy area around a pond. A dozen thirsty horses jostled for room at the water's edge.

"That's a fine-looking band of mustangs," Gram said. Then she added, "Oh, look, there on the ridge."

Sam followed Gram's gesture. She stared past the pond and up the hillside and then sucked in a breath. On a ridge marked by wind-twisted pine trees, the silver stallion stood guard.

From here, he was just a proud outline against the blue summer sky, but Sam recognized her horse. The pine ridge looked so high, windy, and far away, Sam wasn't sure the drinking band and stallion were together.

Gram swerved to the roadside. She shut off the engine, opened her car's glove compartment, and withdrew a pair of binoculars.

Distance made him no more than a sparkling toy, but Sam knew the Phantom by his kingly stance.

"Oh my, it's him, isn't it? Your little lost colt, all grown up." Gram's voice held a mixture of awe and disappointment.

Had she been hoping Sam would really give in to that old idea of out of sight, out of mind?

Gram sat up straighter and angled the binoculars down. Sam figured Gram was studying the mares and foals. Though they looked like miniatures from here, Sam recognized two distinctive blood bays and a mouse-colored horse she'd noticed in the Phantom's band before.

"And who's this, I wonder?" Gram asked.

At Sam's mew of frustration, Gram passed her the binoculars.

"I've never been able to focus these silly things," Sam muttered.

"Take your time," Gram said.

Easy to say. Mustangs could vanish as you stared right at them. It had happened three times with the Phantom.

"Oh, come on," Sam growled at the binoculars. She pressed them too hard against her eye sockets, then held them too far back, so her eyelashes ticked across the eyepieces.

This was important. *Who's this?* Gram had asked, and her voice had sounded suspicious.

The first horse to come into focus had tiger-striped front legs.

"Yeah." Sam sighed. She remembered the dun with the prehistoric markings from her visit to the Phantom's secret canyon.

The mare stared across the pond and shook her ears. The other horses moved into a tighter bunch around her, then fell back as she trotted around the end of the pond. *She must be the herd's lead mare,* Sam thought.

Then the mare proved it. She flattened her ears, bared her teeth, and made a threatening run at an intruder.

"The hammer head!"

"The what?" Gram's dubious voice told Sam she'd spoken aloud.

"That other horse." Without lowering the binoculars, Sam pointed at the heavy-headed stallion. "I've seen him before."

She didn't dare say she'd seen him at midnight the night before on River Bend Ranch, but she was almost sure he was the same horse.

His big head, long mane, and stocky conformation were unusual. By daylight, she could see he was the color of jeans that had been washed about a million times. A blue roan.

"Whoever he is," Sam said, "he thinks he's pretty hot stuff."

The stallion pranced toward the lead mare as if she should bow down and kiss his hooves. The tiger dun wasn't impressed.

As the mare attacked, the stallion dodged. He moved like a cutting horse, removing the troublesome mare from the herd as he headed toward the other mares and foals, who stood watching, wide-eyed.

Suddenly, he was distracted. Sam had to hunt with the binoculars to see what had made the blue roan swing away from the mares.

The Phantom trotted off the ridge and down a hidden path. He seemed to float toward the herd. Head tilted to one side, tail swishing, he looked only curious. Sam guessed he didn't see the other stallion as a threat.

Full of confidence, the blue bowed his head in a move that puffed up his already thick neck. He pawed the sand, glanced back at the watching mares, then strutted a few steps like a bad boy showing off for the girls. Then he charged.

The Phantom stepped aside. The blue stumbled in surprise, but he didn't fall—just ran a few steps and swung back around to face the silver stallion.

A breeze caught the Phantom's white silk mane and it fluttered around him. The blue's head bobbed in three fierce nods; then he launched a second attack. Once more, the Phantom stepped aside, but when the heavy horse gathered for a third try, the Phantom lost patience.

His ears flicked back, and he planted each hoof with determination.

The blue stallion stopped. He lowered his head and swung it just above the dust. The Phantom had treated him like an unruly youngster, and the blue roan looked ashamed. Finally, without another glance toward the mares, he sprinted away.

Sam saw him go over a hill. She waited. The disgraced stallion had to emerge on the other side, didn't he?

"They vanish just like that," Gram said, snapping her fingers. "Don't they?"

When the blue roan still didn't appear, Sam felt suddenly hot and sweaty. The backs of her legs stuck to the Buick's upholstery.

She'd wanted the Phantom to win, but it hadn't been a fight. More of a scolding. Sam remembered the blue roan's huge hooves slamming the River Bend's fence in a burst of temper and wished he hadn't lost to the Phantom so completely. What if the blue roan's pride was hurt? Would he return for a rematch?

Sam shivered, though the August heat rippled through the open car window.

The Phantom's band milled around the pond as if nothing had happened, but the stallion didn't return to the ridge.

"I wonder if that was a bachelor stallion, looking to steal mares," Gram mused, "or just a young horse trying out his moves."

"He looked serious, but the Phantom didn't," Sam said.

"The Phantom. Why do you call him that, even though you, Jake, and Wyatt all think he's Blackie?"

"He doesn't look like 'Blackie' anymore."

"That's true, but if he was your colt, he's not the Phantom."

Chills scurried down Sam's arms. Gram couldn't believe in the legendary white stallion, could she? He was imaginary. When cowboys told ghost stories around the campfire, they wove tales about a pale spirit horse that melted through fences. He floated above the ground, outrunning any mortal horse. He passed through lassos and moved with cloudlike silence. But everyone knew the stories sprang from a family of fleet gray mustangs that lived in the Calico Mountains.

Still, Sam wasn't sure what to say. She couldn't remember Gram ever doing anything more superstitious than crossing her fingers for luck.

Down below, the Phantom lifted his head and stared toward the road, as if he'd finally noticed them.

"He is a beauty," Gram said.

"Then won't you let me go out at night and wait for him? He always comes by midnight, and I promise I won't try to ride him, and—"

"Samantha," Gram's tone cautioned her.

"But, Gram, if I planned to ride him, I would have tried to get Dad to adopt him." Sam thought she sounded quite sensible. "I wouldn't have encouraged the BLM to turn him loose."

"Dear, I know you believe that *now*. But if you go out and see that horse every night, if he lets you get close, pet his neck, and maybe he even starts to follow you around, the next natural thing is trying to ride him. And you cannot tell me," Gram said, pointing her index finger at Sam, "that it isn't exciting to think of riding through the night with the wind in your hair on a mustang stallion no one else can even touch."

Sam couldn't say the idea wasn't thrilling. Would she risk being grounded for one wild night ride? She looked away from Gram, because the answer was yes.

Gram tapped Sam's arm, and she looked back.

"Sam, you know I have a soft spot for animals, but I have a softer spot for you." Gram's blue eyes looked into Sam's brown ones. "I hope you never have to sit in a hospital waiting room, head in hands, praying a child will live. After that horse threw you and kicked you in the head, I made a vow you'd never ride him again. And I'll keep that promise with the last breath in my body."

If Gram had been weepy and emotional, Sam might have reminded her that he hadn't hurt her on purpose. She'd fallen from Blackie, and he'd been running away in fright when his hoof grazed her head. But Gram was speaking in a level tone, without a hint of tears. Sam knew, today, she couldn't win.

Sam looked down the two-lane asphalt road ahead

and saw a car coming toward them. It glittered like glass, and that was the hint that told her it was Linc Slocum's big beige Cadillac.

The city slicker had purchased everything from a cattle ranch to spurs, trying to fulfill his dream of being a cowboy. Still, he had the Cadillac washed every day by a ranch hand, instead of driving a car coated with desert dust like a real cowboy would.

Slocum didn't mind folks calling him a show-off or frowning at the rodeo-trophy belt buckle he'd purchased, not won. The thing that did drive Slocum crazy was his inability to buy the best Western trophy of all: the Phantom.

Three weeks ago, instead of putting the Phantom up for adoption, the BLM had freed him. The government agency was protecting the Phantom, hoping the stallion would mate with wild mares and improve the mustang breed.

But why tempt fate? Sam didn't want Linc Slocum to even see the Phantom.

"Gram, go," Sam said. "Here comes Linc Slocum, and

I think it would be really bad if he saw the—uh, Blackie."

It took Gram a minute to remember Sam's conflict with Slocum, but then she revved up the Buick's engine. She looked back carefully before pulling from the roadside onto the street.

Run, boy, run. Sam stared at the stallion and sent her thoughts winging toward him. *Go, now.* The Phantom circled his mares at a nervous trot, and the tiger dun followed.

Sam stared down the road. Slocum's Cadillac was gaining on them, about two city blocks away. If he looked over the edge now, he'd see the mustangs for sure.

Gram pulled onto the road, and still the horses stayed clustered by the pond. Sam had to do something.

She'd never uttered the stallion's secret name within human hearing. Jake had taught her techniques from generations of Shoshone horse tamers. He said a secret name bonded one horse to one rider. Sam could see no harm in thinking the name, so she did.

Run, Zanzibar, run.

As if she'd screamed the words, the stallion bolted.

The tiger dun wheeled away from the water and darted toward the hills. In a tight knot, the other mares followed. The Phantom circled behind, nipping their haunches, pushing with his mighty chest until the last mare crested the hill.

Just like the blue roan, the horses vanished. A plume of dust rose, then drifted on the desert air.

Chapter 3

LINC SLOCUM MADE SURE GRAM STOPPED. HE stepped into the street and waved his arms frantically.

By the time Gram pulled back onto the shoulder and halted directly across the street from him, she and Sam could see his emergency was minor. Slocum was squatting next to his Cadillac's rear tire, and it wasn't even flat.

Sam shook her head in disgust. In San Francisco, the crime rate was high. People were suspicious. They'd see this for what it was: a setup.

In rural Nevada, folks lived by the code of the West,

which said you *had* to be neighborly to everyone. That included a villain like Linc Slocum.

Even the U.S. government agreed Slocum was bad news. The BLM had denied Slocum the right to adopt a mustang. Slocum had admitted he hadn't reported the harassment of a wild horse. That was grounds for denial.

What Slocum had really done was worse. With a truck, he'd chased the Phantom for miles. As the stallion began to tire, Slocum roped him. The stallion might have won the tug-of-war, except that the end of the rope was tied to a barrel full of concrete. Only luck kept the Phantom's neck from snapping when he hit the end of the rope. The stallion fought and bucked and lunged until, at last, the rope broke.

Though local ranchers scorned Slocum, no one could confirm what had happened. They *believed* it happened, but no one had seen it with their own eyes.

Now Slocum looked at Sam and Gram and waved.

Slocum was a big man, at least six feet tall and egg-shaped. His hair was slicked back, flat and shiny. His jeans and plaid shirt pulled tight as he squatted. He probably hoped the position made him look like a cowboy ready to brand a calf. But it didn't.

Slocum flashed his toothpaste-commercial grin as he called across the road.

"If it ain't my two favorite ladies come to rescue me." He gestured with a little metal tool. "This tire keeps on going flat, so I'm checking how much air I've got."

Slocum stood, wedged the tool into his pocket, and walked across the road. He jingled as he walked, and Sam wondered why he wore spurs to drive a car.

Slocum put both hands on the Buick's driver's-side window frame. Gram drew back a little.

"Hi there," Slocum said. His fake smile flashed across to Sam, but it showed a little confusion. "Haven't seen you in a month of Sundays, little lady. How long's it been?"

Slocum's outdated Western expressions made even his own cowboys laugh, but he didn't care.

Sam shrugged as if she couldn't remember either.

Slocum kept a hand on Gram's window frame as he glanced back toward his polished Cadillac. "It's time to replace that car. I don't like wondering if I can make it all the way home."

Sam pictured Slocum trying to walk the ten miles from here to Gold Dust Ranch in his high-heeled boots. Then she imagined him squeezing into Gram's car.

Oh no. No way. Sam wished Gram could read her brain waves as well as horses could. Gram glanced in the back seat at the bags of new clothes. Sam was afraid Gram was about to ask her to move them into the trunk.

"That tire does look low." Gram sounded as if, for the first time in her life, neighborliness would be a chore.

"If you could follow me back to the ranch just to make sure I get there," Slocum said, "I'd be awful grateful."

Did Linc Slocum hear Gram sigh in relief? Compared to being his chauffeur, it seemed like a fine idea.

"I'd be glad to do that, Linc," Gram said, "just so long as I get home in time to start dinner."

Uncertainty about his car didn't slow Slocum down. At first Gram tried to keep up, but then she let him pull away.

"Imagine replacing a car because its tires are old."

Gram chuckled, but she didn't sound amused.

Since Sam had returned home, Dad and Gram had made her sit through discussions of ranch finances. Sam found the talks boring, but she understood why Linc's remark made Gram envious.

They drove another couple of miles.

"We wanted to spend more," Gram said suddenly.

"What?"

"On your school clothes."

"Don't worry about it, Gram. Really." Sam patted Gram's arm, hoping her frown would disappear. "I haven't even unpacked the box of stuff Aunt Sue mailed me."

Sam had left most of her school clothes in her room in San Francisco. Since the box had arrived, the weather had been stifling hot. The idea of trying on wool slacks and pullover sweaters was repulsive. "Besides," Sam said, just in case Gram was thinking that would be a good way to end the day, "clothes aren't a big deal to me."

Gram looked skeptical. "When you're starting your

first year of high school, clothes are important."

Was Gram trying to make her feel worse? Sam didn't have time to worry about clothes or money, when the blue roan and the Phantom might harm each other. But Gram wouldn't stop.

"There's a darn good reason we're careful with our money." Gram made a hushing movement when Sam tried to interrupt. "We won't make much from fall cattle sales. Drought means sparse grass, and that translates into thinner cattle. And, of course, we get paid by the pound."

Sam cringed inside, but she didn't say a word.

If her orphan calf, Buddy, hadn't stepped into a pool of quicksand and had to be rescued, she'd be out on River Bend lands right now, fattening for market.

Sam's stomach twisted with nausea.

It could still happen. Sam couldn't make herself ask Dad if she could keep Buddy as a pet.

"And then there's the BLM," Gram went on. "It takes twenty acres to support a cow and her calf, so we have to use federal land to graze our stock. When they raise grazing fees for every cow who roams on land that's not strictly River Bend—" Gram stopped talking. "I'm sorry, honey. It's useless to complain and worse to be angry at Linc Slocum for having money."

Linc turned the Cadillac toward huge ornate iron gates. Beyond, Sam saw acres of pastures that looked almost neon green compared to the endless expanses of gray-green. In a desert state, water to keep things green didn't come cheap.

"I wonder how he made so much money," Sam mused.

"Honey, it wouldn't be polite to ask."

Sam had hoped they'd see Slocum to his gate and leave, but as the big iron gates swung wide via remote control, Slocum beckoned them to follow. Gram did.

The last time Sam had been on this property, the ranch had belonged to the Kenworthys. Lila and Jed Kenworthy were nice people with a daughter Jennifer, who was about her age. Sam hadn't gone to school with her, though, because Jennifer's mother had taught her at home.

Gram's Buick rolled through the soaring iron gates

and into a Western wonderland. Flowers flanked the freshly paved road. White wooden fences marked off velvety pastures full of Black Angus and Dutch Belted cattle, animals that were black in front and back, with a wide band of white fur around their middles.

Sam was sure none of those things—especially the remote-control gates—had been on the ranch the last time she'd been here.

Gram nodded at the Dutch Belted cattle.

"Linc told your dad he bought a hundred head of them because they reminded Rachel of Oreo cookies," Gram said.

Rachel, Sam remembered, was Slocum's daughter. He'd mentioned buying her a dressage horse. Sam hadn't met Rachel yet, but Jake had told Sam that Rachel was more interested in gossip and the latest color of nail polish than she was in horses.

There were plenty of horses on Slocum's ranch. A herd of Shetland ponies scampered along the fence on the left. On the right, Sam saw a dozen lean-limbed horses that had to be racing Appaloosas.

In the last pasture, a dozen assorted horses left off grazing. Tails swishing, grass dripping from their muzzles, they watched the car drive by. Sam would bet they were off-duty cow horses.

A line of redwood hitching posts, polished and fitted with brass tie rings, led them farther up the driveway.

Sam finally recognized a high-sided round pen that had probably been here years ago when she'd visited. Its size and weathered wood made it a twin to the one Dad and Jake used for training. An animal moved inside, but she couldn't see through the closely placed rails.

The strangest addition of all lay ahead. Atop a hill stood a mansion that looked like it belonged on a Southern plantation, not a ranch.

Before Sam had a chance to comprehend the sight, Slocum parked and climbed out of his car before walking over to Gram's window.

"You're a horsewoman, Grace," he said. "Would you mind looking at something and telling me what you think?"

Neither Gram nor Sam could resist such an invitation.

Slocum led the way to the round corral, opened the gate, and nodded them in before closing it.

The mare was the red of a summer sunset. No more than fourteen hands high, she moved with deerlike quickness, trotting away. Her hooves floated in a haze of dust. With her shoulder pressed to the fence at the far side of the pen, the mare curved her neck and studied the unfamiliar humans.

Slocum strolled toward the horse. Her sorrel skin shivered as if shaking off flies. When Slocum reached for her halter, the mare moved off. That was when Sam noticed her flank was stamped with the River Bend brand. "Is she ours?" Sam whispered.

Gram shook her head. "She was, but Wyatt sold Kitty to Jed Kenworthy right after"—Gram drew a breath—"your accident."

Sam's hands covered her stomach as if she'd been socked. *Princess Kitty.* No wonder the mare looked familiar. She was Blackie's mother.

Why had Dad sold Kitty? Why would he sell a

Quarter Horse mare with super cow sense, who produced beautiful foals?

Right after your accident, Gram had said. She couldn't mean Dad had sold Kitty because she was Blackie's dam, could she?

Slocum quickened his steps; then he jogged, but the sorrel stayed a few steps ahead.

"The marks on her haunches, Linc?" Gram called to Slocum. "Is that what you wanted me to see?"

Puffing and out of breath, Slocum returned to stand beside them. "Yeah," he said. "What do you think?"

Sam recognized the marks at once. They were the same nips and teeth rakings she'd seen on Ace.

"Do you think they're claw scratches from a cougar?" Slocum asked.

"Oh, no," Gram said. "They're bites from another horse."

"That's what Kenworthy said, too, but it's strange. The mare was gone from the saddle horse pasture yesterday morning; then we heard her neighing from outside the front gate." Slocum pointed toward the fancy iron entrance.

Sam knew it was rare for a captive horse to leave guaranteed food and water, but it wasn't unheard of.

"We did turn out range horses for a few years, and I've no doubt they ran with the mustangs," Gram said. "Maybe Kitty just took it into her head to try it again."

"That doesn't explain the bites, now, does it?" Slocum's tone turned mocking, and his eyebrows arched.

He clearly had an explanation in mind, but Gram refused to play along.

"I guess you'll never know," Gram said.

"But I do know. Kenworthy found strange hoofprints, *unshod* hoofprints, in the flower beds along the road." With a triumphant laugh, Slocum turned toward Sam. "The Phantom came in here and tried to steal her."

"No, he didn't," Sam snapped. At Gram's sharp intake of breath, Sam made a polite addition. "I'm sure you must be mistaken, Mr. Slocum."

"I tend to agree, Linc." Gram shook her head. "I've lived here all my life. In sixty-five years, we've never had a wild stallion up near the house, unless we roped him and brought him in."

Oh yes, we have. Sam thought of the blue roan. He'd been after the Phantom's mares today. And she'd seen him right outside the kitchen door, but if she said that, she'd be grounded.

"I hate to contradict a lady," Slocum said. "But I know for a fact that white stud's been on River Bend property."

Sam suspected Slocum of lurking on the ridge above the River Bend at night, spying with binoculars. But Sam kept her lips pressed together hard and lagged behind Gram and Slocum as they left the round pen.

Gram was quiet until they reached the Buick.

"If you're talking about the gray mustang," Gram said, once more refusing to call him the Phantom, "I don't think he's been any closer than the river. Am I right, Samantha?"

"Absolutely." Sam tightened her hands into fists.

"Well, we'll see. We'll certainly see." Slocum nodded four times. "I've got expensive bloodstock on this ranch. My herd of Shetlands, Quarter Horses, a couple Thoroughbreds, a Saddlebred, and a dressage horse, just to name a few." Slocum let out a breath as if listing his possessions wearied him.

"Kitty's a good cow horse. You're lucky she found her way back," Gram said, sympathizing. "I know she was one of Wyatt's favorites."

Slocum dismissed the mare with a wave of his hand. "I've got a blue-blooded Appaloosa filly on her way here from Florida, so I need to be extra watchful."

Sam had already opened the car door when she felt Slocum watching her. It made her cold, as if she were being watched by a snake.

"If a wild horse trespasses on my property, especially if he's trying to steal my mares, I'll get him declared a nuisance. You're a smart girl, Samantha. You know what that is. A troublemaker." He watched Sam, but she stayed frozen. "Once that's done, BLM has to catch him."

Sam's mouth was so dry she could barely pronounce the words. "And relocate him."

Slocum chuckled.

"You might want to check your facts, little lady. BLM's short of funds just now. They can't be relocating nuisance animals or keeping them locked up and eating at government expense.

"BLM *can* send that horse out of state for adoption, but that's pretty pricey, too. No, when an animal's already proven unmanageable, there's only one financially sound solution. BLM can spend a nickel on a bullet and put that stallion down."

Chapter 4

IT WAS NEARLY FOUR O'CLOCK WHEN GRAM'S car bumped back across the River Bend bridge and Sam heard her horse calling for their afternoon ride.

Ace's sorrowful neigh turned to joyous snorting as Sam climbed out of Gram's car. No matter how full the days were on the ranch, Dad made sure Sam had time to ride.

After two years in the city, Sam had to admit her horsemanship needed polish. Dad agreed, but he assured Sam her skills would come back with practice.

If he noticed she was still a little nervous since the accident, he didn't say a word.

Sam ran to her room and piled her purchases on her bed. She changed into riding clothes and had nearly reached the door before Gram caught her.

"Sam, I know you're in a hurry, but please check for eggs first. They were downright sparse this morning." Gram handed Sam a basket. "Wyatt's been craving a yellow cake with brown-sugar frosting. With him so worried over stock prices, it's the least I can do."

Sam took the egg basket and hurried to the door. She'd already fed the hens and checked their nests this morning, but fresh cake meant the delay was for a good cause.

"Oh, and as long as you're going," Gram said, pulling a tin colander from a shelf, "pick us some sugar snap peas."

Sam didn't growl aloud, but she wished she could. As the screen door slammed behind her, Ace's nicker carried over the quiet ranch.

She smooched in his direction and called, "Soon, boy."

River Bend's garden provided enough food to last all winter long, with few trips to the grocery store in Darton. As summer tapered into fall harvest, Sam couldn't go more than two hours without fetching and carrying baskets and colanders full of produce for Gram.

It took forever. The cowboys had already ridden in, giving her tired waves, by the time Sam presented Gram with sugar snap peas and eggs.

Sam jogged by the pasture on her way to the tack room. Ace had given up on her. He'd fallen to grazing again and didn't even look up.

Inside the barn, Sam heard the radio before she got to the tack room. It wasn't playing music. She heard the rustle of newspaper pages, and when she walked in, Sam could see Dad wasn't reading the comics. Dad looked up to smile, but his index finger tapped his lips, hushing her. As the radio station from Reno gave the latest stock prices, he frowned.

"Hey, girl," he said, snapping the radio off. He pushed the newspaper aside, too, and rolled his shirtsleeves down to cover red scratches on his forearms. "Back from town?"

"Yep," Sam said. She took her saddle blanket from its perch and flung Ace's bridle over her shoulder. "What did you do to your arms, Dad?"

He shrugged. "Fool bull calf got himself stuck in the blackberries, down on the other side of the river."

"Ouch," Sam said.

"Range cattle have no sense once we bring them to summer pasture," Dad mused. "They know how to find water and graze, how to kick cougars and coyotes, but give 'em something simple as a hedge full of stickers, and they only see the sweet berries. One calf—Pepper calls him Baby Huey—just won't learn. His little pink nose is *all* cut up."

Sam made a humming sound as she backed out the door, balancing her saddle. She hoped it sounded like an interested hum, but not too interested. The sun showed a copper edge above the hills, hinting she should have been loping away by now.

"But Baby Huey won't be our problem for long," Dad said, turning back to his newspaper.

As if they'd suddenly frozen, Sam's hands clamped on the saddle. If Baby Huey, a spring calf, was old enough to be sold for beef, so was Buddy.

"He won't be going to market, right?" Sam asked.

Dad gave an impatient shake of his head. "Bull calf auction," he said.

Gram, or even Jake, might have picked up on Sam's hint, but Dad didn't. Instead, he came up with another chore.

"As long as you're riding out, check for Baby Huey. Then I'm counting on you to put Ace and Sweetheart—"

"I remember," Sam interrupted, even though she'd almost forgotten. "But how do I recognize Baby Huey?"

Dad stared at Sam as if she'd asked how to tell a horse from a handsaw.

"He's bigger than the other calves, but for crying out loud, Sam, if you see *any* calves tangled in the blackberry bushes," Dad snapped, "yank 'em out!"

"Yes, sir."

Oh, the joys of country living, Sam grumbled to herself. At Aunt Sue's house in San Francisco, she'd only had to make her bed and set the table. On a cleaning day, she might have had to dust the piano and feed the goldfish, too.

Ace's nicker made Sam look up. Her bay gelding had braved the teeth and heels of other horses to sidle toward the gate. Before she could open it, he nuzzled her neck, tickling her with whiskers and his grass-sweet breath.

"And *that*," Sam said, kissing a muzzle so dainty it could sip from a teacup, "is why I don't live in San Francisco."

Once astride Ace, Sam felt free.

She kept her reins taut. Though Ace was a cow pony, used to working on loose reins, he felt tight beneath her. Sam had learned her lesson. When Ace felt restless and ready to run, she didn't dare let her mind wander. Bucking was Ace's favorite way to make her pay attention to him.

After they'd crossed the bridge and headed north, she would let him run. When he'd settled down, they would check the blackberry bushes for cattle.

Finally, Sam leaned forward, firmed her legs, and

gave Ace's ribs a tap of her heels. Even though she'd braced for Ace's sudden lunge forward, Sam grabbed the saddle horn.

No! Darn it. She only scolded herself for a second. Then, as Ace settled into a smooth run, she relaxed, swaying in the saddle as if she'd been born to it. Which she had.

His pace lulled her. Sam breathed a summer wind scented with pine, sun-yellowed grass, and an edge of evening cold. The ground underfoot slanted down into a damp hollow thick with coarse grass. A few yellow flowers no bigger than raindrops clustered together. She'd bet an underground spring ran just below the surface here.

Wings flapped and a sage hen burst from the grass to flutter right under Ace's nose. Hands steady on the reins, Sam didn't panic. *I trust you, Ace.* Her thought matched the quick stutter step that interrupted Ace's run. As Sam caught her breath, Ace swung back into a gallop. Head level, he watched the cattle that were now about a block away.

Sam slowed Ace to a jog, then a walk, and finally reined him to a stop. As Sam praised Ace by rubbing his neck, a group of white-faced Hereford calves wearing the River Bend brand sighted them. They ran bawling, brown tails straight up, to their mothers.

They were only pretending to be afraid. The calves bumped each other, detoured around a rock, then kicked their heels skyward. The calves had been around riders for weeks. They weren't a bit scared. They were playing.

Buddy would love to romp with these calves, but their fun might not last long. Some bull calves would be sold as soon as Dad found a buyer paying top price. This time next year, all the males would be on their way to market. Sam watched the calves scatter and rejoin a herd of about thirty cows.

Buddy wasn't unhappy at the ranch. Sam served as her mama, although now that she usually munched grass instead of taking a bottle, mothering mostly meant rubbing Buddy's bony head. Buddy didn't lack for playmates, either. She chased Blaze, the ranch dog, with the same zigzag silliness these calves were showing.

Eyes on the vanishing sun, Sam hurried to the hedges. She dismounted, ground-tied Ace, and checked each tangle of blackberry bushes. No sign of Baby Huey.

Angling her hand around the wicked thorns, Sam plucked one fat blue-black berry and popped it in her mouth. Oh, wow. Sam grabbed another one, closed her eyes, and let the sweet juice fill her mouth. No wonder Baby Huey had been trapped so often.

Sam had caught up her reins and started to mount when she spotted another possible hiding place.

Ace hung back at the end of his reins as Sam peered into a cave-like opening in the hedges. No calf hid inside, but one might have fit. She couldn't go in, but—

All at once, Sam felt as if an icy finger had trailed down the nape of her neck. Shivering, she looked over her shoulder.

No one was there, but Sam sensed someone was watching. Could it be Slocum? Not likely. And she'd seen all the cowhands ride in before she'd left the ranch. And neither Gram nor Dad would come after her. They knew she'd be home in time for dinner.

Sam shrugged her shoulders so high, they nearly reached her ears. She felt cold. She studied Ace, but his eyes only scanned the terrain, showing no margin of white around the brown. He wasn't frightened, then, but Ace wasn't the most reliable watchdog. Sam wished she'd brought Blaze along.

Sam felt better once she remounted. She thought of the roast beef sandwiches, homemade french fries, and fresh steamed peas Gram was making. And the cake.

She also remembered she had to swap Sweetheart and Ace into the small corral and turn Buddy in with the horses. That could take a while, especially since she needed to be sure everyone got along. If they didn't, more than feelings could get hurt.

Sam urged Ace into a trot toward home. A rider was less vulnerable than a pedestrian. Afoot, she wasn't very fast. On Ace, she'd be tough to catch.

If she hadn't been watching for the flowers, Sam might have missed the horse's hoofprint. The flowers were a yellow smear, and the hoof mark, distorted by the mud, looked huge.

Ace veered around the place and his pace stiffened. Sam knew a stallion had been watching her. Had it been the Phantom or the blue roan?

Gram wakened Sam early.

"Get up, sleepyhead," Gram said. "Berries are sweeter if you pick before the sun warms them."

In the dark, Sam gathered eggs and filled water troughs for the horses and hens.

In the barn corral, Ace and Sweetheart stood side by side, calm shadows against the graying sky. They looked like friends. Using her cold fingers more than her eyes, she inspected Ace for new wounds. She found none. As they'd hoped, the two horses were getting along just fine.

Filled with relief, she forked hay to Sweetheart and Ace, then scattered the grainy feed called chick-scratch for the hens.

The hens were making cautious, questioning clucks as Jake rode into the yard.

Witch, Jake's explosive black mare, looked like a

dragon. She snorted hot breath into the chilly morning and her roached mane stood up in a crest. Witch stood still as Jake dismounted, but she fidgeted and stretched her nostrils toward the sky when he tied her.

Sam knew Witch was a horse she could not ride. The black mare pulsed with restless energy, ready to leap and run, even though she'd loped at least five miles from Jake's ranch.

Jake gave Witch a pat, then turned toward Sam.

"What a terrifyin' sight," Jake said, bumping his Stetson back and blinking as if he couldn't believe his eyes. "Samantha Anne Forster doing work before sunup."

"I did it on the cattle drive every day," Sam reminded him as they walked toward the kitchen. Side by side, she tried to match his steps. "I've been storing up sleep for school and—"

"Biologically speaking, I don't think you can store sleep," Jake said.

If she hadn't been carrying a delicate cargo of eggs, Sam would've elbowed Jake. All her life he'd pretended to know more about everything than she did.

"Besides," Sam told him, "sleeping until seven as I usually do isn't exactly a life of luxury."

Jake gave a skeptical grunt. He opened the kitchen door, nodded her through ahead of him, and took off his hat before entering.

Gram looked up from washing dishes and frowned at the paltry number of eggs. Dad gave Sam and Jake a considering look before setting down his coffee cup.

"Jake, I want you to take the morning off from working horses," Dad said.

Jake's jaw dropped. Then he looked wary. No other chore came close to working horses. Jake believed he had the best job ever awarded to a teenager.

"Unless you have an objection?" Dad said.

Sam saw Jake's chest expand, as if he wanted to spout off a dozen objections, but he said, "No, sir."

"Go pick some berries with Sam," Dad encouraged him. "Work'll wait, and maybe Grace will convince you to stay for some of her cobbler."

"I'll do better than that," Gram interrupted. "Leave Witch to spend the night and I'll drive you home with a couple pies. With school starting and her classes to prepare for, your mom sure won't have time to bake."

"So if Gram's going to please your mom and your stomach," Sam said, "how can you say no?"

"Never planned to," Jake muttered.

Gram didn't give Jake time to change his mind. She handed them long baskets. "Fix these into the panniers on one of the pack saddles."

Sam felt that too-familiar uneasiness of not quite remembering something everyone assumed she knew. What were panniers, and were the pack saddles in the tack room with all the other horse equipment?

From the corner of her eye, she saw Jake nod. Reassured, Sam kept listening as Gram rattled off instructions.

"Don't get greedy," she said. "Pick as many berries as you can, but if they're green, leave them. Indian summer usually gives us a second harvest."

"Take Banjo," Dad said. "Work some of the orneriness out of him."

In minutes, Jake had the pack saddle cinched onto Dad's big, stocky bay. Dad didn't believe in coddling his favorites. If Banjo had enough energy to bully Ace, he could use it trudging along at the end of a rope, carrying berries on his back.

Sam smiled and held Banjo's head as Jake settled the baskets into side pockets on the pack saddle.

"I like you fine," she said to the Quarter Horse. "But maybe you'll think twice next time you consider beating up on Ace."

"Let's go," Jake said. And they did.

On the way out, Sam echoed Jake's silence. They crossed the River Bend bridge on foot. All the time they walked, Sam watched the Calico Mountains for a flicker of silver. At first the mountains were ink blue against the sky, but as the sun rose, their peaks glowed yellow, then gold.

The cattle had moved farther down the river. A few lifted their heads to watch the humans, but most took little notice. Humans on foot weren't a threat to their serene grazing.

By the time the mountaintops turned the color of orange marmalade, they'd reached the berry bushes. There'd been no sign of the Phantom.

They worked without talking, but it was a comfortable quiet surrounding them with birdsong and the lapping of the river. They ate berries as they picked. Sweet and tart at the same time, the berries tasted like summer.

The end of summer, Sam corrected herself, and couldn't help but think of school.

"Who am I going to hang around with?"

"What's that?" Jake blinked, as if she'd awakened him.

"At school," Sam explained. "According to Gram, all the girls I was friends with are gone."

"The Greens sold out and moved to Oregon before they went completely broke," Jake agreed. "Linda Dennis's folks took jobs up at Lake Tahoe, running a fancy riding stable. And the Potters?" Jake shook his head. "Their spread near Darton's been subdivided for houses. Six per acre. It went for near a million dollars, I heard, so they could be living anywhere they want."

Sam felt a pulse of loyalty for her elementary school friends. "You can't blame them. This is a hard way to make a living."

"No kidding?" Jake's voice oozed sarcasm; then he yelped. "Ow!"

She was tempted to tell Jake he'd gotten what he deserved. Pricking himself on a thorn after acting like such a big shot seemed like justice.

"So I guess you can't answer my question." Sam slipped another handful of berries into the basket. When an especially juicy one stuck to her palm, she ate it.

"How would I know who you'd hang around with, Brat?" Jake sucked the finger he'd stabbed.

Sam fanned her face. The sun was well up now, but she didn't take off her sweatshirt because she didn't want long scratches like the ones she'd seen on Dad yesterday.

She was fanning her collar to cool herself when Jake finally ventured an opinion.

"I don't see you with Rachel Slocum's crowd," he said.

"Linc Slocum's daughter? You've got that right."

"She's cute, really popular, and she dresses like girls

on TV." Jake listed those traits as if Sam might be swayed by them.

"So? With her dad, I can't think she'd be very nice. I know that's not fair, but—"

"She's nice to the right sort of people, and I doubt you'd qualify. Darrell calls her the ice queen."

Sam paused in her picking. *I doubt you'd qualify.* She shouldn't let that remark bother her, but it did. She'd spent two years away at school in San Francisco. Wouldn't that impress the queen of Smalltown, Nevada?

Then the rest of Jake's sentence sank in.

"Isn't Darrell the one who taught you how to disable the engine of Gram's car?" Sam asked.

She recalled Jake's head under the hood of the old Buick. Jake had pulled something loose, so the car wouldn't run. It had blocked the road and she'd beaten Slocum to the Willow Springs wild horse corrals.

Jake frowned. "Since you've got such a great memory, you should remember I told you Darrell isn't a guy you need to know."

"So why is he your friend?"

"That's different," Jake said. "You just worry about what you're going to wear and how you're going to remember your locker combination. Freshmen are always late to class because they're out crying by their lockers, trying to get their books."

Sam pictured herself in a long, empty hall. Since she wasn't especially good with numbers, she'd have to write the combination on her hand until she memorized it.

With the baskets nearly full, they'd started toward River Bend when Jake said, "Hey, you could hang around with Jen Kenworthy. Remember her? Light hair, glasses, supersmart?"

"Sure," Sam said, "but I thought she was homeschooled."

"She was, for elementary school, but she started going to middle school in Darton about the time you left."

Jake's brown face took on the guilty blankness it wore when he remembered her accident and his part in it.

"I thought they owned the Gold Dust," Sam said, "but we stopped by there yesterday, and things had really changed."

"They had to sell out, and Slocum made them a good offer. He paid off their debts and kept Jen's dad on as foreman. Anyway, she'll be at the bus stop."

Just yesterday, Gram had pointed out the bus stop. She or Dad would drive Sam that far each morning, but Sam would have to walk the mile home after school.

Again, Sam's imagination went to work. She pictured herself standing there Monday morning, at sunrise, with Jen Kenworthy, a stranger.

"Jake, won't you be at the bus stop?"

Jake stopped walking. He turned toward her with the superior, tomcat smile he saved for occasions he really wanted to lord over her.

"I ride in with my brother in his Blazer."

Jake kept walking. So much for having an ally at Darton High School. Still, she couldn't give up.

"Couldn't I, maybe, ride with you? I wouldn't mind being squished."

Jake laughed, as if she'd only be able to count on his support if her life depended on it.

"No way," he said. "Freshmen take the bus."

Chapter 5

THE NAVY-BLUE HORSE VAN, PIN-STRIPED IN teal, glittered like a mirage. By the way it leaned to one side, the mirage had a flat tire.

DAVISON'S HORSE TRANSPORT read the small script lettering on the door. ESTABLISHED 1975.

Dressed in business clothes and a tie, the driver stood outside the horse van, consulting a clipboard.

"Almost made it," he called out to Sam and Jake, smiling. "The Slocum place is only about five miles up the road, right?"

Sam and Jake glanced at each other, surprised a man with a flat tire appeared so composed.

"Right," Sam answered. "Is Mr. Slocum getting a new horse?"

She knew he was. Slocum had mentioned a blue-blooded filly on her way from Florida. Sam couldn't see inside, and the van didn't shift from side to side like a horse trailer, but she heard muffled movements within.

If the horse van's inside matched its outside, the filly probably stood in a stall lighted by a crystal chandelier. Nothing but the best for Linc Slocum.

"You betcha," the driver said. "His report on the terrain made me believe I'd be another two hours getting here. The road's a little rough but nothing like what he described. I've got time to fix this flat and still arrive early."

Jake shifted from foot to foot, eager to get on his way.

"You kids wouldn't want to walk the filly around for a few minutes, would you? She'd probably like to stretch her legs."

Banjo pulled against the lead rope and nickered

toward the van. Jake didn't show the same curiosity.

"I've got to get back to work." Jake's voice fell short of being rude, but Sam knew he didn't like being called a kid.

Jake can have his pride, Sam thought. There was no chance she would turn down the opportunity to be first to see Slocum's filly.

"I'll help," Sam offered, and when Jake cleared his throat to protest, she added, "I'll see you back at the ranch, Jake."

"Whatever," he said, then gave a tug on Banjo's lead rope and walked away.

A flood of air-conditioning and an inquiring nicker accompanied the opening of the van's back doors.

Sam would bet her allowance the filly had the bloodlines of a racing Appaloosa. From her cocoa-brown head and neck to her milky body scattered with cocoa spots and barely visible striping on her hooves, the filly showed the best of her Appaloosa and Thoroughbred heritages.

On top of that, the filly's soft brown eyes, alert ears,

and the way she crinkled her satiny neck to watch Sam and the driver showed she liked people.

"She's gorgeous." Sam sighed. "You're sure she belongs to Linc Slocum?"

"'Apache Hotspot,'" the driver read from his clipboard. "'Two-year-old filly by Scat Cat out of Kachina Dancer, bred at the Spanish Moss Plantation in Longview, Florida.' Bought and paid for—" He opened a door inside the van to show a mini-apartment with champagne-colored carpet and tiled walls. "And I do mean *paid* for!"

"What's that?" Sam pointed inside the van, above a clean-scrubbed feed manger. "It looks like a video camera."

"Closed-circuit TV," the driver said, nodding. "I have a screen up front, so I can see what she's doing at any moment during our drive."

"Wow," Sam said.

With ease, the driver backed the Appaloosa from the van and handed her lead rope to Sam.

"Be out in a minute," he said, ducking toward the

mini-apartment. "Gonna put on a coverall, to change that tire."

The Appaloosa was tall. Nearly sixteen hands, Sam guessed, and she moved with a spirited strength that made Sam keep both hands on the lead rope.

The Appaloosa scanned the open terrain and trembled. She stared at the flat, sage-dotted range, at the red-winged blackbirds balancing on tall grass, at the oatmeal-colored hills clumped along the horizon. Clearly, Hotspot wasn't used to open spaces. Head held high, she neighed after Banjo.

Her neigh was like music. Heading home, Jake fought to keep Banjo moving in the opposite direction. As the filly neighed again, Sam knew she'd never heard anything like the melodious sound. Any horse within hearing distance would yearn to investigate.

Sam could hear the clink of metal tools as the driver worked on the tire and hummed.

Hotspot skittered in an arc, trying to scan all the hills at once. The effect was like a dog winding its leash around its walker. Was the driver watching? Sam backed away from the horse, trying to guide the filly as if she were on a longe line.

"Hey, girl," Sam said. "You're fine."

She couldn't let the horse hurt herself. Wrapped for travel, Hotspot's slim legs looked even more delicate.

Sam was about to call the van driver and turn responsibility for the costly filly back to him, when Hotspot stopped. She flung her head so high, Sam stood on tiptoe to grip the rope beneath the filly's chin. Her nostrils quivered with a sweet nicker.

Sam didn't have the Appaloosa's acute sense of smell nor the fine hearing that kept horses ahead of predators, but she could feel the morning grow still around her.

Small stones rattled down the hillside. Sam stared until her eyes burned, knowing what she'd see if she was patient. At last, he appeared.

The Phantom didn't move. Like a statue carved of silver-flecked marble, he stood camouflaged against a granite boulder.

Hotspot gave a worried nicker. The filly from

Florida had never seen a wild stallion. Her muscles bunched to run.

Sam slid one hand down the lead rope, closer to the filly's nose. If Hotspot bolted, what should she do? Sam tried to remember. Maybe bend the filly's nose toward her barrel? Or call the driver if she had time. Sam couldn't tell if Hotspot was frightened or excited.

Still motionless, the Phantom studied the van, filly, and Sam. Finally, he decided to prance closer. The play of muscles seemed to polish his hide from the inside. The Phantom arched his neck until his chin bumped his chest. Dark eyes peered through the forelock cascading over his face.

Show-off, Sam thought, but she didn't speak.

Since his rough capture, she'd only seen the Phantom once, when the blue roan stallion attempted to take the Phantom's mares.

Would Sam see the Phantom only when other horses acted as bait?

Oh no! Sam's attention had wandered, and the filly *did* bolt! She urged the filly into a tight circle, spinning the end of the rope to turn Hotspot's gaze away from the Phantom.

"What's up?" The driver slid from beneath the van, still holding a wrench.

"I—" Sam kept her back to the hillside. *Don't look behind me. There's no beautiful wild stallion there.*

Sam swallowed as the filly slowed.

Don't look, she thought. How could she explain Hotspot's excitement without pointing out the Phantom?

She must think of something. If the driver saw the silver stallion, he'd surely mention him to Slocum. That would convince Slocum that the Phantom had slipped in and tried to steal Kitty.

Slocum was already convinced a renegade stallion would seek out his blue-blooded mares. News of this encounter would only increase his worry.

Sam resisted the urge to look back over her shoulder. She kept her eyes on the driver. His frown faded as the filly calmed down. Sam did what she could to draw the rest of his attention.

"Wow!" Sam brushed dirt from her jeans. "I think all

this open space scared her." She stroked Hotspot's satiny neck. "Do you think that's possible?"

The filly sneezed at the dust she'd stirred, then struck out with one foreleg.

"Could be." The driver walked closer, and Hotspot extended her muzzle for rubbing.

"She seems fine now," Sam said.

Then, since the driver's attention was fixed on the filly, Sam sneaked a look at the hillside. Rocks. Dirt. Sagebrush. No Phantom.

A breath sighed through Sam's lips as she returned her attention to the Appaloosa. Again, she thought how suited this driver was to his job.

He let the filly lip his empty hand. He didn't seem to mind that she smeared him with horse spit.

"You're just a pet, aren't you?" he asked the horse. "I hope this Slocum knows how to treat a lady like you."

Pictures of bloody spurs, cruel bits, and the Phantom's scar flashed through Sam's mind. What she hoped was that Slocum hadn't purchased this sweet filly for himself.

A thunderstorm ruined the last day of summer vacation.

Dad roused Sam early to ride out with the cowboys because he needed another pair of eyes to spot all the cattle and chase them out of the canyons and draws.

During droughts, storms like this could cause flash floods. Sudden rains filled low spots, overflowed them, then followed long valleys. When the water crested, it created furious rivers. Each year, cattle drowned. They were safer on the flats, near the ranch. This year River Bend couldn't afford to lose even one.

In spite of the rolling booms of thunder, the rain was only a light sprinkle. The cattle stayed together, and the job went fast. By eight o'clock in the morning, Sam stood on River Bend's front porch, peeling off her yellow slicker.

This time tomorrow, she'd be walking into her first high school class. Sam hung her slicker on a hook and wondered if she'd like Darton High.

She pushed back her damp hair and wished she could shake dry like Blaze.

Sam noticed Gram standing near the counter, regarding the half-full egg basket.

"Thanks for taking care of the chickens, Gram," she said.

"You're welcome, but I'll tell you, Samantha, something's wrong. Six eggs for fourteen hens is just not normal." Gram shook her head and scooped a serving of warm blackberry cobbler from a square ceramic pan.

"Oh, yum." Sam watched Gram drizzle fresh cream over the top. Sam took the bowl of cobbler, even though she'd eaten so much pie last night that she'd vowed not to touch another blackberry until next summer.

"Have you seen any tracks around the chicken coop?" Gram asked. "Skunk or raccoon tracks? Blaze would wake us if a coyote was getting in."

Sam didn't admit she hadn't thought to search out tracks. "Maybe the hens are sick," she said. "Or getting old."

Sam hesitated to make such suggestions, since Dad insisted every creature on the ranch needed to contribute.

"It's a sad fact that when chickens get sick, they usually die," Gram said. "There's rarely time to call the vet. And those are young hens. Many times, Wyatt's said he won't run a home for old chickens."

A thunderclap rattled the windows. Sam looked out to the big pasture, suddenly worried for her orphan calf. She spotted Buddy instantly. She was running, jumping, and landing in mud puddles for the sheer fun of making a splash.

Still, Sam bit her lip with worry. If Dad wouldn't run a home for old chickens, he probably wouldn't run one for pet calves. Sam half turned toward Gram, then lost her nerve. She just couldn't ask.

Just the same, Gram met her eyes.

"No way you can put it off any longer," Gram said.

Sam's heart vaulted up. The final bit of cobbler wobbled on the spoon, then fell back into the bowl with a plop.

"This mess"—Gram gestured toward rain rivulets on the windows—"probably won't let up until late afternoon, and then you'll want to ride. You'd better get upstairs and try on those clothes from Aunt Sue."

Gram couldn't have picked a more effective way to get Sam moving. For one horribly long second, she'd thought Gram wanted to discuss Buddy's future as hamburger.

"Yep, you're right," Sam said, rinsing her bowl at the sink. "I'll get up there and try on every single thing."

"Call me if you need help making any decisions," Gram called after her, but Sam was fleet with relief, and barely heard.

At the end of an hour, Sam had no doubt she'd grown since coming home. All her jeans were too short. In fact, only one pair of pants fit.

Sam frowned at the gray cords she couldn't remember choosing. She guessed she'd have to learn to like them.

Most of her blouses were snug in the shoulders, maybe because she'd developed muscles lifting hay bales, carrying saddles, and juggling her squirmy calf.

She had an almost-new, hippie-style skirt she'd bought in San Francisco, but she couldn't imagine wearing it to school in Darton.

Sam stood in front of the mirror on the back of her bedroom door. The skirt was crinkly and dark green. Maybe she could wear it for a holiday party, but she couldn't remember anything more festive than going to Christmas Eve service at the Methodist church in Darton.

Sam gave the mirror a more intent look. She liked her slightly wider shoulders, new height, and general fitness. She was glad her waist curved in, and she had a chest that was *there* but not to an embarrassing extent.

She hated her hair. Sam leaned close to the mirror and made a face. Instead of making her look older, it made her look ready for Halloween.

That hair would ruin her first day of school, no matter what she wore.

Unless . . .

Sam took a strand of damp hair and pulled it straight. It reached just below her cheekbone. Gram probably wouldn't approve. Jake's reaction didn't bear imagining. Dad, on the other hand, might not holler if she cut it again.

Sam held her breath and squinted her eyes at the mirror. A new start and a new look.

Gram had said to call if she had trouble making any decisions, but Sam didn't. She walked downstairs, pretending she had a short, boyish cut.

Maybe, she thought with each step. *Just maybe.*

By the time she reached the kitchen, Sam had made up her mind. The announcement burst from her lips, almost without her permission. "I hate this weird hair, and I'm chopping it off!"

"All right, dear," Gram said. She sat at the kitchen table, across from a younger woman with a long red braid. "But first you might say hello to our guest. You remember Miss Olson from the BLM, don't you? She's come to talk with you about that mustang you call the Phantom."

Chapter 6

BRYNNA OLSON, DIRECTOR OF THE WILLOW Springs Wild Horse Center, wore a crisply pressed khaki uniform and a name tag. Her red hair was confined in a no-nonsense French braid. The only thing interfering with her professional appearance was the big bowl of blackberry cobbler centered before her.

"Hi, Samantha." Miss Olson's tone was warm but only for an instant. "Your grandmother says you've heard Mr. Slocum's concerns about a mustang stallion trespassing on his property and stealing his mares."

Miss Olson's expression didn't betray her feelings about the accusation, but Sam could guess what they were. After the Phantom's capture, Miss Olson had watched the stallion's untamed fury with the understanding of a horsewoman.

"There's no way it was the Phantom." Sam defended her horse by reflex. "What does Slocum"—Sam shook her head as Gram cleared her throat—"*Mr.* Slocum expect you to do?"

"I'm holding him off for now, but he wants action." Miss Olson pushed her bowl aside, as if she'd lost her appetite. "Since I disqualified his application to adopt a wild horse, Mr. Slocum is unhappy. He doesn't care for me and doesn't respect my position with the federal government."

Sam stared out the kitchen window, but she didn't say what she was thinking.

Outside, rain dripped from the eaves of the white ranch house. Sam knew many ranchers distrusted the BLM. Ranch families were independent minded. They didn't like government rules telling them how to live on land they'd ranched for generations.

Slocum despised the BLM for a different reason than most.

The rain increased, but it fell so slowly, Sam could almost count the drops. The sky was blue-gray, still deciding whether the storm had ended.

When Sam turned back to Miss Olson, the BLM official's half smile said she didn't expect Gram or Sam to defend her or the government agency. Besides, Sam was pretty sure Miss Olson could stand up for herself.

"Respect me or not, Mr. Slocum wants the BLM to catch the wild horse he feels is stalking his mares."

"Are you going to do it?" Sam asked.

"We're not convinced there is a renegade stallion," Miss Olson said. "The teeth slashes on his mare could have come from any horse.

"He said she's been wandering the range. Folks aren't supposed to turn domestic stock out, but they do. Some escape or are stolen, too." Miss Olson turned to Gram. "I had an email this morning from one of our California offices. A valuable stallion is missing and presumed stolen. His owner's frantic, hoping he's on the loose."

"Horse thieves even in these modern times," Gram said, shaking her head.

Sam wished she could tell the stallion's owner not to give up. After all, everyone had believed Blackie was gone for good.

"More than likely"—Miss Olson's tone sharpened—"the sorrel was bitten by one of Slocum's own horses."

Sam nodded and kept her lips pressed together.

"Before we waste manpower setting a trap for a trespassing stallion that may not exist, Mr. Slocum has to give us some evidence he's right."

"Like tracks?" Sam asked.

"That would be a start," Miss Olson said, "but there's no shortage of unshod horses around here."

Gram took a sip of her coffee, then frowned. Sam could see Gram was so intent on listening, she'd let her coffee grow cold.

"From what you've seen of the Phantom"—Miss Olson watched Sam with such intensity, Sam wanted to say no to whatever she asked—"would he enter an enclosed area like Slocum's ranch?"

Sam stared at the tabletop. She pictured the remote-controlled iron gates, the grassy approach to the pens, ranch house, and mansion.

Up until today, Sam would have sworn Phantom wouldn't enter such an area. But after he'd materialized out of nowhere to eye Hotspot, could she be sure?

"He's never crossed the river," Sam said. "The closest he's come is halfway."

Chills covered Sam's arms as she thought of the beautiful stallion, silvered with moonlight, as he swam out to her. The Phantom remembered he'd once been her colt, and he remembered his secret name.

Sam sighed. Though Miss Olson took the sound as sadness, she didn't turn all sensitive and gooey. She merely agreed.

"Based on what I saw when he was in captivity, that stallion wouldn't willingly enter any fenced area. He showed more resistance to confinement than I've witnessed in any mustang."

"What will you do if Mr. Slocum comes up with some sort of evidence?" Gram asked.

Miss Olson looked thoughtful. She didn't seem to notice she'd pressed her palms together and matched her fingers as she tapped them against her lips.

"We're shorthanded because we lost Flick."

The glance Miss Olson shot Sam asked if she remembered the cowboy who'd used his position with the BLM to capture the Phantom for Slocum. Sam nodded.

"And the college kids who were working for us are on their way back to school." Miss Olson turned in her chair to watch the weather outside the window. "I should get back," she said, standing, but her expression said she'd rather stay in Gram's warm kitchen.

"Frankly, it's hard to find people with the expertise to track and capture horses." Miss Olson raised one eyebrow as she looked at Gram.

"I wish I could help," Gram said, "but the only folks I know who are good at that sort of thing are Jake and Wyatt."

Miss Olson looked sheepish, but she said, "It pays a lot more than you'd think."

Gram made a considering sound, but Sam didn't know why. Dad wouldn't take a job with the BLM unless he was in danger of losing the ranch.

Money. Why did every conversation lead back to money?

Sam was sure Gram had already forgotten her "I hate my hair" outburst as she'd come pounding downstairs. Apparently, Miss Olson hadn't.

With her hand on the doorknob, Miss Olson stopped. She turned so quickly, her braid snapped from one side of her neck to the other.

"Well, shoot," she said. "It's too late to go back to Willow Springs now. Samantha, I might be able to help you out. When I was going to college, I was the dorm queen at cutting hair. If your grandmother doesn't mind, I'd be glad to"—she searched for the right words—"even things up a little."

"Miss Olson, that would be awfully nice of you," Gram said. "And you'll just have to stay for dinner."

"I'd love to if I didn't have so many hungry animals

waiting at home," Miss Olson said. "But if Sam grabs a pair of sharp scissors and leads me to a mirror, I'll see what I can do."

By the time she'd dampened, combed, and snipped at Sam's hair, Miss Olson's voice had turned less formal.

"This is embarrassing to mention, but I liked it better a couple weeks ago when you called me Brynna."

Sam's brown eyes tried to catch the redhead's blue ones in the mirror, but they only darted away.

"Okay," Sam said.

Brynna worked along Sam's neck for a minute before she spoke again. "And since you're tuned in to the way wild horses think, I'd like your opinion of what's going on with Slocum's mare."

Sam thought of the aggressive blue roan. She thought of the Phantom coming to see Hotspot. It wasn't safe to mention either.

This time Brynna did meet Sam's eyes in the mirror. "Please, I'd like to get this cleared up as soon as possible," she said. "If it's a secret, I'll take it to my grave."

Brynna looked sincere. Sam could explain how the blue roan had swum the river, waded ashore, and trotted right up to the corral fence, but stubbornness kept her quiet.

Brynna seemed nice enough, but Sam couldn't shake off years of hearing that the BLM rarely worked in the best interests of ranchers.

And yet Brynna had kept the Phantom free.

A knot of confusion tightened in Sam's stomach. Maybe she should talk with Jake.

"Have you heard unexplained sounds, especially at night? Any sign of an intruder?"

"Gram thinks a skunk might be getting in the chicken coop," Sam offered.

Brynna grumbled, but she kept combing and cutting. At last Sam decided she could tell half the truth. After all, she'd been with Gram when the blue roan challenged the Phantom.

"On the way back from Darton, we saw the Phantom," Sam said.

"You did? Where was that?" Brynna stayed calm,

but Sam could tell she was hoping for a revelation.

"Near War Drum Flats," Sam said. She'd bet Brynna was calculating how close that was to Slocum's ranch. "He was running off a bachelor stallion trying to steal some of his mares."

"Nothing unusual about that." Brynna sounded disappointed.

"He's a blue roan."

Brynna shrugged. "I'll keep an eye out for him, but—"

"About fourteen hands, with a hammer head," Sam said, but Brynna didn't take the hint.

"We're looking for a mustang that doesn't fear human habitation. That points to your colt."

Sam stared blindly into the mirror, until Brynna touched her shoulder and asked, "So what do you think of your hair?"

Sam studied her reflection. Her red-brown hair lay in neat, glossy wisps around her face, and her bangs were layered so they poufed up just a little.

It was a plain haircut that didn't draw attention to

itself, but it did make her eyes look bigger.

"Thanks, Brynna." Sam touched the tendrils that curved against her neck. "It looks great."

"That's an exaggeration," Brynna said, heading toward the stairs, "but I'm glad you like it."

Sam walked Brynna downstairs and past Gram, who still wanted her to stay for dinner.

Sam grabbed her slicker and followed Brynna through the kitchen door. Outside, a fine rain came down, making a hissing sound. Tiny raindrops hit the dirt and bounced up like powdered sugar.

They were halfway to the white government truck when the woman shooed her off.

"Go on back," Brynna said. "And have a good first day at school."

"I will!" Sam shouted over another clap of thunder.

She'd started back to the house, when movement drew her attention to the barn.

Light shone golden and cozy from the open barn where Dad stood. His dark silhouette showed one hand planted against the doorway. The other hung loose as he looked through the curtains of misty rain.

Was Dad angry because they'd invited the BLM official in from the storm? Did he suspect Sam was engineering a secret wild horse adoption? Was he too tired to make a polite trip across the yard to say hello?

Sam quit guessing. She must be mistaken, because from here, it looked like Dad was staring after Brynna with something like a smile.

Sam's alarm was set. Her clothes hung on her closet door. A backpack stuffed with notebooks, pencils and pens, and a tiny tub of lip gloss sat by her bedroom door. Everything was ready for her first day of school, and still she felt restless, as if she'd left something important undone.

Sam stared at her ceiling. Twice, it turned pale, brightened by faraway glimmers of lightning.

The house stood so silent, it was creepy. Sam held her breath, listening. She heard the kitchen clock. A floorboard squeaked. That would be Blaze, chasing dream cats while he slept in front of the empty fireplace.

The only sounds came from outside. The rain had stopped, but thunder grumbled in the clouds. Sam couldn't tell if the storm was moving away or coming back.

She hoped it had gone, because it was one more thing Dad worried about.

After she'd gone to bed, Sam had overheard Dad talking with Gram about hay. Dad always counted on a September harvest. Now, because of the rain, he was afraid he wouldn't get it. So far the rain had been light, but he didn't want to risk a long wet spell. Wet hay could rot. If it did, they couldn't afford to buy good hay from someone else.

She'd heard him slap his palm against the table.

"A single hundred-degree day is all I need. We could cut and dry that entire field of alfalfa one day and bale it the next."

The numbers on Sam's watch glowed blue-green in the darkness. Midnight. This was the time the Phantom had come to the river.

He hadn't come since his capture, and she had no

reason to believe he would come tonight. He couldn't know tomorrow was special to her. Even if he did, what would a first day of school mean to a horse?

The thunder boomed. Closer. *Rain, rain, go away. Come again another day.* The nursery rhyme meant something to a rancher's daughter.

Blaze's toenails clicked across the kitchen floor, and then Sam heard him drink from his water bowl. By the sound of his lapping, he didn't have much left.

Grabbing at the excuse, Sam swung her legs out from under the covers. Quickly and quietly, she moved through the dark house to the kitchen and refilled Blaze's water bowl.

With the dog's noisy drinking to cover her movements, Sam opened the door and slipped outside.

Mud-scented wind blew Sam's nightgown behind her, but nothing else moved. Holding on to a porch post, she leaned out as far as she could, staring toward the river.

Starlight showed the sway of a few trees. If the clouds blew aside, unveiling the moon, she might see the

Phantom standing on the other side of the river.

Of course, that idea made no sense. When even night birds were tucked into dry nests, why would the stallion be out?

A crack, a sizzle, a glare of white-gold light ripped a crooked path across the black sky. Sam smelled a metallic heat. Then she saw him.

The Phantom reared on the other side of the river. Like a frosty tree turned upside down, branches of lightning ran jagged behind the stallion.

The Phantom had come back!

Sam's arms clamped around herself. She was scared and excited, and she had no choice. The stallion had returned. She couldn't leave him rearing alone in the darkness.

Sam had lifted the hem of her nightgown and her toes had pressed into the squishy mud, when the porch light flashed on. For an instant she imagined it was more lightning, but Dad's solemn voice left her no escape from the truth.

"Samantha, get back inside."

"But, Dad—"

"No excuses. We'll talk about this tomorrow."

She'd been caught. She'd be grounded. Worst of all, the Phantom would go on waiting in the darkness, thinking she'd forgotten.

Chapter 7

SAM WAS ALREADY SITTING ON HER NEATLY made bed, dressed and ready for school, when her alarm went off.

If she had just one friend, today would be easier. If Dad weren't angry and likely to lecture her while he drove her to the bus stop, today would be easier. If she could go for a gallop on Ace after school, today would be easier. But none of that would happen.

Face it, Sam told herself as she switched off her shrilling alarm clock, *today is* not *going to be easy.*

Breakfast was not on the table. Nothing sizzled on the stove. Yes, she'd told Gram she only wanted cereal and toast on school days, but this felt wrong.

Dad stood at the window, staring out at the gray morning.

"Dad, I—"

"Eat some breakfast. Gram's out doing your chores."

A lump swelled in Sam's throat. Worry over last night had knocked thoughts of morning chores right out of her head. Out in the wind-tossed yard, Gram was filling water troughs, feeding Ace, finding eggs.

"I've still got time." Sam glanced at her watch. "I'll go stop her."

"She's doing it as a favor. Just for today. Now, get something to eat."

"Okay," Sam said.

Even though he wouldn't turn to look at her, Dad didn't sound too angry. Still, he wouldn't change his mind about grounding her. Dad was stubborn and so darn sure he was right.

The only question was how long she'd be grounded.

Sam poured milk on her cereal and considered Dad's stiff back. The smartest thing she could do was wait for him to explain her punishment, instead of harassing him about it.

Sam tried to be patient. She finished her cereal, managed to eat some toast, then rinsed her bowl. When Gram came back inside, Sam kissed her good-bye, climbed into the truck, and held her backpack on her lap while Dad drove toward the bus stop.

The rain-washed sky spread bright blue above the Calico Mountains, but Sam's chest felt tight. Her teeth hurt from clenching. She knew that if she didn't ask Dad about being grounded, she'd burst into tears when the first little thing went wrong.

She couldn't let that happen on her first day at the bus stop. Even if she ended up waiting there alone, she'd be examined as a newcomer as she entered that bus. How cool would it be to appear with red, swollen eyes, looking like a kindergartner afraid to leave home?

Sam took such a deep breath, Dad must have heard her question coming.

"For how long?" she asked. "How long before I can ride Ace?"

"We'll start with a week and see how it goes," Dad said.

A week. Seven days. That wasn't so long. She could stand it.

"And the fall drive? Will I be able to ride in time to help bring the cattle in?"

"No."

Seven days. Not so long, but time enough to keep her from riding Ace, her hat held down by its stampede string as the wind whistled past. Long enough for her to miss a once-a-year event.

"Since you're already mad at me," Sam began, and noticed Dad didn't correct her, "are you going to butcher Buddy?"

The truck slowed as if Dad had lifted his boot from the gas pedal.

"What in—" He twisted toward her. "What in the *world* are you thinking, Samantha?"

"About money," she said. "I'm thinking that we need every dollar we can make from the hay and the cattle."

Dad shook off his surprise, and the truck surged forward again.

"First off, we only raise enough hay for our own stock. I don't like to buy it over the winter. Second, when we get so poor one pet calf would save us—" Dad's mouth curved up at one corner, but his expression wasn't quite a smile. "Well, let's just say I'd put you to work long before that happened."

"I'd go to work," Sam offered, "if it meant keeping Buddy. Sure, I would." She pictured the mall at Darton and wondered how old you'd have to be to work in the food court. "I bet I could find a job after school. Do you want me to do it?"

Sam couldn't interpret Dad's expression. It flickered somewhere between proud and embarrassed.

"I'll let you know," he said.

The truck slowed again. The bus stop was just ahead.

Dad braked, turned toward Sam, and leaned across to touch her cheek.

"Your hair looks real cute that way, Samantha." Dad nodded three times.

Sam knew he wanted to add something else. She glanced down the road. The bus wasn't in sight, so she waited.

"Honey, there's not a darn thing wrong that time won't fix," Dad said. "Now, you go on and have a nice first day."

Sam walked toward the girl standing at the bus stop. Uneasy because she knew the girl was watching her, too, Sam tried not to stare.

The other girl was thin. Not model trim or athlete lean, but downright gawky. She wore dark-framed glasses, and her white-blond hair hung in skinny braids. They ended in tassels that made them look like exclamation marks.

She wore a hot orange T-shirt, jeans, and black high-top tennis shoes. Showing through the mesh pocket of her backpack was the most complicated-looking calculator Sam had ever seen.

Sam gathered her courage, trying to think of something to say, but the other girl beat her to it.

"Hi. I'm Jennifer Kenworthy. If you're Samantha Forster, I think we've met before, a long time ago."

"I am," Sam said. "And I sort of remember that, too." But this wasn't the timid girl Sam recalled. "I usually go by Sam."

"Good. I go by Jen, or Jennifer, but never Jenny—except to my mom."

They both smiled; then Jen's face took on a puzzled look. "Why did Jake tell me your hair was kind of punk-looking?"

"He didn't know any better," Sam said. "It was, until last night. I had a trim, and he hasn't seen it yet."

Jake didn't take change in stride. Sam thought of the morning after the Phantom had accidentally given her a black eye. When she'd tried to cover it with makeup and a bold attitude, Jake had exploded.

"That's pretty dramatic," Jen said. "All I did for the first day of school is break my poor mother's heart. Not really. That's just what she said, because I insisted on dressing like a normal kid. Last year, when I started going to public school, my mom made me wear skirts and twinsets. This year I'm dressing myself."

About time, Sam thought. She'd been selecting her own clothes forever. But she only said, "Looks good to me."

"Thanks," Jen said. "Mom said I was dressed to go muck out stalls, but I stood firm. The thing is"—Jen lowered her voice—"I don't really care."

"So, you have horses?"

A queasy look crossed Jen's face, and Sam worried that she'd ended the friendship before it had begun. How could she have forgotten what Jake had told her? The Kenworthys had been on the verge of losing their ranch when Slocum offered to buy it.

"Well, yeah," Jen said. "You remember—"

"I do. Sorry," Sam apologized. "I forgot."

"No big deal." Jen ducked her head. "After all, *I* forgot you, uh, didn't have a mom to say stupid things to you, like mine does."

Silence simmered between them for a minute. They'd both messed up and admitted it. That seemed a fine beginning for a friendship.

"But yeah," Jen said at last, "we still have a few horses.

Mine is Silk Stockings, but I call her Silly. She's a truly ditzy palomino mare." Jen shook her head, then added, "I plan to be a vet, though, and she's better than a textbook on horse neuroses."

"She'd probably get along great with Ace, my little mustang. All the other horses like to push him around." Sam met Jen's eyes. Clearly, they both loved their horses, no matter what.

"We should go ride sometime," Jen suggested.

The roar of the yellow school bus ended their conversation, so Sam didn't mention the ride would have to wait until she was out of trouble. She only gave an excited nod.

The morning hours were filled with slamming lockers, ringing bells, and shouting voices. Guided by a useless photocopied map, Sam navigated miles of mazelike halls. She made it to each class on time, but Jake's warning about weeping freshmen kept her from visiting her locker until lunch hour.

Arms aching, Sam approached her locker, carrying every book from each morning class. In little, tiny ink numbers, she'd written her combination on the inside of her wrist.

Her locker opened like a dream. Sam arranged her books inside, closed it, and opened it again, this time without consulting the numbers on her wrist.

When a group of laughing girls passed by, Sam looked at her watch, pretending she had someplace to go. She didn't. She'd had English class with Jen, but Jen hadn't mentioned meeting for lunch. And Sam hadn't seen Jake.

Did she have time to find the library? Not if she figured in time to wander around and get lost. Instead, she pulled an apple from her backpack, wishing the break would end. She practiced opening her locker again. She had journalism after lunch. She'd been on the newspaper staff in middle school, and her teacher had said she had talent. Sam was excited to give it a try in high school.

She might meet some people, too. Although a lot of the other students were strangers to each other, Sam had felt too shy to speak to people in her other classes. She hoped journalism was less formal. Maybe there she could relax and make some friends.

Sam closed her locker. She turned the dial very deliberately, in case anyone was watching.

At last the bell rang. A stampede of students filled the halls, but it was a knot of rowdy boys she noticed. As they forged a path through the other kids, Sam saw Jake. The quietest of them all, he moved along in the center, grinning.

Until he saw Sam. Then Jake came to such a sudden stop, another student rammed into him from behind. Jake staggered forward a step, but his eyes stayed on Sam.

Jake hated her short hair. That was clear. He kept going—without waving, without saying hi, without recognizing she was alive.

He'll get used to it, Sam told herself. It wasn't like she'd planned to tag along with him at school. She'd see him at home, and he could spout off about the mistake she'd made.

Right now she'd better hurry to class.

"We've got to hit the ground running," said Mr. Blair.

Sam's journalism teacher looked more like a football coach as he fired off orders. Half the students loitered near a row of computers. The other half sat at attention in desks arranged in straight rows.

The students whispering by the computers must be the veterans, Sam thought. The students who were seated and attentive, Sam admitted, looked like freshmen.

"Class time is for putting out a newspaper. The textbook is for teaching you how to write. Here's a schedule." Mr. Blair flapped a sheaf of papers. "Do two chapters each night and turn in the work every day when you get to class." Mr. Blair took a breath, then pointed. "What did I say?"

"I, uh—" said a boy wearing a black T-shirt.

"That's what I thought." Mr. Blair turned toward Sam and pointed. "What did I say?"

"We're putting out the newspaper during class and reading the book at night." Sam rattled off what she remembered. "We turn in the work—" When Sam saw Mr. Blair's eyes narrow, she hurried to correct herself. "We turn in *two* chapters' worth of work every day."

"Okay." Mr. Blair turned toward a bespectacled boy who sat with his feet atop a big wooden desk. "RJay, give this girl a story." Mr. Blair jerked his thumb toward Sam, then asked, "Name?"

"Sam," she said, lacing her fingers together in her lap to keep her hands from shaking. Then, as Mr. Blair scanned the student list in his hand, she added, quietly, "*Samantha* Forster."

"Hmm. A freshman." Mr. Blair stared so long, Sam thought it very possible he was trying to read her mind. "Give her a story anyway, RJay."

The teacher shooed her toward RJay.

Feeling singled out, Sam crossed the room. She tugged at the hem of her scoop-neck white shirt, even though she knew it looked fine with her new jeans. Today she'd seen a hundred girls dressed the same way, but Sam still felt awkward as she stood before RJay. She guessed he was the editor of *Dialogue*, the Darton High newspaper, but he said nothing to confirm it.

"Go see Rachel," RJay said, and then he, too, pointed.

At first Sam didn't recognize the name.

Rachel looked like a model. Her sleek hair was the dark brown of coffee. She wore a short, trendy plaid skirt with suspenders. On most girls, it would look silly. On her, worn over a crisp white blouse, it looked great.

Rachel let Sam stand and wait while she talked to a blonde in a cheerleader's uniform embroidered with the name *Daisy*. Gradually, Rachel turned.

Her rose-gold fingernails skimmed the wing of hair slanting across her forehead, lifting it away from her eyes. She scanned Sam from head to waist but still said nothing.

Sam turned hot with embarrassment. She felt like such a reject, but she had to say something.

"RJay said you'd assign me a story," Sam explained.

"Back-to-school interview with Ms. Santos." Rachel

ran the words together, sounding bored and faintly British.

Sam frowned. *Ms. Santos.* Her ignorance only deepened her blush. "Where would I find her?" she asked. After she found her, maybe she'd figure out who she was.

"Oh." Rachel stretched the word so that it sounded like *ow.* Did Rachel have an English accent, or was she pretending? Sam couldn't tell, but all at once she remembered. When they were out picking berries, hadn't Jake said Linc Slocum's daughter was named Rachel? Hadn't he said Slocum was divorced and that Rachel and her brother spent summers in London with their mother?

"Oh," Rachel said again, eyes sliding toward the cheerleader. "I guess the little cowgirl"—she pronounced it *cow gull* and studied Sam's shoes as if looking for traces of manure—"can't be expected to know Ms. Santos is our principal."

Cowgirl. Sam swallowed hard. At River Bend Ranch, she would consider that description a compliment. Here at school, from Rachel, it clearly wasn't.

On the other hand, cowgirls were tough. They stood

up to trouble. "You're right," Sam said, lifting her chin just a little. "I've been going to school in San Francisco, and I don't know a lot of the local people."

"San Francisco?" asked the cheerleader.

"San Francisco isn't London, honey," Rachel said, but the snub fell short when Mr. Blair interrupted.

"Rachel's grasp of geography is quite astounding," he said. Then he glanced at the classroom clock and back at Sam. "Run over to the office and schedule that interview."

Sam grabbed her notebook, wondering what in the world she'd ask Ms. Santos if she was available.

Think fast, Sam ordered herself. She'd been on her middle school newspaper. She could do this.

So what if she didn't have time to make a list of questions or review what a "back-to-school" interview should include?

With determined steps, Sam headed toward the door.

"Don't be surprised if she puts you off until tomorrow," Mr. Blair called. "I have a feeling Ms. Santos is rather busy today, Samantha."

Sam was headed toward the door, when Rachel's silky laughter came after her.

"*Samantha*. See, Daisy, you lose. You thought she was a boy."

Chapter 8

SAM WAVED GOOD-BYE TO JEN, THEN STARTED the long walk home.

Late-August sun shone on the bare nape of her neck as if yesterday's storm had never happened. It didn't feel like the one-hundred-degree day Dad had wished for, but it was plenty hot.

Sam grumbled to herself. This walk ought to count as a chore. It wouldn't, of course. She'd need to check the hens' nests for eggs and make sure the animals were fed. Monday was also laundry day. Even though Gram had a perfectly good clothes dryer, she hung fresh laundry on a clothesline. She expected Sam to take it down and fold it. Sam lengthened her stride, hurrying. She had to admit that her sun-dried sheets always smelled better than those tumbled in the dryer.

Something moved.

Sam stopped. Because it could be the Phantom, she didn't turn to face the movement. Instead, she stood still, letting her eyes search until they found a rabbit crouched on its haunches, watching. It was close enough that she saw its nose twitch.

When Sam started walking again, the sand-colored rabbit launched itself across the desert in the opposite direction.

It could have been the Phantom, but it wasn't. Sam's heart sank as she remembered last night. The Phantom had come to her, rearing against a turmoil of stars and lightning, but she hadn't been able to go to him.

How unfair. Sam lengthened her stride as she grew angry. Not only was she grounded, but she hadn't even done the thing she was being punished for.

There was no use talking to Dad. She could only hope the Phantom spotted her on one of these afternoon hikes toward home.

Thoughts of the stallion pulled at her heart.

She remembered the tickle of his whiskery muzzle as he'd nuzzled her hand when they both stood in the river. She remembered that amazing day at the Willow Springs corrals, when he'd put aside his hatred of humans to rest his great, heavy head on her shoulder.

Sam was almost home when she heard hooves and saw Buddy streaking toward her.

"What are you doing out here?" she shouted.

The calf kept coming at a clumsy run, her front legs slanting to the right while her rear legs swung left. Ross, a River Bend cowboy, rode behind her at a lope.

Sam realized the big-eyed calf had no intention of stopping, so she braced her feet apart. Even though Sam was standing firm when Buddy plowed into her, the calf nearly knocked her down.

"Settle down, girl," Sam said.

Buddy curled around her, streaking Sam's new jeans

with dust. The calf walked two laps before stopping. She pressed against Sam's side and faced Ross.

"Good girl, Buddy," she crooned. "You're safe."

Sam slung her arm over Buddy's neck, brushing her fingers over the plush red fur. The calf trembled.

As she looked up at Ross, Sam wondered if he was shaking, too. She'd never met anyone so shy. Ross's downcast eyes told Sam she might have a better chance of getting an answer from Tank, Ross's flop-eared bay horse.

"What happened?" Sam asked.

"Got out," Ross mumbled.

Sam nearly laughed. It had cost the big cowboy so much to tell her what she already knew.

"It's a good thing I came along when I did," Sam said.

The cowboy nodded. "Want a rope?" He touched the lariat coiled and strapped to his saddle.

"If you go ahead of us, back to the ranch, I think she'll follow me in," Sam said.

Without a word, Ross spun the cow pony away.

In appreciation, Buddy rubbed her muzzle against

Sam's white shirt. Sam looked down at the smear of grassy slobber.

"Yeah, you're welcome," Sam said.

She finished the long walk home with the calf tagging along at her side.

At dinner, Gram and Dad asked endless questions about her first day of school.

"English, history, and journalism, I feel fine about," Sam told them. "And I had a good Spanish teacher last year in San Francisco."

"That will be a help," Gram said, passing Sam another slice of the whole wheat bread she'd baked that afternoon. "Did you see Maxine Ely?"

"She's my history teacher," Sam said. "She must have recognized me. She sort of smiled when she called my name during roll."

"She's a good woman," Dad said, but he sounded preoccupied.

"Don't you have a few other classes?" Gram insisted.

Sam knew what Gram was asking. During the last two years, when they'd communicated by letters, Sam hadn't been shy in telling Gram she was a terrible, hopeless, thickheaded math student.

"P.E. and algebra," Sam admitted.

In fact, she dreaded her gym class almost as much as math class. Darton High required students to shower after gym. Both Rachel and Daisy were in Sam's P.E. class, and she had no desire to stand in the same locker room with those beauty queens.

"You be sure to ask for extra help in algebra," Gram said, "if you need it."

Sam knew she'd need it. Still, she couldn't help being irritated that Gram was waiting for her to fail.

A wave of weariness washed over Sam. She stifled a yawn. She had finished the first two chapters in her journalism book during study hall, so her only other homework was to cover her textbooks. After that, she wanted to climb into bed.

"Buddy got out again," Dad said.

Sam's weariness vanished as if Dad had tossed a bucket of water her way. "I know. I caught her."

"Next time you might not," Dad said.

"I don't think—" Sam began.

"Now, hush," Gram said. "It wasn't your fault. That calf's just trying to do what's natural. She wants to be with the other cattle."

Most of the other cattle will die soon, Sam thought.

"But Buddy's different," Sam said. "Dad told me so, just this morning." She stared at her father for confirmation.

"I did," Dad said. "But that doesn't mean I'm soft-headed."

"Just softhearted," Gram said, looking amused.

Dad ignored her. "Buddy needs branding."

Sam shivered, remembering the smell of the small fire of dried sagebrush and the sound of white-hot branding irons clinking against each other. As a child, the stink of burning hair hadn't bothered her as much as the bleating of the calves. She'd imagined they were crying to their mothers.

Now she was Buddy's mother.

"It's going to hurt," Sam said, wincing.

"It always does," Dad said, "but just for a minute and

not nearly as much as getting caught up with someone else's herd and butchered."

That was the point of a brand. Thousands of red, white-faced cattle wandered the range. Even when they were gathered together, they were impossible to tell apart. Cowboys might remember a steer with a crumpled horn or a cow freckled with white, but such differences were rare.

A brand guaranteed each rancher moved his own cattle to summer pasture.

"If you're serious about keeping her," Dad added, "we should do an ear mark, too. That way riders can see who she belongs to from horseback, when the herd's packed together tight."

"I'm serious about keeping her," Sam said.

"We'll do it this weekend." Dad pushed his chair back from the table. Sam heard him plop into his recliner in the living room.

Sam felt the prickle of tears. Sure, Dad could just go off and forget. Branding Buddy meant nothing to him.

She knew it had to be done to protect Buddy, but

when they seared the calf's skin with a branding iron, they were burning her and creating a scar.

"You know," Gram said, as the television clicked on in the other room, "it would only take him a few minutes to brand Buddy while you were at school. He's waiting for the weekend so you can comfort her when it's over."

"I know," Sam said. "And I know it has to be done, but I don't have to like it."

By the time she finished washing dishes, dusk had fallen, but Sam still went out to visit Buddy.

Buddy didn't want to visit. In the middle of the pasture, she stopped grazing, looked at Sam, and flicked her tail as if shooing a pesky fly. But the calf didn't move a step closer before turning her attention back to the grass.

"Okay for you," Sam muttered, then walked toward the small corral beside the barn.

Ace nickered when he saw her coming.

"No carrots," Sam confessed, holding her palms open as she approached.

Sweetheart blew through her lips and shuffled away from the fence rails, but Ace remained.

He looked a little scruffy. Since she hadn't ridden him today, she hadn't brushed him, and the little mustang loved the massage of the rubber brush.

"You are spoiled, you know." Sam led him into the barn, turned on the light, and began grooming.

As she brushed, Sam turned from telling the bay gelding how pretty he was to confiding her worries. She could tell Ace her troubles and not worry that he'd tell anyone else.

"I suppose I should ask Jake about the blue roan," she murmured to Ace. "I want to, but he'll think of some reason to worry. He's so protective, you'd think he was my brother."

Sam smoothed the brush along Ace's back, thinking. The hammer-head stallion was young, but he had a broad chest and the muscled haunches of a mature horse.

Sam had seen small bands of bachelor stallions cast out of their herds as potential challengers to the ruling stallion. But they tended to be gangly youngsters.

Sam would bet the hammer head was at least five years old. He might have lost his harem of mares to another stallion, or maybe they'd been captured in one of the BLM's wild horse gathers.

When Ace stamped, Sam realized she'd been so deep in thought, she'd stopped brushing.

"Sorry," she told the gelding. "But the more I think about him, the more I believe Hammer is trouble."

Ace swung his head around, and his eyes met hers.

"That's what I've been calling him in my head," Sam explained. "Hammer, because of his big head and the way he kicked that fence."

Ace's brown eyes stayed fixed on her, as if he expected more. "That's not silly, is it?"

Ace bobbed his head, and his forelock fell away from the white star on his forehead.

"Too bad," Sam said, laughing, but she didn't give Hammer another thought until morning.

Sam and Jen were waiting for the bus when a baby-blue

Mercedes-Benz swished past, carrying Rachel Slocum to school.

"Wave to the princess," Jen said, lifting her arm so high, her raspberry-pink T-shirt cleared the top of her jeans.

Sam loved Jen Kenworthy's sarcasm, but as she stared after the car, she pictured the mansion at Gold Dust Ranch. The Mercedes must have passed within yards of the foreman's house.

"I can't believe they'd drive right past your house and not give you a ride to school." Sam took the snub personally. "What do they think," she sputtered, "you—you've got cooties?"

"Don't bring out the elementary school insults on my account," Jen said, but her eyes sparkled behind her glasses. "I mean, I *am* just the foreman's daughter. The housekeeper wouldn't expect to drive me to school. Besides, Rachel and I don't exactly belong to the same clique."

"I don't care," Sam said.

"Linc told my mom that Rachel rides alone because

she can't be distracted. She uses the drive into Darton to do her homework."

Jen twirled the end of one blond braid. Though she smiled, Sam could tell Jen didn't like being shunned.

"Home. Work." Sam pronounced the words slowly. "Do you think Rachel hasn't quite figured out the concept?"

Jen gave her a grateful grin. "I don't want to be her friend, anyway. In fact, if Dad didn't love the ranch so much and if it weren't for the horses, I'd like to move."

"I believe you."

"You know, when Linc Slocum had his well drilled, it ended up draining too much water from ours. My mom can't do laundry some days, and we have to be careful when we take showers."

"Did you tell him?"

"My dad did, but that was over a year ago. Nothing's changed, and I don't expect it will." Jen shrugged. "He had a bulldozer scrape dirt into a pile, so he could be king of the mountain, where there wasn't even an anthill before!

"Every night before sunset, that huge house casts a shadow over ours." Jen's voice faded to a whisper. "I don't like living in Slocum's shadow."

A crow glided overhead, cawing. Jen looked up and pulled the neck of her T-shirt to cover her lips.

"You're right," she called after the bird. "Blah, blah, blah."

Sam bit her lip. Everything Jen said made Sam like her more. They valued the same things. Since she'd come home from San Francisco, she'd learned that sunsets were more important than fancy houses.

She needed to cheer Jen up.

"Speaking of homework, do you know how to work that fancy calculator of yours?" Sam pointed to the complex grid of buttons and arrows showing through the mesh pocket on Jen's backpack.

Sam could tell by the sudden glow on Jen's face that she'd hit the right topic.

"How to work it? To put it humbly, my dear Samantha"—Jen made a mock bow—"I am a math goddess. My mom quit homeschooling me because I passed her in geometry when I was in fifth grade. This year I'm taking calculus."

"I'm taking algebra for dummies," Sam told her.

Jen tilted her head to one side, and sunlight glazed the lenses of her glasses.

"You can't be taking honors English and remedial math."

"Yes, I can," Sam said, surprised she didn't mind exposing her shortcomings to her new friend. "I am truly *un*gifted with numbers."

"Well, girl," Jen said, giving her a playful punch in the arm, "today's your lucky day."

Chapter 9

SAM'S FIRST WEEK OF SCHOOL ALMOST ENDED well.

She'd been on time for each class. She'd turned in every bit of homework. She liked her teachers, especially Mrs. Ely and Mr. Blair. She'd interviewed the principal, Ms. Santos, and discovered she had humor and a flair for lively language that made writing the interview easy. RJay, *Dialogue*'s editor in chief, read the story and flashed Sam a thumbs-up.

And Sam's locker only jammed once.

The week had grown hotter each day, and no rain was predicted. Dad went about his work with a smile, getting ready to pounce on the one-hundred-degree day when it dawned.

As Jake had said weeks ago, the fall roundup paled in comparison to the cattle drive to summer pasture or the spring roundup. In a single day, the steers vanished off the home range. Dad and Dallas, the gray-haired foreman, shipped them off to market the next day. Now Dad waited for the final tally saying how much they'd earned from the range-fed Herefords.

Best of all, Dad said Sam could ride, come Sunday. The announcement launched her into a dozen daydreams of taking Ace out over the foothills with Jen and her palomino.

In all, the week had been great, except Sam *did* wish Jake hadn't been so busy. With the beginning of school, things had been bound to change, but she was surprised by how much she missed him.

Her spirits lightened, though, when she remembered Jake's birthday. It was still six weeks away, but Sam knew she could count on Gram to do something special, even if they couldn't afford an expensive gift.

Standing at the bus stop on Friday morning, Sam wore a sleeveless blue blouse, but she was already flushed and warm. Dozens of mouse-colored clouds hovered overhead, refusing to offer the coolness of shade. They just made the morning dark.

Sam pulled the pale blue collar away from her neck as she and Jen planned a Sunday ride to War Drum Flats.

The bus was coming. The girls settled their backpacks in place as the diesel huff of the bus drew near. The familiar sound was interrupted by a sudden squeal of tires and screeching brakes.

The murky sky made the car's headlights glare red-gold. The lights veered from side to side, as if pushed by a demonic wind. Sam recognized the car.

Linc Slocum gunned his Cadillac until it lurched within feet of the bus's back bumper. He swerved into the lane for oncoming traffic, then angled across the bus's path and sped forward, toward Jen and Sam.

Sam's hand flew up to cover her lips. Her pulse beat

in her wrists and ankles, even behind her knees, as her heart pounded out a warning. Jen looked suddenly pale but joked through her fear.

She shaded her eyes and squinted at Slocum's car. "As my daddy would say, 'There's a man mad enough to kick a hog.'"

Sam tried to answer in kind. "I can't repeat what my dad would say if he saw Slocum cutting off a school bus."

If only Dad were here.

The bus pulled up beside the Cadillac as Slocum climbed out and rounded the front of his car. The bus driver opened the bus door and shouted, but Slocum paid no attention. He stormed toward the girls, shaking his fist.

In the instant before she understood Slocum's words, Sam saw faces press against the bus window, watching.

"That renegade, that mongrel, that *mutt* of a horse has trespassed"—Slocum took a loud breath, as if the morning air held too little oxygen for his ranting—"on my property. That menace has ruined my investment—"

He must be talking about the Phantom. Had the

mustang destroyed a fence or some rosebushes? What was Slocum yelling about? And why was his shirt buttoned crooked and his jeans hanging over bare ankles and bedroom slippers?

"Mr. Slocum," Jen said quietly. "We don't know what you're talking about."

Slocum kept his back to Jen. He loomed over Sam. She saw sweat beaded on his upper lip, and she heard bus windows slam open so everyone could listen. Oh, great.

With his fingers formed like a child pretending he held a gun, Slocum yelled, "*You* know what I'm talking about. This time it's not some cow pony your silver menace stole. Apache Hotspot is the cornerstone of *my* new breeding program." Slocum's fist struck his chest when he said *my*. "That mare's the investment of a lifetime!"

Finally, Sam understood. Slocum hadn't just purchased the sweet chocolate-and-white Appaloosa as a gift for Rachel. The mare was an investment. And she was gone.

"I want you to call that stud! Call the Phantom!"

Past Slocum, Sam saw Jen's jaw drop in amazement.

Good. Let everyone on the bus see how insane Slocum was. She couldn't call the Phantom. Not really.

"Mr. Slocum, I'm really sorry your horse is—"

"Don't give me that," he snarled. "I want that mustang down here, this minute!" Slocum's face twisted with rage. Any second now, he'd burst a blood vessel.

Sam shrugged out of her backpack and let it drop. There was no place to hide, but she was darn sure she could outrun Slocum. She'd done it before.

From inside the bus, there came a sound like a telephone receiver slamming down. The bus driver tramped down the stairs, and the sound of his approach made Slocum glance back.

"Thank goodness," Jen whispered.

"Sir? I've radioed the sheriff," said the driver. "I think you'd better get back in your car and wait for him."

"The sheriff? Of all the idiotic—" Slocum stopped blustering and took a breath. His tactics changed when he faced an adult. "Guess I did get a little loco, didn't I? Shucks, when a man works hard and sinks his money into a fine piece of horseflesh, it's just downright disappointing to lose it."

Sam shivered. Slocum was talking like a Hollywood cowpoke. The sudden change was spookier than his clenched fist.

The bus driver looked confused, but he motioned the girls toward the safety of the bus and held his other arm out, barring Slocum from following.

The bus swayed as students returned to seats on the opposite side of the bus. Both Sam and Jen noticed and met each other's eyes. Sam hesitated before stepping up.

"There are at least twenty kids on that bus," Sam whispered wildly to Jen. "If each of them gets off at school and tells one person what they saw, that's forty people who know, and if each of them goes to class and tells—"

"I can do the math, Sam. You're right, they'll gossip. But we didn't do anything wrong. We're the victims—or nearly were—of Rachel's nutty father." Jen flinched as Slocum's car door slammed. "The man doesn't do well when he doesn't get his way."

Sam remembered Slocum's rage when Brynna wouldn't allow him to adopt the Phantom. Jen was right.

They spotted an empty double seat about eight rows back from the front of the bus. Jen and Sam took it. For a minute, all was quiet. The bus doors closed. The driver put the vehicle into gear and pulled back onto the road.

Sam kept her eyes focused on the seat back in front of her, until a boy across the aisle poked her arm.

"Hey, what was wrong with him?"

Sam shrugged. "I guess he lost his horse."

From the corner of her eye, Sam saw Jen smile, but then an avalanche of questions began.

"Was he talking about the Phantom?"

"Did he think the Phantom stole something?"

"Yeah, like a ghost cares about mortal mares." That speaker wore glasses and pushed them back up his nose in a superior fashion.

Sam's relief froze. Did everyone know the legend? She racked her brain for a clever answer.

"I don't know," she said.

A girl with a pierced nostril turned in the seat just

ahead. Sam searched her mind for the girl's name. Callie, that was it. The girl was in her Spanish class.

"It sounded like he thought you were a witch," Callie said. "Like you could conjure the stallion to come to you."

"Now, *that's* crazy talk," Jen said.

"But she is from San Francisco," Callie pointed out.

Jen laughed. "They carry briefcases there, Callie, not magic wands."

The remark got a laugh. As the tension around her evaporated, Sam looked at her watch. She shook her wrist. She couldn't believe it was only eight o'clock.

Sam took the glass of lemonade Gram handed her as she walked into the kitchen after school. She felt light-headed and weird after the long, hot walk home, but not so weird she didn't notice four unbaked pies and six pans of lasagna crowded side by side on the kitchen counter. Oddest of all was Gram's expression.

"What's wrong?" Sam asked. She held the glass against her cheek instead of drinking.

"The check Dallas brought home for the cattle wasn't much," Gram said. "We barely broke even."

Sam sipped the lemonade.

"What does that mean?" she asked. "That we can't pay back the loans from last year?"

Gram nodded. "We'll talk tonight. Your dad's doing that last cutting of alfalfa with the hands. He left a message on the Elys' phone, too, hoping Jake and his brothers can help. Wyatt's worried it will start pouring and hurt the hay."

"*Pouring?* It's like an oven out there," Sam said. "Dad wanted a one-hundred-degree day, and this is it."

"Look at that sky, young lady." Gram pointed toward the window. "It's tight as the head of a drum. The weather stations say this is a window between two storms."

"If it starts to rain now, is the hay ruined?"

"Not necessarily. Once the hay is cut and baled, a single hot day can dry it," Gram said. "Your dad's got it cut. If they can get it baled today, we might be all right."

Gram sipped her own lemonade before adding, "I just hope my old granny wasn't right. She said when hens left off laying for no good reason, they were predicting hailstorms."

Sam rubbed her hand across her eyes. She'd really wanted to tell Gram what had happened this morning.

The halls had been abuzz before Sam even reached her first-period class. By second period, people were outright staring at her and Jen. When Rachel Slocum had left school "sick," everyone pitied poor Rachel, whose father was out of control. By the time her last class began, Sam had heard gossip saying he'd run the school bus off the road into a ditch.

With rumors flying, Sam longed to tell Gram the truth before she heard something worse. But Gram and Dad were fretting over money and weather and saving the hay crop. This might not be the best time to mention she hadn't had such a great day either.

"If I don't put on shorts, I'll pass out." Sam stood up and headed toward her bedroom, but stopped before she reached the stairs. "I bet there's something I should be doing to help."

"See to the animals, then come help me cook."

Gram gestured toward the pans of lasagna. "The cowboys will eat here tonight, and if the Elys come, that makes seven extra men for dinner. Even with a small cutting, they'll work up an appetite." Gram fanned herself with a dish towel.

Sam had jogged halfway up the stairs when she heard Gram mutter, "And I don't know where I'll find the strength to turn on that oven."

Buddy didn't seem to think the storm would hold off another day. Or maybe she'd picked up on Sam's worry over the branding.

The calf mooed and pressed against the fence rails, trying to follow Sam as she did chores. When the skies darkened and a tumbleweed skittered across the yard, Buddy bucked and bawled, certain the weed had blown in off the range to devour her.

Finally, Sam put Buddy inside the barn. She was scattering extra straw in the box stall when she heard a truck.

Sam sprinted outside. Jake was alone in the truck. Maybe he'd already dropped his brothers at the hay field. It didn't matter. All week she'd wanted to ask Jake if he'd rope Buddy tomorrow for the branding. Not only was he skillful with the lariat, but Jake would be gentle.

If she said that, he'd be embarrassed.

Jake reached inside the truck for his Stetson. Ready for hot-weather work, he wore a sleeveless white undershirt and jeans. As he pulled his Stetson down low, Sam saw the wind catch the long hair he'd tamed with a leather thong. He slammed the door of the pickup and glanced toward the house but kept walking her way.

Sam swallowed hard. This was really stupid. She shouldn't be so glad to see Jake. Or so uneasy. When he got close enough to take her in a one-armed bear hug and walk her back inside the barn, she was happier than she'd been all week.

Jake bumped up the brim of his hat to get a better look at her. "So, how was your mornin', Brat?"

"You heard?" she asked, though she doubted anyone at Darton High hadn't.

"Do I have ears?" Jake waited, thumbs hooked in his belt loops.

"Linc Slocum is not a healthy man," she said.

"He's a real self-centered son of a gun." Jake stared at the barn floor as he spoke. "I know that for a fact, but don't tell me he laid a hand on you or Jen."

When Jake looked up, his eyes were hard.

"He didn't," Sam said quickly.

"Good thing."

Sam didn't ask why. She could figure it out for herself. Though their parents didn't approve, the Ely boys had reputations for settling disputes with their fists.

With a yap of greeting, Blaze bounded into the barn. He stood next to Jake, bumping against his leg, inviting a pat. Jake slid his hand down the dog's back, then straightened.

"My brothers are helping your dad. My dad will be along soon. I better hightail it down there." Jake didn't move, though his bootheels creaked as his weight shifted.

"I've got to help Gram make garlic biscuits to go with the lasagna." Sam didn't know what she was waiting for. Then she blurted, "We're supposed to brand Buddy tomorrow."

"There's no cause to be sentimental over that." Jake squared his shoulders and looked down on her like he had since she was five years old.

"It's not that I'm sentimental over Buddy," she tried to explain. "It's all this other stuff."

Jake brushed her off with a single word. "Yeah," he said. "Gotta go."

He did.

Sam held Blaze's collar to keep him from following. As he started the truck and drove off, Sam sent a frown after Jake.

"Thanks for nothing, you turkey." Sam released the dog's collar, made sure Buddy's stall was latched, and headed for the house.

Hot wind spun the dust from Jake's tires in a whirlwind. It danced across the ranch yard, causing horses to pin back their ears in warning.

Chapter 10

THE HAILSTORM STARTED AND ENDED before dark.

While Gram showered, Sam put two pans of biscuits in to bake. First, she heard a pinging sound, then a tapping, next a rattling like machine-gun fire in a movie.

Sam hurried to the window. In the ten-acre pasture, the horses galloped like a wild herd. Heads and tails flung high, they raced around the pasture as if trying to outrun the hail. For five minutes, ice pellets showered from the sky, bouncing like Ping-Pong balls as they hit the ground. Minutes later, the storm stopped, leaving the evening sky blue-gold and scoured clean.

"Is something burning?" Gram called from upstairs.

Sam jerked the biscuits from the oven, then waited for Gram to tell her what the hailstorm would mean for the hay.

"Not good." Gram rushed into the kitchen in a pink gingham blouse and fresh jeans. She tugged one end of the kitchen table and added another leaf to make it longer. "Not good at all, but Wyatt should have it baled by now, and he's got tarps to cover the hay. It won't dry out there now. He'll just have to bring it in and feed it. Or sell it right away."

With company coming for dinner, Sam wanted to change out of the red tank top and white shorts she'd put on after school. But there was no time.

All of a sudden, trucks came roaring in, and men in cowboy hats were everywhere.

Sam lifted the kitchen curtain just enough to watch them wash up outside and use a big purple first aid kit from the Elys' truck to bandage Seth Ely's hand. Their voices drifted through the open window.

"Whoee, that thing's so purple, it could blind a man," Dallas joked.

"Yeah," said Luke, Jake's father. "But if a man needs a first aid kit, he doesn't want to spend all day looking for it."

When the men began stomping mud off their boots on the front porch, Sam moved away from the window just in time. All at once a cluster of men followed Dad inside. Each hung his hat on the hat rack, until it was full. Then they used the coat rack.

Sam hustled between the stove and the table, carrying the full platters Gram handed her. She slipped into her chair just before Dad said grace, but her eyes were only half-closed. Dad's forehead furrowed as he thanked God for the food and the safety of the men who'd helped with the haying. While Dad prayed, Dallas rubbed his temples and sighed.

Then, like in a scene from a movie, the subdued meal was devoured to the clatter of knives and forks. In those movies, the farm wife didn't sit down and eat, but Gram pulled up a chair long before the meal ended.

Sam wanted to catch Jake's eye and get a feel for just how serious things were, but each time she tried, Jake's brothers noticed. So did his father.

Luke was a handsome but harsh-looking man. Like most of the others, he didn't say a word during dinner, but Sam couldn't help comparing him to his sons. His face had more sharp edges than Jake's, but when Sam brought him pie and coffee, Luke's smile made her grin right back.

As if the smile loosened his jaw, Luke said, "I could use some of that hay if you come up with extra."

Dad's mouth lifted at one corner, but the expression wasn't a smile. Why not? Sam wondered. Dad needed to use or sell the hay before it spoiled.

"Thanks, Luke." Dad sounded as if Luke had offered a favor.

"I haven't shipped my herd yet. You raise high-protein feed. I could use some," Luke repeated.

One of Jake's brothers, the one with the bandaged

hand, spoke next. "I have a friend who trains jumpers up at Lake Tahoe. She's always looking for high-quality hay. I could drive some up to her if you can spare it."

"Go ahead and call her," Dad said. He held a fork, but he hadn't yet cracked the crust of his pie. "If the flatbed can make it up there, that'd be fine."

Dad flushed as if he were embarrassed, but Sam didn't understand why until the men rose to leave.

Sam blinked at all the tall, browned men. It was as if a redwood forest had sprouted in the kitchen.

The boys walked ahead, but Dad paused in the doorway and shook Luke Ely's hand.

"It's not so humiliatin' when you're bailed out by good friends," Dad said.

"Don't know what you're talking about, Wyatt. You're the one doin' me a favor." Luke clapped Dad on the back with the same energy he might've used to appreciate a horse.

It was easy to see Luke's generosity and know that when the time came, Dad would help the Elys, too.

The brothers clambered into the truck bed,

haggling for the best seats, and Sam hoped only Jake would hear her.

"Jake?" She tried to call quietly, but all the Elys looked.

Even though there were no lights in the ranch yard, Sam's white shorts made her all too visible. Jake's brothers elbowed him, joshed him, and one mimicked Sam, calling his name in a high voice. All the same, Jake walked with solid steps back to meet her.

"Yeah?" he said, holding his hat and looking at her sideways, as if she'd scold him.

"Could I ask you a favor, please?"

He nodded with long-suffering patience.

"I've been thinking about this all evening, kind of rehearsing, so I don't do anything dumb like cry," Sam said. "Tomorrow, when we brand Buddy, could you—do you mind—" She stopped, made a smoothing motion with her hands as if steadying her mind was that easy. "Would you please be the one to rope Buddy?"

Sam remembered the way a rider roped a calf's two

hind legs, then dragged her the short distance to the branding fire. Done correctly, it was quick. But Sam had seen ropers catch only one hoof or lasso the calf's tail along with a leg. Often, horses took a while to get into position, and cowboys ended up chasing the calf until it was terrified.

But not Witch and Jake. Together, they were a synchronized roping team. She trusted them.

"Why me?" Jake asked.

"Because you'll get it right the first time," Sam said. Jake looked bashful, and she was afraid he'd refuse out of modesty.

"Because if you do it," Sam added, "Buddy won't be scared any longer than she has to be."

Jake groaned.

"Samantha, you drive me crazy." He shook his head and glared at the night sky as if the stars ought to help him out. "What if I miss?"

"You won't!" Sam took two light steps away. His disgusted expression said she'd better escape before he changed his mind.

From the front porch steps, Dad called, "Fire ought to be ready by seven thirty, Jake."

Dad had been listening all along. Drenched with embarrassment, Sam looked at Jake, spreading her hands in a gesture of helplessness.

"Yes, sir," Jake called, and he seemed just fine as he strode back to his father's truck.

Sam didn't feel fine.

"There's no privacy around this place," she said, letting the door slam behind her as she entered the kitchen. "Not a bit!"

Dad didn't look properly ashamed.

"Sure there is, honey." Gram sounded sympathetic, but her smile held some sort of trick. "Your dad and I are going into the living room to watch a little television."

Gram untied her apron, handed it to Sam, and nodded at a sink stacked high with dirty dishes. "You can have the kitchen all to yourself."

Sage-spiced smoke made its way into Sam's bedroom, waking her with thoughts of branding. It was Saturday.

She *could* sleep in, but then she thought of Buddy. The calf had no idea what the day held for her. Suddenly, Sam was wide awake.

She swung her feet out of bed and stood. Through her nightgown, Sam touched her hip. She'd hate to have a scar burned on her skin.

Dad expected her help. She, Dad, and Jake would do the branding. Once the iron was heated, Jake would ride into the ten-acre pasture and rope Buddy. Sam would swing open the gate, let Jake ride through with the calf, slam the gate, then run to where Dad waited with the branding iron.

Sam didn't feel like eating. She skipped breakfast and went outside. The hens fluttered at the sight of her and scurried away. Dad squatted beside a little campfire.

He didn't give orders, but Sam knew what to do. She gathered an armload of sagebrush and stacked it near the fire. After a few minutes, Sam realized she and Dad both stood with arms crossed, staring down into the flames. Dad seemed even quieter than usual, probably because of the hailstorm and lost winter fodder.

Dad scooted the business end of the branding iron into the fire. After a while, he rotated it a turn. He did that every so often, sometimes pulling it from the fire and blowing on the iron to scatter the ash. He checked the iron's progress as it turned from black to gray to red.

Sam snapped a piece of twisted gray sagebrush into small lengths and dropped them into the fire.

"That's enough," Dad said.

Sam realized she was feeding the fire to keep from imagining the searing pain from that hot iron.

From the instant Jake loped over the wooden bridge and into the ranch yard, he and Dad communicated in silence. Though they didn't wiggle their ears at each other like horses, Dad used only a few gestures to outline the plan he'd explained to Sam last night. And Jake nodded.

It was clear to Sam that both men wanted this operation over with quickly. So did Sam, but she had the feeling Dad and Jake felt embarrassed about making such a fuss over a solitary calf.

She knew they were doing it for her.

At last Dad drew the branding iron out, blew on it, and looked up at Sam.

"That's what we've been waiting for," he said, showing her the metal had turned gray-white.

As Jake limbered up his rope and Witch danced in excitement, Sam jogged to the pasture and opened the gate. The horses stopped grazing to watch Witch lope past, and Buddy glanced up. Grass fell from her lips. She looked to the horses for advice and then, bewildered, jogged in the direction Jake herded her.

Sam blinked back tears. She refused to cry, but Buddy's confusion made Sam's heart ache.

Closer and closer Jake herded the calf. Was he going to ride past the open gate and rope the tiny black hooves somewhere farther out? At last, just before the gate, Jake leaned forward and gently cast the loop over Buddy's hind legs. She fell almost at Sam's feet, and Jake rode through, dragging her mere yards to where Dad waited.

Sam latched the gate and sprinted after them. She

knelt at Buddy's head, steadying her, looking into the calf's frightened eyes.

"It's okay, Buddy," she crooned, and then there was a sizzle, a thread of pungent smoke, and the branding iron was lifted.

"Go," Dad said.

The rope that was stretched tight between Buddy and Jake now slackened as Witch stepped forward.

Quick as her shaking fingers could move, Sam slipped the loop from Buddy's legs.

She rocked the calf. "You can get up, baby."

Buddy scrambled to her feet, staggered a step, then stampeded toward the barn, her tail held straight up.

"Go on after her," Dad said. "You can sleep in the barn tonight, too, if you want."

Amazed but afraid to stay around in case he changed his mind, Sam followed Buddy.

Last night Dad had told her that mother cows always rushed to nurse their calves after the traumatic experience of branding.

Though Buddy ate mostly grass these days, Sam had

left a bottle in the box stall, just in case. What worked for other calves might work for Buddy.

It did. As soon as Sam offered the bottle, Buddy latched her lips around the nipple. She tugged and sucked, gazing up at Sam with accusing eyes. "It's okay, baby," Sam said. "Now you won't get lost, ever."

At last the calf's eyes closed. She drew on the nipple more slowly, and her tail stopped switching from side to side. Buddy's knees buckled wearily. With a shuddering sigh like a baby who's cried itself to sleep, Buddy collapsed into the straw. Her long white eyelashes fluttered, and then she napped.

Sam felt almost like she'd been napping when she emerged from the dim barn. When she saw Dad standing with his arm around Brynna Olson, she knew she was dreaming.

From the small corral, Ace nickered.

"Tomorrow, boy," she said.

Ace stamped his hoof impatiently. For the first time since she'd come home, Sam didn't answer the gelding's summons. She had to see what was going on with Dad and Brynna.

A quick glance showed her the white BLM truck. Another look, as she walked closer, showed Sam her imagination had run away with her.

Dad's arm lay along the top fence rail, *not* around Brynna Olson. Still, Brynna stood pretty close. She was talking to Dad and having to look up at him. Dad was looking down and listening intently.

Sam paused next to the big flatbed truck Dad had pulled out of the barn. She wasn't spying on them, exactly, or even hiding. She just happened to stop and tie her shoe where they wouldn't see her.

Sam crouched there, listening. The conversation she overheard was definitely not romantic.

"Wyatt, I do believe you're the most bullheaded man I've met," said Brynna Olson. "This is a great job, with a terrific salary, using horseman's skills you've mastered. Your contract would run from November to March—months your cattle pretty much take care of themselves—and still, you turn me down."

Brynna had gone from leaning on the fence beside Dad to standing in front of him, hands on her hips.

"Just tell me why," Brynna demanded.

"I work for myself—no one else," Dad said. "And for darn sure, not for the government."

Brynna threw her hands in the air with a strangled little scream of frustration. Sam covered her mouth, smothering a giggle. She'd never heard an adult make that particular sound, but she knew exactly how Brynna felt.

Dad's jaw was set hard, and he wore his stubborn-mule face. No one would be able to budge him.

"Part of this is selfish," Brynna admitted. "I need to go to Washington for some meetings. I'd like everything *not* to fall apart while I'm gone." She tilted her head to one side, as if she were talking to a small child or a smart dog. And she waited.

"Yeah," Dad said.

"Someone from Las Vegas will fill in for me while I'm gone." Brynna let that sink in for a minute. "I don't want my replacement to hand this wrangler's position over to some dude who doesn't know how to ride, or worse, some yahoo who treats horses like machines!"

Brynna was so wound up, she missed it, but Sam saw Dad nearly laugh out loud. That was why he was nodding, all serious, as he looked down at the boot he was scuffing in the dirt. Yep, Dad thought "yahoo" was pretty funny.

"You know, Brynna—" Dad began.

Whoa. When did Dad start calling Miss Olson 'Brynna'?

"—I appreciate the offer, but you're not going to change my mind."

"Because it's a government job."

"Because it's working for somebody else."

Sam couldn't figure Dad out. Had he forgotten about the hailstorm, about the drought-thin cattle that sold for next to nothing, about the school clothes and horse vaccinations and windmill parts he couldn't afford?

Out of nowhere, a hand clamped over Sam's mouth. A strong arm jerked her backward. She slammed down on the seat of her jeans in the dust. And then she was looking up into Jake's mischievous brown eyes.

She tried to shake her lips loose from his hand as he whispered, "Getting yourself quite an earful, Brat?"

Chapter 11

"WHAT ARE YOU KIDS DOING?" DAD'S VOICE boomed like an explosion, when their scuffling drew his attention.

"You are so dead," Sam said. Since she barely breathed the words, Sam wasn't certain Jake heard, but she'd bet her eyes were shooting fire. Even Jake wasn't too dense to understand *that*.

Together, they stood. Sam waved, but Dad didn't look amused. By the time they walked within range, Brynna Olson saved them from making excuses. Brynna knew they'd been eavesdropping. She showed it by blushing to the roots of her red hair, but she refused to let her humiliation last.

"You two know about Slocum's Appaloosa, I suppose."

"Yeah," Jake said. "I've seen rails down on his fences. She could've been restless in her new corral and walked off."

"It's possible," Brynna said.

"I know Slocum thinks the Phantom stole her," Sam said, "but it wasn't him."

"Just how do you know what Linc Slocum's thinking?" Dad said the words slowly, warning Sam he wasn't happy.

"He, uh, talked to me at the bus stop yesterday."

"So I heard." Dad's voice dropped even lower. "I don't like being the last to know an adult threatened my daughter."

"He didn't. Not really. He never said he'd hurt me," Sam assured her father. "He just loomed over me and Jen. He had the crazy idea I could whistle and the Phantom would come running. With his Appaloosa, I guess."

Although no one turned to look at the river, Sam was pretty sure Jake, Brynna, and Dad were listening to the La Charla's rushing, remembering she'd met the Phantom there, more than once.

"I wanted to tell you and Gram," Sam defended herself. "But things were complicated yesterday—with the haying and storm and ten people for dinner."

"Doesn't matter," Dad said. "If Slocum—if anyone—does something like that again, I want to know right away. No matter what."

There was a moment's silence before Brynna spoke.

"Of course, Slocum wants the bureau to catch the horse. He called yesterday, after his chat with Sheriff Ballard." Brynna hid her smile. "He demanded I catch this renegade stallion. In all probability it *is* a mustang, and I'm trying to hire a wrangler to trap the stud." Brynna brushed a wisp of red hair back toward her French braid. "But I'm not having much luck."

The Phantom probably wasn't to blame, but if it did turn out to be him, Sam couldn't hope for a better wrangler than Dad. If Dad trapped the Phantom, he'd treat him with respect, not violence.

Sam glanced Dad's way. As if he could read her mind, he crossed his arms. Tight.

Brynna Olson probably had a better chance of changing Dad's mind than Sam did. The best thing she could do was vanish and hope they worked it out.

"Dad, is it okay if I go to Alkali with Jake to pick up some chick-scratch?" Sam noticed, from the corner of her eye, that Jake looked completely confused, so she rushed on. "Gram forgot to get it when we were in Darton buying school clothes and . . ."

"Go ahead." Dad extracted several dollar bills from his wallet. Sam had started picturing cheeseburgers at Clara's coffee shop when he said, "Gas money. That Buick drinks like a fish."

"Thanks," Sam said.

She was leading a baffled Jake away when she heard Brynna say something softly. As always, conversation that sounded like a secret caught Sam's attention.

"That's assuming it was a horse that stole his new Appaloosa."

"Wasn't it?" Dad asked.

"Slocum made a big show of buying that mare and having her delivered. Transport in that horse van cost a thousand dollars a day. He pointed out that Sam had talked with the driver about the Appaloosa's registration and pedigree."

"Don't tell me he thinks Sam had anything to do—"

Even though it was a bad idea to interrupt her father, Sam couldn't stop.

"What?" Sam whipped around and marched back toward the two adults.

"Samantha, eavesdropping is a nasty habit," Dad cautioned. "You rarely hear anything good about yourself."

"But wait—now I'm a *horse thief*?"

"Sam." Brynna used a soothing tone. "It was mentioned in anger. I don't think Mr. Slocum is going anywhere with the idea."

"He'd better not!" Sam's pulse pounded in her temples. "I'll—I'll—"

To save her from figuring out what she'd do to Linc Slocum, Jake snagged Sam's elbow and tugged her toward Gram's boat of a Buick.

"Sit in the car and polish your six-shooter, Calamity Jane. I'll go get the car keys from your grandma."

It turned out Sam wasn't the only one Linc Slocum had threatened. The Phantom had a price on his head.

In Alkali, Jake and Sam split up to do errands, but they discovered Slocum's campaign against the stallion almost at the same time.

Jake saw the first wanted poster as he paid for a bag of chicken food at Phil's Fill-Up. After reading the poster, Jake hurried from the store, slung the burlap bag into the Buick's trunk, then rushed to tell Sam.

He found her right where she was supposed to be, in Clara's coffee shop buying sodas and french fries to go.

A bell jingled as Jake entered the diner, but Sam didn't notice. She stood reading another wanted poster taped next to the cash register.

A full-color picture of Apache Hotspot topped the

poster. Sam finished staring at it to glance at Jake and then began to read the print aloud.

"'Five-thousand-dollar reward for information leading to safe recovery of Apache Hotspot, three-year-old running Appaloosa mare, white with liver chestnut markings.'" Sam grabbed Jake by the shoulders and tried to give him a shake.

"I know," he said, glancing at Clara, who stood at the open cash register, ready to take payment for the food. "I saw—"

Sam released her grip and tapped the bottom half of the poster, illustrated with a charcoal sketch of a rearing wild horse that looked like the Phantom.

"But wait," she said. "He can advertise for his own horse. What he *can't* do is this." Sam read, "'Five-thousand-dollar additional reward for capture of stallion implicated in theft of aforementioned mare.'"

"Honey, you gonna give me that money or stand there clutchin' it all day?" Clara tugged the dollar bills peeking from the fist Sam had crumpled them in as she read the poster.

"Oh yeah." Sam surrendered the money. "Sorry."

Jake carried the fries and sodas toward the door. Sam followed, her mind spinning with questions.

Wasn't it illegal for Slocum to distribute or put up that poster? What would Slocum do with the Phantom once he had him? Turn him over to BLM for relocation?

Sam stopped in the middle of the sidewalk, remembering what Slocum had said. BLM wouldn't relocate a known troublemaker. BLM would shoot him.

"Sit." Jake nodded at a wooden bench in the sunshine.

"I'm not your dog," Sam reminded him.

"True, but you're walking like a zombie." He nodded at the box of fries. "Dr. Jake's fat, salt, and sugar diet ought to fix you up."

Sam ate.

She worried about Buddy.

She drained her soda.

She watched three cars cruise down Alkali's main street.

She saw a cat on a fence post cleaning her paws and whiskers.

After all that, she knew what they were going to do.

"I've got a plan," Sam said, using a fry to pick up a few stray crystals of salt.

"I was afraid of that."

Sam turned to see why Jake's voice sounded muffled. He leaned back on the bench, Stetson pulled down to cover his eyes.

She couldn't believe it. Nearly every rancher around here was broke. They'd all try to win that money from Slocum before BLM stopped him from handing it out. The cruel, old-fashioned mustanging tricks would be used in secret if the price was right. How could Jake take a nap when the Phantom's life was at stake?

Sam snatched his Stetson.

"I'm awake." Jake sat up, blinking. "I could hear you getting yourself all worked up, Samantha. So, what's your plan?"

"First, we'll call Brynna and tell her what Slocum's doing. This encourages people to do the same kind of harassment of wild horses that kept Slocum from being able to adopt a mustang, right?"

"You know she's left River Bend by now, and it's Saturday. The Willow Springs office won't be open. Do you have her home phone number?"

Sam glared at Jake. "No, but I'll call her on Monday. Anyway, here's part two. You and I will find that stallion."

"Super." Jake grabbed his hat off her lap. "I'm sure the idea hasn't crossed anybody else's mind."

"Jake, why are you giving me a hard time?"

"I'm not, Sam. Just trying to offer a little common sense. Besides, I'm surprised you want him caught. You're the one who convinced Brynna to let him go." Jake gave a disappointed shrug. "Guess it is a lot of money."

"Do you think I'd sell him out for money?" Sam crumpled the cardboard french fry box.

Insulted and angry, she stormed down the sidewalk to a trash barrel. When Jake didn't come after her, she walked back.

"I wouldn't sell *you* out for money," she told him. "And you deserve it."

Jake considered her words as if she'd spoken in another language. "I don't know what that means," he said.

"Never mind." Sam sighed. "The point is, the stallion Slocum wants isn't the Phantom. It's Hammer."

Once Jake pledged his silence, Sam told him about the blue roan she'd seen running along the pasture fence at River Bend. She described Hammer's attempt to take the Phantom's mares, too.

"He's the one," she said.

"You're probably right, but Slocum won't go for it. He's wanted the Phantom ever since he heard about him. This is just another way to get him."

Sam placed her hands on her knees and frowned down at the sidewalk between her shoes. Slocum had convinced himself the Phantom had Hotspot, but she had to prove him wrong. Just next to her shoe, a red ant scuttled along the hot concrete, carrying a piece of straw ten times longer than its body. If it could do that, she could do this.

"Got it," she said, smiling at Jake. "We catch them both. We track, then camp out as long as we have to, or use relays of horses to chase them. If Hotspot and Hammer are together, he's the thief, right? Slocum would have no choice but to believe us." Sam rubbed her hands together. "Then I'll give Dad the ten thousand dollars and he won't have to worry about money for a while, and he'll be so grateful, he won't even consider grounding me again."

Sam sighed with pleasure. She held her face up to the sunlight and basked. She imagined plunking down the money for the beautiful bridle she'd seen at Crane Crossing. She could see herself helping Jake buckle it onto Witch's shining black head. Then she realized that even for Jake, he'd been quiet too long.

Sure enough, when she looked over, Jake was smirking.

"What?" Sam demanded.

"I just noticed this little problem you have," he said.

"Oh, really?"

"Yep. For a girl in honors English, you have this weird little sentence structure defect."

"Defect?"

"Sam"—Jake sounded sympathetic—"I'm not sure what else to call it. All along, while you're talking about stalking the stallion and catching the stallion and dragging the stallion and Hotspot back to Slocum, you're saying 'we.' Then, when you reach the part about spending the reward money, all of a sudden, it's about you."

Jake planted his hat on his head before striding to Gram's Buick.

Sam sighed. Had she really hurt Jake's feelings, or was he teasing? Sometimes she just couldn't tell.

This time it might be better to give in, because Jake was right. She had forgotten about splitting the reward money.

Sam jogged to catch up with him. "Jake, of course we'll share. I'm sorry I forgot."

"Just thought I'd mention it," he said. "'Cause I've got my eye on something a mite more stylish than this"—he patted the top of Gram's Buick—"and five thousand dollars would make a mighty nice down payment."

She had Jake on her side, Sam thought as they drove toward home. Now only two barriers stood between her and that $10,000: Dad and Gram.

Sam thought of the ant. Of course she could convince Gram and Dad that the money was worth the puny risk, but just in case she was wrong, she'd wait until tomorrow to ask.

It was a good thing she was sleeping in the barn, so she wouldn't be tempted to ask too soon.

Chapter 12

IN SAM'S DREAM, THE BARN COLLAPSED. Boards groaned, broke, and rained down in dagger-sharp splinters, making the horses scream.

Her eyes opened to the interior of the dark barn. She made out Buddy's silhouette just as the calf stepped on her arm.

"Ow!" Sam yelped, and the calf jumped over Sam's sleeping bag to stare, trembling, at the barn door.

Horses *were* screaming. It wasn't just a nightmare.

A low, guttural neigh vibrated through the night.

Hooves struck the small corral. A familiar whinny made Sam struggle out of her sleeping bag and run toward the danger.

"Ace!" Sam kicked through the deep straw, past Buddy, and shouldered through the barn door.

Something huge as a polar bear sideswiped Sam. She grabbed at air, then fell as the thing crashed into the fence.

Rocks stabbed Sam's knees, and she crossed her arms over her head, protecting herself, even as she begged her eyes to pierce the darkness and see what monster was scaring the horses.

Slats of wood crashed inward.

Sweetheart squealed. Heavy bodies rubbed against the fence. The low, guttural neigh mixed with Ace's clear mustang call, and Sam knew.

Hammer! The blue roan had come for Sweetheart, but Ace wouldn't let her go without a fight. Sam heard teeth clack. Ace's slim shadow rose, and by the arch of his neck, she guessed the gelding's jaws closed in a savage bite on the stallion's withers. Hammer wrenched loose and wheeled away. Hooves thudded on hide. A confusion of sounds came all at once, and then there was the sound of galloping.

They swept by. Two horses running. A third fought free of cracking wood and launched an awkward jump over the downed fence rails.

"Ace, no! No!"

A starred forehead swung toward her. Ace slowed, hooves stuttering on the hard-packed ranch yard. The porch light flashed on, etching him in a dark silhouette.

For an instant, hesitation made Ace beautiful. His body aimed for the mountains, but his head, with delicate, inquiring ears, turned toward her. "Get inside!" Dad yelled from the porch.

His voice held a kind of command she'd never heard before. And his hands carried a rifle.

Sam ducked back inside the barn, but she didn't close the door. Heartbeat battering her ribs, she flattened herself beside the doorway. From there, she could sort of see and definitely hear what was going on.

Dad rarely took the rifle from the locked gun case.

All the commotion must have convinced him she was in danger.

But she wasn't. And she must keep Ace safe.

"They're gone!" she yelled to Dad. "It's just Ace—and me!"

Outside the barn door, hooves tapped and circled. Then Ace swung his head over Sam's and snorted.

"Ace, here boy." Sam reached up. Her hand grazed the flat fur of his cheek, and Ace lowered his head to nuzzle her.

Breath sweet with alfalfa, Ace moved his lips over Sam's face, then her neck. Then he nosed her hard, maybe irritated that she'd halted his headlong run into the mountains.

"You wouldn't have liked it," Sam told him. "Hammer would have hurt you if you'd tried to go with him and Sweetheart. You know that, don't you, sweet boy?"

As she calmed Ace, Sam realized Blaze had been barking from inside the house for a long time, and Dallas had shouted, "Boss?" from across the ranch yard more than once.

Then Sam heard the crunch of Dad's boots, and he asked, "Who're you talking to, Samantha?"

"Ace." Sam braced for the remark that she babied her horse, but the comment didn't come. "The stallion—it wasn't the Phantom. You could see that, couldn't you?"

Dad shook his head. What did that mean?

"Is he all right?" Dad extended a hand toward Ace, but the gelding shied. "Let's get some light on."

"Hush, Buddy," Sam told the bawling calf. Buddy stumbled along behind her.

"Dad, couldn't you tell it wasn't the Phantom?"

Dad crossed to a light switch and the barn brightened, but he didn't answer.

"Dad, did you see—"

"Let's help the horse who depends on you."

Sam winced at Dad's words.

Mustangs usually took care of themselves. But when Hammer attacked, Ace had been penned, unable to use speed to escape.

She haltered Ace and stood beside him, stroking his

cheek while Dad examined him. Hammer's teeth had slashed five rips on the gelding's rump.

"Just when you were all healed up," Sam said. She let Ace nibble her fingers, glad he couldn't see the new injuries over the old scars.

"They don't look bad," Dad said. "We'll clean them up and cover them with some antiseptic salve, and he'll be fine. I'm more worried about this tenderness."

Ace pulled away as Dad touched his chest.

"He was fighting to keep Sweetheart."

"I heard him." Dad straightened and kneaded the skin at the base of Ace's ears. The gelding blew breath through his lips, relaxing. "He's a good pony, this one."

Out in the yard, the Buick's engine roared to life and sped away. Sam looked at her watch. It was three o'clock in the morning, and even Buddy had decided to go back to sleep.

"Where's Gram going?"

"She's going after Sweetheart." Dad sighed. "But I think that stud will herd Sweetheart clear out of here."

Dad glanced after the Buick's red taillights. "I told your gram so, but she has other ideas."

With two rails broken on the small corral, it was safer to leave Ace inside the barn. Dad tended to Ace's injuries and whipped up a warm bran mash for the gelding, and they left him in a box stall next to Buddy's.

Since Dad had cooked for the horse and Gram was still out searching for Sweetheart, it was only fair that Sam made breakfast. She watched Dad walk out to the road to get the Sunday paper. Letting the door slam behind her, Sam hurried to the kitchen and rubbed her hands together. Even if it didn't measure up to Gram's cooking, Sam knew she could have a meal ready—or at least started—when Dad returned.

She used packaged biscuit mix instead of measuring flour and baking powder. The biscuits were already baking as she heated a skillet and broke two eggs into its center. Sam hummed and the eggs sputtered. She was well on her way to making fried eggs just the way Dad liked them, until she reached the flipping-over part. She ended up serving them scrambled, but Dad didn't seem to notice.

"Good job, Sam," he said, from behind the newspaper.

Yawning with satisfaction, Sam was just loading strawberry jam onto a biscuit when Dad gave a long whistle of amazement.

His eyes were on the Darton newspaper as he folded back pages to show her a large advertisement.

Sam put the biscuit down and stared. Slocum had gone one step further in his campaign against the Phantom.

"Is this advertisement the same as the posters you and Jake told me about?" Dad tapped the sketch of the Phantom.

Sam nodded. Exactly the same, except she'd bet the Darton paper went to hundreds, maybe a thousand subscribers.

"This just won't do." Dad sat back, frowning. "The range is gonna be crawling with bounty hunters trying to lasso every mustang out there."

Sam decided the time was right to mention her plan.

"We should hop in the truck and get a head start," Sam said. "Jake and I discussed it yesterday. He's a great tracker. I've got pretty good horse sense and—" Sam checked Dad's expression and saw he wasn't going along with her. "At least that's what you said, didn't you—that I had good horse sense?"

"*Pretty* good," Dad said. "But, Sam, it's flat illegal."

"Only the mustang part," Sam contradicted him, then hurried to agree. "Probably BLM should know about this."

"Probably they already do," Dad said.

"Just in case they don't, I thought I'd call Miss Olson tomorrow, as soon as the BLM office opens."

"Why wait?" Dad surprised Sam by opening a drawer and extracting a business card with a phone number and the word *cell* inked on the back. A question flickered across Sam's mind. Why did Dad have Brynna's cell phone number? Was he considering the wild horse wrangler's job after all? The answer didn't matter today, and as it turned out, neither did having the number.

All day long, Brynna Olson's telephone rang and rang, but no one answered.

Sam could remember one other time she'd seen Gram this cranky. That time she'd been worried over Sam. This time she feared for Sweetheart. Gram had found no sign of the horses, and she didn't want to discuss her search. Instead, she instructed Sam to clean up the kitchen, do her outside chores, fold laundry, and finish her homework before riding with Jen.

Complaining would soak up valuable minutes, so Sam didn't do it. Even more than she wanted to meet Jen, Sam longed to reach War Drum Flats. Because it was visible from the highway, the flats were an unlikely place for Hammer to keep his mares. Still, the pond provided fresh water, and she'd seen him there before, challenging the Phantom.

At last she had permission to go, but Dad talked her out of riding Ace. "If you kept him to a walk, there'd be no problem." Dad pointed out a swollen muscle under Ace's sleek hide. "No, you'd better take another horse."

"But I—"

"You and Jen will want to gallop." Dad shrugged. "Take another horse, or call off your ride." Dad didn't sound mad, just sensible.

Dad was right. She looked after him as he strode across the ranch yard toward Dallas.

The change in mounts made Sam nervous. There was Tank, Ross's cow pony, but he was so big she wasn't sure she could get a saddle on him. Dad might need Banjo, and though he rode Jeepers-Creepers, the Appaloosa, as a backup, both horses were pretty spirited. Amigo, Dallas's sorrel, was sweet-tempered and levelheaded.

"You're probably my best choice," Sam muttered when the sorrel stamped a front hoof and blinked at her.

But Amigo belonged to Dallas, not River Bend. By the time she asked permission and got Dallas's tips on riding the gelding, she would have wasted half an hour.

She *had* ridden Strawberry. So, even though Ace neighed his jealousy, Sam decided she'd saddle the mare.

"It's for your own good," Sam told Ace as she retrieved her saddle and Strawberry's bridle.

She'd ridden almost every day since she'd returned from San Francisco, but Sam still doubted her ability. That accident two years ago had shaken her confidence.

Not that Sam questioned her skill at understanding horses. Each flicker of ears, each sidelong glance or movement of lips, told her something. And she trusted her ability to ride Ace. Still, fear of falling, far out on the empty range, never left her. It was a secret she'd told no one.

With a saddle blanket smoothed on the mare's freshly brushed back, Sam hefted her saddle. Strawberry swung her hindquarters to the right, putting her back out of reach.

"Hey," Sam said. She carried the saddle three steps closer. The mare moved away again. Finally, Sam got close enough to fling the saddle in place. Sweetheart flinched at the flapping stirrups and cinch and then flashed an accusing look at Sam.

"If you'd stayed still," she began, but then stopped. "We'll share the blame, okay?"

Strawberry blew through her lips.

Reins gripped tightly, Sam prepared to mount

Strawberry. Freshly brushed, the mare looked pink and innocent, but she stood just over fifteen hands tall.

Sam reminded herself how well she and Strawberry had done during the cattle drive. The day she'd let Ace rest by walking the trail riderless with the remuda, she'd had no problems with Strawberry. Had she?

Sam swung into the saddle and turned Strawberry toward the bridge. "I'll be back before dark," she called, but no one watched her ride out.

Pine-spiced wind blew down from the ridge and across War Drum Flats.

Strawberry moved with stiff, tight steps, but Sam couldn't tell why. A few sagebrushes trembled as the wind blew past, but that shouldn't spook the mare. No mustangs clustered at the pond. More disappointing, no silver stallion stood guard on the ridge. Strawberry pulled at the bit, indicating she wanted to stop and drink from the pond. The pond's bank was muddy. Apparently a few days of sunshine hadn't been enough to bake it hard after the storm.

Sam scanned the landscape all around. She didn't want to dismount, stand on the slick bank, and let Strawberry drink. She also didn't want to ride to the water's edge and lose contact with the mare's mouth while Strawberry leaned down to drink.

A breeze moaned through the wind-twisted pines up on the ridge. Somewhere up there lay Lost Canyon.

In childhood stories, she'd heard that this pond was the site of one of the last conflicts between the U.S. cavalry and the Native people who lived here. She couldn't recall details, but she thought the Natives had swept down from the hills as the cavalrymen watered their horses. No one died—at least that was the story she'd been told—but the soldiers had been left afoot when the Shoshone herded the cavalry mounts into Lost Canyon.

Nothing about the old story made her nervous, but Strawberry did.

The mare sidestepped, stretched her neck toward the water, and gave a low whicker, asking how Sam could be so cruel.

"Oh, all right, girl." Still mounted, Sam let the mare walk into the water. "Jen should be along in a minute, anyway."

Strawberry had taken two loud swallows when she jerked her head away from the water. Too late, Sam tightened her grip on the reins.

On the ridge above them stood Hammer and Sweetheart. Sweetheart, a mare. Slocum's Appaloosa, a mare. Bold and successful, Hammer was building a family band of his own, and here she sat on Strawberry. A mare.

No real cowgirl would have made such a silly mistake. What would keep Hammer from stealing Strawberry right out from under her?

The blue roan sampled the wind, searching for the scent of a stallion that might interfere with his plan. His mane flapped as his head bobbed in satisfaction, and then he was running.

Hammer stampeded down the trail, nipping at Sweetheart's heels as they came. Strawberry's front legs lifted in a half rear, and Sam was falling.

Sam grabbed at Strawberry's mane as the mare lunged

toward the other horses. Strawberry was drawn by the sight of Sweetheart, her pasture buddy, but she flattened her ears at the aggressive stallion. Sam couldn't predict Strawberry's movements from one second to the next.

Sam had almost regained her seat when Strawberry slipped in the mud, clambered upright, and then made for open ground. The mare's serpentine gallop kept Sam from settling into the saddle. She sagged to the right.

Suddenly, Strawberry gave a seesawing buck, then another.

Sam grabbed for the horn but missed. Could she ride this out? Not if Hammer rammed into them.

"Go!" Sam clapped her heels against Strawberry. "Go, go, go!" The mare bolted into a run, and for a minute, it seemed she'd mistaken Sam's shouts for authority, but then Strawberry made a sharp turn.

Sam's head snapped back on her neck as Strawberry ran back toward the other horses.

"Nope!" Sam shouted. She was half out of the saddle and holding the horn along with the reins, but there was no way she'd surrender Strawberry to Hammer.

An experienced cowgirl would stay in the saddle, but if Strawberry bolted again, Sam knew she'd fall. Instead, Sam slid down Strawberry's left side, keeping her body pressed close to the mare, gripping the reins. Once her feet hit the dirt, Sam gave a quick jerk on the reins. The mare wheeled around to face her, and Sam felt a pulse of hope. She had Strawberry's attention.

"You're not going anywhere," she told the mare, as the heavy-headed stallion approached at a walk.

Hammer left Sweetheart drinking from the pond. Some distance away, two other mares waited. Hotspot and an aged bay, whose head hung low, as if she were winded, made up the rest of Hammer's harem. Where had she come from?

Neck arched, forelock tangled over his eyes, Hammer came at them, set on increasing his band.

"Back off," Sam shouted, but he was a wild thing, unafraid of human threats.

His skin shivered. Her noise irritated him. Nothing more.

Strawberry lunged. Sam held on, even when the small

bones in her hand grated together. A muscle binding her arm to her shoulder stretched.

Oh no. She must hang on, no matter what, but if her arm was pulled from her shoulder socket, her determination would count for nothing.

Hammer came on. From the ground, his chest looked broad as the front of a car. She was all that stood between him and Strawberry. If he knocked her out of the way, his heavy hooves would trample her and he would take what he wanted.

If she waved her arms, he'd shy. But she couldn't take a hand from the reins. Strawberry was already dragging her around like a toy on a string. If Sam loosened her grip, the mare would be lost.

Strawberry dodged behind Sam, and Hammer's attitude changed. His ears flattened. His head lowered, swinging side to side, flinging froth on the dry desert floor.

"Get back!" she shouted, but the blue stallion came on.

He'd decided she was his enemy.

Chapter 13

FOR AN INSTANT SAM BELIEVED THE THUN-der of hooves came from Strawberry. But the sound was all wrong, and the pull to look back was irresistible.

The Phantom galloped to Sam's rescue. Head high, mane floating like white flame, he carved a half circle around her. With the whirlwind of his passing, Sam knew the Phantom had marked her as his. The explanation was hard to believe, but it was the only idea that made sense.

He'd come running from the ridge before, blocking

Hammer from stealing a single mare. This time, none of his mares were here. Only Sam.

In Hammer's eagerness to steal Strawberry, he'd forgotten to be watchful. His stride shortened at the sight of the other stallion.

Proud of himself, the Phantom turned his back on Hammer. He settled into a fluid, carefree trot as he came back toward Sam.

She couldn't banish the fear she'd felt looking into Hammer's eyes. The Phantom was faster, more experienced, and probably smarter, but Hammer was thicker, desperate for a band of his own. His neck had never known the touch of a girl's hand. To the blue stallion, gentleness meant weakness.

The Phantom trotted closer to Sam. His ears twitched at the sound of her voice.

"Don't underestimate him," she muttered to the silver stallion. "Be ready, boy."

Maybe Hammer couldn't bear the memory of his other humiliation. His hooves sprayed earth as he swung back with the agility of a cutting horse.

The blue roan stopped long enough to scream a challenge. He held a grudge against the silver stallion, and this time he wouldn't run.

The Phantom wheeled around to face him.

Sam held her breath. The mares turned as still as horses carved of stone. No birds warbled. The wind stopped.

Sam wanted to throw rocks. She wanted to shout, to order her horse away from here. But the Phantom wasn't her horse anymore.

His neigh pierced the quiet, returning Hammer's challenge. If the blue wanted a fight to the death, the Phantom would give it to him.

As if guided by knights carrying lances, the stallions trotted forward. Their strides lengthened, flowing into a lope, a gallop, and then all grace fell away.

The stallions slammed together. In that first contact, they grappled to bite, to rip, to raise battering forelegs.

Sam backed off, towing Strawberry away from the sounds and lunging bodies. Speed was the Phantom's favorite weapon. He broke free of Hammer's teeth, spun away, watched for an opening, then darted in to bite and retreat once more.

What Hammer lacked in speed, he made up for in weight. His massive shoulder clipped the Phantom's. His muscled haunches launched deadly kicks.

The two horses twisted in a haze of dust. Blood streaked their necks. Sweat marked them in dark swathes. Rage deepened their short neighs.

Please let him win. Please, if it's a fight to the death, let my horse live.

Sam covered her lips, muffling sounds that might distract the Phantom. As she did, she realized she held only one of Strawberry's reins. The mare wasn't pulling, wasn't looking. Neither was Hotspot or the bay. Was this what wild mares did? Wait for the victor to take over?

Despite her efforts, Sam made a moan of distress, and the Phantom glanced her way. It was a terrible mistake.

Hammer launched himself onto the Phantom's hindquarters, and both stallions crashed down into a snapping tangle of sagebrush.

No, no!

Bleeding, Phantom fought free of the brush.

Hammer shook his head, dizzied by the fall.

Then, as if he'd been hoarding more strength, the Phantom attacked.

Ears pinned hard against his neck, he rushed in, then sprinted away. The blue stallion returned each charge, but the Phantom kept Hammer spinning, first this way, then that. Hammer didn't get a second chance to crush the light-boned silver stallion.

At last, staggering with weariness, the blue made a final effort. Hammer swung his massive head, trying to slam it against Phantom's delicate face.

He missed, the Phantom leaped past, and the effort cost the blue everything. He fell to his knees, beaten.

Blood made jagged paths over the Phantom's silver hide as he trotted around the beaten mustang. Phantom blared a victorious neigh, but Sam saw a stiffness, not yet a limp, in his gait.

Would he kill Hammer? Sam bit her lip, thinking. She knew about the survival of the fittest. She knew if they were on some isolated wild horse island, it would be right for Hammer to die. The Phantom's foals would be faster, smarter, stronger.

But Nature wasn't the boss on this range. Humans interfered with the wild scheme of things. Hammer's herd might have been scattered by helicopters or run to death by kids on motorcycles. Hammer's only crime was following his instinct to have mares of his own. He didn't deserve to die. Hammer regained his feet. His ears flicked toward Hotspot and the old bay. Then, without a backward glance, he bolted to them. Sweetheart followed him.

The silver stallion trembled with tension. Should he pursue the challenger or guard the ones he'd protected?

Sam knew the answer. More fighting, even with a weakened enemy, could hurt her horse enough that another stallion might defy him and win.

She didn't expect the Phantom to understand why the battle must end. She only hoped he'd listen.

"Zanzibar," Sam whispered the horse's secret name.

The tired stallion didn't look at her, but a soft nicker rumbled from him.

"Sweet boy," she said. After the fury and violence, no one would think her words made sense. But no one else could hear.

Hammer led his mares up a trail and vanished.

The silver stallion breathed deeply, searching for Hammer's odor. When he could catch it no more, he turned to Sam.

She fought back a cough. Dust stirred by the fighting horses still hung on the air, but she squinted through it, judging her horse.

He liked to hear her talk. It soothed him, reminded him of the bond they'd forged in the warm stalls and lush pastures of River Bend Ranch. So Sam talked.

"Hey, boy," she said. "Yeah, I hear Strawberry behind me, and I see you looking, twitching your pretty ears. I think she's had enough of stallions today."

Strawberry pulled, tugging Sam away from the Phantom, and Sam released the single rein. It was a risk, but she had to move closer to the stallion.

"There, good boy, good Zanzibar."

The Phantom's nostrils fluttered, sucking in her scent. Once he'd been tricked by a sweater bearing her smell. Slocum had stolen the sweater and used the familiar scent to soothe the stallion. But no one could use the secret name to fool him, because no other soul on earth knew it.

He scuffed forward. Used to the crisp clip of his hooves, Sam looked down. Crimson blood welled from his left rear fetlock. He favored it as he walked.

"Hey, boy, does your leg hurt?" Sam kept talking as the Phantom approached. She wanted to bend and examine the wound, but she'd have better luck staying still. "You wouldn't allow it, would you? You'd snort and tell me a big, strong mustang like you takes care of himself."

Sam's fingers moved, wanting to touch him, and the stallion noticed. He braced for an instant, then realized he had nothing to fear. At last she could feel the warmth of his battle-weary body radiating toward her. Sam lifted her hand.

The stallion nuzzled it. The velvet of his muzzle and the prickle of his whiskers made Sam's heart sing.

"There's my beauty, my Zanzibar."

Sam closed her eyes as the horse lifted his head and rested it on her shoulder.

The stallion's pulse beat in his throat, through her shirt, and Sam's heart kept time with his.

Magic. Sam wished time would stop. She would stand like this, wrapped in this haze of enchantment forever.

Together, they heard the clink of a shod hoof on rock.

She felt the weight of the Phantom's head lift. By the time her eyes opened, he'd moved off a dozen yards.

The gray snorted, staring across the flats. Sam followed his gaze, but she didn't see a thing.

When she looked back at the Phantom, no drowsiness showed in his eyes. No weariness marked his movements. In one long leap, he passed sage and piñon and glinting desert rocks. He took the hidden path up to the ridge, and then he vanished.

Sam's hands shook as she swung back into Strawberry's saddle. The rider on the horizon had to be Jen.

"Get a grip," Sam scolded herself, but the mare's ears swiveled to listen. "Not you, Strawberry. You're doing fine, but you can't breathe a word of this adventure to anyone, got it?"

Thank goodness Jen had been too distant to see the Phantom. Sam just couldn't explain. Not until she knew Jen a lot better.

As Jen rode closer, Sam could tell why the palomino was named Silk Stockings. Her body shone dark gold except for front socks that reached her knees and emphasized her gait, making her look as if she were dancing.

"Sorry I'm late," called Jen.

"No problem. I just got here," Sam said. "Your mare is beautiful."

"Don't flatter Silly. It goes straight to her empty head." Jen didn't stop the mare from rubbing her cheek against Sam's leg. "See?"

"I wouldn't call you Silly if you were mine." Sam laughed, petting the mare's neck.

"Oh yes, you would," Jen said. "If not the first time she bucked you off at the horror of seeing a grasshopper, then you would when she dislocated your arm, shying at a paint chip on a fence."

At the reminder of Strawberry jerking her around like a rag doll, Sam rubbed her shoulder. Carrying a backpack tomorrow would ache.

"That's not Ace, I bet," Jen said, eyes sweeping Sam's mount.

"No, this is Strawberry," she admitted. "Ace . . ." Sam paused, but there was no point in hiding this information. Dad would report it to Brynna Olson tomorrow. "Got a little banged up last night."

"What happened?" Jen asked. Behind her glasses, Jen's blue eyes were concerned.

"The renegade stallion struck again and took Sweetheart, Gram's mare. Ace tried to stop him."

"Oh wow. What did he—"

"He got a couple bites that didn't amount to much, but the stallion rammed him up into the corner of two fences, and Ace hurt his chest."

"Poor guy," Jen said, rubbing her own breastbone, but Sam saw Jen's curiosity beyond her sympathy. "Did you see the stallion? Was it the Phantom?"

"I saw him, and it wasn't. It was a blue roan. He has draft blood for sure, and the Phantom looks like an Arab, you know?"

"Of course I don't know," Jen snapped in exasperation. "For most of my life, I thought he was a ghost story. Now, all of a sudden, everybody's seeing him, blaming things on him, and Linc Slocum thinks you're a witch who can snap her fingers and have him appear."

"Well, I'm not," Sam said. "Or I'd conjure up gold instead of wishing my dad could have gotten a loop on that blue stallion, so we'd be rich."

"I saw that ad, too. *I'm* dying for the money, but my parents think Slocum will be arrested before anyone can cash in on his offer." Jen's head bobbed from side to side as she considered that possibility. "Which wouldn't be all bad, either."

Sam laughed. As the mares jogged along side by side, she decided she liked Jen's sense of humor.

"Do you think he'd believe me if I told him it wasn't the Phantom?" Sam asked.

"I'm no expert on Slocum psychology," Jen said, "but I think he'd say something like, 'You'd say anything to protect that stud.'"

Sam turned in the saddle. "Why—"

"I heard him say something like that to my dad. Slocum is convinced the Phantom was yours."

Was he? Jen didn't ask, but the question vibrated in the air between them.

Although it felt like telling a secret, Sam said, "I had a colt who ran away—"

"Sam, everyone knows about your accident."

"Okay, well, it might be my colt Blackie, all grown up."

"Slocum claims you were up at BLM's Willow Springs holding pens, just riding that stallion around"—Jen spun her hand in the air—"like a carousel pony."

Sam's bark of laughter scared both horses. "Riding him around?"

Jen's smile said she hadn't really believed the story.

"Wanna gallop?" she asked.

Sam barely had time to nod.

Jen's palomino burst into a rollicking gallop, and Strawberry followed as if she'd been waiting for this all day.

Chapter 14

MONDAY MORNING, DARTON HIGH SCHOOL was covered with campaign posters.

"I don't know why we don't do these elections in the spring, like other high schools," Jen grumbled as she and Sam entered the school. "Starting the year with a popularity contest doesn't seem like a good idea."

"On the other hand," Sam said, nudging her friend with an elbow, "you're a freshman, so what do you know?"

"How do I keep forgetting?" Jen asked, pretending to

strike her forehead in frustration. She turned left toward her locker. "See you in gym."

"Bye." Sam scanned the campaign posters as she walked to her own locker. The posters were much the same as those in her San Francisco middle school.

The candidates' appeals were painted on construction paper or butcher paper, sometimes decorated with glitter or clever slogans.

Sam had almost reached her locker when a swarm of students blocked her way. They stared at something on the wall.

Rachel Slocum's campaign poster was different.

Five minutes before the first class of the week, Rachel was already drawing a crowd. The banner looked like a glossy magazine page, featuring four full-color photographs of Rachel. Though the poster was big as a double bed, Sam had to jostle through the crowd to see.

Rachel as treasurer . . . will root for you promised hot-pink script across a cheerleader-skirted Rachel leaping in the air. *Rachel as treasurer . . . will shine for you* said letters across homecoming queen Rachel, hair spilling in a coffee-brown waterfall down her back. *Rachel as treasurer . . . will work for you* showed her bent over a notebook, wearing glasses and a flattering little frown. The last picture, a computer-generated composite of real Rachel and towering stacks of cartooned gold coins and dollar bills, had students chuckling and pointing. *Rachel as treasurer will save every dime for you*, it pledged.

"She'd know about money, all right," a lanky boy said with grudging admiration.

The first bell shattered Sam's contemplation. She sprinted for her locker, dialed her combination, and tried to review her history homework. There was no reason to waste brain time on Rachel. But Sam would bet Rachel had recovered from her convenient Friday illness, and those expensive posters were the price Linc Slocum had paid for embarrassing his little princess.

Gym class was an all-grades torture session. Freshmen had lockers next to juniors. Sophomores averted their eyes when they showered with seniors. Only luck gave Sam and Jen P.E. lockers in the same row.

Now they gossiped as they dressed for a one-mile jog followed by flag football.

"The ranch was her mom's dream," Jen whispered as she pulled on green shorts. "Slocum just went along at first. Then he got hooked by the"—she paused, and a sly smile claimed her face—"charm of the Old West."

Sam glanced all around before she asked, "So where's the mom now? England? Really?"

"She remarried, a baron or something, and lives on a horse farm outside Nottingham."

"Wow." Sam gave a final tug to her tennis shoelaces. "So when Rachel's there, do you suppose she has tea with the queen?"

Jen sputtered with laughter. "You're turning evil, Sam. I don't think I'm a good influence on you."

The locker-room crowd had thinned by the time they bolted toward the athletic field.

Rachel Slocum stood, framed in the doorway, waiting for them. Outside, Sam saw girls jogging around the track, ponytails bouncing, but Rachel didn't seem to care if she was late.

"If you keep gossiping about my dad or do anything to damage my campaign," Rachel said, "you'll be a social outcast this fast." She snapped her fingers beneath Sam's nose.

Sam felt a hot blush claim her face. Last week she'd been the only one in school *not* spreading rumors about Linc Slocum.

Very slowly, Sam tucked a lock of auburn hair behind one ear. She wasn't feeling scared, she realized, just surprised by Rachel's ambush.

"I'm not gossiping about your dad," Sam said.

Rachel fluttered her rose-gold fingernails just inches from Sam's cheek, as if shooing her away.

"In fact," Sam pressed on, "I'm kind of insulted you think I have nothing better to do than spend time thinking about your dad. If he didn't keep showing up where I was, I wouldn't even know him."

"It's that horse." Rachel shuddered. "He's no different from all the others, I'm sure. They're all dirty, smelly, and big enough to hurt you but so stupid they don't realize it. If they had an ounce of intelligence, they'd realize they don't have to carry people around on their filthy backs."

"This horse is wild, Rachel," Jen interrupted.

"So? This time my father's obsessed with a wild horse. Before that it was spotted horses. Who cares? It's his hobby."

Outside, a whistle shrilled as the teacher called the girls together.

"Excuse me," Sam said, slipping past Rachel.

"There are *no* excuses for you, cowgirl," Rachel snapped. "Just remember that."

During lunch, Rachel's campaign drew even more attention. Instead of handing out paper badges or campaign buttons, Rachel passed out dollar bills. Stamped across George Washington's face in hot-pink ink were the words RACHEL FOR TREASURER.

Sam and Jen heard talk of the tactic, but Sam didn't see it with her own eyes until she filed into journalism class and Daisy handed her a dollar.

"Rachel would just love to have your vote," Daisy gushed.

Don't react, Sam told herself. *Don't sneer or fling it back in her face.*

She managed to appear calm, but Sam couldn't stop herself from thinking of Dad's disappointment over the few cents per pound they hadn't made on the cattle.

She kept her feet moving away from Daisy, but Sam still pictured Gram brooding over each new batch of bills.

Sam had almost reached her desk when Rachel squirmed into her path.

"Here, cowgirl." Rachel pressed another dollar into Sam's hand. "You look like you could use an extra."

"Rachel, I'm pretty sure this is illegal." RJay's bellow was so well timed, Sam wondered if the student editor had overheard Rachel's insult. "From what I've heard," he said, examining one of the bills, "you're not going to like prison."

Rachel's fingers went gliding through her hair as she gave a theatrical sigh. "As long as they have MTV and a decent manicurist, I'll manage."

Sam didn't want to laugh, but she did. Was it possible a decent human being lurked beneath that catty exterior? Probably not.

She forgot about Rachel during the quiz on the weekend's homework. Her fingers were aching from writing fast, when Mr. Blair called time.

"Pass 'em up and listen," Mr. Blair yelled above the complaints of those who hadn't studied for the quiz. He put the papers aside and crossed his arms. "As students from last year know, we've got three cameras for staff use. Nikons donated by the *Darton Review-Journal*. Donated," Mr. Blair emphasized, "but very expensive to replace.

"Since last year's staff only produced one decent photographer and he's now editor in chief"—Mr. Blair paused as RJay bowed to nonexistent applause—"I'll let new students try out as photographers."

Excitement rushed through Sam's veins.

"If you're interested, check one out overnight, shoot one roll of film, then submit it to me and RJay. Impress us," Mr. Blair hollered, "because we will decide whose work earns the right to keep the camera for the first semester."

Murmurs rustled as students turned to each other, but Sam didn't talk. She focused on the plan forming in her imagination.

"Class? One more thing. You'll treat these cameras like delicate baby birds. Do not harm them in any way. Got that?

"If they break, I won't care whose fault it is." Mr. Blair paced the front of the classroom, pointing at students during his tirade. "If *your* mama breaks it or *your* dog eats it or *you*, Miss Forster, get abducted by aliens—*you* pay the five hundred dollars to replace the camera."

Sam smiled at her journalism teacher. It didn't matter that Mr. Blair had singled her out. Her idea was bubbling like a shaken soda—sweet and ready to explode.

Mr. Blair's glare swept the entire class. "You break it, you buy it. No excuses."

Sam's nerves hummed with excitement. She'd be

careful, all right, because one of those black-and-silver cameras would help her earn that reward money and prove to Linc Slocum the Phantom was not to blame.

Shooting the test roll of film wasn't easy. She took a few shots at school, but she was afraid they wouldn't turn out. Only after Sam got the camera did she realize photography wasn't a simple point-and-shoot operation. There were shutter speeds to consider and focus to figure out.

Sam was growling with frustration by the time she really listened to Gram's suggestion.

"Just call Maxine," Gram said. "Maxine Ely is a talented photographer. Her work wins blue ribbons at the state fair, and the Darton library has framed prints of her pictures hanging on the walls."

Sam bit her lip, listening, but too sheepish to do anything.

"She's Jake's mother, for heaven's sake, not just your history teacher," Gram said. "She's known you since you were in diapers."

"That doesn't make it better, Gram."

But Sam's determination to get the reward from Slocum won out over her fretting.

She called.

Three times. Each time, Mrs. Ely acted as if helping Sam was the highlight of her day. *She must really like photography,* Sam thought.

And it was sort of exciting. Sam jogged from place to place on the ranch. She took a picture of Buddy trying to scratch her nose with a rear hoof and one of a rusty hinge that had always looked too fancy for the gate. She gave up trying to make a portrait of Ace. The gelding was so friendly and curious, he kept nuzzling the lens.

"You are too cute for your own good," Sam said. She kissed his tender muzzle, then jogged toward the River Bend bridge, imagining the last picture she'd take before darkness fell.

Sam's last thoughts as she fell asleep were, as always, of the Phantom. In the sparkling mist of a dream, he ran toward her, ears cupped to hear her voice, dark eyes soft and filled with her face.

Oh no. Sam sat up. She'd forgotten to call Brynna Olson.

How stupid was she? Sam buried both hands in her short hair and pulled. *Idiot.* Nothing was more important than protecting him.

Dad had gone to bed an hour ago. Sam listened intently. Was that the clink of a spoon on pottery? Hadn't Gram said she might stir up a batch of sourdough bread and let it rise in the refrigerator overnight?

Sam pattered down the stairs so fast, she was actually breathless when she came into the kitchen.

"Did Dad call Brynna about Slocum's posters and that ad?"

Gram nodded. She pulled plastic wrap over the top of the bowl, then did it again, tighter.

Sam nearly shouted in frustration until it hit her. This wasn't going to be good news.

"What?" Sam croaked.

"Brynna left Sunday for Washington. She'll be gone at least a week." Gram paused to let that news sink in.

"Wyatt spoke to her replacement, a gentleman from the BLM office in Las Vegas."

Las Vegas? Sam's mind spun with flashes of neon lights and tuxedoed gamblers. She'd never been to Las Vegas. What she was thinking was probably unfair, because she was thinking Brynna's replacement couldn't possibly understand wild horses.

"What did he say?" Sam heard her voice crack.

Gram sighed, closed the refrigerator, then leaned against it. "He said it was 'bothersome,' but he was sure it was a difficulty that would blow over without his interference."

Sam couldn't sleep. She resented the night, because she had to move fast. Without Brynna's help, her plan might be the only thing between the Phantom and capture. She tossed and turned all night, picturing the stallion's injured fetlock. If it made him slow, some cowboy could lasso him.

She dreamed of Flick, the cowboy with the drooping handlebar mustache. He'd worked at Slocum's Gold Dust Ranch before his temporary position at the

Willow Springs Wild Horse Center. While working for the BLM, Flick had illegally roped the Phantom and Brynna had fired him. Flick had disappeared after that, but Slocum would know where to find him. Sam was sure of it.

The next morning before classes began, Sam tracked down Mr. Blair and handed him the camera and the film.

"Overachiever, huh, Forster?" he asked.

"I guess so," she answered, but she could tell his gruff question had been a compliment.

Mrs. Ely pulled her aside after history and made her promise to stop by after school and show her the pictures.

"I don't think Mr. Blair will have had time to develop them," Sam said. "And I can't miss the bus after school."

"Mr. Blair might surprise you. He's in the school darkroom as much as he's in class. And after school—"

Mrs. Ely glanced over Sam's shoulder for a second. Sam turned, too, and saw Rachel pretending to gather her books, though she was clearly eavesdropping.

"—I can always give you a ride home," Mrs. Ely continued, "if you miss your bus."

"Thanks. I'll bring them if I can," Sam said.

Her spirits soared as she hurried to her next class, even though Rachel pushed past her with a sour expression. Rachel always looked that way in history. After all, she was a sophomore taking a freshman class. She must have flunked last year.

Sam had just swallowed the last of her peanut butter sandwich and walked toward the journalism classroom, when she saw Mr. Blair, waiting outside the door. Her heart plummeted, and she had to force her fingers out of the fists they had curled into.

What stupid thing had she done? Left the lens cap on so that the entire roll of pictures turned out blank? Broken some mechanism she hadn't even noticed?

Her steps must have slowed, because Mr. Blair shouted down the hall, "Too late now, Forster." His voice caused a dozen heads to turn and stare. "Come in and face the music."

Mr. Blair had used the school darkroom to develop and print the photographs, which were now spread over a table in the back of the room. Those who'd arrived early were already looking at them, and Mr. Blair didn't make them leave as he gave Sam an evaluation of her work.

"This one shows evidence of nearly every mistake a beginner can make." Mr. Blair tapped a picture Sam had taken of a reflection on a watering trough. "This is better, but you've got to read up on lens openings and shutter speeds." His finger skimmed above a photograph of two Herefords at dusk.

"Your people pictures are the best," RJay said as he scooted one photo away from the others.

Sam bit her lip in surprise. It was one of the after-school shots she'd taken before her telephone tutoring from Mrs. Ely. She'd lucked out on this one.

In it, Ms. Santos was tapping at her computer keyboard with one hand, a telephone clamped between her ear and shoulder, smiling and beckoning a student into her office.

"We'll use this for the next issue," RJay said, and Mr. Blair nodded.

She felt dizzy, as if she hovered above the whole scene. Other students studied the photos and gave her sidelong glances that could have been admiration or amazement that she'd done something noteworthy.

Maybe she had, and maybe it could help her save the Phantom.

And then Mr. Blair held up the one photograph she'd wanted to erase as soon as she'd snapped it.

In it, Rachel stood by one of her campaign posters. Her forced toothpaste-commercial smile looked just like her dad's. One hand was perched on her hip and the other hand flicked out, the light caught on her glittering fingernails as she made a point to a bedraggled-looking freshman boy.

"This one is priceless," Mr. Blair said.

Laughter sparked all around her, but Sam only felt the hot stare of Rachel's eyes on the nape of her neck.

RJay took the photograph from Mr. Blair and pretended to make up a caption for it. "'In honor of my campaign, dahling, I'm wearing my new fuchsia-periwinkle nail enamel. So very chic, don't you know.'"

For a minute, Sam felt sick, but when she finally risked a look, Rachel was smiling. She was a better sport than Sam would have thought.

"I think, Miss Forster, you should take the camera for another night and see if you can refine your touch with lighting," Mr. Blair said. "Come back at the end of the day to pick it up."

When the last bell rang, Sam jumped from her seat and got to Mr. Blair's classroom as quickly as she could. She didn't have much time to get the camera and make it to the bus on time.

Mr. Blair was waiting for her at his desk.

"Try playing with the aperture," he told her, "to alter your depth of field."

Sam glanced at the classroom clock. Jen would be saving her a seat on the bus. If she talked fast, she might have time to ask a few questions.

Mr. Blair answered every question, then paused.

"You seem awfully interested in shooting in low-light situations," Mr. Blair said.

Carefully Sam looped the camera strap over her neck.

"I am, sort of," she admitted. Sam checked the clock and saw she had no time for half-true explanations.

She couldn't tell anyone about her plan to take pictures of the thieving blue roan.

"Thanks for the help," Sam said, and hurried away.

With the camera around her neck, she didn't dare run, but the smell of diesel fumes from the idling buses made her walk in long strides.

Sam would have made it to the bus if Mrs. Ely hadn't leaned out from her classroom door.

"Come tell me," she said.

Sam couldn't resist telling Mrs. Ely how much her advice had helped.

"He loved them," Sam said. "Well, except—"

A desk moved in the front row of the empty classroom. What was Rachel doing here again?

Mrs. Ely followed Sam's glance. "Rachel thinks a pen might have rolled out of her backpack during class, so she's searching for it."

Bent to look under a desk, Rachel flashed a lopsided grin.

"Got it," she said, but she didn't leave.

"So, you're in a hurry and don't have the photographs with you." Mrs. Ely summed up the situation. "I'll let you run, but first there's a photography book you should have. I want you to borrow my copy, but it's up there." Mrs. Ely rushed across the classroom to a soaring bookcase crammed with books. She pointed to the top shelf. "I think you can reach it better than I can."

Sam smiled. It was funny being taller than her teacher. It would only take a minute.

"Okay," she said. Carefully, Sam removed the camera from around her neck. She looked around for a place to put it. Mrs. Ely's desk was sort of a mess.

"I'll hold it for you," Rachel offered.

Sam's hands tightened on the camera. She told herself her paranoia was just plain childish. She handed the camera to Rachel and went to stand beside her teacher.

"It is kind of high," she said, standing on tiptoe.

Sam's index finger locked on the book's spine, and it plummeted to the floor. An apology was forming on Sam's lips when she heard the sound.

Metal slammed against tile. A fraction of a second later, there came the tinkling of glass.

Without meaning to, Sam covered her ears. She didn't have to turn around to identify the sound. She'd just heard the shattering of her dreams.

Chapter 15

"SAMANTHA, OH MY GOSH." RACHEL'S HANDS covered her mouth in mock horror. "There must have been something slippery on it. That camera just slid right through my hands."

Rachel's eyes showed no sympathy as she looked at Sam and shrugged. "Wow, you know what Mr. Blair said. Those cameras cost five hundred dollars, and if it's checked out to you, it's your problem. No matter what."

Mrs. Ely had already picked up the camera. She turned it carefully, looking through the viewfinder.

"Ta-ta until tomorrow," Rachel chirped, and her perfume lingered in the room like a taunt.

Rachel broke the camera. Sam knew it, and by her jerky movements, Mrs. Ely knew it, too. But their certainty wouldn't matter to Mr. Blair. *You break it, you buy it. No excuses.*

This is what it feels like to be in shock, Sam thought. She took the camera from Mrs. Ely and wandered down the empty hall.

No buses remained outside Darton High School. The only moving vehicle was Rachel's baby-blue Mercedes-Benz.

Sam stood there, priming herself to refuse Rachel's offer of a ride home. She had dropped the camera on purpose. It would feel good to refuse to even be in the same car with her.

When Rachel drove off without a backward look, Sam felt her backpack's weight would drag her to her knees. She could call Gram or Dad to come get her, but then she'd have to tell them about the camera even sooner.

A sigh lifted her chest and gusted out. How could she pay for the camera? She loved her life at River Bend, but there were no luxuries to give up.

In a single swoop, Rachel had robbed her of Mr. Blair's respect, Gram's and Dad's approval, the Phantom's rescue, and money. Lots of money.

"I suppose those useless sons of mine are long gone." Mrs. Ely was suddenly beside Sam. She wore fresh red lipstick, and her blond curls bounced as she scanned the parking lot and jingled her car keys. "They're more fun, but I have a nicer car."

Sam stared at Mrs. Ely, knowing she should say something.

"Come with me," the teacher said, and beckoned Sam toward a green sedan.

Sam felt boneless, but she managed to climb in and fasten her seat belt. As they drove, Mrs. Ely talked about school. She described an upcoming history project she hoped would be fun. When Sam only nodded, Mrs. Ely gave up on conversation in favor of the radio news. After a few minutes, she snapped off the radio.

"Can we pretend I'm not your teacher?" she asked.

"What?" Sam shook her head in confusion.

Mrs. Ely kept her eyes on the road, but she extended her right hand toward Sam. "Glad to meet you. I'm your neighbor Maxine. Jake's mommy. Our cows sure are loving that alfalfa we got from Wyatt."

Sam laughed. The out-of-order sign on her brain could be removed. Suddenly, she understood that Mrs. Ely wanted to say something un-teacherly. Sam hoped it was something vile about Rachel.

"Do you think it was an accident?" Mrs. Ely asked.

"Maybe," Sam said. "I wasn't looking."

"It looks like the mirror is broken. That was the tinkling sound, but I didn't want to take it apart and check. That's work for an expert."

Sam felt her scalp tighten against her skull. Experts were always expensive.

"If Rachel broke it, she should pay for it," Mrs. Ely said.

When Sam explained what Mr. Blair had told the class, Mrs. Ely's expression darkened.

"That could be sticky, since he took a stand in front of the class," Mrs. Ely admitted. "Still, if I told him the truth . . ."

Mrs. Ely's voice trailed off. Neither of them had *seen* Rachel do it.

"Mr. Blair said we were responsible, no matter whose fault it was," Sam repeated.

They drove in silence a while longer, but Sam suspected Mrs. Ely was having a serious talk with herself. She frowned, then nodded, raised one blond eyebrow, and then her frown vanished.

"So what is it you're yearning to photograph?" Mrs. Ely asked. "You wouldn't be shy if you knew what I like to shoot best."

"Your family?" Sam guessed.

"Sometimes, but it's tough to catch them being themselves. Those men of mine work hard at being stoic." Mrs. Ely lowered the car windows to let the late-August breezes surround them. "No, I like to photograph windows. Windows that reflect faces or mountains, windows that let you see inside to a family dinner table—" She shrugged. "Just windows. Nothing could be artier than that."

"Wild horses," Sam admitted. "At night."

The invading breeze ruffled the ungraded papers Mrs. Ely had tossed in the back seat. Sam noticed a flash of yellow on the road ahead. They'd catch the school bus soon.

"Oh, Sam," Mrs. Ely said, staring ahead. "What an incredible idea. I wonder," she mused, "what kind of equipment you'd need to do it right."

"Well," Sam said as they drew alongside the bus, "a camera would be a start."

Sam saw Jen and leaned forward. She waved, trying to catch Jen's eye. Once she did, Jen looked puzzled, then angry.

Oh no. Sam just knew Jen was thinking she'd stood her up.

Sure enough, Jen straightened, pressed her shoulders against the seat back, and turned away.

Oh great, Sam thought. *This day just keeps getting better and better.*

When it seemed nothing else could go wrong, they arrived at River Bend. Mrs. Ely switched off the engine, said, "Be right back," then hurried to tell Dad what had happened.

Surprised and horrified, Sam froze next to Mrs. Ely's car.

Near the barn, Dallas and Ross were conspiring with Dad to shoe Tank, Ross's bald-faced bay. Dad hated shoeing horses in general and Tank in particular. It took two men to hold Tank while a third wielded the hammer and horseshoe nails.

Mrs. Ely crossed the ranch yard in her tidy slacks and blazer, then folded her arms and stood talking.

From here, Sam couldn't tell if Dad had finished shoeing Tank before he laid the hammer on the ground and walked away. Each step was firm and deliberate, but Mrs. Ely followed him. Sam wondered if Jake's mom was doing more harm than good.

She didn't have to wonder long. Mrs. Ely came storming back, shaking her head.

"Never marry a cowboy, Samantha," Mrs. Ely said. She leaned against the car next to Sam and stared toward the Calico Mountains. "Pride is their downfall, and that's for sure."

"Am I grounded until I'm eighteen?"

"No." Mrs. Ely looked over at her suddenly. "Oh, Samantha, of course not. You're not in trouble. I just suggested Wyatt make a private arrangement with Slocum, to cover his daughter's carelessness. You'd think I suggested something illegal."

Sam felt relieved she wasn't in trouble but was not surprised at Dad's reaction. "Yeah, Dad's like that."

"Aren't they all." Mrs. Ely rubbed her hands together. "The men of Three Ponies Ranch are exactly the same as those at River Bend."

Mrs. Ely took the camera from Sam and looked at it once more. "Well, maybe the repair won't be too expensive. Until it's fixed, though, the least I can do is lend you a camera."

"It wasn't your fault," Sam protested, taking the Nikon back.

"She heard me ask you to come in after school. Then she arranged to be there, too." Mrs. Ely's red lips pressed together, but she just couldn't stay silent. "Of course, I'm not suggesting Rachel would do something destructive because you're getting lots of attention from your teachers and classmates. What kind of teacher would even hint at such a thing?"

"Not you," Sam said.

"Not me. I'm glad we've got that straight," Maxine Ely blurted, but she was laughing as she climbed back into her car. "Jake'll be over with that camera. Soon."

The phone was ringing when Sam walked into the white ranch house. "It's Jennifer Kenworthy." Gram extended the telephone receiver toward Sam, then whispered, "She doesn't sound very happy."

"Hello?" Sam let her backpack down to the floor.

"So, you got a better offer and ditched me?" Jen meant her tone to be sarcastic, but it sounded hurt. "Next time let me know, so I don't feel dumb saving you a seat."

"I missed the bus." Sam tried to keep the weariness from her voice, but a glance from Gram said she wasn't doing a good job. "Because Rachel broke the camera Mr. Blair loaned me."

Jen gasped as if someone had poured cold water down her neck. "The Nikon?"

"The Nikon."

"I suppose Mrs. Ely was your escort home because the school police think you're a flight risk. So are you making a run for the border?"

"Jen, this isn't funny." Sam smiled in spite of her gloom.

"I know." Jen took a breath, then asked, "How much?"

"I don't know yet. It makes a tinkling sound when you shake it."

"That doesn't sound good," Jen said. After a few seconds of silence, she asked, "How deep?"

Sam took a glass of lemonade from Gram and repeated, "How *deep*?"

"Yeah, how deep are we going to bury Rachel's body?"

"You are really awful." Sam wavered between laughing and crying. "But you're not still mad at me, right?"

"Not this time," Jen said. "Even though you probably want to put off our ride for a really interesting family discussion."

"Oh yeah," Sam said, looking at Gram's impatient expression. "Interesting."

Sam braced herself for further explanation, but as soon as she hung up the phone, it rang again. Because her voice was still unsteady, Sam let Gram answer.

"Hello," Gram said. "Oh, Maxine."

Wow, Jake's mom had made record time getting home to Three Ponies Ranch. What kind of workaround did she want to discuss with Gram, since Dad had refused to listen?

Sam lifted the cookie jar lid quietly so she could listen. She loaded three raisin-fat oatmeal cookies onto a saucer.

"Is that so?" Gram said. "A knack? He said 'promising' and that little—" Gram broke off. "Samantha, please take your snack upstairs and get started on your homework."

Sam trotted upstairs. At least Gram and Dad didn't

seem mad at her. She could be grateful for that, because her stomach wound into one big knot when she thought about facing Mr. Blair.

A shrill wind chased around the house, banging the shutters on Sam's window.

It was almost dinnertime, but she heard Jake pull up in his dad's truck. As she folded away her biology worksheet and stacked her books, Sam could hear past the wind and knew Jake was talking to Dad and Gram.

When Sam came down the stairs, she could tell he'd laid out some sort of plan.

Jake wore a brick-colored shirt that Sam hadn't seen before. It was tucked into faded jeans. The scuffed toes of his boots showed as he leaned against the kitchen door, but Jake smelled like soap and his black hair was shiny.

Something was up, and Sam felt uneasy.

"You want to drive down by War Drum Flats, lie low, and see if some stallion shows up with Sweetheart and that Appaloosa of Slocum's?" Jake asked.

Sam's glance flew to Dad, then Gram.

"I packed some sandwiches and a thermos of cocoa, so you can get there before dark." Gram indicated a brown paper bag. "If the lead mare sees you there as part of the scenery, she'll be less spooked than if you drive up later."

It made sense, but Sam wondered why Gram and Dad were going along with this scheme.

"But it's a school night," Sam blurted. Jake groaned an instant before Dad spoke.

"That's right," Dad said. "You've got a watch, and you'd better use it. I expect you in bed by ten o'clock."

"Yes, sir," Sam said.

Gram handed Sam the bag and kissed her cheek. "See if you can find Sweetheart for me, dear."

"Okay, Gram."

Jake opened the door, lifted her sheepskin coat from a hook, and shoved it toward her. Nights on the range could turn cold, even after ninety-degree days. Sam took it, then hurried, before Gram and Dad changed their minds.

"Don't ask me," Jake said, as Sam fell into step beside him. "It's Mom's doin', and I'm just your chaperone."

Sam's mind spun as they left the ranch, crossed the River Bend bridge, and headed into the wind toward War Drum Flats.

She hadn't told Maxine Ely the details of her plan, just that she wanted to photograph horses at night. Somehow, though, Maxine had figured out Sam wanted to photograph the thief stallion with his mares, and she'd sent Jake to help.

Jake on a horse *might* help by roping Hammer, but this Jake—looking mature and in charge at the steering wheel—could just as easily get in her way.

Sam crossed her arms in determination.

"Your hair's okay," Jake said, without looking at her.

"What a relief," Sam said. So much had happened since Brynna had cut her hair, Sam had forgotten about it. "You can't imagine how many nights I've stayed awake worrying that—"

"Don't annoy the driver," Jake interrupted. "I just thought I'd mention I'm getting used to it." He switched on the truck's heater. "You should know, though, guys always think it's a mistake when girls cut their hair."

"I'll write it in my diary," Sam sneered, but they both relaxed after that.

As the sun dropped behind the mountains, the glow from the instrument panel made the truck's dark cab almost cozy.

"Remember when we were little kids and you used to tell me stories your grandfather told you?" Sam asked.

"I remember that you were a pest and I could bore you into falling asleep so you would leave me alone."

Sam shivered. "I was never bored," she said, pulling her sheepskin coat closer. It was a good thing she'd brought it, since the truck's heater barely did its job. "How many of those stories were true?"

"Lots of them are legends. People all over the country substitute the names of their own tribal heroes. I don't know." Jake shrugged. "Mom could tell you better than I could."

When Jake still didn't offer a story, Sam began planning. "Can you park the truck off the road? Then I'll walk down by the water. Like Gram said, if I'm just sitting there—"

"We."

"What?" Sam felt a shimmer of irritation.

"If *we're* just sitting there, the horses are more likely to approach."

"Thanks, Jake, but you can stay in the nice warm truck. All I'm going to do is take a picture—"

"With *my mom's* camera, *if* I decide to give it to you."

"Don't be bratty, Jake."

"Try 'sensible,' Pest." Jake glanced into the rearview mirror, then pulled the truck off the street, onto a dirt road.

"Explain why it's more sensible for both of us to sit in the cold, waiting for mustangs that probably won't show up."

"If you scare them," Jake said patiently, "you could be hurt. Horses, you might've heard, are really big."

Sam folded her hands. He was so annoying, it was a challenge to stay calm.

"If the horses spooked, they'd run away from me.

And if they accidentally ran my way, do you think you can single-handedly stop a stampede? If you can, so can I." Sam took a long breath, thinking of how she'd freed the Phantom from the Willow Springs corrals. "Sometimes I don't mess up, Jake. Sometimes, I do things right."

Jake let her words hang there between them.

Sam didn't force him to reply. She just bounced against her seat belt as he guided the truck over the rutted road. It was five minutes before he slowed down.

"Let's eat before we go down there," Jake said. "My mom sent food, too."

As the truck stopped uphill from the pond, behind a screen of wind-tossed piñons, Sam let Jake believe he'd won. It would be good for his digestion.

Using the big purple first aid kit as a picnic table, they feasted on roast beef sandwiches, corn chips, and cocoa from Gram, and Swiss cheese on rye, carrot sticks, and bottled water from Jake's mother.

They chewed in such companionable silence, Sam was reluctant to rekindle their fight. She searched for words that weren't a declaration that she was, by golly, going out there alone.

The evening had turned midnight blue around them, but a smudge of tan showed against the eastern hills.

"Does that trail lead to Lost Canyon?" Sam asked.

Jake followed her pointing finger and nodded.

"Why's it called that, do you know?"

Jake narrowed his eyes, as if she were trying to trick him.

"What?" Sam demanded.

Jake settled back against the driver's door and rolled a bottle of water between his palms. "I'll only tell you this story because I'm too full to move."

"Oh, good." Sam leaned against her own door and nestled into her coat. She pulled the sheepskin collar against her cheeks, still watching the window behind him, in case mustangs appeared.

"A band of Shoshone—not a hunting party or families with tents, but warriors—holed up in Lost Canyon with their war ponies. Stories say they had a hundred of the West's fastest horses, and each night they led them down to water."

Jake pointed at the pond. "In those days, that was a huge lake, blue as a bowl full of sky, with water so pure and sweet the horses craved it more than grass.

"After the Civil War, cavalrymen posted at the remount station by Alkali had little to do. Through the war, they'd captured mustangs, broken them to saddle, and sent them off to Southern battlefields.

"After the war, they were ordered to clear the Shoshones and Paiutes off this land for farmers.

"Hoofprints told the cavalrymen that the one hundred Shoshone ponies were no tall tale, so the soldiers set a trap. Why didn't the warriors see it?" Jake wondered. "Was it a foggy night? Were the horses thirstier than usual and less wary? No one knows."

Outside the truck, Sam heard an insect, but nothing else moved.

"They captured the men and corralled the ponies. The horses could have made a run for it. They might have escaped, but herd instinct is stronger than anything. If a horse is left behind, he's prey to coyotes and cougars. Safety is with the herd. Usually."

Sam hugged her knees to her chest. She didn't want to hear the rest of the story, but she wouldn't make Jake stop.

"These soldiers were cavalrymen. They understood the superiority of a mounted warrior over a man on foot. So they took what the Shoshone valued more than life—their war ponies.

"The shooting started at dawn. It's said all the penned ponies screamed each time a rifle cracked and the next horse fell. By noon, the soldiers were sickened by the blood-slick ground and frightened by warriors chanting death songs. But their orders said to slaughter every pony and they did.

"They released the Shoshones. Why shouldn't they? The Natives' power lay stinking on the desert floor, dinner for vultures. With the cries of dying horses still echoing from the hills, the cavalrymen watched the Shoshone warriors walk the long trail to Lost Canyon."

Wind made the truck shudder, and Sam rubbed

her arms against a sudden chill. It was lucky she wasn't superstitious, she thought. A more fearful person might mistake the wailing wind for the sound of ghost ponies, crying for their lost companions.

"Releasing the Shoshones was a mistake," Jake said. Even in the darkness, Sam could see his faint smile.

"One man and three ponies had stayed behind. Three ponies is a small fighting force, for sure, but the warriors petted them and trained them. They strengthened them with war paint. Red prints marked their shoulders and blue rings circled their eyes. The warriors fasted, prayed, and vowed to wait.

"One day, a small cavalry patrol trotted across the desert. Confident they could pass in safety, they dismounted and let their horses drink. When they heard Shoshone drums, they laughed. What would the brave warriors do? Chase after them on foot?"

"But wait." Sam remembered. "The last battle in Nevada was fought on War Drum Flats, right?"

"Not much of a battle." Jake's tone turned casual. "Not a single man died, but somehow the Shoshone warriors took the horses and left the cavalrymen to walk back to the fort, proving the power of one man and three ponies."

"And that's how your ranch got its name," Sam said.

"I guess." Jake shrugged. "You ready to walk down there?" He turned on the headlights to light their way.

Sam started to reply, then stopped. She blinked, making sure the combination of moonlight and headlights hadn't fooled her eyes.

"Behind you," she whispered.

For a second, Jake turned to stone, then smoothly and slowly his head swiveled to look out the window.

Down the trail from Lost Canyon came the Phantom's herd, without him.

Chapter 16

"IT'S THE PHANTOM'S HERD, BUT WHERE IS HE?"

In the darkness outside Jake's truck, Sam made out the lead mare with zebra-striped forelegs. She spotted one of the blood-bay mares, too, but the silver stallion was missing.

"Relax." Jake jiggled her arm in a way he must think was calming. "You're breathing too fast for someone just sitting in a truck."

"Jake, a couple days ago, the Phantom was in a fight. He won, but he was injured."

Cautiously, always keeping a quarter mile between themselves and the truck, the mares made their way to level ground, headed for the pond. The wind blew from behind them. Their wild manes and tails streamed forward, and the scent of humans hurried ahead of them.

"Blackie's been doing this for years, Sam. He knows how to take care of himself."

Sam nodded, a little surprised Jake still thought of the stallion as Blackie, the colt she'd loved and lost.

Sam stayed quiet. She didn't want to frighten the mares. Still, she worried about her horse. Injured, he'd be prey for another stallion or coyotes. His own herd might outrun him.

"I've seen him up on the ridge," Sam whispered to Jake. "He stands guard between those wind-twisted pines while the mares drink."

Together they watched for the Phantom. Jake didn't approve of her obsession, but he knew that when she was worried about the stallion, nothing else mattered.

Sam was about to suggest they douse the headlights, when suddenly the Phantom was there.

Up on the ridge, moonlight struck his coat, turning it bright as liquid silver. The wind tossed his mane around his neck and shoulders.

"He looks fine," Jake said.

"No, he doesn't."

The stallion's head wasn't high-flung and eager. He held it level with his shoulders. Though his ears pricked forward, alert, he rocked awkwardly as he took steps toward the path.

"Left rear leg?" Jake asked as the stallion came down the mountain.

"Yes, just at the fetlock. I think some sagebrush stabbed him. Jake, he's really hurting. Look at him."

Head angled toward the truck, the stallion hobbled into the pond.

Jake drew a breath. "He's coming a lot closer to us than the mares did," he whispered.

Sam felt sure the Phantom had scented her.

She wanted to get out of the truck and go to him, but she let him drink and cool his injury.

"He's favoring that leg, but I don't think he's sick

yet." Jake leaned nearer the windshield. "I bet it could be swabbed clean, disinfected, and—oh no." Jake's head snapped Sam's way as if he'd heard her thoughts.

"Tell me, Jake. I'm going out there. You can help me or not, but I'm going."

"Don't dare me, or I'll drive away from here so fast it'll make your head spin."

"You won't," she insisted, "because it's not the right thing to do. Because you might be responsible for his death."

"Better his than yours."

"Will you get over that?" Sam didn't mean to shout, but she must have. The stallion's head left the water's surface so quickly, moisture scattered like diamonds.

"I am over it," Jake said. "That doesn't mean you shouldn't be careful."

"Of course I'll be careful. I'll get out of the truck, walk toward him, and if he wants my help—and he *has* before—I'll look at his fetlock."

"And then what?"

"If there's, like, something sticking out, I'll pull it loose."

"And leave him with an open wound? An invitation to infection? Great plan, Sam."

"No." Sam pressed her hands down on the purple first aid kit. "I'll use whatever you tell me to, from this."

Jake's breath rushed out. He muttered, "No, no, no." At the same time, he started assembling what she'd need.

"Listen to every word, Sam."

"I will." She watched him, knowing her mind had never been more alert. "But remember, I can't carry too much. He always watches my hands. And I don't think he'll like this coat."

As Sam shrugged out of her sheepskin coat, Jake rubbed his forehead, but he didn't give in to frustration. He lifted the purple lid slowly, so the hinges wouldn't creak.

"We'll drench this gauze with water," Jake said, reaching to the truck floor to shake a plastic water bottle. "Good thing you didn't finish yours. If he lets you close enough, go to his near side and face back, toward his tail, to clean that wound."

"Facing back? Are you sure?"

"I'm—" Jake hesitated. One other time he'd been sure, and caused her accident. "I think his kick would have the least strength from that position."

"I'll do it. What next?"

Sam listened, shoving gauze and a needleless syringe of Betadine into her pockets. Last, she tucked a disposable diaper—a perfect lightweight bandage—into her jeans' waistband.

Before she could climb out, the Phantom summoned her. "Jake, look."

The Phantom limped toward the truck. He left the mares behind and halted about four car lengths away to stand in the headlights' beam. He tossed his head in three quick jerks and stood, ears swiveled toward her. Then, looking right at her, he nickered.

"If I get out now, he won't run." Sam put her hand on the truck door, then stopped. The Phantom trusted her to do what was right. "Is this all I need, Jake?"

"I'm trying to think—" Jake rubbed the back of his neck. "Aw shoot, it can't hurt. Here."

Confused, Sam watched as Jake reached into their

sandwich sack and sorted out a small piece of plain bread. "My grandfather used to make bread poultices for horses. To draw out infection, he said."

"Bread," Sam repeated.

As Jake dampened the bread with water, Sam listened to his directions, but she kept watching the Phantom.

"Do you know what's going to happen to me if you get hurt?" Jake muttered.

His words wrenched her attention away from the stallion.

Sam bristled with anger. "I know I'm getting really sick of you expecting me to fail," she said, and scooted toward the door.

"No, I don't think you'll fail, or I wouldn't let you go," Jake snarled. Sam saw Jake really didn't care if they kept fighting. "Now, get him back in the water."

"What?" Sam barely got the word out. Jake couldn't change the rules at the last minute.

"You tamed him in the water. He trusts you in the water." Jake's voice was level and calm. "Get him back in the water or the deal is off."

Forget it, Sam thought. She opened the truck door as silently as she could. Then she glanced back.

"My hand's going to be on the horn," Jake said, demonstrating. "If the safest thing for you is to scare him away, I'll lean on this horn with everything I've got."

Sam didn't utter another word. It wasn't worth the time wasted.

She moved toward the pond. The mares scattered farther up the hillside, but the Phantom stayed quiet. As she passed, his head bobbed, scattering his mane and forelock free of his brown eyes. His weight rested on his three good legs. Maybe that, and pain, made it hard for Sam to read his body language.

Would he follow? He hadn't since he was a colt.

The sound of following hooves did not come. Sam glanced back over her shoulder. Every line of the stallion's body showed his puzzlement. Whenever he'd come to her before, she'd met him. Now she was walking away.

"Come on, boy." Sam swung along at a casual pace.

Icy water slapped over her tennis shoes and soaked

her socks. She waded out three steps, four, five . . . and heard the splash of hooves behind her.

Yes. Sam felt a smile lift her lips. This stallion was the most wonderful horse in the world. Sam wanted to throw her arms around his satiny neck, but when she turned, the night wind pierced her T-shirt, awakening her to the fact that this was no dream.

The stallion was curious but cautious. He whuffled his lips, switched his tail, then stamped a forefoot. When he stamped, his balance shifted and he stumbled a step.

"Poor boy."

The stallion sighed as Sam edged closer. She held her hands out to him. Up the hillside, the clustered mares raised their heads. The stallion sniffed her hands, then turned his attention to her pockets and waistband. Maybe he couldn't see the supplies she'd hidden, but he knew they were there.

"We haven't done this in a long time, boy." Sam walked past the horse's front legs, dragging her hand along his sleek hide. "I'm going back here, okay? I'll pet you as I go, so you know right where I am. Full hand, okay, boy? No tickly stuff."

He kept the injured leg clear of the water. Sam half squatted, and he allowed it. "Good, good boy."

He let her touch his fetlock. Just as Sam realized it felt hot, he jerked away from her shaking hand. She tried again, and he let her dab at the wound with the gauze.

Sam had faced his tail, just as Jake ordered, but now she looked over her shoulder. The Phantom was watching. He blinked, looking nervous, but no more than a domestic horse would.

Sam hurried. Once the hair was washed free of dirt, she noticed a nub of sagebrush protruding from the wound. It was just what she'd expected, so why hadn't she brought tweezers?

Sam's knees shook, but she kept her hands steady. She knew what she had to do.

"This is the test," she crooned to the horse. "I'll get it right the first time, but it's going to hurt. Zanzibar, good boy, just let me do it and you'll be better."

Using her fingernails like tweezers, she jerked the

sagebrush free. *Don't honk, don't honk,* Sam thought, and Jake didn't, though the stallion bolted a splashing step forward.

The Phantom stopped, shuddering. "That was the hard part, boy."

Sam edged back into position. The stallion's head swung back and nuzzled her shoulder. He didn't want her facing away. She let him lip her shirt, hoping it would distract him when she squirted a stream of disinfectant on the wound.

His skin shivered, but he didn't move away.

"The medicine's just cold, right, boy?" Sam's own teeth were about to chatter, but it had nothing to do with the temperature.

Fingers flying, she molded the damp bread against the stallion's fetlock, glad he held the hoof above the water. The Phantom seemed to relax.

"You like that, boy? It's supposed to draw out the infection. That's what Jake's grandpa said. You remember Jake, don't you?"

The stallion didn't respond, and he didn't trust the

disposable diaper. At the first crinkle of plastic, his ears flattened. He walked out of the water, and this time Sam followed. Jake had better not honk. The disposable diaper and the pond water were a lousy combination. He ought to have the sense to see that.

Once out of the water, the stallion circled back. Clearly irritated, he swung his head in her direction and snapped his teeth.

"'Just get it over with,' is that it, boy?" Sam kept her voice low and worked quickly.

She pressed the bread poultice more firmly into place, wrapped the plastic diaper around the stallion's leg, and fastened the tapes.

As her fingers left his leg, the stallion launched himself away. By the time Sam regained her feet, he was gone.

Sam got the truck door open. She sat in the doorway, unlaced her shoes, and poured out the water before stripping off her socks. By the time she closed the door, Sam was shaking so hard, she couldn't get her arms into her coat sleeves. Once she quit struggling, she noticed Jake's silence.

"Didn't you even watch?" she asked.

"I watched."

Sam waited, excitement fading. "Wasn't it incredible?"

"He remembers you, I guess."

"Why are you talking like a robot?" Sam asked.

"I'll stop." Jake started the truck and drove back toward the main road.

Sam crossed her legs and wiggled one bare and freezing foot. It seemed unlikely that Jake was waiting for a compliment, but she gave one anyway. "Everything you told me to do worked."

Jake just kept driving.

By the time the truck tires bounced off the dirt road and back onto the asphalt, Jake still hadn't spoken.

"Why are you acting so weird?" Sam demanded.

Jake looked over. His expression mirrored the Phantom's as he'd pinned his ears back and glared.

"I hate feeling afraid," Jake said as if she'd dragged the words out of him. "Half the time I'm around you—"

He didn't finish. He waved one hand in dismissal and leaned closer to the steering wheel.

Sam let him drive. He'd only had his license for a month, and it was a bad idea to distract him.

His reaction wasn't a surprise. Her accident had changed their friendship. Sam tugged her coat cuffs down and pulled her fingers up into her sleeves. She didn't want Jake to worry, but she wasn't going to sit home playing video games or doing her nails either.

Facing forward, Sam rolled her eyes to peer at him. The dashboard lights lit his hard-set jaw.

Let him sit there, Sam thought. *She* sure wouldn't talk first.

River Bend's porch light was visible miles before they crossed the bridge and rolled into the ranch yard.

Sam had hopped down from the truck and started to close the door when Jake's voice stopped her.

"Here's Mom's camera."

He dangled it by a leather strap, and Sam wanted to refuse. Why hadn't he given it to her earlier, when they were on the range with the horses? That had been the plan.

As she took the camera, Sam felt an odd satisfaction.

Jake hadn't forced it on her earlier, because he'd known she was watching for the Phantom. "See ya at school," she said through a tight throat.

"Yeah." Jake sounded resigned. "I'll see ya."

Sam was asleep when the telephone rang downstairs in the kitchen. With a half-formed idea that it was Jen, Sam swung her feet to the floor and raised her nightgown hem so she wouldn't trip. She ran down the stairs, vaguely aware of Dad lumbering along behind her.

Sam had reached the kitchen when Dad spoke. "I'll get that," he said. "Get on back to bed."

Sam let Dad lift the receiver.

"Hello," he said, but nothing in Dad's expression told her who'd called so late. She moved slowly, listening. Near the top of the stairs, she heard half a sentence.

"—businesswoman would have a phone that took messages . . ."

Businesswoman? The only businesswoman she knew was Aunt Sue, in San Francisco.

Curiosity boiling, Sam sat on the top step.

". . . wanted poster . . . stallion . . ." Dad's voice

rose, then faded. He had to be talking about Slocum and the Phantom.

Like a latch clicking into place, she knew it must be Brynna Olson.

Sam tiptoed back to her room, mulling over that possibility. Was Brynna back already? Did anyone go from Nevada to Washington, DC, for a single day?

No.

And Washington's time was three hours ahead of Nevada's. Sam rolled back into bed. Why would Brynna call Dad so late at night?

Brynna calling Dad. Sam stared at her bedroom ceiling until she saw a haze of spots, feathery horses, and flying arrows.

Brynna could be urging Dad to take that job. Dad might have left a message with the Willow Springs office about Slocum's posters. Or maybe . . .

Sam flopped over and buried her face in her pillow.

Maybe she needed to go into Darton and see a movie before her imagination ran away from her completely.

Chapter 17

SAM'S HEAD SNAPPED BACK, AND HER EYELIDS sprang wide as Dad braked at the bus stop.

"I don't want you falling asleep in class, now," Dad cautioned.

"I won't," Sam promised.

She felt cranky. She'd asked Dad about his talk with Brynna, but Dad only said Brynna was gone for a week of meetings. She already knew that.

Since Jen wasn't at the bus stop yet and Sam didn't

want to wait alone, she tried once more to lever information out of him.

"Exactly what did she say about Slocum's posters?"

Dad thought a minute, then recited, "Soon as someone at Willow Springs heard about the posters, they should've had a ranger call on Slocum to educate him about the Wild Horse and Burro Act."

Again, Sam thought. She'd been sitting next to Slocum when Brynna had explained it the first time.

Slocum knew he was breaking the law. He just didn't care.

"Can they arrest him?" Sam asked.

Dad didn't sugarcoat the truth. "Nope, not until something happens to an animal."

As soon as Jen arrived at the bus stop, she told Sam the stallion had been sniffing around Gold Dust Ranch the night before.

"My dad thinks he's come back for Kitty," Jen said as the bus arrived.

Once they were seated, Sam looked at Jen and decided to trust her with the truth.

"Jake and I saw the Phantom last night," Sam whispered. "He's hurt. So it couldn't have been him."

Jen sat up so suddenly, her glasses slipped down her nose. If intelligence could show in someone's expression, Jen's blue eyes glittered with brainpower.

"He's hurt?" Jen whispered. "If you don't want to call the BLM to take care of him, I could help." Jen had her heart set on becoming a veterinarian.

"I wish you had been there last night," Sam said. "But I think he's going to be all right."

Sam's mind churned. She had Mrs. Ely's camera around her neck. If Hammer really had been at the Gold Dust Ranch, he might come back tonight. If she were there, she could prove her point right away.

Sam had just drawn a breath to test her plan on Jen, when a boy's shout cut her off.

"Look at those fools!"

Every student on the bus watched a black truck swerve across the range, raising a rooster's tail of dust. A skinny, shirtless guy stood in the truck bed, hugging the cab for balance. A lariat dangled from his hand, but he was hanging on too hard to use it.

"They're chasing a horse," Jen said, pointing. "It must be for the reward. Look, the truck has Idaho license plates."

But Sam couldn't look away from the horse. Long-limbed and root-beer-colored, he raced toward the school bus. Their driver slowed to let him pass.

As he did, Sam noticed the animal wasn't young. His muzzle was gray and the bridge of his nose had been rubbed bare by years of wearing a bridle.

"He's not even wild," Sam gasped.

"He looks like an old saddle horse someone turned out after years of ranch work," Jen agreed. "Some reward."

"I'm phoning the BLM as soon as I get to school," Sam said.

"Your dad already did," Jen reminded her. "It didn't do any good."

Although Sam blamed the men in the black truck for their actions, Slocum had created this craziness by dangling a reward.

"I'm calling the BLM again," Sam insisted as the truck drove out of sight. "And I won't hang up until someone listens."

Jen nodded, then withdrew a pen from her backpack, grabbed Sam's hand, and began writing on it.

"What's that?" Sam asked.

"The truck's license plate number." Jen shrugged at Sam's amazement. "Numbers just stick in my brain."

Things could go wrong in such a hurry.

As soon as Sam arrived at school, she jogged to the journalism room. Mr. Blair let her use his telephone and listened while she talked.

After she reported the men harassing the horse, an efficient voice at the Willow Springs holding pens thanked Sam and explained that a ranger had already been dispatched to deal with the situation.

Sam's next ugly chore was to tell Mr. Blair about the camera. He didn't seem shocked. In fact, he was almost sympathetic as he looked the camera over and agreed with Mrs. Ely's diagnosis of a broken mirror.

"You'll have to pay for the repair," he said. "But it shouldn't be more than a couple hundred dollars."

Before Sam could hit the floor in a faint, Mr. Blair explained how she would go about earning money to pay for the repair. That was when Sam felt the icy fingers of panic.

"One of those sandwiches and one package of—no, two packages of corn chips."

Halfway through her first shift in Darton High School's snack bar, Sam had reached three conclusions.

One, teenagers really did have lousy diets.

Two, she must earn good grades and attend college to avoid long-term snack bar employment.

Three, if another dollar bill stamped with Rachel's name smeared pink ink on her hands, she would scream.

This was Mr. Blair's remedy for penniless wrongdoers. She worked in the school snack bar but never saw a dollar of her wages. The Darton High bookkeeper deposited Sam's pay directly into the school newspaper's bank account.

Sam stared through the order window, trying to enjoy the sunlight and forget tomorrow's algebra test.

The job wasn't too bad. Jen had come by to sympathize and so had Jake's friend Darrell, though he was mostly interested in negotiating a deal on sunflower seeds. That meant Jake would know about her humiliation soon.

All at once, her view of the school courtyard vanished.

"Samantha Forster." Rachel strained to put a British slant on the name. "Whatever are you doing here?"

Sam couldn't think of a clever answer, so she extended a cellophane-wrapped dessert.

"Want a Ding Dong, Rachel?" Sam thought how appropriate it was that she'd been basking in the sunshine streaming through the snack bar window until Rachel blocked it.

"What I want is for you to explain why a ranger showed up at my house this morning." Rachel's expressive hands reminded Sam of rosy talons.

"Hurry," urged a voice from behind Rachel. "The bell's gonna ring in a minute and—"

Rachel swung to face the impatient customer.

"Do you mind?" Her icy tone sent the boy running.

Sam looked after the guy, grateful he'd distracted Rachel.

"Go ahead and play innocent," Rachel snarled when Sam didn't speak. "But you've declared war on the wrong family. You have no idea how unpleasant your life will be if you decide to stick around." Then she flounced off without buying a thing.

Sam and Rachel ignored each other during journalism. In fact, the newspaper staff labored toward a deadline in near silence. The only sounds were tapping computer keys and rustling paper.

Three minutes before class ended, Mr. Blair approached Sam. She braced herself for the possibility that the camera was ruined.

"Forster, are you still interested in night shoots?" he asked.

Night shoots. Sam's relief was so great, it took her a few seconds to understand. Then she nodded vigorously.

"Do you think I can do them with this?" Sam held up Mrs. Ely's old Pentax.

"Sure. It'd be easier with one of those little point-and-shoot jobs you see on television, but you wouldn't learn anything.

"Quick lesson." Mr. Blair glanced at the clock. "Listen up."

As he explained, Sam took notes on the back of an algebra worksheet. The grade on the front side wasn't worth saving.

Most of Mr. Blair's directions made sense. She hoped she understood enough to carry out the plan she and Jen had put together.

Sam checked her watch and counted. In four hours, she should be arriving to study algebra and spend the night at Jen's house. In five and a half hours, Jen's parents should be driving off for their weekly "date" in Darton. Just after that, Sam would be crouched and ready for the blue stallion's appearance.

A day or two later, she figured, she'd be rich.

"Hey, Forster, no daydreaming." Mr. Blair snapped

his fingers. "Don't be afraid to *shoot*. Keep shooting as long as there's something to see."

The bell shrilled, class ended, and Sam rushed out. She needed to find Jen and work out a few more details.

They spent so long conspiring at the bus stop, Sam and Jen both had to jog home before someone came looking for them.

Dressed in jeans and a white blouse, with her hair in a tidy knot, Gram waited for Sam at the door.

"What did your teacher say about the camera?" Gram asked.

Sam explained and prepared to launch her plan, but when she entered the house, she was nearly sidetracked. A meringue-topped lemon pie sat on the kitchen table.

She loved lemon meringue pie and Gram knew it. Since Sam had worked through the lunch hour, she was hungry. She could almost taste the sugary meringue and lemon tartness on her tongue.

But some things were more important than food. Like saving her horse. Sam turned her back on the pie and met Gram's eyes.

"Gram, I got a C-minus on my algebra pretest today." Sam saw Gram wince. "Tomorrow is the real test, and Jen offered to help me study. I know it's a school night, but numbers just come naturally to her and I really need the help."

"Why didn't you girls get together right after school?" Gram asked.

"I had my chores to do." Sam gestured toward the pasture and barn. Though Buddy's brand and Ace's bites were almost healed, Sam still checked them. And of course there were chickens to tend and water troughs to check. "So can I please spend the night?"

"I guess it wouldn't hurt," Gram said, "if you two don't stay up too late."

"We still have to catch the bus in the morning," Sam said, and Gram nodded. Sam figured she could sleep in this weekend.

If there was a truer test of friendship, Sam couldn't imagine it. Jen offered to help Sam study the material for her algebra test. Instead, Jen ended up teaching.

"You really don't get this, do you?" Jen was mystified.

"I really don't, but you make more sense than any teacher I've had so far."

"Cool," Jen said. "Wait until you see me on linear equations."

At last Sam declared her brain was full, so the girls baked frozen pizza and drank sodas. After washing the dishes, they picked the perfect spot for Sam and her camera.

The sorrel mare, Kitty, had been trotting along the fence since dusk. Her high-strung actions convinced the girls that Hammer was near.

"I know it will work," Jen said. "It's not like you're trying to catch him, just photograph him. What can go wrong?"

"Your parents could come home early."

"They won't," said Jen. "Statistically speaking, it cannot happen. My parents are creatures of habit."

Because she planned to be tucked up inside the house watching television while Sam shivered behind a tree stump, Jen refused to share the reward money. She did agree to let Sam buy her a poster of her hero, mathematician and scientist Albert Einstein, if everything went as planned.

Now Sam crouched next to Kitty's corral, reviewing Mr. Blair's advice on shooting in the darkness. When she tired of that, she watched Kitty. She couldn't ignore the Phantom's mother.

Clean-limbed and graceful, Kitty trotted around the corral, then stopped a few feet from Sam. When Kitty cocked her head to the side, as if wondering what Sam was up to, a lock of flaxen mane veiled one eye.

Sam smooched at the mare. Kitty's ears flickered back and forth; then she struck at the dirt with a foreleg. Sam had seen the Phantom do the very same thing. Had he learned it from his mom? When Kitty lived at River Bend, she and her son had shared the same pasture for two years.

As the mare sidled near, Sam reached out. Kitty shied and bolted across the corral.

"Hey, girl," Sam said. "Don't be afraid."

Seconds later Kitty returned, alert ears turned to catch

Sam's voice. "Your baby's turned out real nice," Sam told the inquisitive mare. "He's a stallion with pretty colts of his own. You'd be proud of him."

Sam tried to shake off a wave of sadness. She needed to look through the camera's viewfinder. This was no time to let her eyes blur with tears simply because she missed her own mother.

The next time Kitty shied, Sam didn't move a muscle.

It must be him. The sorrel's head lifted. Her nostrils sampled the wind. Kitty stared into the darkness. Sam followed her stare but saw nothing. The mare snorted. Her legs were braced straight as broomsticks. Something was there.

A hoof clacked on asphalt. The Shetlands near the front gate moved across the frosty grass, and nickers floated on the night air.

Hammer, Sweetheart, and Apache Hotspot drifted like ghosts up the driveway.

Patience. Let them get closer, Sam told herself. Her fingers trembled. She'd done everything Mr. Blair suggested, except brace the camera against something solid. For that she'd have to wait until the horses moved into position.

The blue looked sleeker than before. Jets of steam huffed from his nostrils. His massive head swung from side to side, checking each shadow in the ranch yard.

Hammer didn't move as if his fight with the Phantom had lamed him. With rippling stealth the blue stallion drew closer, looking prehistoric and tough.

His shoulders churned as he came on. Ranch lights glimmered on wisps of hair under his chin, making the stallion look like a bearded unicorn. Sam remembered how Hammer had turned on her, treating her as an enemy, threatening to run her down just before the Phantom appeared. She didn't look forward to startling him.

Tonight the Phantom couldn't save her. If the blue stallion heard the click of the shutter, he'd be in her face or gone.

Just a few feet away sat a series of flat-topped redwood hitching posts with brass rings. As the stallion passed the farthest one, Sam thought she might use the nearest one to prop her camera on.

Almost there. Almost . . .

Far out, car headlights slashed across the desert. The electric gates whirred, responding to a remote-control opening the entrance to the Gold Dust Ranch.

Hammer hesitated, and Sam knew what she had to do.

She ran into the stallion's path. He reared. *Click*. He threatened her with his fury. *Click*.

Sam braced against the redwood post, following the stallion's rising torso and flailing forefeet. Then, as the Kenworthys' headlights lit the horses from behind, Sam took a final shot of the rearing stallion with the red-eyed mares behind him.

She expected the stallion to turn and run. Instead, he bolted straight toward her. Flint-hard hooves reached forward, pulling his body after. Sam ducked behind the redwood post and rolled to the ground, clutching Mrs. Ely's camera to her chest.

Eyes wide open, she saw the shaggy belly pass overhead. She heard the crash of his hooves landing, running past Sam, past Kitty, past Slocum's mansion on the hill, and into the night.

Chapter 18

SATURDAY MORNING, THE DAY AFTER SAM'S photograph ran on page one of the Darton *Review-Journal*, the newspaper still sat on the kitchen table.

ROGUE STALLION REVEALED! shouted the headline.

While Jake and Dad fought to read the follow-up article in today's newspaper, Sam ate the cinnamon toast Gram had just served and studied her picture again.

In rearing close-up, Hammer looked like a Wild West bronco. The mares behind him looked terrified. Sam almost wished the stallion captured on film had been the Phantom. At least it would mean he was alive.

It had been three days since she'd seen him, wounded and limping. Her amateurish vet care might not have been enough to save him from infection.

Sam shook her head against her gloomy thoughts and straightened the wrinkles in the newspaper. She'd studied the picture so often, it hardly seemed to be hers anymore, but the tiny type under the photograph read, PHOTO BY S. FORSTER.

Sam remembered how Mr. Blair had interrupted Mrs. Ely's history class to show Sam the picture as soon as he'd developed it.

Mr. Blair and Mrs. Ely had encouraged Sam to submit the photograph to the *Review-Journal*. They'd claimed the recognition would build her self-esteem, but Sam knew the truth. The teachers thought Linc Slocum would try to wriggle out of paying the reward.

That was exactly what he was doing.

The newspaper across the table rustled fiercely as Jake demanded their attention.

"Listen to this," Jake said, reading. "'The reward of

ten thousand dollars has yet to be paid. According to local rancher Lincoln Slocum, who offered the reward, "My posters clearly state the reward will be paid for the stallion's capture and information leading to Apache Hotspot's return. The filly is still out on the range. As far as I'm concerned, after running with that wild bunch, she can stay there.""

Gram, Dad, and Jake grumbled in disapproval.

Sam had another hope, though. She'd heard a helicopter making sweeps overhead all morning. Perhaps the BLM was on the stallion's trail.

"Never thought I'd be glad to hear those choppers." Dad echoed Sam's thought. "But that son of a gun Slocum owes you a college fund."

"And Sweetheart should be back here where she belongs," Gram said.

"I just want to hear Slocum tell Sam thank you." Jake laughed.

"But he is right." Sam went to the refrigerator for the pitcher of orange juice. "He—" Sam broke off when the phone rang. "I'll get it."

"Good morning, Samantha. This is Brynna Olson. Sorry to call so early—"

"Brynna? When did you get back?" Sam looked up. Jake met her eyes and began punching the air. He must think Brynna could force Slocum to pay up. Sam crossed her fingers.

"Yesterday. And I bet you can guess what I found on my desk when I went in to work."

"The newspaper?"

"Yesirree." Brynna's voice sounded young and completely unprofessional. "Congratulations on that super photograph and on snagging the reward."

"But, well . . ." Sam's voice faltered. She didn't want to drain away Brynna's excitement. "In today's paper, he says—" She broke off, realizing Brynna wasn't listening.

"What are you doing for lunch today?" Brynna asked. "Do you think you could make it to Clara's in Alkali at about noon?"

"I'll see." Sam felt awkward as she turned to Dad. "I don't quite understand what's going on, but Brynna is"—Sam spun her hand next to her head—"pretty excited. In fact, she's downright giddy, and she wants us to meet her at Clara's today at noon."

Dad drained his coffee cup and set it down hard. His face held no more expression than the tabletop as he said, "Tell her we'll be there."

Sam stared in amazement. Saturday was a serious workday on the River Bend Ranch. They never went out for lunch. Something was going on.

"Brynna? Dad says we'll be there."

"I don't suppose Clara serves champagne," Brynna said, laughing.

"What?" Sam wondered what had happened to Brynna in Washington.

"Never mind. Just plan on pineapple upside-down cake for everyone. And, Sam, you know what?"

Sam was almost afraid to ask, but curiosity won out. "What?"

"It'll be your treat."

The blue stallion didn't enjoy the party held in his honor. He kicked the tailgate of the horse trailer parked in front of Clara's Café.

Inside, the jukebox played, and Clara dealt out plates of cheeseburgers and fries to the table of rowdy customers celebrating Sam's victory.

But Sam stood over by the window, beside a young woman watching the horse trailer.

Rosa Perez had midnight hair and the flavor of New Mexico in her voice. "He is such a bad boy." Rosa tried to glimpse the horse inside the trailer, then turned to Sam with a smile. "And I am so glad to be taking him home."

Sam's photograph had helped the BLM capture the horses from a ravine on the other side of Lost Canyon.

Now Apache Hotspot and Sweetheart were back in their home corrals. And even before the horses were found, Brynna's first look at Sam's picture convinced her he was no mustang. Her second look revealed a half-grown-out body clip that some riders used to help endurance horses stay cool.

After that, a phone call and a risky peek at the tattoo inside the blue roan's upper lip verified it. "Hammer" was the California endurance champion Brynna had heard about by email weeks ago. Within hours, Rosa Perez had started driving to Willow Springs to be reunited with her beloved Diablo.

"I hope he didn't cause you any harm," Rosa said now. "I know he has a bad habit of charging."

Sam pictured the horse bearing down on her, ears pinned back, but she only shook her head.

"I bought him from a logger, who used him for pulling and, I think, whipped him a lot." Rosa looked back at the trailer and smiled. "He's mild as a dove with me."

"Some horses just bond with one person," Sam said, understanding.

She gazed at the road beyond the horse trailer. Any minute now, Linc Slocum was supposed to arrive with a check, making everything perfect.

All the same, Sam wasn't as happy as she should be. She missed the Phantom.

Since she'd bandaged his fetlock, there'd been no sign

of the mustang. Sam tried to think positively, but she couldn't stop worrying.

Laughter boomed from the table where Jake, Gram, Dad, and Brynna sat talking. Applause greeted a tray of Clara's pineapple upside-down cake.

Everyone was having fun, but Sam wouldn't really celebrate until she'd seen her horse, whole and healthy. The quickest way to do that was to retrace her steps to the Phantom's haven. Soon. It was only August, but the high pass and stone tunnel leading to the wild horse hideout could be blocked by an early snowfall.

"Sam! Come eat!" Jake held up a plate of cake.

"In a minute," she said. Sam noticed Dad had a little smear of pineapple next to his mouth. If she timed it right, maybe he'd say yes when she asked to return to the Phantom's home. Of course, that meant telling him about it.

From outside the café, Sam heard the blare of country music. She and Rosa squinted at sun glaring off the beige Cadillac. Slocum had arrived.

"Oh my," Rosa said.

Linc Slocum heaved himself free of the car and straightened the coat of his Western-style suit. The suit was purple as plum jam, but his Stetson was white and he wore a bolo tie set off by a polished rock.

Although neither Sam nor Rosa could hear what he said, they saw Slocum lean toward the horse trailer and speak to the stallion.

Diablo kicked the tailgate of his trailer with renewed vigor. Rosa reached into her purse for her car keys.

"Thank you again, Samantha, for everything." Rosa gave Sam a hug that said more than words. "I think I must leave before my endurance horse can endure no more."

Rosa waved and slipped through the café door. As Slocum tipped his Stetson after Rosa, Sam hurried back to the table and plopped into the chair next to Jake's.

"Mr. Slocum." Dressed in her khaki uniform, Brynna greeted the rancher strutting toward them.

Sam uncrossed her arms and legs. A second later, she realized she'd crossed them again. Slocum had an oblong piece of paper in his hand. It was really going to happen.

"Hello, folks," he said. "I figured—"

Slocum blushed. All his bluster was costing him a small fortune. Sam tried to feel sorry for Slocum, but she couldn't.

"That is, Miss Samantha—"

Then Jake caught Sam's eye. In a subtle movement, Jake rubbed the side of his neck, reminding Sam of the Phantom's scar. Sam straightened in her chair and met Slocum's bashful expression with a glare.

Since Slocum couldn't pay the stallion for the pain he'd inflicted, the next best thing was paying someone who loved him.

"Yes, Mr. Slocum?" Sam stood.

"Well, I know Wyatt is just as happy as a dog with two tails to wag, so I won't take up your time. Thanks for finding that filly of mine and getting her home, uh, safe."

Sam knew why Slocum hesitated over the last word. The vet who'd checked the animals after capture suspected Hotspot was in foal.

Slocum ran his fingers through his slicked-back hair

until it stuck out at odd angles. "In fact," he said with a short laugh, "I may just insist you take a bonus with your reward check. How 'bout you keep one stall open, Wyatt? This baby may not fit in with my Appaloosa breeding program. Still, with those two for parents, you might end up with a colt who's fast as a caged squirrel."

As those around her laughed, Sam took the check. This skinny piece of paper would pay Mr. Blair for the camera, put in new fence rails where Diablo had broken them, and replace River Bend's aged pump. Dad was making her save the rest for college, but she planned to keep back a few dollars for a present.

Jake looked over in surprise as Sam squeezed his hand. She couldn't help thinking about his October 1 birthday and the beautiful bridle just waiting in Tully's Western Wear.

Frost clung like silver icing to every twig and branch as Sam rode Ace away from the Calico Mountain camp the next morning. An early cold snap made frozen brush sparkle as the sun rose. It was all the more beautiful because Jake had let her come alone.

Trusting her, even though she wouldn't tell exactly where she was going, Dad had allowed Jake to drive Sam back to the Phantom's territory. He'd instructed Jake to let her approach the stallion's secret haven alone.

Sam checked her watch. It was five a.m.

Jake had driven to the site where they'd held the cattle during the cattle drive. That night she and Ace had been kidnapped by the Phantom.

As soon as they'd arrived, Sam had unloaded the horses while Jake built a campfire, positioned his sleeping bag next to it, then crawled inside.

Leaning on one elbow, he'd rattled off orders.

"You've got two hours to get there and get back, or I'm coming after you," Jake insisted. "Witch can catch your old pony without even trying."

Sam was counting on Ace to help find the mustangs' hideout. Everything looked different than it had in early summer.

A crystal forest of cottonwood trees crowded around

her, and the broad plain seemed smaller. Was Ace taking a different approach to the stone tunnel and wild valley?

The footing turned steep. That seemed right. Sam recalled shale shaped like dinner plates, but she didn't see it as they climbed upward.

Sam kept her weight balanced, sparing Ace. The little mustang snorted and looked from side to side, more watchful than ever.

"Do we need the Phantom to lead us back, boy?"

Ace shook his head so hard, the buckles on his headstall clinked. Sam loosened the reins, wishing the stallion would appear.

Fear hovered over her like a storm cloud. What if she found the way back and her horse wasn't there?

All at once Sam saw the faint path Ace was following. It was no more than a dust smear through silver-green sagebrush. Though it ran along a cliff, Ace's delicate hooves navigated it with ease.

"Good boy," Sam whispered, and then she saw what the uncertain light had hidden. A steeper path climbed a cleft between two rocks, and suddenly they moved into darkness.

Ace stopped. His hooves echoed as he shifted from hoof to hoof on the slick rock, but he didn't go forward.

Sam listened. She dismounted, then ground-tied Ace, as if the act of holding the reins could distract her from something she must hear.

The tunnel turned from brown-gray to black just ahead.

"You stay, boy. I'll be back."

Sam walked into the gloom. She wouldn't think of bats, of earthquakes, of tons of stone hanging overhead.

The way ahead was silent. Cold shimmered from the walls. She could not hear the rushing stream in the Phantom's hidden valley, nor the squeals of hungry foals. She heard no hooves striking rock, telling her the stallion was coming to meet her.

Was she lost? Sam wrapped her arms around her waist, shrinking away from the narrowing stone walls. Could this be the wrong tunnel?

Up ahead, brightness flickered. Cheered as if sunlight

warmed her, Sam recalled a crack in the tunnel roof. That must be it.

But it wasn't formless daylight. The pale shape wavered like a ghost. Zanzibar?

It couldn't be. No matter how wild, no animal could move so silently. Then she said the word aloud. "Zanzibar."

In this lonely cavern, it must be safe to speak a secret name.

For a heartbeat, Sam blinked against the brightness, and then her stallion stood before her, whole and healthy.

His front hooves lifted off the stone floor, spinning in a blur. He would have reared in greeting if not for the low stone ceiling.

His back hooves pranced with no trace of a limp. *No limp.*

This time Sam didn't think. She embraced his silvery neck, and though the stallion lifted her briefly off her feet, he didn't run. He didn't flinch. He didn't bowl her over or neigh a protest.

The stallion stood, head over Sam's shoulder, chin moving up and down her spine, as if he hugged her, too.

"You're safe." Tears stung her eyes, but Sam blinked them away. She refused to miss an instant of magic.

It was a good thing, because Zanzibar leaped backward. Head tossing, he gave her chest a push. Off-balance, Sam retreated a step. With the persistence of a father moving his child along, the stallion urged her back another step, toward Ace, still ground-tied and waiting.

Sam stepped backward until Ace's whinny vibrated through the tunnel. For only a second, Sam looked behind her.

When she turned to face the stallion one last time, shadows had taken his place.

"He was here, Ace." Her voice echoed around her, and the gelding nickered in agreement.

Zanzibar was alive. He'd come back to tell her so.

As Sam walked out of the darkness, love bounded up in her like a fountain.

Read on for an excerpt from Sam's journal!

Dear Mom,

Tomorrow I start a new life at Darton High School. I'm excited and worried.

I won't know anyone except Jake. I don't expect him to hang around with me. People would think we're a couple and NO, we definitely are not. Plus, he'll be happy to see his own friends.

I'm not sure what to wear, but I'm trying to remember all the advice Aunt Sue gave me last year in San Francisco. And at least I want to be here in Nevada. I did not want to be in San Francisco.

Aunt Sue understood that clothes were important to feel like I sort of fit in. We looked at the school's website and then looked at my clothes to pick something not too dressy and not too casual.

She told me to sign up for every sport or club or activity that caught my interest, and it worked. Basketball is where I made my first friends. Gram and Dad don't understand. "What are you worried about? You've only been gone for a couple years."

Socially, a couple of years might as well be twenty. There's a big difference between eleven years old and thirteen, and I'm sure anyone I <u>did</u> know back then is totally aware of why I've been gone. Head injury.

Will signing up for stuff work like it did in San Francisco? I have ranch chores and I want to get home to ride Ace, not plan school dances or assemblies.

But this is what I can do: write down all my

questions, even silly ones like how many minutes do I have to get from one class to another. To find answers, I'll start with going through that orientation packet the school sent me. Gram has been nagging me to read it, and she might be right. Knowing answers to my questions could make me less nervous.

 P.S. Mom, please don't think I'm complaining about chores! If you had to leave, you left me in the perfect place. Blue skies on forever. When there's dust on the horizon, there's always the chance it will be wild horses. I have everything I love except you. I bet you miss the smells of fresh straw and saddle leather and the brush of a hen's soft feathers on the back of your hand as you reach under her, into her nest, to collect smooth brown eggs. I love you and I miss you and I would do anything to feel your hug wrapped around me again.

Dear Mom,

When horses are the most important thing in my life, why am I still making mistakes about them? I always thought when cowboys called a horse a "hammer head," it meant that it had a big head. I was wrong.

    A mystery stallion is slipping like a shadow into River Bend and Gold Dust ranches. I'm the only one who's seen him. He's no taller than Ace, but his muscles are compact where Ace's are long. I've been calling him Hammer because my first glimpse in the darkness made me think his head was a bit too big for his body. So, a hammer head. But today I noticed Dallas shaking out his saddle blanket by the tack room, and he looked at me and waved me to come over. When I got right by him, he asked what I meant by "hammer head."

I froze. I knew he wouldn't ask if I hadn't made another tenderfoot mistake, but I had to answer.

"It's a horse with an oversized head, right?" When Dallas stayed so quiet that I could hear the pigeons in the barn rafters, I tried a second guess. "Is it a not-very-smart horse?"

"Nope. Neither one, Sam. Let me show you something."

Dallas reached toward a toolbox on the tack room floor and lifted out an actual hammer.

He held it up, ran his hand along the part you grip, and said, "Some horses are born with short necks. They don't curve all graceful like Ace's or Sweetheart's or even Amigo's. Doesn't mean they can't be good to ride, but when a horse's head juts straight out from his neck," he said, moving his hand up to the metal part of the hammer, "that's when he's called—" Dallas paused like a teacher trying to get the right answer from me.

"A hammer head," I said.

Even though I know Dallas was trying to keep me from being embarrassed later, I feel my face blushing right this minute.

Dear Mom,

I did another embarrassing horse thing. No, not just embarrassing. It was dangerous. I'm glad that no one was there to see what happened.

Today Ace needed a rest and Dad gave me a choice of any of the saddle horses to ride out to meet Jen. He trusted me to make a good choice and I thought I had. But no.

I picked Strawberry because I'd ridden her before, on the cattle drive, and we got along just fine, even though Strawberry considers herself the boss of all the saddle horses—the lead MARE.

Now, because you know horses, you're probably thinking about the blue roan mystery stallion that's been skulking around River Bend and Gold Dust ranches stealing MARES.

I didn't realize my mistake until I'd ridden Strawberry all the way out to War Drum Flats. There I was, just sitting there, waiting for Jen, when I looked and—ding, ding, ding—saw Hammer standing on the ridge with Sweetheart and Hotspot, Linc Slocum's Appaloosa mare.

Yes, Hammer tried to steal Strawberry away from me. No, I wasn't hurt. Yes, Strawberry was pretty interested in having a playdate with Hammer. No, I didn't let her go. I brought her home safe and sound.

The only thing that makes me feel a teeny bit better about my mistake is that my new friend Jen, a real cowgirl, rode her palomino mare Silk

Stockings out to meet me, and she knew that stallion was on the loose too. So there.

Dear Mom,

Gram says I never really had a hobby as a little kid. Instead, I had collections of rocks, colored pencils, and pocket-sized pony toys.

    Wait! I just looked up at the top shelf of my desk, and the rocks and ponies are lined up along it, and right here, where I'm writing, there's a red mug full of colored pencils! How weird that I just noticed that Gram saved everything!

    So, September of my freshman year, I do have a hobby: photography. It took me until now to appreciate how I can catch a moment and keep it forever. You knew Jake's mom, Maxine Ely, didn't you? She's helping me with my photography. I've been writing down all her tips. When Mr. Blair saw them, he asked me to make a handout he could give to other students. You should have seen Rachel roll her eyes. She's Linc Slocum's daughter. Be glad you never met her. She thinks her superpower is fashion. I think it's hearing anyone getting recognition, so she can belittle them.

    My list so far:

    Be patient.

    Sunrise and sunset have golden light.

    Get close to your subject (physically or with a longer lens).

Look for clean backgrounds to simplify your photo.

Look for moments between people or animals when they're communicating.

If you're at a crowded event and everyone's looking in the same direction—like at football games, parades, assemblies—turn around and photograph expressions on people's faces.

Dear Mom,
I don't think Hammer is a wild horse! When he was so close to me and Strawberry at War Drum Flats, I noticed something, but it didn't sink in until now. His whiskers were really, really short! I think they were shaved off and they're growing back.

Remember that day when I was feeding Sweetheart apple slices and got prickled by whiskers? I must have been really young, because I had to stand on tiptoe to touch the white heart shape on her brown body.

I was whining about her prickly whiskers, and you told me she had them for a reason. You said even though horses' eyes are on the sides of their heads, they have two blind spots. One spot is right behind a horse's tail, and that was why I should never walk up and surprise a horse from that direction. But the other blind spot is directly in front, and horses use the stiff whiskers (not the long, silky chin hairs) to test out whether it's safe to eat something that they can't see!

So Hammer, if he were wild, would have

whiskers. But I also know that some people shave off whiskers because they think it makes their horse's muzzle look neater.

I wonder if he's some kind of show horse. He doesn't act like it, but he's not afraid to come onto the ranch with all its fences and human smells, and he sure wasn't shy around me, so I think it's possible!

Dear Mom,
The Phantom was hurt, and he trusted me to help him. He fought Hammer and won, but that's not the point. He let me touch his blood-crusted, swollen fetlock. It was hot and feverish, and it had to hurt, but he believed I'd help him. It was his left rear leg.

I washed it and he stayed on three hooves, keeping watch as I worked on him.

Each time I glanced up, his brown eyes gazed back at me through his forelock. Our eyes only left each other's for seconds at a time. I was crouched at the feet of this powerful stallion. I had to be hurting him, but he trusted me. How did he know that I only hurt him to help him?

I was almost finished molding a bread poultice to his leg when I felt a squeeze in my chest and realized that I was so completely myself. I wasn't being a daughter, a student, or a friend. He was a horse. I was a human. We two creatures made a language with our eyes, and it was better than any words could ever be.

Sam's Dictionary

DARKROOM: These special little rooms used to be vital to every newspaper and magazine. All photographers ducked into these dark rooms, lit only by red light, to develop film. Only then could they see if they'd caught the image they wanted! Now darkrooms are antiques. The one at Darton High School is about as big as the inside of Gram's car. It has a revolving door that sort of rolls you into the space where red light keeps pictures from being overexposed. We use digital cameras

SAM'S DICTIONARY

for almost everything, but students in journalism have to turn in five darkroom photographs each semester. Mr. Blair, my journalism teacher, says students learn a lot using photosensitive paper to produce a unique photograph. He says we should be <u>exposed</u> to the artistic side of photography.

CORPORATE RANCHES: Big businesses—corporations—own lots of land in the West, but they make their money from oil, prescription drugs, computers, and other kinds of companies. Money is what makes them different from River Bend Ranch. Dad and Gram make our money—all our family earnings—from River Bend's cattle, horses, and horse training. We worry about storms ruining our hay crops or a fire burning a barn. Corporations buy ranches to get tax benefits from the government, and Dallas says corporations can make more money in bad years than good. Movie stars and people like Linc Slocum buy ranches too. Some want to live like cowboys or get away from

SAM'S DICTIONARY

their city lives. Whatever their motivations, when a family ranch isn't making enough money to support the family, Gram says there's always a big business or multimillionaire ready to "swoop in like a vulture" and buy it.

Acknowledgments

Just as Sam discovers a love for photography in this book, I've discovered an overwhelming appreciation for photographers and photojournalists while writing the Phantom Stallion. In high desert heat and mountain snows, they've brought wild horses stampeding into my real life and imagination. With them I've crept through sagebrush, waited for dawn light, witnessed the tenderness of wild stallions with their foals and the matriarchal wisdom of lead mares. Photographers document the cruelty of wild horse roundups, the heartbreak of the auction ring, and, for a few lucky horses, a second life with a family band of humans.

You and I can view wild horses on our phones, laptops, or in framed photos on our walls because these people use their skills for us. They believe that people can't care about the lives of horses if they can't see them.

ACKNOWLEDGEMENTS

I've spent months adding to my list of image-makers, but I have no doubt that I will still miss some! Please know that my gratitude is no less genuine for those I've accidentally left out.

Richie Asencio, Cheryl Broumley, Jim Brown, Mary Cioffi, Kimerlee Curyl, Mary Dibble, Margaret Dziolek, Melissa Farlow, Mary Hone, John Humphrey, Ginger Kathrens, Cat Kindsfather, Laura Leigh, Maria Marriott, Deborah Sutherland, Mark Terrell, Carol Walker, Scott Wilson, and Marty Wright

Read on for a sneak peek at the next book in the Phantom Stallion series: *Dark Sunshine.*

THE SWEET SMELL OF HORSES AND HAY CARried to Samantha Forster on an early morning breeze. She eased the front door closed behind her. Everyone inside was asleep. By rising at four o'clock, she'd beaten even Dad out of bed.

Sam stifled a yawn. She could have slept in on this September Saturday, but she and Jen planned to unlock the secrets of Lost Canyon before the sun rose.

Strange things were happening in Lost Canyon. Weird white plumes rose skyward. Were they dust, smoke, or spirits, as some Shoshone elders hinted? And what about those eerie screams?

Standing at the bus stop just the other morning, Sam and Jen had heard the faraway wails. Though they'd agreed those sounds weren't the cries of Native ponies slaughtered there a hundred years ago, she and Jen had scared each other with other "what-ifs." They'd been rubbing gooseflesh from their arms when the school bus finally arrived.

Now Sam moved silently across the front porch of the white, two-story house. She carried her boots and walked in stockinged feet. With Gram and Dad still asleep, River Bend Ranch was all hers.

Darkness cloaked the neat pens and corrals, the barn and bunkhouse, and the surrounding rangelands where Hereford cattle grazed, but Sam knew it was all there waiting for her.

As she pulled on her scarred leather boots, Sam glanced toward the river. Across the current, on the wild side of the river, the Phantom could be waiting. But he had never come to the ranch this near sunrise and probably never would.

Sam hefted her saddlebags and canteen and walked toward the barn.

Blaze woofed from his post outside the bunkhouse. The Border Collie's bark startled a horse. Its hooves went thudding across the ten-acre pasture.

A few steps from the barn, a neigh challenged her.

"It's only me, baby," Sam whispered. She hurried. Once Ace knew it was her, he'd set up a ruckus.

Fingers flying, Sam drew the bolt on the door connecting the barn and corral. Ace followed as Sam flipped the switch for the overhead lights. The little mustang nudged Sam until he backed her against the barn wall.

That nudge, what Dallas, the ranch foreman, would call misbehavior, she called love.

"You are too sweet." She caught Ace's muzzle between her hands and gave it a quick kiss.

Sam dragged a curry comb over Ace's already glowing coat. He wasn't crosstied or tethered; he just stood with eyes half-closed as he enjoyed the massaging movements of the brush.

When Sam stopped, Ace looked back over his shoulder as she smoothed on the blanket. Next, she saddled him and replaced his halter with a snaffle-bitted bridle.

Sam shivered. She should have remembered a jacket. Since she hadn't, she snatched the faded green sweatshirt she kept hanging from a nail in the barn. Before pulling it on, she dropped Ace's reins, ground-tying him.

Like any well-schooled cow pony, Ace understood the signal to stand and wait. He snorted with impatience, though, as Sam tugged the sweatshirt over her short reddish hair.

"Sorry." Sam's muffled voice came from inside the sweatshirt.

Ace pawed the barn floor, stirring dust until she led him into the yard.

Before she could mount, Ace raised his finely boned, almost Arabic head. His nostrils flared as he gazed at the Calico Mountains, where a rim of midnight blue showed above the peaks.

Sam swung into the saddle.

The Renegade

Also by Terri Farley

The Wild One
Mustang Moon
Dark Sunshine

The Renegade

ALADDIN
New York London Toronto Sydney New Delhi

If you purchased this book without a cover, you should be aware that this book is stolen property. It was reported as "unsold and destroyed" to the publisher, and neither the author nor the publisher has received any payment for this "stripped book."

This book is a work of fiction. Any references to historical events, real people, or real places are used fictitiously. Other names, characters, places, and events are products of the author's imagination, and any resemblance to actual events or places or persons, living or dead, is entirely coincidental.

🪔 ALADDIN
An imprint of Simon & Schuster Children's Publishing Division
1230 Avenue of the Americas, New York, New York 10020
First Aladdin paperback edition March 2024
Text copyright © 2002 by Terri Sprenger-Farley
Cover illustration copyright © 2024 by Louise Meijer-Åström
Map on pages vi–vii copyright © 2024 by Francesca Baerald
Illustration of notebook on pages 296–307 by aopsan/iStock
Also available in an Aladdin hardcover edition.
All rights reserved, including the right of reproduction in whole or in part in any form.
ALADDIN and related logo are registered trademarks of Simon & Schuster, LLC
Simon & Schuster: Celebrating 100 Years of Publishing in 2024
For information about special discounts for bulk purchases, please contact Simon & Schuster Special Sales at 1-866-506-1949 or business@simonandschuster.com.
The Simon & Schuster Speakers Bureau can bring authors to your live event. For more information or to book an event contact the Simon & Schuster Speakers Bureau at 1-866-248-3049 or visit our website at www.simonspeakers.com.
Designed by Tiara Iandiorio
The text of this book was set in Adobe Garamond Pro.
Manufactured in the United States of America 0124 OFF
10 9 8 7 6 5 4 3 2 1
Library of Congress Control Number 2023948709
ISBN 9781665916417 (hc)
ISBN 9781665916400 (pbk)
ISBN 9781665916424 (ebook)

The Renegade

Chapter 1

IN RIVER BEND'S BIG PASTURE, THE HORSES waited for rain. Cottonwood branches danced overhead, but instead of rustling, the dry leaves clacked. The horses stood with heads up and nostrils wide, searching for a trace of moisture on the breeze.

Across the dirt driveway, near the house, Sam did the same. She stood in the vegetable garden, where she was supposed to be turning over dirt to mix parched cornstalks and empty vines with the earth. Instead, she leaned on her shovel and wished she'd brought a water bottle outside with her.

Two sparrows dove for a worm her digging had uncovered. The birds cheeped and quarreled, then flew off in a flurry of feathers, leaving the lucky worm untouched.

Sam looked skyward. The sun was sealed down by a lid of gray clouds.

Irritated whinnies and the thud of hooves came from the big pasture. Banjo, Dad's roping horse, bolted across the sparse grass. Teeth bared, Strawberry sprinted after him.

Except for a few hammering rainstorms that ran off the drought-hardened land, it hadn't rained since spring. Now it was October. Every creature was edgy with waiting.

More hooves thudded inside the round pen, but these made a soothing sound, just like the voice that directed them.

"Other way," Jake said. "Good horse."

Friday after school, Jake had mounted Teddy Bear for the first time. Now it was Saturday morning, and the colt was already responding to the bit and reins.

THE RENEGADE

The morning quiet didn't last for long. Blaze burst barking from the barn, and Sam noticed a plume of dust approaching the ranch. The roar of an overtaxed engine told her who was driving even before the beige Cadillac crossed the bridge too fast and skidded into the ranch yard.

Sam dropped the shovel. For their neighbor Linc Slocum, everything was a crisis. Still, it was always possible it was a real emergency.

The Cadillac's horn blared, even though Gram had already appeared, wiping her hands on her apron. Dallas, the ranch foreman, had emerged from the shady barn, blinking against the sunlight.

Jake slipped out of the round corral and beat everyone to Slocum's side.

"Rachel's missing," Linc said as Sam got close enough to hear.

Gram patted Linc's arm as the man removed his oversized cowboy hat and sighed.

"I don't know what to think," he explained. "I'd just got back from riding with Jed." Linc scanned faces, making sure they recognized the name of Jed Kenworthy, his foreman. "But he stayed out with the other hands and I came back. Otherwise I sure would've got him helping me."

"How long has she been gone?" Gram asked.

"Hard to say. Let's see." Linc squinted as he tried to recall. "When I got back home, Rachel was lazing around her suite, and then I had a snack and after that I sorta dozed off." He shook his head. "I'd say at least a coupla hours."

Sam's eyes slid toward Jake. Jake was only sixteen, but he spotted trouble better than anyone Sam knew. And he didn't look worried. In fact, when he crossed his arms over his belt buckle, he seemed to be telling Linc to get to the point.

"Thing is," Slocum said, sounding as if he were about to make a confession, "she was perturbed about something. In fact, she's been sort of put out—say, how long has it been since I had the rodeo stock contractor over to the house?" Slocum mused a minute. "All week. Yessir." Linc sounded amazed. "She's been perturbed all week long."

THE RENEGADE

For an instant, Sam wondered how he could tell perturbation from Rachel's usual attitude, but then she understood his amazement. How could Rachel be dissatisfied for a full week? She wore the finest clothes and makeup. A driver took her to school in a baby-blue Mercedes-Benz, and her bedroom suite included a hot tub and state-of-the-art entertainment systems.

Rachel was her father's princess, and she pretty much ruled Darton High School as well. Her face, hair, and figure might have been composed by a computer designing the perfect girl.

Too bad no one had pushed the button marked PERSONALITY, Sam thought.

"Could the stock contractor have said something to upset her?" Gram asked.

"No, no way." Linc actually blushed. "We were cutting a deal for my Brahmas, that's all."

Did Linc redden because the stock contractor had rejected his bulls? City-bred Slocum really didn't know what he was doing when it came to animals, Sam thought. He just liked playing cowboy.

"Where do you think she's got off to?" Dallas asked. He sounded more sympathetic than Sam felt.

"Did she take a car?" Jake added. Though Rachel didn't have a driver's license, she wouldn't let such a formality stop her.

"No, she didn't, and no one came to pick her up or I would've heard tires." Linc wedged a thumb into the tooled leather belt that strained around his middle. "But my horse is missing too."

"Why would she take Champ? Rachel hates horses," Sam blurted.

"Well, now—" Slocum frowned.

"She does," Sam insisted. "She says they're dumb and dirty, and she can't understand why anyone likes them."

Gram made a cautioning sound, but Sam knew she was right.

"I don't mean to be rude, Mr. Slocum, but she told me all that herself."

"My ex-wife made the twins ride for three hours every day when they were little," Slocum said. "Ryan took to it and Rachel didn't. Maybe that's why he's in England.

Now that his mom's married that baron, or whatever he is, they have stables packed with horses."

Slocum sounded wistful. For about two seconds, Sam felt sorry for him. Then she remembered the spade bit he used on Champ, his gentle-natured palomino. In the hands of an excellent rider, the bit could work. Hauled on by an angry girl who didn't like horses, that bit could do terrible damage to Champ's tender mouth.

"Let's go find her," Sam said.

"I'll be glad to pay—" Slocum began.

"Land sakes, Linc, will you hush?" Gram snapped. One of her hands darted out as if she wanted to give Slocum a pinch. Instead, she shook her finger at him. "We'll help because we're neighbors, not because you have money."

Gram took Western neighborliness seriously. Her tirade made Linc look sheepish.

"Wyatt's checking the herd with Ross and Pepper," Gram said, "but the rest of us will saddle up. I don't imagine she's gone far. Have you called over to the Elys'?"

Gram gestured toward the Three Ponies Ranch, Jake's home.

"No," Linc said. "I think Rachel would be embarrassed. Mainly I came for Jake."

Jake shrugged modestly. Sam wished she had a skill she could be humble about. Jake was a first-rate tracker. Local ranchers, the Bureau of Land Management, and even the sheriff's department knew it.

"Sure," Jake said. His eyes darted skyward at a rumble of far-off thunder. "I'd want to start at your ranch, though."

"You do that," Gram said. "And, Linc, we'll go up the ridge trail, since it runs behind your place, ours, and Three Ponies." Gram removed her apron and started for the barn and her mare, Sweetheart.

"Hop in, Jake." Slocum gestured toward the Cadillac, but Jake glanced at the round corral, where Teddy Bear stood saddled and curious.

"I'll take care of the colt," Dallas said. "You go on."

Sam bit her lip. Jake had teased her forever, calling her a tagalong brat, but she couldn't help it. "I'd really like to watch you track," she said.

Jake didn't reply. Did he suspect she also wanted to see Rachel uncomfortable?

Sam stared hard at the back of Jake's head as he unstrapped the short, fringed chaps called chinks and slung them over the top rail of the corral.

Finally, her brain waves must have penetrated his thick skull.

"You might as well come." He didn't even look her way. "Rachel might not be so embarrassed with you there."

He was right, Sam thought as she climbed into the Cadillac's back seat. She brought out Rachel's natural snobbishness. Rachel couldn't believe there were people who actually liked "the little cowgirl," as she called Sam.

Sam tightened her seat belt, as Linc Slocum drove fast and recklessly. If he was so worried, why hadn't he gone looking for Rachel himself?

Jake grabbed an armrest as Slocum swerved around a turn. Sam hoped Linc wouldn't hit anything. She'd hate to miss a chance to see Rachel in trouble. After the mean things Rachel had said and done, it would be sort of satisfying to see her squirm.

But that wasn't going to happen. Rachel wouldn't be punished for causing Linc to worry, and Sam knew why. When they found Rachel, she wouldn't be sunburned or dusty. Every hair would be in place, and she'd blame someone else for her troubles.

When they reached Slocum's Gold Dust Ranch, he surprised them by saying he wouldn't come along.

"I'll stay by the phone," he said. "You just take any horses you want. The tack shed's over there."

Any other time, Sam would have rejoiced. The Gold Dust Ranch was home to dozens of expensive and beautiful horses. But Jake was in a hurry. He flashed her a look that said she'd better not knock on the door to the foreman's house and tell her best friend, Jen Kenworthy, what was happening.

Sam and Jake took the mounts easiest to catch, then rode past Linc Slocum's pillared mansion and up the ridge trail.

The mare Sam rode was a sturdy paint with a scar on one knee. Jake's horse was a bay Thoroughbred she'd seen Slocum ride only once before.

Jake rode automatically, attention directed toward the dirt as if he could read it like a book.

"Tell me how you do it," Sam urged after about ten minutes.

"Noon's the hardest time to track," Jake said as they rode side by side. "With the sun directly overhead, tracks just disappear. See how there are no shadows in the hoofprints?"

Jake didn't slow his horse as he pointed. Sam looked down. The ground looked bare as concrete. Except for a few drought cracks, she saw nothing.

"What hoofprints?"

Jake smiled. "Never mind. We don't have to look for clues, just a horse."

Sam didn't like Jake's superior smile any more than she liked the sweat trickling down the back of her neck.

"Don't tell me 'never mind,'" she insisted. "Tell me what to do, so when I have to come looking for *you*, it won't take so long."

This time Jake laughed aloud. "Dreamer."

Sam glared at him, but Jake wasn't looking. He told

her how to judge the age of a print and the weight or speed with which it had been made, but then he went back to reading the earth, as if she'd interrupted him while he was reading a good book.

They rode in silence for a while, and Sam welcomed the sounds of thudding hooves and the gabbling conversation of two ravens that passed overhead. She hadn't seem the Phantom for weeks, but here in his world, she could daydream about him.

Everything reminded her of the great silver stallion. The rocks and ridges around her seemed painted with his shadow. When she heard the rasp of a tool from Slocum's ranch down below, it sounded like the Phantom's neigh of surprise.

As the trail twisted around the mountain, rising higher, Sam looked down on River Bend Ranch and the silver-brown glitter of the river. The stallion's vast territory spread from here to the Calico Mountains. She looked east, past War Drum Flats. That wisp of white on the mountain was probably a thin curl of cloud, but it could be the Phantom's windblown mane and tail.

THE RENEGADE

Jake must have taken her silence for pouting, because he reined in the Thoroughbred and started an exasperated lecture, as if she'd been silently begging him to do it.

"Okay, if Rachel had been lost overnight," Jake said, "there'd be more of us in the search party. We'd form groups, divide up the area, and check each section on foot. Or maybe we'd use airplanes and ATVs. We'd check every little splinter road. . . ."

Jake's voice trailed off as something drew his attention away from the trail and down the hillside toward a clump of brush.

"What?" Sam asked.

"Nothing. And since the horse—and not Rachel—is probably in charge, he'll stick to the path, where the footing is easy. Here, look at this." Jake reined his horse back the way they'd come and dismounted.

He walked along, pointing. "See, the hoofprints are pretty close together and pretty distinct, and then there's this big mishmash of tracks."

Sam climbed off the paint, squatted next to Jake, and

stared. Finally she saw horseshoe prints, one on top of the other. "Yeah," she said.

"Something scared Champ. I'm thinking maybe deer, down in that brush. Rachel probably wouldn't think of trying to pet him and calm him down. So he stayed scared, she couldn't handle him, and look—" Jake pointed to widespread hoofprints. "He's running, kind of off-balance, and pretty soon we'll see where she fell."

"How can you be so sure? Linc said she had riding lessons."

"Well, she's forgotten what she learned." Jake's finger moved through the air. "Champ's veering left, right, all over the place. She's jerking him around. Pretty soon he'll get sick of it, or the bit will hurt enough that he'll decide the deal is off."

With horses, it was all about trust. That was what Sam had been taught since she was old enough to listen. Dad said horses were big, strong animals who agreed to do what you wanted them to do as long as you knew what you were doing.

Rachel clearly wasn't doing her part.

Suddenly, Sam could see where Champ had balked. Four hoofprints were planted in a square, as if someone had used a kitchen table like a stamp.

"Bet she went over his head," Jake muttered as they remounted.

They'd ridden only a few minutes when the trail split. Jake chose the path that slanted down and left. Soon Rachel's voice, distinctive because of its faint English accent, soared toward them.

"Get away from me, horse. *Away*, I said, or you'll be sorry."

Jake gave Sam a smug look, congratulating himself on picking the right path, just as Rachel stormed into view.

Her coffee-colored hair lay in a shiny wing across her forehead. She wore a red silk blouse and tan boots that looked as soft as the nose of the palomino following her.

But Rachel's designer jeans were ripped to show bloody knees, and the palm pushing her hair back looked raw, as if she'd used her hands to break her fall.

"Rachel, are you okay?" Sam asked.

Rachel stopped. Champ halted behind her, though his bobbing head said he wanted to touch noses with the other horses.

"Aren't you rather far from your 'spread'?" Rachel's lips twisted as if Sam and Jake were viruses that had escaped from a lab.

She didn't seem happy to be rescued. Jake darted a glance at Sam. She didn't think he was surprised by Rachel's ingratitude. Then he frowned past Sam, toward the mountains.

Maybe if Rachel understood the worry she'd caused, she'd be nicer.

"Your dad was afraid you were lost, so we came looking for you," Sam explained. "My grandmother and Dallas are searching too."

"Clearly, I am not lost." Rachel understood, all right. She just didn't care.

"Sorry for interrupting your walk," Sam said, pretending to turn the paint mare back toward the Gold Dust Ranch.

"I'm not lost," Rachel said loudly, "but I am frustrated with this horse. He wouldn't let me remount after I, um, climbed down to admire the view."

The only view Rachel had been admiring was one of the earth rushing up to meet her hands and knees, but Sam didn't say so.

Rachel stumbled forward as Champ nuzzled her backbone. The horse wasn't holding a grudge, but Rachel was. She whirled around to scold him just as Jake leaned toward Sam and whispered, "Don't look behind you."

When they were little, Sam had told Jake he had "mustang eyes." Sometimes the label still fit. Dark brown, half-wild, and hypnotic, his eyes managed to hold hers now, but barely.

Behind Sam, the trail dropped off to a steep hillside. What was there? She hadn't heard the whir of a rattlesnake, but it could be a cougar or a bear. Sam felt an almost irresistible pull to do the opposite of what Jake had ordered.

"I'm going to do something loud and obnoxious." Jake barely moved his lips. "Then you can look. Got it?"

Sam nodded, but it was Rachel who spoke first.

"It's hardly polite, talking about me in whispers." Rachel faced them with one eyebrow arched.

"Not going to be using that horse anymore? Is that what you said?" Jake asked.

Rachel looked a little sickly. "If you could just hold him while I get back up—"

"No need," Jake said. He forced his horse forward, made a loud coyote yip, and slapped his hat on Champ's hindquarters.

The palomino bolted past, headed toward home, away from Rachel's squeal of outrage.

And that was when Sam looked.

Hidden up to his shoulder in a thicket of sagebrush, the Phantom was watching them. His perfect Arab ears were pricked to catch Sam's voice, but his intelligent eyes surveyed the scene and judged it too risky for approach.

Still, he didn't flee. Instead, the stallion tossed his thick white mane in greeting, and his eyes were set on Sam.

Chapter 2

JAKE HAD PROBABLY WANTED HIS WHOOPING shout and Rachel's running horse to make the Phantom stampede back the way he'd come from. But he didn't.

At first, Sam admired the stallion's intelligence. The mustang knew he wasn't in danger.

Then she felt a warning chill. He shouldn't be so trusting. There was no telling what Rachel would do. And Jake had sworn he'd never give the stallion another chance to hurt Sam.

The Phantom should never trust a human. Ever.

Once before, the Phantom's love for her had been responsible for his capture. She couldn't let that happen again.

"Now what?" Rachel demanded.

Sam wrenched her eyes away from the stallion and looked at Rachel. Hands on hips, the rich girl stared up at the riders.

"I found her," Jake said. "So you deal with her."

"Like I couldn't have just ridden along this trail and blundered into her?" Sam asked.

Hoping Rachel was distracted by their bickering, Sam dared a quick glance at the Phantom. He sidestepped off a few feet, eyes rolling white at her sharp tone.

"No, you couldn't have found her. Not without a bloodhound," Jake said. "Or me."

"Hello?" Rachel snapped her fingers. "Ex-*cuse* me? Will one of you dismount so I can ride home?"

"No," Sam and Jake said in unison.

At least they could agree on that.

"Then how do you expect to take the credit for 'saving' me?"

Rachel had a point, but Sam didn't tell her so.

"You'll have to ride double with one of us." Jake's voice cut off Rachel's whining.

Saddle leather creaked and a blue jay squawked, laughing at their predicament.

"No way," Rachel said. "Samantha, just get down and give me that horse. She belongs to me, after all, and if you can ride her, so can I."

"I'm not the one who ended up on the ground."

"You stupid girl." Rachel's eyes narrowed. "I could tell you something you'd pay your whole pitiful allowance to hear."

Like fashion advice? Or Queen Rachel's tips on snagging the popular crowd's adoration? Sam kept her lips closed and wished Gram hadn't handicapped her with good manners.

"Both of you hush up," Jake said.

"What did *I* say?" Sam cried.

Jake kicked loose from his left stirrup and pointed.

"Rachel, put your foot in there, swing up behind me, and hang on."

The bay shied at Rachel's approach, and she hesitated.

"Do it now." Jake calmed the horse with a pat. "If I don't get my work done before sundown, I don't get paid."

The instant Rachel followed Jake's instructions, he set the Thoroughbred loping away.

Like something from a movie, Rachel's glossy hair swung from side to side.

As her accented voice floated back to Sam, it was clear Rachel was mulling over what Jake had said.

"That hardly seems fair." Rachel seemed puzzled by the idea of doing a fair day's work for wages.

Jake laughed. Sam tried to join him but failed.

She could disregard Jake's amusement and ignore the fact that he'd asked Rachel to climb up behind him. What Sam couldn't overlook was the way Rachel Slocum had her arms wrapped around Jake's waist. She was doing a lot more than just holding on for balance.

Sam was so hot with jealousy, she forgot to look back for the Phantom. When she finally remembered, he was gone.

THE RENEGADE

When they rode into the Gold Dust ranch yard, Sam expected to see Linc Slocum waiting for his daughter. After all, Champ had run on ahead, and a saddled but riderless horse was rarely good news.

Champ had taken the right path home, but he was sweating and still saddled. Bloody foam clung to the corners of his lips, but he looked happy as he stretched over a fence to touch noses with a huge Brahma bull.

All three of them had dismounted, and Jake had begun unsaddling the tired palomino when Slocum finally appeared, tucking a cell phone into his pocket.

"Soon as I saw you coming, I phoned River Bend to call off the search," Slocum said.

"Thanks," Sam said.

"Wyatt had just come in and was wondering where everyone was." Slocum gave a strained chuckle.

He looked even more out of place than usual in a pale green shirt and matching pants. Without his cowboy hat and boots, he looked a lot like a golfer.

Sam tugged at the paint mare's cinch while peeking

over her back. Linc Slocum was approaching Rachel, and Sam couldn't help being nosy.

"What were you thinking, honey, to go riding off without telling me?" he asked.

Maybe his daughter's ripped jeans and the fear that she'd been hurt explained why he sounded like he was apologizing.

Rachel squared her shoulders and looked down her nose as if addressing the lowliest freshman.

"I don't want to discuss it," she snapped, then walked right past her father.

As Sam pulled the saddle off the paint's back, she listened for Linc to call Rachel back and scold her.

"Rachel, honey, I wish you'd tell me what has you so perturbed," he said.

"Later." Rachel kept walking.

Sam was amazed, but she just balanced the saddle blanket atop the heavy Western saddle, slung the bridle over her shoulder, and walked to the tack room.

The tack room smelled of fresh-cut pine boards, tended leather, and buckle polish. Sam would bet it was the result of Jed Kenworthy's work, not Slocum's.

"Nothing happened to her when she sassed her father." Sam couldn't help sharing her surprise when Jake came through the door with tack from Champ and the Thoroughbred.

"Uh-huh."

"She just walked off." Sam followed Jake. "And he didn't say anything."

"Yep." Jake hung the bridles on spindles.

"She could have ruined that horse. Don't you think I should tell him so?"

"Suit yourself," Jake said, but now he was looking at a shelf of horse medicine.

When he unscrewed the lid on a tin of salve and sniffed it, Sam wondered if Jake was just stalling to make her mad.

"You're too chicken to do it, right?" she teased. Nothing. "Or maybe you like her."

Instead of rising to the bait, Jake glanced in a mirror on the tack room wall and adjusted the angle of his Stetson.

She'd been joking, but Jake never looked in the mirror, never took pains with his appearance. He showered, and that was it. What if Jake really *did* like Rachel? At school, dozens of guys flocked around her. They walked her to class, brought her sodas, and shared their homework.

Sam replayed the image of Jake riding double with Rachel. *Oh please, not Jake, too.*

When they came out of the tack room, Slocum was standing near the big Brahma as if he was waiting for them. He should have at least offered to help with the horses, but he hadn't. He hadn't said thank you, either.

Filled with irritation, Sam walked right up to him.

"Mr. Slocum, Rachel could have hurt herself and Champ, riding off the way she did."

"I know." Slocum tried to hang his thumbs in his pockets as Jake did, but they wouldn't quite fit.

Sam waited. Gram would say she'd already been impolite. "Guess I'll just hope she doesn't," Slocum continued. "She never has before."

Sam bit her lower lip to keep her mouth closed.

She couldn't say another sassy word. Slocum might

be smiling, but he was angry. If he talked to Gram or Dad, she was already dead.

"I'll have to be sure someone's around to unsaddle horses, so she'll leave them be." Slocum seemed to be talking to himself. "Or maybe take her mind off horses altogether and buy her that red Porsche she's been wanting."

Sam couldn't believe her ears.

From the corner of her eye, Sam saw Jake shake his head as if she should know better than to take on another lost cause. She ignored him.

"Maybe," she suggested to Slocum, "you could talk with Rachel about—"

A sudden threat flared in Slocum's eyes. She stopped. She glanced at Jake. Of course he hadn't noticed. When Sam looked back to see what Slocum would do next, she decided she must have imagined the look. Slocum just shrugged and gave her a dopey smile.

"You're right, Samantha. I guess what I really need around here is a smart girl like you to tell everyone exactly what they should be doing."

"I'm sorry, Mr. Slocum." Sam hoped her sincerity showed. "I guess I got a little carried away, but Rachel fell, you know, and Champ's mouth is torn up."

"Jed keeps medicine for that," Slocum said.

Slocum watched Jake move close to the haltered and tied palomino. Gently, Jake dabbed on the salve he'd brought from the tack shed.

"I see Jake found that medicine. Good. And you don't go worrying, Samantha. You didn't hurt my feelings."

Sam didn't believe him. She felt like the sun had moved closer and the lid of clouds had pressed down tighter.

"In fact, my son, Ryan, is coming home soon. He'll help keep everything straight. Though he's more of a horseman, he's agreed to help with my new hobby."

Champ snorted and pulled against his tie rope as Slocum approached the pen that held the tiger-colored Brahma bull.

Glossy orange and black hair swirled with creamy white over the bull's saggy skin. A hump wobbled where his neck flowed into his back. He had such large, gentle eyes, he wouldn't have looked fierce at all if it hadn't been for his markings. Black tiger stripes made a mask around his eyes. Each side of the mask pointed back to his short, sharp horns.

"Meet Maniac," Slocum announced, "part of my new bucking Brahma program."

As Slocum gestured in fanfare, the bull wrenched his massive head away from the fence. Strings of saliva swung from his jaws, but he didn't bolt in fear. Once Maniac backed out of Slocum's reach, the big bull held his ground.

Sam swallowed hard. What was the bull doing? Most of the time, she could think like a horse. That made it easier to know when Ace or any other horse might spook. Range cattle seemed to react the same way. Horses and cattle loved the safety of the herd, and most chose to run away from danger.

But Maniac seemed different. His chocolate-colored eyes were watching for a challenge, but his drooping ears belonged on a velvety toy.

"He doesn't look too mean," Sam said.

"Not mean?" Slocum roared, making his voice loud enough to provoke the bull. "Watch this."

He waved his arms, too. The bull shook his head and pawed the earth once. Sam could read that message. It meant, *Back off.*

Before Slocum goaded the bull further, Jake sidled in and pulled the rope tethering Champ. The knot slipped, as intended. When he walked the skittish palomino past, Jake glared at Sam.

What? If he thought she'd purposely egged Slocum into making a fool of himself, Jake was wrong.

"Hey, you two-thousand-pound cheeseburger," Slocum shouted, "show the little lady what you got!"

Flinging his bulky body toward the fence, Slocum started to climb.

Maniac didn't warn again. He trotted two surprisingly graceful steps, feinted his horns to the left, then slammed forward into the fence.

Slocum fell. The side of the corral was still shuddering when he stood, dusted himself off, and gave a breathless laugh.

The bull stood huffing, eager for another dare.

"I guess you're right," Sam said quickly. She didn't want him to tease the bull anymore. "He's fierce."

"Darn tootin' I'm right. And I'm not the only one who thinks so." Slocum beckoned Sam to come closer.

Struggling to be polite, she moved toward him.

"Last week, d'you know who I had out here?"

Sam shook her head.

"Karla Starr, of Starr Rodeo Productions. She's just getting started and you might not have heard of her yet, but you will." Slocum rubbed his hands together. "She's a cowgirl. Just a little bit of a thing, not much bigger than you, but tough. Oh my, yes, tough as a bootheel and ready to go up against the big boys who breed rough stock for rodeos. That's bucking bulls and horses," Slocum added, "in case you didn't know.

"Karla gets rough stock the old-fashioned way. She doesn't breed 'em on a big fancy ranch. She buys renegade horses and outlaw bulls from cowboys—and ranchers like me."

Sam could tell he liked the sound of that. Puffed up

with pride, Slocum gave the words "ranchers like me" a chance to echo around the hot, silent ranch yard.

If only he knew how ignorant he sounded.

Renegade horses weren't born man-haters. Most had been ruined by careless, impatient humans. Sam wouldn't be surprised to learn it was the same with "outlaw" bulls.

Some of the old ways had died out because rodeo fans couldn't stand such cruelty. In the past, hundreds of mustangs were trapped, crowded into high-sided trucks, and driven hours across country. Once they reached a rodeo arena, the thirsty animals stampeded out of the truck, only to be roped and blindfolded while men slammed saddles on their backs.

Men were injured once in a while, but others usually twisted a mustang's tail or bit his ear—anything to paralyze the horse with fear until a cowboy was jammed into the saddle. Sam imagined the horses could only compare men's weight and spurring to a cougar attack.

Those were the "good old days" of rodeo. Slocum should be smart enough to know they'd ended for a reason.

THE RENEGADE

"Karla Starr thinks Maniac and some of my other Brahmas could be rodeo celebrities." Slocum savored the syllables as they rolled off his tongue. "She's willing to give my critters a try in a late-fall rodeo in California—if I sweeten the deal a little."

Sam noticed Jake was still nearby, listening, but since he didn't ask the question, she did.

"What does that mean, 'sweeten the deal'?" Sam asked.

"Well, she was looking for light-colored bucking horses, mainly. Had her eye on the palominos, but Kenworthy won't sell."

Sam wondered where Slocum had found the nerve to even ask the Kenworthys to sell the last of their palominos. Before they went broke and sold out to Slocum, the Kenworthys had been known not only for their prime cattle but also for Quarter Horses with palomino coloring.

Only four of the horses remained. Two were mares, Mantilla and Silk Stockings, the skittish horse Jen called Silly. The other two were geldings. Jed Kenworthy rode

Sundance in cutting competitions, and Gold Champagne was the horse Slocum now owned and called Champ.

Sam was afraid to ask why Slocum hadn't sold Champ to Karla Starr, but he must have read her frown.

"I would've thrown Champ into the deal, but he just won't buck no matter what you do to him."

The words made Sam sick. So how had he convinced the stock contractor to take a chance on his untrained bulls? She had to know.

Sam thought of a fancy tea party with china cups and white gloves and made her voice polite enough to match.

"Gosh, Mr. Slocum, so how *did* you 'sweeten the deal'?"

"We're still working out the details, but Miz Starr won't be disappointed."

There it was again. Slocum's sneaky half smile hinted that he was hiding a dark secret.

Sam tried to shake off her paranoia, but Slocum was worrying her.

"So, you'd sell Maniac?" she asked. "I thought he was going to be part of a breeding program."

"He was," Slocum agreed. "But breeding Brahmas takes time. And, shoot, Maniac could be famous now."

"But in the future—" Sam began.

"Samantha, let me tell you a fact of life. When you have money, the future takes care of itself." Slocum gave her a pitying smile. "I could sell every Brahma I bought for the breeding program, then just get more of 'em before Ryan comes home, so we'd have some cows to play with. It's simple."

Just like buying Rachel off with a sports car so she wouldn't sneak Champ away. Just like buying Jed Kenworthy's ranch so Slocum had a place to play cowboy. Just like stripping all the old pine trees off the mountainside so he had a place to put his mansion.

"Mr. Slocum?" Jake shifted his weight toward Slocum's Cadillac.

"That's right. You'll be wanting to get back to the River Bend and that colt you're riding. Must be a lot of fun, showing a banker like Mr. Martinez what you can do."

"Most fun work there is," Jake agreed. "And college won't come cheap, so it's lucky I like it."

"College? I thought you'd be saving for a fast car," Slocum said as they climbed into his Cadillac. "When I was your age, that's all I did—race when the cops weren't watching."

Slocum's voice implied that Jake was a wimp if he wasn't longing for a hot car.

"He wants a car, too," Sam said, but Jake, sitting in front beside Slocum, stayed quiet.

As they pulled away from the Gold Dust Ranch, Sam looked back at the bare ridges behind Slocum's mansion. According to Gram, the piñon pines had been there for hundreds of years; they helped slow the snowmelt and kept the ranch from flooding.

Jen said that since Slocum had built his huge, flashy house, mud puddles and mosquitoes had marred the ranch until May.

Slocum probably didn't understand why. He wouldn't believe that he couldn't buy off nature.

As they drove past War Drum Flats, Sam looked for the Phantom.

A dozen times, near dawn and dusk, she'd seen wild

horses watering at the little lake down there. Now, in the heat of the day, nothing moved.

Suddenly, Slocum's chuckle interrupted her thoughts.

"When they caught rodeo stock the old way, those range rats musta put on quite a show."

It was probably coincidence, the way Slocum narrowed his eyes toward the water hole she was watching for the Phantom. But his words made Sam uneasy, just the same.

Chapter 3

TWO NOISY HORSES AND A BARKING DOG competed for Sam's attention as she climbed out of Linc Slocum's car.

"Blaze, simmer down," Dallas called from the bunkhouse porch. The Border Collie frisked around Sam's legs a minute, then obeyed, but no one could quiet the horses.

Dark Sunshine whinnied from the big pasture. While most of the horses crowded into the shade beneath the big cottonwood tree, the tiny buckskin trotted along the fence. Her black mane and tail billowed around her, and her eyes watched Sam.

"She sounds better, doesn't she?" Sam asked Jake.

"Lots," Jake agreed. "That sound she used to make gave me the creeps."

Just weeks ago, the mare's neigh had chilled them all. Mustangs were usually silent, but abuse and neglect had made Dark Sunshine's neighs sound like screams.

Although Sunny was the wildest horse on the River Bend Ranch, she'd adopted the herd of saddle horses as her family. Only Popcorn matched her explosive energy as she ran laps around the ten-acre corral, and she always outlasted the albino, showing how much she missed the open range.

To help calm her, Sam made time every day after school to pony the mare. Sunny trotted alongside as Sam rode Ace, happy to stretch her legs.

Dad and Dallas were pretty sure Dark Sunshine was in foal to the Phantom, so it was important that she exercise and become gradually more accustomed to people.

Everyone understood this—except Ace.

The bay gelding paced along the barn corral fence. Every so often he halted, pawed impatiently, and aimed a summoning snort toward Sam.

"If I believed in such things, I'd say that gelding of yours is psychic," Gram said as she walked toward them from turning Sweetheart into the pen with Ace. "He started fussing about five minutes before Blaze barked to tell us Linc's car was coming."

Sam smooched toward the corral. Ace stopped. He tossed his head so that his forelock flipped away from the white star on his forehead.

"Quit embarrassing him," Jake said. "No working cow pony likes to be treated like a pet."

"Shows how much you know," Sam said.

She would have gone to Ace right away if Jake hadn't disappeared into the barn just as everyone else asked for details about the search for Rachel.

"Found her okay, I guess," said Dallas. The gray-haired foreman sat on the front step. He looked tired.

That morning, Dad had confided to Gram that Dallas's arthritis was acting up. Though Dallas would resist, Dad planned to ask him to do work that would keep him around the ranch.

Sam sat down beside him on the step. She tried not to be judgmental in telling how they'd found Rachel, but she couldn't resist adding a few sentences about the surprising treatment Rachel had received when she reached home.

Dad, Gram, and Dallas all shook their heads.

Gram said, "In rough country like this, someone needs to know where you are."

Sam agreed, for Rachel. But Gram and Dad wouldn't have to worry about Sam. "If there was an emergency," she began, "and I had to leave without—"

"No excuses," Dad said. "Not now and not when you're twenty-one. Never try a fool stunt like that."

"I'm not like Rachel."

Dad nodded, looking satisfied. He wouldn't say anything bad about a neighbor, but she could tell he didn't approve of bribing your child to make her behave.

"Good thing," Dallas said, pulling himself to his feet.

"Because you've got a chore that needs doing. Before you went tearing off after Jake, I planned for you to check the feed room for mice. That means moving everything in there."

"But, Dallas, Sunny and Ace haven't been out today. They need exercise."

"That can wait. You're taking tomorrow morning to ride out with the Kenworthy girl. Isn't that right?"

"Yes, but—"

"I saw something out the corner of my eye this morning in the tack room. We can't have rodents eating the winter feed."

"Dad," Sam appealed to her father. Instantly, she saw it had been a mistake.

"Dallas is the foreman. You know that."

"Yes, sir," Sam said, but as she trudged toward the barn, Sam couldn't help thinking everyone was happier when Dallas was out on the range, where he belonged.

One side of Ace's corral allowed him inside the barn. He trotted in just as Sam entered, and she couldn't resist giving him the hug he wanted.

THE RENEGADE

Ace swung his head over the top fence rail, and Sam wrapped her arms around his sleek bay neck. Eyes closed, she let his coarse mane rub her cheek while his lips whuffled her shoulder.

"You are such a good horse. I'm sorry you're bored."

Ace drew a deep breath, inhaling her scent before he relaxed against her.

"Tomorrow we'll go on a good long ride." She tightened her hug for a minute, then gave him a pat and pulled back to look at his serious brown eyes. "Until then, you can watch me look for mice. How's that for excitement?"

Sam gave Ace's nose a kiss, then turned on the radio in the tack room and considered her job.

For as long as she could remember, Dad had talked about pouring a cement floor in the feed room. Until then, mice could burrow up from under the wooden floor in search of tasty grain.

Dad kept grain and corn in shiny aluminum garbage cans with tight-fitting tops. They should be mouseproof, but the mice remained hopeful some grain would be spilled or someone would be in a hurry and not wedge a lid on tightly.

While she worked, Sam's mind gnawed on her own problem.

Where was the Phantom? What would Slocum do if the stallion he'd always wanted was nearby? She'd looked away from him so Rachel wouldn't see him and tattle.

But looking away had worked too well. When she'd looked back, the Phantom had vanished. Was he still on the ridge trail above the Gold Dust? Would whatever lured Rachel up there in the first place make her return and notice him?

Sweating and troubled, Sam was trying to distract herself by singing along with the radio when she heard footsteps.

Dallas stood in the doorway. Just behind him stood Ace.

"Sam, you're going to have him right in here with you if you let him wander like this. It's a bad habit." Dallas shooed Ace with a brush of his hand, and the gelding drew back, insulted. "If a lid's ever left off one of these cans, he could get in here and eat himself to death."

Sam knew it was true. Horses were grazing animals. Most would eat as long as there was food.

"But I didn't let him out."

"The inside corral gate is open and unlatched. And here he is," Dallas said.

Sam approached Ace and touched his neck as if he had the answer. He probably did, but he just swished his tail and looked up at the rafters.

"I did hug him," Sam admitted. "But I didn't go inside the corral, so I couldn't have left the gate open, even accidentally."

Dallas gave her a frown full of disappointment.

"Well, who'm I supposed to believe, Samantha? You or my lyin' eyes?"

Even if Dallas's arthritis was making him cranky, he had a point.

"I'm sorry," she said, and hustled Ace back into his pen.

Sweetheart gave them both a scolding look.

"Yes, you stayed in like a good girl," Sam told Gram's pinto. "But how did this bad boy get loose?"

She considered the inside latch. It was open, all right. She supposed Ace might have rubbed against it, scratching an itch, until the latch opened. Or it was barely possible Gram had forgotten to lock the pen when she put Sweetheart inside.

With both latches in place, Sam tugged at the gate from outside. It held.

Ace nudged the finger she shook at him. He knew she was joking. "No kidding, Ace. Don't go getting us both in trouble."

Just after midnight, a horse woke Sam. She sat up in bed, fingers curled into her quilt, waiting for the sound to come again.

A joyous whinny drifted through the night. She knew it was Dark Sunshine because she'd heard that sound before. When the mare first came home from running with the mustangs, she'd used that same greeting to Popcorn.

But Popcorn and Dark Sunshine were both in the ten-acre pasture.

Sam's heart thudded. It was him.

Cautious not to make a sound, she slipped from bed and tiptoed downstairs. The stove clock and refrigerator hummed in the dark kitchen as Sam let herself out into the night.

Across the ranch yard, Blaze stood and shook himself. Then he decided he was too sleepy to come along and flopped back down.

Good. Sunny's racket was enough to wake Dad and Gram, but they might roll over and go back to sleep. If Blaze started barking when he saw the Phantom, they'd both be up and notice she wasn't in bed.

The moon was a smudged thumbprint, offering little light, but Sam had made this midnight expedition to the river often enough that she knew where to place her bare feet to avoid rocks. The dirt underfoot felt powdery and warm, and though it made for easy walking, it felt wrong.

Not wrong, she told herself, just bad weather for ranching.

Even though she couldn't see the Phantom, she knew

he was there. When she reached the bank, Sam stopped and waited.

She could hear cattle lowing not too far away.

River Bend's white-faced Herefords had made their way out of the sage-covered foothills, closer to the main ranch and the river. Beyond the mooing cattle, Sam heard nothing. And there was no sign of the Phantom.

For a minute, she watched stars sparkle on the river's rills. Then she closed her eyes. If her sight adjusted to the darkness, she might see him.

When her eyes opened, Sam saw a flicker on the far riverbank. Like a pure white wing, the Phantom's mane flared away from his neck.

Sam held her breath until it hurt. Tonight, he was magical. The moon emerged just for him, making the stallion's coat shimmer with silver light.

Gone was the mischievous horse who'd played hide-and-seek with her on the ridge trail that afternoon. Tonight the Phantom hadn't uttered a sound, yet he'd pulled her to the river.

THE RENEGADE

Only one thing puzzled Sam. Why wasn't he wading toward her?

She grabbed a handful of nightgown in one hand, held it clear of the water, and started forward.

Usually, the stallion met her halfway. The first time she'd mounted him, as a colt, she'd done it in this river. She believed that memory made him return here. But tonight, he made her come to him.

Sam was shocked by the shallow water. Halfway across, it barely reached the middle of her shin, and it was tepid, warmed through by the day's sun.

That was when she knew she could wade all the way across. La Charla was only about a city block wide, and tonight the current was sluggish and slow.

Now she heard the thud of his hooves, trotting down the bank, wheeling, and trotting back.

Sam slogged closer. She should feel dumb, wandering so far from home in her white nightgown. What if she fell and broke her leg? But she didn't feel dumb, just entranced, like a sleepwalker called from bed to do something important.

Sam didn't look back. If the porch light was on and Dad or Gram was watching, she was already sunk. Better to have time with her horse than get in trouble and not even get a chance to touch him.

She didn't slip on the rocks underfoot. When she reached the other shore, the Phantom stood off and watched her. Sam lowered her eyes, wringing out the hem of her nightgown, even though she'd have to wet it again going home. As she twisted the water out in a splatter on the parched ground, she heard the stallion come closer.

Warm breath sighed over the nape of her neck. Sam shivered as gooseflesh raced down her arms.

Veiled by a thick forelock that parted only over his eyes, the stallion settled back as Sam straightened.

"Hey, boy," she crooned to him. "C'mere, boy."

The stallion blinked but didn't come within reach.

"Do you think I was ignoring you this afternoon, hmm? Is that why I'm getting the cold shoulder?"

The stallion stretched out his nose, then jerked it back, shaking his head.

"I was trying to keep Rachel from seeing you, that's all. She's self-centered and unpredictable, boy, and if she knew you were right there on their ranch, who knows what would happen?"

Sam remembered Linc Slocum's voice, bragging about his deal with a rodeo stock contractor. For one ugly instant, she imagined the Phantom exploding out of a bucking horse chute into an arena filled with cheers and music.

That would be illegal, of course. The Phantom was a free-roaming mustang, and it would be against the law for Slocum to capture, sell, or trade him to Karla Starr. But Slocum had proven before that he placed his own desires above the law.

As the image of a high-spurring cowboy faded from her imagination, Sam noticed that the Phantom stood beside a boulder just the perfect height for a mounting block.

The Phantom didn't belong to her, either. But once he had. And tonight he seemed lonely and almost tame. Temptation told her the stallion might let her ride him into the night.

"One day, a long time ago, you let me on your back, boy." Sam edged closer. "You know I wouldn't hurt you."

The stallion flicked his ears but trusted her to come closer.

As she put one foot on the rock, the Phantom turned to watch. When both feet were up, Sam bit her lip.

"Zanzibar . . ." She sighed his secret name, and the stallion answered with a nicker.

A wild horse shouldn't be so trusting. She wouldn't try to climb on tonight.

But if she only did it once . . .

No night birds called. La Charla ran as quietly as unfurled satin. The entire world held its breath, waiting to see what she would do.

"Zanzibar, could I try? Please? You know I won't hurt you."

Sam leaned one palm on the stallion's back. It felt smooth and muscular. She placed her other hand there too, then smoothed her hands together along his back.

The Phantom sidled just out of reach. Sam felt her chest deflate.

"Not tonight?"

As if he understood her disappointment, the stallion lowered his head. His lips whuffled along the ground as if he'd lost something, and Sam knew just what it was. For a minute, they'd both lost their good sense.

Then, just like the playful colt he'd once been, the Phantom surprised her. Head still lowered, he grabbed the ruffle at the hem of her nightgown and tugged until the ruffle ripped.

Then the stallion released the fabric and shook his head.

For the space of three heartbeats, he rubbed his velvet muzzle against her neck. He uttered a deep nicker that was so much like language, Sam tried to understand the words.

And then he trotted away. Light as a ghost horse, he drifted over a series of trails and shortcuts up the mountainside.

By road, the way to the Phantom's valley took close to four hours. Riding Ace and following the Phantom's path, Sam had made it once in two.

She wanted to follow him. Instead, Sam watched the silver stallion until he was out of sight. She didn't cross back to River Bend until even the sound of his passage had died into silence.

Finally, she walked home. With each step away from him, Sam felt a tearing in her chest. Her head believed it was time to go back to bed, to pretend the night hadn't been interrupted by magic. But her heart knew better.

Together, she and the Phantom had woven a spell that let them read each other's minds. And tonight, Sam had the awful feeling that the stallion had been saying good-bye.

Chapter 4

SHE DIDN'T GET CAUGHT RETURNING TO HER room on Saturday night, but Monday afternoon was a different story.

Journalism was Sam's last class of the day and her busiest. Mr. Blair expected the Darton High *Dialogue* to be a real newspaper, so he treated students like real reporters. If they didn't turn in daily homework, meet deadlines, and follow the direction of student editors, they didn't get "paid" with passing grades.

The classroom buzzed with the sound of tapping

computer keys, rustling papers, and a ringing phone, but Sam often escaped to the photo lab.

Eerie red light that wouldn't damage exposed film glowed over the darkroom sinks where Sam developed the film she'd shot for a story about overcrowded classes. Little string "clotheslines" held wet prints of Friday night's football game.

In spite of the smelly chemicals used to develop the film, Sam smiled at her handiwork. Everything about film photography was fun. She loved getting down on the football field, far closer than the fans and cheerleaders, and crouching to catch the action with her camera. When grunting players crashed into each other, the ground shook as it did when wild horses galloped.

Sam stared at the sink before her. There was a different sort of excitement to this moment. In an almost supernatural way, images turned from vague blotches into pictures.

It was quiet inside the darkroom. The revolving door, designed to keep light from invading, grated as it opened, acting as an alarm.

She was expecting the sports editor, who was itching to see if Sam had caught a particularly great run by a lumbering linebacker, so she didn't glance up from her work when she heard the door turn.

"This seems a place where we'll have a bit of privacy."

The British accent gave her away. It was Rachel. Why would the rich girl want to talk with her in private?

Unless, Sam speculated, Rachel planned to get rid of witnesses to the disgrace of ripping her designer jeans and skinning her knees.

"What's up?" Sam asked as she sneaked a glance at Rachel's knees. It was easy to do, since Rachel wore a plaid sundress that barely reached mid-thigh.

But the uncertain red glow in the darkroom showed no harm to Rachel's knees. Of course not.

"I want you to put some polish on my riding skills."

"What?"

"Yelping isn't necessary, Samantha, and there is some need for secrecy," Rachel scolded.

Sam's head was spinning. She would have been less surprised if Rachel had tried to drown her in the sink.

"You want me to teach you to ride?"

"I know the basics. What I need is practice under the eye of someone who can point out ways I can improve. This is important to me."

A little flattered, but still confused, Sam asked, "But why?"

"Did I not say this was important to me?"

"That's not really a reason."

"Let's say *that* information is available on a need-to-know basis." Rachel smirked. "And no one—certainly not you—needs to know."

"Then you don't need my help," Sam said. "Hire someone who does it for a living."

She turned back to her work. The print in the sink was almost ready when Sam realized temper had dictated her words.

What a mistake. Slocum would probably pay her big bucks to teach his princess to ride.

"But I want you to work with me," Rachel said.

That made Sam look up. The reddish light made Rachel's lower lip look even glossier as she pouted.

"You don't even like me." Sam noticed Rachel didn't rush to correct her. "And you don't like horses."

"I must find a way to make this work." Rachel mused to herself. She steepled her glittering bronze fingernails together and pointed to Sam. "You don't have to be very good, just inexpensive."

Sam laughed. "You don't have much experience at kissing up, do you?"

"You needn't act insulted. We both know I could have a superb horse master. Which you are not. However, I must clear purchases over a certain amount with my father."

"So, do it."

"I would." Rachel's face brightened. "Except this is a surprise."

It made sense, Sam supposed. Still, she didn't want to hang around with Rachel. Even in a corral.

Rachel was selfish, conceited, and rude. Sam admired nothing about her. Then she flipped her fingers through her own growing-out cap of hair and looked at the smooth sweep of Rachel's. Almost nothing.

"The only people who'd know about it wouldn't matter," Rachel said.

That meant Gram, Dad, Jake, and Jen. How could Rachel believe they didn't matter? And even if she believed it, why would she say it?

"But Jake doesn't like me," Rachel went on, sounding incredulous. "And if he should hear I made the tiniest mistake, it would be just like him to tell his gang of friends—not that I care what *they* think," Rachel hurried to correct any conclusion Sam might jump to. "But word spreads." Rachel's smile said she felt a little sorry for herself. "Some of us are always the focus of other people's attention."

Yeah, it's real tough being you, Sam thought. But she didn't say it. She was too busy trying to figure out what Rachel was up to.

The story didn't hang together. Sure, Linc Slocum would be happy if his daughter fit into his Western fantasy, but Sam couldn't believe Rachel cared about pleasing him.

"You know that becoming a good rider means work

and getting your hands dirty, maybe even sweating," Sam said.

Rachel didn't rise to the bait. Instead she put on an even more superior tone. "May I be blunt, Samantha?" She didn't wait for permission. "This drought has been tough on all the small ranchers, and it's bound to get worse. Some will certainly lose their property. The pay I give you for this may not help a lot, but the good opinion of my father will."

Someone in the other room tapped on the revolving door and shouted, "Sam? Got those photos yet?"

"In a minute," Sam called, but she was thinking about what Rachel had just said.

This didn't fit with Rachel's personality either. She cared about makeup and fashion, occasionally about winning a school election, but not about weather and agriculture.

"Why would you be paying attention to the drought?"

Rachel gave a half smile as she walked her fingers along the edge of the developing sink. "Just how do you think my daddy got so rich? You don't know, do you?"

"No, I don't. How?" Sam asked.

"Keep wondering, little cowgirl." Rachel patted Sam's cheek and headed for the door. "But don't take too long. The title 'Best in the West' will be mine by June."

Even though she hated to do what Rachel told her, Sam kept wondering all afternoon. It probably slowed down her after-school chores, too, because by the time she had Ace saddled to go ride with Jen, Dad and the hands were riding in from the range and dusk was hovering over the hills.

All four men looked tired and unhappy.

Ace gave a little buck as Pepper and Ross turned their horses out into the big pasture. Usually, they'd tease her. Today, neither seemed to notice. Dallas rode by on Tank. Too weary for a greeting, he just raised a hand and smiled.

Dallas's smile wasn't really for her. It was for the horse he was leading, his old gelding, Amigo. The bay's muzzle was frosted with white and his eyes looked hazy, but he was the best horse Dallas had ever owned. The only horse he'd trust with his life, Dallas always said.

And that was why, on the gelding's twenty-fifth birthday, he'd been turned out to pasture. Only once in a while did bad range conditions force Dallas to bring him in.

Dad drew alongside Sam, on Banjo. His face was grimed with dust.

"Gettin' kind of a late start," he said.

"I know, but I'll be back in time for dinner. And my algebra homework." Sam made a face and Dad managed a smile. "I spent a lot of time with Sunny," she told him. "I don't know if she'll ever settle down."

They glanced toward Dark Sunshine. The mare seemed determined to make Sam wrong. She grazed with the saddle horses as if she'd been born among ropes and fences.

Across the yard, Blaze gave a sharp yap and ran circles around the cowboys as they stomped dirt from their boots outside the bunkhouse.

It was a sight Ace saw daily, but he shied as if Blaze were a werewolf. Sam slipped in the saddle. Embarrassed, she steadied herself.

"Quit that," she scolded Ace.

"It's a lot of work taming a mustang," Dad agreed. "They're always lookin' for trouble. And if it's not there, they'll imagine it."

Sam knew he was talking about Ace as well as Sunny. Dad might be right, but mustangs had to take care of themselves on the range. Of course they watched for danger.

"If you plan to keep that buckskin, gentle her. Otherwise, what's to keep her from passing her wildness on to her baby? Or coming at us hoof and teeth if she needs help foaling?" Dad shook his head. "You better plan on handling the young one all the time."

"You bet," Sam said.

Her heart went zinging skyward at the thought of a wobbly legged foal with Sunny and the Phantom for parents.

"No daydreamin'," Dad said. "Go work the sass out of Ace and get back here in time for dinner. I smell fried chicken, and I'm hungry enough to eat it all, then lick the platter clean."

THE RENEGADE

When she finally met up with Jen, Sam's mind was spinning.

She didn't like keeping secrets from Jen. They were best friends, and that meant sharing everything.

Well, almost everything. As Ace and Silly zigzagged around clumps of sagebrush, Sam decided she and Jen did the same. They detoured around a few private spots. Jen knew Sam had found the Phantom's hideout, but she didn't ask where it was. And though Sam knew Jen's parents fought too much, she didn't ask for details. Both girls considered those topics off-limits—unless there was an emergency.

In the darkroom, Rachel had said there was "some need for secrecy" about her riding lessons. She'd mentioned gossip, and that wasn't a problem with Jen. But what if Rachel was really worried about something else? Sam felt like growling. It wasn't that she felt loyal to Rachel, but this wasn't her secret to tell.

Sam abandoned her thoughts as a shadow suddenly crossed between her and Jen. Both girls looked up.

A red-tailed hawk soared overhead. The bird's rasping scream gave Sam chills. She'd never heard anything like it in the city. The sound was everything she'd missed about Nevada when she lived with Aunt Sue in San Francisco.

"Let's follow her," Jen said. Blond braids flapping and glasses slipping down her nose, she set Silly into a lope.

The girls rode together, keeping the bird in sight to see where she'd nested.

"If she drops a feather, I get it," Sam said.

"For a good luck charm or something?" Jen asked.

"It's almost Jake's birthday." Sam paused. Jen was listening hard, frowning to hear over the clattering hooves.

"Jake wants a feather for his birthday?" Jen asked.

"No." Sam laughed. "But how cool would it look braided into Witch's mane with the new headstall I got him?"

"Wow," Jen agreed. Then she frowned. "She's getting away."

They galloped, rushing into a wind that tasted of sagebrush and rabbitbrush and something tangy Sam couldn't name. The horses ran side by side, surging after the hawk.

If a russet feather fell, Sam knew she would give it to Jake, but she longed to keep it for just a while. Holding a little piece of wildness—not stolen from an animal, but freely given—always filled her with quiet wonder.

But the hawk didn't care what Sam wanted. After leading them on a swooping path toward War Drum Flats, the redtail made a shrugging motion with her wings, banked upwind, and disappeared into the evening sky.

"We've lost her," Jen said.

"I know, and I've got to get home."

"Me too. D'you want to let these two drink a minute before we go?"

"Sure."

The horses followed a well-worn path past a tumble of boulders, toward a dirt road that paralleled the highway. Few vehicles used the road, since it dead-ended near the narrow mountain trail up to Lost Canyon.

The pond was in sight when Jen's palomino reared.

Chapter 5

THE PALOMINO STOOD TALL, WHITE- stockinged front legs flailing in surprise.

"Silly!" Jen shouted. She slammed forward on the mare's neck, forcing her to touch down. "She smelled something, I think. Did you see how she was flaring her nostrils?"

Sam shook her head and stayed focused on Ace. The gelding danced with uneasiness as he watched Silly.

"It's okay, boy," she assured him, but as soon as she saw Jen regain control of Silly, Sam twisted in her saddle, searching for whatever had frightened the horses.

Could it be the Phantom? Sam's glance swept the area around the pond, the path to Lost Canyon, and the giant stair-step ridges and buttes that hid deer trails and passages to the stallion's hideaway.

The stallion and his herd weren't in sight. Neither were antelope, coyotes, snakes, or even a sage hen that might have startled Silly. What else could the palomino have smelled?

Sam knew she and Jen paid attention. Even hurrying, they would have noticed signs of danger. Jen was probably right. It was a sound or scent beyond human senses.

Ace snorted, telling Sam he found her fidgets far from comforting. He shifted his weight to his hind legs before teeter-tottering away from the earth, threatening to rear.

One horse rearing was a mistake. Two horses rearing was an unplanned rodeo, and Sam wanted no part of it.

Using leg pressure and a kick, Sam forced Ace to walk, then trot. Awkwardly, he went.

"That's it, keep going." Sam kept after Ace with her voice and hands. As long as the gelding moved forward, he couldn't rear, so she rode him right into the water.

The pond was shallow and the footing gummy. Ace's hooves made sucking sounds until he stopped to drink. He'd be a muddy mess to clean up, but at least she was still in the saddle.

"What was that all about?" Jen had dismounted to let Silly drink. She stood beside the palomino, holding the reins in two places.

In seconds, both horses had drunk their fill of the cloudy water.

"You've got me." Sam rode Ace slogging out of the pond. His legs were coated with taupe-colored clay.

"These two are going to need a bath, not a brushing," Jen grumbled, and remounted Silly.

All at once, Sam remembered Rachel's taunt about the drought. She hadn't been asked to keep that remark secret.

"Hey, Jen, how did Slocum make his money?"

The setting sun cast a gold glaze across the lenses of Jen's glasses as she tucked back hair that had escaped from a braid.

"Do you know?" Sam prodded.

"Of course. He gets it from people like my family."

"I don't understand," Sam said.

Jen took a deep breath and jiggled one foot in its stirrup. "My dad's been doing some research, and it seems like Slocum is buying up farms and ranches all over the West. He builds houses, malls, sometimes even factories."

Sam tried to unravel Rachel's threat. Of course she wouldn't want River Bend covered with acres of free parking, but Dad and Gram would never sell.

"Dad says Slocum is a genius at finding people in debt. A lot of times drought pushes them over the edge."

Sam felt chills at that suggestion.

"In Montana it was mad cow disease. It was just a scare. The cattle turned out to have something like the sniffles, but the ranchers couldn't *give* that beef away."

It made sense, Sam thought. But Jen wasn't done talking.

"And you know how the ranchers all help each other out?"

"Sure," Sam said, "with roundups and haying and when we had the fire—"

"Well, if Rancher One sells out, he can't help Rancher Two with haying. Rancher Two hires a hay crew, goes broke paying them, and sells out. Then Rancher Three thinks, 'If I moved to the city, I could work nine-to-five in air-conditioned comfort and my kids could play soccer instead of watching barbed wire rust.'"

"Personally, I like watching barbed wire rust." Sam knew it was a weak joke, but she didn't have time to improve it. The horses had begun flicking their ears and acting restless again.

When Ace shied, Sam saw what he did.

She wheeled Ace, dismounted, and kicked at the dirt. Beneath a puff of dust, something glittered.

"What is it?" Jen asked.

Sam picked up the shimmering gold strand and examined it.

"Silky fringe," Sam said, "like you'd have on a fancy shirt or costume."

"*That* couldn't be what scared my big, strong palomino." Jen leaned forward and kissed Silly's neck.

"I don't think so either." Sam shoved it into a pocket as she remounted.

They rode in silence, squinting against waves of dust that came with each gust of wind, until they came to the spot where they usually parted to ride home.

Then Jen cleared her throat.

"There's something I didn't tell you about Slocum," she said. "In one way it doesn't matter. In another way it's really important."

"Okay." Sam found herself swallowing hard.

"The first ranch Slocum bought belonged to two families in Colorado who could trace their roots back to pioneers. They'd helped each other for over a hundred years. Some of their kids had even married, so after a while it was all one huge ranch. But they were in serious debt to the bank."

"Slocum made them an offer and they finally had to take it. And then he sold the ranch to a beer-brewing company and made a ton of money." Jen gave a wry smile. "My dad says Linc has a nose for something dying, and he's no better than a land vulture. That's how he got our ranch."

Jen never cried, so Sam told herself it was probably just a reflection she saw on her friend's glasses. *Some small ranchers will certainly lose their property.* That was what Rachel had said.

Sam's heart hammered as she rode for home. She had to ask Dad if the River Bend Ranch was in danger.

No one noticed she was late.

Showered and wearing satisfied grins, Dallas, Pepper, and Ross were just coming down the steps, leaving the house as Sam ran in from the barn.

That was weird. The cowboys took turns cooking in the bunkhouse kitchen, but they'd definitely looked well fed.

When Sam eased into the house, the kitchen table was so laden with food, Gram and Dad were just looking at it.

Gram's usually tidy bun straggled down her back, but her hands were perched on her hips, and she looked proud.

"I'm trying out fried chicken recipes for the county

fair cook-off," she told Sam. She gestured toward three plates that had probably been piled higher a few minutes before. "I've got their votes. Now it's our turn."

Sam obeyed Gram's taste-test rules, eating bites of mashed potatoes and green beans in between chicken sampling, but her full stomach couldn't chase away thoughts of Slocum.

"Time to vote," Gram said as Dad laid down his fork. "Which is best? The Buttermilk Crunch recipe?" Gram pointed to an empty pink plate. "Cha-Cha Chicken?" She indicated a dish holding a lonely red-flecked chicken wing. "Or Honey Fried?"

"Honey Fried." Dad placed his napkin on the table as if offering surrender.

Gram turned to Sam.

"They were all really good," she said. "But if I have to pick just one, it's the Honey Fried for me, too."

Gram gave them a lopsided smile. "But that's my usual recipe. It's the one I always cook."

"Lucky us," Dad said. He leaned over and patted Gram's hand.

"How did Pepper, Dallas, and Ross vote?" Sam asked.

"Pepper gave half his vote to the Cha-Cha Chicken, but otherwise, same as you," Gram said.

Before they left the table, Sam blurted her question. "How much trouble are we in from this drought?"

Dad's smile melted. "It hasn't helped, that's for sure."

"Really, Dad. Tell me how bad things are."

Dad glanced at Gram, then shrugged. "We've been this close to the edge many times. A lot depends on winter rainfall. We need it now, before all the topsoil blows away."

Sam thought of the curtains of dust she and Jen had ridden through today. "But we aren't farmers. Why is the soil important?"

"Graze for the cattle next spring and then our hay crop to see us through next winter," Dad explained.

"Then, if rain comes all at once, like it does sometimes, even thirsty ground can't absorb it," Gram said. She looked toward the window. "We get flooding, and it washes away what topsoil the wind left behind."

"It's kind of hard to know what to hope for," Sam said.

"Honey, you just leave the worrying to us," Dad said.

Gram nodded but added, "I think it's a real sign of maturity that you're considering the future of your home, Samantha. It shows you're really growing up."

Gram placed a reddened and wrinkled hand on Dad's brown one. Together, those hands had done a hundred years of work. That struck Sam harder than Gram's compliment.

"What brought this on?" Dad asked.

Sam didn't rush to tell the truth. Once she did, she was committed to working for Rachel's money. And didn't *that* sound selfish?

"Rachel asked me to teach her to ride," she admitted.

"I thought she already knew how," Gram said.

Dad frowned, probably trying to see how this fit with Sam's worries.

"She said she'd pay me," Sam explained.

"That's fine, if you want to," Dad said.

"There'll be field trips coming up, and clothes you want to buy," Gram said. "If you earn money, it's yours."

Gram and Dad gave her smiles that said the small

amount Sam earned wouldn't really help the ranch. Still, she didn't know how to translate what Rachel had said about earning Linc Slocum's good opinion.

"Has Mr. Slocum ever tried to buy River Bend?" Sam asked.

Dad slid his chair back from the table with a screech. Even though Sam knew he wasn't mad at her, he looked scary.

"I'd carry this land bucket by bucket and dump it in the Pacific Ocean before I let him have it." Dad started from the kitchen, then turned back, voice even lower. "You can bet on that."

From the living room, Dad's chair creaked, and the television came on louder than usual.

"We're good neighbors to the Slocums," Gram said, "because that's the way things should be. But when he came in here a couple of years ago, flashing his money around, some of us decided to stand firm."

"It was just after your accident, and Linc had the idea we'd want to sell and move out. Even made us feel ashamed for sending you off all alone to San

Francisco." Gram looked up, her expression guilty.

"I had Aunt Sue," Sam protested.

"Of course you did," Gram said. "Linc went to the Potters, the Dennis family, the Greens, and the Kenworthys. In any case, Linc tried his hardest and we shut him down, but"—Gram stood and picked up two platters—"this could be a hard year."

After the dinner dishes were washed and dried, Sam trudged upstairs to do homework.

Television didn't tempt her tonight. Not only did she have algebra homework, but she was trying to figure out the history project Mrs. Ely had assigned.

But Sam's mind wandered. She placed the silky gold fringe on the desk beside her. Something more than this had frightened the horses. Glancing toward her bedroom door to make sure no one could see her, Sam raised the fringe to her nose and sniffed it herself. It might, very faintly, smell like incense.

She put it back down. Who had a shirt with gold fringe?

Slocum was the only neighbor who wore such showy

gear for routine rides. Everyone else saved such finery for rodeo time.

The Darton rodeo had ended months ago, in June, but who knew how long the fringe had been out on War Drum Flats?

Sam forced herself to look at her algebra book. She positioned her paper beside it and copied a problem neatly.

$3x + 11x =$

Sam looked away from the text and gave the fringe a poke with her pencil eraser.

This was so frustrating. She knew the fringe was a clue to something, but it remained a mysterious x to her.

Chapter 6

THE NEXT MORNING, SAM WAS RUBBING HER hands together, wishing she'd worn her gloves to the bus stop, when Jen gave her a shove that spun her toward the mountains.

"Sam! Oh my gosh! Look!"

For an instant, all Sam saw was Jen's breath, hanging before her like smoke in the cold morning air. Then she saw what had startled her friend.

Hooves crunching dry earth, a band of mustangs swirled in an uneasy bunch. The lead mare nipped with flattened ears, keeping the horses on the wild side of the highway. Only the Phantom crossed.

The Phantom. What was he doing down here by the highway? Sam watched with amazement as he approached.

As if the asphalt might splinter beneath his hooves, the stallion took a step, stopped, and squared up. Faint tremors ran over him like water, but his ears pricked forward and his eyes were set on Sam.

She risked a quick glance away from the stallion, at Jen. Her friend watched her with awe and a little suspicion.

"He's coming to you," Jen said.

Sam opened her mouth, then closed it.

There was no use denying the statement. Jen knew horses. She knew the silver stallion wasn't wandering across the highway by chance.

Suddenly, the girls heard the labored downshifting of the school bus. It rumbled their way, with one more hill to crest, and then a dip. When it came up the other side, the bus would be just yards from their stop.

THE RENEGADE

Fear lodged in Sam's throat. She couldn't speak and she struggled to take a breath.

The Phantom didn't notice. If he heard the diesel engine, he was too focused on Sam to pay attention.

A collision between tons of metal and delicate equine flesh flashed in Sam's imagination. She saw him rearing, falling. . . . She had to stop him.

"Get back!" Sam shouted so loudly Jen flinched. "Hyah!" She waved her hands and bolted onto the pavement. "Get out of here!"

The stallion only cocked his head and considered her craziness. His white mane cascaded like a waterfall as he frolicked a step closer.

Jen joined her, yelling and jumping into the air.

They looked back and forth, searching for the bus, staring at the confused horse.

The bus had dropped into the dip. Only an edge of yellow roof moved closer. In a minute, it would be upon them. Why hadn't the stallion spooked? What if the bus struck him?

Something like electricity rushed through Sam's

bones and muscles. She shoved Jen back toward the bus stop and darted into the road. The engine's huff clogged her ears. As soon as the bus crested the hill, the driver would see her standing in his path.

The horn blared, vibrating her insides, just as the stallion's hot shoulder brushed hers. Sam turned to see the Phantom's eyes edged with white, mouth agape.

Clumsy with fear, he almost fell as the bus braked. Scraping hooves and a grunt of effort proved the stallion was fighting to keep all four legs beneath him.

He spun, still skittering for balance, and ran for his herd.

Sam didn't watch the mustangs go. The bus driver stood in front of her, yelling.

"What were you thinking?" His hands flew skyward in frustration. "Of all the— It was a *horse*. Just a horse. I could have killed you."

For a second, the driver's hands covered his face. She'd really scared him, Sam thought, but when he looked up, his fear had been replaced by fury.

"I'm writing you up, Samantha. I'm giving you a cita-

THE RENEGADE

tion that will have you in trouble so deep you won't be able to see out for months! Now, get on that bus!" He pointed as if sending her to her room.

Sam ran up the steps onto the bus. Jen clattered right behind her. From the corner of her eye, Sam noticed Jen had snagged both of their backpacks.

Jen was such a great friend—and Sam knew she was going to need one. Although the bus was filled with people she knew, their astonished faces didn't look sympathetic. Of the thirty kids on the bus, half were gawking, with their mouths wide open.

The driver slammed into his seat and pulled the doors closed. He glared into the mirror and addressed everyone sitting behind him.

"No more distractions," he commanded. "I want it quiet as a tomb. One peep out of anybody and there'll be a pack of you going to the principal's office. Got it?"

Though a resentful murmur rippled through the students, they knew better than to protest.

As the bus jerked back into motion, Sam's stomach rolled with nausea. She closed her eyes, but it didn't help. She made fists until her fingernails bit into her palms. Cold sweat gathered over her top lip, but wiping it away would only call attention to her distress.

She swallowed. Probably, she hadn't almost died. Probably, her mind had exaggerated the nearness of the silver grille on the front of the bus. Probably, Zanzibar would have run away in time.

When Jen's elbow hit her in the ribs, Sam felt as if she'd been awakened. She blinked heavy eyelids and pushed her hair back from her eyes.

Jen had taken a lens-cleaning tissue from her backpack. Methodically, she polished her glasses, held them up for inspection, and let her eyes slide sideways to meet Sam's.

It's okay. Jen mouthed the words silently, then slipped her glasses back on.

Sam really hoped she was right.

By the time they reached school and got off the bus, Sam had to hurry to her locker. Her rush didn't keep her from noticing the eyes that followed her. Up and down

THE RENEGADE

the halls, kids from the bus were spreading gossip about the morning's excitement.

Later, when a student messenger interrupted Sam's history class to give Mrs. Ely a yellow office pass, everyone looked at Sam.

"Sam?" Mrs. Ely raised one eyebrow, and Sam guessed word of her misdeed hadn't had time to spread to the teachers' workroom this morning.

She almost enjoyed her walk to the office. Unlike her three-story San Francisco middle school, Darton High's single story framed a central courtyard. Sam crunched through yellow cottonwood leaves and looked up at the patches of blue sky showing between wind-torn white clouds.

Sam pulled her sleeves down. The breeze cut right through her cotton shirt, feeling like winter, but that was the least of her worries. If she'd known when she got dressed this morning that she'd be talking with the principal, she would've worn her newest jeans. Or maybe even a skirt.

It probably wouldn't have made any difference.

Ms. Santos wore a businesslike beige suit and fooled with a clip-on earring as Sam entered the principal's office. Not until Ms. Santos pointed her toward a chair did Sam notice the principal was on the telephone.

During her first week at Darton High, Sam had interviewed Ms. Santos for the school newspaper. She'd found the principal to be a no-nonsense woman with a great sense of humor. Would she feel that way when she left Ms. Santos's office this time?

Sam waited. With luck, Ms. Santos would just lecture her. There was no reason, really, for Gram and Dad to find out about her reckless behavior.

They worried, and they blamed the Phantom for Sam's riding accident. Even though the stallion had been young and had carried her weight for less than an hour, they blamed him for Sam's fall, for the kick that knocked her unconscious and kept her in the hospital for several weeks.

After that, Sam had been forced to live in San Francisco for two years, just to be near a hospital.

THE RENEGADE

Since the day Sam had returned from San Francisco, Gram had been afraid the stallion would hurt her again. And if Dad thought Rachel's riding off into the mountains was a "stunt," what would he say about this?

Ms. Santos hung up the receiver.

"Sorry," she said. Immediately, her eyes skimmed a form Sam knew was the citation. Ms. Santos frowned, then pushed the form toward Sam. "Look at this."

Sam studied the undecipherable handwriting. She recognized her name and the word "horse," but that was all.

"I can't read it," Sam said.

"Neither can I, and I've never had trouble reading one of Mr. Pinkerton's citations before." Ms. Santos shook her head. "The man's driven a school bus for fifteen years. He doesn't get rattled easily. Tell me what happened."

Sam did. She left out the fact that she knew the wild horse she'd rescued.

"It's not like I'm ever going to do this again," Sam ended her explanation.

"No," Ms. Santos agreed. "Not *this*."

Sam wasn't sure what the principal's emphasis meant. While Ms. Santos wrote on the form, Sam checked the wall clock. She'd missed half of P.E. The bad thing was, it was one of only two classes she had with Jen. On the other hand, it was one of two classes she had with Rachel.

When Ms. Santos finally put down her pen, Sam realized she'd been sitting with fingers crossed on both hands while she awaited the principal's decision.

"You'll need to apologize to Mr. Pinkerton—"

Sam found herself smiling and nodding before Ms. Santos finished her sentence.

"—and find other transportation to school for two weeks."

"You mean, I can't ride the bus?"

"That's what I mean." Ms. Santos glanced at the phone, which had begun ringing behind her.

"But then my dad has to know," Sam said.

"That's right," the principal said.

Sam shook her head. "I'm going to be mucking out

THE RENEGADE

the barn until I'm twenty-one," she moaned.

Ms. Santos laughed, picked up the phone, and waved Sam on her way.

The other girls were already jogging toward the locker room when Sam reached her P.E. class and fell into step with Jen.

"I'm not suspended," Sam said. "Except from the bus."

"Could be worse, but what are you going to do?" Jen used the hem of her gold T-shirt to blot her face.

"You'll be the first to know. Hey, I've got to ask you something."

"Math or vet stuff?"

"What?"

"You must realize that you don't ask my opinion about much of anything except your algebra class and horse medicine," Jen said over the slamming of gym lockers. "On everything else, you just rush recklessly ahead."

"Wrong." Sam shook her head and lowered her voice. "Here's the thing: in the past few days, the Phantom has shown up where he shouldn't have. Before this he's never come near me when other people were around. Now he's done it twice."

Jen nodded, encouraging Sam to keep talking.

"So," Sam whispered, "do you think he could be asking for my help?"

Jen finished dressing, then faced Sam. Jen's expression was owlish. "Would this be a bad time for me to suggest your attitude toward the Phantom is anthropomorphic?"

Sam crossed her arms. "No worse than any other time—if your plan is to make me feel dumb."

They left the gym and walked toward their next classes. Jen was taking so long answering, Sam wondered if she'd used the word on purpose and hoped Sam wouldn't ask what it meant.

"Well?" Sam said.

"It means you're crediting an animal with human feelings," Jen said gently.

"But he does love me, like Silly loves you. And he actually leaves his herd to come see me. And I've helped him before. . . ."

"But does he know that?" Jen asked.

Exasperation made Sam's voice loud. "Of course—"

"Hullo, ladies," Rachel said, suddenly appearing beside Sam. "Am I intruding?"

"Later," Jen said, splitting off toward her class.

"Yeah," Sam said. She quickened her pace, but Rachel kept up. Finally, Sam glanced over at her.

Olive silk pants billowed around Rachel's legs. The matching pullover should have appeared rumpled. Instead, Rachel looked incredible. It just wasn't fair.

"About our business arrangement," Rachel began. "And please don't give my reputation a thought. Since we're keeping this quiet, it won't matter that some might think you're a bad influence." She gestured toward the principal's office.

"You know what, Rachel?" Sam felt her anger building again.

"If this is a bad time, we can talk later," Rachel said.

"No, it's a fine time." Sam paused outside her classroom door. "But you see, I've been suspended from riding the bus. And that means I have to wait for someone to pick me up from school. There's no telling when Dad gets in from the range, and Gram can't always get away either."

"Yes, yes, they work so hard." Rachel rolled her eyes. "But they won't leave you here. You're just saying that to be annoying."

"No, I'm not," Sam insisted. "Some days they can't drive all the way into town until after dark. It's that whole *work* thing, you know? Like Jake was talking about?"

"Ride home with him, why don't you?" Rachel suggested.

"He rides with his brothers, and the Blazer's already too full," Sam said.

Besides, even if they could squeeze her into the Blazer, there wouldn't be room for Jen. Though she was a little ticked at Jen right now for that anthropo—*whatever* remark, they were best friends. They did some of their best talking at the end of the school day, riding home. She didn't want to give that up.

"There's always Mrs. Ely," Rachel suggested. "She seems to like you."

"No." Sam knew Jake's mom would give her rides, but wouldn't she have to stay for meetings and stuff?

Sam ducked inside her class and left Rachel musing over some great idea Sam knew she'd hate.

Rachel ambushed Sam in the hallway just outside journalism.

"It's all settled," Rachel muttered as if she'd planned something shifty. After all, her cheerleader friend Daisy was in journalism too. "You can ride in my car. Our housekeeper doesn't mind."

Once Sam had cooled off, she'd realized that all her mental vows to save the ranch were worth nothing if she didn't teach Rachel, take her money, and get in good with Linc Slocum.

Next, it occurred to Sam that this wasn't an idle wish for Rachel. She wanted this a lot, so Sam could hold out for what she wanted too. And what she wanted most didn't have a single dollar sign attached.

"That'll be fine." Sam gave Rachel a minute of relief

before adding, "And since you drive right by her house, you can give Jen a ride too."

"Jennifer Kenworthy?"

Sam kept her sarcasm trapped behind closed lips.

"She hasn't been barred from the bus, surely?" Rachel scanned the crowded hall. "Jennifer likes riding the bus."

"Rachel, you've never been on a bus or you wouldn't say that. No one likes the smell of old bananas and sweaty socks, and even on a good day . . ." The horror on Rachel's face stopped Sam. "You haven't, have you? You've never been on a school bus in your life!"

"The first few days you were in this class, you were so nice and quiet," Rachel snapped. "Why don't you—" Her eyes closed and stayed that way, as if she were counting to a hundred.

Eventually, she opened her eyes.

"I suppose it doesn't matter." Rachel smiled and smoothed the wing of dark hair as if it had been displaced by her temper, but Sam was pretty sure Rachel hadn't noticed Daisy in the doorway dead ahead.

THE RENEGADE

The cheerleader stared at her friend as if she couldn't be certain Rachel was actually conversing with Sam.

Sam made sure to raise her voice as they approached.

"Thanks, Rachel," Sam said, nudging her. "You're a pal."

Chapter 7

SAM AND JEN EMBARRASSED RACHEL THE MINute they slid into the baby-blue Mercedes after school.

"Hi, Mrs. Coley," Jen said as she fastened her seat belt in the back seat.

"Jennifer, it's good to see you."

The woman who turned away from the steering wheel had boyish short gray hair and a welcoming smile.

"Hi," Sam said, leaning forward with her hand extended. "I'm Samantha Forster. I've seen you drive by, but I don't think we've met." Sam often felt a moment of uncertainty about people she'd known before the accident. This time, Rachel's huffing didn't help, but Mrs. Coley's handshake couldn't have been friendlier.

"Nice to meet you, Samantha. I'm Helen Coley. I know your grandmother, Grace, from church."

Sam squirmed a little. Although both Dad and Gram were devout people, they had an ongoing battle about church. Gram believed folks liked to join together with the minister to pray for rain. Dad thought it gave them false hope, no different from teasing winds, which blew through carrying the smell of wet grass and rain-slick rocks from some luckier place.

"Yes, ma'am," said Sam, but Mrs. Coley had already turned her attention to the parking lot crowded with teenage drivers.

Sam didn't feel smug about riding in Rachel's Mercedes. She felt misplaced and uneasy. Telling Dad and Gram she'd been kicked off the bus would be ugly. They'd blame the Phantom, of course. Just when they seemed reasonable about mustangs, their old-fashioned ranchers' stereotypes cropped up.

As they edged through the parking lot, Sam saw RJay, editor of the Darton *Dialogue*, strolling to his car. When he did a double take at the sight of Sam and Rachel riding together, Sam waved. Rachel might have wanted to fling herself to the car floor, but she only flattened her spine against the seat back as they left Darton High traffic behind.

Sam was just thinking how cool it would be to have a saddle made with the supple leather used for the Mercedes's seat covers, when Rachel's cell phone rang.

Sam and Jen looked at each other. Since they couldn't cover their ears, they shifted away and pretended not to listen.

"Ryan!" Rachel's voice brimmed with happiness, and though Sam knew she'd heard the name before, she couldn't place it until Rachel said, "What's up in Nottingham?"

Her brother, Jen mouthed, and Sam gave a tiny nod.

"Of course, Ry." Rachel's voice returned to its usual mocking tone. "My equitation instructor is in the Mercedes with me now."

Rachel's fingers flipped through her silky hair as she shifted with discomfort. "Anyone can improve. My skills will be top-notch for summer competition— Oh, it is not. It's no more a beauty contest than your steeplechasing."

She laughed at her twin's answer, then turned farther away from Sam and Jen and lowered her voice.

"Just the recognition. I'll donate the scholarship to the needy or something. That's what I was about to say. You always—" She paused, listening. "The advantage of being twelve minutes older, yes?"

Rachel's chat turned brittle again. "My horse? I'll let that be your summer surprise."

During the silence that followed, Sam decided Rachel didn't have a mount of her own. Of course, Linc wouldn't allow that to be a problem for long.

"Not really!" Rachel's gasp was so sudden, even Jen, who'd been politely pretending to study, glanced up at Rachel's red face.

"Christmas?" Rachel pronounced the word as if she'd just learned it. "She is?" Rachel sighed, and though her coloring faded toward normal, her expression was sad. "Switzerland. How nice. Well, then, of course you—and I guess you'll get to see my horse a little sooner than expected. Still, I want to surprise you, Ry. Okay, yes. Ta to you, too. I miss you."

Face to the window, Rachel curled against her side of the car, looking small.

No. Sam would *not* let herself feel sorry for Rachel. She couldn't forget the girl had dropped one of Mr. Blair's cameras and let Sam take the blame. And what about Rachel's mocking laugh as she said Sam looked like a boy? As if that weren't enough, Rachel had also been rude to Jake and Jen, Sam's two best friends in the world.

"Well, cowgirl," Rachel said suddenly. "My schedule's changed and so has yours. You'll give me the intensive course. Starting tomorrow, I'd say, since I must be riding well by Christmas. And you'll need to help me find an appropriate horse."

Rachel's lips formed a witchy smile, as if Sam had no choice.

As Rachel replaced the car phone, Sam considered her unprotected back. Sam didn't think of herself as a violent person, but if Jen's knee hadn't nudged hers meaningfully, she might have explored her desire to give Rachel a punch.

The car's rolling tires were the only sound for a minute.

"Mother calls Ryan the conscience of the family," Rachel said.

Sam imagined Rachel with a cartoon devil perched on one shoulder, an angel on the other. If that was Ryan's duty, he was slacking. Linc and Rachel needed him, big-time.

"I want your assistance too," Rachel said to Jen.

Jen closed her book. "I'm fascinated," she said. "But it depends on what you need."

Rachel wrestled with whether she could admit she *needed* anything from them, then decided to let it go.

"Samantha knows," Rachel said.

"Sort of. You want to improve your riding skills."

Jen's hand couldn't cover her mouth before a laugh escaped.

"I have some skills," Rachel protested.

"What's the competition you want to enter?" Sam asked. "Is it the 'Best in the West' you mentioned?"

"You want to be a rodeo queen?" Jen blurted.

The Mercedes slowed as if Mrs. Coley's foot had faltered on the gas pedal.

Rachel considered her green-and-gold-tinted fingernails.

"Karla Starr encouraged me to enter." Rachel's chin lifted as if the rodeo contractor's opinion was all that mattered. "Once I told Ryan, it became a fact. But I want to keep it a secret from Dad."

"My mom was first runner-up for Best in the West, like, twenty years ago," Jen said, shaking her head. "I don't know, Rachel. You'd have to compete in horsemanship, modeling, and there's a personal interview."

"Riding is only a third of it." Rachel shrugged. "Plus, it would stop Ry from bragging about his silly water jumps, and I *have* been told—by an expert, mind you— that winning would be a piece of cake for me."

The day he'd come to River Bend for help, Slocum

had mentioned that Rachel had been perturbed ever since Karla Starr's visit. Rachel must have seen Champ, saddled and tied, and decided to prove to herself that she could still ride.

Had she made it as far along the ridge trail because she remembered how to ride, or because Champ was a patient, well-schooled horse?

"It would have worked out nicely," Rachel said, "if I'd had the whole school year to train. But Ryan's coming home at Christmas."

Sam felt a pulse of excitement. If Rachel's sense of urgency made her buckle down and work, they might finish sooner.

But was that a good thing? River Bend needed the money.

What would Rachel pay for lessons? Twenty dollars per hour? Thirty? Fifty? Sam knew she could earn enough money to help. She was adding up dollars and basking in possibilities, when Rachel sighed.

"I could pretend I was sick or tell him I changed my mind," Rachel suggested.

"Come on, Rachel," Sam said. "You're not a quitter."

"Certainly not," Rachel said, but she looked surprised.

"If we got together three times a week after school, you'd make progress fast." Sam couldn't believe she'd volunteered to spend so much time with Rachel.

"That's a splendid idea, Samantha, perhaps the best you've ever had."

The shocked expression on Jen's face would have made Sam stop, but River Bend Ranch was at stake.

As they approached War Drum Flats, Sam saw a bachelor band of mustangs.

"Mrs. Coley," she blurted, "if it's not too much trouble—"

Everyone in the car followed Sam's pointing finger.

"Samantha, really," Rachel moaned, but Mrs. Coley was already pulling over.

"I'm another of those ranch women who actually like mustangs," Mrs. Coley said. "I've been watching this bunch for a week or two."

THE RENEGADE

"Are we in a time warp?" Rachel said. "It's taking forever to reach home."

In spite of Rachel's complaint, the Mercedes stopped at the roadside.

Shoulders touching, manes blowing, three young stallions clung together so closely, Sam thought she could measure across all three chests with her outflung arms.

Little bachelor bands like this one were common. When a lead stallion saw them as potential rivals for his mares, he used hooves and teeth to drive young males from the herd. Wandering the range, lonely and yearning for the safety they'd always known in a band, the young stallions formed small herds of their own.

"I call them New Moon, Yellow Tail, and Spike," Mrs. Coley confided.

The first name gave Sam chills. During the new moon, the sky was black. This colt had no white markings. Neither had the Phantom as a colt. In fact, as a two-year-old, he'd looked much like this leggy horse.

Distracted by memories, Sam took a minute to see

how well the other young outcasts matched Mrs. Coley's names for them.

Spike had to be the bay whose mane stuck up almost as if it had been roached, then moussed into place. The sorrel, standing in the middle, had a long flaxen tail that really did look almost yellow. In spite of the warm fall temperatures, both were getting fuzzy winter coats. Only the black, who led the others by a half stride, still shone like glass.

As Sam watched, the black broke away from the others. He arched his neck and executed a sort of bow, inviting his pals into a mock battle.

Like guys sparring because they had nothing better to do, the three pulled each other's manes and tails. They reared and fenced with their front legs, clearly playing.

Sam had seen the Phantom fight a blue roan stallion she'd called Hammer, and this was different. The bachelors were practicing. One day they'd challenge another stallion for his harem. This was a study session for that day.

THE RENEGADE

"If you could have your pick—" Jen began.

"The black," Sam answered without hesitation. "There's something about him. . . ."

Sam's voice trailed off as her mind recognized what her eyes had already noticed.

The black was from the Phantom's herd, perhaps even his son.

Weeks ago, he and several other horses had been trapped by rustlers using Dark Sunshine for bait. The captive mustangs had very nearly been sold for pet food. Detective work and luck had rescued the horses, and they'd been released in the Phantom's territory.

But maybe his absence made the black seem an intruder and the Phantom had driven him away.

Done with their skirmish, the three horses rolled in the dust until they were caked with it.

"How gross," Rachel said. "That black one was kind of pretty, before."

"It keeps off bugs," Jen explained.

"I'd think that was the least of their worries," Rachel said, yawning.

"What do you mean?" Sam tried to keep her voice light, but Rachel had hinted at something secret before. If it had anything to do with wild horses, Sam needed to know.

"With BLM and other people trying to catch them, I just think they'd better watch out," Rachel said.

The mustangs did seem more intent on playing than watching for danger, but Sam knew they could vanish in a heartbeat.

"If they're caught by anyone except BLM, that would be illegal." Jen studied Rachel. "You know that, right?"

Rachel sat back in her seat and gave a superior laugh.

"Of course, and I'll thank you not to lecture me, Jennifer, for the remainder of our little car pool."

When Jen's index finger stabbed her glasses back up her nose, Sam knew her friend was about to declare she didn't want to be part of this arrangement.

With the excuse of showing good manners, Sam tried to make Jen feel too guilty to desert her.

"Rachel, Mrs. Coley, thanks so much for giving me a ride," Sam said. "I'm going to be in trouble, but at least I won't have to ask Dad and Gram to drive me back and forth."

Sam winced as the River Bend bridge came into view. The last time she'd been in big trouble, Dad and Gram had turned her into a hired hand, one less worthy of respect than Dallas, Pepper, and Ross.

"You have no idea how hard it's going to be to tell them what I did. All day long, I've been thinking about the right way to put it."

"Oh, I think you'll be spared that, dear." Mrs. Coley looked up in her rearview mirror. Sam could only see her eyes, but they were sympathetic. "Mr. Pinkerton, the bus driver, has a little romance going with Junie. You know, the waitress at Clara's Café."

"Yes," Sam said, and even she could tell her voice was faint with fear.

"Well, when Jed came back from buying some fuses for me at the Alkali store this morning, he told me all about your wild horse escapade."

"Don't worry, Sam," Jen said. "My dad wouldn't pick up the telephone unless he had to report a fire.

A big one. He sure wouldn't call and tattle on you."

"No, you're right, Jennifer, but he did have a cup of coffee with Dallas while he was there." Mrs. Coley sighed. "He told me how that Junie sure is a chatterbox. Fact is, Samantha, if I know, I expect your folks do too."

Chapter 8

THE MINUTE MRS. COLEY LET HER OUT IN THE ranch yard, Sam crossed her fingers. It was just possible Dallas had decided to keep her secret.

She didn't worry too much about Jake. Although he'd probably heard gossip at school, he wouldn't pass it on to Dad. There was no sign of his brother's truck or Witch, so maybe she'd beat him to River Bend.

The entire ranch simmered silently in the afternoon heat. Even Blaze didn't come running to meet her.

When Sam opened the door, she saw Gram and Dad

sitting together at the kitchen table. That meant a lecture was brewing, but Sam was more worried over the missing snack.

Every day, since the first day of school, Gram had put a plate of cookies on the kitchen table. Today there were none.

And Dad was home in the middle of the day. Though this was a slow time of year for cattlemen, Dad rarely came home before dusk.

Sam shrugged out of her backpack and let it fall to the floor. If she could tell them about the money she'd be making for Rachel's lessons, and about arranging her own rides to school, it would show she wasn't irresponsible.

They didn't seem in a rush to start, so Sam did.

"I guess you heard," she said.

"About the stunt you pulled," Dad said. "Not about your penalty."

"I can't ride the bus for two weeks," Sam answered, "but I—"

"Ms. Santos is too soft," Dad said.

"Or," Gram suggested, "she's left the punishment up to us."

"That *is* punishment," Sam insisted. She drew a breath to steady herself, but it came in all quavery. "Just so you know, I've arranged to ride with Rachel Slocum for those two weeks. Mrs. Coley will pick me up at the bus stop. Uh, Mrs. Coley says she knows you from church."

Gram nodded, but her eyes looked sad. "Seems you have no sense at all when it comes to that horse. Sakes, Samantha, how long has it been since you've known not to run into the middle of a street? That's something a child would do."

"Shamin' her's not going to help," Dad said. "The only thing that will is BLM taking that stallion off the range and shipping him somewhere for adoption."

Sam didn't realize her hands had flown up to cover her heart until Dad looked at them.

"You think that's harsh, but it's the truth. I never thought I'd say it, but I'm embarrassed by you, Samantha."

Sam closed her eyes.

"And I'm scared for you too."

"Dad, you wouldn't have let him get hit by the bus. I know you wouldn't."

"No. I woulda tossed a rock to spook him off the road, not run into the path of a bus."

It seemed so simple when Dad said it.

"I didn't think—"

"That's just what I mean," Gram said. "You're a smart girl, but that horse does something to you."

"You're not doing him any favors," Dad said. "You know how to think like a horse, so ask yourself what he's thinking. Is he a pet or a wild animal? Does he trust you or his own instincts? Being confused in his thinking is gonna get him killed. Or captured."

Still standing, Sam swayed a little at the truth of Dad's words. The Phantom had had two close calls. Though BLM tried to protect all mustangs, they had only a handful of rangers to patrol the whole state.

Plenty of people had dreamed of catching the ghostly white stallion rumored to roam this range. But now they knew he really existed, and Sam blamed herself for proving he was no myth.

"That stallion is depending on you for his safety," Dad said. "If you love him, let him go back to being wild."

"Okay," Sam said.

"To help you keep that promise," Dad said, "you're confined to this ranch. You go to school and home, and that's it."

Sam didn't ask for how long, but she thought of the Phantom coming to the river, waiting for her.

"No slipping out at night, either," Gram said. "Don't make me keep watch, Samantha. It's beneath you."

Sam felt as if all her energy had drained out of her fingertips, but she had one more thing to say.

"If it's okay, Rachel's going to come over and start taking lessons tomorrow. The money's for the ranch."

Gram started to protest, but Dad cut her off.

"Thanks," he said, and the simple word sounded almost like forgiveness.

Thunder rolled and Ace neighed for attention as Sam shooed the hens into their pen. All day they wandered, picking bugs and worms from their hiding places. Gram said happy hens laid more and better eggs, and they rarely had trouble with hawks.

Still, they didn't seem to mind returning to their coop, which was shaded by an old cottonwood tree.

The ranch yard was quiet once they'd fluttered back inside. Teddy was tied by the barn, but Jake was nowhere in sight and Dad had ridden out on Banjo. Right after their talk, he'd mentioned a couple of steers with runny noses. He wanted to check them before nightfall.

Another rumble sounded. At first, Sam thought it was more thunder. Or Dad herding steers across the bridge to be doctored. Instead, a white pickup truck was crossing the bridge. It looked like Brynna's.

Brynna Olson would be a welcome visitor today. Not only had the BLM manager been the first to suggest keeping the Phantom on the range to improve free-roaming herds, but lately she could almost always make Dad smile.

But as the truck drew nearer, Sam saw it wasn't Brynna's. This vehicle was newer, and its doors were decorated with gold stars trailing copper streamers and the words STARR RODEO PRODUCTIONS.

It must be Karla Starr, the rodeo contractor, but what could she want? They didn't have Brahma bulls or unmanageable horses. By Dad's decree, every animal on this place worked. Even Dark Sunshine and Popcorn were part of the HARP program, working to teach at-risk teenagers the patience needed to work with wild horses. So what would bring Karla Starr to River Bend?

Along with curiosity, Sam felt a rush of excitement. For a long time, rodeo stock contracting had been a man's world, but Karla Starr was breaking in.

When Dallas walked out of the bunkhouse, Sam wished he hadn't. Not only had the foreman told on her, but she could tell by the way he fixed her with a grim look that he thought he'd done it for her own good.

And now he was horning his way in on Karla Starr, when Sam knew she could have handled the meeting just fine.

The way Dallas moved was a reprimand for Sam's

irritation. He was in pain, and Gram had explained that his arthritis was aggravated by pinched nerves, a crushed disk, and vertebrae rearranged by a life he shrugged off as "rugged."

Now he stood near the truck door, and Sam thought he was trying to get rid of Karla Starr.

"As Wyatt told you on the phone, ma'am, we just can't help you."

The woman climbed out of her truck anyway. She bowed a little to Dallas as if he'd welcomed her.

"Well, I heard through the grapevine that you've got title to a few mustangs, and sometimes they can make pretty good bucking horses." Karla Starr flashed a smile toward Sam.

"That's true," Dallas said, "but these horses are workin' a special sort of job."

As Dallas described the HARP program, Sam studied Karla Starr.

She was probably younger than she looked. About thirty, Sam guessed, but her body looked hard as a stick, and her skin was leathery. Her eyes were a lively hazel, though, and they bounced from Dallas to Sam to the ten-acre pasture, taking everything in.

And then there was her hair. Sam decided it was show-business hair. It flipped away from her face in a sort of ruffle, and it looked as if Karla Starr had gone into a hairdresser's salon with a shiny new penny, pointed to its pinky-bronze glitter, and said, "That's it; I want my hair that color, exactly." And it was.

But it wasn't her hair that fascinated Sam. The thin woman wore a black shirt with curlicues of fancy stitching across the yoke. Below that, slanting down from her collarbone, were twin rows of gold fringe that shimmered and swayed with her every movement.

Sam knew that if she could run into the house and grab the glittering strand from her dresser upstairs, she could prove the fringe on Karla Starr's shirt matched the one she'd found at War Drum Flats.

Karla Starr had been there, where the three bachelor stallions rolled in the mud, where Ace and Silly had shied with fear, but why?

The address on her truck door said Mesa Verde,

California, but Karla Starr had been spending a lot of time in this part of Nevada.

"I see," the woman said, then glanced at her watch. "But don't rule me out. Even if you don't have any now, I want to get dibs on any broomtails too ornery to use with children."

"Someone's led you astray, Ms. Starr," Dallas said. "We only have two horses for that program."

"Which would those be?" Karla Starr turned to Sam as if she'd just recalled she was there. "And you're the young woman who can talk to wild horses."

Karla's smile was warm and friendly, as if she wanted to give Sam a girlfriends-only hug.

"That's an exaggeration," Sam said, wondering where the woman had heard it. She pointed to distract the woman. "The albino," Sam said, "and the buckskin are mustangs."

"She's a beauty." Karla Starr's eyes flicked over the horse. "Tiny for a bucking horse, though, and a little soft in the belly."

"She's in foal," Sam said.

"Too bad." Her expression faded. She glanced at her watch again, then lifted one shoulder in a shrug. "In my business, there's no such thing as a long-term investment."

"Aw now, do you mean to say you don't breed bucking mares to bucking stallions?" Dallas asked.

"Never. I buy rough stock, buck 'em out, and resell when they lose their edge. A mare might go through her entire rodeo career before that one's ready for the arena."

Sam met Dallas's eyes. Neither of them knew what to say.

"And the albino?" Karla Starr raised one brow. "He's tall enough, but he doesn't have the look. Still, there's no telling what he'd do in the arena, properly prepared."

"Properly prepared with drugs, shocks, burns—" Dallas used a casual tone for such horrors, but Karla Starr stopped him.

"Of course not. Those are tricks from the old days."

"Not so old," Dallas said. "When I worked for Slim Perkins, he was the only man raising stock instead of buying outlaws and terrifyin' them into bucking."

"I thought Slim Perkins was dead." Karla Starr laughed.

"He is, ma'am." Dallas looked hurt.

Why didn't Karla Starr go keep whatever appointment had her checking her watch every couple of minutes? There was nothing for her here.

"I can guarantee you my animals love to buck," the woman said, as if realizing she'd alienated them both. "It's play for them. Who wouldn't like a job where he only worked a couple of weekend afternoons a month?" She winked at Dallas. "Wouldn't take too long to get the cricks out of your back that way, would it?"

Dallas wasn't taken in. "These are lifelong cricks, ma'am, and I love my life the way it is. Just like these ponies do."

Karla Starr smiled as if she were indulging Dallas; then she looked past Sam and raised her auburn-penciled eyebrows in surprise. "Well, now, who's this?"

Sam heard hooves right behind her. They were determined but not collected like a horse under saddle. Even before she saw him, she knew it was Ace.

"Hey, runt," Karla Starr said, pretending to joke

with the gelding. "What're you up to? Is he just an old pet?" She reached to touch Ace's nose, and he swung his head away.

"He's one of the best usin' horses on the spread," Dallas said. "He's a little spoiled, but—"

"Babying animals ruins them," Karla interrupted, grabbing on to something she and Dallas had in common.

How had Ace escaped his corral again? Sam couldn't figure it out, but when he nuzzled her palm, she let him.

"You spoil him with sugar cubes," Karla said.

"Almost never," Sam said.

"He's sayin' otherwise." Karla laughed, then sneaked another glance at her watch before looking toward the range.

"He's not supposed to wander," Sam agreed. "But since school started, he hasn't been getting as much work as he needs, and he's been getting out of his corral."

"An escape artist." Karla looked at Ace with new eyes. "Usually means they're pretty smart."

A torrent of wind slashed through the ranch yard and

Karla's copper curls blew in her eyes. She looked ready to go, and then Dad came loping across the bridge into the yard.

"Now, there's a horse," Karla said.

Dad rode Banjo, and the Quarter Horse looked great. Collected and gleaming on his neck and shoulders, the gelding was all a working horse should be.

Karla Starr could just eat her heart out, Sam thought, because Dad would never sell Banjo.

"I should probably go, but I'd really like it if you could introduce me to your dad first."

Karla caught Sam's questioning look and laughed.

"I knew because you two look just alike," she said.

Sam motioned for Dad as he brought Banjo down to a trot. Her father looked impatient, displeased to have company, and downright peeved over Ace.

"Mr. Forster, I'm Karla Starr," she said before Sam could perform an introduction. "I love that gelding you're riding. He'd make a great pickup horse—"

"Excuse me." Dad made an apologetic gesture. "Samantha, what is Ace doing loose?"

THE RENEGADE

"Dad, I think he's figured out how to work the latch—"

"That's clear. I want you to fix it. And when you start those lessons tomorrow, use him. That horse is bored."

Karla Starr gave a between-us-adults chuckle, but Dad ignored her.

Sam thought of Rachel hauling on Ace's tender mouth and knew there was a better way to end his boredom. She needed to take him out and run him. She *was* grounded, but maybe Dad would agree—for Ace's sake.

A raindrop struck her eyelid. Sam blinked. Could those clouds really be ready to give them the rain they needed? A storm would excite Ace. He'd really run for her then.

"I know you all are busy," Karla said, "but I mean what I said. I'd pay top dollar for a horse like your gelding. He's strong enough to carry one rider and pick up a cowboy when his bronc or bull ride is over."

"I'll remember," Dad said, but he was looking skyward and holding back a smile.

Now, while he was pleased, Sam tried to ask.

"Dad, I know if I took Ace out now, I could take the edge off his energy and he'd stay put."

Wind rushed through the cottonwood trees, and the horses in the ten-acre pasture began to run.

All at once, there was a tapping sound as rain hit the brim of Dad's Stetson.

Ace tossed his head up, nostrils eager for the rain-sweet air. Then he neighed so loudly Sam covered her ears.

"Please, Dad?"

"Get him tacked up and run him into the wind," Dad said. "But just for a little while."

"Thanks—"

"Don't thank me. Your horse needs work. Take Jake with you and put both those ponies into a good gallop." Dad gestured toward the barn where Teddy Bear was tied. "Get after it, and don't be late for dinner. I'm sure Ms. Starr will excuse you."

"Of course." The woman slid her fingers into her pocket and withdrew two business cards, one of which she gave to Sam. "Sam, people would pay good money to see Ace do what he's getting in trouble for."

Then, looking at Dad, she added, "I don't love my animals. I let them feel useful." Then she handed him the second card. "Just in case you change your mind."

There was something flirty in the gesture that made Sam wish Brynna Olson were there.

Dad nodded politely, and Karla Starr was already driving away when Sam noticed the dog in her truck.

An Australian shepherd stared through the truck's back window. Its one white eye made the dog's stare eerie.

For close to an hour, the dog had stayed silent in the truck cab. If Karla Starr didn't love her animals, how had she trained the dog to be so patient?

Sam didn't want to know.

"C'mon, Ace." She led the gelding by a handful of mane.

Sweetheart was kicking fence rails in the barn corral. Out in the small pasture, Amigo arched his neck and pranced like a stallion ready to do battle. Teddy Bear, tied to the hitching rail, jumped back against his reins as Jake hustled out to plop Sam's saddle into her arms.

"I heard what he said, and this is a fool idea."

"Jake, he'll be fine. Ace always behaves."

Jake ignored her, shaking his head as he frowned after Dad.

"I think your dad was just glad you got away with all your fingers and toes."

Sam smoothed on Ace's saddle blanket. "What are you trying to say? I don't get it."

"That Karla Starr gives me the creeps," Jake said. "She's after something."

"It's just like you to see a competent businesswoman as a threat," Sam told him, even though she didn't trust Karla Starr either.

"Competent? Is that what you call it?"

"Sure," Sam said. Without being asked, Ace opened his mouth for the bit.

"And she didn't give you the creeps?"

"Okay, it did bother me when she was sizing up the mustangs as bucking prospects."

"And flashing her business cards around."

"That didn't bother me," Sam said.

"It did," Jake said, "but you won't admit it. I listen to

THE RENEGADE

my instincts." Jake pulled Teddy Bear's reins loose from the hitch rail and mounted. "Want to know why?"

"No, but you're going to tell me anyway."

Sam rode beside Jake. By silent agreement, they kept the horses to a walk as they crossed the ranch yard.

"One night, I was trying to get to sleep. I was tossing and turning, feeling like bugs were crawling on me. I knew it was my imagination, 'cause I wasn't camping, just lying in my own bed. Finally one of my brothers—Nate, I think—yelled at me to settle down.

"I did, but I kept feeling like something was trailing on my arm. Really quiet, 'cause I didn't want Nate to beat the tar out of me, I kind of flipped my arm to the side."

Even now, Jake shuddered.

"Something hit the floor. Nate came roaring out of bed and I turned on the light, and there was this ugly black scorpion scuttling across our bedroom floor."

Rain was falling for real now, and Sam pulled up the hood on her slicker.

"You get the point, Brat?" Jake said.

"Yeah, yeah, instincts," Sam muttered.

Jake rode close enough to grab Ace's cheekpiece. Because it was Jake, Ace didn't shy, only stopped and flicked his ears in curiosity.

"No, the moral of that story is: if you think something is creeping up to do you harm, don't wait till it fills you with poison."

Chapter 9

RAIN CAME IN SHEETS, WAVERING IRIDESCENT in the dusk. The sagebrush glowed silver-green as sunset sifted through thunderclouds. The land Sam had known all her life looked alien and exotic.

Jake took the lead, and Sam let Ace follow at a gallop. The wind whipped something past Sam's face. She thought it was a wildflower stalk, until Jake turned to look back over his shoulder. It must have been Jake's leather string, the one he used to tame his long hair, because his black hair looked more like a mane than ever, blowing in the wind.

A smile showed in his rain-wet face. Thoughts of wild horses made her think Jake shouldn't be confined either.

Jake liked school and excelled at everything that would make him the good rancher his family wanted him to be, but he wanted to be a police tracker. Sam thought that kind of far-ranging work would suit him best.

A rasping cry sounded overhead, and Jake looked up. The hawk had no time for dropping feathers today. Her rounded red tail shifted like a rudder as she sought the safety of her nest.

"Did you send a wish?" Jake shouted, but Sam shook her head. "Hawks carry hopes and prayers to the sky spirits, then bring back blessings. That's what the elders believe."

Jake's words were proof he was feeling as wild as the storm winds. He rarely mentioned his Native heritage, and Sam knew if she asked him a question now, he'd shrug off the hawk as just part of a story.

The horses galloped through groups of cattle running in sheer joy. With rain spattering their red backs, calves cavorted, holding their tails straight up in the air.

Sam knew she should be afraid to gallop. She wasn't the world's greatest rider, and much of the topsoil had blown away, leaving slippery clay underfoot.

They headed away from the highway and the trail to War Drum Flats. Jake still rode ahead, but now his black hair hung below his Stetson, lying straight and wet to the middle of his back. Teddy's hair was wet too, and his Bashkir heritage showed in the little C-shaped curls on his rump.

The trail to the canyon was narrow and rough, no place to take a young horse like Teddy.

"Let's turn back," Jake shouted over the hammering rain. His voice was serious.

A single bolt of lightning zigzagged overhead, turning the world aquarium green. Teddy fought for his head, pulling against the reins Jake kept snug.

There wasn't a trace of fun on Jake's face anymore. He concentrated on telling Teddy what to do.

Sam slowed Ace, giving Jake room to work.

Once he had Teddy's attention, Jake forced him back

in a straight line, to sidestep, anything to remind him his rider was in charge.

Squinting through the rain, Sam saw Teddy begin to relax. Fear drained out of him as he did as he was told. Each time he followed Jake's instructions, Teddy was rewarded. The reins loosened, the bit sat lighter in his mouth, and Jake praised him.

"There you go, partner. Let me do the worryin'," Jake said.

Teddy did, and soon Jake moved him through his gaits with fluid grace, then kept him at a jog.

"That," Sam told Ace, "is the difference between a rider and a horseman. Stick with me a few years and I might be one-tenth that good." She rubbed Ace's neck.

Only after they'd jogged through the rain for five minutes did Jake glance back at Sam.

"Keep your hood up, since you didn't have the sense to wear a hat." He tugged down on his own hat brim but didn't give her time to argue. "We need to get in before there's more lightning."

Jake let Teddy gallop. Ace followed, lining out like a

racehorse, legs reaching, head level. Sam trusted Ace to find the best footing. Unlike Teddy, Ace's life had once depended on his instincts.

Still, Sam reminded herself to sit back in the saddle. She was too far forward. If Ace veered or stumbled, she'd fall and Jake would be halfway home before he noticed she was missing. At this pace, they'd cover the five miles to River Bend in no time.

The sky brightened as if lightning was racing above the clouds.

Jake let Teddy out another notch and angled him away from the path home.

It must be because of the lightning. Sam knew you were supposed to stay away from trees, from telephone and power poles, and seek low ground.

That was just what Jake had done, she saw now. He'd steered Teddy into a dry riverbed.

Usually dry. Sam looked around at the low, sandy area. This cloudburst had already turned a few of its dips to puddles. As a child, she'd heard TV broadcasts interrupted by high-pitched signals and announcers warning against flash floods. She knew they'd cautioned that rainwater could gather in low-lying areas like riverbeds.

Ace's gait turned choppy, responding to the worry that had tightened Sam's grip on the reins. Starting at her head, working down through her neck, shoulders, and arms, Sam forced her muscles to loosen. Dad had trusted Jake to bring her out here.

"Just follow them," she told Ace. "We'll be fine."

The riverbed narrowed and the banks were nearly as high as the horses' backs.

Dead ahead was a boulder. Sam saw it an instant before Teddy jumped. Ace knew his legs were too short for the leap. He cut through a narrow detour and sprinted ahead. Sam glanced back in time to see Teddy fall.

His jump had been fine. Teddy had cleared the boulder easily, but his front-off hoof struck a puddle. Teddy slid, hundreds of pounds of horseflesh sliding on watery mud.

Jake shifted his weight left, trying to give Teddy the help he needed to get centered. Nothing helped.

"Get off!" Sam screamed.

Jake could have, poised to the left as he was, but he stayed with the falling horse. As Teddy's hooves slipped away, his barrel slammed against the right bank. Muscle and bone splattered damp dirt. Teddy grunted, breath knocked from his lungs. Jake's head—tucked in, chin to chest—said he'd been hurt. The fall smashed his leg between the horse and the riverbank.

Sam pulled Ace to a stop, though she wasn't sure what to do. All four hooves had slid from beneath Teddy. Since Jake had stayed astride, he must be okay. But Teddy's legs thrashed. Was one of those legs broken? Had Teddy ruptured an internal organ or stabbed himself on broken brush? Or was he just struggling to get up?

Only five miles home, she'd thought a minute ago. Now five miles seemed an impossibly long distance.

Jake stayed on as Teddy heaved himself up to stand. Jake's hat was gone. He stared down at his saddle horn, and his arms looked boneless, swaying as the horse trembled.

Sam tightened her legs, but Ace didn't want to go closer.

"C'mon, boy, nothing to be afraid of." Sam kept her voice strong. "Teddy needs your company. You're a levelheaded guy. C'mon, Ace."

Thunder grumbled as she reached them, but no lightning flashed. There was just enough light to see rain running down Jake's forehead into his eyes. He did nothing to stop it. A knot of muscle stood out under his skin, showing how hard his jaw was clenched.

"Jake, what hurts?"

It must be everything, she thought, because Jake kept his jaw locked. Or maybe he was afraid that if he opened his mouth, he wouldn't be able to stop yelling.

"My horse okay?" he asked finally.

"Sure. He's up. He's fine." Sam dismissed his question, until she noticed Jake's boot hanging free of his stirrup. "What about your leg?"

"Check him." The effort it cost Jake to say the words made Sam do it.

There was no sense arguing. Jake's concern for

himself would wait until he knew Teddy was safe.

Sam turned Ace. They circled Teddy, and though the cloud-strained evening light made everything look black and white, she could tell he was only a little scuffed.

"A cut on his fetlock and lots of mud. That's it," Sam reported, and then her breath caught.

She saw blood. It was Jake's. A dark patch about the size of her fist had welled through the denim covering his right thigh, and it was spreading fast.

"You must have cut your leg when you fell."

She wished Jake would talk. When one corner of his mouth jerked, she thought he was about to laugh, but he only nodded.

"Do you want to stay here while I go get Dad and the truck?"

Jake was shaking his head no before she finished asking.

"Don't be stubborn, Jake. I can tell you're in pain."

He went back to staring at his saddle horn as if it were the most fascinating sight on earth. He took a deep breath, like someone preparing to jump off a cliff, but only uttered a few words.

"Flash flood could come up," he managed. "Or lightning. Don't think—" He looked up at Sam with dark eyes that begged her not to reveal what he was about to say. "Don't think I could handle him."

"Then get down and wait," she demanded.

"Don't think I can do that, either."

Dizziness spun through Sam. Jake was in trouble. He must have done more than cut his leg. He might have struck his head. He might have some injury he was hiding from her.

Sam didn't know how to assess his injuries, but she knew she was in charge and they were wasting time.

"Okay," she said, but then she felt a flash of pain. If his leg *was* broken, the bone ends would grate as Teddy moved. Jake would be in agony.

"I can ride. Just get my hat," Jake whispered.

Sam slid off Ace, keeping a grip on the reins as she snatched Jake's Stetson from the mud. She brushed it off, only smearing it worse, then handed it up.

Jake didn't notice.

Sam remounted, reined Ace close, and leaned over

to put Jake's hat on his wet hair. A wave of tenderness shook her, but Sam refused to let Jake see her distress.

"Typical cowboy," she muttered. "The world could be coming to an end and you wouldn't go outside to watch without your hat."

"You got—" Jake grimaced as Teddy shifted. "Got that right. Now lead us outta here."

Chapter 10

JAKE'S TRUST MADE SAM CAREFUL.

It was up to her to make sure everything turned out all right.

Sam kept Ace at a walk and searched every inch of earth and sky for danger.

Familiar clumps of pine and rock outcroppings passed in slow motion. Though no sensible snake would be out in this downpour, she watched for them. The frolicking Herefords posed no threat. They'd formed into tight, unhappy herds. One group moved toward the ranch, driven by the rain. A few more stood in a miserable cluster, tails clamped down, white eyelashes blinking.

"I guess no one's come looking for us since we're such hotshot range riders," Sam mumbled to Jake. "Why should they worry?"

Jake didn't answer.

Sam rode another few minutes before it struck her they'd be plenty worried if a horse came home riderless. Sam thought it through. What if she climbed down, gave him a swat, and Ace still didn't leave her?

And Jake wouldn't get off Teddy, even if he could. Pride wouldn't let him lie suffering in the rain until help arrived.

Suddenly Jake was beside her instead of following.

"Faster," he croaked. The bloodstain on his jeans was spreading.

Sam wanted to argue, but his eyes warned her it would be a waste of time.

Sam clapped her heels to Ace, hoping he'd leap straight into a lope. He did, and Teddy imitated him, skipping the hammering trot that Sam knew could finally break Jake's will.

After what seemed like an eternity, a welcome sight appeared on the horizon: smoke, puffing from the chimney at River Bend.

"We're going to make it, Jake."

Sam didn't expect an answer. Only once, when Teddy nearly stumbled, did Jake groan as if the sound had been wrenched from him.

Finally, she let the horses settle to a weary walk.

Just ahead, the bunkhouse windows glowed yellow. All the hands were in from the range, probably eating dinner.

As the horses clopped across the bridge, Sam thought she saw Gram's face peer from the kitchen window.

Jake held Teddy on a tight rein, refusing to let him pass the front porch for the barn.

As Sam slid from Ace's back, the front door opened and Dad stood there.

"Everything all right?" he asked, looking past her.

THE RENEGADE

"Jake's hurt, Daddy. He's really hurt."

It seemed like Dad reached her in a single stride.

For the first time since that awful sound of bone smashing into the riverbank, Sam let herself cry.

The next afternoon, the baby-blue Mercedes was silent. The windshield wipers swished, but no one talked.

Jen stayed quiet, thinking her own thoughts, because that was just Jen. Rachel kept her fuchsia lips pressed together as if she couldn't believe she was sharing the same air with two lowly freshmen. Sam was simply exhausted.

Somehow, she had made it through her morning classes. By lunchtime, though, Sam needed some calories to substitute for sleep. The cafeteria was packed with students wearing new sweaters and jackets it had been too hot to wear until now, and the food lines were disorderly and loud.

All the noise and high spirits reminded Sam of the calves' reaction to the rain. Everyone was glad the drought had broken.

Sam and Jen were balancing their trays and searching for a few feet of table space when Jake's friend Darrell snagged Sam's elbow.

"Hey! I need this hamburger," Sam snapped. And then she recognized Darrell.

He was the kind of guy Gram labeled "bad company," but Sam knew only two things about him. First, he'd taught Jake how to disable a car by pulling loose strategic wires under the hood. Second, Jake didn't want Sam to know him.

Today, defying the rain and school policy, Darrell wore an orange tank top and sunglasses. Where was Ms. Santos when there was a real delinquent around? Sam wondered.

"What happened to my man Jake?" His index finger hooked the hinge of his sunglasses and pulled them down so he could watch Sam. "I'm hearing bad things."

"What have I missed this time?" Jen despaired.

"I was going to tell you when we found a quiet place," Sam said.

"This looks quiet," Jen said.

THE RENEGADE

It was, because when Jen slammed her tray down next to Darrell's, Jake's usual crew made room with amazement as the girls sat down.

For strength, Sam took a bite of her hamburger, then summed up yesterday's disaster. She had to explain it quickly. If she pictured the fall and that tortured ride, she'd get weepy all over again.

"Jake's horse slipped in the mud and crunched his leg, but Jake insisted on riding back to our place. And so," she finished, "he had a compound fracture—"

"Ahhh, man"—Darrell drew the words out in twisted admiration—"like where the busted bone shoves through the skin?"

"Right." Sam nodded.

Her stomach didn't turn over as it had the first time Dad told her what Jake's bloody jeans had hidden. That was progress. And she tried not to recall how they'd made Jake swallow a dose of pain pills and wait for them to take effect before Dallas and Dad moved him from the saddle to the back seat of Gram's Buick.

"And so?" Darrell encouraged her.

"The emergency room doctor put him in a cast and said he'd be down for a while. The Elys were all there by then, so Dad left before they talked about when he could ride."

Darrell made a waving motion as if that didn't matter.

"What about driving?" he asked. "We're supposed to go to Cimarron for the midnight drag races next week."

"I don't know. What are drag races?" Sam pictured draft horses pulling heavy loads, but she had a hard time believing Darrell was bereft at the thought of missing such a competition.

"Like with two cars . . . going fast as they can in a straight line?" Darrell studied Sam for comprehension. "You know."

"Not really," Sam said. She noticed her hamburger was getting cold and began eating again, feeling more ravenous than before.

"When is he coming back to school?" Darrell asked, with no concern at all for her meal.

Sam shrugged and kept eating. She wished the crowd

of boys would go away so she could talk to Jen, but it was their table.

Satisfied that they'd leeched the choicest information from her, Darrell and the guys leaned together, talking.

For a minute, Sam wondered if Jake was still in the hospital. She remembered how scared she'd been in a big white hospital bed after her accident two years ago.

She'd been younger, of course, and Jake might not be scared, but he'd hate the limits on his movements. He'd get cranky and restless, though the doctor had said it wasn't an especially bad break.

"So that's where you were when I called last night," Jen said.

"Yeah."

"Your gram said you were out riding, so I figured you hadn't gotten into trouble." Jen looked at her meaningfully. "You know, over the incident?"

Sam stared at Jen.

"The *school bus* incident?"

"Oh. Yeah." Sam hadn't forgotten really, but the shame she'd felt yesterday had faded. "I'm grounded."

"Even after what you did for Jake?"

Sam considered the question. Her thoughts felt like they were swimming through honey, but she was pretty sure of the answer.

"All I really did was ride along with him, and even if it had been more, well, I can't see one teensy act of heroism erasing what Gram and Dad see as a gigantic mistake."

The end-of-lunch bell rang through the cafeteria. Sam swallowed the last of her soda and stood. "Better go," she said. "Who knows what they'd do to me if I added tardiness to my criminal record?"

It was a crummy day to teach Rachel to ride.

When Sam arrived home from school, Gram was in a chatty mood. She announced that Jake had been released from the hospital and was resting in his own bed at Three Ponies Ranch. Of course, Sam couldn't go see him, since Rachel would be arriving soon.

Gram told Sam that Dad and Dallas were on the range, checking the runny-nosed steers. They could have used Sam's help, since Jake was missing from the crew, but they'd ridden out without her because she'd still been at school.

Gram was most excited about her weekend plans. She, Dad, and Brynna were going to the county fair. Gram would compete in the fried chicken cook-off and Dad would meet Brynna's parents.

Sam felt herself staring dully at Gram. She knew it was significant that Brynna wanted to introduce Dad to her parents, but she had no comment. All this information was making her tired. Her eyelids drooped, begging for sleep.

Instead, Sam stood in the drizzle, watching Rachel try to corner Ace and halter him. She felt impatient with them both.

"I don't see why I can't use the pinto one." Rachel stood in the barn corral. Sweetheart crowded up behind her, and Ace was doing everything he could to escape the halter Rachel was pushing at him.

"Because you can't," Sam explained. "And if you expect to get out of there anytime soon, you need to put the lead rope over his neck, like I told you, and reach over the top of his head, like I told you, and slip his nose into that round part. He's not going to do it for you."

Rachel wasn't used to following orders, that was for sure. Even as she did what Sam asked, sort of, she grumbled. "I'd rather ride a 'loud-colored' horse. That's what I read attracts attention to a queen candidate. Ha!"

At last she'd buckled the halter over Ace's head. The glare the gelding gave Sam didn't need words to explain how annoying he found this entire exercise.

"For what I'm paying you," Rachel went on, "the least you can do is have the horse saddled and ready when I get here. And I'd prefer one without a scar on his neck."

A dozen responses hammered through Sam's mind, but she picked the calmest one as she opened the gate.

"This builds the horse's confidence in you, so he'll do what you ask later. Lead him through, Rachel."

Sam figured there was no reason to explain that Rachel would never earn the trust of a smart horse like Ace.

"Besides," Sam said as they went to the hitching rail, "I don't think they just present you with a horse—hold the rope with two hands, one closer to his chin—and tell you to do your stuff when you're trying out as a rodeo queen."

"I should find out," Rachel said. "That could save a lot of time. Where's the saddle?"

Sam took the lead rope from Rachel and tied Ace. "In the tack room," she said. "I'll show you."

Sam piled the saddle and blanket on Rachel's arms and slung Ace's bridle over her shoulder.

"I am not a pack animal," Rachel said, her British accent surfacing with scorn.

This is not going to work. Sam gritted her teeth to keep from saying it. Only the tiny possibility that she'd be more patient when she'd had more sleep kept Sam from telling Rachel to go home.

And the fun had just begun.

Ace planted a hoof on the toe of one of Rachel's new boots. She whimpered.

Ace sidestepped, eyes rolling white. Rachel dropped the saddle.

Ace flung himself to the end of the lead rope, pretending the snaffle was a terrifying foreign object. Rachel recoiled from slimy horse spit.

A long forty minutes later, Ace stood saddled and bridled.

"If you think I'm going to do this every time I come for a lesson, you're delusional," Rachel said as she checked the polish on her fingernails. "I do not like to perspire."

"Could you girls use some cookies and cocoa?" Gram stood on the porch, smiling.

This was what she needed to keep in mind, Sam told herself. Gram cooking happily in the kitchen, the wide ranch house porch, and horses all around. Money made it possible, and that was all she needed from Rachel.

"Let's take a break," Sam said. "Then we'll get you up on Ace."

Sitting on a step, sipping cocoa, Sam stared off toward the ten-acre pasture. Buddy was getting big. Dark Sunshine's pregnancy was beginning to show. Popcorn grazed beside her, looking content.

THE RENEGADE

"Karla Starr is looking for attractive bucking horses," Rachel said.

"I know. She was here just yesterday," Sam said, but she was wondering if the steers with the runny noses had something contagious. She'd ask Dad if Buddy needed an inoculation.

"Sam."

Sam stared. Rachel had never called her that.

"Yes?" Sam watched Rachel watch her. "I heard you. Karla Starr is looking for rough stock. We don't have any."

"I'm just saying . . ." Rachel ran her fingers over the pattern on her cup. She glanced up at Sam, then gave her head a faint shake. "Why should I bother to do you a favor?"

"Rachel, I don't mean to be dense." Sam brushed her bangs away from her eyes. "But I don't know what you're hinting at."

"Karla Starr told my father—oh, this is utter nonsense," Rachel said. "Let's get back to it, shall we?"

By the time Mrs. Coley came for her, Rachel had made some progress in mounting and dismounting from Ace, but Sam had made none in figuring out the clues Rachel had given her.

She trudged toward the house. Maybe Rachel's hints would make sense in the morning. Just now, all Sam knew for sure was that she needed a warm bath, cozy pajamas, and sleep.

Chapter 11

THURSDAY WAS JAKE'S BIRTHDAY.

As Gram drove her over to the Three Ponies Ranch, Sam was not only glad to be getting some time with Jake, but she was glad to have a reason for skipping Rachel's lesson.

Only Jen knew how much Sam disliked having to fit in the after-school chore.

But it wasn't for either of the reasons Jen suspected.

True, yesterday Ace acted like a brat-horse around Rachel. He sprinted for the fence rails and tried to rub

Rachel off whenever he felt Sam's attention wander. And Rachel was no better. She protested the lack of a covered arena, whining that any civilized ranch needed one for winter. But Ace's tricks and Rachel's stuck-up attitude weren't what made Sam nervous.

Rachel's unending hints were the problem.

She was trying to say something about Karla Starr, but what? Sam tried to connect Rachel's clues with the fringe from the watering hole and her constant, gnawing worry over the Phantom.

She was hoping that Jake would help her understand. Together, they'd been able to figure out almost anything.

"Welcome to Jake's lair," Mrs. Ely announced as she led Sam to the sunporch, where her son sat. "He's cranky as a bear, Sam. We throw him a chunk of raw meat a couple of times a day, but in honor of your visit, I put some iced tea and chips on the table there." Mrs. Ely hesitated. "You're the only one he's agreed to see."

"I'd be flattered," Sam joked as Jake glared past her at his mother, "except that he knows I bought him a cool present back when I got that reward."

THE RENEGADE

As Mrs. Ely and Gram moved off, talking about the county fair and harsh weather, Sam tossed the big, brightly wrapped present toward Jake.

He caught it, but barely, and Sam understood why her friend was so down.

He was embarrassed. The cast held his leg straight and jointless. Energetic Jake, who was always bounding off somewhere, couldn't move without help. His jeans were split to go over the white plaster, and he wore no shoes.

Had she ever seen Jake's feet before? Bare and pale, they made him look kind of defenseless, so Sam tried not to look. Instead, she took in the wide windows and cascading ferns of the sunporch. And the crutch leaning in one corner.

"Out here, you can pretend it's still summer," she said.

"It's better than my room."

"And you get to skip school."

Jake shook his head, and Sam saw how it was. She didn't know how many brothers shared Jake's room, but she could imagine the quiet after they'd all dressed and left him behind.

Sam poured iced tea for both of them. She stared at the slice of bobbing lemon in her glass and resolved to cheer Jake up.

"After you open your present, I have something else for you too."

Jake's expression said he didn't want to be pitied.

"Open it, Jake. I've been waiting months to see it again." Sam had had the saddle shop wrap the gift in its special packaging. The cardboard was printed to look like hand-tooled leather stamped with the shop's exclusive brand.

"Need some help with that tape and tissue paper, or what?"

"Shut up, Brat," Jake muttered, but then he pushed the wrappings away and stared. He looked up at her, speechless.

"I'm going to put it on Witch for you," Sam said as if she gave hundred-dollar presents every day.

"She'll eat you alive." Jake fingered the split-ear headstall with something like respect.

"Yeah, and I'm such a good friend, I'll let you watch."

Jake smiled, but it didn't last long.

Sam was glad she'd anticipated this. She'd known that right after he admired the headstall, he'd be sad he couldn't ride with it right away.

"And that's not all." Sam dug into her backpack. "This isn't a present exactly, more like a contribution to your secret ambition."

Jake struggled to sit up straighter. The box and tissue paper slipped away from him before he could grab them.

Pretending she'd intended all along to clear it out of the way, Sam pushed the wrapping aside with one foot and scooted her chair closer to hand him the printouts she'd made.

"The Shadow Wolves," she announced in a dramatic voice.

"Thanks." Jake's tone was careful, as if he was trying not to hurt her feelings.

"It's not science fiction or any kind of fantasy, Jake. It's a group of Native trackers—from several tribes—who help the government catch smugglers. Mostly in the Southwest deserts, but—it's *you*. Take a look."

She'd found the perfect way to end Jake's mope. Once he began reading, he was transformed from sulky to studious.

Outside, the sun ducked behind a cloud. The sunporch grew dim, but Jake didn't notice. He hardly breathed as he entered the world of men and women whose ancient skills worked better than modern technology to catch criminals sneaking across the desert.

"I didn't know," he muttered, but Sam could tell he wasn't talking to her.

The minute he quit reading, he'd want her gone so he could search the internet for details she'd missed.

Sam smiled. It was working out just as she'd hoped. She couldn't give Jake mobility, but she'd given him hours of daydreams.

Somewhere in the ranch house, a window was open. Wind gusted, slamming a door, even as it brought the scent of more rain.

Jake finished reading, then paged back to a photograph illustrating an article.

Gram would want to leave before the roads got too

slick. Sam bit her lip. If she was going to ask Jake about the clues, it was now or never.

"I have this situation," she began.

"Figured as much." Jake set the papers aside. "You've been fidgeting for five minutes."

As rain pinged on the aluminum overhang outside, Sam told him everything. His head tilted to one side as he stared out the window.

"You're not stupid, Sam. You just don't want to face facts."

Her heart hammered. She'd counted on Jake to tell her she was just being paranoid.

"Rachel overheard something. She's telling you Karla Starr's after the Phantom."

"But why would she do that? Rachel can't stand me."

"Don't ask me to look into her head. I don't want to be there." He pretended to shudder. "But the horses, now . . ."

Jake's eyes lost focus as he sank deeper into the chair.

"The key to how Karla Starr is catching horses is in the way Silly and Ace reacted at the water hole. They're domesticated. A trap shouldn't scare them." He rocked forward and his fist struck the table in frustration. "If I could get out there and look around—"

"You wouldn't find a darn thing, because it's been raining for days. So forget that."

"Don't get uppity or I'll hit you with my crutch."

"You will not." Sam didn't feel like joking. She warmed her arms against a chill that had nothing to do with the rain. How could she help the Phantom?

"Tell Brynna." Jake turned one hand palm up, as if the solution to Sam's worry was obvious. "If I could ride, I'd go check it out with you. That terrain's too rough for you alone, but she can send a ranger or wrangler up to the high country to look for him. It'd be best, you know, if you told them exactly where to find him. There's nothing else you can do."

Jake was wrong. She could ride Ace to the Phantom's hidden valley. He might even come to her. Being grounded would make it tougher, but Gram and Dad were going to the county fair. They expected her to go along, but maybe she wouldn't.

"I can see the wheels turnin', but with that river rising, it's too dangerous to risk going alone. Don't cross your arms and get all huffy with me, Brat."

Jake was trying to tease her. He knew he couldn't stop her himself, and he didn't want to tell on her. But he would. He'd done it before.

Sam heard footsteps approaching. She stood to go, feeling more irritated and confused than when she'd arrived.

Jake grabbed her sleeve, and his voice turned gruff.

"Get it through your thick head, Sam. Rodeo season's nearly over. If Karla Starr wants the Phantom, she probably already has him."

When she got home and jogged into the barn, Sam expected to see Ace waiting impatiently for her.

Instead, she saw Brynna Olson kissing Dad right on the lips.

Sam froze. As far as she knew, they'd only been on one date. She had caught Dad talking on the phone to Brynna a couple of times, but still . . .

They were in the barn, just outside the tack room.

Even though Brynna wore her red hair in a tight braid and had on her BLM uniform, she looked anything but professional. And though Dad's hands rested on each of her shoulders, he was not pushing her away.

And then they noticed her.

Dad had the decency to look embarrassed. Brynna blushed, then giggled. "We didn't hear you."

"No kidding?" Sam itched to inform Brynna a thirtysomething woman shouldn't giggle. But she couldn't do it.

She liked Brynna in most ways, and Dad's expression warned Sam that her tone had come close to crossing the line.

Since no one seemed to know what to say, Sam turned to Ace.

His head hung over the fence facing into the barn. He tossed his forelock, showing off the white star between his eyes.

Sam stood close and let him nuzzle her neck. She closed her eyes, and though she heard Dad and Brynna talking about the county fair and Brynna's parents coming to meet Dad, she was thinking of the Phantom.

Sure, she was mad at Brynna, but Brynna cared about her job. And her job was to protect Nevada's wild horses.

"I think Karla Starr is trapping wild horses," Sam said loudly.

Dad's eyes narrowed.

Brynna turned, took in his expression, then faced Sam. "Who's Karla Starr?"

"She's a rodeo contractor—" Sam started.

"Strictly small-time," Dad interrupted, but Brynna was still listening to Sam.

"She's said things that sort of sound like she doesn't think the law applies to her." Sam hadn't put the thought into words before, but she felt it was the truth. Like Slocum, Karla Starr thought she could make herself an exception to the rules.

"Anything else?" Brynna looked willing to be convinced.

"Rachel Slocum has been hinting that her father told Karla Starr about the Phantom to 'sweeten the deal' he was making to sell her some of his Brahma bulls."

Brynna nodded, encouraging her. "What else?"

"Isn't that enough?" Sam demanded, as Brynna looked at Dad.

"Wyatt?"

"I don't know why she'd do that if she wanted to stay in business."

"And out of jail." Brynna was actually smiling.

"Because she thinks she can get away with it!" Sam snapped.

Karla Starr *would* get away with it too, if Dad and Brynna didn't pay attention instead of making goo-goo eyes at each other.

"What exactly did Rachel say?" Brynna asked.

"Just a bunch of stuff." Sam's frustration swelled as Brynna glanced at Dad again. "I didn't write it down, okay?"

"Okay," Brynna agreed. "Sam, you were right about Slocum before, and I trust your judgment. You want what's best for the horses, and so do I. I'll tell the rangers to keep an eye out for any unusual activity—"

"I have her business card," Sam said, but Dad had

already taken his copy of the card from his wallet.

Brynna studied the card. "We'll check her out."

"You can have someone keep watch on the Phantom, too, can't you?"

"I wish I could, but I only have two men to patrol ten thousand acres." Brynna's weight shifted toward Dad.

It must have been some kind of cue.

"Tomorrow night we're driving in for the fair," Dad said. "We figured you'd want to come along and watch your gram win a blue ribbon for her fried chicken."

We figured. Sam ran the sentence over in her mind. Dad and Brynna. Together. Overnight. They'd be with Gram, but it still sounded awfully serious.

"Maybe," Sam said. "I have a history project I need to work on, though."

Sam waited for Dad to tell her she didn't have a choice. After all, it was pretty clear he was going. And not to watch Gram, either.

She looked him straight in the eyes. Arms crossed, he mirrored her own stubborn stance. But he'd never left her alone overnight. Would he do it now?

"Suit yourself," Dad said.

"I will." Sam gave Ace a pat and started out of the barn.

She couldn't believe this. How was she supposed to feel?

They were watching her. Every step seemed to take forever. She'd longed for Dad to trust her enough to leave her alone overnight, but now he was doing it for all the wrong reasons.

"She'll get over it," Brynna whispered.

And though the angel on Sam's shoulder was assuring her that Brynna meant it in the nicest way possible, her little horned conscience was saying, *That settles it. I'm doing this my own way.*

Chapter 12

THE WIND SHRIEKED SO LOUDLY, RUSHING around the ranch house all night, not even Blaze heard the hens squawking when half their house was smashed to splinters beneath the cottonwood tree.

Sometime after midnight, a combination of drought, rain, and wind had forced the tree to tip over. When Gram and Sam walked out to hurry through morning chores before Gram left for the fair and Sam for school, the cottonwood tree was tilted, branches down, roots up.

"Oh my goodness!" Gram's hand covered her lips, but

only for an instant. "Help me count them, Samantha."

Since there was nothing to be done about the tree, Sam did as Gram asked, counting the Rhode Island Red hens who had hopped over the flattened fence.

"At least they were smart enough to stick around," Sam said, and when they'd both counted twice, it turned out she was right.

Three hens had been trapped inside, unharmed, and the rest had decided freedom wasn't worth drowning for. They huddled clucking and complaining near their house, waiting for Gram to do something.

Would Gram stay home after all?

Sam looked at the tree roots, skeletal and black against the gray sky. Was this a sign that she shouldn't ride out to check the Phantom even if Gram and Dad were gone?

"Well, ain't that an awful-looking thing?" Dallas had come from the bunkhouse. Hatless and smelling of maple syrup, he stood with his hands on his hips. "The other boys are still eating, but we can get this put together in no time."

"I don't know," Gram fretted.

"Don't even think about skipping your trip," Dallas scolded. "All we was going to do today was push those heifers back uphill again. Seems they remember grazin' down here when winter's coming on, so they want to stay down, no matter if higher ground is safer with all this rain.

"You and Wyatt go on. Nothing here the rest of us can't take care of. Isn't that right, Samantha?"

Sam swallowed hard and nodded.

Dallas's question and her own uneasiness kept Sam in a haze of guilt all day. Gram had kissed her good-bye, promising to call both Friday and Saturday nights. Dad had told her to let Dallas and the hands worry about the chores. All she had to do was study and enjoy having the house to herself until they got home Sunday evening. When he'd given her a hug that lifted her off her feet, Sam almost cried.

As the school day passed, evidence kept piling up to convince Sam she'd make a lousy criminal.

She was gathering her book and notebook at the

end of history class when Mrs. Ely asked what she had planned for the weekend. Sam panicked.

"Why? What do you mean?"

"I just thought you might come over and keep Jake company." Mrs. Ely looked up from her grade book, eyebrows raised.

"I'm working on my history project." Sam fell back on her cover story without thinking that Mrs. Ely was the one who'd given the assignment.

"Oh. Good." She looked surprised. "How great that you're getting an early start."

At lunch, Jen asked the same question.

"Why do you want to know?" Sam demanded.

"Don't jump down my throat. I was just going to see if you wanted to come over for popcorn and movies, since your dad and you gram are going to be gone."

"How did you know?"

"You told me," Jen said patiently. "And you talked about it with Mrs. Coley this morning in the car, remember? Because she's going to the fair too, and my mom's picking us up?"

"Oh. Yeah. No, I can't come over. I'm working on my history project."

"Fine." Jen held her palms out as if her agitated friend might charge. "I guess you're trying to get off restriction early by getting good grades."

The bell rang.

"Right," Sam agreed, but as she walked to class, Sam decided there was another reason to get good grades. If she flunked out of high school and turned to a life of crime, she'd be down at the police station confessing before she did one thing wrong.

Sam had never really considered Jen's mom, Lila Kenworthy. If she noticed anything about her, it was her faint Texas accent and her tendency to look tired. But not today.

When Lila pulled up in the Darton High parking lot, driving the Mercedes in place of Mrs. Coley, even Jen noticed the difference.

Jen slid into the back seat first, and Sam heard her ask, "Are you—are we going somewhere, Mom?"

"Jen." Mrs. Kenworthy's voice held a gentle reprimand.

"Thanks for picking us up," Sam said. She noticed that Mrs. Kenworthy's short blond hair was poufy and she wore eye makeup.

"No problem," she said, but her attention seemed focused on Rachel.

Rachel entered the car wordlessly. She wore jeans, a white top, and a long, canary-yellow cardigan that kept the outfit from looking casual. She fastened her seat belt, then waited a few seconds to see if someone would trot around and close the door for her. When no one did, she sighed, leaned out, and pulled it closed herself. But she didn't say a word to Jen's mother.

"Did Dad get Maniac loaded all right?" Jen asked, then added for Sam's benefit, "He's entered in the best-of-breed competition at the fair."

Sam guessed that was another difference between Linc Slocum and Dad. If Dad wanted to show an animal in the county fair, he loaded it into a trailer and drove it there himself.

"They came to an agreement after a while," her mother said.

Sam didn't envy Jed Kenworthy the task of convincing the tiger-faced Brahma bull to enter a stock truck.

They were on the highway, headed for home, when Jen's mom spoke again. "So, Rachel, I hear you want to be a rodeo queen."

Sam had expected Jen to keep Rachel's secret. Judging by Jen's open mouth and wide eyes, she'd hoped her mom would keep it too.

Rachel straightened with the grace of a cat and gave Jen a look such as a cat might give a mouse, but her voice sounded polite.

"Why, yes, Mrs. Kenworthy, that's so. I've been toying with the idea, although I'm discovering it's not as easy as it looks. Jen tells me you competed."

"I did, and that's why I brought it up. I'd be glad to help if I can."

Jen stared at the back of her mother's head as if she'd begun speaking Swahili. From what Jen had said before, Sam knew the Kenworthys and Rachel exchanged fewer than a dozen words each month.

"I do have one advisor who's competed more recently." Rachel blinked in a leisurely manner that showed off her eyelashes. "However, I'd appreciate your impressions. Especially what you learned from the experience."

Sam had never seen Rachel's charm in action. She knew some people—even teachers, who should be wiser—liked Rachel, but since the rich girl had never tried to impress her, Sam hadn't seen this side of her.

"What did I learn?" Mrs. Kenworthy relaxed into the driver's seat. When she talked next, there was a smile in her voice. "I learned to put on mascara in a moving truck. I learned to go to school in hand-me-down clothes because anything I bought new had to have sequins. I learned to make a loop of duct tape, stick it to my forehead, and press my hat against it so it didn't blow off as I galloped around the arena.

"You'll lose points for that, you know, when you're being judged." Mrs. Kenworthy's dancing eyes glanced at Rachel. "Girls these days can use double-sided tape."

"Double-sided tape," Rachel repeated, touching her forehead. "But doesn't that irritate your skin?"

"It leaves a red line, but nobody'll see it except your horse, because you're never without your hat."

Jen seemed to be studying her mother, weighing her words. Sam wondered if the woman was trying to discourage Rachel or just give her a reality check.

As they passed War Drum Flats, Sam looked out the window for mustangs. The entire area was a different color than usual, darkened by days of rain, but there wasn't a horse in sight. Lila Kenworthy drove in silence for a few miles, and Sam saw only a few cattle searching for grass.

"Honestly, though, Rachel," Jen's mom continued, "the two big things I learned were to ride any horse they pushed at me—sometimes you'll ride one belonging to the stock contractor, you know, and not your own—and to get along with people."

"Now, that's a valuable skill." Jen seemed set on interrupting her mother's lecture.

It almost worked.

With the River Bend bridge in sight, Mrs. Kenworthy added, "At least your dad won't have to take out a loan on your house to pay for cases of hair spray. My dad was always joking about that."

The horses had congregated on the far end of the ten-acre pasture and made no move to greet Sam. Beneath overcast skies, the ranch yard stood gray and empty.

The cottonwood tree had vanished, and the ranch hands had done such a good job of repairing the henhouse and fence, Sam had to look carefully to see where they'd patched and nailed.

When she started up to the house, Sam smelled the fresh-sawed wood. The tree had been cut into lengths for the fireplace and stacked neatly on the front porch to dry.

Sam shrugged off her backpack, but before she went into the empty house, she checked on Ace. She'd only just made her decision to ride into the Phantom's canyon alone. She hadn't been able to give Ace the endurance preparation he deserved for such a long, hard ride.

"I'm counting on your mustang toughness," Sam told Ace when she reached the barn. Ace shoved his chest against the fence. "No, you rest."

"What for?" Dallas shuffled into the barn.

Sam let out a squeak of surprise.

"Sorry, didn't mean to startle you, hon," he said. "Guess you and Ace were having a personal conversation."

When he patted the gelding's neck, Sam noticed Dallas's knuckles were swollen. And yet Dad had given him and the other hands her weekend chores so she could "study."

"Why don't you quit work early today, Dal?"

"Been doin' that all week. This rain's like a vacation, 'cept for resetting fence posts that are washing out of where they're set." Dallas shook his head. "This ground's soaked up about all the water it can hold. You be careful if you go out riding early."

Sam smiled, but she felt a little sick. Dallas himself had supplied an excuse for her absence. Hadn't Dad told him she was grounded?

Straw rustled in a stall that was usually empty. As Sam moved to look inside, Dallas explained.

"It's Buddy. Thought you might like to help me give her that inoculation. Just a precaution, but your dad likes to be careful with her."

"Sure," Sam said. In fact, she didn't want to help give Buddy a shot, but Buddy would appreciate her nearness.

When Dallas came with the syringe, Sam wrapped her arms around Buddy's furry red body.

"It'll just take a minute," she crooned to the calf as Dallas held up the syringe and flicked it. "Just a minute, and you get to stay in this nice warm stall."

Buddy gave a surprised bleat at the needle prick, and her ears flapped, but that was all. She twisted to get free and Sam released her.

"No problem," Dallas said. "Guess your bulldoggin' career is over."

Reminded of rodeos and Karla Starr, Sam took a breath. Dallas had worked for a stock contractor. That made him an expert. She had to ask.

"Dal, there's talk . . ."

THE RENEGADE

"There always is." The foreman's gray-haired head came up as he said it, though, and his expression turned attentive.

"Do you think it's possible Karla Starr would catch mustangs to use as bucking horses?"

"Possible? Sure. And that gray stud you like would be a prize. He'd be a real crowd-pleaser 'cause he's pretty, and a real arm-jerker 'cause he's strong. A cowboy could earn a lot of points if he stayed on. And if he didn't—well, that's every rodeo fan's fantasy, to see a horse that's never been rode."

Sam's spirits fell lower than ever, until Dallas crossed his arms as he leaned against Ace's corral. "Now, is that likely? Not if she's just starting out and wants to stay in business. There's ways to catch mustangs, of course, but to my way of thinking, it's just not worth the risk."

"That's what Brynna Olson thinks too. And Dad."

Sam relaxed, feeling like she'd just climbed into a warm bathtub. Obviously, Karla Starr wouldn't do such a thing. The Phantom was probably holed up in his cozy canyon with his mares and foals, waiting out the storms.

Sam might have given up her whole plan if Dallas hadn't started nodding and added, "Then again, some folks think they can get away with anything and not get caught. Heck, sometimes they're right."

Sam paced. If she was going to go, she should go tonight, right after Gram called, so she'd be back by the time Gram called again Saturday night.

She warmed up the dinner Gram had left for her. When she realized it was only four o'clock, Sam left the meal on the counter, ate three cookies, and drank some milk.

This was stupid. It wasn't raining now, but it was wet, and she'd seen Teddy go down in slippery footing. She shouldn't endanger Ace. Or herself.

She unloaded her backpack onto her bed, then scurried around the house. She gathered a flashlight, matches, granola bars, and an apple, and put everything in plastic bags inside her backpack.

Would it be safer to ride out tonight or leave before daylight tomorrow? She couldn't decide.

Then Sam remembered telling Dad she wasn't like

Rachel, who'd snatched Champ and sneaked away. Sam dumped the supplies out of her backpack. She was *not* going.

Without reheating it, Sam ate the meat loaf and mashed potatoes Gram had left. She ate standing, staring at the kitchen clock, and remembered the Phantom in the BLM corrals. Mane tangled, eyes huge with fear, he'd slammed himself bloody against the fence rails. How much worse would he feel after being trucked from rodeo to rodeo, when men tried to ride him? Would he remember how she'd led him gently to the river and climbed on his back long ago? Would he blame her somehow?

Sam ran down to the barn and grabbed a slicker. It was dusk, and the smell of spaghetti sauce came from the bunkhouse kitchen. The hands were having dinner, so they hadn't seen her. Probably. But why had she brought the slicker to the house? She should have left it in the barn, near Ace, so she could wear it when she rode out. If she rode out.

By the time Gram called, Sam had changed her

mind a dozen more times. Gram asked if she'd eaten. Sam rinsed her dish as she told Gram the meat loaf was great. As Gram told how they'd stopped for lunch in Darton, how they were meeting Brynna Olson's parents for dinner at a steak house, Sam wanted to scream with tension.

"The first round of the chicken cook-off is at nine tomorrow morning—Samantha, is everything all right?"

Sam looked at the telephone receiver. She didn't know what to say. "Everything's fine. I miss you guys."

"Well, we miss you, too. I'll call you tomorrow night and tell you what we won. Good night, sweetie."

It was the right thing to say, because Gram hung up happy.

Sam walked out to the front porch and faced into a warm breeze. She heard a night bird's call, but not a single splat of rain dripping from the eaves. Dark and light flickered inside the bunkhouse, where the hands were watching television.

Sam stared into the night sky. She could see stars, not clouds. Maybe the storms had gone east. Maybe the wind and rain wouldn't return for weeks. If she left tonight, she'd have plenty of time. She wouldn't rush or make mistakes.

In ten minutes, she'd pulled on her boots, hat, slicker, and backpack full of supplies. She left a few strategic lights and the television on and started toward the barn.

Ace's neigh floated through the night, urging her to hurry, and Sam felt better. Ace wanted to go.

Soon enough, they'd both be in the canyon. Ace would be home, and she would be relieved, watching sunbeams turn Zanzibar's coat to silky silver.

Chapter 13

ACE KNEW HE WAS GOING BACK TO HIS FIRST home. He loped through starlight, head high, breathing the fragrance of sagebrush and creosote bush. A few hours without rain had improved the footing. His hooves struck the dirt in a smooth rhythm as he swooped to miss puddles.

They headed toward War Drum Flats, cut left through a brushy ravine, and traveled up through a series of switchbacks. Ace negotiated the zigzags with such precision, Sam felt light-headed by the time they reached the boulder that nearly blocked the tunnel to the valley.

They slipped past it, and Ace's hooves echoed on the rock floor. Sam pressed her cheek against his neck, staying low to avoid hitting her head on the stone ceiling. Along here, somewhere, cracks crossed the ceiling. She'd seen light shine through them before, sparkling on the Phantom's coat.

Tonight there was only darkness.

"Whoa. Ace, ow! That was my head. *Whoa.* I'm getting off."

The gelding danced in eagerness, so Sam kept a grip on the reins as she climbed down. She heard faraway sounds that could be questioning nickers or water running over rocks.

The Phantom had always greeted them before. Ace had bowed to the stallion's authority and followed at his kingly pace. This time, Ace's hooves clipped her boot heels, and he shoved her along with his chest.

"No!" She turned to face him but could barely see his outline. He filled the gloom as he tried to shoulder past.

"Ace, you're only here for a visit." Sam gave a light tug on the reins, reminding him he wasn't returning to the wild.

The gelding blew through his lips and followed Sam.

She saw stone walls soar against a black sky strewn with a million diamond stars. She saw shadowy horses, alert at this invasion, and then the stallion trumpeted a challenge and charged.

He wasn't the Phantom.

In the instant before she clambered atop a boulder and pulled Ace around it out of harm's way, Sam knew it was a different horse. This stallion was taller, darker, younger.

"Hey!" she shouted.

The horse veered, unnerved by her human voice.

Sam squinted, wishing she could see more than a murky shape, but as she huddled against the boulders, waiting for the light, it was enough to know the Phantom was gone.

Sam stared at her glowing watch dial, trying to guess when it would be light enough to see the entire herd and know for sure the Phantom wasn't there.

She knew the charging stallion hadn't been him, but what if the horse had defeated the Phantom and left him injured?

Sam rubbed her cheeks to keep them warm. Rain was pelting down again. She sat under a shelf of rock as she made a plan.

If the Phantom wasn't there, Karla Starr probably had him. Sam tried to accept that fact without imagining details. Her job was to hurry home and call Brynna so that she could track down Karla Starr now.

If that failed, she'd call the number on Karla Starr's business card and find out which rodeo—if any—the woman had supplied with stock this weekend.

"And then—" Sam saw Ace look her way.

Intimidated by the new stallion, the gelding had stayed nearby, even after Sam turned him loose.

"—I'll get Dallas to drive me to her ranch, or the rodeo, and I'll get the Phantom myself."

At last morning was brightening the sky, and though her horsewoman's heart rejoiced at the beautiful animals before her, Sam closed her eyes.

He wasn't there. Sleek and wet, dozens of horses moved through the grass with their foals. Brown, red, gray, and tan coats shone darker from days of rain. The tiger dun mare stood guard, watching the new stallion. Her caution said she didn't trust him completely, and Sam realized why.

He was one of the bachelors, the young black horse that Mrs. Coley had called New Moon. A son of the Phantom, he'd returned to the herd and discovered his father gone. Without a fight, he'd taken over.

Sam tacked up Ace and hurried toward the tunnel. Before she left the enchanted valley, she looked back.

"Don't get too comfy, Moon. I'm coming back, and when I do, I'm bringing your dad."

Going back through the tunnel was even scarier than usual. Sam imagined the tons of rocks overhead. An earthquake could bring them crashing down, or an avalanche could sweep the entire tunnel off the mountain's face.

When she reached the mouth of the tunnel, she

couldn't believe the water. It was like facing a waterfall.

Sam looked back into the tunnel. Should she stay until the downpour slacked off or risk Ace's legs on the shale-shingled mountainside?

If Dallas had come over to the house, he'd see the lights she'd left on and hear the television. If she didn't answer his knock at the door, he might think she was sleeping. Or he'd notice Ace gone and know she'd ridden out.

"What do you think, Ace?" Sam stood next to him, arm slung around his neck. His body warmed her, even through the slicker. "You know the desert better than I do. I sure wish you could talk."

Since he couldn't, Sam swung into the saddle and tried to read her horse's movements. His ears pricked forward, seeming eager to go, and he moved out. For a few steps his head lowered, trying to escape the pelting rain. When he found that impossible, he ignored it, picking his way down the hillside on a path only he could see. Somehow, he seemed to miss most of the plate-size disks of slate that could slide them in directions they didn't want to go.

Far below, she saw the river. It looked wrong. Not placid and blue-green but squirming across the range like a chocolate-brown anaconda.

Sam looked away.

About halfway down, Ace couldn't sidestep the storm's damage. Water had run in the mustang trails, making them into channels, then overflowed, branching into many-fingered streams and connecting the paths. Lower down, water had cut through shelves of dirt and crumbled them off in chunks.

They were almost down when the trail began collapsing at the touch of Ace's hooves. Just ahead lay War Drum Flats, but it didn't look right. The water hole was filled. It had overflowed its banks and washed out the dirt road leading down from the highway.

"Back up," Sam told Ace. "We'll just have to forget about the path. We'll go along the hillside and look down for a place that's not too steep."

When they crashed through the brushy ravine where mustangs hid, they found it full of cattle. Ace tossed his head up and balked, but the white-faced animals didn't spook. In fact, when Sam reined Ace aside, the cattle followed him.

If he hadn't been so tired, Ace would have resisted as more lowing cattle and their calves fell in around them. He snorted, knowing he should be chasing them, not the other way around.

Sam understood. Riders not only herded the cattle to better pastures, but they'd brought the Herefords out of dangerous situations before. These cattle were insisting—in loud, bawling voices—that she should get busy helping them now.

One heifer with a face splotched brown and white made a panicky sound like a cuckoo clock.

Ace pinned his ears and lunged at her, teeth bared, before Sam could rein him around.

"*Whoa*, darn it! We've got bigger trouble than her. Aren't we right across the river from the ranch, Ace? Where is it?"

Sam stared into the rain, which had softened into a wet fog. She couldn't see the bridge or the lights she'd left on upstairs or a place to cross. The flood had washed away landmarks. The one willow tree she thought she recognized had stood on the wild side of the river. Now it stood at midstream.

There. At last she saw the house and barn. They were on higher ground. If she could just get the cows and calves across the river, they'd be safe—if crowded—in the pens.

And it looked like there might be a place to cross. Sam tried to understand what her eyes saw. Just upstream from where the bridge should be was a spit of land. It was shaped sort of like a cooking spoon, except with handles on both sides. And the farthest one—the bridge of ground leading home—was skinny.

As they rode closer, Sam was amazed. The water was so churned up it really looked like cocoa covered with foam. Uprooted sagebrush rode the waves. A board, painted yellow and hinged, hit a submerged rock and launched into the air.

Sam pulled Ace back a step. His hooves splashed. Water was everywhere.

Suddenly, the brockle-faced heifer dashed past. Ace

was still gathering himself when the cow belly flopped into the river.

Sam jerked Ace around, using his brown body to keep the other cattle from following. She flapped her hat toward the eye-rolling white faces. They didn't follow, only looked after the heifer. She wasn't swimming. She was being swept downstream by a surge of muddy water.

"Poor silly thing." Sam blinked then, suddenly aware of what she was seeing.

She was a rancher's daughter, and the ranch was already in trouble. One heifer lost was a heifer who wouldn't calve, who wouldn't go to market, who was a loss the River Bend could not afford.

All week Dal and the hands had herded cattle to higher ground. But this contrary bunch had returned to the riverfront pasture.

Now, no matter how much she wanted to get back home, it was Sam's turn to herd. For the animals' own good, she must scare the heck out of them and hope they ran for the mountains.

Sam loosed the rope on her saddle and shook out a loop. She had no intention of lassoing a single cow. She couldn't, with all her shivering. But the cows didn't have to know that.

Sam whooped. She flashed the rope at the cows' pink noses.

"Git, git, git!" she shrieked.

The cattle understood exactly what this meant, and so did Ace.

"Go on, cows!" Sam yipped like a coyote and snapped the rope at furry red haunches.

The cattle crowded away, rolling their eyes and making short, hooting bellows.

Ace grunted, shoving the cattle before him while Sam wielded the rope like a bullwhip.

They bolted and ran. One calf slipped, righted herself, and crashed into her mother in her rush to escape the wailing human on her heels.

Ace chased the herd until they were running toward the Calico Mountains.

I should follow them. That would be the safest move.

But even as Sam thought it, she was pulling Ace into a wide turn back toward the river.

If Pepper, Ross, and Dallas thought she was in danger, they'd come after her. For their safety, if not to stay out of more trouble, she must try to cross that spoon-shaped spit of land.

She wasn't the only one with that idea.

Dead ahead were more cows. While her back had been turned, a handful of cattle had tried the same thing, then stopped.

"We'll take them home," Sam told Ace. "B-B-Buddy will enjoy the company."

Not only was she shivering, but her head hurt as if she were getting sick, and icy rain sluiced down her neck. She should put her hood up under her hat, but her hands were so numbed with cold, she was afraid she'd drop her hat.

What was that sound? As Ace poised himself to step on the land bridge, Sam thought the bumpy brown earth looked like the spine of a sunken dinosaur. And that grinding sounded like something with stone teeth. . . .

Stop it, Sam told herself. She clucked to Ace, and he walked calmly toward the milling cattle crowded on the little hilltop that had turned into an island.

Then Sam saw the source of the sound. There was no dinosaur in the river, but the truth was almost as bad. The mighty current had scoured the range and swept everything along. Now it was bouncing boulders along like basketballs.

River Bend was close; the thought of home had never been more welcoming.

"Let's go home, Ace," Sam said.

As the gelding moved, two Herefords rushed away from him. Clumsy from fear, they hurried side by side along the dirt tightrope to shore. It crumbled beneath them.

With the instincts of a great cow pony, Ace tried to go after them. Sam yanked her reins tight. She wouldn't risk him, no matter the cost.

A whirlpool spun the heifers until they couldn't tell which direction to swim. Sam was glad the foggy rain hid them from her before she had to watch them drown.

She and Ace must weigh less than the two summer-fat Herefords, but should she risk it or go back? Sam looked over her shoulder. The way back was twice as long, and fingers of muddy water were spreading across it.

She could stay where she was with seven panicky Herefords and her horse. If she stayed, she might still be there when the water covered the little island completely.

Sam leaned forward and hugged Ace hard. She had to decide for both of them.

And for the Phantom. If something happened to her, the BLM might not know for years that he'd disappeared.

They had to go on and hope the cattle didn't try to follow. Once she got across, she'd try to rope each cow and pull it to shore.

"We can do this, Ace." Sam gathered her reins and analyzed the path leading home.

About as wide as her rib cage and two car lengths long, it wouldn't challenge Ace at all if it weren't for the roaring river and forlorn cows.

"We'll be back for you, ladies." Sam hoped it was true.

She balanced in the saddle, trying to make her position perfect for Ace. "Step lightly, boy."

Before Sam gave Ace the cue to move, a voice came through the stormy commotion.

"Samantha!" She knew the voice, but she couldn't see the speaker.

"Stay put for a second. I'll toss you a loop and you'll knot it around your waist."

A shadowy horse and rider took shape in the distance.

"Tie it right. You know how. Then put Ace to that little dirt trail. He's a good pony. But if he falls, I'll pull you to shore."

It was Dallas. He sounded young and sure. Sam brushed aside thoughts of his stiff walk, his arthritis, and his bad back. She hoped he felt as competent as he sounded. Her life might depend on it.

Chapter 14

A LARIAT SANG OUT OF THE MIST AND HIT Sam's shoulder. She grabbed the riata before it could fall.

Dallas's braided rawhide rope felt almost alive in Sam's hands. She flexed her cold fingers before passing the rope around her waist, then tied the same knot she used to hitch Ace. No doubt there was a better knot for this job, but she didn't know it, and there was no time for Dallas to shout instructions.

Sam jerked on the riata. The knot held.

She waved her arm to tell Dallas she was coming over, then smooched at Ace to go ahead.

The rain had slacked off, but the wind had picked up. It blew Ace's forelock straight back, out of his eyes.

Good, Sam thought. *We need all the help we can get.*

Sam kept her eyes fixed on the opposite shore. Jake had always told her a rider should look where she wanted to go. It was important to do things right. So, even though Sam worried about the cattle shuffling behind her, she looked ahead.

A windblown wave gobbled the last few yards of the path. As it turned to dirt, then slurry, then liquid, Ace leaped.

Hind legs thrust them forward. Front legs straightened and reached. They touched, but his body was too short. As Ace's forelegs scrabbled on shore, his hind legs slipped.

The riata tightened. Sam's legs and Ace's hindquarters plunged into a cold tide that yanked and tugged, determined to wash them downstream.

Ace's neck whipped forward, straining to bring the

rest of his body along. It didn't help. The mustang refused to give up, but his loud panting said he was exhausted.

Sam felt Dallas's riata tighten yet again. The foreman was giving Ace one last try before jerking Sam free. It would save Sam, but the sudden imbalance would surely send Ace spinning down the river.

Ace's hind legs kicked. Sam felt his haunches dropping, hooves seeking earth to brace against. He found nothing but fast-moving water.

The riata closed hard on Sam's ribs. She grabbed onto the saddle horn. She would not leave her horse.

"Come on, boy. You can do it, Ace."

With a mighty heave of shoulder muscle, Ace rose and hurled his body forward. Something sang in the air and Ace slid forward on his belly. Snakelike, he was gliding on the muddy riverbank, closer to the bridge.

And then he stopped, beyond the reach of the flood-frenzied river.

Confused and breathless, Sam rolled free of Ace. She worked the riata over her head before turning to see Ace boost himself to all four hooves and shake like a giant wet dog.

Dallas rode toward them, slowly gathering the slack from a second rope.

"Easy, horse, that's it." Dallas clucked as he rode closer. The other end of the rope he was coiling had caught Ace just behind the forelegs, around the barrel. "Surprised that worked." Dallas chuckled. "If he hadn't reared up that way, I'd've laid the loop over his neck, but..."

Sam knew what he didn't want to say. With the river pulling one way and Dallas the other, Ace might have strangled.

Black dots swarmed over Sam's field of vision. Her knees unlatched and her legs wobbled.

"Sam!" Dallas shouted. "Stay with me, girl."

She straightened and stared at him. Dallas's blue eyes were the only color in the gloomy day.

"Take this knife." He extended it toward her. "Open it, and cut that rope."

Sam took the knife and staggered toward Ace. She

would have steadied herself against him, but Ace pinned his ears back, warning her away.

"Just cut it, Samantha. That pony's had enough aggravation."

Sam sawed at the rope. A few strands twisted loose.

"Don't give up on hacking that," Dallas said. "If you reach down and try to take that loop off, he might just decide to give your head a kick for getting him into this mess."

Finally freed, Ace trotted toward the barn. He glanced back only once, shaking his ears at Sam as if he'd understood Dallas's idea and liked it just fine.

"Dallas, I'm sorry." Sam's words came out on a shaky breath.

"Wait." Dallas urged Amigo toward the raging water, though the old horse was trembling from the exertion of pulling Ace and Sam up the bank.

Milling and mooing, the cattle were wondering what to do. Dallas frightened them into action.

"One more time, old friend." Dallas spun his riata at the cattle. "Hunt 'em down."

The words were a signal. Amigo crouched, head level and threatening. He looked vicious, as if he'd savage any stragglers that didn't run.

The cattle burst into a rocking, splashing gallop. Like tightrope walkers, they balanced side to side, heading for the safety of the wild side of the river.

As soon as the cattle ran, Dallas spun Amigo on his hind legs, then dismounted. He set the reins over the horse's head.

"Go on home, 'Migo."

The old horse moved off at a shambling trot, and Dallas watched every step.

"Now," the foreman said, "tell me about that 'sorry' part while we walk back to the ranch."

After they rubbed down the horses, Dallas went to the bunkhouse to change and told Sam he'd meet her in the ranch house kitchen as soon as he had.

It was only one thirty in the afternoon, but overcast skies and a power failure made the house feel as if night were coming on.

Sam grabbed a flannel shirt and fresh jeans and turned the shower on full blast. She took off her muddy clothes and stepped into the shower, turned her face to the spray, then lathered her hair.

It might be her last peaceful moment for a long time. Even if Dallas didn't know she was grounded, he had to tell Gram and Dad she'd almost drowned. Or did he?

A flash flood was an act of nature, totally unpredictable, right? She sighed. She knew the answer was no.

Sam was ready to rinse the suds from her hair when the water slowed, dwindled to a stream no bigger than a pencil, then stopped altogether.

Why? She'd never been alone when this had happened. She'd left this sort of problem to Dad. She concentrated.

Their water heater ran on propane, but . . .

"The pump runs on electricity, stupid!" Sam's voice echoed around her.

Only the water left standing in the pipes had run out in the shower, and she'd used it up fast. She was clean enough, but what was she supposed to do with her soapy hair?

"How long have you lived here?" she muttered to her foamy-topped reflection in the mirror as she climbed out of the shower.

Blaze's toenails came clicking upstairs. He stood panting outside the bathroom door.

Blaze hadn't let himself into the house, so Dallas must be downstairs waiting. She'd have to hurry if she didn't want to make him even more annoyed.

In three minutes flat, Sam was dressed and downstairs with a towel wrapped turban-style around her hair. Her stomach was growling so loud, she wondered why Blaze didn't answer it.

She brought a plate of cookies to the table. She had just put a cookie in her mouth when Dallas asked, "Was he there?"

Shocked, Sam stopped chewing. Dallas seemed to know exactly where she'd gone, and why.

"That's all I'm going to ask." He stared down at his folded hands. "And if you decide to tell me anything else, I might have to call Wyatt. Otherwise, I'm thinking you went out riding this morning, got caught in a flash flood, but had the good judgment to try to take care of seven or eight head of cattle and wait for help."

Sam's tired brain sorted back through the list. Riding. Flash flood. Cattle.

"That's right," Sam said, and it was so. There wasn't a single lie in Dallas's list—if he didn't ask where she'd ridden out *from* this morning. "But I—"

Dallas held a palm toward her, and Sam stopped talking. The foreman knew that the Phantom's freedom, and maybe his life, were at stake. He cared, but he didn't want her confession.

Sam fidgeted in her chair. Would any harm be caused by keeping where she'd been a secret?

"No, he wasn't there." Sam circled back to Dallas's question. "I think Karla Starr's got him."

"She might."

"And since that's against the law, and BLM is in charge of watching out for mustangs, I think I should call Brynna Olson and tell her that I saw the Phantom's herd and he wasn't with them."

Dallas nodded.

"And then . . ." Sam wondered just how much of a buddy Dallas was willing to be. "And then, I thought I'd figure out which rodeo Karla Starr is supplying stock for this weekend"—Sam met Dal's blue eyes; he hadn't said no yet—"and have you, uh, drive me there?"

"Right now. During a major storm. Without Wyatt's permission."

"No, we could call Dad first."

"And you think he'd say it's fine and dandy?"

"Well, if they weren't too far away." Sam counted three cookie crumbs on the table. "And if I was with you." She used her finger to herd the crumbs together. "Yeah, I think he'd say it was all right."

Dallas shook his head. "You know, I remember when you couldn't hold up your head. Now you're maneuverin' me into running all over the countryside on a wild-goose chase."

The electricity chose that moment to return. If the

lights hadn't flashed bright and the television clicked on with a chorus of recorded laughter, things might have been different.

But Sam took the sudden gaiety as a sign. And so, it seemed, did Dallas. Or maybe he was simply too tired to argue.

"Okay." Dallas pushed back from the kitchen table. He took a green coffee can from the cupboard and ran water into a small tin coffeepot. "Get on the phone, sweet talker, and let's see what you can work out."

Chapter 15

OF COURSE, NO ONE WAS PICKING UP SAM'S phone calls.

Even if they'd heard about the flash flood, it was Saturday. Gram would be frying chicken in her neat white apron. Dad would be riding Banjo in lazy figure eights, warming him up for the roping competition. So Sam left a message.

"Dad, please tell Brynna the Phantom isn't with his herd." Sam's voice stayed level. Since Dallas had agreed to help her, she felt strong.

"There's a young black stallion who thinks he's in charge. He must be the Phantom's son, because he looks just like Blackie did." Sam thought for a few seconds.

"That's all, I guess. There was kind of a lot of flooding, but Dallas can tell you about that tonight. Bye. I love you."

Sam ran upstairs and rinsed her hair. Then, still hungry, she put a frying pan on the stove, turned on the burner, and made a grilled cheese sandwich.

"Are you sure you don't want one?" she asked as butter sizzled in the hot pan.

"Not good for my old heart." Dallas shook his head and sipped his fresh coffee. "And you seem dead set on testing it."

While the bread browned and the cheese melted, Sam called the number of the BLM corrals at Willow Springs. No one answered, since it was Saturday afternoon.

Sam wasn't surprised. She'd known since daybreak that Brynna was her only hope. Brynna wanted the stallion left on the range to improve the mustangs of the

Calico Mountains. And Brynna had the authority to notify rangers when something was wrong.

Dallas munched an apple while Sam ate, and together they listened to the radio. No flash flood or storm warnings were reported, and even the storm watch had ended. Dry and clear on Sunday, the weatherman said, with temperatures predicted to be around 68 degrees.

Outside the kitchen window, though, it was still windy and gray.

Sam started for the sink to wash her dishes.

"Leave those for now," Dallas said.

"Really?" Sam backed away from the sink.

How cool of Dallas to let her relax. Maybe she'd kindle a blaze in the fireplace and start on that history project for real. It would be cozy, sipping hot chocolate and reading while the fire baked the rain chill from her bones.

"You can do dishes later." Dal took his hat from the hook by the door. "We've got near three hours of daylight left. Before we go gallivantin' off to rodeos, we gotta make those cattle as safe as possible. I'll catch Strawberry and Jeepers. You be out front in five minutes."

From the River Bend bridge, Sam saw that the river had receded faster than it had risen.

Sculpted by floodwater, the riverbank dirt wore ripply patterns. In low places, puddles shone. Sticks, rocks, and clumps of brush were strewn at the high-water mark.

The cottonwood tree was missing a few lower branches, but once more it stood beside the river, instead of in the middle. Two jays hopped on its branches, squawking.

Sam surveyed the ranch. If this flood had rushed through San Francisco, she and Aunt Sue would be staring out the apartment window, looking down on cleanup efforts. Red and amber lights would flash, backup warnings would beep from emergency vehicles, and workers in hard hats would string cables everywhere.

Here, nature had started healing both animals and land.

Sam's heart hurt as she remembered that the Phantom wasn't out there, tending his herd.

Hooves splashed, and for one soaring second Sam hoped the stallion had come to prove her wrong. Instead, she saw Pepper and Ross riding toward her and Dallas.

"Been upstream as far as Three Ponies?" Dallas asked.

Ross nodded. "Just—" He pointed at the debris left behind, indicating there was no more serious damage.

Sam pushed her damp bangs out of her eyelashes. If she hadn't been so tired, she would have teased Ross. The shy cowboy never wasted a word when he could use a gesture.

Pepper, all red hair and energy, sat on a fretting Quarter Horse named Nike. Pepper wasn't much older than Jake, but he was a full-time cowboy and proud that he'd bought the lanky horse he called a "ruby bay" with his own earnings. The animal suited him, Sam thought. Neither of them ever settled down.

Just now, though, Sam felt Pepper checking her out.

"Hey there, cowgirl, you look pretty done in."

It was as close as Pepper would come to questioning Dallas's judgment about making Sam work. Always the boss, Dallas just turned Jeepers downstream and rode on.

"'Course, we don't have Jake." Pepper reined Nike into step with Strawberry. "I guess we can make do with you."

Sam smiled. It was the kind of compliment only a cowboy would give, and she accepted it with pride.

The four riders fanned out across the range on both sides of the river. Their eyes searched everywhere for cows in trouble.

They didn't see many. After days of being herded to higher ground, most cattle had stayed in the upper valleys, even though it contradicted their usual grazing patterns.

Sam surprised five deer drinking from a puddle that a red-winged blackbird was using as a bathtub. The does raised their muzzles, judging Sam with gentle eyes before they pranced away. And then she saw the dead heifer.

Sam didn't want to look. She tried to believe the bloated cow was something else. A rust-colored sofa, maybe, jammed there between a ripped-off branch and a boulder.

Was it her fault? Was this one of the two heifers who'd leaped ahead of her and Ace, then been snatched off their hooves and washed downriver? Why did she have to find this corpse?

It wasn't fair. She wasn't a cowboy, she was a kid. Then Sam reminded herself that this wasn't punishment. It was part of ranching. Here, even a teenager had to pitch in and help.

Sam urged Strawberry forward, overriding the mare's caution.

"Pepper!" Sam yelled to him, since he was nearest. "Want to give me a hand?"

Coming at a jog, Pepper limbered up his rope. He'd already seen the cow. He didn't offer Sam a word of sympathy, but she heard it in the respect he gave the dead animal.

"I'll just put a loop on this old girl and bring her back where she belongs." Pepper sent his rope flying.

Though it took several tries, a loop finally tightened

around two stiff hind legs. Eyes rolling, nostrils fluttering in disgust, Nike pulled the awful burden to shore.

By dusk the cowboys had dragged home three dead Herefords wearing River Bend brands.

When Sam stood in the ranch yard at last, exhaustion hit her. Her arms were noodles, too limp to lift the saddle from Strawberry's back. She did it anyway.

"It's a sad business," Dallas admitted. He looked out to the far pasture, where Ross was using their beat-up bulldozer to bury the dead cattle. "But we didn't find that calico-faced heifer you mentioned. Maybe she grew fins."

Sam managed a smile just before she heard the phone. Thinking of the Phantom, she ran for it.

"'Bout time you got in." Dad sounded mad. "What's all this about a flood, and how is it you're not sitting home studying so you can answer the phone?"

"They needed me—Pepper, Dallas, and Ross did—and I—" Sam shrugged out of her slicker and let it fall on the kitchen floor. "Some of our cows drowned, Dad, and—Ace did his best, you know? We tried to keep them from jumping in, but—"

"You were out there on Ace?" Dad's voice shook.

"—there were pieces of fence and branches and whirlpools." Sam kept talking, trying to make him understand. "They couldn't swim because the water was going so fast, even where it was only a few inches deep. It looked like chocolate milk, all churned up, and it snatched their feet right out from under them."

Dad had stayed quiet too long. Sam picked up the slicker from the floor and hung it up, as if he were watching. Had he figured out from her message that she'd ridden alone to the Phantom's valley?

The long-distance line crackled with static.

"Did you and Gram win?" she asked weakly.

"Samantha, you're not making one bit of sense. Let me talk with Dal, if he's there."

"Yes, sir, he's just outside. I'll get him."

I'm dead. Sam laid the receiver down and shuffled outside.

She felt dizzy. Pepper and Dallas looked like a black-

and-white photo of the Old West. Standing in the dusk, they looked at her over the backs of tired horses.

"Dallas, Dad wants to talk with you."

Both Blaze and Dallas followed Sam inside, and Sam kept walking. She sat on the living room floor in front of the television. She stared at the screen without noticing what she was watching and petted Blaze's head until he fell asleep.

Something in Dallas's tone changed, attracting her attention.

"Three. She was right," Dallas said. "Yeah, she got a good scare, but . . . Naw, she's fine. Could use some sleep.

"The thing is . . ." Dallas's voice dropped almost to a whisper for what seemed like a long time. ". . . Sweetwater, Riverton, and someplace near Salt Lake. 'Course, that one's out."

As Sam pushed off the floor and tried to stand, her knees stuck. Her leg muscles trembled too. Without thinking, she must have clamped them hard around Ace to keep from falling into the raging waters. Poor Ace.

She wobbled toward the kitchen and braced herself in the doorframe. Why pretend she wasn't eavesdropping? Dal knew she was, or he wouldn't have whispered.

Water had dripped off Dal's slicker and made a pool around his boots. He must have been concentrating awfully hard not to have noticed.

"Weather station says it's passed on through." Dallas was nodding. "Nothing the boys can't handle. Okay, you have yourself a nice evening, now. Eat some of that fettuccine Alfredo for me, and don't worry about a thing. I'll send her off to bed early and see you all sometime tomorrow night."

Dallas hung up.

Sam waited.

Then all the wrinkles on Dallas's tanned face lifted, and he gave Sam a thumbs-up and a smile that made her whoop for joy.

Dad had said they could go.

She crossed all her fingers on both hands. This time tomorrow, the Phantom could be home, safe and sound.

THE RENEGADE

Sam had turned off her reading light. Her eyes were closed and her mind drifting, when the telephone rang. She stared stupidly at the numbers on her watch. Nine o'clock. She peered toward the dark outside her window. Nine o'clock at night. She'd understandably conked out early after getting no sleep the night before.

Oh, ow! Sam tottered across her bedroom floor and into the hall, but her leg muscles were so stiff she had to cling to the banister to make it downstairs.

The phone was still ringing when she entered the kitchen, so the call must be important.

"Hello?"

"You sound outta breath." Jake's lazy voice made Sam sure he'd taken all those naps she'd only dreamed of today. "Were you in the barn?"

"No, I was in bed."

"Are you okay? Did you hurt yourself in the flood?"

"Did *I* hurt . . . *myself*?" Sam's fingers clamped hard on the telephone receiver. "Let me think."

She thought of shale sliding on slick mud, of cattle

rocketing against Ace so he nearly stumbled into the wild river, of wind and rain that might have added up to hypothermia.

"No, I didn't hurt myself. Thanks for asking."

"Whew, you've sure got your cranky pants on tonight."

"My, my—*what?*"

Jake laughed at Sam's outrage. Then he used an adult voice meant to put her in her place. "I only called to see how Teddy's doing."

Sam winced. She should have thought sooner of the curly Bashkir colt Jake was schooling. The two-year-old was at a critical stage in his training, and no one had ridden him since Jake's accident.

"He's fine. We put him in the ten-acre pasture, and he's getting along with the other horses. In fact, he and Jeepers are sort of palling around together."

"That's good. I was thinking . . ." Jake's voice trailed off. He cleared his throat.

"My alarm is set for four a.m.," she said, "so if this is going to take long—"

"Zip it, Sam. You know I'm bad at asking for favors. What I was thinking, though, is that Monday, if I can get Nate or somebody to drive me over, you could work Teddy while I tell you what to do."

"Like *that* would be a new experience."

"Forget I asked."

"No, I won't." Sam wondered if she could use this as an excuse to put off Rachel's lesson. "Of course I'll do it. I'm flattered you asked."

"Who else is there?"

Sam laughed in spite of herself. "You're a great guy, Ely, but I'm going back to bed. Good night."

The receiver was almost down when she heard him ask, "Where are you going at four a.m.?"

For some reason of its own, Sam's brain flashed a picture of Rachel's arms linked around Jake's waist as they rode double.

"To my friend Duncan's house," Sam said.

"Duncan? Duncan *who*?"

Sam hung up the phone. She didn't go back and answer its ring as she walked upstairs, either.

Of course, she didn't have a friend named Duncan, but that didn't matter. It served Jake right.

Ahh. Sam's shaky muscles unfurled as she got back into bed. When her head touched the pillow, she was in heaven.

Even though her alarm was set for four a.m., Sam's lips curved in the biggest grin she'd worn all day.

Chapter 16

SAM CAME DOWNSTAIRS BEFORE DAWN AND found Dallas hunched over road maps of California, Nevada, and Utah.

"We'll be going places where your silly cell phone coverage won't work," he said. "A paper map won't let us down."

Sam watched Dallas trace a finger on one of the maps. If they were traveling rural roads, his distrust of electronics was probably justified.

"Last night I called the stock manager at Karla Starr's

ranch. I told him we had animals she might be interested in—which is true."

Sam nodded. If Dark Sunshine hadn't been in foal, would Karla Starr have made an offer? Or was the fierce little mare too small to be a bucking celebrity?

"Her manager says Karla moves around a lot—one step ahead of the law, I'm guessing."

Dallas's guess brought Sam fully awake. If Karla Starr had the Phantom, he'd be stolen property.

"In any case, the manager doesn't keep close tabs on her. Just feeds broncs and bulls, but he had a few hunches where she might be this weekend."

Dallas positioned the map so Sam could see.

"We'll be checking the Sweetwater Rodeo first," he said, "since it's closest."

The next closest was a hundred miles beyond Sweetwater, at the Wild West Days rodeo in Riverton, California.

"Third place is a college rodeo in Tower Mountain, Utah, but that's too far to check and still be back in time for school Monday morning."

THE RENEGADE

Dallas folded the map and swigged down the last of his coffee, and ten minutes later they were on the road.

Sam had never seen a more beautiful sunrise than the one over the rodeo grounds in Sweetwater, Nevada. The glitter of sun on windshields in the contestants' parking lot made yesterday's storm seem like nothing but a bad dream.

Although the rodeo wouldn't start until noon, cowboys and cowgirls were crawling out of campers and motor homes, checking on their horses, and looking for breakfast.

Some followed their noses toward the pancake breakfast served after a church service held in the arena.

"Kinda peaceful, isn't it?" Dallas stretched as he climbed out of the truck.

Sam nodded. She'd never been to rodeo grounds before the action began. A folded event program somersaulted in the wind, blue pennants flapped on a food truck showing a CLOSED sign, and the grandstands overlooking the arena were empty.

"You'd never guess at all the music, yelling, bucking, and bellowin' that'll be startin' up soon," Dallas mused. "But this is a good time for us to look around, see if we can find Karla Starr's fancy rig or anything else with her brand on it."

He strode past a maze of metal fences and gates, and Sam followed.

"All those go somewhere," he said. "The trick is to get the bulls and broncs headed for the right chute and the cowboy who drew 'em."

Dallas explained that a cowboy registered for an event, and then his name was randomly matched with a certain animal.

"At small shows like this, their names are probably just drawn from a hat."

"Does it really matter which one you get?"

"Sure does," Dallas said. "If you get one that bucks and you stay on, you make lots of points and money. A stock contractor's dream is an animal that bucks hard every time. All the cowboys want to draw him."

Sam closed her eyes in dismay. The Phantom would buck until his proud heart broke.

"Over here." Dallas steered Sam around a bare-chested cowboy whose ribs were being wrapped with yards of white tape. "Those are the holding pens."

A dozen horses raised their heads from a pile of hay. Still chewing, they regarded Sam and Dallas.

"Those don't look like wild horses."

"They're not on the job," Dallas explained, then added, "And not one of 'em looks like your Phantom."

He was right. Except for one black and one paint, all the horses in this pen were bays and sorrels.

"So, do we give up and go on to the next one?" Sam asked.

"Not just yet." Dallas's hands perched on his hips. He scanned the closed concession booths painted with pictures of cotton candy and corn dogs.

Professional stock contractors, he explained, had many responsibilities and lots of rules to follow at sanctioned rodeos.

But this wasn't a sanctioned rodeo, and Karla Starr fell short of being a professional.

"Sanctioned means approved, right?" Sam asked. "Who sanctions them?"

"At small, end-of-the-season rodeos like this one, it's hard to tell. All those the manager mentioned were connected with county fairs and such." Dallas shook his head as if he'd expected as much. "The bigger rodeos, though, for cowboys who're tryin' to make a living, are sanctioned by professional cowboy organizations. That's how they get points and honors and whatnot."

The aromas of sausage and pancakes made Sam hungry, but keeping up with Dallas kept her from thinking about it too much.

Cowboys and cowgirls were lined up at a folding table shaded by a picnic umbrella. They were paying entry fees and getting starting times for the day's events, Dal explained.

Every time they saw the bobbing ears or shiny hindquarters of a horse, they detoured to take a look. The rodeo grounds were growing busy. Trucks and cars pulled in. Trailer gates were opened and restless horses unloaded. Dogs and children scattered, looking for companions.

Once, Sam sprinted toward a rearing gray horse, only to find she was really an Appaloosa.

"She hates having her legs taped," a girl explained to Sam. "But it keeps her from getting banged up."

Next, they passed a bullfighter. He wore clownish clothes and makeup, but his leg was extended, and a woman dressed like a paramedic was wrapping it with tape matched to his athletic shoes.

"Everywhere I look, somebody's getting bandaged up," Sam said. "It looks like a hospital back here."

"Rodeo's a rough game," Dallas agreed.

Before they gave up, Dallas even checked the chutes that opened into the arena. They were empty, but Sam couldn't help noticing that inside them, the wooden walls were gouged through the paint, down to bare wood.

"Some poor horse—"

"Or some poor cowboy," Dallas corrected her.

"Yeah, but the cowboys have a choice."

"Ya got me there," Dallas agreed, but he seemed to be thinking of something else.

Sam crossed her arms and considered a pen of bucking bulls. They looked healthy and well fed. One dozed in the sun.

She wished she could sleep through these mixed feelings. She'd always loved the popcorn smell and excitement of rodeos, but the thought of the Phantom, terrified and confused, changed everything.

"I have one more idea." Dallas strode toward a man with a clipboard and a walkie-talkie. "Excuse me, can you give me an idea of when the wild horse race starts?"

The man didn't bother consulting his papers. "We don't have one here at Sweetwater, but you could probably catch the one in Riverton. I hear they've put all their local businessmen in teams of three to compete against each other." He chuckled and swept a hand over the small, busy fairgrounds. "That'd give us about one team."

Sam tried to talk with Dal as he hurried toward the truck. "What's a wild horse race?"

THE RENEGADE

Now the smell of onion rings mingled with the smell of pancakes and sausage, making her even hungrier, but Sam still caught Dallas's answer.

"You'll see when we get there," he snapped, and something in his tone told Sam she wouldn't like what she saw.

Halfway to Riverton, Dallas stopped for gasoline. Inside the convenience store, he bought them microwaved burritos and colas.

"For heaven's sake, don't tell your gram."

"I won't," Sam promised. Gram thought fast food was corrupting the younger generation.

"You want one of those fried pies, too?" Dallas pointed at little greasy things that didn't look anything like Gram's pies.

"Can I have ice cream instead?" Sam felt greedy after she said it.

"I don't mind spoilin' you some." Dallas laughed. "You were a big help yesterday. Get anything you want, just so long as you can eat it in the truck."

Riverton's Wild West Days rodeo was in full swing when they arrived. They hurried to the arena just as saddle bronc riding was announced.

A pale horse spun in the middle of a dust cloud. With the sun shining through, Sam couldn't tell the color of his coat.

When the buzzer sounded, the cowboy's free arm stopped waving and a pickup man swooped in on a sturdy Quarter Horse. Smoothly, he yanked at the bronc's flank cinch and helped the rider to the ground.

The bronc stopped bucking and ran for an open gate. His coat was a creamy palomino.

"I thought for a minute . . ."

"Too polished," Dallas said. "That palomino's been in a chute more than a time or two."

The announcer boomed the name of the next cowboy and a horse called TNT, but there was a commotion in the chute and they didn't emerge.

Maybe, Sam thought, *maybe this is him.*

It wasn't. The horse exploding out of the chute was dark bluish black, the color of a bruise. He seemed to fly.

"A sunfisher," Dallas said. "See how he twists up in the air so the sun shines on his belly? And that"—he pointed as the cowboy flew off over the horse's tail—"is called goin' out the back door."

Sam admired the skilled horsemanship of the pickup men. She appreciated Dallas's explanations and his offer of cotton candy, but she was losing hope.

Dallas must have noticed.

"I'm thinking the Phantom—if he's here at all—will be in the wild horse race. He'd be a devil to get in one of those chutes, and besides"—Dallas looked around the fairgrounds as if instinct was whispering to him—"they might not be too careful checking brands on horses that're supposed to act wild."

Sam and Dallas left the stands to search the holding pens.

They wandered through the dust, checking everywhere.

Unlike the Sweetwater Rodeo, action was all around them here. Ropers practiced on anything that moved. A barrel racer's horse, eager to dash into the arena, nearly trampled them. As they sidled into an area behind the chutes, a cowboy grunted. Sam snuck a look just as he leaned down to check a bull rider's spur that had been molded on as part of a smudged and autographed cast.

"Can you believe that?" Sam gasped. The cowboy clearly had a broken leg, and yet he planned to ride.

"Sure." Dallas nodded. "Jake'd ride, if he could get away with it."

Sam guessed he was right, but as they walked among the men preparing for the bull-riding competition, she decided they were insane. She could imagine riding a bucking horse. In fact, she'd done it, just not on purpose.

But bulls scared her. The best were "rank," Dal said. They spun, fought, twisted, and kicked, then chased down the riders with murderous rage.

Sam was listening to a cowboy with a black eye brag that he'd earned it when a bull's horn hooked him, when Dal's voice interrupted.

"You feel like a break?"

For the first time all day, Sam really looked at the

foreman. There was a gray cast to his skin, and he shifted from boot to boot, as if neither foot was up to bearing weight.

She'd been selfish, but if she fussed over Dallas, he'd keep going, even if he was ready to drop.

"Yeah, I could really go for some lemonade, and maybe we could sit in the shade for a few minutes."

Dal's raised brow made Sam worry that she'd overdone the pitiful act, but he jerked a thumb toward one of the booths.

It was three o'clock, and Sam had started worrying about Ace—the gelding was bound to be as sore as she was—when a voice announced the wild horse race.

"How they do it," Dal explained carefully, "is put men in teams of three behind a rope barrier. All the wild horses are put in a chute. There's a whistle, usually, and then the men and horses kinda meet up in the arena."

Sam and Dal found seats in the stands, and before Dallas finished, the announcer's booming voice explained that each team had to stop a wild horse and saddle him. Then one man had to ride the horse over a finish line.

Three against one, Sam thought as eight horses charged into the arena. None were grays and none looked like mustangs. Probably, they were saddle and bareback broncs, just called "wild" for this event.

No fair. Sam noticed that each horse wore a halter with a trailing rope. It made them easier to catch, but when the men grabbed the ropes, holding them out, Sam was afraid one of the spooked horses would come barreling through, trying to escape a pursuer, and trip.

A perfect event for the Phantom. No experience required, just energy and speed.

One team had its horse. The paint struggled as a man hung on to his head and another chased him with the saddle.

Sam didn't realize she was holding her face in her hands until the third man dodged the paint's heels and twisted its tail. Pain made the horse still, and the saddle crashed down upon his back. Before any of the men could mount, Sam covered her eyes.

"I don't think he's here," Dallas said, standing up. "'Bout time for us to be going anyway."

Dallas led the way back to the truck. They were already on the freeway, headed home, when Sam spoke.

"I don't know what to hope—that Karla has him but just didn't bring him to this rodeo, or that the black stallion killed him, or that he just deserted his herd...."

"Not likely." Dallas stared at the road ahead.

Sam knew she should let him concentrate. He didn't drive in heavy traffic very often.

"If I turn on the radio," Dal said, "think you could still grab some sleep?"

"Sure," she said, but it didn't happen. When Dallas spoke again, Sam was still awake.

"You and me don't have the manpower to go after Karla Starr the way she deserves," Dallas said, as if he'd been thinking about the Phantom for the whole hour they'd been driving. "Much as I hate to say it, BLM might be the stallion's best hope."

"Maybe." Sam looked out the window. As they traveled on, she saw mud on the pavement, and water ran in channels next to the road.

There would still be flood damage to deal with at home. She'd have lots to think about besides the Phantom, but she still felt like she'd failed him.

What's next?

Sam didn't know she'd whispered the words until Dallas answered.

"What's next is this: get that Brynna Olson on your side. Wyatt says she's half as obsessed with that stallion as you are, and that's enough to defend him like a mother bear."

Chapter 17

GRAM AND DAD STILL WEREN'T HOME FROM the fair when Sam and Dallas pulled into the ranch yard long after dark, but Pepper met them with good news.

"All night long the local TV news has been sayin' Darton High School is closed Monday." Pepper was hatless and his red hair stuck out in clumps, but he looked happy for her.

"Why is it closed?" Sam rejoiced at the chance to do her homework tomorrow, instead of doing it half-asleep tonight. Then an awful thought cropped up. "The library's not flooded, is it?"

Though most of Darton High was ordinary, Sam loved the library. Tall windows kept it sunny, and a librarian with a green thumb coaxed ferns and flowers to brighten every corner.

"They didn't mention it." Pepper rubbed his eyes, then yawned. "Just said the road was washed out, like it is lots of places in town."

"Thanks for staying up to tell me. Now I can go out and check on Ace."

"He's fine. They're all fine, and 'cept for those three heifers, the cattle seem to have made it through."

Sam's arms felt heavy, and the barn looked far away.

"Sam, honest." Pepper must have seen her weariness. "I looked Ace over."

"I know," Sam said as she started walking, "but he needs to know I'm home."

Ace neighed a sweet welcome, and Sam ran the rest of the way. "You look pretty good, but you wouldn't turn down a massage, would you?" She took up the rubber curry comb and worked it over Ace's coat. He shook his mane as if her touch gave him chills of delight.

"I didn't find the Phantom," Sam confessed. "Ace, what if I never do?"

She kept brushing long after his bay coat shone. Then she told Ace the truth that had ached inside her for three long days.

"It's my fault. I let him become too tame." Sam remembered how close the stallion had come that day when Rachel had been lost. "Dad was right, but I didn't believe him until it was too late. The Phantom would be curious about Karla and get too close. Then I bet she caught him herself."

Sam dropped the curry comb and leaned against Ace's back. "I'm to blame," she whispered, "and I don't know what to do."

Ace didn't have any answers, but talking to him helped more than crying. Finally, Sam went to the house and left the front porch light on. She was ready for sleep.

Gram woke her with a kiss and a glass of orange juice.

Sam struggled up onto her elbows. Gram snatched a T-shirt from Sam's floor and straightened some papers that didn't need straightening. Sam had missed her.

"You won, huh?"

Gram turned, a towel dangling from her fingers, and smiled. "I did, and not only a blue ribbon, but two hundred dollars' credit at the new superstore in Darton."

"That's great. What are you going to buy? A rice cooker?"

Gram had been reading up on those appliances for months. She loved making Asian food, but she just didn't have the knack with rice that she had with potatoes and bread.

"Land sakes, no. I'll just put it toward our monthly food bill, and it'll be gone quick enough." Gram's words drifted back as she bustled out the door.

Sam slipped out of bed and dressed, thinking about Gram. The trip and the blue ribbon were reward enough for her, it seemed, but shouldn't she buy herself a treat too?

"Wyatt's in the barn," Gram said as Sam poured her cereal. "He wants to talk with you."

"About what?"

"You'll have to ask him." Gram frowned at Sam's breakfast. "You should have some fruit on that, at least. And some whole-wheat toast." Gram held out a hand to ward off Sam's protest. "Even if you're not hungry."

Dad was in the barn talking with Dallas, but Tank stood saddled at the rail, so Dad had probably already ridden out to look over the storm-damaged range.

Sam heard his voice before she saw him.

"It wasn't a decision I made quick, but what he offered for Banjo, after we won, was just about the price those three heifers would've brought at market. And that's if it had been a good market."

"You sold Banjo?" Sam stepped into the barn. She couldn't believe Dad had meant what he'd said.

He didn't answer right away, and maybe it was a good thing. The look he gave her was complicated, and it took her a minute to figure it out. His expression said he was glad she was alive, that he would've liked a greeting instead of an accusation, and that her eavesdropping was out of line for a thirteen-year-old.

But all Dad said was, "Yes, I did."

"But, Dad, you love that horse."

"No. I love this ranch and the people on it." Dad's eyes wouldn't let her wiggle away. "Banjo's a good horse, but I have others. He made lots of contributions to this ranch."

"I heard he won," Sam admitted, "and you got enough to balance things."

"More than that. After I sold him, I felt sorta at loose ends. Your gram was in a runoff for first place." Dad's grin flashed, then faded. "I went to a workshop the county was givin' and learned about drought-tolerant hay and grass seed that grows in poor soil."

"I'm sorry, Dad." Sam saw Dallas slip out of the barn to give them privacy. "I didn't mean to sound—" She shrugged. No word really fit.

"It's hard. I know." Dad placed a hand on Sam's shoulder. "And I'm sorry as I can be that your Phantom's gone."

"You know what, though?" Sam felt suddenly excited.

THE RENEGADE

Now that Brynna was back, things might change for the better. "Dallas said I should get Brynna busy on this. Do you think it's too early to call?"

"She'll be in her office by now." Dad smiled, looking a little awkward. "Sam, about Brynna. We need to talk."

"I know. Me and my big mouth. Dad, I'm really sorry I was rude to her the other day, but I do trust her. I think she's the only one who can help."

Dad took off his Stetson, smoothed his hair, then put his hat on again. "Go ahead and call her."

Brynna was at Willow Springs, but she took ten whole minutes to come to the phone.

"Sam." Brynna sounded exasperated when she finally picked up. "If it were anybody but you, I'd tell you to go fly a kite. I'm awfully busy with the Red Rock horses we had to bring in because of drought, and now there's another twenty or so on their way—in bad shape from the flood."

"Gee, I'm sorry. If I can—"

"So what I'm saying, Sam"—Brynna's tone was

half impatience and half amusement—"is, 'Spit it out, honey, or I'm going to hang up this dang phone.'"

It wasn't the encouragement Sam had hoped for, but she tried. "You got my message about the Phantom, right?"

"I did. I feel awful." Brynna paused before her brisk professional manner kicked in, full force. "But I must rule out natural causes—predators, injuries, and the like—before questioning Karla Starr."

"I already did that—ruled out other causes."

"No offense, Sam, but no, you have not. And it's going to be a solid week before I can release rangers for that purpose. I'm sor— Just a minute."

Brynna muffled the mouthpiece, then returned. "Sam, I've got to go. If it's possible, I'll be out at River Bend tonight and we'll talk more." She paused as commotion continued in her office. "I may be late."

Dallas needed Sam's help riding upstream. A big piece of bank had caved in, narrowing the river's flow, and Sam spent most of the afternoon with a shovel.

Only when she saw the baby-blue Mercedes bumping across the bridge did she realize Rachel had come for her lesson even though school had been canceled.

Sam didn't allow herself to complain, even mentally. Gram was using her prize money for groceries and Dad had sold Banjo to cover the cost of the lost cattle. The least she could do was watch Rachel trot around in circles on Ace.

Dallas saw the car and waved Sam toward home.

"C'mon, Strawberry." Sam urged the mare into a lope toward the house. "I'll work on my blisters later."

Sam figured she must have been too busy shoveling mud to see the Elys drop Jake off, but there he was, laughing and talking with Rachel.

Sam drew rein and watched.

Hopping around on his good leg, Jake had managed to saddle Teddy, and it looked as if Rachel had been mirroring his efforts with Ace. She sure didn't laugh like that when Sam told her which strap went through which ring. And she'd never saddled up so fast.

Okay, so Jake had been cooped up for a week. Even

Rachel probably seemed like good company after that.

Ace neighed a welcome, although Sam felt invisible to Jake.

"Glad you made it back." Jake frowned as if they'd had an agreement to meet at a certain time.

As if he had so many important engagements to keep.

But Sam didn't say anything out loud. She wasn't sure why, but it had something to do with Rachel.

"Let me slip Strawberry's bit out and loosen her cinch." Sam swung down and loosened things, so the mare would be more comfortable while she waited. Dallas had said they might have to go out again later.

It was bad enough that Rachel wore perfect jeans and a pink blouse with little pearl studs for buttons, while Sam had mud caked on her shirt cuffs and probably in her hair.

"Jake tells me *he* is going to act as master of the horse today." Rachel batted her eyelashes at him.

She really did.

Sam sighed and mounted Teddy, wishing Jen had been there to see this. And she couldn't wait to tell her how Jake had put Rachel in her place. Except . . . Jake didn't.

Things got worse as the lesson progressed.

"Good job taking him through the barrels at a walk, Rachel. Now try lifting his head a little. No, it's not your fault. He's just being lazy."

Lazy? Ace? But when Sam would have said something, Jake waved a hand her way.

"Keep Teddy back a little."

No *please*. No *thank you*. Just do it, and Jake made no mention of her superb handling of Teddy, a half-trained colt.

"Jog now," Jake ordered.

Where did he think he was, in a show ring?

"Rachel, you'll need to sit down right in the saddle. That's it." Jake leaned against his crutch, smiling.

"No posting in Western, Rachel. I know it's a little uncomfortable at first, but your seat needs to be right in the saddle."

"Rachel's already ridden Ace at a trot," Sam pointed out.

"That's right, I have." Rachel repositioned herself

with a thump. Ace braked to a stop and Rachel fell off.

Sam wasn't sure how it happened, but Ace didn't walk off, and Rachel didn't stand up, so Sam dismounted and went to her.

"Why did you do that?" Sam asked.

"Oh, shut up." Rachel's British accent had never sounded so lofty. She took a quick glance at Jake, then lowered her voice. "You think you're so smart about horses. Well, why didn't you brand that stallion if he was yours?"

Sam stood speechless for a minute. Rachel had to be talking about the Phantom, but why?

"I wanted him wild," Sam snapped, even before she could question Rachel's sudden change in topic.

"Well, if you wanted him at all, you should have bloody well done it."

"Ladies?" Jake called. "How 'bout another ride along the rail, then reverse and . . ."

If the baby-blue Mercedes had been bringing serum for a fatal disease, Sam couldn't have been happier to see it.

THE RENEGADE

She only wished Mrs. Coley would take Jake away too.

Alone, Sam unsaddled all three horses and brushed them. Before putting Ace away, she checked his feet and found a pebble in his off hind hoof. Of course Rachel wouldn't have noticed.

Sam had put Ace in his corral and was leading Teddy and Strawberry out to the ten-acre pasture when Jake finally fell in beside her. She slowed down a little so he could keep up.

She turned both horses out and watched them run. With manes and tails lifting on the late-afternoon wind, they were so beautiful, Sam wanted to cry. Instead, she turned on Jake.

"You don't even like Rachel!" she snapped.

Jake gave a self-satisfied smile.

"You're only nice to her because she's cute!"

His smile got a little broader.

"And I'll tell you, Jake Ely, one more clever remark about her *seat* and I would have lost my lunch!"

Jake was trying not to laugh, but he failed. Sam socked him in the arm.

"Ow," he said, and laughed harder.

She stared at him, hoping he'd be embarrassed once he got over being so terribly amused.

"You're right. I don't like her." Jake rubbed his arm. "I'm only nice to her because she's paying *you* money, and for crying out loud, do you just ignore her posting?"

If she hadn't heard Mrs. Ely's car coming across the bridge, Sam might have hit him again. For making sense.

Jealousy and Rachel's slashing remarks about the Phantom came together into something dark and mean inside Sam.

"I'm not speaking to you anymore, Jake Ely. Find someone else to make fun of, okay?"

She turned and walked toward the house.

"Oh, Brat, come back here."

Sam lengthened her stride. She held her head up as if a string ran straight up to the stars pricking through the dusky sky.

It felt good to pay him back.

Chapter 18

BRYNNA CAME FOR DINNER AND STAYED TOO long. Sam was in no mood to watch her and Dad give each other slow, meaningful smiles. Gram must have noticed Sam's irritation, because she asked if Sam wouldn't like to take her dessert upstairs and finish her homework.

Just perfect, Sam thought. Her algebra homework was as baffling as this entire day. She was concentrating so hard, she didn't even hear the phone ring.

Dad came upstairs to tell her, "That was Jake on the phone."

Sam almost snapped that she wasn't speaking to Jake Ely. Ever again. But Dad's formal tone stopped her.

"It was?"

"Yeah." Dad stared at a glass horse on one of her shelves. She'd bought him when she was ten, because he looked like Blackie. "Honey, he has a video he thinks we all should see."

Sam had never left for a neighbor's house this late. Driving through the darkness on a school night might have been fun, except that Brynna was explaining while Dad drove.

"The Elys get the sports channel on their big satellite dish, Sam. Apparently they taped a weekend rodeo wrap-up that included all kinds of highlights, even from dinky little rodeos."

Brynna waited for Sam's brain to brace for what was coming. Finally, she understood.

"Oh no." Sam wanted to cover her ears. "No." She wanted to tell Brynna to stop.

"I'm reserving judgment until I see the tape, but Jake has a good eye for horses, and he thinks, well,

THE RENEGADE

that there's something that needs investigation."

"Enough," Dad said. "We're here."

Once, Sam had been to a gathering after a funeral. Sober-faced ranch families had gathered in a living room. They'd balanced plates of food on their knees, but otherwise it had felt just like this.

All the Ely boys sat straight-backed on chairs and couches. They nodded at Sam. A big wooden bowl filled with popcorn sat, forgotten, as they faced the blank TV set.

Mrs. Ely gave Sam a one-armed hug. Jake's dad, Luke, watched her as if he was afraid she might stumble and break into a million pieces. Of course she didn't stumble or break anything. Unless her heart counted.

First the tape showed clips of a bucking bull spinning until it staggered with dizziness. It showed a calf roper sail over his horse's head and outdistance the running calf.

Those were supposed to be funny, but Sam was so busy lacing her fingers together, to keep them from shaking, that she barely heard the TV announcer's lead-in to the next clip. He said something, she thought, about a young man who'd been injured in a college rodeo.

"This is it," Jake said. "The wild horse race."

Sam wouldn't need a video to remember the Phantom's eyes. The photographer had shot from an odd angle, but the stallion's brown mustang eyes, frightened and accusing, stabbed right through her.

And then the camera pulled back. The Phantom was rearing, reaching for the sky, and the rider was falling. *A rider.* Someone—that boy, that stupid, stupid boy—had been on the Phantom's back. Once the boy fell, the Phantom came back to earth.

It made sense. He'd dislodged the attacker.

Except that the boy wouldn't give in. He made a grab for the Phantom's tail and caught it.

Sam heard a gasp, but she didn't look away from the screen. The Phantom whirled. Mouth agape, he grabbed the boy by the shoulder like he would a misbehaving colt and shook him.

They'll kill my horse, Sam thought. After that, they must have shot him.

Sam felt Dad standing beside her as the screen was filled with the face of Karla Starr. Suddenly, Sam knew that the Phantom was more valuable than ever before.

"Starr Productions regrets the injury to Ben Miller." Karla Starr wore thick eye makeup and red lipstick. Fair flags flapped behind her, but her hair didn't move, and Sam remembered what Jen's mom had said about rodeo queens and hair spray. "We deny any accusations that the Renegade is a man-eater. Such things don't exist in the horse world."

Karla Starr moved closer to the microphone and turned steely eyed. "Rodeo fans can rest assured that when Renegade appears in next Friday's wild horse race, we will prevent such an accident from occurring again."

"Where? *Where?*" Brynna shouted at the television. "Sorry," she said, then threw her French braid over her shoulder and rubbed her palms together before looking at Jake.

"We've played it over and over, Ms. Olson. They don't say."

Sam let Brynna talk to Jake and Nate. She let her consult with Jake's father, who'd spread their coffee table with schedules and charts. He'd already been on the internet and had Karla Starr's next move narrowed down to five West Coast rodeos.

Sam couldn't stop seeing the Phantom's outrage. The boy had climbed on his back, then grabbed his tail. The stallion was a king in his world. He should never be treated like this.

"Wait." Gram spoke for the first time. "Why don't you just go to her ranch?"

"We will. Tomorrow, first thing." But Brynna was shaking her head even as she said it. "If she has any sense at all, and I'm afraid she does, she won't be there. Or the horse won't.

"We're talking about a federal crime. I don't think she'd hand herself and the stallion to us on a silver platter."

Sam woke the next morning, feeling like her head carried an invisible metal helmet. She wanted to stay home from school, but Dad and Gram said no. It was already Tuesday, they reasoned. In just four days, Karla Starr could be trapped—if she was greedier than she was careful.

It would be better, Gram said, if Sam thought about something else. Like school.

But how could she?

Before facing a breakfast she didn't want, Sam fed the hens. How quickly they'd gotten over the loss of the cottonwood tree. Last week, half their world had turned upside down, and they didn't even remember.

Sam wasn't so lucky. She made it through her morning classes. At lunch, she told a shocked Jen what had happened. But when Mr. Blair gave the journalism class a current events quiz, Sam knew she'd flunked. He'd included no questions about drowned cattle, suffering horses, or people who'd do anything for money.

At home, Sam had a message to call Brynna.

"She's not stupid." Sam could hear Brynna tapping a pencil on her desk at Willow Springs. "Her ranch is in good order, and she's got bills of sale on every animal there."

"So, she has him someplace else," Sam said dully.

She hoped the Phantom couldn't wonder why this was happening to him.

"Apparently," Brynna said. "We didn't tell her we had come looking for him. In fact, my ranger just went along with a Humane Society official, as if it were a routine inspection. That way, she may let her guard down and not hide him at the rodeo."

"Do you know which one yet?"

"We're still working on that."

"I want to go with you," Sam insisted.

"Sam, I'll be working."

"If you find him, he'll— Nobody will be able to handle him except me." Sam heard the begging in her own voice, but only part of it was aimed at getting to go. The rest was hope that the Phantom would still love her enough to let her near him.

"I'll talk to your dad," Brynna said finally, and Sam knew that was the best she could hope for.

The Cimarron County Fair had a great carnival. From miles away, Sam and Brynna saw the neon lights marking the spokes on a Ferris wheel and the swoops of a roller coaster.

As they left the BLM truck in the parking lot, they could already smell hot dogs and funnel cakes and hear the happy shrieks of children on thrill rides.

Brynna wore a pale blue shirt and jeans. A cell phone holster was clipped at her waistband. Even out of uniform, she looked official as she surveyed the fairgrounds.

"If we get separated," she told Sam, "this is the midway, there's the exhibit hall, and over there, on the other side of it, are the grandstand and arena. Rodeo security has an office over there."

"I'm not a little kid. I won't wander off." Sam tried not to sound impatient, but Brynna was taking this standing-in-for-Dad responsibility way too seriously. Then again, maybe they were both nervous.

BLM still hadn't found the Phantom. Karla Starr had been contracted to supply stock for the small Cimarron rodeo, but neither she nor the horse she'd called Renegade had been spotted, so rangers had spread out through three states to watch for the stolen silver stallion.

Brynna was working with local law enforcement, and she really didn't want Sam around during her meetings.

"How 'bout if I buy you dinner?" Brynna looked at the watch she'd actually insisted Sam synchronize to hers. "I've got ten minutes before my meeting, twenty until the grand entry, and another hour or so until the wild horse race. We've got plenty of time."

Sam was scanning the throngs of kids clutching strands of ride tickets. She spotted a familiar face.

Darrell wore a yellow jersey, a backward hat, baggy pants that showed his boxer shorts, and a kid attached to one hand. His irritated expression lifted a little when he saw her.

"Hey, Sam, is Jake with you?"

"No, I'm here with—" Sam caught Brynna's frown. Probably she didn't want Sam to be too specific, but Sam knew she was an awful liar. "With my, uh, aunt."

"What a coincidence. I'm here with my cousin."

THE RENEGADE

Darrell held up the hand locked to a freckled boy with untied shoes.

"I wanna go on the Mad Mouse," the child informed Sam.

"That's nice." Sam took a step back. She had on her favorite red blouse, and Darrell's cousin was sticky with what probably had been cotton candy.

"And how old are you?" Brynna asked, but her eyes were sweeping Darrell with disapproval.

"Wanna ride the Mad Mouse," the cousin said again.

"I don't even know what it is," Darrell said. "I'm just here for the drag races after the stupid rodeo ends. This is all Jake's fault, you know. If he was with me, they wouldn't have made me babysit."

The child looked up at Darrell. "I wan-na"—he pronounced the words slowly—"go on—"

"I know, I know," Darrell said. "We'll find it. See ya, Sam."

"About dinner," Brynna said. "I don't feel much like it either, but how about a soda?"

Sam agreed. She watched people throw baseballs at

wooden milk bottles and line up for a haunted house that had walls painted with purple-skinned witches.

Finally, Brynna returned with two cherry Cokes and a cardboard envelope of fried artichoke hearts.

"No thanks," Sam said, but Brynna looked so disappointed, she tried one. They weren't bad.

Brynna kept looking at her watch. Sam tried to count people turning green on the Tilt-A-Whirl instead of wondering where Karla Starr had stashed a stallion who should be running wild.

"I've got to go meet Sheriff Rayburn." Brynna tapped her watch face. "Why don't you go wander around the exhibit hall?"

Sam couldn't imagine anything more boring than looking at peaches canned and squares crocheted by 4-H kids she didn't know.

"I think I'll try that for a little while." Sam pointed at a booth where you could throw Ping-Pong balls at bowls and win the goldfish inside.

Sam saw Brynna hesitate. "I have money," Sam assured her.

"That's not it." Brynna looked around as if she expected a pack of Darrell look-alikes to swagger up.

"I'm thirteen. As long as we have a place and a time to meet, Dad would let me stay." Sam wasn't sure that was true, but it might be.

"In twenty minutes, I'll meet you right there at the gate." Brynna pointed. "There, where they let the barrel racers in and out, where the grand entry—"

"I see it, and I'll be there in twenty minutes. I promise."

"Karla Starr will probably ride in the grand entry, and I need you to help me spot her," Brynna explained.

"I will. I want to catch her more than anyone does. See you later."

"Samantha, I don't feel good about this." Brynna walked away, still talking. "I'll send rodeo security after you if you're not there."

Heads were turning, so Sam just waved. Brynna had gone past responsible and reached obsessed.

Sam had just decided she'd better quit throwing balls, in case she really did win a goldfish and had to take it home balanced between her ankles on the floor of the truck, when someone tugged on her shirt.

It was Darrell's cousin, and he was crying.

"Are you lost?"

Oh no, don't let him be lost. Sam looked at her watch. Eight minutes until she was supposed to meet Brynna. The cousin kept crying and held his arms out for her to pick him up. What was his name, anyway?

Over the merry-go-round music, she shouted, "Where's Darrell?"

"Mad Mouse," the child moaned, and flung his arms toward her more demandingly.

"Did he leave you at the Mad Mouse or what?" Sam picked up the little boy. When he cuddled his head into her shoulder, she couldn't be too mad at him. But she was going to strangle Darrell.

She balanced the child on her hip and jogged toward the arena. She'd passed the exhibit hall when she heard the rodeo announcer.

"And now for our grand entry."

"Let's go see some horses," Sam said, but running

this way was hard, and she wasn't the only one hurrying toward the arena.

Maybe Brynna could send security after Darrell, or have an announcement made. Except that she didn't see Brynna. The chutes were packed with horses for the first event, saddle bronc riding, and though there were plenty of cowboys stretching their legs, rubbing rosin into their gloves and even praying, she didn't see Brynna.

Sam moved toward the grandstand steps and climbed a few for a better view. No Brynna, but out in the arena the equestrians lined up with flags for the national anthem. There, mounted on a big Quarter Horse, sat a rider in aqua sequins with a shooting star on her back.

Karla Starr.

Sam ran back down the stairs.

"Don't bounce!" the child ordered, but she had to find Brynna now.

The arena gates were wide open for the riders to leave the arena, when Brynna shouted and Sam turned.

"There you are! Is that her?" Brynna pointed.

Sam nodded furiously, but the child had her around the neck now, and she could hardly talk.

"Yes," she croaked.

The riders came galloping out and Sam dodged behind Brynna. If Karla Starr saw her, it would be a warning.

When the riders were all through, the gates slammed closed.

"And now, folks, a little change in our program. The Cimarron County rodeo is pleased to have Miss Karla Starr, former Best of the West rodeo queen and current president of Starr Rodeo Productions, as contractor for our little show. Miss Starr is proud of her stock, and because of some unfortunate publicity about her stallion, Renegade—"

"He's here!" Sam gasped.

Brynna was already shouting into her radio, trying to be heard over the noise all around.

"—directly across the arena, you'll see our cowboys all lined up. Give 'em a hand, folks, and watch the gate swing open for our rough-and-tumble, best-ever wild horse race!"

Chapter 19

HEAD HIGH, MUSCLES PUMPING, THE PHAN-tom exploded into the arena. The silver stallion claimed the attention of every person sitting in the stands.

At once, the crowd recognized the difference between a bucking horse and a wild mustang. He fled the dark, skyless place in which he'd been kept, following the wall of the arena as he would the high cliffs of home.

His desire to escape hardened every line of his body, making him beautiful despite his matted mane and dirt-smeared coat.

But he was muzzled.

Sam's head snapped back. They'd muzzled the great stallion like a dog.

It seemed she'd watched him for only a minute, while the world spun around her in a blur of color and music, but two of the teams had saddled their bucking horses and crossed the finish line. The others had given up.

One man in a blue shirt threw his hat in the dirt as the Phantom rounded the arena again. The stallion shied from the hat and ran toward a weak barrier where a calf-roping horse stood waiting. It must have looked like an opening, but it wasn't.

As the Phantom slowed, the man in blue saw his chance and grabbed the rope trailing from the stallion's muzzled head. Another man joined him, and then there were three, hanging on to the rope in a tug-of-war as the stallion bucked.

It was unfair, until the Phantom charged.

Dropping the rope, the men scattered with the stallion in pursuit. Others reached hands down for the men to grab. Two of the men were pulled over the fence to safety.

A neigh floated across the arena, and the voice of that bucking horse made the Phantom swerve.

Was it an offer of help? Sam didn't know, but the stallion answered by galloping in that direction, even when he could see no way out. As his broad chest slammed into the chute, Sam felt it in her own heart.

Enough. She had to help him.

"Here." Suddenly aware of the child she was still holding, Sam shoved Darrell's cousin at Brynna.

"Sam, you're not—"

Some instinct made Brynna drop her radio to keep the child from falling. Relieved, Sam loosened her grip and escaped before Brynna could stop her.

She ran. Past all the closed arena gates, past the faces of people she squirmed between. Sam ran until she could duck under a metal fence, into a maze of rails.

Brynna wouldn't follow her down this channel to the bucking chutes, because she wouldn't know where it led. These were just like the chutes she and Dallas had inspected at the Riverton and Sweetwater rodeos, only these were empty.

Sam heard the thunder of the Phantom's hooves. She was getting closer. She had to get into the arena before he hurt someone. What if he'd already trampled the man on the ground?

The smell of animals and manure told her she was getting closer. And still no one had followed.

All at once, Sam saw why.

A Brahma bull filled the space between the fences so completely, he couldn't turn. But he knew she was there. He bucked up, looking over the hump of flesh on his back to fix Sam with a glare.

"Maniac!" Sam gasped, transfixed by the mask of black and orange stripes on the bull's face.

She didn't have time to think what it meant, that Linc Slocum's bull was here. So was Karla Starr. And the Phantom. It all fit together somehow.

Maniac uttered a rumbling protest. Did he think she was attacking him from behind? Whatever the massive bull thought, he was furious. He loomed over her, coming as fast as a truck in reverse, intent on running her down.

"It's okay, boy," Sam shouted. "It's okay."

Conversation wasn't going to work. He had no reason to think a human meant him well, she guessed, so Sam jumped for her way out.

Her fingers locked on a metal fence rail; then she pulled herself up, hand over hand, tennis shoes searching for each foothold. Maniac backed past her. She knew by the warm blast of breath and the splatter of moisture on the back of her favorite red blouse.

Over the top. Sam sprinted across the next narrow chute, over one more fence, and slid down the wall into the arena.

The Phantom saw her at once. The nervous pacing that had taken him around and around the arena stopped. He was still for only a minute, and then he rushed across the arena.

Sam heard gasps from the grandstands and shouts summoning help, but she watched her horse. He galloped, head swinging from side to side, then lowered in a snaking, herding motion.

The Phantom stopped about six feet from her, and though every proud line of his body told Sam it was him, something was wrong. The stallion's head cocked to one side, then rose, eyes rolling, as if he couldn't see her clearly. Every sign of horse language she'd learned to read was scrambled.

More commotion rustled through the grandstands as the stallion arched his neck and pranced a circle around her. Some people caught their breath with awe. A few even clapped, thinking this was a performance.

In a way it was, but Sam turned, always facing the stallion, because she knew what came next. She'd seen this ritual both times the Phantom had fought Hammer.

There. A front leg struck out in challenge, and then he charged. Sam didn't close her eyes. He passed within inches, head swinging out as if to bite, and the metal muzzle slammed into Sam's shoulder. She felt the impact, no pain, and a fierce stab of shame that the stallion might have bitten her if he could have.

The Phantom ran past, and from the corner of her

eye, Sam saw a pickup man on a big dun horse, poised to help. She swallowed hard.

The Phantom pivoted and walked back. He looked calmer and he talked to her in a low, rumbling nicker, but his eyes still rolled, showing white around the brown.

Sam's world shrank to just this moment, just this horse. Everything depended on her skill at understanding him.

The stallion's forelegs braced apart, and his head hung, mane falling forward, forelock covering his eyes. Sam made a quiet smooching, and he staggered forward a step.

Inside the metal muzzle, the stallion's velvety lips moved. He lifted his head as if he might have nuzzled her if he could.

"Zanzibar, boy, what have they done to you?"

Grandstand sounds covered her voice, but the stallion's ears pricked forward. He heard her. He knew her. He tried to come to her, but he had taken only two steps when he fell to his knees.

Unafraid, Sam ran to him. She ignored the rope trailing

from his halter. Instead, she placed a hand on his withers.

"My poor boy," Sam murmured. The stallion's skin shivered at her touch, and he lurched up again.

With careful movements, Sam reached over the stallion's crest and lifted the halter over his ears. As it fell off his nose, the mustang shuddered. Sam wanted to grab the awful thing and throw it as far as her strength would let her. But that would shatter the Phantom's calm, so she just stroked him silently.

Through her dismay, Sam heard Brynna's voice.

"Sam, over here."

A gate swung open on oiled hinges, revealing a small pen. Seeing a way out, the stallion made for it.

The arena was silent as the stallion swayed step by step. Twice, he fell to his knees. Both times, Sam stood with her hand on his mane, talking, encouraging.

When the Phantom reached the enclosure and the gate closed behind him, his head flew up. A low cry said he recognized this final trap. In despair, he fell to his knees, to his side, and lay still.

Brynna grabbed Sam before she could get in the way of the team of vets who stood waiting. They swooped down upon the gray stallion, rolling back an eyelid, hydrating him, monitoring his pulse and heartbeat.

Sam didn't know how long she watched before Brynna tried to explain.

"Drugs," Brynna said as she turned Sam to face her. "Karla Starr uses drugs to sedate her stock and to make them perform. She gave the Phantom something she calls Mad Dust. She cups it in her palms and blows it toward their nostrils."

Sam closed her eyes against an image of the copper-haired woman working black magic on the mustang.

"She claims it's legal. She also claims Slocum told her the stallion was his, and if she could catch him, she could have him—if she made Maniac a champion."

"He's here," Sam whispered. "Maniac, I mean." But she was watching the Phantom's legs twitch.

One of the vets spoke soothingly, though the stallion was unconscious. The vet's kindness made tears start up in Sam's eyes.

"We've impounded Maniac." Brynna's professional tone fell away for just a moment. "Tell me I didn't see right, that you weren't actually in the same chute with him, Samantha?"

Sam shook her head, and Brynna sighed.

"Never mind. The important thing is, you're all right, and Karla Starr will have a lot to answer for in court, and the bureau will pursue this case. I know it."

But that wasn't the important thing to Sam. She put her hand out to still Brynna as the Phantom's legs churned more vigorously.

The kind vet she'd noticed before rose from his place beside the horse and came toward them. He was young and blond, with black-rimmed glasses, and his expression was full of hope.

"So far, so good," he said. "It's a blessing, really, that he's out, so we can work on him without causing further stress."

"Will he—" Sam couldn't ask the questions tumbling through her mind.

"His respiration is fine, and his reflexes, though delayed,

are improving. My name's Glen Scott, by the way."

He shook hands with Sam and Brynna, then glanced at the stocky woman who still sat by the horse while she talked on a cell phone. Just then she gave him a thumbs-up.

"We've got a horse ambulance on the way, and if the stallion keeps improving, we'd recommend releasing him back to his environment as soon as possible."

"Dr. Scott"—Brynna's tone was hesitant—"don't you think he should be kept someplace overnight, for observation?"

Glen Scott shook his head and pushed his black glasses up his nose. Sam almost smiled, because he reminded her of Jen.

"That would mean more captivity and even more drugs." He looked earnest and determined to convince Brynna. "Get another opinion if you like. But after what he's been through . . ." The vet shook his head.

"What about a week or two at the holding pens in Willow Springs? That would be safer," Brynna suggested.

"The life of a wild animal is never safe." Dr. Scott

scanned the nearby pens, seeming to weigh the lives of the captive animals around them. "I think it will do more harm than good to keep him locked up. Why not drive all night, let him wake close to home, and release him?"

Home. Sam could picture the stallion, suddenly freed and galloping on the range where he belonged. The Phantom would face a challenger in his valley, though, and New Moon was young and strong.

Brynna turned to Sam. "It's your call, honey. What do you want for him?"

Safety or freedom? It should have been a simple choice. Safety meant the stallion's life would be filled with longing. Freedom might mean Sam had lost him forever.

She moved away from Brynna and crouched beside the Phantom. She'd never seen him down like this. It frightened her. She laid a hand on his neck. Beneath the sweat-stiff hair, his tiny blood vessels pulsed.

She'd heard of people who'd faced a firing squad and not been shot. Some never lost the fear they'd felt when they'd believed death was certain. Would the Phantom be the same? Would he have the strength to drive New Moon away when the young horse had already served as king?

The Phantom lifted his head. His eyelids fluttered, and then he lay still again.

"Bad dreams," the vet said. "His vital signs are improving all the time. Don't worry."

The Phantom trusted her. Terrified and filled with drugs, he'd come to her, allowed her to lead him from the arena by a piece of mane and the gentle pressure of her hand.

"Let's take him home," Sam said.

She leaned down and pressed her lips to his silver neck. It was a good-bye kiss. The Phantom would be safest if she never touched him again.

One mile past War Drum Flats, the sun rose and the desert turned tawny orange.

They'd driven all night. With the light, Sam saw frost edging the sagebrush at the roadside. It was cold out there and warm in the cab of Brynna's truck, but Sam shoved the door open and ran to the horse ambulance the minute the vehicle braked to a stop.

Hooves pounded inside, and the Phantom screamed. Sounds that would have horrified her two weeks ago made Sam glad. He was awake and strong and ready to be free.

Dr. Scott met Sam behind the vehicle. The stallion's neigh vibrated the ambulance. His kicks rocked it. The vet rubbed his hands together and blew on them. Cold, but heartened by the mustang's vigor, he smiled as he surveyed the high desert landscape.

"It's gorgeous out here," he said. "And I think this mustang smells home."

Sam nodded and followed the vet's glance as he watched Brynna stride nearer.

"Last chance to take him up to Willow Springs," Brynna told Sam. "We could keep him there until we've removed the black from the herd. Kind of ease the transition."

Staring at the dark road, their headlights the only

light for miles, they'd talked about this for hours last night, and Sam's answer never changed.

"No." She shook her head. That would mean revealing the Phantom's hideaway. Never again would his mares and foals be safe. "It's time."

Metal bolts clanged. Hinges squeaked.

The stallion backed out, kicking. Brynna, Sam, and the vet stepped away, but not far enough. The Phantom's head snaked toward the humans, scattering them farther off.

Sam didn't speak. She didn't try to soothe him. That part of their friendship was over.

The great silver stallion swung to face the mountains. He took a single breath, loosed a mighty neigh, and launched himself away. In what felt like seconds, only a white spiral of dust nearly a mile away suggested that a mustang traveled a narrow zigzag trail.

The stallion didn't look back and Sam didn't cry.

She didn't reply when Brynna spoke to her either, or join in her thanks to Dr. Scott, although she wanted to.

Instead, she stared at the ground, where a faint sifting

of sand had caught the Phantom's running hoofprints. Shallow and far apart, they held morning light and tiny shadows. She walked the path he had taken until the ground hardened and she lost her way.

Behind her, Sam heard Brynna tell Dr. Scott the BLM would be in touch regarding the cost of doctoring the mustang. She should go back, but she wanted to hang on to the Phantom for just a few minutes more.

Sam heard a screech and looked up. She squinted, letting her eyelashes filter the brightness enough that she could watch the red-tailed hawk wheel in a dark silhouette against the morning sun.

A messenger to the sky spirits. That was what Jake had told her just before the flash flood struck. She hadn't wished then, but now she did.

"I don't want him to be gone forever," Sam whispered. "I just want to see him. I love his wildness. I'll never try to take it away."

She closed her dazzled eyes. A frenzy of multicolored lights from staring at the sun made her dizzy. When she opened her lids, the hawk was gone.

THE RENEGADE

Sam trudged back toward Brynna's truck. The horse ambulance was bouncing away, leaving twin wisps of dust behind. Brynna must be waiting in her truck.

There was no sense putting it off. It was time for her to go home too. Sam hurried, then hesitated. She detoured just a little to her right, to see what lay on the ground.

Was the sun still playing tricks with her vision? Sam refused to believe her eyes until she stood right over it. Between her dirty tennis shoes lay a feather. It glinted red-brown and glossy against the white desert floor.

She smiled and bent to pick it up. Between thumb and forefinger, she held the feather's spine, then smoothed her fingers along the perfect plume.

The red-tailed hawk had given her a sign.

Sam's wish for the silver stallion had been heard.

Read on for an excerpt from Sam's journal!

Dear Mom,

What is wrong with the Slocum family? Jake and I rode to Rachel's rescue today, and not only was she ungrateful (it's not like I wanted a reward, but a sincere thank you would've been nice), but her dad didn't seem to be grateful either. Rachel took off on Champ because even though she's told me horses are dumb and dirty, she wants to be a rodeo queen. She talked to Karla Starr, a rodeo contractor, and then all of a sudden it's Rachel's goal to see herself in sequins, riding into an arena of cheering fans. She says it's a way to surprise her dad and show her twin that she's as good as he is. I should think that's pitiful, but I don't. When Jake was reading hoofprints and came to a spot where he said Rachel probably went over

Champ's head, I thought it was funny. Of all people, I shouldn't think a fall from a horse is something to joke about, but the picture of Rachel sitting in the dust in her designer jeans made me smile.

Besides, she was riding beautiful palomino Champ with a spade bit. Jake and I could tell from the blood on Champ's mouth that Rachel didn't know how delicate, how careful you have to be with that bit. It's supposed to be used so gently, no one can even see your hands move. It's a beautiful bit with etched silver shanks—really a work of art—and I bet that's all Rachel saw. But that's on the outside. Inside, there's a piece of metal that rests against the horse's tongue until you pull the reins, and then it rocks up against the roof of their mouth. You probably know that, Mom, but I'm sure Rachel never thought to look.

Rachel can't say a word without acting superior. I told Gram that Rachel said one of us should dismount so she could take the horse one of us was riding to get home. I also told Gram about Linc.

When I sort of hinted that he should teach Rachel to handle Champ (like he'd know, but there's Jen, her mom, and her dad), he got all squinty-eyed and said yeah, that's what they were missing around there, a smart girl like me to tell everyone what to do.

You know that's not what I meant. Gram knew it too. At least I thought so, but she kept quiet for so long I wasn't sure and I asked, "Do you think she just gets it from her father?"

Then Gram was STILL quiet, like she was telling herself, "If you can't say something nice, don't say anything at all."

Finally she said, "Samantha, the way that family acts? It's not about you."

Dear Mom,
Today Dallas was sweet-talking his old horse Amigo. He's a pretty sorrel, but his coat is starting to look kind of dusty, with gray around his muzzle and eyes. I don't know how long Dallas has had him, but I can remember a time when my eyes were even with Amigo's knees, so you probably knew him too. Dallas put Amigo out to pasture when he was twenty-five

years old, because we have plenty of working horses and Amigo deserved a rest. But Dallas told me that Amigo is the only horse in the world he'd trust with his life. I guess that means if I see him riding Amigo, I should worry!

Dear Mom,
I wish you were here to help me figure out why the Phantom is acting so weird. I also wish I knew whether you could see everything going on down here. Should I blame myself for making the Phantom too tame? I really don't think so. He's not trotting up to me like a pet pony. No. He popped up when Jake and I were rescuing Rachel

and just stared at me. I don't count any time he comes to La Charla at night, because that's our place and time together, but today he came to the BUS STOP! He had to feel the asphalt under his hooves and feel the wind as a car went rushing by. He must've heard the kids inside the bus pounding on the windows, even if it was kind of muffled. And Jen and our bus driver were right there. You know it's true: that's just not a situation a wild horse would put himself in on purpose unless there was some reason! If he was hurt, it might make sense. Blaze comes to us and whines and holds his paw up when he gets a sticker in it. But the Phantom looked totally fine. I feel like he wants something from me, and I don't know what it is.

Dear Mom,

Today was almost the worst day of my life. If I'd messed up, Jake could be dead. Gram says I should be proud of myself, but how? I can't make my hands stop shaking, and I keep taking these shuddery breaths, and proud is far, far away. I'm just working toward relieved.

    It was raining so hard, and Teddy galloped, and I keep hearing his hooves splatting on the ground. I think that dirt was clay or something. And then Teddy was sliding. The impact of Teddy, that whole horse slamming down on Jake—I don't think I'll ever forget it. Jake didn't yell or gasp or anything, but I knew it was bad.

    I've never felt so helpless, but I couldn't be

helpless because I was the only help Jake had, the only one standing out in the rain looking down at him. His eyes were closed and his hair was spread out, all black over the blue-brown mud, and when his eyes did finally open, he looked at me with this confidence. Like he knew I could help! ME! The one he treats like a tenderfoot and is always calling "Brat."

Maybe this is how fate works. Jake had to take care of me when I fell off Blackie, and today I had to take care of him.

This page is probably going to rip. It's all wet.

But I didn't cry then. The first aid class I took at the Y in San Francisco came rushing back. Was he breathing? Yes. Was he bleeding? Oh, heck yes. His pant leg was soaked with blood. Could I give treatment in a safe place? Ha! If this place was safe, Jake wouldn't be under a horse! I took calming breaths. I heard him try to do the same. I kept asking him questions, but inside I was screaming. The way his jaw was clenched told me he was in terrible pain.

But then he asked about his horse. And his hat. Oh, Jake, your hat?

And we did it. Jake and Teddy, Ace and I made it home. Jake is going to be okay. He'll be in a cast for his birthday, but who cares?

Dear Mom,
I can't go to sleep. I close my eyes and I see Jake on the ground in the ranch yard.

"How long ago did it happen?" Dad's asking me.

Jake's eyes are open, looking up into the gray sky. Raindrops hit his face and he says, "How long? Well, Sam didn't dillydally around."

Dillydally. He knows how I hate that fake Western talk, but I couldn't get the words out to tell him to shut up.

And then Teddy snorts and yanks back to the end of his reins as Dallas is coaxing him, trying to lead him to the barn. Jake turns to look just like I am, but he gasps. Still, he isn't done acting all tough. "Sam cowgirled up and got me here before—"

"That's enough, Jake," Dad tells him.

"—before the m-mud dried..."

And then Gram shows up holding a blue-speckled mug full of water. I see two oblong pills cupped in her hand. Jake coughs taking them and reaches for his leg instead of his throat. In a couple of minutes he looks almost limp. They load him into the Buick and take him to town.

Mom, why wouldn't they let me go with him? I'm shaking again. But I wanted to squeeze myself into the back seat, or crouch on the floor. I wouldn't have jostled him and made him hurt. I just think Jake might've felt better if I was there with him.

Sam's Dictionary

PONY: This means leading a horse—of whatever size—while you're riding another horse. It's not as easy as it sounds, because the rider has to pay attention to two horses. With luck, you're riding the calmer horse. You might want to do this if you're leading a child's horse with the child onboard or giving an untrained horse like Dark Sunshine some exercise outside a corral.

HIGH-SPURRING COWBOY: In rodeo competitions, riders wear metal spurs on the back of their boots. The instant the gate to the chute opens, the rider has to touch the spurs above the horse's shoulder and then rake the spurs down. Dallas says some horses are trained or bred to buck, but the high spurring above the shoulder makes them buck harder. Rules for professional rodeos say any rider wearing spurs that will cut the horse will be disqualified.

RIATA: This is a braided rawhide rope. Dallas is the only cowboy at River Bend who uses one. They're usually twice as long as the ropes most cowboys use, and working with one takes a lot of skill. The name comes from Spanish, because the first riatas were used by California vaqueros.

OFF AND NEAR HOOVES: The horse's left is his near side, the right his off side. We lead horses, do up their tack, and mount from the near side. Believe it or not, this all goes back to the days of wearing swords on horseback.

LOUD-COLORED: A horse's coat color doesn't really have a sound, but if a horse is pinto, paint, or Appaloosa, it's considered loud-colored. Some people use "loud" for buckskins and bright red or blue roans, too, or any horse that isn't bay, black, or sorrel.

Don't miss the next Phantom Stallion

READ & LEARN
with *simon* kids

Keep your child reading, learning, and having fun with Simon Kids!

A one-stop shop where you can **find downloadable resources, watch interactive author videos, browse books by reading level, and more!**

Visit us at
SimonandSchusterPublishing.com/ReadandLearn/

And follow us @SimonKids

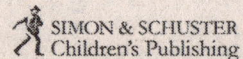

The Wild One

TERRI FARLEY
PHANTOM STALLION

The Wild One

ALADDIN
New York London Toronto Sydney New Delhi

If you purchased this book without a cover, you should be aware that this book is stolen property. It was reported as "unsold and destroyed" to the publisher, and neither the author nor the publisher has received any payment for this "stripped book."

This book is a work of fiction. Any references to historical events, real people, or real places are used fictitiously. Other names, characters, places, and events are products of the author's imagination, and any resemblance to actual events or places or persons, living or dead, is entirely coincidental.

ALADDIN
An imprint of Simon & Schuster Children's Publishing Division
1230 Avenue of the Americas, New York, New York 10020
This Aladdin paperback edition March 2023
Text copyright © 2002 by Terri Sprenger-Farley
Cover illustration copyright © 2023 by Louise Meijer-Åström
Map on pages vi–vii copyright © 2023 by Francesca Baerald
Illustration of notebook on pages 281–300 by aopsan/iStock
Also available in an Aladdin hardcover edition.
All rights reserved, including the right of reproduction in whole or in part in any form.
ALADDIN and related logo are registered trademarks of Simon & Schuster, Inc.
For information about special discounts for bulk purchases, please contact Simon & Schuster Special Sales at 1-866-506-1949 or business@simonandschuster.com.
The Simon & Schuster Speakers Bureau can bring authors to your live event. For more information or to book an event contact the Simon & Schuster Speakers Bureau at 1-866-248-3049 or visit our website at www.simonspeakers.com.
Designed by Tiara Iandiorio
The text of this book was set in Adobe Garamond Pro.
Manufactured in the United States of America 0223 OFF
10 9 8 7 6 5 4 3 2 1
Library of Congress Control Number 2022933538
ISBN 9781665916325 (hc)
ISBN 9781665916318 (pbk)
ISBN 9781665916332 (ebook)

This book is dedicated to Barbara and
Bob Sprenger, who let me talk to horses

Chapter 1

AT FIRST, SAM THOUGHT SHE WAS SEEING things. The windshield of Dad's truck was pitted by years of windblown dust. Maybe she'd been away from the ranch so long, the desert sun was playing tricks on her eyes.

Suddenly, she knew better.

Mustangs stampeded over the ridgetop. They ran down the steep hillside. As their hooves touched level ground, a helicopter bobbed up behind them.

It hovered like a giant dragonfly.

As she watched the herd, Sam saw one creamy mane flickering amid the dark necks of the other horses. She saw a black horse shining like glass and two roans running side by side. Here and there ran foals, nostrils wide with effort.

Sam wondered if the men hovering above could see each running horse, or only a flowing mass of animals.

The mustangs ran for the open range. Sam knew the horses would find little shade and less water ahead, but they seemed to think of nothing except outrunning the men and their machine.

The herd swung left. The helicopter swooped, ten feet off the sand, to block them.

The herd galloped right. With a whirring sound, the helicopter followed.

Then, from the back of the herd, a silver stallion raced forward. Sam never imagined a horse could be so beautiful, but there he was. He nipped and screamed, turning the mares in a wide U back under the helicopter's belly, running to the hills and safety.

The helicopter pulled up. It banked into a turn and followed, but it was too late.

"Wow! Where did they go?" Sam's thigh muscles tensed. She sat inside her dad's truck, but her knees shook as if she'd been running with the wild horses.

"Mustangs have their secret getaway trails. They go places even a chopper can't." Dad took one hand off the steering wheel to pull his Stetson down to shade his eyes.

Sam cleared her throat and looked out the window at dull, brown Nevada. Could she have felt homesick for this?

Yes. Every day of the past two years, an ache had grown under her breastbone.

She just wished Dad would talk more. She wanted to hear about the ranch and the horses and Gram. But the nearer they got to the ranch, the more he acted like the dad she remembered. Relaxed and quiet, he was completely *un*like the awkward man who'd come to visit in Aunt Sue's polished San Francisco apartment.

Since he'd picked Sam up—literally off her feet in the middle of the airport—their conversation had bumped along just like this old truck. Slow, but sure.

"Shouldn't use helicopters and trucks," Dad muttered. "They just don't savvy mustangs."

Translated, that meant he had no respect for men who didn't understand the wild horses they were capturing and taking off the range.

Dad really talked like a cowboy. And his first name was Wyatt, a cowboy name if she'd ever heard one. Plus, he walked with the stiff grace of a man who'd ridden all his life.

When he'd first sent her to the city, Sam had been so angry, she'd tried to forget Dad. For a while, it had been easy.

After her accident, the doctors had said Sam might suffer "complications." When a girl fell from a galloping horse and her head was struck by a hoof, that was bad. When she lost consciousness as well, they explained, it was far worse.

Fear made Dad agree to send Sam away from the ranch to live with Aunt Sue. In San Francisco, she was only two minutes away from a hospital instead of two hours.

First Sam had begged to stay; then she'd turned stubborn and refused to go. But Dad was just as stubborn. He wouldn't take no for an answer. Since she'd barely turned eleven, Dad had won.

After a few lonely weeks, she'd learned to love San Francisco. Aunt Sue's willingness to take her everywhere and show her everything eased the pain of leaving home, but it couldn't make her forget Blackie.

Blackie had been the first horse who was all her own. She'd raised him through a rocky colthood, gentled him to accept her as his rider, then made a terrible mistake that injured her and frightened him into escape.

Each time Dad called her in San Francisco, Sam asked for word of Blackie. But the swift two-year-old had vanished.

In time, Sam stopped asking. She and Blackie had hurt each other. She'd been unable to go after him and touch him and explain. So Blackie had followed his mustang heart back to the wild country.

Although Aunt Sue didn't ride, she did share Sam's passion for movies. Sam made friends at her middle school, too, and played basketball in a YMCA league. It wasn't long before the months had added up to two years.

Still, movies and basketball couldn't measure up to Sam's memories of riding the range, fast and free. Sam never stopped loving horses and missing them. When Dad announced it was safe to come home, Sam had started packing.

Now Sam sneaked another look at Dad. In San Francisco, she'd been embarrassed by him. She'd worried that her city friends would hear his buckaroo slang, or take a good look at his face, all brown and lean as beef jerky. If they had, they would have known Dad for what he was: a cowboy.

But here in Nevada, he fit in, and it was easier for her to see she had a lot in common with him. They were both skinny, tanned, and stubborn.

"You really liked living in San Francisco?" Dad asked.

"After I got used to the fog and traffic, I loved it. I jogged in Golden Gate Park with Aunt Sue and we saw at least three movies every weekend."

Dad glanced her way with eyes as cold as a Hollywood gunfighter's. He hated the city.

Sam shrugged as if she didn't care. If he'd left the ranch more often to visit her, this wouldn't be so awkward. She and Dad might have a lot in common, but when he asked questions like that, hard-eyed and expecting a certain answer, Sam felt like a stranger.

She crossed one knee over the other and jiggled her foot. She ignored Dad's frown, which said he was disappointed that his daughter had become such a city slicker.

"Not far to River Bend, now," Dad said.

As if she didn't know they were near the ranch. She couldn't wait to see if it was the horse paradise she remembered. She only hoped she could still ride like she had before the accident.

She remembered so little of that moment. Falling. Breathing dust. Impact just over her right ear. The sound of Blackie's hooves galloping away, fading, gone. The accident wouldn't keep her from riding, because she wasn't afraid. She *wasn't*.

Sam fanned herself, wishing she hadn't worn black

jeans and a black T-shirt. What was fashionable in San Francisco might be considered weird in rural Nevada.

She blew her bangs out of her eyes. Using Aunt Sue's sewing scissors, Sam had cut off her reddish-brown ponytail. She didn't want to look like the child Dad had sent away.

She straightened to look at herself in the truck's mirror. She'd accomplished her goal, all right. She didn't look like a little kid; she looked like a teenager with a bad haircut.

Sam shifted against her seat belt, stared out the truck's back window, and blinked.

Half-hidden in dust stood a horse. His powerful shoulders glittered in the sun, convincing her he was the silver stallion who'd turned the herd, but he had the dished face and flaring nostrils of an Arabian. She hadn't seen a horse that perfect since—

"Sam?" Dad's voice hit like a bucket of cold water. "What are you staring at, honey?"

Sam looked at Dad. Then, before she told him, Sam turned back around to make sure of what she'd seen.

"Uh, nothing," she said. The horse had disappeared. Had it been a mirage?

Never mind. In minutes she'd be at River Bend and she'd have a horse of her own again.

Still, Sam couldn't help glancing back over her shoulder one last time. The first place she'd ride would be here, wherever *here* was, to find that ghost horse.

Sam saw a metallic glint against the sky. The helicopter was still searching.

Sam worried about the mustangs. Even a city girl knew how some cattle ranchers accused mustangs of eating all the grass and drinking water holes dry. A newspaper article she'd taken to class for Current Events had told how wild horses roaming Nevada's range were rounded up with government helicopters, then penned until they were adopted.

Sam remembered that half the girls in class had waved their hands over their heads, volunteering to take wild horses into their apartments or carports. Now here she was with wild horses practically in her front yard.

"I can't wait to get you up on Ace." Dad nodded,

smiling. Apparently, he wasn't holding a grudge because she liked San Francisco. "You two are a match for sure."

Ace. Could there be a more perfect name for a cow pony? Sam had to smile. Dad said Ace "stuck to a calf like a burr on a sheep's tail." She supposed that meant Ace was a good cutting horse, able to separate the calves from the herd.

"I wish you had a picture of Ace."

Dad laughed. "And have him get conceited around the other horses? That'd mean trouble for sure."

Dad squinted through the windshield as a flashy tan Cadillac drove straight at them, honking.

"Speaking of trouble . . ." Dad shook his head and coasted to a stop.

"Who is it?" Sam tried to read Dad's face. "Don't you want to talk to him?"

"I'd rather take a shortcut over quicksand."

The Cadillac's window eased down, revealing the driver.

"Hey, Wyatt." The driver had slick hair and a toothpaste-commercial grin. His cowboy hat was as big as one of Dad's truck tires. "This must be Samantha. Welcome, little lady."

No one called her Samantha—just Sam—but one thing Dad insisted upon was being courteous to adults. Sam smiled and wondered if she was supposed to recognize this guy.

"On your way to town?" Dad sounded neighborly, but his back looked stiff.

The man slumped back in his seat, all relaxed, and Sam nearly groaned. A horse of her own waited at the ranch. She wanted to see Ace, run her hands over his neck and smell the alfalfa sweetness of his soft nose. And this guy looked like he'd settled in for a long chat. When he lit a cigarette and threw his match on the desert floor, she knew she was right.

"Sam, this is Linc Slocum." Dad sighed.

"I'm your new neighbor, Samantha." The man nodded. "Even though we've never met, I've heard lots of stories about you and that one-man horse of yours that escaped."

One-girl *horse*, Sam corrected silently. Blackie had

bonded with her, because she'd used the Shoshone horse-taming tricks her pal Jake Ely had taught her. She'd breathed into the colt's nostrils so he'd know her scent, she'd mounted him for the first time in water, and she'd called him by a secret name.

After the accident, lying in a hospital bed, Sam had worried that no one could call Blackie back. Her mind kept replaying the sound of his hooves galloping, then fading away, but she'd told no one the colt's secret name.

How could a stranger know Blackie had been a one-girl horse?

Dad's voice interrupted her memories. "Nice seein' you, Linc, but we'd better head on."

Even when Dad started to drive, Linc kept talking. That's when Sam knew Linc Slocum was no cowboy. Real cowboys hardly talked, even when they had something to say.

"If it hadn't been for that danged Jake—"

Confusion nipped at Sam's memory. She'd let *Jake* down, failing to ride Blackie right, but it sounded like Mr. Slocum blamed Jake for the accident.

Clearly, Dad didn't like Linc's implication.

Dad bumped his Stetson up from his brow and faced Linc Slocum head-on. Sam couldn't see Dad's expression, but Slocum pulled back like a turtle jerking its head in.

"Old news," Slocum said, but his smile slipped.

Sam shivered as if someone had sprinkled a handful of spiders down the neck of her shirt.

"Maybe he'll come home," Linc said.

Sam bit her lip. She knew better, but Dad's words still hurt.

"Don't get your hopes up," Dad said. "The wild ones never come back."

Chapter 2

BOARDS RUMBLED UNDER DAD'S TIRES AS HE crossed the bridge over the water that gave River Bend Ranch its name. Sam breathed the scent of sagebrush as they rolled under the tall wooden rectangle marking the ranch entrance.

A black dog with a white ruff ran barking toward the truck.

"That's Blaze," Dad said. "He sleeps in the bunkhouse most of the time, but it looks like he's come to welcome you."

THE WILD ONE

A cowboy yell split the summer silence.

Sam glanced left. She saw only a huge grassy pasture and horses grazing peacefully.

"Come on, now!" the same voice shouted again.

To her right, Sam saw the ranch house, white with green shutters. White curtains billowed from the upstairs window of her bedroom.

But all the racket was coming from a round corral straight ahead.

As Dad pulled up next to the corral, Sam heard thudding hooves. She climbed down from the truck in time to see her old buddy Jake fly over a horse's buck-lowered head. Jake cartwheeled through the air and skidded to a stop on the seat of his jeans. Dust rolled around him.

Sam peered through the log fence rails, then planted one shoe on the lowest one and climbed until she saw over the top.

A sassy paint mare stamped and snorted in the corner. Her intelligent eyes studied the rider she'd thrown. Then she blew a whuffling breath through her lips.

Jake ignored the mare and looked toward Sam. The

instant after she realized he'd turned handsome, Sam remembered how Jake used to trick her, tease her, and stare down his nose as if she were a lower life-form.

And she'd deserved every bit of bullying. Jake lived on the nearby Three Ponies Ranch and only put up with her because he liked riding. Jake was the youngest of six brothers. At home, the oldest boys had dibs on fun chores, like working horses. As the youngest, Jake had to collect hens' eggs and mend wire fences. So he chose to ride over to River Bend each morning, where Dad let him train young horses.

Something about Jake just brought out the pest in her. There he sat, bucked off before her very eyes. Sam was usually speechless around cute guys, but she couldn't resist teasing him.

"Oh, Jake, what's wrong?" Sam said in a singsong voice, like the little kid she'd been.

Dad slouched against the fence rails beside her and chuckled. "I'd say you just missed a good chance to keep your mouth shut, Sam."

Behind her a screen door closed. Hens scratched

and cackled. The scent of cooking wafted on the wind.

When Jake stood up, he looked a lot older than sixteen. He was almost smiling as he slapped his cowboy hat against his leg, knocking off dust. Then he resettled it on the black hair he'd pulled back with a leather shoelace.

"Well, if it ain't Samantha." Jake walked toward the fence. He wore chinks, fringed leather leg coverings like short chaps. "Still skinnier than a wet weasel, aren't you, Sam?"

Jake *had* to remember his fake drawl made her crazy, but it was weird that Linc Slocum's respectful "little lady" made her bristle and Jake's insult made her laugh.

"Jake, you leave Sam alone till she's had a chance to catch her breath." Grandma Grace slipped around the side of the corral. She wore a denim skirt with a pale blue blouse. Sam noticed its pattern of little red hearts just before a hug closed around her.

"Gram." Sam's throat felt tight, but she fought back tears. She didn't need to look like a wimp already.

Gram had emailed Sam every week she'd been

gone. Almost all the ranch news Sam had received came from Gram.

"Besides, Sam looks like a nice young lady. Not a weasel." Gram touched Sam's hair, reminding her of the mistake she'd made cutting it. "You'll see that for yourself, Jake, when you've showered up for lunch and washed the dust out of your eyes."

When Dad hefted her backpack and duffel bag, Sam wished he'd put them down. She could wait to get inside the house. She could wait to breathe the remembered smells of woodsmoke and coffee and to fling herself down on the patchwork-quilted bed she knew Gram had kept ready for her. She could *not* wait to see her horse.

"Where's Ace?" she blurted.

"Let me drop these inside and I'll show you." Dad shrugged the backpack higher up his shoulder and walked toward the house.

"You're givin' her Ace?" Jake shouted after Dad. *"Ace?"* Jake yelled again, but the screen door had slammed closed. "You gotta be kidding." Jake rubbed the back of his neck, then faced Sam. He looked her over for just a second too long. Then he said, "Ace's smarter than you and me put together."

"Then he and I ought to do just fine." Sam looked down at Blaze. Since the Border Collie was begging her to rub his ears, she did.

"Yeah? You're quite some rider, are you?"

Sam looked up. She thought Jake's eyes clouded with something like worry, but she must have misread his look. He was taking in her black T-shirt, black jeans, and black sneakers.

"Excuse me." Sam placed a hand against her chest and pretended to apologize. "Guess I've been in civilization so long I just plumb ran out of cowboy duds."

She didn't mention she'd only ridden four times in two years, and all four times had been in a stable's riding ring. She sure didn't tell Jake he'd hit on the one thing she was really worried about.

"You kids knock it off," Dad said as he returned from the house. He sounded amused, though, not a bit mad.

"I was only telling Sam how glad I am to see her."

Jake's arm circled Sam's shoulders. Although his voice brimmed with sarcasm, Sam felt a genuine warmth in Jake's hug.

This might turn into her best summer yet.

Ace was runty. Fourteen hands at best, he stood alone.

When Sam came to the fence, the other horses lifted their heads and swished their tails with faint interest. A little grass fell from their lips before they went back to grazing.

Not Ace. If a horse could put his hands on his hips and look as if he were asking "And what do *you* want?" that's exactly what Ace did.

His hide glowed a nice warm bay and he had neat white hind socks, but a scar made a long line of lighter hair on his neck.

"Ace!" Sam held out a hand and smooched to him.

For a heartbeat, Ace was a horse transformed. His tiny head tilted sideways. His back-cast ears pricked up, black tips curving in. He pranced forward with the fluid grace of a dressage horse—until he saw that Sam's hand was empty.

Ace planted all four legs with a stiffness, which showed he was insulted.

"Told you he was smart." Jake laughed.

"I wasn't trying to trick him!" Sam said. "I just wanted him to come over and let me rub his ears."

From the ranch house porch, Gram clanged something metal against a triangle. She *didn't* shout "Come and get it," but they all hurried in for lunch. Except for Sam.

She stalled, thinking Ace might come to her if the others left. She was wrong. Ace looked at her, shivered his skin as if shaking off a fly, and yawned.

Mashed potatoes sat next to a mound of green beans fragrant with onions and bacon. Dad plopped a slab of beef on Sam's plate. All this for lunch.

Sam glanced around the kitchen. White plastered walls and oak beams made it cozy and bright at the same time. She wondered about the cardboard boxes stacked against the wall.

"I know he doesn't look like much, Sam," Dad said. "But Ace is a great little horse."

Before she answered, Sam noticed Jake kept a sidelong glance aimed her way as he reached for a platter piled with biscuits.

"I'm sure he's super," Sam said.

It wasn't that she minded Ace's size. She was barely five feet tall herself. She could mount a small horse more easily. But that scar. And his *attitude* . . .

"What about that mark on his neck?"

"The freeze brand?" Jake held his butter knife in midair, and Sam knew she'd surprised him.

Sam looked from Jake to her father.

"That's what it is," Dad agreed. "Ace is a mustang. He used to run with the herd you saw today."

Gram made a hum of disapproval, but Sam didn't try to decipher it.

"After wild horses are rounded up and vaccinated, they're branded with liquid nitrogen," Dad explained. "That freezes the skin temporarily, the horse's fur turns white, and—"

"Really? He was wild?" Sam's mind replayed the gelding's attitude. Ace hadn't been rude. He just had pride.

A stab of disloyalty deflated Sam's excitement as she remembered her lost colt.

"I wonder if he could've known—" Sam hesitated. "If he could've run with Blackie."

"That's a fool thing to say." Jake rocked his chair onto its back legs.

"It's not, is it?" Sam appealed to her father.

Dad blew his cheeks full of air and shook his head.

"Jake, put all four chair legs back on the floor, if you please," Gram ordered.

Jake's chair slammed down, but his face was flushed crimson. Did he hate her for losing the horse they'd worked so hard to train? Or did Jake's blush mean what Linc Slocum had implied: some folks blamed Jake for Sam's injury?

It didn't matter. The accident had happened years ago. She wanted to know where Blackie was *now*.

"What about that stallion we saw turning the herd away from the helicopter?" Sam's hands curled into fists. She kept them in her lap. "That was the Phantom, right? What if Blackie's running with the Phantom?"

Were they just going to let her babble until she ran out of breath?

"Now, Sam, first off, there's no such thing as the Phantom. There's been a white stud on this range as far back as I can recall. Dallas—you remember Dal, our foreman?"

Sam nodded, but her fists tightened with impatience.

"Well, he claims that sometimes, when he's up late playing the guitar in front of the bunkhouse, he's seen a shadowy horse just across the river. He thinks it's the Phantom, drawn by the music." Dad shrugged, but Sam felt chills at the picture his words painted.

"Folks always call him the Phantom. But it's not the same horse year after year. He's a . . ." Dad put down his fork and rotated one hand in the air. "You know, like a local legend."

I know that, Sam wanted to interrupt, but Dad was trying to be nice, so she just listened.

"There's fast blood in one line of light-colored mustangs, that's all," Dad continued. "They haven't been caught because they run the legs off our saddle stock. Not because they're 'phantoms.'"

"But aren't white horses unusual? I mean, maybe it *is* the same horse. Maybe he's really old." Sam cut a green bean into four neat sections.

"Remember Smoke, Blackie's sire?" Dad asked. "That old cow pony was a mustang, and he was dark as Blackie when he was a yearling. He turned gray by age five, but he was snow white by the time he died last spring. That's the way it is with most white horses, if they're not albinos, and that's all there is to this Phantom."

So quick that it startled them all, Gram stood up. She lifted the coffeepot, poured a cup for Dad, and set it before him.

"Who wants dessert?" Gram went to the counter and came back with a pie. She placed it on the table.

"I don't know." Sam wondered if she could eat another bite.

"No excuses, young lady." Gram's thick-bladed knife split the golden crust. She served Sam along with everyone else.

"And second, Sam"—Dad watched her over the top of his coffee cup—"we've watched for your colt and haven't seen him. With all the trouble these horses are into—"

"And Linc bein' loco to catch the Phantom," Jake added.

"What he thinks he'll do with that stud is beyond me," Dad said, shaking his head.

"Wyatt, it's clear as glass what he intends." Gram sat down with her own pie. "Linc Slocum moved out West to play cowboy. He bought a ranch. He hired men to teach him to ride and rope. He bought clothes to look the part of a working buckaroo, but he only looks like he's wearing a costume.

"Folks still see him as an outsider," Gram said, mostly to Sam. "So he wants a wild white stallion that stands for everything he *can't* buy."

"Capturing the Phantom won't change what folks think of him," Jake said.

"And it'll land him in jail if the Bureau of Land Management finds out," Dad added.

THE WILD ONE

Sam fidgeted with her napkin. Linc Slocum gave her the creeps.

"If Blackie joined a herd headed away from here, it would be for his own good," Dad said, then swallowed his last bite of pie.

Sam thought for a minute, counting the years. Blackie would be almost five by now. A stallion. With his mustang bloodlines, he could survive in the wild.

"Blackie's got a herd of his own now," she said, and crossed her arms. "That's what I think."

By the time Sam left the table, the snap on her jeans was pushing against her stomach. She felt stuffed and a little sleepy, but she could hardly wait to go ride Ace. Still, she tried to be polite.

"Want me to wash dishes?" she offered, then crossed her fingers. *Please let Gram refuse.*

"No, you'd better go try out your horse." Gram stacked the dishes.

Sam knew it wasn't fair to leave Gram indoors while she, Dad, and Jake escaped into the June afternoon.

"Maybe I'll unpack first." Sam fidgeted near Gram's elbow.

"Don't do that." Gram slipped the plates into a sink full of soap suds. "It'll just be a waste of time."

"Don't unpack?" Sam bit her lip. "Why not?"

Jake slid his chair away from the table with a screech and said, "You won't be staying long. That's why not."

Chapter 3

SAM COULD HAVE SWORN THE ROAST BEEF wiggled in her belly. What did Jake mean when he said she wasn't staying long?

"What Jake means," Gram said, "is we'll be leaving in the morning, so it makes no sense to unpack and repack." Gram watched Sam with gentle eyes. "I'll help you go through your clothes, though, and make sure you have what you'll need."

"Need for *what*?" Sam's shout surprised her as much as it did everyone else.

"Wyatt!" Gram tied her apron strings with a jerk. "Don't tell me you didn't explain."

"It was gonna be a surprise." Looking embarrassed, Dad turned to Sam. "We're moving the cattle from their winter pasture near the Calico Mountains up here to River Bend for the summer. It will take about a week and a half because we do it the old-fashioned way, on horseback."

"It's easier on the calves," Jake added.

"Besides," Dad said, "it'll be a good way for you to get to know Ace and get back into the habit of riding."

"About *ten* hours a day!" Jake laughed.

Sam swallowed hard and returned his idiot grin, but she wasn't at all sure she was up to such riding. If only Jake hadn't said it like a dare.

Gram gave Sam a gentle push toward the door. "With all that riding ahead, you'd better get acquainted with your new horse."

Like Sam, Ace had good manners. Sam bridled Ace as Dad watched, and the gelding accepted the bit as if it were candy-coated. He didn't puff up his belly when she saddled him either, or move off while her left foot fumbled for the stirrup.

Sam and Ace circled the pasture with precision. Walk, jog, lope. The little bay made her look like an expert. All she had to do was stir her legs and the horse moved as she asked. And he was a *mustang*? Jake and Dad must be joking.

"You know what this is like?" Sam whispered, and the gelding's ears flicked back to listen. "Like you're just babysitting me, Ace."

Sam drew back on her reins and Ace stopped. He didn't shift from leg to leg, didn't pull against the bit. He did turn his head, noticing that Dad and Jake had walked away from the pasture fence. The gelding blew a breath through his lips as if he were bored stiff.

Far off, Sam heard a neigh. Ace tossed his head and looked toward the foothills. Sam looked too. She saw nothing, but Ace vibrated beneath her, nickering. Sam collected her reins an instant before Ace lunged from a standing stop into a full gallop.

Oh no. Sam crashed back against the high Western

cantle. Her teeth clacked together. She grabbed handfuls of Ace's coarse black mane and tried not to lose her stirrups.

The horse ran faster. Surely Ace wouldn't crash through the other horses clustered near the fence. Would he?

Sam leaned low against his extended neck and inched her hands down the reins, closer to the bit. As she remembered the last time she'd galloped this way, her pulse pounded in her neck. This time, she would *not* fall off.

Wind whipped Ace's mane into Sam's eyes. He was running away. Sam pulled the reins tighter, afraid she'd hurt his mouth. Ace ignored her. Then she tugged.

As if they'd run head-on into a brick wall, Ace stopped.

Sam slipped forward. The saddle horn poked her stomach, but that was all that kept her from sliding down his neck like a kid going headfirst down a playground slide. Thinking fast, she wrapped her arms around Ace's neck. Tight.

When Ace coughed, Sam made herself uncoil one

arm. She really hoped no one was watching. Finally, she took the other arm from around the gelding's neck.

Drawing a deep breath, she sat up, straightened her reins, and flexed her fingers. Her hands might be shaking from the pressure she'd applied to the bit, but she was pretty sure she was trembling because Ace had scared her half to death.

Could she ride this horse for ten days, with witnesses?

Beyond the pasture, near the barn, Jake waved. Sam pretended not to notice. No way was she going to take a hand off the reins to wave back.

Ace stamped one hoof and slung his head around to look at Sam. His big brown eyes glowed with intelligence and an equine sense of humor. For the first time, she noticed the white star high on his forehead.

"I apologize for thinking you were boring." Sam dismounted, keeping a grip on the reins. Her knees wobbled as she rubbed the gelding's warm neck. "You're a good boy, Ace."

The horse tossed his forelock to cover the star, then he followed obediently as Sam led.

Dismounting in the middle of the pasture might be silly. Leading Ace back to the barn instead of riding him might confirm Jake's opinion that she was a wimp. Still, there was no way in the world Sam would risk another one-horse stampede. Ace had proven he had the pride of a mustang.

A white quilt decorated with a patchwork star covered Sam's bed. The mattress was perfect—not too hard, not too soft. The pillow wasn't too puffy or too flat. Still, Sam couldn't sleep.

The full moon turned her bedroom wall into a movie screen. At least, that's what she'd thought as a child. Sam remembered staring at it, imagining stories in her own private theater.

In the best one, Blackie had worn the red and green Christmas ribbons she'd plaited into his mane. Together, he and Sam had rescued Mrs. Ott, her teacher, from stampeding buffalo. Sam had been too young to know that Nevada had no buffalo.

Sam stared at the wall, trying to recall the exact shape

of Blackie's face. And then she knew why she couldn't. In the stories she'd told herself at night, she'd called the colt by his secret name.

A secret name, Jake had confided, was a code between human and horse. It would bind the colt to her so that even in darkness, he'd know her. But horses heard many words, so the secret name had to sound like no other.

Zanzibar. Though the name was too fancy for a ranch horse, it had been their secret, and the colt had answered to it.

Down the hall, Dad and Gram slept. Outside Sam's window, the river sighed and coyotes called from the hills. They yipped, barked, and then joined in a community howl.

Sam tried to enjoy the coyotes' wild song, but their nearness frightened her a little. One more thing she'd have to grow used to. Her bedsheets twisted around her legs. She kicked loose and rolled over onto her stomach.

It wasn't late, but they'd leave for Red Rock, where Dad's cowboys were holding the cattle herd, by six a.m.

Sam reached for the wristwatch she'd left on her

bedside table. Its numbers glowed in the dark. Ten o'clock. What would Aunt Sue be doing? Since it was summer, she'd have no papers to grade. She might be watching the news or reading. Maybe worrying about Sam.

When Sam had worried that her fall and Blackie's kick might have injured her brain and made her forgetful, Aunt Sue had urged her to make lists. When Sam missed the ranch, Aunt Sue had brought home a huge plush horse for her to cuddle. The strongest reason Sam missed Aunt Sue was because she was Sam's mother's sister, and the closest Sam would ever come to knowing her mother, who'd died so young.

Sam had been almost five years old when Mom died in a one-car accident. Skid marks showed she'd swerved to miss an animal, and her VW Bug was upside down near an antelope migration area.

Sam remembered how Mom's auburn hair looked in braids with daisies stuck through the ends. She remembered her laughing and clapping in excitement. And later, she remembered someone saying, "Louise just shoulda hit that critter," and someone answering, "Louise always had too big a heart."

Sam rolled back over and pulled the sheet over her face. She listened to her eyelashes tick back and forth.

She had a horse. She had Jake to remind her how to ride like a buckaroo. She had Dad. Why couldn't she be satisfied?

Sam threw back the covers, pulled on her pink robe, and crept down the hall. Quietly, she left the house.

As Sam closed the front door, the river shushed her. Crickets stopped chirping as if they were holding their breath.

River Bend Ranch had no outside lights, and she'd left the porch light off. Little by little, Sam's eyes grew used to the dark. A full moon turned the ranch grounds the black and white of an old photograph.

Sam stepped off the porch. Ahead, the sand-and-gravel driveway unrolled like a white velvet carpet, leading to dark hills beyond the ranch gate. Night sky arched overhead with stars so bright, Sam picked out the Big Dipper instantly. A low nicker drew Sam's attention to the ten-acre pasture. It lay in a dark rectangle, and horses moved across it in dreamy slowness.

And then a shower of gravel against rock made the horses jerk alert. One snorted. Another shied. They all looked toward the river.

Sam ran on tiptoe, wincing as pebbles jabbed her bare feet. The horses moved in a silent wave toward the far end of the pasture. Sam's toes jammed against a round rock and she almost stumbled. The horses broke into a trot and Sam ran faster, ignoring the stabbing stones.

The river rushed like wind as she neared it. When she saw him, Sam stopped.

Floating like a ghost, the stallion picked his way down the hillside on the other side of the river. His mane and tail rippled around him. His hooves were so soundless, he seemed to drift above the ground.

The stallion reached the river and stopped.

Would he clop across the wooden bridge or wade across the river? Would he jump the fence into the pasture?

Sam's pulse pounded. She couldn't believe this. The

moonlight must be magical. She'd read myths of maidens who summoned unicorns, but Samantha Anne Forster was no fairy-tale princess.

The stallion didn't care. He splashed into the water, coming to her.

His hooves grated on river rock. Halfway across, he stood still, knee-deep in his own reflection. This close, Sam could see the stallion wasn't white. His hide was dappled gray and silver, like the surface of the moon. He was the same stallion who'd rescued the herd this morning.

Sam didn't move. She barely breathed.

The stallion's nostrils flared, drawing in her scent. For a moment, he lifted his head, testing the breeze, and then his eyes returned to her.

Sam's heart thudded so hard she feared the stallion could hear it. Only one horse had ever studied her with such friendship.

If this was a dream, Sam never wanted to wake.

The stallion arched his neck and pawed three times.

Water drops scattered like diamonds.

What did he want? He was a mustang, a wild thing. If she whispered or held out her hand, he'd run. Then it struck her. What if he was hers? What if he was Smoke's son, a black colt turned white?

Sam had no chance to find out. As if he'd read her mind, the stallion flung his head high. Water churned as he wheeled on his hind legs and launched onto the bank in a single leap.

Mist hung where he had been. The river flowed smooth again and the crickets chirped.

No one could know the stallion had stood there.

Except for Sam. She knew the truth. The truth was, her dream had come true.

By moonlight, Zanzibar had returned to her at last.

Chapter 4

GRAM PULLED THE PILLOW OFF SAM'S HEAD and kissed her cheek. "Good morning," she said.

Sam wasn't so sure. When she gazed out her bedroom window, it still looked like night.

Minutes later, Sam sat beside Gram in the white van, which served as a modern chuck wagon. Sam focused on the red taillights bobbing on the road ahead. Jake and Dad drove the truck and pulled a horse trailer big enough to carry Ace; Dad's horse, Banjo; and Jake's black mare, Witch.

Sam stayed awake long enough to drink the cocoa Gram had insisted she bring. As soon as her eyelids closed, though, she imagined a silver stallion. Wild as the wind, he'd returned to River Bend on the same night she had. *He was Zanzibar*, she thought drowsily, *and he was real.*

Sam slept through much of the drive to Red Rock, where Dad's three cowboys had joined Linc Slocum's men to gather range cattle from both ranches into a single large herd.

When Sam awoke, they'd arrived and Gram was hustling her out of the van.

Hundreds of cattle, mothers and calves with fuzzy red-brown fur and white faces, were mooing and bawling, worried by the two trucks and the men on horseback.

Sam climbed out, feeling a little shy. She shouldn't. Many of these cattle belonged to her family, but she'd been too young to go on drives before. Now her time in the city made her feel like an outsider.

Then Gram stood beside her, indicating which cowboys rode for Dad.

"Dallas has been on the River Bend for years," Gram said. "You probably remember him."

Sam did, and she smiled. The gray-haired man was the only cowboy on foot. He stood talking to Dad. Sam thought his bowed legs looked better suited to gripping a horse than walking.

"And that's Ross." Gram nodded to a man sitting tall in the saddle of a Quarter Horse. "That man is so quiet, he hardly talks to anyone, even your father."

Pepper was the youngest cowboy, nicknamed for his chili-pepper-red hair. He glanced at Sam, then looked away.

"How old is he?" Sam asked. "He looks like a kid."

"A year older than Jake," Gram said with a sigh. "That boy ran away from his home in Idaho. Far north in Idaho, near the Canadian border. Said it was too cold." Gram smiled and lowered her voice. "He has no idea your father tracked down his parents to tell them he was okay."

As Sam pulled on her favorite black sweater, she felt a surge of pride in her father. She ran the names through her mind once more. Dallas. Ross. Pepper.

They'd all eat dinner together tonight and she'd have to start learning the other cowboys' names too.

Gram would cook for all of them. Each day, she'd drive the van to the place where the crew would camp for the night. She'd arrive hours before the slow-moving cattle.

Gram would get the gear down from the carrier atop the van and she'd pitch the tents. Next, she'd build a campfire. She'd roast meat over the fire, but she'd cook the rest of the meal on a stove in the back of the chuck wagon. By the time the herd arrived, the cowboys would just have time to clean up for dinner.

Gram's job sounded like a lot of work. Riding Ace all day and watching the cattle trot back toward their summer pastures at River Bend sounded like a vacation.

"Hey, princess." Jake's joking voice made Sam turn. "Think you can give me a hand with these horses?"

The cowboys were watching. Sam could feel them wondering how Wyatt Forster's city-slicker daughter would do.

What if Ace tossed his head too high for her to reach?

Or refused the bit? If he planted a hoof on the toe of her new boot and wouldn't move, could she keep from yelping?

The River Bend cowboys might not mock her, but Linc Slocum's men could be a different story.

Sam shot a quick glance their way. She probably just imagined their sneers.

Jake had unloaded all three horses and tied their lead ropes to rings on the trailer. Now he carried a saddle on each arm, as if they didn't weigh an ounce. As Sam moved in next to him, Ace swung his head around as far as the rope allowed. His warm breath clouded the cold morning air. He nuzzled her arm.

Surprised and pleased, Sam rubbed the gelding's brown neck. He knew her.

"Good boy," she said, then turned to Jake. "Where's Ace's bridle?"

Sam reached up to lift the halter off the bay's head.

"Put that back on," Jake ordered as he handed her Ace's bridle. "Put this on over the halter and get a bit in his mouth before you untie him." Jake shook his head.

"You don't want him hightailing it out of here before you can say good-bye."

"I don't need lessons," Sam muttered.

She did it Jake's way, even though Ace was so well behaved, she didn't need to.

With the feel of eyes watching each move, Sam smoothed on Ace's saddle blanket. Bracing her arm muscles, she grabbed the saddle and swung it into place on Ace's back.

As she tightened the cinch, she felt smug.

As she tucked her boot in the stirrup, she was confident.

But when she placed all her weight on that stirrup and started to vault up into the saddle, it slipped sideways. The cowboys laughed, and Sam wished she could turn invisible.

Though she jerked her boot free of the stirrup and hopped back quick enough to keep from falling, she must've looked real funny.

"Happens all the time, honey." Dad was beside her right away.

"I know," Sam said. She didn't want sympathy.

"Oldest trick that pony has," Dallas added.

"I know that," Sam repeated. And she did.

Yesterday, she'd checked Ace's belly to see if he'd puffed up so the cinch would hang loose when he released his breath. Today, she'd trusted him.

She bent to lift the saddle. When she heard movement, she looked over her shoulder to see Jake step forward, as if to help.

"Don't even think about it," she muttered.

Jake held his hands up as if holding off an attack, then stepped back again.

Sam didn't need a mirror to know she was blushing.

Once she put the saddle right, she tapped Ace's belly to make him exhale, then pulled the cinch snug. Ace stamped one hoof and swung his head around to give her a glare.

She looked him right in the eyes.

"Look insulted all you want," she whispered. "But if you won't trust me, I can't trust you."

Ace's black-tipped ears flicked back and forth,

waiting for another word. But Sam was done talking.

Once in the saddle, she consulted her watch, just to avoid the cowboys' amused eyes. It was only seven o'clock in the morning.

Because her face was still so tight and hot that it hurt, riding out on her first cattle drive wasn't as much fun as she'd expected.

Gram waved, and the cows and calves increased their calls to a moo racket Sam never could have imagined. All the animals wore brands, either Slocum's double-*S* brand or the backward *F* for Forster. The herd strung out across the range until they stretched about a quarter mile in front of Sam and Ace. The riders moved into a rough formation around the herd.

Dad rode in front on Banjo. A few cowboys rode on each side. Sam, half-hidden in dust, brought up the rear.

A few times, she tried to ride closer to the other riders, but Linc Slocum's big palomino struck out a hoof, trying to kick Ace.

"Sorry, little lady," Slocum said with his toothpaste-commercial grin.

Slocum wore snakeskin boots, brass-roweled spurs, and a long, brown duster more appropriate for Hollywood than rural Nevada.

His too-friendly attitude might have bothered her more, except that other riders were unwilling to talk. And when she rode too close to Jake, Witch whirled with her mouth open, looking as if she'd peel Ace's nose with her bared teeth.

Sam reined Ace in, urging him away from danger. He thanked her by giving a buck. Sam's teeth clacked together. Before she remembered not to, she grabbed the saddle horn for balance. By the time Ace quit pulling against the bit, dancing as if he wanted to run for home, they were bringing up the rear again.

So this was her dream come true. Samantha Forster, the boss's daughter, blinked against the dust raised by hundreds of hooves. She stayed in the back of the herd all morning as they headed east, toward the Calico Mountains.

Sam had just looked up at the sun, directly overhead, when Jake appeared, making Witch walk beside Ace, whether or not she wanted to.

"We're not stopping for lunch," Jake said. "I have some jerky in my saddlebags, though, if you're hungry."

"I'm fine," Sam said, even though she had nothing but the water in her canteen, and it tasted metallic and warm.

She didn't care about lunch. She only cared about riding well enough to return to the range in search of the Phantom. So far, she wasn't doing so well.

Since it was getting hot, Sam wiggled out of her black sweater and tied it around her waist. She settled her old brown felt cowboy hat with one hand. It still fit after two years. She peered out from its shade.

Sam tried to read Jake's expression, but his jaw stayed in its usual set position and he looked straight ahead. Would he mention her terrible morning and say she had a long way to go before she was the rider she used to be?

Sam wouldn't give him a chance.

"How old are these calves?" she blurted, pointing at the leggy babies walking beside their mothers. Most weren't as tall as a Labrador Retriever.

"A couple months old," Jake said. "We wait till they've all been dropped before we move them."

To Sam, *dropped* seemed a strange word for being born, especially because cows were such gentle mothers.

Now, for instance, she saw a cow stop and use her huge pink tongue to wash her calf's face. The herd flowed around her on both sides, but she cleaned her baby as the other cattle passed her by.

As soon as the cow and calf stood alone, Ace bolted forward as if to chase her, and Sam drew the reins tight.

"You need to keep loose reins on a cow horse. Remember?" Jake said. He still didn't look at her, and he said it so quietly, no one else could have heard.

"Every time I loosen up, he goes his own way," she admitted.

When Jake said nothing, she decided he was only trying to help. She bit the inside of her cheek and loosened the reins.

Ace bolted into a jouncing trot.

"Relax. You're not riding in a horse show. Don't grab that horn again, Samantha. What are you thinking?"

She was thinking that her new horse hated her.

Ace veered away from the herd and lengthened his stride. Sam jerked the reins tight again.

She didn't speak when Jake stopped his horse too. She couldn't risk sounding weepy.

Jake bumped his black hat away from his serious brown eyes.

Mustang eyes. When they were kids, Jake had told her Shoshone tales. One story described the old times when humans were animals. Ten-year-old Jake, with his glossy black hair and lively leaps, just knew he'd been a mustang back then. He'd been equally convinced Sam was once a mosquito—a buzzing, troublesome pest.

Now Jake looked at her with frustration, as if he might still believe it.

"What?" she demanded. After a single day on the ranch, she was sick of trying to prove herself.

"Nothing."

"It's not *nothing*. Didn't you outgrow that?"

He shrugged with a teasing grin, as if he remembered

their kid days too. Half of Sam wanted to go back to being playmates. Half of her wanted to confide in Jake. He was older, and a wizard with horses. He'd know what to do about the silver stallion.

But she'd waited too long. Jake tugged his hat back over his eyes. All business, he nodded toward her horse.

"Ace is testing you is all," Jake said. "Hang in there."

He rode on ahead.

Any curl that had ever been in Sam's hair was gone. The short wisps hung into her eyes. She needed lip balm for the dry skin on her mouth, and her cheeks felt chalky with desert dirt.

At first, she thought the white triangles ahead looked like teeth poking up out of the sand and sagebrush. She squinted and blinked. Finally, she recognized the tents and Gram's chuck wagon. Then she caught the aroma of baking biscuits.

This time when Sam loosened her reins, Ace read her mind. He trotted past the cattle, past the cowboys, past Dad, whom she hadn't seen since morning.

With a rolling hand motion, Dad was instructing

the cowboys to urge the cattle into the tight herd they'd been in this morning.

Rejuvenated by the smells ahead, Sam winked at Dad and pointed at the herd.

"I'm going to leave this to you professionals," she said. As she moved off, Dad gave a short laugh.

Longing for a cold soda, Sam let Ace swing into a lope and settled back into the saddle. This time, the signal made him stop short in a haze of dust.

"Careful of my campfire," Gram scolded, but she didn't sound cranky. She looked neat, with a white apron over her jeans, as she pointed toward an enclosure made of portable plastic fence. "Follow Pepper," she added.

The young red-haired cowboy had dismounted. He unsaddled his dun gelding next to the corral and left his reins trailing on the dirt. *Ground-tying*, Sam reminded herself. That's what it was called. Cowboys trained their mounts to stay around without being tied, but Sam didn't think it would work with Ace.

Before she could give it a try, Jake appeared to stand at Ace's head.

"Thanks," Sam said, but she got the distinct feeling that Jake was babysitting her. She'd swung one leg toward the ground when she heard him mumble something that sounded like "Long ride," but she wasn't sure enough to answer.

He added something she did hear.

"Your knees are apt to be a bit wobbly."

"I'm fine," Sam insisted.

The warning irritated her, mostly because it was true. She'd been in the saddle for nine hours and Jake knew she wasn't used to it. As her boots touched the ground, her legs felt liquid and unsteady. She hated to use Ace for balance, but it was better than falling over backward.

The chores of checking Ace's feet, unsaddling, and juggling that floppy gate before she turned him out loomed like the task of climbing a mountain.

"I'll take him," Jake offered.

"Fat chance," Sam said. As she lifted her chin to look up at him, her hat slipped off her hair. She caught it and slammed it back on her head.

"If there's one thing I know, it's to take care of my

horse before I pamper myself," she said. "It doesn't matter how much I want to pry off these boots or wash my face. Ace comes first."

For a minute, she thought Jake would give her a pat on the back. He didn't, but the satisfied look on his face was enough.

As Sam squatted to lift Ace's hooves and check them for stones, she felt so pleased, she forgot to worry about all the other cowboys she'd have to face at dinner.

Chapter 5

THE JOSHING STARTED AFTER DINNER, AS SAM swallowed a last bite of peach cobbler. Dad stood with one boot on a tree stump, staring into the fire. Jake stood a few steps away, leaning against the chuck wagon. Sam sat perched on a rock between them.

She looked past the men eating around the campfire, off into the desert painted lavender by the setting sun. The herd was still restless, but a few mounted cowboys circled them, turning back cows trying to make a break for the familiar territory they'd left behind.

The cattle wouldn't be left unattended for a minute until they reached home pastures at River Bend and Slocum's ranch.

Sam wanted to do her part, but she felt tired down to her toenails. She hoped Dallas wouldn't tell her to "nighthawk." If she rode four more hours tonight, she'd be facedown in her mashed potatoes by this time tomorrow night.

One of Linc Slocum's cowboys set his plate aside and looked her way. Named Flick, the man was renowned for his roping skill and his long, drooping mustache.

"That pony was doing his best to keep the herd together," Flick said.

Sam couldn't pretend he wasn't talking to her. Everyone knew he was. And his comment awakened her to the reason Ace had kept bolting.

A cow pony was like a sheepdog. Ace's job was to keep the herd together. When that cow had stopped to lick her calf, Ace had thought she was lagging. Sam had been so set on controlling Ace, she'd stopped him from doing his job.

Apologies streamed across her mind, but she didn't utter them. This was a test. The cowboys were waiting to see if the city girl would act offended or burst into tears.

Neither.

Suddenly, Sam knew what to do. A cowboy wouldn't make a fuss explaining.

"Yep," she said, nodding. "He was."

Had she heard her father chuckle?

"Sam's been gone awhile, but she's on the comeback trail," Dallas said as he whittled a stick.

Sam would bet everyone was remembering the accident.

Linc Slocum confirmed it. "Can't wipe out that mustang blood in one generation," he said. "I heard the horse that throwed you was a mustang."

"Half," Sam said, though she hated to give Slocum an instant of satisfaction.

"Range rats," muttered Flick.

Sam couldn't resist answering that too.

"You know, 'mesteño,' the Spanish word that 'mustang'

comes from, just means 'strays,'" Sam pointed out. "So some will be good horses, and some ordinary."

"Smoke, her colt's sire, was the best working horse I ever had," Dad said. "He was a mustang. Same color as an iron skillet and just as tough. Smoke could stay out all day and be fresh at night. He was kinda wise, from looking out for himself on the range."

"Seems to me there's a mustang you've been trying to put a rope on, Linc," Jake said.

Slocum stood up, as if he'd been insulted. He made a big show of lighting a cigarette and threw his match on the ground.

Jake poured more coffee from the pot suspended over the campfire.

When Slocum figured out Jake wasn't worried that he'd offended him, Slocum gave a short laugh.

"That Phantom's the only one out there worth anything," Slocum said.

Sam shivered. When she'd met Slocum, he'd known a surprising amount about Blackie. Could he suspect her lost colt had grown up to be the silver stallion?

"Those broomtails eat like vacuum cleaners," Slocum complained. "I wish they'd take 'em all off the range and keep it for cattle."

"Your herd looks fine, Linc." Dallas stood and stretched. He started giving orders. "It's eight o'clock. Time for me, Jake, and two of your boys to give those riders a break." Dallas gestured toward the herd. "If the night riders get sleepy, your fat, sassy heifers might lope out of here. Rest of you, turn in. Nighthawk shifts change at midnight and four."

Slocum tried to finish his argument over the sound of men putting tin dishes in the dishpan.

"It's pure luck it's been a wet year," Slocum shouted. "With plenty of graze . . ."

When his voice trailed off, Sam thought no one noticed.

She was wrong. Later, Sam went to find Gram and found her tidying up. Gram looked glad for the company, but she tsked her tongue and nodded toward Slocum.

"This time last year, the closest he'd been to a cow was a T-bone steak."

Sam laughed and admired Gram's skill. She'd already set the chuck wagon back in order. Potatoes and onions sat in mesh bags next to a burlap sack of rice. Cans of fruit, beans, and coffee shared space with soap and first aid supplies. But there was much left to do.

"Can I help you wash dishes?" Sam offered.

"I don't mind doing them. My hands are a little stiff from driving. Warm water will feel good." Gram smoothed her hand over Sam's chopped-off hair. "You'll have plenty to keep you busy this week without doing my chores too. Might as well crawl into your sleeping bag now. I'll try not to wake you when I come to bed."

As Sam moved away from the campfire, it got darker. Still, she knew Jake was following her before she made it to the tent she'd share with Gram.

Sam didn't remember noticing Jake wore spurs, but they rang in the darkness as he took long strides to catch up with her.

"What'd you do with your gear?" he asked.

"My—?"

"Saddle, bridle, saddle blanket?" Jake gave her ten

seconds to think. "You left them on the ground, Sam. You're in charge of your own tack, so go pick it up, clean it off, and put it where you can find it." Jake gave her shoulder a shake, and Sam wondered how he could still have so much energy. "Nothing says 'tenderfoot' like being the last one saddled up in the morning."

Though she yearned for the warm cocoon of her sleeping bag, Sam borrowed a flashlight from Gram and found the spot near the corral where she'd dropped her gear.

Crickets chirped as she shook out her saddle blanket, turned her stirrups, and cleaned her bit. Suddenly, every horse in the makeshift corral threw a drowsy head up, ears pricked to attention toward the dark shape of the Calico Mountains.

Sam listened. The crickets had hushed, so she heard the movement of cattle, but nothing more.

It couldn't be Zanzibar. Gram had said they'd driven seventy-eight miles this morning, and traveling cross-country, they'd herd the cattle fifty miles back to the ranch. A horse couldn't cover that much territory in a day. One who could had to be a ghost.

Sam's knees creaked as she stood, slowly and silently.

"Sam?" Dad's voice came through the darkness.

So much for quiet. Oh well, the horses had probably only heard a coyote or deer.

"Over here." Sam picked up her gear, determined to take it into her tent for the night.

"How're you doing, hon?" Dad's voice told Sam he'd worried over her, but he hadn't let the other cowboys know.

"I'm fine." Sam settled under Dad's arm as he took her saddle in one arm and hugged her against his side with the other.

"I wanted to give you time to get used to being home, but your grandmother said no. She said this would show our neighbors you were home for good, and that I, well, trusted you."

Dad stopped walking for a minute, and Sam wished she could see his face.

"Every calf will be worth his weight in dollars come market time. The sooner we get them home, the less chance harm can come to them."

When she'd been eleven, Dad had never mentioned money. Or maybe money hadn't seemed important to her. Now Sam heard the worry in his voice.

"I won't do anything to slow you down, Dad."

"You're doing fine, Sam. It's just—" Dad cleared his throat. "Every small rancher in Nevada feels the land vultures circling, looking to buy failed ranches. We can't afford any mistakes."

"No more tenderfoot mistakes," she promised. "I'll watch you and Jake and the other hands and do what they do. I promise. You can assign me to nighthawk, even."

"Dallas is the trail boss. He decides who does what."

"Why? If you're the owner, shouldn't you be in charge?"

"We're doing this drive with Slocum." Dad's voice turned hard. "In case of conflict, if the two of us claim an unbranded cow, for instance, we need a man in charge who doesn't stand to profit."

Dad stood with her outside the little white tent and waited for her to understand.

"I get it," she said, but a yawn clouded her words and Dad chuckled.

"Enough heavy talk. Hop in bed, sleepyhead. Dawn comes mighty early on the range."

Next morning, Sam woke to the sound of lowing cattle.

She pulled jeans past aching muscles, yanked boots over her warm socks, and managed to devour a stack of hotcakes with maple syrup before she and Ace put on a rodeo.

Mindful of Jake's warning, Sam was first to catch her horse and saddle him. Even in the crowded corral, in half-light, Ace was easy to find. He cowered in the far corner, facing the other horses.

Soon she found out why. She smoothed the saddle blanket on his back and gave his flank a pat. Her hand came back sticky with blood.

"Oh, Ace, poor baby." She pressed her cheek against the gelding's neck as she remembered Witch lunging at Ace with bared teeth.

In spite of the bites, Ace still had the spirit to try

puffing his stomach against the cinch. When that trick didn't work, he kept his teeth closed, refusing the bit.

"You're like a little kid who won't eat his vegetables," Sam whispered as she slipped her thumb into the corner of Ace's lips to lever open his jaws.

Once Sam mounted, Ace settled down. Since the other cowboys were just finishing breakfast, she considered what to do.

What if she rode up to the chuck wagon and asked Gram for a cup of coffee? She didn't really like coffee, but it might look cool to sit there on Ace with one of those blue-speckled mugs.

That was how Sam came to be right near the chuck wagon, where everyone could watch, when Ace bowed his head between his front hooves, kicked out his hind legs, and began to buck.

As her chin flew forward to strike her breastbone, Sam's hat flew off. It cartwheeled right under Ace's nose. He reared as if it were a demon, and Sam's head snapped back. Then he did it all over again. Sam heard voices as if someone were switching between stations on a radio.

"Sam—"

"Ride 'em—"

"—away from the—"

"Holy Hannah, hang on!"

The loudest voice was the one in her head. *No more tenderfoot mistakes.* She must stick to Ace no matter what.

As Ace began running, Sam tightened her reins. But when she saw he meant to jump the campfire, she gave him his head.

Up, stretch, over.

In a flurry of hooves, he headed for the tents. Before he reached them, Ace bucked some more. Brown hide, gray dirt, blue sky . . . She caught swinging views of the world before memory told her what to do.

Sam leaned back, grabbed the right rein, and pulled it toward her hip. Ace couldn't help turning in a circle. He didn't like being dizzy, and finally stopped. For a minute, his legs stayed braced apart. His sides heaved with effort. Then he shook like a wet dog, swished his tail, and waited, ears up, for directions.

For a minute, Sam wondered what to do. *Jake.* As temporary wrangler, he'd be over by the corral. Maybe he could explain why Ace had chosen this morning to go insane.

Dallas gave an approving nod as Sam and Ace passed. Another cowboy winked. Pepper handed Sam her hat. She must have done all right. At least that's what Sam thought until she saw Jake.

"Jake?"

Down on one knee, he didn't look up from checking a horse's pastern, even though he must have heard her voice.

"Hey, Jake," she said again, aware she sounded breathless.

"Don't talk to me, Samantha."

Sam froze in surprise. Even though she hadn't fallen off, she'd committed some awful tenderfoot sin.

"Why are you mad?" Sam felt a clutch of guilt. "Was it—Did I pull on his mouth too hard?"

"No. Nothing like that."

"If you think I was mean to him—" Sam pictured

the scene all over again. "Honest, I couldn't think what else to do."

Jake wouldn't face her. Staring at the back of his head told her nothing.

When Jake looked sideways, she followed his glance. At a distance, she saw Dad, tight-lipped and white-faced. They were both mad, though she'd hoped to make them proud.

Confused, Sam rode over to Dallas. As the trail boss, he handed out work assignments. Maybe he'd explain where she'd gone wrong.

Sam only had time for a sigh before Dallas began talking.

"You did fine," Dallas said. "Don't pay Jake and Wyatt any mind. You scared 'em, that's all."

Sam didn't think that made sense, but Dallas hadn't asked for her opinion.

"You and Ace came to a fork in the road," he said. "And you took charge."

"Thanks, I—"

"That's that. Now, you ride drag again. You've got a

bandanna. Today, wear it against the dust. And if Ace wants to cut off strays, you let him.

"You know how to ride, Sam, but that fall's made you skittish. Just keep your reins low and loose in your left hand, and let the palm of your right hand rest on your thigh. Sway with him and he'll do the rest. You're not going to fall."

Sam took Dallas's advice to heart, and the second day of the drive was better than the first. It was a breezy day, but hot enough to roll up the cuffs of her pale blue shirt.

She and Ace had reached an agreement. Sam went along for the ride as he dropped into a low, stalking-cat posture to turn back cows. In return, he followed her directions on everything else.

The compromise turned yesterday's stiff trot into a smooth jog. Relaxed, Sam wondered if Dallas was right about that other thing. Had her wild ride scared Dad and Jake because they still worried over her accident?

"Well, they'd better get over it," Sam told Ace.

At noon, Dallas directed her to change horses. She'd need Ace fresh tonight, he explained, for nighthawking.

"You're a sight better rider than Slocum and he's next in the rotation after you." Dallas glanced toward Slocum where he sat, smoking, on a red dun horse.

The sun's angle turned Slocum's belt buckle to dazzling silver, and Dallas made a sound of disgust.

"I'd bet my next three paychecks he bought that trophy buckle in a pawnshop," Dallas said, then looked Sam straight in the eye. "Sam, some things can't be bought. You were born to ride, so get out there and do it."

Sam felt such a zing of surprise, she had to concentrate as Dallas went on.

"Jake'll wake you at midnight when he goes off shift," Dallas said. "Get to bed early and rest up."

Sam changed her gear to a roan mare named Strawberry and wondered if Ace would enjoy the break. Turned in with the group of spare horses, the remuda, he'd still walk along, trailing the herd, but no rider would tell him what to do.

Pulling her cinch snug, Sam thought about tonight. When Jake came to wake her, she'd make the most of the quiet time while the rest of the camp slept. She'd find out what had made him mad, even if she had to tickle it out of him, as she had when they were kids.

Sam's heart lifted at that idea, then skyrocketed as she thought of something even better.

Oh, wow. For four hours, she and another cowboy would ride in opposite directions around the herd. They would pass each other only once in a while. If the feeling she'd had last night was real, the Phantom had followed her to the desert. Maybe he'd spot her, riding alone.

It was improbable, but not impossible. Dad had told her mustangs had hideaways and trails that no people knew.

The thought gave Sam chills. As soon as the first star of evening glowed in the sky, she'd wish upon it, wish that her lost colt would come to her again.

Chapter 6

SAM TURNED UP THE COLLAR OF HER FLEECE- lined jacket. She couldn't find her favorite black sweater, or she would have worn it, too. Saddle leather chilled her knees even through her jeans. It might be summer, but nights in the high Nevada desert were cold.

Ninety percent of your body heat escapes from your head, or so Dad had told her years ago. Sam tugged her Stetson down tighter and Ace sidestepped.

"Settle down, boy." Sam adjusted her hat on its new string.

The narrow leather strips, smoothly braided into a single strand by Pepper, were knotted a couple of inches below her chin.

"Stampede string," Pepper had said as he helped her attach it after dinner. "So you don't lose your hat next time."

Smiling, Sam patted Ace's neck. Her watch said it was after three. Ace should be tired. She couldn't imagine why he kept arching his neck, or why his barrel vibrated with low nickers.

Then she saw the Phantom.

The desert floor stretched around him, level and smooth as a marble dance floor. The stallion snorted plumes of breath into the night. Starlight caught the dust, which drifted from each hoof to create a shimmering trail behind him.

Sam held her breath, joining in the silence. He was the most beautiful thing she'd ever seen, a silver dragon horse, spun of moonbeams and magic.

Suddenly, the stallion's low neigh shattered the quiet. He reared, shaking wild torrents of mane, then launched himself toward them at a run.

He wasn't going to stop. From afar, he'd looked fine-boned, but as the horse thundered closer, Sam saw Phantom had the broad, powerful chest of a mature stallion. He galloped straight for Ace, ready to ram.

"Go!" Sam leaned low on Ace's neck. She clapped her heels against his sides, asking, then *telling* him to run.

Even when she smacked his hindquarters with her palm, Ace only moved a few stiff-legged steps. Hopeless, Sam tried to discourage the stallion.

"Stop!" she shouted.

The Phantom faltered a step, struck Ace a glancing blow, then turned to lay his muscled neck over Ace's back.

The horses stood together and the stallion's head was so close, Sam could have touched him—but she didn't. She was a little afraid. This must be some sort of dominance move, because Ace didn't fight.

The stallion was big. And this close, Sam couldn't deny he was real. He smelled like an animal who'd run long and hard. Though his hide glowed silver with an overlay of dapples delicate as gray lace, much of his fur was rough with dried sweat.

THE WILD ONE

The horses drew apart. Together, they tossed their muzzles skyward. It must have been a signal of agreement, because suddenly, they were running.

With a peculiar rocking movement, the two horses ran side by side. Sam had ridden galloping horses before, but this was a faster gait, unnamed by man. Ace flung his legs out to their limits, and the stallion matched each movement.

I'm being kidnapped, Sam thought. It would be foolhardy to jump, but she couldn't catch a breath.

Night wind roared into her face, sealing off her nose and lips, ripping the hat from her head and flinging it to the end of the stampede string, where it flew like a kite.

Ace ignored the gentle pressure on the reins. Sam increased the pull and settled hard in the saddle. Nothing worked. Ace was running away.

Fear and enchantment battled for Sam's emotions. She didn't dare fall. At this pace, she'd break an arm, leg, or ribs for sure. The sharp and heavy hooves might miss her, but her head would crash against the desert floor. Again.

And yet, Sam couldn't suppress her excitement.

Eight hooves pounded a rhythmic drumbeat. Night wind sang past her ears and tugged her hair. The scents of sagebrush and horse flooded her senses. This was the wildest adventure of her life. She only hoped she lived long enough to brag to Jake.

When the stallion put on a burst of speed and cut across their path, Ace followed. The ground beneath grew steeper and rockier. The Phantom swerved onto a secret trail.

If they turned back now, could Ace find his way back to the cattle?

They'd galloped at least three miles, maybe five. Could she return alone, if Ace dumped her and traded his bridled days for life as a mustang?

As the stallion crowded in front, his hooves rang on smooth rock. If she could see her surroundings, Sam thought she'd wheel Ace and force him back toward camp. But she couldn't see. They might be on the edge of a meadow or a cliff.

The darkness broke. Moonlight glowed on the

stallion's muscled haunches, but just for an instant. The trail had become a tunnel. Stone grazed Sam's knuckles as Ace pressed against the rock wall on the right.

In a shaft of light, Sam saw the stallion's pale head lower. Ace ducked too.

Just in time, Sam imitated them before a cold stone ceiling scrubbed her shirt back and grated over the bumps of her spine.

Ace moved slowly, carefully, but the Phantom bolted ahead. The sounds greeting him told Sam that she knew exactly where they were, though she'd been here only in her dreams.

One neigh was followed by another, and another. A foal squealed and horses swished through grass. The stone ceiling ended. When Sam stared up, she felt dizzy. It looked as if a huge bowl full of stars had been clapped over the top of this mustang hideaway.

She had only seconds to marvel before Ace bucked.

"Steady," Sam said, but she gave up without a fight.

As Ace came to a nervous stop, Sam knotted her reins

together. Then she scrambled down, kicking free of her stirrups before he bolted away.

Dark horse shadows rippled against the moonlit cliffs, looking huge, then merging with the night. Sam knew it was too dark to try to leave. She didn't want to anyway.

Sam worried about getting back to camp. She worried the cowboys would come searching, find her, and call her worse than a tenderfoot.

But who cared? What was a tenderfoot anyway? It wasn't like Westerners went around barefooted to get calloused feet. Sam believed few humans would ever experience a night like this, and she wouldn't give it up.

As she settled against a boulder, hoofbeats told Sam that the Phantom was circling his herd, checking. She heard a foal nursing and the quiet rushing of a stream.

Sam snuggled deeper into her coat. She felt surprisingly warm and satisfied. Ace was home. It was only fair that she give him a chance to enjoy it.

Faint sunlight shone through Sam's closed eyelids, but she didn't open them. As soon as she did, the dreamy valley of wild horses would probably vanish. She'd be back in the tent she shared with Gram. Maybe even back in Aunt Sue's San Francisco apartment.

Then Ace whuffled his lips across her hand and Sam opened her eyes. She took a deep breath, let it out, and for the first time, she understood what it meant to "feast your eyes."

She couldn't count all the mustangs, but she tried to memorize them. Bays and blacks, red sorrels and honey chestnuts grazed beside buckskins, duns, and grays. More lean and muscular than even hardworking ranch horses, they looked wild, but their coats gleamed with health.

As if he felt her watching, the Phantom strode forward, standing between Sam and his mares and foals.

Protective and wary, the stallion squared off, ready to fight for his family.

Sam knew she should leave. Dad and Jake were probably looking for her and they could find this haven. Worse, Linc Slocum could find it—Dallas had told her that Slocum had the nighthawk shift after hers.

Sam stood and the mares scattered. Reins trailing, Ace moved along behind her, willing to carry her home. But Sam had to try one thing before she mounted up.

She walked toward the stallion.

"Zanzibar," she whispered.

His neck arched until his chin bumped his chest, but his eyes stayed fixed on Sam. His ears strained so far forward, they nearly touched at the points. His skin shivered as if he felt the same goose bumps she did.

"Zanzibar, remember me?"

The stallion tilted his head, listening. A clump of silver mane fell aside, exposing a scar on his neck.

Pitying him for whatever accident had caused the scar, Sam held out her hand.

"Poor boy," she murmured, but her move was a mistake. *Too much, too soon.*

The stallion backed away. As his band scattered, Sam noticed a buckskin with a black dorsal stripe and a dun mare and foal with dark slanted stripes on their legs.

They could be throwbacks to ancient horses. Prehistoric horses had such markings, but Sam hadn't known horses lived in this valley. Sam felt a surge of affection mixed with loyalty. She'd come here by accident, but now it was her duty to protect these animals and their home.

She must leave without startling them into a stampede. Ace stood nearby, apparently willing to go, but she'd misread his equine mind before. If he put up a fuss, the herd might run from the valley—right into Slocum.

Sam decided to lead Ace instead of mounting.

"Ace?" She patted her leg to get his attention. The gelding stepped forward.

His willingness tugged at Sam's heart. Ace still had welts from the bites in the camp corral. He couldn't want to return. Yet here, too, Ace was an outsider.

Sam caught the reins and vowed to talk with Jake about horse behavior. She'd help Ace if she could.

Sam moved as if she wore ankle weights. She had to go, but longed to stay. She stepped carefully and kept her eyes fixed on the passage ahead. That tunnel would lead her out of the valley. Ace lagged at the end of his reins as she led him.

Ace stopped, and Sam heard the thudding of other hooves. She looked back in time to see the Phantom touch noses with the gelding.

Entering the passage was easy, but the rock tunnel closed around her, dark and creepy. Sam blinked, wondering how Ace walked without hesitation. She could see nothing. It smelled damp, like a cave. She imagined bats sleeping just overhead, and her boots slipped on the smooth stone underfoot.

By the time Sam and Ace emerged from the tunnel, daybreak had turned the sky peachy pink. The high desert lay silent and calm, but Sam wasn't sure what to do.

They stood atop a hill. Not a huge hill—it was about the size of three houses piled one on top of another—but it was steep, and she could see no way through the sharp-edged shale covering it all the way down to level ground.

There must be a way down. In last night's darkness, the horses had jogged up with so little hesitation, they might have been traveling on a bridle path.

Sam decided to trust Ace. She swung into the saddle, gave the horse his head, and prayed he wouldn't fall.

As Ace started down, Sam stared between his ears and swayed in the saddle, trying to ride loose. Even when Ace's hoof made something skid away, starting an avalanche that sounded like a crash of dropped dishes, she didn't tell Ace what to do.

Dad had taught her that horses were prey animals: Their brains believed that something fast and hungry was always lurking nearby. If a horse shied at a blowing branch, it was because a crouching cougar might have caused that movement. If a horse refused to cross a creek, it was because his legs moved slowly in water and something on the bank might notice and come after him.

Horses knew pursuit could happen anytime. Speed was their secret weapon. They fought to stay on all four fleet feet. So Sam trusted Ace to pick his way down the hillside safely.

With Ace picking their path, Sam should have noticed the approaching rider, but she didn't until they reached level ground.

"Samantha!" Linc Slocum's bellow surprised two sage hens into flight.

Sam ran a hand over her short hair. Its tousled appearance was a dead giveaway that she hadn't just gone out for an early ride. Sleeping against a rock had left her hair mashed in some places, sticking out in wild swoops in others.

Sam hoped her hat would cover the worst of it.

"Where have you been?" Slocum yelled, when he was still a city block away.

Sam cupped her hand at her ear as if she couldn't quite hear, giving herself time to think.

"Where were you?" Slocum asked. "If Jake hadn't said he knew where to find you"—Slocum smirked, glad to have proven Jake wrong—"your dad would have sent out a search party."

Sam still didn't answer, because she was distracted. With their horses just feet apart, Sam saw Slocum's big palomino chew at his bit. Foam had gathered at the corners of his mouth, and he rolled his eyes.

"This is pretty rough country for a newcomer," Slocum added.

"I was born here, Mr. Slocum."

"So, where have you been?" Slocum squinted past her, but Sam didn't turn to see if the silver stallion had followed.

If he had, she'd chase him away herself. The Phantom was one trophy Slocum would never have.

"I woke up and decided to go for a ride," she said. That much was true. She hadn't mentioned *where* she'd awakened.

Sam's chin lifted as she waited.

"No one came to wake me for the four o'clock shift," Slocum said. He sized her up, then looked Ace over. "I think you were out looking for trouble."

"Sorry, sir." Sam shrugged. "I wasn't looking for anything but the way back to camp."

Slocum shook his head. "You expect me to believe that?"

Why was Slocum so suspicious? Sam wondered. Unless he was stalking the stallion by night, he couldn't know the Phantom had come to her. She wouldn't give Slocum any reason to think such a thing.

"I'm a lousy liar. Ask my dad." Sam looked away

from Slocum as another rider came toward them at an easy lope. "Or ask Jake."

Sam watched Jake approach. Her friend rode with a fluid grace she could only admire. Even if she rode for another fifty years, she wouldn't look that natural on a horse.

Jake's mount slowed, stopped. Jake flashed her a look that said she had some explaining to do.

"Morning, Sam," he said. His voice was lazy.

"She says she was just out for a ride." Slocum sounded like a tattletale.

"That's pretty much what I figured," Jake said.

"The way she was speaking up for mustangs the other night, I figured she went looking for some," Slocum said.

Sam's heart hammered so hard, she could feel it in her throat.

Slocum winked at Jake. "Better bait than hay with sweet molasses, that's how young girls work on horses."

"You sure that's not with unicorns?" Jake asked without cracking a smile.

"I hope Gram wasn't worried," Sam blurted.

"No problem. Grace put some biscuits aside for your breakfast. I told Wyatt I'd get you a fresh horse and help you catch up with the herd."

Jake's expression didn't change, but the heat in his eyes told Sam that Dad had taken lots of convincing.

Slocum looked between the two as if he expected an argument. Sam knew that might come later, in private, but not in front of Slocum, who seemed to yearn for division between them.

When nothing happened, Slocum gave a disgusted grunt.

"I'm headed back. You two can ride in together." Slocum jabbed ornate spurs at the palomino's sides and galloped away.

"No reason to run," Jake yelled after Slocum, then mused to himself, "He's just the sort who'll cuss his horse if it steps in a ground squirrel hole."

Sam and Jake sat in silence, broken only by the creak of saddle leather.

"Ever hear your dad call me a good tracker?" Jake asked finally.

He stared off at the horizon. Sam knew Jake wasn't bragging, just hinting he knew the truth and giving her a chance to confess.

"He says you're a *world-class* tracker," Sam admitted.

"I was ten when I trailed Smoke to a wild bunch."

"I know," Sam said.

"And you remember Buck Henry."

"Sure." Sam swallowed hard.

Buck Henry was a hermit who'd broken into Jake's dad's meat house and made it look like the work of a bear. Only Jake hadn't been fooled. He'd trailed Henry to his mountain cabin and knocked on the door before the man could fry a single stolen steak.

"I don't suppose you know about the cattle thieves." This time Jake gave her a quick sideways glance.

"Gram emailed me about it, show-off. She told me you were in Darton after school one day," Sam said, "and identified tire prints from a truck that had driven off with some of our stock. You got them arrested." Sam urged Ace toward camp. "So, what's your point, Jake?"

She wouldn't lie to him, but she wouldn't give away the Phantom's hiding place either.

"You think I don't know what happened?" Jake asked.

"I think that if you bothered to look at our tracks, you know exactly what happened," Sam snapped.

For Jake, it would be as if she'd left a note saying she'd galloped off with a wild horse.

"You want to talk about it?" Jake pulled his fingers through his rein ends.

"Not now," Sam answered.

"That's what I figured, but there's two things I need to tell you. First, if you've seen the Phantom, you know he has a scar on his neck. Slocum put it there."

Sam caught her breath and felt dizzy. "How?"

"Slocum roped him from the back of a moving truck. The other end of the rope was tied to a barrel full of hardened cement."

Sam covered her lips to keep a gasp inside. She thought of her colt's delicate neck, of the concrete snubbing him to a stop.

"He couldn't get away, but he tried, flinging himself

against the rope even though it was choking him."

Sam could almost hear the echo of the stallion's terrified scream.

"But Slocum got greedy. He left Phantom fighting the barrel and went after an Appaloosa mare running with the herd. By the time he got back, the Phantom was gone."

Sam thanked the instinct that had forced her out of the valley and away from the wild horses before Slocum found her.

"Slocum asked me to track the Phantom." Jake gave a cold smile.

"But you didn't," Sam said.

"The blood trail would've made it easy, and he offered me a couple hundred dollars," Jake said. "But I was too busy with school and stuff like that."

Sam wanted to tell Jake she was proud of him, but her mind kept replaying the stallion's screams. She rode beside Jake in silence, wondering what kind of monster would leave a wild horse alone and fighting, with every chance of breaking his neck.

Only the plastic corral and Gram's chuck wagon marked the place where camp had been. The herd of red-and-white cattle had moved on.

Before they rode in, Sam pulled Ace to a stop. "You said you needed to tell me two things. What's the other one?"

"Just this: You got hurt before because I wasn't watching you close enough." Jake raised his voice, refusing to let Sam contradict him. "This time, I'm going to stick to you like glue, Samantha Anne. Slocum's dead serious about catching that horse. He'll do whatever it takes—including using you as bait. But I'll do whatever I have to to keep you safe."

Then Jake touched the brim of his hat and galloped away before Sam had time to say a word.

Chapter 7

JAKE HAD A LOT OF NERVE. HE'D "STICK TO her like glue," would he? In Sam's opinion, she'd proven herself halfway to being a cowgirl.

As she rode drag on Strawberry, Sam wondered why Jake still worried over a fall that had happened years ago. *She* thought about it because it had, after all, been her head Blackie had kicked as he escaped.

You got hurt before because I wasn't watching you close enough, Jake had said. Had someone blamed Jake for her accident, or was he blaming himself? Sam made a mental note to ask Gram.

Sam glanced up toward the front of the herd of cattle, but she couldn't spot Jake's black hat and paint cow pony. After the drive, she and Jake must talk this out. She wanted a friend, not a watchdog.

They'd ridden for about an hour when Strawberry's gait changed. Had she picked up a rock? Sam stopped, ground-tied the mare, and patted down her leg to lift a rear hoof and examine it.

In the quiet, wind rattled the buck brush and cattle calls drifted back to her. No rock was lodged in the hoof, and the stop had cost her only a couple minutes.

She gave Strawberry a pat before remounting. As Sam swung into the saddle, she glanced ahead to see if she'd have to hurry to catch up. That's when she noticed him.

Slocum had dropped back too. Through the rolling dust, he sat watching her and scanning the open range.

Jake had said Slocum was using her as bait, but did

Slocum expect the Phantom to come galloping to her side?

Sam waved at Slocum to let him know she'd noticed his spying. He didn't wave back, just let his horse walk on, as if he'd never stopped.

Maybe Jake wasn't being paranoid. Still, if he thought he could stand between her and the Phantom, just to keep Slocum away, Jake was dead wrong.

Sam pushed aside thoughts of Slocum and concentrated on tomorrow's crossing. They would be crossing the playa. Sam knew "playa" was Spanish for "beach." Thousands of years ago, most of Nevada had been covered by ancient Lake Lahontan. Over centuries, the waters had dwindled and a crust had formed over the muddy pools left behind.

The men had warned that the crossing could be treacherous. This time last week, a risky crossing for Sam would have meant sprinting across Market Street ahead of a cable car or taxi. Tomorrow's crossing would be something new. Dallas had ordered an early stop today so they could cross the playa in daylight.

THE WILD ONE

When Dallas trotted back to join her at the rear of the herd, Sam grabbed her chance to ask questions.

Trying to act unconcerned, she wondered aloud if the crust always held up under the weight of the cattle.

"Not always," he said. "And the animals know it. They've got an instinct for when it's gonna break, and any sound can cause them to stampede."

The crust could crack beneath a single hoof, he added, sending a cow and calf or horse and rider into the quicksand beneath.

"See you at camp," he said, then put his horse into a lope so he could catch the leaders.

Sam shuddered and wished the playa wasn't too huge to detour around.

The drive was over for the day. By the time Sam reached camp, the lead cows had made a muddy mess of the water hole. Some cattle had waded in up to their bellies. Others hung back, keeping calves apart from the crowd until it was safe to drink.

Strawberry was thirsty, but she and the other horses

weren't interested in a water hole packed with noisy cattle.

Sam didn't know Jake was behind her until his voice startled her.

"There's a pond up the hill where the mustangs drink," he said. "Let's take the horses up there, after dinner."

"Quit stalking me," Sam snapped at him.

Jake rode past, but he glanced back over his shoulder and smiled. Though she didn't catch all he said, Sam heard the words "like glue."

She couldn't imagine a more annoying friend.

After chili, cornbread, and a mound of green salad, Sam didn't feel like riding to the mustangs' water hole. Just lifting a saddle onto a horse's back seemed like work.

Jake looked her way and must have seen her weariness.

"Forget it. They can drink down here," Jake said. "You didn't sleep much last night, what with nighthawking and all."

Sam was tempted, until she thought of the two bottles of clear, cold water she'd chugged with dinner.

The horses had worked a lot harder than she, and only had a few sips of muddy water.

Dallas must have seen her hesitation. "Sam, you go on ahead to bed and catch up on your sleep," he said. "I'll get one of the boys to help Jake."

One of the boys. Something in Sam growled at Dallas's offer. His words were like a dare, and Jake was about to laugh.

"Give me five minutes and I'll meet you at the corral," she told Jake, then turned to the pot suspended over the campfire. "Gram, do you mind if I take a little of this before it turns into dishwater?"

"Help yourself, dear," Gram said.

Sam washed her face, then considered her reflection in the little mirror Gram had hung on the back of the chuck wagon.

Her sunburned cheeks felt worse than they looked, but blowing dust and short hours of sleep showed in her bloodshot eyes. Sam longed for some lip balm, and she wished she hadn't chopped off her hair. Braiding it might have made her feel tidy. She leaned close to the mirror and fluffed her fingers through her bangs.

It sure was a lot of trouble, proving she was tough enough to belong.

Finally, Sam tucked her hair behind her ears.

"Best I can do," Sam said as Gram's reflection appeared alongside hers.

"You look like a cowgirl, and that's all the horses care about." Gram kissed her cheek, then stood back as if she had more to say. "I know Jake gets on your nerves sometimes."

"It's worse than that." When Sam noticed she'd put her hands on her hips, she let them slide off. "He either ignores me or acts like a mother hen."

"Don't you think that's natural? After your accident?" Gram asked.

"I don't know what it is, Gram." Sam leaned over and whispered loudly, "But he's driving me nuts!"

Sam waved good-bye and took two minutes to rummage through the tent for her black sweater. No luck. She jogged to the corral and arrived as Jake rode by, herding most of the saddle horses in front of him.

"I left Ace and Strawberry for you," he said. "Just take the path up that ridge."

His gesture was easy to follow, and Sam had no doubt she could handle the last two horses.

After a lazy day just moving with the remuda, Ace rushed the fence, seeming glad to see her.

"Hi, good boy," she said, stroking the velvety nose he thrust over the fence. Ace nodded until his forelock uncovered the white star high on his forehead, and she rubbed that, too.

Sam considered the short ride up the ridge and decided to ride Ace bareback and lead Strawberry.

Jake had said he'd taken all the other horses, but as she entered the corral, Sam noticed a third horse tied nearby at the same time that she smelled cigarette smoke.

The brown Thoroughbred had the long legs and deep chest of a steeplechaser. Double sets of saddlebags hung from his saddle, and the man drawing his cinch tight was Linc Slocum.

Everything about the horse and saddle made Sam nervous. She bridled Ace, thinking that Slocum was prepared for more than nighthawking. Just the same, Sam returned Slocum's wave before leading Ace from the corral.

"I'm giving you a break from that heavy saddle," Sam muttered as she vaulted onto Ace's back. "Don't dump me and make me look bad."

Aunt Sue would have said the gelding acted sweet as a lamb. As Ace plodded up the trail, Sam watched the sky. Dark clouds hung over an amazing sunset. Often over the past two years, Aunt Sue had coaxed her to watch San Francisco Bay turn gold as it swallowed the setting sun. The scene was always nice, but for Sam it fell far short of entertainment.

Today, Sam had seen the sun rise and set. No one had prompted her to watch. The fiery tangerine color flooding the desert foothills made Sam understand Aunt Sue's enjoyment.

Then she heard him. Sam knew, even before the horses' ears pricked forward, that the Phantom had returned. His nicker floated around her like the words to a secret song.

"Where is he, Ace?" Sam whispered. "Where?" She twisted at the waist, scanning every rise and dip of the land around her.

Somewhere, hooves skittered on rock. Sam urged Ace and Strawberry up the trail for a better view, but still there was nothing, except Slocum's shout.

"I knew it!" His words carried from below.

No! Slocum must have spotted the stallion first. His Thoroughbred leaped into action, covering yards of desert, stretched low as a greyhound.

Ace pulled at the bit and danced in place, eager to join the chase, but Sam kept him reined in. Still she saw nothing.

"You okay?" Jake was suddenly there on foot. He grabbed her reins near the bit and gave a tug to make Ace settle.

"I'm fine, but Slocum—"

Jake pointed and Sam's eyes followed. The Phantom was leading the Thoroughbred across the desert.

A pale wisp, he teased Slocum's mount. Phantom let the Thoroughbred draw close enough that he must have felt the Thoroughbred's breath on his tail. Then the stallion jumped a clump of sagebrush and doubled back with impossible agility.

More ghost than horse, the mustang disappeared in the middle of a hillside with Slocum still thundering after him.

Sam told herself everything would be fine. The Phantom would escape. But that night in her dreams, she saw the stallion dashing through snowdrifts, past a candy-cane North Pole, while Slocum followed in a sleigh, face fringed with a beard of ice.

Thunder woke Sam before dawn. She wriggled deeper in her sleeping bag and listened to the lowing of restless cattle. Raindrops pattered on the canvas tent. In the dimness, she saw Gram's bed, neatly tied in a roll.

Dallas called, "Boots on the ground, we're burnin' daylight."

"*What* daylight?" Jake's voice came from somewhere nearby. His spurs chimed and a horse snorted its bad mood as its hooves sucked across wet ground.

Sam heard bacon sizzling.

Moving like an inchworm, she scooted to the tent flap and pulled it back.

"Psst," she whispered.

Jake heard her over the hissing curtain of rain and stopped.

"Is Slocum back?" she asked him.

Rain dripped off Jake's black hat brim as he shook his head and kept riding.

Slocum had been out all night after the Phantom.

Sam pulled on her jeans. Four days of riding had finally caught up with her. She ached all over, and the contortions required to tug up her socks made Sam bite her lip against a whimper.

Dad was waiting by the campfire. He gave her a wink and a yellow slicker. Once she'd struggled into the raincoat, he offered her a warm pottery mug. Steam curled up from the creamy combination of cocoa and coffee, and Sam sighed with delight.

The cold sneaking between her upturned collar and pulled-down hat made the hot drink taste even better.

Pepper approached the other side of the fire and

rubbed his hands together. He wore a long duster that must have been oiled, because the water beaded on it.

The bad weather had put him in a playful mood.

"Great day for crossin' the playa," Pepper said with a wicked grin. "Rain pourin' down from on high and water bubblin' up underfoot."

"Is it really?" Sam asked. She tried to look out of camp, past the herd, to the playa.

"You bet. Think of a hard-boiled egg. Y'know how you give it a whack so you can peel off the shell?" Pepper asked, and Sam nodded. "Well, the playa's like that. Little cracks all over the place, with quicksand underneath, just waiting to suck in your horse's hoof and pull you down, down, down."

As Pepper's voice quavered into the creepy tone you'd use to scare a child, Sam knew she'd been had.

"Hey, you don't want to go scaring a dude like that."

Dude? Sam looked up to see which of Slocum's cowboys had put her down as a wannabe cowgirl. She thought it had been Flick. Not that it mattered. They were all laughing at her.

"Quicksand doesn't suck you under," Dad said, sipping at his coffee, looking patient. "It's just a thick combination of sand and water. It doesn't have a mind of its own."

"I know," Sam said, but she didn't.

"The main thing's to keep the herd together and quiet. Don't do anything to spook 'em."

Dad glanced at her, confirming that she knew what he meant. Cattle, horses, even people got edgy during a storm. The least little thing could spook them into doing something stupid.

"If a cow does go through," Dad added, "we can rope her and pull her out."

Sam hoped he was right, but she remembered an adventure movie in which the villain had died struggling in quicksand. The last shot had shown his hat sitting on the surface of the gritty ooze. But she didn't bring that up.

"Think you all have time to quit joshing and move some cows?" Dallas asked.

The men mounted up. Sam gave Gram a stiff smile

and went off to get Ace. She imagined the earth cracking and a black goo swallowing her without a trace.

As always, Jake read her mind. "You can swim right out of it," he said quietly. "If you don't panic."

"You take care of your little girlfriend, now." Flick grinned at Jake. "Even if they have good bloodlines, dudes scare real easy."

Sam ignored Flick, just like she would any smart-mouthed jerk at school.

"Sam's no dude," Jake responded. Sam felt herself relax before he added, "More of a *dudette*, I'd say."

Jake wheeled Witch away from the other riders, away from Sam. That was a good thing too, Sam thought as Witch splashed away with Jake into the gray morning. She still had an empty mug in her hand and could barely suppress the urge to fling it at Jake's head.

Stop. Go. Stop. Go. All morning they followed the cautious cattle through the rain, never pushing, just watching.

Dallas hadn't asked her to ride drag today. He assigned her to ride on the right side of the herd. She knew better than to ask why. Ranch hands never questioned the cow boss.

Thunder rumbled overhead and a cold wind blew.

Sam hunched her shoulders inside her slicker and pulled her brown Stetson lower on her brow. Her cheeks were cold, but rubbing them with her gloved hand didn't help.

"Hey dudette, how's it goin'?" Pepper called from the other side of the herd. He sounded good-natured, but Sam didn't answer.

Whether it was Pepper's shout, the thunder, or her bovine imagination, a big brindle cow wearing Slocum's brand spooked. She bolted away from the herd, just yards in front of Ace.

Ace tensed to follow, to gallop after the cow and return her to the herd. Sam clapped her heels to the gelding's sides and let him fly off in pursuit.

Dudette, am I? Sam stayed loose in the saddle as Jake had told her to do when riding a cutting horse. But the brindle cow didn't want to go back.

"Hey!" Sam shouted. No way was this cow going

to slip past her. Holding her reins in one hand, Sam snatched off her hat and flapped it at the cow, trying to scare her back toward the herd.

Mouth wide in a bellow, the cow bowled past Ace.

Humiliation made Sam glance back to see if any of the cowboys had noticed her failure.

What she saw made her sick.

Chapter 8

FRIGHTENED BY THE BRINDLE COW'S BEL-lows, the rest of the herd split off in all directions. Some trotted with their heads held high, ears swiveling in confusion. Others galloped, eyes rolled white. Big red bodies slammed each other as the cattle ignored everything but fear. Though the cowboys kept their horses at a walk, trying to regather cattle without scaring them even more, Sam knew what had happened. She'd caused a stampede.

Once she returned the brindle cow to what remained

of the herd, Sam rode at the edge of the restless bunch. She surveyed the playa, hoping she'd see no animals sunk in quicksand.

What she did see was Jake, shepherding about thirty cows her way.

Sam braced herself, but Jake didn't yell, didn't accuse, didn't even give her a hard look. He kept his eyes on the herd.

Somehow, that was worse.

"Jake, I was stupid," she said. "I was trying to show off, to prove I knew what I was doing, and I did just the opposite. I moved too fast. I didn't think—"

Jake's mouth was set in a hard line as he nodded. Agreeing. He sent Witch off at a gentle jog after two cows with calves.

It took the experienced cowboys about twenty minutes to regather the herd, but to Sam it felt like hours.

Stupid, stupid, stupid. So the cowboys had joked with her. So they'd called her names. Big deal. Now her inexperienced look-at-me action had ruined everything. She had acted just like a dude.

The cowboys riding around her, even Dad, would forget she'd ridden out Ace's bucking fits. They'd forget she'd risen from her warm sleeping bag to nighthawk at midnight. They'd forget she'd helped take the horses to water, even when she was bone tired.

Rain pounded down, bouncing up like popcorn from the cows' backs. When she glanced at a squishing sound, Sam saw Dad riding toward her on Banjo.

As he stopped beside her, Sam drew Ace to a halt.

"What happened?" Dad asked.

Sam took a breath. She couldn't deny the stampede had been her fault, but she could keep herself from crying. She cleared her throat and leaned forward, pretending to straighten the headstall behind Ace's ears.

"A cow spooked and broke from the herd. I let Ace go after her." Sam bit her lower lip, then corrected herself. "I made him go after her."

Dad put Banjo into a walk and shook his head. "That wouldn't do it. It must have been something else." He gave her a sympathetic smile. "It wasn't your fault."

It would be easy to accept his mistake, but it wouldn't be right.

"I'm pretty sure it was me," she said. "I yelled at the cow and flapped my hat in her face."

Dad gave an astonished laugh, which did not sound amused. "That'd do it, all right."

As they rode, Sam waited for Dad to say something else. Up ahead, Ross tucked his bandanna inside his slicker, as if the sight of its ends blowing in the wind could spook the cattle. Sam did the same.

"No harm done, this time." Dad's sober look said there'd better not be a next time. "No legs broken or calves lost, far as I can tell."

"I'll stop being so sensitive," Sam said.

Dad nodded. "Good. They don't joke with folks they don't like. They just ignore them."

Sam wondered if Dad was referring to Slocum, whose own cowboys rarely spoke to him.

"I'm sending a couple riders forward to the chuck wagon to help your grandmother set up camp," Dad continued. "In this wind, the tents will be more than one person can handle. We'll need to trench around them too, so rain doesn't flood us out of our sleeping bags. Do you want to go?"

Dad was offering her a chance to escape. Unlike the cowboys, Gram wouldn't fix her with eyes that accused her of causing extra work. On the other hand, riding away seemed a lot like surrender.

"Not unless you need me to go," Sam said. "I'll probably be living this down till I'm fifty years old, right?"

"Possibly," Dad said. "But there's always a chance they'll forget. You might save Flick when he's treed by a grizzly."

Sam savored the image a minute, then cocked her head to see her father's face under his hat's broad brim. "There aren't any grizzlies around here," Sam said.

"You're learning." He laughed, then squinted toward a rider coming up from behind the herd.

As the rider drew close, Sam saw that it was Pepper, his dun horse black with exertion.

"Boss," Pepper said, a little breathless himself, "we've got some trouble."

Dad sent the herd on with the other hands, but Jake accompanied Sam and Dad as Pepper led them to the trouble.

A tiny calf was trapped in a mire of quicksand. His bleating had turned gruff, as if he had a sore throat from calling his mother.

"Where's your mama, little guy?" Dad's voice was gentle, but he kept his distance. "Sam, stay back." Dad held out his arm as if stopping traffic. "This crust is thin."

Lunging to escape the quicksand, the calf had cleared an area big as a bathtub. If his struggles had done that, the desert floor certainly wouldn't hold a horse.

Dad's rope whirred through the air and settled. The lariat looked huge around the calf's neck.

"Better make this quick," Dad said, then spurred Banjo into a jump forward.

Instead of letting himself be dragged free, the calf tried to swim. His flailing forelegs broke through the crust again and again.

Dad backed Banjo and let the rope go slack.

"If I could get a loop past his front legs, around his

whole front end, he'd slide right out," Dad said.

But that wasn't going to happen. They could all see that.

Weak with fatigue, the calf gave a cranky bawl, then pillowed his head on the quicksand, sinking until his neck and the rope were submerged.

Jake rode a wide circle around the calf. "It's not like a mom to walk away, unless she thought he was—" He shrugged.

Dead. Sam gazed at the calf's closed eyelids and white eyelashes. The little animal was helpless.

Both Jake and Dad looked as if they'd given up hope. She knew orphan calves required lots of time and trouble. Sam also knew the whole summer stretched ahead of her. She could help.

"If we can get him out, I'll bottle-feed him," Sam offered.

Dad gave her a sad smile. "He's all worn out. He couldn't keep up with the herd."

"I'll carry him across my saddle."

"Honey, sometimes you lose one. It's hard, but you'll come to grips with it, living out here."

Looking thoughtful, but a little hesitant to offer advice to his boss, Pepper said, "I know what we'd do if he'd fallen through the ice."

Sam's pulse pounded fast. Years of cold had made Pepper leave northern Idaho. She'd bet he knew all about ice rescues.

"Go ahead," Dad encouraged him.

"The lightest one of us goes flat on the ice, or the crust, I guess, and kind of wiggles toward the opening. The idea is to keep the weight distributed over as broad an area as possible. You can't do that on a horse, or walking, but spread-eagled on your belly, it works." Pepper looked away from the calf to Sam. "We'd probably want a rope around her waist, just in case."

Her waist. Sam waited for Dad to protest that the scheme was too dangerous. When he didn't, she felt a little dizzy.

"Then," Pepper continued, "she'd get a good grip on the calf and we'd pull 'em out."

Dusk and rain clouds grayed the desert all around.

THE WILD ONE

The quicksand looked thick and clammy. A coyote called, trying to gather friends to go hunting. Sam shivered at the lonely sound.

"Let's do it," Sam said.

Trying to look confident, she dismounted and tossed Ace's reins to Jake.

He caught them, but flashed a questioning look at her dad. "Wyatt?"

It was the first time she'd heard Jake address Dad by his first name. Some man-to-man protectiveness in Jake's tone irritated Sam.

"It's up to Sam," Dad said.

Sam liked being her own boss. For the last year, she'd argued with Aunt Sue over whether she was mature enough to make her own decisions. Right this minute, though, she wished Dad had taken charge.

"Shoot, he's half-dead already." Jake sounded disgusted. "There's no branded mama around. Why, there's no telling if he's even a River Bend calf. He could be Slocum's."

"Of course I'll do it." Sam warmed her palms against

the front of her jeans. Jake's worry actually made her feel stronger.

"You're not going to let me drown," she explained to Jake. "And the calf's not going to hurt me. I'm going to hold on to that baby so tight that even if you have to drag me to San Francisco, he won't get loose."

Jake looked away, fed up with her.

Within five minutes, Dad's rope was looped around her waist and Sam lay on the surprisingly warm desert floor. She inched her way toward the calf. He was wide awake now and squirming out of her reach.

"It's okay, little guy. I won't hurt you."

Sam was dimly aware of the men barking advice, but her world had narrowed to the calf bawling and bucking in front of her.

"How about some nice warm milk?" she crooned.

The calf's ears fluttered her way. *Now!* Then she pounced.

She hunched her shoulders forward. Keeping her legs still, Sam plunged her arms through the quicksand. It felt like cold oatmeal. She caught the calf in a bear hug.

THE WILD ONE

Maaaaa, maaaaa.

She could swear the calf called for his mother, but Sam held tight. His front legs tap-danced against her chest. The rope jerked her middle up. They began to slide backward. Fast. And then she stopped.

"You can let go. Sam, let go!" Jake squatted beside her, prying loose the arms she'd locked around the calf.

By the time Sam wriggled free of Dad's rope, she noticed Jake had a smear of blood on his cheek.

"What happened?" she asked.

"Your little buddy butted him in the nose," Dad said. He gathered his rope in, fastening it in a loop on his saddle.

Sam felt happy. She felt shaky. And when Pepper helped her balance the calf across her saddle to ride back into camp, she felt proud.

That night, Sam shrugged off the cowboys' jokes about the stampede. She was too busy trying to save the calf's life.

For a while the calf remained limp, then thrashed and fought as Sam introduced the bottle Gram had fixed.

"Come on, little guy," Sam grunted.

She knew Pepper had stopped to watch her, but she didn't look up, even when he said, "Maybe she's mad cause you're calling her a guy. That little critter's a female."

Sam didn't care. She only knew that for an animal no bigger than a dog, the calf was incredibly strong. The rope burn around Sam's waist stung as she tried to drip milk past the calf's tightly shut pink lips. By the time the calf figured out she wanted the milk, Sam's arm muscles had stretched like rubber bands and her hands trembled.

Once the calf fell asleep beside her, Sam slurped down the soup Gram made her eat. She sighed, feeling better, and looked around. The campfire crackled orange and bright against the darkness. Except for Gram, she was alone.

"Time for bed." Gram untied her apron and yawned.

"I can't leave her," Sam said. "Can I sleep out here?"

"It's not good for either one of you, but your dad already said you could." Gram tsked her tongue. "You'll probably get sick, but we're almost home. You'll be sleeping in your own bed tomorrow night."

Gram was doing a good job of talking herself into it, so Sam didn't say a word except "thank you" when Gram brought out her sleeping bag.

The calf lay beside Sam, exhausted. Her thin eyelids twitched. What did calves dream of?

Sam knew that if she dozed, she'd dream of the Phantom.

Today she'd had a rope around her middle. Through her clothes, it had sawed a sore abrasion, even though Dad had been quick and gentle. She thought of the Phantom, caught by a rope and that barrel of cement. There'd been no worry over his suffering and pain.

Now Slocum was after him again.

Sam stroked the calf's fur and tried to think of something else. The little animal had grown used to her touch so quickly, she didn't even wake.

Sam stared into the satiny flames of the campfire. She thought back to how Pepper had suggested her for a dangerous job and Dad had let her make up her own mind. Sam looked down at her hands and wondered if she'd ever get the dirt out from under her fingernails.

She hadn't seen Jake since they'd returned to camp. She remembered his gentle firmness, removing her arms from the calf's neck. There'd been a smear of blood on Jake's cheek.

What was it Dad had said? Oh yeah: *Your little buddy butted him in the nose.*

Sam petted the calf some more. "How about if I name you Buddy? I don't see why it couldn't be a girl's name, do you?"

Since the calf made no protest, Sam settled down to rest. The tendons holding her head up relaxed.

She was almost asleep when she heard a disturbance at the corral. Hooves churned and horses nickered in greeting.

At the edge of the firelight, a rider appeared.

Slocum slumped on the brown Thoroughbred, looking around. Sam was pretty sure he didn't see her there in the shadow of the chuck wagon. Sam didn't move, didn't say a word.

THE WILD ONE

Slocum had returned empty-handed.

Sam felt a quick surge of pleasure, until Slocum hauled on his reins, turning the Thoroughbred. In the firelight, Sam saw dried foam around the horse's bit. Behind his cinch, long bloody gouges had been raked by Slocum's spurs.

Chapter 9

"NO ONE LIKES HOUSEWORK, YOUNG LADY," said Gram. "That's why TV commercials have singing scrub bubbles and dancing toilet brushes."

Gram stood with her hands on her hips. She'd caught Sam trying to slip out the front door on cleaning day. That had not put Gram in a good mood.

Sam had no chance to offer an excuse. Gram kept talking.

"I'm giving you a choice. Stay indoors and help me, or hightail it out to the barn and clean out a winter's worth of straw and manure."

THE WILD ONE

Mentally, Sam compared the smell of ammonia and glass cleaner with the scents of a summer barn. Kind of a toss-up. Though it was cool indoors and hot outside, in the barn she'd have Buddy for company. The calf would be in a better mood than Gram.

Sam rubbed her eyes. This would teach her to sleep in.

Each night since they'd been home from the cattle drive, she'd crept out of bed about midnight and waited, watching by moonlight for the Phantom. If she'd awakened early, she'd have ridden out with the cowboys. Dad, Pepper, and Ross hated riding the fence line and mending breaks the cattle might escape through, but Sam knew it was more fun than housework.

Jake couldn't offer any distraction either. He'd stayed home to help his dad with an irrigation problem. To Sam, even standing knee-deep in water sounded like heaven.

"Take your pick." Gram tapped her foot.

"The barn," Sam said, and made a run for it.

Sam stabbed a pitchfork under a dusty layer of straw and lifted.

Blaze, the ranch dog, lay in the shade of the barn, watching. His tail thumped in greeting, but he didn't get up. As Sam dropped the straw into the wheelbarrow, Blaze sneezed.

Sam stopped, pushing back the locks of hair that curved on her cheeks as her short cut began to grow out. She'd been working for an hour, and the chore wasn't as gross as she'd feared. Still, the most exciting part of ranching was over for this year.

The cattle drive had been the high point, and this was, she hoped, the low point.

Once again, Sam filled the wheelbarrow and rolled it out into the sunshine. Buddy did her best to make the job fun, frolicking beside Sam as she passed the corrals and dumped the dried straw and manure on a growing hill. Instead of buying garden fertilizer, Gram used this stuff.

After just a few days at the ranch, Buddy was peppy and healthy. She twirled her tail in a corkscrew, then made little hip-hop bucks. She was pretty happy for an orphan.

"And pretty lucky," Sam told her. Slocum hadn't claimed Buddy, and Dad hadn't said they should turn the calf out with the beef cattle. "Stay runty and maybe you can spend your life as a pet," Sam added.

Buddy spooked and ran around to Sam's other side, ears cupped toward the pasture. Blaze got to his feet, stretched, and then, ears alert, made an inquiring noise deep in his throat. Ace and a few other horses stopped grazing. They stood statue-still, attention aimed toward the river.

Chills sprinkled over Sam's scalp and down her shoulders. The Phantom wouldn't come to the ranch in the daylight, but she'd never seen the other horses act this way except when he was around.

Sam scanned the wild side of the river but saw nothing. She was imagining things. Why would the stallion come back again?

Sam rolled the wheelbarrow back to the barn and bent to her task. She didn't *want* to give up hope the stallion would return, that was all.

She kept after her work, back and forth from the barn. All the while, she imagined the stallion watching. He wasn't, of course. The last time he'd come to her, Slocum had chased him day and night. Had his lungs burned? Had he wondered why one of his own kind joined a man to hunt him? And before that, when Slocum ripped his flesh with ropes and weights, what had the Phantom thought, under those crashing waves of panic?

Men had done nothing but hurt him.

Sam leaned the pitchfork against the wall and appreciated the clean barn and stall she'd tidied for Buddy. Then she heard a splash. Sam turned and looked out the wide barn doors. Against all logic, her horse had returned anyway.

Sam walked from the barn. She moved smoothly, reaching out to the stallion with her thoughts. *I'll never hurt you.*

The horse gleamed like polished ivory. His hide glimmered at each flex of muscles as he lifted his knees through the silver sluice of water. Even when Sam

THE WILD ONE

reached the bridge, he kept coming, fording the deepest part of the river with his broad chest.

Sam's heart threatened to beat free of her own chest.

"Zanzibar," she whispered as the stallion looked left and right, as if he'd cross the river and walk right up to her.

He shouldn't. *She* wouldn't hurt him, of course, but she was human. Humans would always want to capture and cage a wild animal as beautiful as Zanzibar. He shouldn't trust her.

And yet he swam. Head surging forward, nostrils distended to show pink inside, he came to her. Sam thought of a myth she'd studied in English class. Poseidon the ocean god had driven horses whose white manes blew back on the wave crests.

River Bend might be just a small ranch in a desert state, but Zanzibar was a stallion fit for a god.

His hooves grazed river rock and he stopped, still knee-deep in water. For a minute, he looked away, but one ear turned in Sam's direction. Each second, she thought he'd bolt, but he didn't. He blew through his lips, opening his mouth as if to speak, then closing it as if he were too shy.

Sam tried to understand. Instead of reaching out to the stallion with her mind, she used her heart. He remembered the ranch, but how did his equine mind remember her?

The stallion lowered his muzzle almost to the water. Instead of drinking, he uttered a low rumble that begged her to reply.

"I took care of you, Zanzibar. When you were a foal and just weaned from your mom, I stayed with you, didn't I, boy?"

The stallion kept his head low, but the angle of his ears told Sam to keep talking.

"Remember that thunderstorm when you were a yearling? It shook the barn walls and Dad let me stay, petting you all night until my fingers were stiff. I fell asleep and missed the school bus. Dad said when he came into the barn, you were standing over me like a big guard dog. So I guess you took care of me, too."

He was a stallion now, an adult. What help could she give that he couldn't get from his herd?

Her silence broke the spell. Zanzibar became the Phantom once more. The stallion backed three splashing steps away, then lowered into the current, silver dapples glinting as he struck out for the other shore.

What did the stallion want? He had a lush valley full of mares and foals. They were his family. She could offer him nothing but captivity. Even if Jake helped her use gentle ways to bring the stallion in, the Phantom would hate her for it.

Sam stared at the hills long after the horse vanished. Half of her wanted to hug this secret close. Half of her wanted to tell Jake.

Buddy nuzzled her hand, then licked her palm with a long tongue, reminding her it was time to eat.

They returned to the barn, where Sam had stowed a full bottle. The calf tugged at the nipple. Her eyes rolled back and her tail switched in pure delight. Sam remembered when helping Zanzibar had been this simple.

Things had changed so much in two years. Now Sam didn't know what to do.

The next morning, Sam ran out to the barn before breakfast. She fed Buddy and turned her into a pasture adjoining the barn. The calf had the grassy enclosure to herself. Though she looked small out there alone, the calf would have a good time until she returned to the barn for a midday bottle.

Sam went back to the house and washed her hands.

"Can I help you with anything, Gram?" she asked.

If Gram answered, Sam didn't notice. What she did hear was Jake's spurs chiming before he sauntered through the kitchen door.

"You're in for the time of your life, Samantha." Jake took his hat from fresh-washed hair and snatched a piece of bacon from the plate Gram placed on the table. "Wyatt's going to let me drive his truck up to the mustang corrals at Willow Springs."

"The mustang corrals?" Sam felt excited and worried all at once.

"Willow Springs is where the Bureau of Land

Management holds wild horses until they're adopted," Jake explained. "And you"—he used his bacon like a scepter—"get to come along."

"Lucky me," Sam said. She wasn't sure she liked the BLM, because they took wild horses off the range, and she was half-afraid Jake would act overprotective around even captive mustangs.

Jake ignored her sarcasm and added, "'Course, Wyatt's coming too, since I only have my learner's permit."

Sam drained the rest of her orange juice and watched Jake. Should she tell him about the Phantom? Maybe she should wait until no one else was around.

"You are lucky," Gram told her. "Wyatt doesn't have much use for the Bureau of Land Management." Gram glanced over as the door opened to show Dad stamping off his boots. "You'd think visiting their corrals was paying a call on the Devil himself."

"Them talking about raising grazing fees again isn't improving my attitude," Dad said. He looked over Gram's shoulder as she flipped two pancakes at once.

He licked his lips, then added, "I can rein in my tongue long enough to take Sam up there. She's been a big help at home while we've been riding fence."

Sam felt a burst of pleasure at the compliment. Dad was taking a day off from ranch chores just for her.

"Thanks, Dad," Sam said.

"You've earned it." Dad's voice said he wouldn't tolerate any sentiment. "Let's just hope Jake gets us there in one piece."

Gram handed him a cup of coffee. "I wondered if you were ever coming in," she said. "I thought I was going to have to feed these pancakes to the dog."

Sam wondered why Gram sounded cranky. She'd just cooked those pancakes, so they weren't the real problem.

For two days in a row Gram had acted like this, and it was out of character. It had also made it impossible for Sam to ask Gram why Jake seemed to feel guilty over her accident.

"You be careful driving, Jake Ely, even backing out," Gram said. "I love that Buick, and if you hurt it, your folks are footing the bill."

"Yes, ma'am," Jake said.

Jake looked puzzled by Gram's mood too, and her attachment to the long yellow car, which must be two decades old.

Jake grabbed a chair, turned its back to face the table, and straddled it.

"For heaven's sake, if you come to my table, sit right," Gram snapped.

"Yes, ma'am," Jake said again, but this time he sounded humble. He switched the chair to its proper position.

As Gram walked away, Jake's eyes asked Sam what was going on. Sam shrugged.

"BLM is pretty much done gathering horses for the year," Dad said. His sudden change of topic made Sam think he was trying to distract them from Gram's mood. "Those up at Willow Springs have been there a while."

"I'm glad they're done," Sam said. "But why?"

Dad sipped his coffee. "Usually, they won't gather when there are foals. Unless there's an emergency." Dad gestured toward the range. "I expect they'll tell us that bunch we saw them trying to round up the day you came home was in a real dry area and they didn't want 'em to go thirsty."

Jake continued Dad's explanation. "They use helicopters to drive them into traps. Then they truck them off the range, vaccinate and worm them, and give them some vitamin-laced feed while they're waiting for adoption. Or whatever."

Jake's tone was ominous. What did he mean?

"See where my grazing fees are going?" Dad grumbled.

Sam wondered why they couldn't just leave the horses alone. Mustangs had survived droughts without human help for a long, long time.

"It is expensive stuff," Jake added. "Just putting a helicopter and pilot in the air has got to cost thousands of dollars."

Sam stared out the kitchen window, but she wasn't thinking of money. She imagined herself as one of those horses. She heard the helicopter's racket overhead, felt herself slam into a corral and then a truck with other mustangs.

It must be terrifying, and yet she'd read that fewer mustangs were injured with helicopter herding than when men chased them on horseback. She wasn't sure she believed it.

"Does that mean," Sam said slowly, "we can just drive there, pick one out, and bring it home?"

"Yep. If you've got the money to buy it and a decent place to keep it," Dad said. "But don't bring your allowance, Sam. We're just window-shopping."

Window-shopping. Did that mean Dad might allow her to adopt a mustang later? There was only one mustang she wanted, and the prospect made her heart beat faster.

"Might want to bring a sweater," Dad said, standing. "We could be back late." He turned to Gram and added, "I talked with Dallas. He and the boys will take care of the evening chores. You just enjoy your day."

Sam didn't mention she had not been able to find her favorite black sweater since the cattle drive. That sounded careless. Now that Dad was treating her with respect, she didn't want him to change his mind.

As Dad followed Jake out the door, Sam hustled from table to sink, clearing plates. The curtains at the kitchen window moved in the early-morning breeze. Outside, Dad directed Jake in backing up the truck.

"Come on back, come on," Dad said, motioning.

Sam smiled. Soon, Jake would be testing for his driver's license, and Dad didn't miss an opportunity to teach him.

"Honey?" Gram put a hand on Sam's shoulder.

Sam turned. Gram's concerned expression reminded Sam of Gram's bad mood, but Gram reached a gentle hand to brush Sam's hair back from her eyes.

"What do you do when you leave the house so late at night?"

Relief rushed through Sam.

"Nothing," Sam said. "When I get restless and can't sleep, I go out and listen to the coyotes, watch the horses in the pasture, and—" Sam told the truth. "I've seen some wild horses at the river."

Gram still looked skeptical.

"What did you *think* I was doing?"

"Never mind. Sorry I've been such a scold. I do that when I'm worried." Gram kissed Sam's cheek as Jake honked the truck horn outside. "You run along now, and have a good time."

Sam bolted out the front door and nearly collided with Dad.

"Gram talk to you?" Dad nodded toward the kitchen.

"Yes," Sam said. "But I don't know what about."

Dad gazed toward the river, looking embarrassed. "She thought you and Jake might be up to something."

"Jake," Sam said slowly, "and me?" A blush heated her cheeks. *"Jake and me?"*

Why would Gram think she was sneaking out to meet Jake? Jake was like a brother. Almost.

"Guess she was way off base." Dad pulled at his hat brim.

"I was looking at the horses, Dad. It's the horses I missed while I was in San Francisco."

Dad smiled and opened the truck door. "It'll be a tight squeeze, but the three of us can fit. Slide on in," he said, indicating she'd be sandwiched between him and Jake in the truck cab. "And hang on tight."

Jake wasn't a bad driver, but the road to the Willow Springs Wild Horse Center made Sam appreciate her seat belt. The road's surface was like rock-hard corduroy, and her teeth hammered together as they swooped through the high desert.

"Dad," Sam said suddenly, "I forgot to ask Gram to give Buddy her bottle."

"I'm sure she'll think of it when that calf starts bawling." Dad must have thought she looked worried, because he added, "Gram's working out in her vegetable garden. That's not far from the barn. I think she'll hear Buddy just fine."

"Yeah." Sam bit her bottom lip. She didn't tell Dad she'd put Buddy out into the pasture, but since it was only a few yards farther from the garden, it probably wouldn't matter.

Suddenly the road slanted uphill.

"This next part's called Thread the Needle. We're almost there," Jake said. He slowed slightly as the road narrowed, leaving just enough room for the truck as steep cliffs fell away on each side. "Look hard and you'll see River Bend." Jake took a hand from the steering wheel to gesture down the cliff.

Sam didn't enjoy looking down, but she saw the river, glinting silver-blue in the distance. Between here and there, a maze of trails marked the steep hillside.

"Antelope paths," Dad said, his finger showing how they zigzagged through sagebrush and rocks.

Then the road slanted downhill and the Willow Springs Center was spread before them. To Sam, it looked like a patchwork quilt with pipe fencing for stitching.

Sam's stomach tightened as they drove slowly past the pens. On her right, horses moved away from the fences. On her left stood an office building and a parking lot for three white trucks with U.S. GOVERNMENT stenciled on their doors. Ahead, horses waited as a huge, bearded man broke open bales of hay.

Why did she feel nervous, when everything seemed normal? The pens looked clean. The horses weren't crowded. A hill in each corral ensured rain would run off before the mustangs stood in deep mud. Nothing was wrong.

Sam noticed two mares standing head-to-tail, eyes half-closed as their tails swished flies from each other's faces. Then she recognized what was wrong. These "wild" horses looked tame.

A door slammed and a trim red-haired woman in a crisp khaki uniform left the office building.

"Hey," she called to a bespectacled man standing at a corral with a clipboard. "We have thirty head coming in from the Calico Range."

"Ready," he answered, gesturing toward three empty corrals.

Sam heard Jake draw a breath. Clearly, he'd listened too. Something the two BLM officials had said surprised him.

"What is it?" Sam asked.

Jake lifted one shoulder in a shrug.

"Since our cattle drive ran right along the Calico Mountains," Dad said, "I suppose he's thinking the wild band you two saw has been trapped. Is that it, Jake?"

Sam's mind swarmed with images of the Phantom running across the range with Slocum in pursuit.

"Could be," Jake said, but before he went on, the red-haired woman interrupted.

"Hello," she said. "Are you thinking about adopting a wild horse?"

Now that the woman stood closer, Sam saw that her name tag read "B. Olson." She had freckles. The sun lines around her blue eyes said she spent more time outside than in the beige office building.

"Just looking," Dad said.

The woman glanced away to take in the truck's Nevada license plates.

"We don't get many adoptions from local people," said B. Olson.

"We have a fair number of mustangs running on our ranch," Dad explained.

The redhead picked up on Dad's apologetic tone. "Have a look around," she invited, pointing out which corrals held mares, foals, and stallions. "And if you have any questions about the animals, just ask."

"Are they all *wild* horses?" Sam blurted.

Dad and the BLM woman looked puzzled.

"Yes, BLM is only charged with protecting free-roaming horses and burros." The redhead spoke slowly, as if she didn't want to mention Sam wasn't too smart.

Sam felt embarrassed, but she needed a plan before explaining her question.

At the risk of sounding even dumber, she asked another question. "What if a horse was free-roaming but not a mustang?"

"Like a domestic animal turned free?"

"Or one that escaped," Sam said.

The woman nodded, catching on. "We look for signs of domestication. Marks from the nose band of a halter, maybe." She sounded so proper, it surprised Sam when the woman rubbed the bridge of her own nose. "And a brand inspector comes with us when we capture horses. Branded animals are declared 'estray.' A second brand inspector checks horses before they're adopted, too, just to be sure."

THE WILD ONE

Sam pretended to study a sorrel mare with white socks, but she was thinking, *The Phantom may not have a brand, but he's mine.*

"And if there isn't a brand?" Sam heard Dad's boots shift as he listened.

"No lip tattoo or ear crop either?" the woman asked, and Sam nodded. "The person claiming the animal might supply registration papers if the horse were a purebred—or convincing photographs."

Sam's spirits soared, then crashed. She had a photograph taken when her colt was eighteen months old, but she wouldn't call it convincing. In that picture, his coat was coal black.

"What about a scar?" Jake asked. Sam knew he'd remembered the mark from Slocum's rope. "Could someone get a horse back by explaining a scar?"

"Not a chance." The woman brushed away the suggestion as if it were a pesky fly. "Anyone could tell a story about a scar." She peered past the three of them toward the road, then turned to Dad. "You must be missing a horse."

"Not a one." Dad didn't give Sam a stern look, but she heard displeasure in his voice.

Miss Olson shrugged, then glanced toward an approaching cloud of dust. "That rumbling means it's time to return to work. This drought's caused us a couple of emergency gathers. If you'll excuse me."

Sam watched the woman go. Sam didn't trust her formality and she didn't like the way Miss Olson kept referring to horses as "animals." Even though they were.

As everyone turned to see the vehicles, Sam noticed a cowboy who looked familiar. Not the bearded man she'd started thinking of as Bale Tosser, nor the clipboard man, but another man. His long, drooping mustache reminded her of someone, but she couldn't recall whom.

A huge truck labored up the road, but another smaller truck pulling a roomy gooseneck horse trailer came first. Miss Olson started to walk away, then paused.

"The stallions are in the gooseneck," she said. "The mares are in the semi. You might enjoy watching us unload."

Dad glanced at Sam. She nodded, though something told her it wouldn't be fun.

The smaller truck backed the gooseneck trailer into position for a loading chute. Sam heard horses shifting, stamping, snorting. The stallions demanded release.

Men in cowboy hats checked the chute, tested gates, and unlocked latches. A few held long flexible whips with pieces of paper attached to the tips, probably to hurry the horses along. If they ever emerged.

Sam didn't know whether she longed for their appearance or dreaded it. Especially when she squinted at the horses jostling inside the trailer.

Like most horses, mustangs were usually bays and sorrels, but through the side of the trailer, Sam saw one creamy horse.

Miss Olson joined the man with the clipboard. They stood where they could see each horse appear.

It took forever for the trailer door to swing open.

A neigh echoed. Hooves stumbled. More whinnies were followed by the snapping of teeth.

One horse slammed against the side of the trailer.

When he tossed his head in distress, Sam saw it was the pale mustang.

Please not the Phantom, please.

Sam hadn't spoken aloud, but she realized her hands were clenched in fists when Jake grabbed one of them. He unfolded her hand, gave it a squeeze, and held it as the first stallion bolted out of the trailer and into the sunlight.

Chapter 10

THE FIRST STALLION WAS THE COLOR OF orange sherbet mixed with whipped cream.

He was not the Phantom. Not even a gray. Sam sighed as if a metal band had been cut from around her chest.

The stallion had the thick neck of a mature horse, but he stood only a little taller than a pony. His long forelock swept back from his eyes as he charged into the empty corral. Then he trotted along the fence line, anxious for the company of other horses.

When he was joined by a leggy bay, taller but

younger, they circled the pen together, forming a herd of two.

With all eight stallions penned, the truck full of mares was unloaded into a larger corral.

The stallions seemed to ignore them, until the bay veered too close to the side of the pen nearest the mares. At once, the cream-colored stallion charged, reared, and came down to give the bay a savage bite on the crest.

Surprised and hurt, the bay fled to the opposite side of the corral. He stood trembling among the other stallions, while the pony-sized bully held his ground.

"It happens once in a while." Miss Olson stood next to them again. "But not often. Sometimes there's one horse just itching to prove he's in charge."

"Just like people," Jake said.

Sam thought of Slocum.

"Precisely," said the woman. Then she glanced at Sam. "We've got a vet who'll check that bite."

Sam held her breath. Miss Olson must have noticed Sam looked worried, but she couldn't know why. Sam was imagining a fight between the cream stallion and the Phantom. She had a feeling it wouldn't end so quickly or quietly.

The Phantom was used to surviving in the wild and fending for himself. In a place like this, challenged by other stallions, surrounded by fences and unfamiliar humans, he might believe he was fighting for his life.

Sam ducked her head a little, hoping to hide her eyes. It didn't matter, because Miss Olson's attention had moved on.

"Don't all those horses, loaded with potential, make you want to go on a shopping spree?" Miss Olson asked, and Sam realized she was trying to sell Dad a horse.

"Not hardly," Dad said, but he looked amused.

"What about that black mare with white socks?" Miss Olson turned toward Sam and Jake. "Don't you kids think she'd be just right for your mom?"

Their voices overlapped in response.

"He's not my dad," Jake corrected.

"My mom's dead," Sam said.

"I'm sorry," the woman said. She took a while to put together an explanation. "A man with two teenagers—" she began.

"Understandable," Dad said, but Sam thought he let the woman off the hook too quickly.

Sam couldn't believe Miss Olson didn't just slink off to her office. But she didn't. She hadn't finished trying to find homes for the horses. Next, she sized up Jake.

"That buckskin filly is quick as a cat. I bet you could school her into a fine cutting horse."

Jake shook his head, and the woman sighed.

"If I didn't have two mustangs and a wild burro already, I'd take her home with me."

Sam considered the woman's freshly pressed uniform and short, scrubbed fingernails. Sam couldn't imagine her working in a dirt corral with dust settling on her perfect French braid.

Dad squinted toward the corral, not the woman. When he nodded, Sam considered the horses again.

The buckskin had clean lines and a sloping shoulder

for smooth gaits, and she wanted to belong. Separated from other mustangs, she might allow a human to substitute for her herd.

Grudgingly, Sam admitted to herself that Miss Olson had some horse sense. And she was trying to get these mustangs out of their pen and into real homes.

Sam scanned the newly arrived mares. If she were going to pick one for her own . . .

Then she caught herself. She had a horse. Besides, she didn't approve of the BLM. Wild horses should be running free.

Dad looked restless. Sam checked her watch and found they'd left home nearly two hours ago. Dad never spent this much time just hanging around.

"Best be going," Dad said. "Sam, Jake." He nodded toward the truck.

"Before you leave, I should introduce myself." The redhead extended her hand. "I'm Brynna Olson, director of the Willow Springs facility. Bring a horse trailer next time you visit, Mr.—"

"Wyatt Forster," Dad said. As he shook the redhead's

hand, Sam thought his tone was too friendly for a man who criticized the BLM so often.

Miss Olson leaned toward Sam. "Call me if you have more questions." Her voice dropped, as if the two of them might conspire against Dad. "Willow Springs is in the phone book under 'U.S. Government.'"

Back at the truck, Dad held the door so Sam could slide inside. As she climbed up, Sam saw Dad look back toward the corrals. Something told her he wasn't picking out a mustang.

"She only mentioned 'our mother' to find out if you were married." Sam couldn't believe the sneering voice was her own.

Still, she knew she was right. And even though Mom had been dead for eight years, she didn't like strangers bringing it up.

Dad's face turned crimson, and his expression looked more angry than embarrassed. Dad didn't speak to her, though; he just looked across the truck cab at Jake and said, "I'll drive."

Jake glared at Sam as if it were her fault he'd been

demoted to the position of passenger. Once inside, he leaned against the door, as far from her as possible.

As they rattled along the road back to the ranch, Sam felt ashamed. If Brynna Olson *had* been flirting with her dad, why should she care?

Sam looked sideways at him. Dad's amused expression had turned into a frown. His hands gripped the steering wheel, hard, and his hat brim cast his face in shadow. He didn't look her way, even when Sam sucked in her breath as they drove through the narrow, dangerous pass Jake called Thread the Needle.

She glanced to her right. Jake wouldn't meet her eyes either. He had one arm on the open window, and his face leaned into the wind.

As soon as the truck reached pavement and they picked up speed, Dad let her know he hadn't liked her remark.

"It wasn't a museum or a movie, but I thought you'd get a kick out of those horses," he said.

"I did."

She sure hadn't acted like it, his silence told her.

Sam knew she owed Dad an explanation. Just because she felt worried and confused over the Phantom, she didn't have to drag Dad down with her.

She thought of the quicksand. That afternoon, she'd acted like an adult. She'd given Dad a reason to be proud of her. It was time to do it again.

"Please pull over, Dad," she said. "We need to talk."

Sam told Dad and Jake everything. She listed each time the stallion had come to her and described the way he'd acted. She revealed everything except the hidden valley of wild horses and the Phantom's secret name. By the time Sam finished, even Dad suspected she was right.

"So you think it's Blackie," Dad said.

"It has to be."

"Jake, you've had a look." Dad stared past Sam to Jake. "What do you think?"

Jake looked uneasy with the burden of Dad's trust.

"Couldn't say, based on the look I got. But if even half of what Sam says is true, I'd bet my college fund on it."

"Sam, are you exaggerating?" Dad asked.

Sam thought hard. "I can't read his mind or be sure he recognizes me, but he's come to the river twice. And I saw him two times on the cattle drive." She remembered the magical night ride with Ace and the Phantom racing side by side. "Once, he was almost close enough to touch."

"At the ranch and out there, it was the same horse," Dad said. "You're sure?"

"The same exact horse," Sam insisted. "Silver-white with gray dapples and a scar on his neck."

"I rarely see mustangs. Once in a while around the water hole, and then I run 'em off," Dad mused.

Sam felt startled, until she reminded herself that Dad might like wild horses, but he was a rancher first. Every meal on the table and tank of gas in the truck depended on fat, healthy cattle. River Bend would die without them.

"If you've seen the same horse four times in a couple weeks," Dad continued, "that's just too often to be chance."

They all sat quietly. The smell of hot sagebrush blew through the truck window. A meadowlark caroled liquid notes. A minivan from Vancouver rushed by, and a crow jabbered as it hunted among weeds at the roadside.

"And there's not a darn thing we can do to get him back," Dad said.

"Not according to Miss Olson, but maybe some BLM hotshot could help," Jake suggested. "Do you know anyone, Wyatt?"

"Never had much use for the BLM," Dad said, then threw Sam a guilty look. "They're all just doing their jobs, but they make it tough to keep doing mine."

"I don't want him back," Sam blurted.

"What?" The word erupted from both Dad and Jake.

Sam had even surprised herself. She'd never thought it through this far. But suddenly, Sam knew it was true.

"That's right," she said. "I don't want to tame him. I've got Ace to ride. I had a chance to make Blackie mine and I blew it. Now he's learned to be free."

THE WILD ONE

Sam smiled at Dad, too worried about sounding sappy to wonder why Jake's eyes closed as if she'd socked him in the stomach.

"You want him to stay on the range," Dad said.

"Unless Slocum—"

"Call him *Mr.* Slocum," Dad said. "Or *Linc* Slocum, at least."

Sam couldn't believe it. Just when she got to thinking how cool Dad was, he reverted to some code of the Old West. On this issue, she could not go along with him.

"Slocum doesn't deserve my respect," Sam insisted. Then, in spite of the confinement of the truck cab, she folded her arms.

Dad prepared to wait her out. His eyes stayed steady, and Sam folded her arms even tighter.

Not for a second did she wonder which of them would win the stare-off. They might be equally stubborn, but she was *right*.

She would have outlasted Dad if Slocum's flashy tan Cadillac hadn't appeared just ahead. Honking a long blast, it swerved across the street's white center line and stopped beside Dad's truck.

Western music thumped from the car, even though the windows were closed. Then the driver's window slid down, releasing a blast of air-conditioning into the high desert heat.

Linc Slocum's slicked-back hair and toothpaste-commercial grin reminded Sam of the day she'd met him on her arrival home. This time he wore mirrored sunglasses and held a cigarette in one hand.

"Been up to Willow Springs?" He shouted over the music instead of turning it down, and he didn't wait for an answer. "Find any range rats worth the drive?"

Range rats. Oh, sure. If that's what Slocum thought of wild horses, why had he spent two days chasing the Phantom?

Sam glanced out the truck's back window. Black asphalt stretched off to a heat-wavering horizon. They'd come a long way since they turned off the dirt road from Thread the Needle and the BLM corrals. How could Slocum know where they'd been?

"Fraid we're coming home empty-handed," Dad said. "Just wanted to show Samantha what the government's built since she's been gone."

"There's nothing up there I want," Slocum said. "Even if they bring that white stud in—"

"Gray," Sam muttered to Jake.

"—I'm not sure I'd buy him. Although"—Slocum took off his glasses and settled back in his seat—"there might be some Quarter blood in him. And maybe some Arab."

Sam felt a pang of surprise. Slocum was right. Blackie's sire, Smoke, had been a full-blooded mustang with the build of a Quarter Horse. His mother, Princess Kitty, had been a racing Quarter Horse, but she'd had the fine-boned head of an Arab. Somehow, she hadn't expected Slocum to know that much about horses.

Even though Smoke had been Dad's horse, even though he knew Slocum was right, Dad didn't encourage the man's speculation.

"Hard to say." Dad's response sounded like a dismissal,

but as he started the truck's engine, Slocum kept talking.

"Not that I'd put him to my registered mares," Slocum mused.

Dad shifted uncomfortably.

"Still, he'd be good for breeding cow ponies. Those mustangs have good hard hooves, don't they?"

"Yeah," Dad said.

Why didn't Dad speak up and say there was more than hard feet to admire in a mustang? Why didn't he ask why Slocum needed cow ponies when he had more land and fewer cattle than any rancher in northern Nevada?

But even if Dad didn't want to chat, Slocum did.

"You heard what I'm doing, just before school starts?" Slocum rambled on, as if Dad had begged for details. "I'm getting both my kids new horses."

Sam made a mental note to ask Jake about Slocum's kids. How old were they, she wondered, and did they take after their dad?

"Yes sir," Slocum continued. "An Irish heavy hunter for Ryan and an English Thoroughbred with bloodlines from Queen Elizabeth's own stables for Rachel to use in dressage."

"That's great, Linc," Jake said. "But I thought Ryan was learning to rodeo."

"Not if his mother has anything to say about it. And she does." Slocum frowned.

Did Slocum scowl because of the topic, or because he didn't like talking to Jake, a teenager who'd stood up to him?

Aunt Sue had always advised Sam to give people a chance. The better she got to know Slocum, though, the worse he got.

". . . keep that loco range rat away from the real horses—" Slocum sneered.

"I don't know about loco, Mr. Slocum. I can't help thinking how smart a mustang would have to be." Sam kept her voice sweet, not mentioning how often the Phantom had outsmarted Slocum. "A mustang has to provide food, water, and shelter all for himself."

He was unprepared for the interruption. The way Dad's eyebrows shot up to disappear under his hat, so was he. But Sam had heard enough about range rats.

Sam took a breath, hoping Dad would notice her use of "mister."

"You'd think it would work that way, wouldn't you, little lady?" Slocum said. "But it just doesn't. Still, I could turn a good old-fashioned bronc buster loose on that Phantom. In an hour, he'd be thrown, hog-tied, sacked out, and taught some manners. Then I might make something of him."

Sam only understood half of what Slocum suggested, but she knew it was evil. He wanted to terrify her horse into obedience.

What she wanted was to dive headfirst out the driver's window and make Slocum shut up. But Dad moved to block her view of Slocum and Jake muttered, "Cool it," just loud enough for her to hear.

"You might have a good point, Samantha," Slocum said. "Dumb or not, those horses are tough. And cheap."

When Slocum pretended to contemplate their combined wisdom, Sam felt sick. And Slocum's scheme only got worse.

"Since my wrangler, Flick, is working up at Willow Springs, trying to earn a few extra dollars, I'll have him watch for that stud."

Now she remembered the cowboy with the droopy mustache. On the cattle drive, Flick had joked that even dudes with "good bloodlines" scared easily.

In the lull between two guitar-twanging tunes on the radio, Sam heard Slocum chuckle, and now she knew he was baiting her.

"Yep, that guarantees I'll be the first to know the stud's been captured, and the first to show the legendary Phantom who's boss."

Chapter 11

DAD REFUSED TO HEAD FOR HOME. HE SAID Gram wanted the entire day alone to work in her garden. Dallas, as foreman, could see that the evening chores were done.

Instead of cooking, Gram planned to build wire cages to hold up gangly tomato plants. Instead of washing clothes, she wanted to kneel in the dirt and pull weeds while the sun warmed her back. Most of all, she wanted to hollow out basins around her thirsty vegetables so precious desert water could wait in little pools before soaking slowly to the roots.

Sam understood and promised she wouldn't interfere with Gram's day off.

"I just want to check on Buddy," she told Dad. "I won't get in Gram's way or ask for a single thing."

"Nope. I promised to keep us gone all day," Dad said. "So we'll stop at Clara's for dinner."

Clara's Café looked like the 1950s diners Sam had seen in movies. It sat next to two houses and Phil's Fill-Up, a gas station that also stocked hardware and groceries. The settlement of Alkali had few citizens, but it was a friendly place and the only civilization between River Bend Ranch and Darton, where local kids went to school.

Inside, five tables crowded together and six round stools faced a counter. As Dad and Jake hung their Stetsons on a rack by the door, Sam read a faded banner stretched across one wall. It read HOME OF THE BEST PINEAPPLE UPSIDE-DOWN CAKE IN THE WORLD!

Dad ordered giant cheeseburgers and a mound of french fries. Sam ate quickly, but she waited for Dad to finish before asking more questions. When he folded his paper napkin, Sam asked, "How can we keep Mr. Slocum from getting my horse?"

"What makes you think he'll be caught?" Jake asked. "Blackie, I mean."

Sam refused to be sidetracked. She needed Dad's opinion.

"If he is caught," she asked, "what should we do?"

Dad sighed. "We'd have to adopt him, and that means money."

"I know, but Aunt Sue could send my birthday present early. You know she would, and she always gives me a hundred dollars."

Dad shook his head. Without his hat, he looked exposed. He'd never accepted the embarrassment of Aunt Sue giving Sam so much money every year.

"That wouldn't pay the adoption costs, let alone his feed." Dad lowered his voice as the waitress brought the bill for lunch.

"I have my savings account," Sam began, but when

Dad pointedly plopped his hand down on the bill, she closed her lips.

"I'll think about it, but if I'm going to be forking hay to an animal all winter long, he must be good for something. Handling cattle. Dragging in firewood. Riding out to check fence, even.

"On a ranch, we all earn our keep. You do chores, I see that the cattle operation turns a profit, and Gram does everything no one else has time for. Jake here"—Dad jerked a thumb in Jake's direction—"does as he's told."

"Yes, sir." Jake laughed.

But then Dad's smile faded. "I don't see a four-year-old stallion who's been running wild doing much but causing trouble."

Dad stood, dug in his pocket, and then tossed some dollar bills on the table.

"You kids have some dessert and pay the bill. I'll be back after I see if Phil has a part I need for the well pump. That well needs to be redrilled," Dad said, almost to himself. "But until we can afford it, I'm going to patch it together for one more year."

Sam thought of San Francisco, where water gushed every time you turned a handle. People complained about the cost each month when they paid bills, but the water never ran red with minerals and no one wondered if the supply would run dry.

Dad looked old and tired when he talked about money. When the restaurant door closed behind him, Sam sat looking at her folded hands.

"Just get me a candy bar," she told Jake as he walked toward the cash register.

A candy bar was half the price of pineapple upside-down cake, but did it matter if she saved Dad a dollar? *I'll think about it*, he'd said, but logic wouldn't solve this problem. She had to come up with something creative. Something no one else had considered possible.

Jake returned with two candy bars. Since the coffee shop was cool from the big-bladed fan overhead, and the only other person inside was the waitress eating her own lunch and reading a magazine, Sam and Jake stayed.

"Making that stallion useful would mean training him," Jake said.

"You're good at working with horses, Jake. I've been watching you with Piper. I know you could help me school him. You did it before."

Jake ignored the compliment. "It would mean gelding him too."

Sam noticed the scuffs across Jake's knuckles as he unwrapped his candy slowly, giving his words time to sink in.

"But he would have such beautiful colts," she said.

"I don't think Wyatt has much use for a breeding stallion around the place. They're unpredictable." Jake cleared his throat. "Besides, you've heard Slocum criticize mustangs, and what he says is mild. Lots of ranchers think they should be gunned down on sight."

Sam blocked the mental flash of a rifle shot and horses falling.

"You're saying no one would pay to breed mares to him," Sam said. "No matter how strong, fast, and smart he is?"

"I know it sounds harsh, but it's true."

"Besides, he'd be miserable," Sam said.

"*Dangerous*, Sam. When that stallion is scared, he's dangerous. Got it?"

"Yes, I've got it."

Sam glanced over to see if the waitress had looked up from her magazine at the sound of their bickering. She hadn't.

"You might be right," Sam admitted. "Think of that little stallion staking out his territory in the Willow Springs corral."

"I didn't say a stallion like him, Sam. I said *that* particular stallion. The Phantom. Blackie. Whatever you call him, he nearly killed you."

This time, Jake didn't look guilty; he looked mean.

"He wasn't trying to—"

"Sam. Shut up." Jake reached for Sam's wrist but she jerked it out of his reach. "Sorry. I didn't mean 'shut up.' Could you just listen a minute? This talk between us has been a long time coming. Can we have it now?"

Sam didn't want to have a serious talk. Nothing Jake said would convince her Blackie had meant to hurt her. And what had he meant by reaching for her wrist? She realized she still held her arm up in the air, fingers closed in some kind of hammer fist. She swallowed and lowered her arm to the tabletop, and Jake took the move as a sign of agreement.

"Most of the time, I don't think we should even hang around together." Jake looked at her from the corner of his eye, like a nervous horse. "I can't help teasing you, and you take it as a dare. That's why you keep getting in trouble."

"I get in trouble on my own," Sam said. "You've got nothing to do with it."

"Don't try to lead me off the subject, Sam. We're going to talk about that day."

Jake was right. She did *not* want to relive that day. In her lap, Sam's hands curled into fists and her fingernails bit into her palms.

"When I tried all that Shoshone horse taming stuff with Blackie—"

"It worked," she interrupted. "It wasn't 'stuff.' It was traditional . . ." Sam searched for a word. "Skill." She put her fingers over her lips. "Sorry, I'll be quiet now. But it *did* work."

"Yeah. Most of it I'd do over again. Some of it I still do with rough stock your dad turns over to me. When you gave him a secret name, sighed your breath into his nostrils, and mounted him for the first time in the river, it all worked."

Jake's eyes grew dreamy as he remembered. "That colt was yours, body and soul."

He looked up then, sharply. "But he's still got a horse's brain. We couldn't trust him to think for himself."

"It was my idea to leave the ranch grounds," Sam said, remembering the second day she'd ridden Blackie.

"I was older. I knew better."

"I remember begging," Sam said.

"So what? I shouldn't have given in to a little kid."

The wind had come up outside the restaurant. Dust pecked at the window. There were no trees and few other buildings to slow its force.

It had been a windy day at River Bend when she'd talked Jake into letting her ride Blackie.

He'd agreed, but only if she met his list of requirements. Jake told her to ride bareback, so she did. He insisted she use something soft for Blackie's first bitless bridle, so Sam fashioned an outgrown red flannel nightgown into a headstall and attached cotton rope reins.

As they'd set out, the colt looked flashy and responded like a dream. He'd welcomed Sam's small weight on his back and her hand resting on his withers. His wide eyes took in everything and his slim black legs pranced as they passed the ranch house, angled through pastures, and headed for the open range.

"Everything was going fine." Jake's voice narrated the pictures in Sam's mind. "You followed my directions exactly."

"Because I looked up to you, Jake, even though you called me a brat and a tagalong and teased me unmercifully." Sam was joking, but Jake's downcast expression said she'd made him feel even worse.

"I only planned to take you out a mile or so, but

Blackie was doing so great, we just kept riding."

"It showed how much time we'd taken gentling him," Sam added. "You taught me a lot, Jake."

Jake didn't seem to hear her.

"The whole way out, I opened the gates and closed them behind us. I don't know why I thought that was such a chore."

From her earliest days, Sam had known that major ranch rule. If a rider came to a gate that was open, the gate was left open. If it was shut, the rider had to ride through, then back his horse and close it.

"Coming back, I let you ride ahead so you could maneuver Blackie to open the gate. You'd only been riding him for one day, though, and it was windy. Blackie was already starting to spook at blowing sagebrush. What was I thinking making you fight those gates?"

Sam thought she'd forgotten most of that day, but details came back with the remembered scent of dust on summer wind and Jake's shout.

"Ride in parallel to the gate," Jake had yelled. "Parallel, Brat. Get him to face the hinge. That's it. Now rattle the

THE WILD ONE

gate. Whoa, keep him together. Now ride back and do it again. Parallel. Rattle it. See? He's not as scared this time."

Blackie had tensed beneath her. She'd felt his sweat soak through her jeans. But he'd trusted her. By the third time Sam rattled the gate, the colt didn't tremble.

But holding the gate open and getting the horse through wasn't easy. By then, Sam was sweating too.

"Pull the gate toward you. Don't take your hand off it."

"Jake, it's too hard. He's scared."

Sam could still hear her quavering voice, and she'd known that her hands, shaking on the reins, only made the colt more afraid.

"Just back him through, or turn him." Jake's impatience made Sam feel clumsy. "Don't take your hand off the gate, I said. Sam, get a grip."

The black colt had danced in place, tossing his head. His black mane stung her cheeks and her arm ached from holding the gate open. Her legs quivered from urging the horse to obey.

"Jake, he's really scared," she said over Blackie's snorts. "You have to get this gate. I can't."

All right, you baby. The words echoed in Sam's mind. Had he really said them? Sam looked at Jake across the table and asked.

"Yeah, I said it," Jake admitted. "And as soon as you twisted around in your saddle to start yelling that you'd slug me if I didn't take it back, Blackie fell apart. He charged into the gate. You lost your hold on it and Blackie thought he was trapped.

"His shoulders were only pinned for a minute, but he reared to escape. I tried to ride in and help, but he bolted backward, slamming into my horse. You stayed on, until he took off for open range."

That's when she'd lost her reins. Sam remembered leaning against the colt's neck, looking down at the gray-green desert floor speeding by in a blur as the ropes swirled around the colt's running legs.

Why hadn't she just held tight and ridden out his fear? Why had she stretched, reaching down to grab them? It made no sense to her now, but she had.

"And when you leaned down on the left to grab your reins, he caught a glimpse of you and veered hard right.

You went one way, he went the other, and his off hind hoof caught you in the head."

Like a drumbeat she'd never forget, Sam heard those hooves pounding away. She felt weak, as if she'd lived it all over again. As if she were lying shaken on the ground.

"I don't remember much after that," she said.

"You were unconscious. Your head was bleeding. I knew head wounds bled a lot. I knew it, but it was *your* head. And there was so much . . . blood." Jake separated the last two words with silence. "I didn't know what to do."

What *should* he have done? Sam was thirteen now, the same age Jake had been then. Sometimes she thought he shouldn't have left her on the range to get help. If he'd stayed with her, he could have stopped some of her bleeding. But if he hadn't left, how long would help have been delayed? Even now, sitting in Clara's with no blood in sight, she didn't know what Jake should have done.

Sometimes Sam thought she had trouble remembering things. Was that Jake's fault?

Water rushed against a metal sink as someone washed

dishes in the restaurant kitchen. The waitress closed her magazine, stretched, and carried her plate across the room on squeaky tennis shoes.

"Can I get you two something else?" she asked.

"No, we're just going," Jake said.

What should he have done? Sam swept the candy wrappers into a pile. Then she and Jake stood and headed for the door. Jake took his black Stetson from the rack as she threw the wrappers away.

Sam squinted against blowing dust as they left Clara's and walked toward Phil's Fill-Up.

"It was the hardest thing I've ever done, galloping away, leaving you there all alone."

Sam tried to catch Jake's arm. She wanted to tell him that he couldn't help being a dumb kid, that he had no right to keep shouldering this guilt.

She felt Jake's bicep tense as he shook free of her hand, refusing comfort. He kept striding toward the gas station, and Sam rushed to keep up.

"I'd heard not to move folks who were badly injured, so I didn't. But the whole way back to River Bend, and the entire trip riding out, leading your dad to you, I kept promising God that if you weren't dead, I'd watch over you better."

Sam bit the inside of her cheek. She certainly didn't want to interfere with Jake's bargain, but she didn't want a constant watchdog either. And there was probably nothing wrong with her head.

"I wasn't dead. Which is great." Sam made her voice cheerful. "And I'm a big girl now, so I can take care of myself."

Jake stopped. He faced her in the middle of the sidewalk.

"A promise is a promise, Sam. Get used to it. I won't let anyone, including Wyatt, give that horse a second chance to kill you."

Chapter 12

IT TOOK SAM MORE THAN A FEW STEPS TO shake off Jake's announcement.

They had almost reached the truck when she saw Dad hold up a small cardboard box. The pump part must have been inside, because he looked pretty happy.

When Jake gave Dad a smiling thumbs-up, the tension waned and Sam finally asked the question that had nibbled at her all afternoon.

"If Buddy were crying for her lunch from the pasture

and Gram was in the garden, she'd hear, wouldn't she?"

"I don't know," Jake said. "Which pasture? Did you put her out with the horses?"

"No, the other pasture."

"Right by the barn?" Jake shook his head. "If you got those rails back up alone, you're stronger than you look, Wonder Woman."

"Rails?" Sam's stomach sank.

"The fence rails. We lowered them to back the truck in with hay last week. I should've had them back up by now, but since we weren't using it . . ." Jake's words trailed off as he watched her.

"I hope Buddy didn't find the opening in the fence."

"She couldn't have missed it, Sam. How could you not see the rails lying in the grass? They opened a hole big enough to drive a truck through."

"I was in a hurry this morning." Sam's lips felt numb as she mumbled the words.

On the ride home, neither Sam nor Jake mentioned her mistake. Jake had changed a lot. Two years ago, he would have rushed to Wyatt to announce her blunder.

Hurry, hurry. It can't be too late. Oh please, let it not be too late. Sam leaned forward in her seat, as if she could make the truck move faster.

As late afternoon grayed into dusk, Dad offered to drop Jake at home. Jake said he'd ride Witch from River Bend.

"Suit yourself," Dad said. "But it's coming on dark."

By the time the truck rumbled over the River Bend bridge, the sky had turned ink blue. Only the bottoms of the clouds were orange from the setting sun.

When the truck headlights showed Gram, dressed for riding and leading Ace, Sam's dread turned to fear. Had she saved Buddy's life just to lose her now?

She glanced at Jake. So this was how it felt to be guilty and totally to blame.

"What is it?" Dad called out the window before he stopped the truck.

"The calf's disappeared. I didn't go in for lunch until quite late. Then I noticed her bottle in the refrigerator. I'd forgotten all about it," Gram said. "I was surprised she hadn't reminded me with her bawling.

I've scouted all over on foot, calling for her, and I was just getting ready to ride out."

"Let me go." Sam was out of the truck, reaching for Ace's reins. "Please."

"In a minute," Dad said. "First explain how this happened."

Sam knew she had no choice.

"This morning, before I knew we were going to Willow Springs, I turned Buddy out into the pasture."

"Which pasture?"

Sam glanced at Jake. "The one with the rails down."

"Did you put them back up?" Dad looked at Jake as if he might have helped.

"No. I, uh, didn't notice they were down," Sam admitted. "About an hour ago, I mentioned what I'd done to Jake, and he told me the rails had been down for a week."

Sam felt herself shrink as Dad stared at her.

"Better get going," he said finally. He shooed her with one hand, as if he wanted her out of his sight.

"I'll get Witch and ride along," Jake said.

"No, you won't," Dad barked. "That calf was Sam's responsibility, Jake. Let her go."

Sam didn't know where to start, but she didn't ask for help. Instead, she tried to think like a cow. She started at the downed rails and rode through every gate that stood ajar, zigzagging on a path that led toward open range.

The afternoon's breeze had turned into a cold night wind, but Sam wouldn't turn back for a jacket.

Buddy could be lost. Her soft fur could be snagged on barbed wire. Those delicate legs could be trapped between rocks in a ravine.

The calf was a baby, too young to be out alone. Whatever happened to her, Sam would be to blame.

When Sam heard a quick series of yips, she stopped Ace. She watched the gelding's ears. They swiveled forward, locating the coyotes, but he didn't turn skittish, so Sam rode on.

Dark clouds blew across the moon's surface, dimming light that might have helped her search. Sam stopped and stared into the near darkness. Dad must be terribly angry to let her go out in the dark, alone, where anything could happen.

Ace heard Buddy first. The gelding froze, head level and ears pricked forward.

Sam heard the calf bawl, but then the sound cut off. Why?

With nightmarish uncertainty, Sam rode another step. Stopped. Rode a step. Turned her head to listen. She couldn't give up, but she couldn't tell where Buddy's cry had come from either. Finally, she trusted Ace.

"You're the one with the cow sense. I'm just a tenderfoot." Sam rubbed the mustang's neck. "See if you can find her, please?"

She gave Ace his head and he stepped out with confidence. Soon he trotted through the darkness, jumpy but unafraid.

Two coyotes had Buddy cornered. With her tail flat against a fence post and her head lowered for a charge, the calf did her best to protect herself.

It wasn't good enough.

One coyote rushed in to nip the calf's flank. When

Buddy faced her attacker, the other coyote darted for her shoulder.

"No!" Sam shouted. She clapped her heels against Ace's sides and sent him running forward.

The gelding liked nothing about this. Not the calf bawling toward the sky. Not the coyotes, who'd paired up and backed off a few yards. The gelding slowed into a shambling gait, but he didn't refuse to run between the calf and the coyotes.

When Buddy saw yet another monster, Ace, bearing down on her, she sprinted past.

The coyotes followed the calf.

"Stop it! Go on, get away!" Still holding her reins, Sam slid from Ace's saddle. She picked up a rock and heaved it.

The coyotes dodged, then stood watching her. Moonbeams broke through the clouds, spotlighting them for a moment. Absolutely doglike, the coyotes stood with heads tilted, confused by Sam's screaming.

"Get out of here!" Sam's voice rasped this time.

She was breathless and scared, and the coyotes knew

THE WILD ONE

it. They trotted only a few steps before looking back. Sam tried to take a deep breath, but it hurt. The coyotes probably thought they could take Buddy away from her. And they were right.

Desperate, Sam held her arms out wide, flapped them, and rushed forward.

Apparently, the coyotes didn't want to try their luck against a crazy person. They broke into an easy lope and didn't even break stride as they ducked under a fence. Before Sam's eyes, they disappeared on the sage-spotted plain.

At last, Buddy recognized her. The calf meandered closer, snuffling, then leaned against Sam's legs. All she had to do was get the calf up across Ace's saddle, and it would be a short ride home. Dad would be proud of her. Or at least not quite so angry.

And she'd do it. In a minute.

With one hand, Sam rubbed Buddy's ears. With the other, she held her reins, so she couldn't cover her mouth when she yawned.

"You don't care, do you, Ace?" Her yawn-muffled

words came out in a roar, and suddenly, Ace was done cooperating.

He backed to the end of the reins. His ears tilted out until he looked like a mule. When Sam lifted Buddy and staggered forward, Ace continued backing, shaking his head.

"C'mon, Ace," she puffed, but the gelding refused to stand still. He tugged against the reins, jerking Sam off balance.

When Sam tripped and fell on top of the exhausted calf, Ace snorted and pawed the ground.

Sam struggled back to her feet and faced the horse. She shouldn't give in to him. If she did, he'd learn misbehaving got him what he wanted. But Sam was too tired to fight.

She wanted to be home, warming the backs of her legs in front of the fireplace before she crawled into bed.

"Okay, you win." Sam took the rope from her saddle, settled a loop gently around Buddy's neck, and led her home.

Buddy's bottle was in the barn, waiting. Once the

calf had suckled and fallen asleep, Sam brushed Ace and turned him loose in the pasture. Then she got furious all over again at the coyotes.

The awful animals had been laughing at her, but they hadn't been playing with Buddy. Although she'd examined the calf and found she wasn't bleeding, Sam knew they would have kept up their in-and-out assaults until the confused calf gave up. Then they would have launched the final attack.

Sam stamped her boots on the wooden porch and flung open the kitchen door so hard it hit the wall.

Dad and Gram turned away from the stove.

"I hate coyotes." Sam swallowed the quaver in her voice. "They tried to eat Buddy."

Sam didn't get the sympathy she expected.

"And whose fault is that?" Dad passed Sam a cup of hot cocoa and stood watching her.

"What do you mean?" Sam croaked, but she knew exactly what he meant.

"It's a coyote's job to feed her young and herself. Mostly she does that by killing old animals and weak ones." Dad's lecturing tone said he expected a response.

"I know," she said.

"I don't like losing cattle to coyotes, but some calves are orphaned and they become prey. The herd moves on too fast for them to keep up, and they starve, all alone. That makes a coyote kill almost merciful, don't you think?"

Dad waited for Sam to nod.

"Mother Coyote doesn't figure on human interference. She didn't know this little one was yours. She never would have laid eyes on it if you"—Dad stared at Sam—"hadn't neglected that calf. So don't go blaming the coyotes."

Dad left. She heard him collapse into a recliner in the living room. Then came the drone of television news.

Sam couldn't work up the energy to feel sorry for herself, or to pull out a chair and sit. She covered her face with her chilled hands until Gram guided her to the table.

Gram placed a grilled cheese sandwich and a green teapot full of cocoa on the table before her.

Never in all her thirteen years had Sam heard her father string so many words together. Dad had chosen every one to prove she was irresponsible. And a disappointment.

If she added together all that had happened today, she should be too miserable to eat.

Sam closed her eyes and saw the horse fight at Willow Springs. Once more, she heard Slocum's leering promise to get his hands on the Phantom. And she felt the helpless guilt of knowing she'd put Buddy in danger.

All the same, Sam was famished. She took a bite of the buttery, toasted sandwich, then sat back, chewing.

"Gram?"

Gram pulled up a chair and sat down. Breaking all her own rules, Gram put both elbows on the table and held her chin.

"Yes, Sam."

"Do you think I'll be grounded until I'm nineteen?"

"No, dear. I think your father was just shocked you'd do something so careless."

"I thought you were on my side," Sam mumbled.

"You know very well this isn't about sides. Next time, your carelessness might hurt you."

Sam wondered if the clock had stopped. It must be later than eight o'clock.

"You'll never know how hard it was for him." Gram took a shuddering breath. "For both of us, when you got hurt. For days, we waited to see if you'd be able to walk or talk again. He doesn't want that to happen ever again."

"Then why did he let me go out there?" Sam waved a hand toward the range. "Gram, it was creepy being out there all alone."

"I'm sure you didn't like it, but if you touched your dad's coat, hanging on the back of the kitchen door," Gram said, "you'd feel it's still cold. You were never alone, Sam."

Sam sagged against the chairback. Her body wanted sleep, but her mind kept chattering.

Gram reached across to pat Sam's hand.

"Your father's a pretty level-headed man. I think he'll get over it."

Gram had hardly finished speaking when Dad stormed back into the kitchen.

"And another thing," he began. "If you aren't mature enough to handle a six-week-old calf, what will you do with a mustang stallion?" Dad paced between the table and the refrigerator, then pointed his index finger at her. "The adoption is no longer open for discussion!"

This time, when he left the room, Dad clomped upstairs.

Gram and Sam exchanged shocked expressions. They both heard the echo of Gram saying Dad would soon "get over" Sam's mistake.

"Then again," Gram said, looking up as something—maybe a boot—hit Dad's bedroom wall upstairs, "I might be wrong."

Chapter 13

LAY LOW.

After her near disaster with Buddy, Sam could think of no other way to avoid her father's anger.

For three days she did chores and kept her room neat. Without being asked she helped Gram in the kitchen and vegetable garden. She folded laundry.

At night Sam studied the mustang adoption application. If Slocum made one move toward adopting the Phantom, she'd try to stop him. Sam paid special attention to the section listing "prohibited acts." If half of what she'd heard about Slocum was true, he was in big trouble.

Sam was a good student, and two weeks without classes made this kind of work exciting, even fun. She filled pages of the purple stationery Aunt Sue had given her with reasons Linc Slocum might be ineligible to adopt. She couldn't wait to pass her research on to Miss Olson.

The opportunity probably wouldn't come soon, because Dad hadn't finished punishing her.

Yesterday when Dad told her to scrub out the watering trough, she'd done it. The backbreaking chore left her arms trembling, but she didn't complain when Dad took one look and sent her back to do it right.

Sam spent two more hours scouring the metal. When she finished, it looked like Dad had bought it the day before. She didn't expect any praise for her accomplishment, and she didn't get any. Still, Dad couldn't conceal his surprise at how good it looked during his final inspection.

Now that Sam had changed the straw in Buddy's stall, she laid down the pitchfork. Standing in the barn door, she glanced around. Everyone was busy outdoors, so Sam sneaked toward the house.

What she was about to do wasn't wrong, but Dad might not like it. She wished she could ask Jake if he thought Dad would be mad if he discovered she'd called the Willow Springs Wild Horse Center.

But Jake wasn't around. Sam hadn't asked why or where he was, but her imagination had supplied lots of answers. Though Jake hadn't caused her to put Buddy in the wrong pasture, maybe Dad thought he'd distracted her. Or Dad might have decided to save money by firing him.

She didn't think he would fire Jake, but she hadn't thought Dad could ever be so angry, either.

As she crossed the yard, Sam glanced toward the river. It was a reflex triggered by the fact that she hadn't seen her silver stallion for four nights. Could the stallion know she'd made a big mistake and didn't deserve his company?

Still, he deserved her protection and she'd give it to him, even if it meant defying Dad.

Inside, Sam heard only the refrigerator's purr and the ticking of the kitchen clock. Two o'clock. Good timing, since the BLM office closed at four.

She'd dialed the number twice before. Each time, Sam had to erase her nerves with a pep talk and a reminder that Miss Olson had encouraged her to call.

The first time, Sam had called anonymously. She'd asked if any new horses had been rounded up. A voice she recognized as Miss Olson's described the herd Sam had already seen at the corral. Reassured that the Phantom was still free, Sam had hung up, satisfied.

Yesterday, when she still hadn't seen the stallion, Sam had called again. Miss Olson's answer was the same: no new horses.

It was getting easier to call, but this morning, she'd begun worrying over Flick. She knew he'd call Slocum the instant the Phantom was unloaded. Sam couldn't take any chances.

She hadn't figured out what she'd do if Miss Olson

said, "Yes, as a matter of fact, we just brought in a splendid silvery-gray stallion."

Sam just had to know.

She dialed and asked the usual question.

Instead of the usual answer, Miss Olson asked a question in return. "May I ask who's calling?"

Sam's hand gripped the telephone receiver and she blurted the truth. "This is Samantha Forster."

"Hi, Samantha, this is Brynna Olson. We met the other day." She sounded as if she'd known the truth all along.

Sam glanced out the kitchen window. No one was headed this way. "Oh, hi," she said as casually as she could.

"You know, we don't do much gathering this time of year," Miss Olson said. "February through July are quiet months, unless there's a problem horse or an emergency gather, like the one the other day. We try to hold off until August so we don't stress the spring foals."

"That's good," Sam said. She was surprised by the BLM's humanity. This also meant she had time to pass on what she had learned about Slocum.

"Samantha, is there a particular horse you're waiting for? Because if there is—"

"No ma'am, of course not." Sam looked out the window in time to see Gram stand and peel off her gardening gloves. "I've got to go now." Gram began walking toward the house. "Thanks for the information."

"But Samantha—"

"Bye." Sam hung up, grabbed a glass, and jerked the ice tray from the refrigerator just as Gram came inside.

"Ice water?" Sam asked.

She hoped Gram couldn't hear her pounding heart. Probably not, since Gram only washed her hands and asked if Sam would help make a sauce for the spareribs they'd barbecue for dinner.

When a white BLM truck rumbled over the bridge to River Bend at five o'clock, it was a complete surprise to everyone except Sam.

Work had ended earlier than it had to today, because Gram, for the first time in Sam's memory, had made a miscalculation. Only after everyone had quit chores to come in and clean up before dinner did Gram discover that the barbecue fire had fizzled before the spareribs were cooked.

Since Pepper, Ross, and Dallas were already eating in their bunkhouse kitchen, and Sam and Dad had showered, there was no sense returning to work. So Gram turned her mistake festive. She restarted the coals, then served tortilla chips, salsa, and lemonade on the front porch while they waited for the ribs to cook.

Before gobbling her own snack, Sam walked down to the ten-acre pasture to give Ace an apple. The little mustang had never been pampered, and he was beginning to like it.

That's where she was when Miss Olson arrived.

Glancing over her shoulder, Sam saw Dad stand and shade his eyes. Her only hope was to get to Miss Olson before he did.

"Hi," the redhead said as she slammed the truck door behind her. "Since you're interested, I thought I'd drop by and do an informal pre-adoption inspection."

Informal or not, the word "inspection" sounded official. Dad wouldn't like it a bit.

With the apple still clutched in her hand, Sam rushed forward. "I can't, you know, make any deals behind my dad's back," she whispered.

Miss Olson surprised her by laughing. Once more, Sam noticed the sun lines around her blue eyes.

"Even if you could hide a horse, you'd have to be eighteen to adopt." Brynna followed Sam's worried peek toward the porch.

"He doesn't miss much," Sam admitted. "And he's dead set against adopting a mustang."

"What about your pal there?" Brynna nodded toward Ace.

Sam saw the little bay had followed her. He stretched his neck over the fence, showing the freeze mark beneath his mane. He extended his head and fluttered his lips, begging for the apple.

"That's Ace."

"He's one of ours, though, right?"

"No." Sam's anger flared. "Ace is mine."

Miss Olson was quiet long enough to retuck her uniform shirt into her khaki pants. Sam felt embarrassed.

Just the same, Sam would not apologize to a woman who worked for an agency that not only leached away Dad's money with high grazing fees but could end the Phantom's freedom in an afternoon.

"I meant, he's a mustang the BLM brought in from the range." Miss Olson turned her head, moving her lips as if she were reading the white hairs in Ace's freeze mark. "Clearly, since he's been captive for two and a half years, he belongs to your family."

Sam's curiosity nearly got the better of her, but she would not ask how to read the mishmash of angles that composed the freeze mark.

"Who gentled him? You?" Miss Olson watched Ace grab the apple in one chomp.

"No, not me. I don't know who did," Sam said.

She knew it had been Jake, but the less this woman knew, the better.

Ace nodded as if he agreed, so Sam didn't mention he was a prime cutting horse, too.

Up and down went Ace's Arab-shaped head, and he drooled as he enjoyed the apple.

"Most of them make the transition quite well, if people take the time to understand it's hard shifting from freedom to captivity."

"If you know that, why do you trap them? Those helicopters, trucks, and pens must cost thousands of dollars—"

"Millions, actually." Miss Olson folded her arms along the top rail to watch the other horses.

"So why do you do it?" Sam found the woman's composure obnoxious. "Just to make them miserable?"

Finally, the redhead stood back and met Sam's eyes.

"Number one, they'd die of dehydration. The range has too little water for ranchers' cattle and native wildlife, let alone horses with no natural predators."

Sam was pretty sure she could disprove Miss Olson's points with some of her own, but she'd have to do some research.

"Number two"—Brynna Olson drew a breath and ticked off a finger for another argument—"they'd starve, because of the competition for graze.

"Number three—and this isn't nice, but you look

like a girl who appreciates the truth—the BLM is charged with *protecting* free-roaming horses from folks who want them dead."

Brynna Olson's argument had been so passionate, Sam almost didn't hear her father's boots crunch the gravel on the driveway.

As Sam watched him approach, she felt the tension of the argument drain away. She was about to watch Dad drive Brynna Olson off his land.

"You ladies having a squabble?" Dad asked.

Oh no, Sam thought. Would this get her into more trouble?

"More of a political discussion," said Miss Olson.

Dad's prickly attitude stayed focused on Miss Olson. "So, did we pass?"

"This wasn't . . ." Miss Olson's voice faltered. "I mean, since you haven't applied for adoption . . ."

Any minute, Miss Olson might give away their secret conversations.

"But if it was an official inspection, would we pass?" Dad asked.

"Looks like it." Miss Olson's poise returned as she looked at the ranch with a professional eye. "Your facilities are adequate. Sufficient exercise space, shelter, good drainage. Is that fence six feet tall?" She pointed toward the round pen where Jake worked young horses.

"Yep."

Brynna smiled as Ace nibbled the collar of Sam's fresh blue T-shirt. "You'd probably pass, *if* you decided to apply."

Sam thought of the folded sheets of purple paper in her room. This was a perfect opportunity to tell what she knew, but she felt sheepish. Sam considered Miss Olson's pressed uniform and the sharp way she'd rattled off the reasons mustangs were gathered. Would Miss Olson think Sam was trying to tell her how to do her job?

Before Sam could puzzle out the possibilities, Gram's voice carried from the porch.

"Wyatt?"

Sam could tell Gram was reminding Dad of something.

Dad looked awkward as he asked, "Miss Olson, would you like to stay for dinner?"

Sam almost chuckled. That *had* to be Gram's idea. Dad would never invite a BLM employee to sit at their table.

"I didn't mean to interrupt your meal," Miss Olson said.

"You didn't. Our barbecue fire fizzled." Sam stopped talking when she met her dad's eyes.

Miss Olson looked at her watch. "I couldn't, really."

Dad didn't press her, only shook her hand and thanked her for stopping by before he walked away, leaving Sam to walk Brynna back to her truck.

Looking at the woman's neat braid, Sam wished again that she hadn't cut her long hair. Sam had hacked it off so she wouldn't look like the kid who'd left River Bend Ranch. How childish was that?

But she was done acting like a kid. It was time to ask Miss Olson for hard facts.

"What kind of emergency made you round up that last herd?"

The woman wet her lips in confusion, then remembered this afternoon's conversation. "Dust pneumonia," she answered. "The herd was in a severe drought area."

Sam thought of the wild horse valley, knee-deep in grass. The Phantom was safe there, but he ranged over a wide area, as he'd shown her by coming to River Bend.

Miss Olson climbed into the truck and slammed the door. She just sat for a minute, and Sam saw that the woman was unwilling to leave things in such a tangle.

"I don't know what's going on with you, Samantha, but I might be able to help, if you would tell me what has you so worried."

Sam bit her lip. BLM was the enemy, but Brynna seemed genuinely concerned. Should Sam believe what Dad had told her, or the evidence in front of her? She wished she knew what to do.

So far, this entire summer had presented her with one decision after another, and her choices hadn't all turned out so great.

Then Brynna seemed to go veering off on a wild tangent.

"I have three horses," the woman said abruptly.

"And you know which one works with me like magic, like we were one animal instead of two? Penny, my little blind mustang."

"I can't imagine anything scarier than galloping into the darkness because the stranger on your back told you to do it," Sam said.

Brynna pointed at Sam, as if she'd gotten an answer right in class. "Penny does it because she trusts me."

The truck's gears made a grinding sound. Brynna backed up the truck a couple of feet before she added, "Sometimes, blind trust can be the most perceptive of all."

Chapter 14

SAM SWUNG HER SLEEPING BAG OVER ONE shoulder.

On this moonless night, she had only starshine to show the way along the gravel driveway, past the pasture, and down to the river's edge.

Things grew quiet behind her. She heard the soft crunch of her tennis shoes, a whicker as Ace, alone as usual, followed along the fence line, and the occasional hoot of an owl.

Since luck was sitting on her shoulder tonight, Sam

had decided to test Brynna Olson's blind-trust theory.

After their picnic supper of spareribs, garlic bread, and salad, the family had enjoyed a long talk. No one mentioned her mistake with Buddy, but Dad seemed ready to believe she'd learned her lesson.

Crickets hushed as Sam picked up rocks to clear a place for her sleeping bag. She savored the plop-splash of each stone she tossed into the river. She didn't miss San Francisco one bit.

Sam smoothed her sleeping bag on the bare ground, but she didn't try to sleep. She sat, tugged the cuffs of her gray sweatpants to cover her ankles, and pushed her feet into the sleeping bag's cozy layers. Then she gazed into the high desert sky.

Blind trust. She wasn't sure what Brynna meant by it, and she was less sure the stallion could feel such faith in her.

As a foal he had, but that was a long time ago. Since then, Blackie had encountered many scary times. Most of them involved people.

She'd been the one astride the young horse as he was

trapped by the gate. Later, a man had nearly strangled him with a rope and weight. Helicopters had pursued him, and he'd run hard and long to evade Slocum and his Thoroughbred.

Zanzibar was a wild thing now. He couldn't trust her as a tame horse trusted its master. He might trust her as a friend.

Sam stared into the darkness, silently calling the stallion. The river ran murmuring by, but she heard nothing else.

For a long, cold time, she stared across the river, glad she'd left her watch inside. She shrugged her shoulders and wiggled her toes, keeping her muscles moving. When she finally burrowed into her sleeping bag, with only her face exposed to the night air, she still wouldn't allow herself to sleep.

And so Sam sang.

Ears pricked to catch each word, the River Bend horses lined the pasture fence. Sam thought her voice sounded pure and almost pretty, as it rose into the black and diamond sky.

Sam had run out of songs with memorable lyrics, when she thought of Christmas carols. Even on the last night of June, "Silent Night" sounded great.

The stallion appeared on the opposite bank, hazy as a chalk outline. Head raised on his graceful neck, he listened.

With a powerful plunge, the stallion rushed into the water, coming toward her, mane billowing on wind created by his own speed.

Spellbound, Sam stopped singing. Then she scolded herself. Last time, she'd frightened him with silence. For some reason, the stallion expected sound from her, so Sam kept singing.

Inch by inch, she slipped out of her sleeping bag, stood, and walked to meet him.

The stallion slowed his swimming.

Did he remember she'd first ridden him in the river? Far back in his equine memory, did the stallion feel the soft flannel halter?

Did he hear echoes of Sam's whispers as she'd grabbed his mane and vaulted softly upon his back?

"All is calm . . . ," Sam sang. She was in the river now, amazed that the water warmed her legs. Underfoot, the stones felt smooth. "All is bright . . ."

As she walked, Sam trailed her fingers in the river. It felt thicker than water. The closer she got, the more certain Sam grew that she could touch the stallion.

Once, he lowered his head and skimmed his muzzle along the river. Water splashed as if he meant to play.

"Zanzibar," she crooned, and lifted her right hand from the river.

He bolted.

For one heart-stopping second Sam thought she'd seen the last of him. At least for tonight. Instead, he scampered like a puppy, moving three watery lunges upstream before prancing back to her, pushing waves before him that crashed over Sam's legs.

"Good horse, Zanzibar."

He stood two horse lengths away. Heat from his silver body made mist that clouded his form in the darkness.

"That's my boy," Sam said, slowly moving toward him.

His head snapped sideways, looking toward the

ridge marking the boundary between River Bend and Slocum's ranch. Light flared like a low shooting star, and the horse trembled before looking back to her.

"Zanzibar," she said to him again, stopping. She kept her hand outstretched but still.

If the stallion lowered his head now, his muzzle would touch her hand. His nostrils distended to study her scent.

Sam knew why. The stallion had seen her in many forms. Sometimes she approached him on Ace, so she'd seem to have a horse's legs. He'd seen her working in the barnyard, afoot. And tonight he must seem legless, flowing toward him like a mermaid.

Only scent promised it was her.

Satisfied, the stallion lowered his head. She felt warmth as wisps of breath floated between her fingers.

He lipped her palm, tickling her with a muzzle that was both whiskery and velvet. Sam let her breath out slowly as he nudged her hand.

"Zanzibar, what do you want, boy?"

A faint brightness washed toward them. Without

turning, Sam knew that either Dad or Gram had turned on the kitchen light. Probably checking on her at the worst possible moment.

The stallion shifted his weight between his two front hooves, aware of the change. The new light let her see the expression in his brown eyes. He was telling her something she was too dense to comprehend.

Sam's mind spun with choices. Was he investigating her as he would any unfamiliar object, or could he be asking her to pet him?

When his muzzle knocked against her wrist, Sam opened her fingers.

Mistake. The stallion acted as if she'd grown the claws of a cougar or bear. He was the Phantom once more. A savage light blazed in his eyes. He made a reckless swoop right, leading with a swing of his head. Heavy bone under smooth hide struck Sam's cheekbone. The impact knocked her off balance. Sam stumbled and drenched herself to the waist.

Headed for the safety of the range, the stallion swept past so near that he might have trampled her, but he didn't. Sam wasn't grazed by even the edge of one hoof.

Rubbing her cheekbone, Sam watched him go. In his first instinctive burst of panic, the stallion had left the river, but once his hooves touched the riverbank, he moved more slowly. He loped a few rocking steps, then settled into a jog, mane and tail drifting as he left her.

Once he was out of sight, Sam felt cold. Her sweatpants sagged in a sodden effort to drag right off her hips, and her toes felt so frozen, they might shatter as she dashed toward the house. At least they were numb, so she didn't feel the gravel's sting. Halfway to the house, she stopped, turned around, and ran back to get her sleeping bag. Boy, it was a pain acting like a responsible kid.

Dad, wearing boots, jeans, and a half-buttoned flannel shirt, had the door open when Sam's feet hit the porch.

Dancing with cold, she slipped past him to land in a kitchen chair.

"Freezing, freezing, freezing," she said, then pulled

both feet up into her lap and rubbed them with her hands.

As she tried to knead warmth into her toes, Sam's mind was flooded with the wondrous thing that had happened. She looked up at Dad.

"I saw." Dad's hands rose and just hung in the air. Even though Dad was a man of few words, he used them well. Now he seemed at a loss.

Sam swallowed hard, caught between crying and laughing. "Pretty amazing, huh?"

Dad nodded. "Was it the light that scared him off?"

So he'd seen her collision with the stallion. Sam had hoped he hadn't. She interlaced her fingers to keep from touching her face. Now that she was warming up, it hurt.

"No, it was my fault. I moved my hands in a weird way."

"And he knocked you down." The awe in Dad's face changed to concern.

"No, I get the blame for this," she said. As she stood, her wet pants made a puddle on the kitchen floor. "I tripped."

She faced her stubborn father. Were they about to clash, again?

"Mm-hmm," Dad said. He slid the pad of his thumb along her cheekbone. "This is starting to swell. I think it's gonna bruise some."

"It doesn't hurt," Sam said. She made a point of raising her chin. "And I wasn't a bit scared."

"He grew up real nice," Dad said, then let out a sigh and hung his thumbs in his jeans pockets. "You want something to eat?"

"No, I'm . . ." Sam stifled a yawn. The skin pulled tight where the stallion's head had struck her. "Just tired."

"Your head feels okay, except for that bump? I know Gram would keep you up a couple hours to watch for a concussion, but I'm inclined to let you get a good night's sleep."

"I'm fine, Dad. I took a lot harder hits when I got knocked on my booty playing basketball."

He smiled, and Sam pressed her advantage.

"Can I . . . Don't you think I should call Miss Olson in the morning and talk to her about Blackie?"

Dad frowned for a second before he shook his head.

"Time to discuss that tomorrow, Samantha. Now, get to bed."

Sam overslept.

Sunshine had painted her white walls yellow by the time she opened her eyes. She might not have awakened then if Gram hadn't brought a glass of orange juice to her bedside.

This time when Sam yawned, it hurt.

"Oh dear, Wyatt was right." Gram clucked her tongue, eyes examining Sam's cheek.

"Don't touch it, please."

"Wouldn't think of it, dear, but you might want to borrow a little makeup." Gram sounded dubious, as if she wasn't convinced makeup was the solution.

Sam blinked. She hadn't worn makeup since she'd left San Francisco. Even then, she'd only worn a little mascara and lip gloss.

"Why?" Sam asked. "Does it look terrible?" She crawled out of bed to consult the mirror.

"You might be able to even out the color a little bit," Gram said. "Try it before you go outside."

Dad's truck idled in the yard and bolts rattled, but Sam didn't pay much attention. She stood in front of the mirror, wondering how a bump on the cheekbone had turned into this.

While Gram went to get the makeup, Sam studied the lumpy purplish distortion taking over the right side of her face. What fool had ever named this thing a simple "black eye"?

Gram returned and extended the bottle. "Do your best, honey, because if Jake sees that shiner, he's likely to have kittens."

A mask might have helped, but the makeup didn't. In fact, Sam thought the flesh-toned foundation made her look even more ready for Halloween.

So what if Jake was back? After twenty minutes of fussing with various combinations, she gave up, washed her face, put on a bright red tank top and white shorts, and strode out into the ranch yard.

Jake had just loaded Piper into a horse trailer. At the

sound of her approach, he turned, smiling. But his smile faded fast.

"You should see the other guy," Sam said, nearly shouting the phrase she'd rehearsed.

Jake didn't utter a sound. He fixed the metal doors tight behind the paint filly, then slid the bolts into place.

"Isn't that what guys say, when they've got black eyes?" Sam kept a boasting tone in her voice.

Jake still faced the tailgate. "In case you hadn't noticed," he said, "you're not a guy."

"Let it be, Jake." Dad moved to touch Jake's shoulder, then pulled his Stetson down a notch instead. "She's fine."

Jake whirled around. His voice was low and hard to hear. "I leave for a couple days, and you get into trouble."

"I said, that's enough." Dad's voice grew stern. "I was watching her all along. If you'd been standing where she was, you'd be the one with the black eye."

"He may get one yet," Sam taunted.

"That goes for you too. Just hush," Dad snapped.

Sam crossed her arms. Jake shrugged. Both times he'd come close to defying Dad had been over her safety. And Dad let him get away with it, as if he and Jake were on the same team or something. She wanted them both to knock it off.

"Gram and I are delivering this filly for Dawn Archer's birthday," Dad said. "You kids take the day off. And sort this out however you want. Short of homicide."

Gram came hustling from the house and deposited a set of car keys dangling from a fluffy neon-green ball into Jake's hand.

"Jake, if there's an emergency or something, you can use the Buick, but be careful."

"Yes, ma'am," Jake said, but he gave Gram's boat-like yellow car the kind of sidelong glance horses gave rattlers.

As the truck and trailer pulled away from the ranch, Dad's arm waved through the driver's window. In a minute, it was across the River Bend bridge and gone, with only a line of dust to show it had passed.

"Well?" Jake said.

Now his arms were crossed and Sam's hands were on her hips, but she wasn't about to waste time fighting.

"Well, I'm going into the house to make a phone call my dad didn't tell me I *couldn't* make," Sam said. "And you, Jake Ely, can just suit yourself."

Chapter 15

SAM LIFTED HER SHOULDERS UP AND THEN rolled them back as she listened to the telephone ring at Willow Springs Wild Horse Center. She tried basketball stretches to work out the stiffness from her fall in the river. She'd already blurted out the details of her encounter with the Phantom to Jake, but telling a virtual stranger and expecting her to believe what had happened would be trickier.

Brynna Olson recognized Sam's voice at once, and she was quite friendly. At first. Sam hadn't figured out how to tell a BLM employee that the Phantom was her horse. Jake, seated at the kitchen table with his chin propped on one hand, wasn't trying to make it easier.

"You've probably heard about the Phantom," Sam began. "He's sort of a local legend."

Jake made a face at that, so Sam turned toward the wall.

"Of course." Brynna's tone encouraged Sam. "The wild white stallion."

"Actually, the horse they're calling the Phantom now is a light gray with dapples. And—" Sam took a breath so deep, it might have fueled a dive into a bottomless sea. "He's my horse. Two years ago, my colt escaped, and this is him."

Sam closed her eyes, wincing, ready for Miss Olson's laughter. Instead, well, she said the same words Dad had, but she sounded suspicious. "You're sure of that, are you?"

"I am sure, but there's no way to prove it. No papers, no recent photographs, no brand, tattoo, nothing." Sam waited.

And waited.

"So you want to claim him?" Miss Olson asked.

"No. Well, sort of, but I just want him running free."

At that, Miss Olson's tone changed a little. "Huh," she said. "Well, if you *could* claim him, and keep him on your ranch lands, that'd be the best solution." Brynna spoke slowly, as if she were devising a plan. "Do you have his sire or dam, or any other domestic horses related to him?"

"Just a second, I'll check." Sam covered the phone's mouthpiece and repeated Brynna's question to Jake.

"I don't think so. Smoke's dead. Blackie was his last foal and your dad didn't breed him often."

"What about Kitty?" Sam asked, remembering the flighty chestnut mare, Blackie's mother.

Jake made a dismissing motion. "Gone," he said, frowning.

"No luck," Sam said, but curiosity spurred her to see what Miss Olson had been considering. "What did you have in mind?"

"DNA testing," Brynna said. "Sounds pretty high

tech for the Wild West, huh? But if the Phantom shared bloodlines with your domestic stock, that might be good enough. Still, those tests are a little pricey when you're testing multiple horses."

Sam thought of Aunt Sue's birthday money. "How pricey?"

"The costs are coming down, but . . . oh shoot, for something as detailed as we'd need, a couple hundred dollars, and if someone wanted to appeal the findings, they could take you to federal court."

Even if she could track down another of Smoke's foals and Dad developed a demented desire to adopt a wild stallion, the Forster family would not go to court over a mustang.

"Samantha?" Brynna sounded as if she thought Sam might have fainted from shock. "It's unlikely we'll even bring him in. Why don't you relax?"

Sam had already disclosed everything except the location of the Phantom's valley, so she confessed her fear, too. "Because I think someone else will try to adopt him."

Papers rustled before Brynna asked, "Would that someone be Lincoln Slocum?"

"Yes." Sam slumped.

"Lincoln Slocum was in the parking lot this morning when I arrived at seven-thirty. He filled out adoption papers, saying he wanted to set things in motion in case a horse came in that he liked." Brynna had resumed a cool, bureaucratic tone. "He expressed a particular interest in grays."

Sam held her free hand over her eyes. She longed to hand the phone to Jake and see if he could make this problem go away. But she knew he couldn't.

"That's really not good," Sam said. The mention of federal court made her purple pages of Slocum's transgressions seem pretty weak.

"Don't give up. Just let me look at this application a minute . . ." Brynna's voice faded.

As Miss Olson looked over Slocum's application, Sam hoped the woman would find something that showed Slocum shouldn't be allowed to adopt a wild horse.

"Never mind," Brynna said. "To discuss this in any

more detail would be unprofessional. I've only shared this much because the man annoyed me. He asked if he could finance a roundup targeting grays."

Sam thought a second. A helicopter, a pilot, wranglers, trailers, and portable corrals were, as Brynna said, pretty pricey. "He wanted to pay for it all? Himself?"

Sam heard an open hand slamming a desktop.

"Can you believe it?" Brynna's voice soared with outrage. "Of course, I told him the federal government doesn't work that way, and then—" Brynna turned businesslike again. "Samantha, please give me your number so I can phone if there are any developments that might interest you."

Sam had barely finished reciting the numbers when the woman said, "You have a nice day."

"Wait, wait! Brynna?" Sam saw Jake raise his eyebrows and silently form the word *Brynna?* She ignored him.

"Yes, Samantha?" Brynna's patience sounded strained.

"I think one of Linc Slocum's cowboys is working for you."

In the moment of silence, Sam couldn't tell if Brynna

was perturbed with her or if she resented the possibility that she'd been used.

"We always have new hires in the summer—" Brynna began.

"His name's Flick."

"—but thank goodness, no one by that name."

And then Brynna Olson hung up.

"I guess I am glad you're back," Sam admitted, after she'd shared the bad news with Jake. "Where were you, anyway?"

"My mom had to drive into Reno for a teachers' conference. It's to help rural teachers keep up with the rest of the state."

Gram had mentioned that Jake's mother taught at Darton High School. Sam was eager to see her again and glad she'd know a teacher at her new school, even if her only memory of Maxine Ely was a small blond woman as vivacious as her husband was quiet.

"It's about a four-hour trip, and Mom thought I could use the driving practice. In fact, I tested for my license while I was there. And passed." Jake looked smug.

"Now, if you only had a car," Sam teased.

"You sure know how to make a guy feel important, Sam. Someday you'll ask me to take you someplace and I'll remind you of that crack," Jake said. "Anyway, since Mom had a hotel room to herself and Dad won't leave the ranch unless it's for a wedding or a funeral, I went and hung around."

"Doing what?" Sam asked.

"The hotel had a gym and swimming pool, and a video arcade. Mainly, I watched a lot of TV."

Sam didn't feel a single twinge of jealousy, but she did feel relieved, and her sigh escaped in a gust.

"Your eye hurt?" Jake guessed.

"No," Sam said. Actually, it *was* sore, and she didn't like being reminded of how it must look. "I thought Dad had fired you."

"Fired me?" Jake laughed. "I guess he could, but that's not really how we work. It's more like, we both make a small profit and a big reputation for turning out good, gentle working horses.

"We go to auctions, buy raw horses, and then school them."

"Like Piper," Sam said. "Weren't you sorry to see her go?"

"A little, but Dawn Archer's a good rider, and her dad's had his eye on that filly from the first. He'll pay Wyatt top dollar, now that she's gentled. And that's how it works. When we sell, your dad deducts the cost of feed, shots, and shoes from the horse's price, and then we split the profit—sixty percent for him and forty percent for me."

"It won't be enough to buy a car, will it?" Sam asked.

"It all adds up," Jake said, rubbing his hands together like a miser. "And it beats working at McDonald's or Phil's Fill-Up."

The ringing phone startled them. It was too soon for Dad and Gram to be calling to check on them, and ranchers didn't hang around the house talking on the phone in the middle of the morning.

"Hello?"

"Samantha, this is Brynna Olson. We have that stallion."

"Now? But I thought you said—"

"Two of our new hires just brought him in cross-tied and blindfolded. They said they got a complaint from a nearby rancher." Brynna sounded doubtful. "What matters is this: The horse seemed pretty calm until they removed this black sweater they'd used to blindfold him. Once he saw where he was, that stallion started screaming. He went insane."

"Oh no."

"Samantha, this is serious. He's rammed a wooden fence. He's bleeding and we can't get close to him. He's reared and gone over backward. Other horses are panicking. A foal may have broken her leg trying to escape. This is serious," she repeated.

Sam didn't allow her heart to break. The Phantom had been tricked and betrayed. She was his only hope.

"I'll be there as soon as I can," she promised.

"I hope it's soon enough." Brynna's no-nonsense

voice was colder than ever. "Because if I can't get him sedated, I'll have to put him down."

Jake grabbed Gram's fluffy key chain before Sam could explain. He went out to start the Buick while Sam scrawled a note to Dad and Gram, grabbed her purple pages, and then ran after him. She had to jump back on the porch, though, when the car careened too close.

"Can you drive this thing? Or—"

"Or what?" Jake demanded.

"Or—" Sam climbed in and buckled her seat belt, then wrapped her arms around her ribs as they bumped toward the bridge. The big car didn't look like it would fit. "Or should I see if I can get Dallas to drive me up there? I mean, you barely have your license."

"No kidding?" Jake accelerated once they crossed the bridge. "And after you found Dallas, do you really think he'd figure this was enough of an emergency to quit working on the pump after he told Wyatt he'd handle it?" Jake filled the silence. "I don't think so."

Jake was right. He was also risking a lot by driving Gram's car with a brand-new license. Sam wondered why he hadn't hesitated to take her to the aid of a horse he feared would hurt her. He must be doing this for her.

"Thanks, Jake."

He grunted and kept driving.

They drove ten minutes without passing another car, and Sam stayed quiet so Jake could concentrate. They slipped through Alkali without slowing down.

Sam wondered if Slocum was in front of them or behind them. Only when they made the hard right turn off the asphalt and onto the dirt road that would take them uphill to Thread the Needle and the Willow Springs corrals did she find out.

Jake sucked in a breath that made Sam worry.

She bit her lip as rocks crunched under the Buick's tires. The big car wallowed in the deep sand, lost traction with one tire, but stayed upright.

"We doing okay?" she asked.

"Fine, but you'd better keep watch out the back window. I just caught a glimpse of Slocum's car."

The tan Cadillac was about a mile behind them.

"He's an adult," Sam blurted.

"So?"

"Neither of us can sign for the adoption."

"Sam, we're not going to adopt the Phantom. We're driving up there to, uh, to try to—just why *are* we going?"

"To keep him from getting hurt."

"Don't tell me you think you can get close to him like you did last night." He glanced away from the road and gave her a grim glare. "Do not tell me that."

Sam stared out the windshield. That's exactly what she planned to do. But Jake had said not to tell him, so she wouldn't.

"Sam? Better answer me, or I'm pulling over right now and waving Slocum good luck as he goes past."

"I'm just going because Brynna said I should," Sam said, and it was only a white lie. Brynna must have wanted her to come, or she wouldn't have called.

Jake swerved around a refrigerator-sized rock. "She has to hold horses till they've been freeze-branded and vaccinated, anyway."

Jake was trying to comfort her, but as Sam shrank

back against the seat, she imagined the Phantom's terror. And though the branding and vaccinating would hurt the stallion, it wouldn't hurt as much as the betrayal. Sam thought about the blindfold Brynna had described. "They used my sweater to blindfold him."

"Yeah?" Jake sawed at the steering wheel as they began a series of switchbacks. "That was a dirty trick."

"They used *my* scent to keep him calm. That flash I saw on the ridge last night was probably Slocum, smoking cigarettes and throwing matches like he always does." Sam shivered. Like a stalker, Slocum had been watching her.

"It means Slocum started planning this a long time ago, during the cattle drive. That's when my sweater disappeared. He's a weird guy, Jake."

"He's also a fast guy," Jake said, eyes on the rearview mirror.

Sam twisted to look over the seat back. Slocum was gaining on them. "Can Gram's car go any faster?"

"Not much, but I have an idea."

Jake punched the accelerator and the car wobbled too

near the edge of the road, but they drew away steadily. They'd almost reached Thread the Needle, and Slocum's Cadillac was just slogging through the switchbacks.

As Gram's car entered the single-lane road, Jake slammed on the brakes.

"What are you doing?" Sam shouted. Since last time, she'd had a creepy feeling about Thread the Needle. "You said there's no way another car can pass here. You can't stop."

But Jake did stop. He switched off the ignition and left the car aslant the road. He climbed out, fiddled with the hood, and opened it.

Sam climbed out too. The desert heat hit her as if she'd opened the world's biggest oven door. For an instant she was glad to be dressed in shorts and tennis shoes instead of boots and jeans.

Then she watched Jake's head disappear under the car hood.

"Jake?"

"Quit shrieking and start running, Brat." His voice was muffled. "I'm pulling out the"—he stretched further into the engine compartment and tugged—"coil to the distributor. My buddy Darrell . . . ," he began, then changed what he'd been about to say, "is someone you don't need to meet, but he always has a trick up his sleeve and this is one he taught me."

With a satisfied sound, Jake reappeared. He shoved a wire, curled like a spring, at her.

"Stick that in your pocket," Jake ordered. "Gram's Buick isn't going anywhere until we put it back."

The Cadillac roared closer. Sam hated to leave Jake to deal with an angry and frustrated Slocum.

"Run, Sam!" Jake gave Sam a shove between the shoulder blades, and she took off. "And don't do anything stupid!"

Chapter 16

SAM'S HEARTBEAT POUNDED IN HER THROAT, in her arms, and in her face. It wasn't the blistering heat that made her run a choppy pace. Sam was afraid.

She slipped on a patch of gravel. Her feet shot out from under her body, and only her hands kept her face from slamming into the dirt.

Sam stood, wiped the dirt and blood from her palms on her shorts, and glanced down the hillside to her left.

Hypnotized by the steep drop-off, Sam couldn't help

but look. Far away, River Bend was arranged like a toy ranch and the river glinted silver blue.

If only the Phantom were down there, playing in the river, safe and sound. But he wasn't, so Sam kept running.

If Slocum got her horse, there were ways to get him back. If Zanzibar died . . .

She quit thinking of the powerful stallion, slamming the door on those nightmare images. Instead, she thought of Jake. Slocum had probably reached him by now. Slocum would be furious. But Jake was younger, stronger, and faster. And hard in a way Slocum could never achieve, even if he spent hours in a gym. Jake worked. Slocum only pretended. Slocum had to buy the trappings of a cowboy. Jake was the real thing.

The rhythm of Sam's steps turned regular. She caught her breath, kept her head level, and aimed her eyes straight ahead.

She heard the Phantom's neigh before she saw him. Raspy, as if he'd screamed his throat raw, his cry and galloping hooves lured Sam to his corral.

People. Sam caught a glimpse of Miss Olson in her khaki-colored uniform. She saw Flick and the men she'd identified as Bale Thrower and Clipboard when she'd visited the corrals before. She refused to let them see her. Or stop her.

Sam ducked and sneaked along the fence, keeping her head low. She couldn't risk walking to the gate and opening it. If Phantom galloped through, he'd be lost in the maze of corrals and easily recaptured. She looked for another way in.

Down a few yards, a bottom rail was missing from the fence. She crept along, determined to reach that gap. Once there, she'd slip under and into the corral before she was spotted.

"The vet's on her way."

Sam recognized Miss Olson's voice. Her tone was so unemotional, Sam couldn't tell if the vet was coming to sedate the stallion or destroy him.

As if he understood, the stallion trumpeted a challenging neigh. Sam had to look. She crouched and peered through the fence rails.

THE WILD ONE

The Phantom was transformed by fury. Dirt dulled his silver coat. His drifting mane lay clumped and matted with mud from dust mixed with his sweat, but he fought captivity with every weapon a wild horse possessed.

He tried speed, galloping around the corral. Stumbling and exhausted, he still tried to outrun the walls surrounding him.

He tried slashing hooves, battering the fence until he dropped back, all four legs spread wide to keep from falling.

He tried screaming with defiance. He was a king of stallions determined to scare his captor.

And then, once more, he ran.

"I want to see you two, now," Miss Olson snapped with authority. She stood with one foot on the porch. From where Sam hid, it looked like there was a pile of rope on the porch. Sam hoped Miss Olson was calling in the two men who'd trapped the Phantom.

"Yeah?" The lazy voice was Flick's. "Ed's gone, but what do you want with me?"

He didn't sound worried. Miss Olson's voice was stern, but Sam didn't listen.

Time was running out. Sam edged closer to the gap beneath the fence.

The faltering stutter of the Phantom's hooves made Sam wonder if the stallion scented her. His dread increased. He ran faster, streaking along the fence line and slamming into a corner. Only then did he turn, run, and ram into the next corner.

Blood ran in rivulets between his churning forelegs. Twists of forelock hid his eyes, but that wasn't why he kept running and slamming into each corner. The royal stallion ran blind with rage.

"He's doing it again." Miss Olson sounded close. "I'm afraid he'll run himself to death."

There were mumbles from Bale Thrower and Clipboard, but Sam heard Flick clearly.

"Hasn't got a brain left in that puny mustang head," Flick said.

"You've got your paycheck," Miss Olson said. "I asked you to leave. Do it."

"Oh yes, ma'am." Flick laughed. "I guess I got what I came for."

Sam knew he didn't mean the money.

Face lowered to within a quarter inch of the dirt, Sam slid under the fence rails. The stallion's hooves came to a halt.

Sam stood. If anyone saw her now, it would be too late. She walked slowly to the middle of the corral. The stallion watched, vibrating with an emotion Sam couldn't read.

This wasn't the river. None of the stallion's movements would be slowed by water. Sam's cheek still ached from last night's accidental blow.

If this horse wanted to hurt her, she couldn't stop him.

If he hurt her, Miss Olson would surely put him down.

With everything at stake, Sam stretched out her hand in a gesture the horse understood.

The stallion froze. His nostrils flared wide from exertion. Sam imagined the feel of velvet muzzle and prickly whiskers, but the stallion didn't lower his head as he had last night.

He straightened to a commanding height, tossed his forelock back, and stared. He blinked once, as if he couldn't believe she'd dare this.

He took two steps forward and as he did, Sam heard Miss Olson gasp. She said something too, but Sam quit listening as the Phantom pinned back his ears and charged.

Sam didn't move, couldn't move, and the stallion passed by. Dust choked her, but she refused to cough. His hooves stamped behind her, and she turned to face him.

Sam reached into her memory, trying to recall the signs of horse language Jake had taught her.

The stallion reared, showing a vast underbelly spattered with mud and blood. He lowered to all four legs, gathered himself into a churning coil of muscle, and charged past again, head snaking out as if he'd bite; but he didn't.

The stallion told her he was confused and angry. He said he wasn't going to kill her, even if she deserved it.

He moved around the pen at a trot and as he turned

gracefully at each corner, Sam sighed. The Phantom was acting like a normal, nervous horse.

Voices attracted her eyes.

Jake was there. "She knows what she's doing. At least *he* thinks she does."

The stallion curved away from the fence and walked toward her. He stopped and stared toward the mountains, with one ear turned her way.

Sam talked to him.

"Hey, boy, I'm sorry. I'm so sorry they hurt you."

The horse shuddered, but his ear stayed turned to catch each word. She knew the sound he was waiting for, and she uttered it so quietly, no one else could hear.

"Zanzibar." Sam breathed the word, hoping it reached his ears.

Her scent had betrayed the stallion. The word was all she had left to offer him. The word held all her love. No one else must hear it. Ever.

The stallion's head swung to face her. He took two steps, then pawed the dirt. His respiration was labored, raising his wide chest. Blood misted from his nostrils.

"Zanzibar," she whispered. "It's okay. I'll get you out of here, I will."

When his lips fluttered, Sam felt his breath. His neck stretched past her hand, lifting. If he bolted now, she'd go down under his hooves and be trampled.

"Zanzibar, I love you, big horse."

The stallion lowered his mighty head to Sam's shoulder. His sigh rocked them both. She saw his muscles loosen, felt his head grow heavy as he calmed.

Neither horse nor girl moved for a very long time.

Slocum's high-heeled boots and broad belly kept him from reaching Willow Springs until after Sam left the Phantom resting in his corral.

As Sam came through the gate, Jake called her nine kinds of fool and ten kinds of idiot, then gave her a hug that nearly broke her ribs.

Miss Olson ordered Sam to sit down on the office stairs until she decided whether to arrest her or award her a medal. Sam gave Miss Olson the purple pages, just in case they could sway things in her favor. The woman skimmed them and folded them into her pocket, but she didn't comment on Sam's hours of work.

When Slocum finally staggered up to the porch outside the office, he was puffing from exertion but doing his best to seem polite.

"Miss Olson." Slocum took her hand in a meaty grip. "I hardly expected to see you again so soon. But it's a pleasure, of course." Slocum paused to breathe. "Excuse me," he said, patting his chest. "I walked all the way up here. Some old clunker of a car broke down on the road and its driver neglected to pull over to the side."

Slocum glared at Jake, then continued, "I hear you were able to recapture my horse."

"*Your* horse?" Sam shot up from her seat on the porch. "What in the world are you talking about?"

"Oh now, sugar," Slocum said, hefting his belt so the trophy buckle dented his overhanging belly. "You're not hoping that's your little black colt all grown up and changed color, are you?" Slocum gave Miss Olson a just-us-adults smile, then studied Sam more closely.

"What happened to your eye, Samantha? Didn't sass Wyatt, did you?"

The insinuation that her father would hit her was like pouring gasoline on Sam's already flaming anger.

"Unlike some people, my father never hurts anyone or anything," Sam shouted. "And he"—she pointed toward the corral—"is not your horse."

Miss Olson made a smoothing motion with her hands. Jake tugged at her elbow.

"Fire coming out of your nostrils there, Brat," Jake said quietly. "Take it easy. I think the law's on your side."

He probably meant Miss Olson, but she wasn't "the law," just a government representative. Still, the redhead's icy expression said she was in control. Sam sat down.

"Miss Olson and I have already talked about the matter of the gray's scar," Slocum said.

Sam met Jake's eyes. If Miss Olson had read Sam's notes, she'd know how folks said Phantom had gotten that scar.

"And I told Mr. Slocum I couldn't accept it as proof

of ownership. If I could accept circumstantial evidence, I'd be inclined to award him to Samantha. She has an amazing link with that stallion."

Sam tried to catch Miss Olson's eye to thank her for the compliment, but the woman didn't seem interested.

"I suppose she demonstrated some of Jake Ely's horse whisperer magic," Slocum scoffed.

Miss Olson left enough silence that even Slocum looked embarrassed. Then she went on.

"As a horsewoman, I was convinced by what I saw. It was better than a bill of sale. As a representative of the federal government, however, it's not good enough."

The redhead leaned against the porch railing with her arms crossed. Even then, her crisp uniform didn't wrinkle. As always, Miss Olson looked detached, but something told Sam the woman was waiting for Slocum to stumble into a trap.

Sam decided to give him a push.

"Mr. Slocum, did you make the complaint about the Phantom?" Sam asked.

"A complaint? Must be some misunderstanding. I did call." Slocum rocked back on his bootheels. "The horse was on my property, and I could've just put my rope on him—"

"Like you did before." Sam nudged him to admit it.

"—but I wanted everything to be official this time."

This time. Bingo. Slocum had just admitted he'd caught the stallion before. Wasn't that illegal?

Sam kept herself from looking at Miss Olson.

Slocum could go to jail for that. Sam was sure of it. She pressed her lips together. It wouldn't do to celebrate.

But Slocum wasn't stupid. He turned shamefaced toward Miss Olson. "I used to have a cowboy who fancied himself a buckaroo. He caught the stallion, once." Slocum looked down at his eel-skin boots and shook his head. "Tempted as I was, I wouldn't keep him. After all, it's against the law."

Jake had heard enough. "Then how come you offered me two hundred bucks to track him down for you?"

"What *are* you talking about, Jake?" He winked at Miss Olson. "These kids."

"They can really get some crazy ideas," she said. "Still, I can't help wondering why you didn't report the harassment of a wild horse. That's a prohibited act under the Wild Free-Roaming Horse and Burro Act of 1971."

Yes, Sam thought.

Slocum only slowed down a minute, then answered, "I wanted to give the young man a chance."

"Even though you knew the horse was bleeding." Miss Olson pretended to wince. "That would count as negligence, another prohibited act."

"Miss Olson, it's not something I like to talk about, but you and I both know horses can bleed all day long and—"

"And you'd noticed the animal's injuries were severe enough to scar."

"If I'd thought he was suffering, dang it, I would have put him out of his misery," Slocum snapped.

"Without permission of an authorized officer?" Miss Olson shook her head. "Another prohibited act."

Snorting like a bull, Slocum dropped all pretense of cooperation. "Lady, you can take your prohibited acts and—"

"Go to court with them, Mr. Slocum?" Miss Olson smiled. "In that adoption application, you can read that the commission of prohibited acts are punishable by fines or time in prison. That's a few thousand dollars for each offense." Miss Olson pretended to calculate. "And how many are we up to now?"

"Three!" Sam said, counting the charges on her fingers. "Harassment, negligence, and destruction, right, Jake?"

"I'm no expert," Jake said. He nodded toward Miss Olson.

"Mr. Slocum, until I have time to do a background check, I'm deferring your application to adopt a wild horse."

Slocum sputtered. "You can't—I'm gonna—When I—" He started three sentences and they all fizzled out.

Finally, he shouted, "I have connections in Washington!"

"Do you?" Miss Olson looked bored. "The fact remains, you need to leave the premises until you're more relaxed."

"I'm not leaving." Slocum paced up and down. He glanced at Bale Thrower with a little concern, then got his courage up. "You're not a cop, Olson, and you can't make me."

Bale Thrower and Clipboard walked a step closer. Jake crossed his arms, looking ready for a fight.

"I could make a citizen's arrest." Sam heard the words tumble from her lips and wondered where they'd come from.

When Slocum sneered, Miss Olson said, "I don't think that will be necessary, Samantha. Hugh, perhaps you'd give Mr. Slocum a ride back to his car."

So the big man Sam had been thinking of as "Bale Thrower" was really named Hugh. He stepped forward with a grin. He'd obviously enjoyed this showdown with Slocum.

Frustrated, Slocum swept off his cowboy hat and hit

it against his leg as he'd seen real cowboys do. Then he pointed at Sam.

"This isn't over, Samantha Forster." He pulled his hat back on. "It is *not* over."

Chapter 17

IF SHE DIDN'T COUNT THE TIME HER FIRST-grade teacher had told her to stop reading storybooks during arithmetic *or else*, Sam had never been threatened by an adult.

Slocum's threat had scared her. She was safe now, sitting on the front porch step of the Willow Springs office with Jake. And Miss Olson was standing by, but what about later?

Sam's hands still shook after Miss Olson disappeared into her office with a promise of lunch.

"Citizen's arrest, huh?"

"Shut up, Jake. It worked, didn't it?" Sam gave him a shove.

Jake's broad shoulders barely moved.

"No kidding, Brat. *I* was terrified."

Sam giggled. The laughter felt good, but it only lasted until Miss Olson came back. She balanced a cell phone between her cheek and shoulder and placed sodas and a box of crackers on the porch between Jake and Sam.

Miss Olson broke off her conversation for a moment. "Is your dad home?" she asked.

"No," Sam said.

Shaking her head, Miss Olson turned away, still talking.

Sam didn't mean to eavesdrop, but she heard words like "stallion," "local girl," and "restraining order."

Sam ate one saltine, then another. When she'd eaten half a dozen and sipped down half of her sugary soda, she felt better.

Miss Olson put her cell phone in her pocket, strolled back to the porch, and sat near Sam and Jake.

"You outsmarted him, Samantha." Miss Olson sounded pleased, but a cautious tone lingered in her voice.

"Please call me Sam," she said. "When you say Samantha, it sounds like I'm in trouble."

"You may be, but not from me." Miss Olson extended her arm for a handshake. "I'll call you Sam if you agree to call me Brynna."

They shook. Brynna looked up at Jake's grunt of discomfort.

"Something wrong, Mr. Ely?"

"Naw," Jake said. "I just want to hear what kind of trouble Sam's in."

Brynna sighed. "Linc Slocum didn't like Sam outsmarting him. He knows no one around here would take his part against her."

"Unless he paid them," Jake said. "Like he paid Flick."

"Right," Brynna said. "Wherever he came from, Slocum could buy what he wanted. In that way, he's different from folks around here. They work for what they want."

"Besides that, he's sneaky," Sam said.

"Right," Brynna agreed. "Even though most Nevada ranchers can't stand the BLM"—Brynna held her hand palm out to Sam and Jake as they shifted—"and we won't discuss why—the fact remains that they're straightforward about their complaints. Slocum lied about the horse. When that didn't work, he gave intimidation a try. And that failed too.

"I don't think he'll hurt you, Sam, but I think it would be wise to make provisions for the stallion. Right away."

Sam's mind spun. What would be best for the Phantom?

"I bet Wyatt would let you adopt him, if we told him what happened," Jake said.

"It's a good thing he wasn't here," Sam said. She'd never seen Dad hurt anyone, but Sam could imagine him slugging Slocum for threatening her.

"Slocum's approach would have been entirely different if Mr. Forster were here," Brynna said, but she refused to be led off the topic. "The afternoon's creeping away from us. We need to help that horse."

Both Jake and Brynna stared at Sam, waiting. And that wasn't the worst of it. The Phantom yearned for the open range and his herd. By placing his head upon her shoulder, he'd said he trusted her to help. If only she knew how.

Jake rubbed the back of his neck, frowning, but Brynna looked eager.

"Any suggestions?" Sam encouraged her.

"Just one, but I think it's a winner." Brynna drew a deep breath. "BLM doesn't put all captured horses up for adoption. We release some because we think there's little chance they'd find a home. Others"—Brynna paused—"we release to enrich existing herds."

Jake must be following Brynna's suggestion faster than she was, because Sam didn't understand why Jake began reciting Blackie's pedigree.

"His sire was pure mustang, but his dam is Princess Kitty, a running Quarter Horse with Three Bars breeding on one side and King Leo on the other."

Brynna and Jake stared at each other as if they were designing a conspiracy.

Slowly, Sam puzzled out Brynna's idea aloud. "So, you're saying you—"

"The BLM," Brynna corrected.

"Okay, the BLM could turn the Phantom loose? Because his colts and fillies would improve the wild herds, they'd set him free? Just like that?"

"Just like that," Brynna said. "I've already checked with one of our wild horse specialists and verified that the gray's herd is the only viable band in the Calico Mountains district. There are a few bachelor bands—young stallions who roam together without mares—but those stallions are small and scrubby. If they took over the gray's herd, we'd end up with fewer adoptable horses."

"Let's do it," Sam said. "Slocum won't have a chance to cause any more trouble."

Brynna didn't look so sure, but she made a promise. "As long as I'm manager here, Slocum won't get a single wild horse."

"I hate to rain on your parade," Jake said. "But we can't just set him loose. Think of the fences between here and the mountains and"—he gestured—"the cars coming up that road."

"It's a long truck ride back to the Calicos, but we could trailer him there and release him," Brynna suggested.

Sam imagined the tight, moving world within a horse trailer. The Phantom had fought the corral as if locked in a death match. Would he survive hours in a trailer?

Jake must have thought the same thing.

"If you could get him as far as Thread the Needle," he suggested, "I bet he'd head downhill toward River Bend."

In minutes, Brynna and Jake spun out a plan while Sam listened.

The stallion had been halterbroken as a foal. And the stallion trusted Ace.

After seeing Sam with the Phantom, Jake believed she could ride Ace and lead the stallion to Thread the Needle.

"I'll go back for Ace," Jake said. "I need to move Gram's Buick anyway."

As Sam worked the coiled car part out of her pocket and handed it to Jake, Brynna stared at it, confused.

"I don't want to know," Brynna said, when Sam started to explain.

"Wyatt's sure to be back with the trailer by the time I get there," Jake said. "Do we need anything besides Ace and a lead rope?"

"I've got plenty of rope," Brynna said. "It'd be best if Sam started working him with the halter right now."

Things were moving too fast. Sam wasn't sure the stallion would recall his halter training. Even if he did, why should he obey?

Sam watched Jake leave. Then, gingerly, she touched her cheekbone. It hurt. And her brain felt like mush. She was probably just tired. Once she slipped back into the Phantom's pen, she'd probably remember how to think like a horse.

There was only one way to find out.

With a soft rope halter and lead, Sam walked to the Phantom's pen. The stallion stood opposite the gate, body hugging the fence. His ears tipped forward at the sound of the gate opening. Otherwise, he didn't move.

Sam entered the corral. He ignored her.

"Hey, boy," she crooned, but for each step she took closer, the stallion moved a step away. He must have listened for each footfall, because he never looked at Sam.

Sam talked and talked. After a while, she spoke not to the stallion, but to Brynna.

"You're an expert. Tell me, why do people want wild horses?"

"Some want to help them, of course—"

"No, I mean, you've read all the old Western stories," Sam said. "For hundreds of years, people have wanted wild horses."

"They look at a wild horse and see beauty, spirit—"

"And they can't wait to take it away," Sam interrupted.

She saw the new rope burns on the stallion's neck and realized he wouldn't willingly let her halter him. But what else could she do?

For two hours, Sam followed the stallion around the enclosure. He never broke into a run, never battered the rails as he had before, and never gave a sign that he heard her speak his secret name.

At last, Sam sat down with her back against the fence. The position was dangerous and she knew it. If the stallion decided to charge, she couldn't move fast enough to escape. But trust must run two ways. Maybe he'd come to her.

A shiver ran over the stallion's body. Keeping his head turned her way, he edged toward the water bucket, lowered his head, and drank deeply. His eyes remained fixed on Sam, and she realized they weren't brown and lively now, but black and questioning.

The stallion hadn't given up hope. He was waiting for her to understand.

She watched every twitch of muscle, every movement of his lips, every shifting of his weight from leg to leg. Even when Dad and Jake arrived, she didn't stop.

"I do not believe what I'm seeing." Dad's voice was low and furious. "Tell me that is not my daughter in a pen—*sitting* in a pen with a wild stallion."

Brynna answered, but Sam blocked out their conversation. She kept watching the Phantom. It seemed the water had revitalized him.

"Okay," she said softly to the stallion. "Okay, I'm getting it."

And then he made sure she understood.

Tossing his mane and forelock in fanfare, the stallion lifted his muzzle and pranced toward the fence. He gazed toward the mountains and uttered a neigh of longing.

Ace stamped his hooves in the confinement of the River Bend horse trailer and answered the stallion with a short burst of whinnies.

In spite of the danger, in spite of what Dad and Jake and Brynna might say, Sam knew what she must do. She walked toward the gate.

"Our idea's not going to work," Sam said, closing the corral gate behind her.

"You are testing my patience, Sam," Dad said, but his arm draped over her like a bird's sheltering wing.

Sam hugged him back, but she didn't let the warmth of Dad's welcome slow her down.

"When Flick and the other guy dragged the Phantom

in here, crosstied, they—I don't know, traumatized him, I think. He's not going to let me halter him or pony him with Ace. And he won't go into the trailer. But I know what *will* work."

"I'm listening," Jake said, but his thumbs were in his jeans pockets and he looked at the dirt, not her.

Sam's stomach dropped away, as if she were rising in a fast elevator, before she said, "We wait until dark."

"Oh, no." Dad crossed his arms.

"I don't know why, but he trusts me more in the dark," she said. "Then Ace and I run toward Thread the Needle and start down the hillside toward River Bend. Just like we were going to, only—"

"Only you don't pony him, you use Ace like a Judas horse." Brynna spoke with a kind of dread, but she understood.

"Yes."

Sam had read how the BLM trapped wild horses, using a keyhole-shaped corral. The mustangs came running, chased by a helicopter, and then, just as the horses might sense the opening to the trap, a domestic horse, who knew a bucket of grain awaited inside, was released. As he ran for his treat, the mustangs followed and the gate closed behind them.

"Only Ace isn't a Judas horse," Sam said. "He's the Phantom's guardian angel, because he's going to lead him out of here."

"And you'll be riding Ace," Jake said.

"Yeah," she admitted.

"That's all fine, but let's go back to the part where you gallop downhill in the dark and break your fool neck!" Jake kept his voice level, until he turned toward Dad. "Wyatt, are you going to let her do this?"

"Dad, I'll only run him there." Sam pointed at the straight road, smoothed by car traffic. "When we reach the hillside, I won't gallop. I'll leave the pace up to Ace.

"Remember what you taught me, Dad? He doesn't want to fall. He wants to keep his four legs underneath him. Isn't that what you've always said, Dad?"

Sam crossed her arms. Dad crossed his.

To Brynna, Dad must look more intimidating. With her hacked-off hair, black eye, sunburned arms, and legs dirty from sitting in a dusty horse corral, Sam knew she didn't look as determined as she felt.

But Jake knew her. He walked away, reached a hand into the horse trailer toward Ace, and left the standoff to the two Forsters.

In the deepening dusk, Sam saw Dad shake his head.

"You could get hurt again," he said.

Sam heard his fear. It made her feel selfish, but she had to do this for her horse.

"Dad, I don't want to get hurt. I don't want to go back to the hospital or to San Francisco. I want to stay here, with you and Gram." She looked toward the horse trailer. "And Jake. But I want to do what's right."

Dad glanced through the fence rails. The stallion looked weary and harmless in the gray failing light.

"I haven't told you this before, Sam, but when you're absolutely sure of something, you look a lot like your mom. She'd get convinced she knew what to do, and usually, she turned out convincing me, too. Like keeping the ranch," Dad said quietly. "Like having a child."

A sweet warmth enveloped Sam. The sun had vanished behind the mountains and the sky had turned dark blue.

"I say it's close enough to dark," Dad said. "Jake, bring Ace out."

On the high road overlooking Willow Springs, Sam crouched in the saddle while Ace danced beneath her.

Metal slammed as Brynna opened a series of interconnecting gates, funneling the stallion toward the road. At first, the Phantom was slow and cautious.

Then he understood. His legs moved more quickly. Picking up speed, he trotted faster until his hooves hammered like gunfire as he came closer and closer.

"Now!" Jake shouted.

Sam clapped her heels to Ace's sides. He leaped forward as the final gate clanged open.

"Go on, Blackie!" Dad yelled.

Behind her, the stallion's hooves stuttered, held, and raced after them.

Sam's heart echoed the thunder of hoofbeats. Both horses breathed loud with excitement, and then the Phantom ran beside them, beautiful once more.

How far left to gallop along this road? Sam knew she had to judge. A half mile? A quarter?

The Phantom held his head high, all senses alert. Eyes wide, nostrils open, he tested the breeze for anything other than sagebrush and juniper. He could have passed them at any time, but he matched strides with Ace, loping with long-legged care, unsure of the earth beneath his hooves.

At Thread the Needle, they slowed.

"Take us home, Ace," Sam said.

She leaned back a little, balancing so Ace could pick his way down the hillside.

The Phantom's warm hide rubbed Sam's leg. Even though the men with ropes had fractured her friendship with the stallion, a link remained.

The stallion moved through the darkness with a girl and a small outcast mustang as his guides.

A warm updraft of wind brought the green scent of the river. The stallion caught the familiar smell. Once the lights of River Bend Ranch were no more than a mile away, the stallion surged ahead.

THE WILD ONE

He left her.

Silent, except for night wind rushing through his mane and tail, the stallion ran, reclaiming his freedom.

Carefully, Sam drew rein. Ace slowed. They couldn't catch the stallion. The little gelding didn't try. His home was a place among fences, with plenty of water and a snug, straw-deep stall when the snows came.

The Phantom crashed into the river. Waves surged for the shore.

At the water's edge, she slid from Ace's back and left him ground-tied as she waded in up to her knees, watching the stallion go.

He gained the other shore and shook the water from his coat. Moonlight turned the droplets into silver dust.

The Phantom whirled, sighting everything around him, assuring himself of safety. Then he made a graceful leap toward the mountains and freedom.

With each of the stallion's steps, Sam felt reality settle around her. Her horse was gone for good.

Summer's magic had ended with Jake's anger, Slocum's threats, and a wild stallion running. Between now and

September she had plenty to worry about: a different school, unfamiliar classmates, and teachers with brand-new expectations.

And then Ace snorted and stared into a darkness with only a twinkling of starlight to show the stallion swinging a wide turn back.

Sam ran, splashing through the river shallows. The current held her back, warning her the water flow was too strong to test. She couldn't go to him, and the stallion had turned too wary to come to her.

He stopped, knee-deep in silver water. His reflection wavered on the rills and ripples. Since they were alone, Sam shouted.

"Zanzibar!"

The stallion rose into the air, rearing as if his forelegs reached for the moon. Sam understood his neigh as if he'd spoken. From the wild side of the river, the Phantom promised to return.

Read on for an excerpt from Sam's journal!

Dear Mom,

I miss you. You're the only one on this ranch who cares about horses the way that I do. Cared. They weren't just useful animals to you. Every day we were around horses together, I felt how you loved them. And me.

You never got to meet Blackie, but I believe you looked down and saw us cuddling in the barn's deep straw. I bet you heard me whisper his secret name, and I'm sure you saw our accident. I'm sorry for that. I wish you'd been sitting with me while Blackie galloped toward the mountains and Jake rode off to tell Dad and Gram that I was hurt. But that's all over! I'm fine! I'm back at River Bend (obviously), and here's what I have to tell you: Blackie has transformed into the horse they call the Phantom. Maybe the Phantom started out as a myth, but he's not anymore. He's a real mustang, but he's something special, too.

Tonight was all secrets, stars, and thinking his horse brain and my human one might understand each other. I mean, a silver stallion stared across the river, focusing his eyes, muscles, and mind on me!

I know Dad, Jake, and Gram would say it's not magic. They'd believe it's just by chance that he showed up here at the same time I came home, and curiosity that makes him return.

If Blackie and I had stayed on the ranch together, we would've communicated with the touch of leather, rope, and hands. Some words, too, but that's not what happened tonight. If it's not magic, it's some kind of super instinct.

As Blackie, he spent two years on the ranch with me. As the Phantom, he's had two years on the range running free. I didn't call him back. I wouldn't even try. I might as well tell the wind when it should gust. All I know is this: my horse has been waiting for me to come back. And I did.

Dear Mom,
Gram and Dad haven't changed much since I've been gone. I guess they tell me more stuff about money and responsibility, which is NOT what I missed about

River Bend. I bet that wasn't the part of ranching you loved either.

Now, Jake. He's changed. I admit that I'd like to walk with him through the halls at my old school in San Francisco and see what my friends say. His sense of humor is the best. You might not agree. He's pretty sarcastic, but in a cute way. He's not really being a jerk to me when he calls me Brat. Besides, Dad trusts him. I wonder if he's popular at school. I'm not looking forward to being the new girl in September. Making new friends is hard, and what if Jake just ignores me?

You know who I wish WOULD ignore me? Linc Slocum. His smoking and swaggering and throwing cigarette butts on Nature is disgusting. Be glad you never knew him. He's cruel to his horses. It's like they're just accessories to show he's a cowboy. Not. Remember how you'd tell me, "If you can't say something nice, don't say anything at all"? The best thing I can say about Linc Slocum is that when he bought the ranch next door, he didn't pave it over or dig it up. He didn't kick out the family that lives there either. The Kenworthys. I don't remember them that well, but Gram says their daughter Jen is my age.

Dear Mom,
Is there such a thing as an omega horse? Like the opposite of an alpha? That's what I THOUGHT Ace was, but now he's got me confused.

In the ten-acre pasture, the alpha is Strawberry. She looks like an ordinary red roan mare, but she is the boss. She flattens her ears at Ace all the time, and most of his bite marks were made by her teeth. She's bossy to Popcorn and Jeepers-Creepers, sure, but she goes after Ace almost every day when all he's doing is standing up for himself. I wonder if it's because he's different, a mustang. Even if he just trots to the fence to see me, she acts like it's HER fence and he gets kicked or bitten.

The weird thing is, Ace doesn't look sad or picked on. His bay coat is red-gold and glossy. He carries his head high and tosses his forelock to show off his white star. And he practically rolls his eyes, not believing me, when I tell him I'm in charge.

On the cattle drive, after his leap over the campfire (which I rode out! I hope you saw that!), I thought we'd worked out a relationship. But then we were riding drag at the back of the herd, just jogging along, and I heard Ace groan. You know how a burro goes "hee-haw"? Well, it was just the "haw" part, a lot like a camel on the Discovery Channel. No one else noticed. Then Ace shook his head, black mane flipping side to side. He lowered his nose, tugging on the bit, sniff-scanning the ground. He pawed the dirt and groaned again. I was so scared he was sick and that it was somehow my fault.

But then he went down on his front knees and glanced back with this—I don't know, SMARTY HORSE look. Then I got it. I remembered that I'd seen him drop to his knees when he had an itchy spot on his back and he was going to roll to scratch it!

Whether I was in the saddle or not, he was going to do just that. Roll!

I kicked my boots out of the stirrups, let go of the reins, and pushed out of the saddle. You bet I didn't want to drop the reins, but I didn't want to pull Ace over on me either. Once I stood clear of him, I should have been proud of my "emergency dismount." But no. I was angry, yelling, "No! Stop! Wait!"

Ace didn't care. He rolled. Lucky I wasn't in the saddle. Lucky he didn't crush the cantle or snap off the horn. Lucky no one was watching. I guess with the saddle on his back, his roll didn't feel so great. It couldn't have lasted even half a minute. When he stood up and gave a good shake, I saw my chance to grab the reins so that he didn't run off. I lunged for them and then held on tight, even though my hands were shaking.

Ace looked totally casual, but I felt my heart ricocheting off my sternum.

Finally, Ace blew through his lips, swung his head toward the cattle moving away from us. Then he turned his steady brown eyes on me like, WHAT ARE YOU WAITING FOR?

As I rode, I thought of the first day I'd met Ace and recognized he had the pride of a mustang. He grew up wild. It's pride that makes Ace stand up for himself against Strawberry. And me.

Dear Mom,

This is something I really wish we could talk about. Aunt Sue did a good job, but she's not here. And bringing this up with Dad, Gram, or Jake? They'd just get even more freaked out about it. My accident. My head.

I am worried now (honestly, it never really goes away) because Buddy walked away from River Bend Ranch and almost got eaten by coyotes. If she'd died, it would've been my fault. I put her in a different pen. And I DID NOT NOTICE that a whole side of that pen was missing. Who does that? Someone who's just distracted, or someone with brain damage?

My worst day in San Francisco was when I

picked up Aunt Sue's laptop to order take-out curry for dinner. I'd only typed the B-A in "Bangkok Cuisine" when I saw what she'd been reading: "Traumatic Brain Injury and Memory Loss."

What?

"HOW CONCUSSIONS CAN AFFECT CHILDREN YEARS LATER."

I sank down on the couch and opened the next tab.

"EVEN MILD CONCUSSIONS CAN CAUSE DEVELOPMENTAL DELAYS IN THINKING."

When Aunt Sue sauntered in talking about noodles, I held the laptop out to her like it was a box of snakes.

"Am I acting weird?" I asked her. "Because if I am, I don't know it. What does THAT mean?"

Aunt Sue said she was doing research, "just in case." It took about a half hour for her to convince me that I should go ahead and order dinner, and another hour after that to persuade me she was telling the truth. She said I wasn't the only "head case"—which was really rude and totally inappropriate—in her life. She claimed she had students who'd suffered head injuries from playing football or crashing their skateboards. She was a "mandated reporter" who had to tell kids' parents if something was wrong. I didn't buy that, because wouldn't the parents know? But that's when she looked at me intensely. Some kids, she said, were injured doing something they loved, so they hid it because they didn't want to stop heading the soccer ball in soccer or riding their favorite horse.

I didn't have to think twice to know that I wouldn't have told anyone about my accident with Blackie if I could have kept it hidden.

"Well, I'm not the one hiding things." I nodded at Aunt Sue's laptop as if the articles were still up on the screen.

Aunt Sue told me she'd saved everything into a folder. She opened it and said I could feel free to read it all. That wouldn't have taken so long, but every time I hit a term I didn't know—like TBI, "traumatic brain injury"—I'd get pulled into another story.

By the time I realized that I was yawning,

Aunt Sue had gone to bed. All the lights in the apartment were off except for one. I was sitting in this little pool of light, remembering all the times I didn't know where I'd put my favorite pen or couldn't remember the title of the book I was reading or couldn't find my backpack. Was I just distracted by other stuff or suffering from "brain fog"? Studies said that even mild concussions could cause loss of memory, focus, and ability to plan and organize! One article said the aftereffects of a concussion could be misunderstood—especially in teens—as drug or alcohol abuse! Isn't that just what I need at my new school!

Aunt Sue took me to all my follow-up doctor appointments and scheduled me for every available test. A psychologist taught me coping skills—like not replaying the accident in my mind. Like making to-do lists, making dictionaries of my school vocabulary words, and writing down ideas that I don't want to forget. And I'm fine. At my last appointment, "my team" gave me a congratulatory chocolate cupcake with an icing unicorn on top.

But still, Mom, how could I NOT have noticed one whole side of a corral lying down in the grass? I feel so stupid. I could use one of your Mama Bear hugs. I really could.

Dear Mom,
I understand that a buckaroo is sort of a super-cowboy . . . one who has pride in his horse, his tack,

and the way he rides, but I overheard Dallas say that a real Nevada buckaroo "won't do nothin' he can't do on horseback. If he's told to mend fence, he'll just pick up his saddle and head on down the road." Does that mean a working ranch like River Bend can't afford to hire real buckaroos? ☹ Dad and the hands are always mending fence, repairing trucks, or hammering something back together. Do you think maybe there are weekend buckaroos? If so, I think Jake is one.

Dear Mom,
I haven't forgotten TOO much about being a cowgirl, but I hate making mistakes in front of

people. I've known my whole life NOT to grab the saddle horn, but I'm still a little afraid of falling. When I did sort of rest my hand on the horn for balance and Jake saw me, he got this disappointed look on his face.

    One morning on the cattle drive, maybe because it was like five a.m. and still dark... Okay, no excuses.

    I know horses can be fussy about the cinch. I get that it's like a belt that holds the saddle on and it's supposed to be snug, but I'm always a little worried I'll get it too tight and it will pinch. Anyway, smarty horse Ace likes his cinch nice and loose, so he puffs out his belly while I'm buckling up. That way, when he breathes normally, the cinch hardly touches. Comfy for him, but dangerous for me. I knew it, but that morning (did I tell you that it was WAY early?), I didn't pull the cinch snug. I put my boot toe in the stirrup and hopped a little on my other foot to mount up and the saddle slipped sideways. "I don't think that's what they mean by ladies ridin' sidesaddle," one of Slocum's cowboys said. And then all the cowboys laughed. My face feels hot even as I write this. I'm only grateful that I wasn't in the saddle when it happened!

Dear Mom,
This is a good thing. I didn't mean to eavesdrop

on Dad and Dallas, but they were standing in the shade of the bunkhouse while I was saddling Ace over by the round pen, and their voices carried. They were talking about me. Dallas said I had "a horseman's hands." Instead of calling out that I was not a horseMAN, I kept listening because Dad was agreeing! Dallas said how he'd noticed that I wasn't holding my reins the way he'd told me to on the cattle drive, but Ace was working better for me. I didn't really think about changing. I just worried about sending the wrong messages to Ace and remembered these girls I saw riding with two hands in Golden Gate Park. I tried it, Ace liked it, and it's not like riding the range is the same as being in a Western horse show, right? I hope I'll get good enough to ride the way Dallas said to, but not yet.

But there was MORE! Gram says "she who eavesdrops never hears anything good about herself," but that's not true. Dad said something about "soft, quiet hands." I thought he was talking about you, Mom, but then he said something like "A rider whose hands fidget around is sending static, but if Sam keeps those soft, quiet hands, they'll serve her well with any horse for the rest of her riding life." Isn't that just the best?

Sam's Dictionary

ALKALI FLATS: If you flew over and looked down, you'd see that this land is flat and white and stretches for miles. Alkali flats exist other places, but the ones near River Bend Ranch are sometimes called the "playa" (Spanish for "beach") because they were the lake bed of ancient Lake Lahontan. The lake spread across the West, covering much of prehistoric Nevada, California, and Oregon. Ichthyosaurs, huge swimming dinosaurs, thrived in that lake, and though there's no water visible now, big animals like horses and cows can break through the crust and get bogged down in the quicksand underneath.

ALKALI THE TOWN: Home to Clara's Café, and a gas station with a mini-mart that stocks chicken feed, cat chow, alfalfa pellets for horses, random ranch equipment, snacks, and drinks. Clara's is where ranch folks go for local gossip, upside-down cake, and biscuits with gravy.

WILD HORSE BANDS and HERDS: A band is a family of wild horses. There's usually a lead mare and stallion, aunts, grandmothers, brothers, cousins, yearlings, and foals. Most of the males in a band are less than three years old. After that, they leave to form bachelor bands. A herd is a whole neighborhood of horses, made up of several bands.

FOAL: A baby horse, male or female, less than one year old.

SAM'S DICTIONARY

CALICO MOUNTAINS: The volcanic mountain range on River Bend's eastern horizon has unusual rock formations—crags, caves, and spires—that soar to about seven thousand feet. In different lights the snow-capped peaks look like ice cream melting down cones of orange, rust, gold, tan, pink, or purple. They are steep, full of wildlife and surprises. Some downhills are simply sandy, but others are covered with overlapping dinner-plate-sized shale that slides under the hooves of horses.

HEREFORD: Sturdy cattle with boxy bodies, brown-red coats, white faces, and brown eyes with white eyelashes. River Bend has mostly Herefords and Hereford crosses. The crosses can be black or brindle. Since they're range cattle and roam for miles, they're branded. That way cowboys won't confuse our cattle with cows from another ranch when it's time to round them up for sale.

PRONGHORN: They're not antelope, though some people call them that. They look like chunky gazelles, with rusty-brown and cream-colored fur. They can outrun all predators, but they're very curious and not the best jumpers, so they still get ambushed and eaten. They live in herds for safety.

TACK: Everything the horse wears for the rider: saddle, bridle, reins, etc. STIRRUPS are the part of the saddle where you rest your feet to stay balanced. The CANTLE is the curved, raised part of the saddle just behind you. The HORN sticks up in front of you. A CINCH is like a belt that holds the saddle on top of the horse. A BRIDLE is the horse's headgear. There are different styles, but all have a piece that slips over the top of the head, goes behind the ears, and then lies along the cheeks before it attaches to the bit in the horse's mouth. REINS are leather strips that go from the bit to the rider's hands.

COW PONY: A horse (not necessarily a small one) that knows cattle and their tricks. If a cow breaks out of the herd during a cattle drive, a cow pony automatically goes after it. If a rider needs to rope a steer, the cow pony puts his rider in position to throw a loop and doesn't spook when the rope goes singing over his ears or a when a cow bucks at being caught. When a cow pony separates one cow from a big bunch of them, that's called CUTTING. Then, there's no rope involved. Just horsepower.

RANGE RATS and BROOMTAILS: Ugly names that some ignorant people call wild horses. (MUSTANG is okay because it just comes from the Spanish for "a wanderer.")

GROUND-TIE: This is like teaching a dog to "stay," and the best cow ponies are trained to do it. When a horse works with you as a ranch partner, sometimes you'll want to do a quick chore, like pull a tumbleweed out of a wire fence, and then get right back on your horse. That's when you just drop your reins and maybe say "whoa," and the horse will stay.

SAM'S DICTIONARY

SAGEBRUSH: This dusty-blue-green plant smells like a combination of lemon, incense, and wind. It's not like the sage you'd use for cooking, but deer, rabbits, and pronghorn graze on it. Mustangs will eat it, but it doesn't seem to be their favorite. Sagebrush grows in small clumps all over the range and even clings to the mountains in some places. When sagebrush grows together in thickets, it's hard to ride through and it rips your pants unless you're wearing chaps. Some explorers called this part of Nevada the "Sagebrush Sea" because the sagebrush grows side by side, rolling off as far as you can see, like rising and falling ocean waves.

Acknowledgments

For years, I tried to leave the River Bend Ranch, but it's a good thing I couldn't. Samantha Forster, the magical silver-gray mustang she loves, Jake, Jen, and hundreds of horses are back.

This book exists because so many people said "Yes" and used their creative skills to help me revisit the Phantom Stallion series. My agent Tim Travaglini's "it doesn't hurt to try" attitude brought the Phantom to Aladdin Books, where editors Kristen Gilson and Jessica Smith (a fellow horse girl) freed my wild stallion to run through new flickers of my imagination. Louise Meijer-Åström (another horse girl) captures the beauty of Nevada's wild horses and wild places with startling insight and Francesca Baerald's map allows readers to follow my stories across the sagebrush sea to ranches, school, and anywhere else my characters roam.

I'm grateful that Tiara Iandiorio, cover and art designer,

ACKNOWLEDGEMENTS

helped us all visualize the Phantom's world and that Aladdin publisher Valerie Garfield was eager to relaunch the series.

Elysa Buckheart (Te-Moak Western Shoshone) of Northern Nevada, read my books through Native eyes and guided me to better paths.

I want to have a relaxed coffee date with the far-flung staff of Simon & Schuster and thank them in person. Until then: thanks to Production Editor Olivia Ritchie, Production Manager Amelia Jenkins, Associate Publisher Anna Jarzab, and Kilson Roque, who helps editors with everything from presentations to ensuring sales people have materials they need.

To Samantha McVeigh and ALL of the publicity team, Marketing Director Alissa Nigro, and the Education & Library and Sales teams: I've amateurishly worked in your fields, and you have my deepest appreciation. Call anytime!

My gratitude requires a little time travel.

I met the real live Phantom Stallion twice, both times after rare Nevada rainstorms.

The first encounter took place at the edge of the Black Rock Desert, near the real-life Calico Mountains. *Nevada Magazine* sent me out on the range to write an article about

ACKNOWLEDGEMENTS

a cattle drive from Soldier Meadows, Nevada, to Ravendale, California. Ten days on a sassy BLM-branded mustang didn't leave me saddle sore, because I was living my cowgirl dreams. The morning after a storm that would have flooded me from my sleeping bag if I hadn't trenched a moat around my tent, we rode in fog. That morning I spotted a lone white horse in a slot canyon. It only took one glimpse for him to firmly plant his hooves in my imagination as the Phantom.

The first books of the Phantom Stallion series had already galloped into the world when I met the Phantom again. My then agent Karen Solem and editor Julia Richardson believed young readers yearned to run free with wild horses, to adventure in today's West. Editors Amanda Maciel and Kari Sutherland were always willing to talk horses as well as words.

My second meeting with the Phantom took place as he stood in a muddy corral on the grounds of the Nevada State Prison in Carson City, Nevada, with his lead mare and their foal.

I learned of his capture from members of the Wild Horse Preservation League. Many of them thought a

ACKNOWLEDGEMENTS

wild white stallion that had roamed the Virginia Range of Northern Nevada for years was the inspiration for my fictional Phantom.

Because his territory was controlled by the Nevada Department of Agriculture, capture could have meant branding, gelding, and a truck ride to an auction yard where he'd be sold for slaughter. No wonder those who'd seen the stallion kept him a secret. The stallion's friends called him the Phantom, and they wanted him to stay free. I joined their plan to spring him from state corrals even before I met him.

I could—and have!—written thousands of words about meeting the real Phantom, but I'll boil it down to this: "At last, with the sun up and the clouds clearing, the Phantom walks right over to the fence where I am standing. I don't think of trying to touch him. I'm close enough, but even if he allowed it, it would be disrespectful . . . the stallion could be the king of the wild horse nation."

Thanks to Diane Nelson of the Wild Horse Sanctuary in Shingletown, the Phantom's family lives free on five thousand fenced acres in Shingletown, California. It was there I met Lauri "Palomino" Armstrong, a rescuer of hundreds of

ACKNOWLEDGEMENTS

last-chance animals, especially wild foals. I'm honored that she's my lifelong friend.

The Phantom Stallion series has put me in good company for over a decade. Librarians, teachers, booksellers, editors, and readers around the world have supported me with letters, emails, and their presence at book signings and author visits. It's a blessing that many young readers learned to love reading and wild horses in the same breath and went on to join the never-ending fight to save America's wild horses.

When Suzanne Morgan Williams persuaded me to join SCBWI, the Society of Children's Book Writers and Illustrators, I had no idea we'd become road trip pals. We've given so many presentations together—in schools, libraries, conferences—that she can recite the Phantom's story as well as I can recite the pants-ripping scene from *Bull Rider*. Together, we've learned there are tarantula stampedes, some ranch dads will drive their daughters four hours to have a collection of Phantom books autographed by the author, and—Yes!—when there's a power failure in 12-degree weather, ice cream will stay frozen in a car.

A loud thank-you to parents everywhere who drive

ACKNOWLEDGEMENTS

young readers to libraries, bookstores, and reading events. They'll remember.

Lyndi Cooper-Schroeder, my best friend in motherhood, teaching, and life insists on supporting me and expressing true interest in my writing no matter where I am on the publishing Ferris wheel.

Most of all, I thank my family. I could go back generations, but I'll spotlight my children Kaitlin and Matthew, who *mostly* fell in with the rule that, while writing, no answer I gave them counted unless I took my hands off the keyboard and met their eyes.

From the beginning, my husband, Cory, has believed telling stories is worth time "away." He's taken up the slack, commiserated, cooked, and really—Cory, no list will come close to what you've given me. I love you forever.

Dark Sunshine

Also by Terri Farley

The Wild One
Mustang Moon

TERRI FARLEY

PHANTOM STALLION

Dark Sunshine

ALADDIN
New York London Toronto Sydney New Delhi

If you purchased this book without a cover, you should be aware that this book is stolen property. It was reported as "unsold and destroyed" to the publisher, and neither the author nor the publisher has received any payment for this "stripped book."

This book is a work of fiction. Any references to historical events, real people, or real places are used fictitiously. Other names, characters, places, and events are products of the author's imagination, and any resemblance to actual events or places or persons, living or dead, is entirely coincidental.

ALADDIN
An imprint of Simon & Schuster Children's Publishing Division
1230 Avenue of the Americas, New York, New York 10020
First Aladdin paperback edition October 2023
Text copyright © 2002 by Terri Sprenger-Farley
Cover illustration copyright © 2023 by Louise Meijer-Åström
Map on pages vi–vii copyright © 2023 by Francesca Baerald
Illustration of notebook on pages 298–312 by aopsan/iStock
Also available in an Aladdin hardcover edition.
All rights reserved, including the right of reproduction in whole or in part in any form.
ALADDIN and related logo are registered trademarks of Simon & Schuster, Inc.
For information about special discounts for bulk purchases, please contact Simon & Schuster Special Sales at 1-866-506-1949 or business@simonandschuster.com.
The Simon & Schuster Speakers Bureau can bring authors to your live event. For more information or to book an event contact the Simon & Schuster Speakers Bureau
at 1-866-248-3049 or visit our website at www.simonspeakers.com.
Designed by Tiara Iandiorio
The text of this book was set in Adobe Garamond Pro.
Manufactured in the United States of America 0923 OFF
10 9 8 7 6 5 4 3 2 1
Library of Congress Control Number 2023942352
ISBN 9781665916387 (hc)
ISBN 9781665916370 (pbk)
ISBN 9781665916394 (ebook)

To all who search for second chances. And third. And more.

Chapter 1

THE SWEET SMELL OF HORSES AND HAY CARried to Samantha Forster on an early-morning breeze. She eased the front door closed behind her. Everyone inside was asleep. By rising at four o'clock, she'd beaten even Dad out of bed.

Sam stifled a yawn. She could have slept in on this September Saturday, but she and Jen planned to unlock the secrets of Lost Canyon before the sun rose.

Strange things were happening in Lost Canyon. Weird white plumes rose skyward. Were they dust, smoke, or spirits, as some Shoshone elders hinted? And what about those eerie screams?

Standing at the bus stop just the other morning, Sam and Jen had heard the faraway wails. Though they'd agreed those sounds weren't the cries of Native ponies slaughtered there a hundred years ago, she and Jen had scared each other with other "what-ifs." They'd been rubbing gooseflesh from their arms when the school bus finally arrived.

Now Sam moved silently across the front porch of the white, two-story house. She carried her boots and walked in stockinged feet. With Gram and Dad still asleep, River Bend Ranch was all hers.

Darkness cloaked the neat pens and corrals, the barn and bunkhouse, and the surrounding rangelands where Hereford cattle grazed, but Sam knew it was all there waiting for her.

As she pulled on her scarred leather boots, Sam glanced toward the river. Across the current, on the wild side of the river, the Phantom could be waiting. But he had never come to the ranch this near sunrise and probably never would.

Sam hefted her saddlebags and canteen and walked toward the barn.

Blaze woofed from his post outside the bunkhouse. The Border Collie's bark startled a horse. Its hooves went thudding across the ten-acre pasture.

A few steps from the barn, a neigh challenged her.

"It's only me, baby," Sam whispered. She hurried. Once Ace knew it was her, he'd set up a ruckus.

Fingers flying, Sam drew the bolt on the door connecting the barn and corral. Ace followed as Sam flipped the switch for the overhead lights. The little mustang nudged Sam until he backed her against the barn wall.

That nudge, what Dallas, the ranch foreman, would call misbehavior, she called love.

"You are too sweet." She caught Ace's muzzle between her hands and gave it a quick kiss.

Sam dragged a curry comb over Ace's already glowing coat. He wasn't crosstied or tethered; he just stood with eyes half-closed as he enjoyed the massaging movements of the brush.

When Sam stopped, Ace looked back over his shoulder as she smoothed on the blanket. Next, she saddled him and replaced his halter with a snaffle-bitted bridle.

Sam shivered. She should have remembered a jacket. Since she hadn't, she snatched the faded green sweatshirt she kept hanging from a nail in the barn. Before pulling it on, she dropped Ace's reins, ground-tying him.

Like any well-schooled cow pony, Ace understood the signal to stand and wait. He snorted with impatience, though, as Sam tugged the sweatshirt over her short reddish hair.

"Sorry." Sam's muffled voice came from inside the sweatshirt.

Ace pawed the barn floor, stirring dust until she led him into the yard.

Before she could mount, Ace raised his finely boned, almost Arabic head. His nostrils flared as he gazed at the Calico Mountains, where a rim of midnight blue showed above the peaks.

Sam swung into the saddle.

"Don't get your hopes up," she told the horse. "We're heading away from his territory."

Sam shifted her weight slightly. Ace started toward the bridge, answering her cue.

"No reason to think we'll see him, boy," she said, but Sam had watched wild horses travel the trail into Lost Canyon.

Once, they'd been led by the Phantom.

Jen and her high-stepping palomino weren't at the pond by War Drum Flats. Although she was disappointed, Sam could guess why.

All week Jen had sniffled and sneezed, but she'd carried a backpack full of tissues and refused to miss a single day of classes. Sam would bet the flu had finally gotten the better of her friend.

She was out here alone.

Then she heard it. The weird warbling was impossible to identify until it changed to a piercing cry.

Through the saddle leather and blanket, Sam felt Ace tremble. They both knew the cry was no cougar's scream. It was the plea of a terrified horse.

Sam wheeled Ace away from the pond and aimed him toward the tumble of boulders and sagebrush leading toward the path. The gelding moved at a stiff-legged trot.

"I know you don't want to go, but that horse is in trouble." Sam wasn't exactly sure how to find Lost Canyon. It lay someplace between here and that highest peak wearing a cap of snow.

"C'mon, Ace. I'd want someone to help if you were crying."

Ace moved into a grudging lope, but the steep uphill path meant he couldn't maintain the pace for long. Just when the footing grew more level, the trail dead-ended into a rock wall.

Water seeped from a crack running across its face.

"Let's try this," she told Ace. Sam almost lost her way when the deer trail crossed a slick stretch of granite.

Sam slowed Ace, stroked his coarse black mane, and listened. She hadn't heard the whinny for several minutes. When she closed her eyes to concentrate, she *did* hear something: a whirring motor, like a chain saw. This high up the mountain, the sound could have carried from anywhere.

"Just a little farther," Sam told Ace.

The gelding picked his way across the rock, then grunted with irritation as Sam urged him onto a narrow ledge.

Ace did as she asked, but he clearly disagreed. The little mustang understood searching for grass and water. He understood people expected him to chase calves. But running toward a place where one horse was *already* in trouble? Ace shook his mane in disgust.

Suddenly the ground turned bare and sandy. But why? A thick stand of juniper lay ahead. Nothing should have rubbed this rugged terrain bare of vegetation.

Sam wished the sun would hurry and rise. The buzzing sound drew closer, but she still couldn't see its source. Ace looked back, and Sam heard the sound of galloping hooves.

"You're right, boy. We're out of here." Sam searched the area and spotted an outcropping of rock. She slid to the ground and jogged toward the rock. Ace followed.

The juniper branches were bare on the side facing the trail, as if something had rubbed the leaves off. Sam had just seconds to hide behind the rock before a buckskin horse exploded onto the trail.

Black forelock blowing back from a golden face, the mustang ran, widemouthed and foaming, eyes rolled white with terror. Her delicate legs pulled her away from the noise, toward the path that narrowed like a funnel into the juniper just ahead.

As the horse passed, Sam saw a red bandanna knotted around the mare's throat.

A trap! Sam knew it an instant before she saw the shambling horses that followed the buckskin. The panicky buckskin was a Judas horse, leading the others into a trap. Necks dark with sweat, the mustangs veered too close to the trail's crumbling edge. One more step would send them plummeting to their deaths.

But the mustangs ran on, fleeing the buzz of motorcycles ridden by men in straw cowboy hats. There were two of them.

The men whooped and yipped over the whining

motorcycles. Horses crashed into each other, into boulders. They feared the men and machines more than the trap.

A dun with tiger-striped forelegs vaulted up a steep path just past the spot where Sam and Ace hid. The path went nowhere. As the mare wheeled and slid back down the path in a shower of rocks, Sam recognized her as the Phantom's lead mare.

Sam covered her mouth. No, no. Just weeks ago, the Phantom had been turned loose by the Bureau of Land Management. He was protected, freed to run wild and strengthen the mustang breed. How could he do that if BLM took his herd off the range?

If she burst out now, the horses would shy off the hillside. The fall might break their legs or necks. She had to wait until they were safely corralled. But this didn't look anything like the government gathers she'd heard about. It was too rough and primitive, too risky for horses the BLM was supposed to protect.

As one of the vehicles roared past, Sam realized it wasn't a dirt bike but an all-terrain vehicle. It was driven by a man in a shirt that looked like army camouflage. Attached to the vehicle was a scabbard holding a rifle.

These whooping idiots didn't work for the BLM. They were wild horse rustlers.

Ace lifted his head. Before he could neigh, Sam grabbed his muzzle and pulled it down. She pressed her cheek against the gelding's.

"You have to be quiet, boy," she whispered. "They're criminals."

Men committing a federal crime wouldn't mind hurting the only witness to their wrongdoing. Sam swallowed hard. If something happened to her, Dad and Gram might assume she'd suffered another riding accident. They might never know the truth.

A sleek black yearling flashed before Sam. A pair of blood bay mares followed. This was definitely the Phantom's herd. How could she save them?

Ahead, inside the trap, the buckskin lowered her head to a bucket so full of grain it spilled over at the thrust of her nose. The mare bolted the food in desperate gulps, ribs working like bellows. The men had starved her. That was how they'd forced the mare to lead the others into the trap.

She was so hungry, she ignored the chaos at the mouth of the trap. Inspired by the attempted escape of the tiger dun, other horses circled away from the ropes that had been strung on each side of the path and camouflaged with khaki-colored garbage bags. If the horses continued down the path, they'd be hemmed in on both sides and funneled into a pen made of metal panels so tall that there was no chance they could leap to freedom.

Sam saw the trap clearly now. So did the horses, but they had no place else to go. The tiger dun wouldn't let them enter, but she didn't know where to lead.

Movement beyond the trap made Sam spot a third man, on a horse. He raised his arm and pointed. For an icy moment, Sam feared he'd spotted her, but then the horseman shouted.

"He's mine!"

Even before she looked, Sam knew.

The Phantom burst into the clearing.

Thick-muscled and furious, the Phantom shone

silver amid the whirlwind of dust. Head held flat on a lowered neck, he slashed the rump of a roan mare, driving her away from the trap, toward a downhill path so steep it seemed to plunge into space.

Swinging his head, the Phantom herded another mare after the roan. When she trotted in place, hesitating, the stallion's teeth convinced her to run too.

Like a striking snake, the silver stallion worked his way through the herd, bullying his family away from the trap that would end their freedom.

"Stop him! They're all getting away!"

"Hey, close the gate!"

The buzzing vehicles only made the herd flee faster. Hooves clattered on rock, and the sounds of falling horses told Sam the descent down the Phantom's escape trail wasn't easy.

The horseman trotted forward, swinging a lazy loop of rope above his head. He wanted to rope the Phantom.

Oh no you don't, Sam thought. But how could she stop the man?

The stallion hated ropes and feared them. The scar

on his neck told why. With a choice between the rope and the cliff, the stallion would leap and die.

The buckskin shied from the horseman. With a metallic banging, she hit the side of the portable corral disguised with juniper. She feared the rope but kept her head down, eating in the midst of chaos as if nothing else mattered.

Only a few horses still milled inside the corral, near the buckskin: an old bay mare, a bald-faced roan, the black yearling, and a chestnut colt. Not enough to sacrifice the herd for, and yet the Phantom stayed.

Run. Go now! Sam sent her thoughts to the stallion as she had before, but he wouldn't leave the others behind.

The loop flew, closed on air, and slapped the stallion's back. The rider swore and jerked the rope away for a second try.

Run, boy, run.

Before the rider threw another loop, the Phantom darted inside the trap.

"Close the gate!"

Sam's leg muscles tensed. She was ready to sprint

from cover, ready to launch herself at the man dismounting from the ATV, but the Phantom noticed the man's approach. The stallion wheeled, herding the colt before him.

Sam made herself wait. *He can do it. He can make it.*

The man in camouflage was closing the gate, but the stallion charged and knocked him aside.

The man reached up, grabbing for the Phantom's mane. He fell before he could touch the stallion.

The chestnut youngster ran on, but the stallion's head turned. His ears flattened to his neck and his eyes narrowed. The man saw what he was risking and stumbled out of range of the Phantom's flashing teeth.

With a whisk of his tail, the stallion leaped after his herd and vanished.

Ace's breath sighed against Sam's cheek. The horse was as relieved as she, but only one danger had ended.

Chapter 2

SAM SQUATTED AND HID. SHE WISHED THE juniper foliage was more dense. She wished daybreak hadn't come while the rustlers battled the Phantom for his herd.

The three horses left behind didn't provide much of a distraction. Sooner or later, the men would see her.

The black yearling trotted a stride ahead of the bay mare and the stocky roan. Together, they formed a small herd and circled the pen made of portable steel panels.

The buckskin shone like a spot of sunlight among the darker horses, but each time they reached her, the three horses veered aside. Just the same, the buckskin always kicked out a rear hoof in warning.

The mustangs showed no interest in her grain. They ran as if they could escape their captivity, and stopped only once, calling after their band mates as if their wild hearts would break.

Sam grabbed Ace's muzzle when his nostrils vibrated in response. He yanked his head from her grasp. For a minute, Sam felt a cold clutch of dread, but the gelding stayed quiet.

"Well, shoot, this wasn't hardly worth the trouble," said one man. He climbed off his dirt bike, then snatched off his straw hat and swatted it against his pant leg.

Though Sam had seen her father make the same gesture a hundred times, on this man it looked wrong. He wasn't a cowboy, just a man dressed up like one.

"Old mare's so bony, I don't think she'll weigh up to a hundred bucks," said the man, and because his wide, freckled face looked good-natured, Sam disliked him even more.

Still mounted, the rider wrapped his rope into a neat coil as he spoke. "What we lose on the old one, we'll make up with the roan. Get 'em loaded. I'll be back."

As he rode away, Sam wondered where he could be going. More than that, she wondered what the men were talking about.

Weigh up to a hundred bucks?

Sam tried to make sense of the conversation. But when the man in camouflage pulled a rifle, her brain could only focus on it. She had to stay hidden. She must keep Ace silent and still.

Sam tried to get a good look at the men. If the police caught them later, she wanted to be able to identify them. It was difficult to see from her hiding place, but she had to try.

Man One wore camouflage and had a broad and freckled face. Man Two had snatched off his hat to reveal bushy white hair and eyes that bulged.

The men began tugging at the edge of a huge sort of

blanket. It looked like a patchwork quilt made of feed sacks. As they pulled it away, Sam saw they'd used it to cover a small stock truck.

A sigh shuddered through Sam, but the men were too busy to notice. The feed-sack quilt made a great disguise. She'd been staring at the hidden truck for at least twenty minutes, but she hadn't noticed it. From the air, it would look like part of the rough terrain. From below, it blended with the rock and juniper.

Although the Ford truck was a fairly new model, it was painted a muddy yellow that didn't shine, even in full sunlight. Hitched on behind was a gray stock trailer. An orange stripe, probably reflective to catch cars' headlights at night, had been painted on its side.

The rustlers would be less likely to be spotted at night, and the trailer was big enough to carry at least a dozen animals. She'd remember that orange stripe.

Sam didn't know how they'd driven the truck up the mountain or how they'd get it back down again, but the men set to work with an ease that indicated they'd done this many times before.

How many horses had they kidnapped off the range, and where had they taken them?

The third man returned and dismounted, and he climbed into the pen with the mustangs. He moved like a cowboy, but he was a reckless one.

Quickly, she saw he had nothing to fear. With each step he took, the frightened horses scattered.

Sam couldn't see his face, but he carried a thick-handled black bullwhip. The buckskin left her food and joined the other horses. Her shrill neighing began. Sam recognized it as the sound that had floated down the mountain as she and Jen had waited for the bus yesterday.

This close, the piercing sound hardly seemed equine.

Mustangs were usually silent, and the BLM freeze brand on her neck proved the buckskin was a mustang. But someone had taught her to scream.

The men on the outside dropped one panel of the corral. All four horses bolted for the opening. When they saw they were stampeding toward the truck ramp, they shied and turned back. But the man with the whip left them no choice.

The lash snaked outward, popping in their faces. The mustangs stopped, sliding back on their haunches, then wheeled toward the ramp.

That quickly, the animals were conquered. Heads low, their mouths made submissive chewing movements. In the language of wild horses, they begged for mercy.

The man cracked his whip again.

Although frightened by the hollow pounding of their hooves on the ramp, the horses went. They didn't know what lay before them, but they fled the whip.

The buckskin was last. Her legs and body trembled so much, Sam feared she would collapse.

Gathering her courage, the buckskin leaped toward the ramp. As she did, the man in camouflage got a foothold on the metal fence, swung up, and leaned toward her. Before the buckskin could swerve away, he grabbed the red bandanna around her neck and tugged it up to cover her eyes.

The mare stopped, standing still as the man laughed.

"She done it again," he said, laughing. "Never quite

figures out she's not goin' with 'em, does she?"

His cruelty almost made Sam burst from her hiding place. Now she understood. The buckskin mare had been starved and used to lure wild mustangs into this trap many times before.

Each time other horses were loaded into the truck, the buckskin thought she'd escape. Each time, she was left behind in darkness.

Sam swallowed hard and made the mare a silent promise.

I'll find a way to get you away from them.

The man in camouflage stowed the rifle on a gun rack inside the truck cab. That made Sam's determination more solid. She'd been quick and agile when she played basketball for her middle school team. Without that gun to fear, she could outmaneuver those men and release the buckskin.

Yes, she might be stealing, but Sam didn't care. She'd just figured out where the rustlers took the wild horses.

Only one kind of business purchased mustangs by the pound—the kind that made them into meat.

The mud-yellow truck swayed from side to side, gears grinding, engine laboring. The horses inside couldn't possibly stay on their feet. The truck's engine made a weird pinging sound as it slogged down the back side of the mountain, safe from eyes that might have seen it go down the front side, toward the highway.

Though Sam had watched all three men climb into the truck, she still didn't move. Where was the horse the cowboy had ridden? Had he loaded it in with the wild ones? Was someone else still around?

She could climb back on Ace and ride fast, back the way she'd come. She glanced at her watch and was amazed to see it was only seven o'clock. She could get home and report the men to Brynna Olson at the BLM and still save the mare.

Unless they delivered the horses to someone nearby and returned to collect the abused buckskin who did her job so well.

Sam started to sip from her canteen, then noticed the buckskin had no water. The corral was empty of anything but the plastic grain bucket.

"That does it," she muttered to Ace. "You've got a new friend, boy."

After all the commotion, it wouldn't be fair to trust Ace to ground-tying. If he had any sense at all, he'd head for home. And she couldn't let him. Sam knotted the reins around a thick stand of brush, then surveyed the area one last time. Nothing moved except the buckskin mare.

"Things could get a little weird, Ace," Sam whispered. "If they do, just think like a mustang, okay?"

She gave Ace a final pat and started toward the corral. Sam walked boldly, wondering how fast she could run back, untie Ace, vault onto his back, and escape if anyone hollered "Stop!"

The buckskin's ears were a beautiful dark gold edged in black, and they swiveled to catch each one of Sam's steps.

Sam paused outside the gate. The man who'd pulled the bandanna up to cover the mare's eyes had done it with little fuss. Sam thought she could probably pull it down, except that the mare wasn't anywhere near the fence.

The bolt on the fence clanged back. If anyone was around, he would come charging out now. Sam held her breath and listened. A shadow surprised her, until she realized it was a hawk sailing on updrafts around the snowy peak.

She left the gate ajar. Running in boots was next to impossible, but if someone appeared, she'd sprint back to Ace. She'd trust her life to his speed and sure-footedness.

She should have been worrying about the mare.

Black forelegs thrashed through the air as the mare leaped toward Sam.

Like a cougar. The words flashed through Sam's mind as she flung herself left, out of the buckskin's path, and rolled in the dirt. Instinctively, her arms came up, shielding her head as the buckskin came even with her. Sam's eyes were clamped shut, awaiting that awful slam of hooves on skull.

Darkness closed around her like a swarm of bees, but Sam didn't pass out and the buckskin's kick never came.

As the buckskin's hooves retreated, Sam rolled and regained her feet. The buckskin was still blindfolded, but free.

Sam worried as she jogged back to Ace. The trail to

the top had been a challenge with her eyes and Ace's working overtime. How could the buckskin stampede down the hill sightless?

Breathing hard, Sam stabbed her thumb on the juniper as she jerked Ace's reins loose. She glanced up to see the buckskin picking her way across the slick granite. Then she started down the twisting trail.

Instinct had kept the buckskin from falling over the cliff, but did she know where she was going?

Sam swung into the saddle. The gelding was eager, but with the buckskin just ahead of her, Sam kept Ace reined in.

"Easy, boy," Sam said, leaning close to his neck. "You're going to have to help me do this."

They followed the mare at a distance, until she stopped at the wide spot in the trail where water seeped from a crack in the rock. Sam remembered this spot. They were almost down.

Still blindfolded, the mare lapped at the moisture.

Sam watched and waited, giving the buckskin a chance to drink.

The mare was tiny, thirteen hands or a little taller. Her black mane tangled down to her shoulder. Her ribs stood out with hollows in between.

Ace nickered, and there was something excited and hopeful in the way the little mare turned to him. She risked a step in his direction, slipped on hooves that hadn't been trimmed in a long time, then took one more step and returned his inquiring nicker.

That's it! She trusts Ace.

Sam remembered Brynna's tale of her blind mustang, Penny, who followed her rider's cues out of trust. And Sam remembered the Phantom, galloping down a hillside in the dark beside Ace, out of trust.

Sam would stay silent. Scary as it was, she'd leave the red blindfold in place and hope the mare followed Ace all the way home.

Sam kept her eyes on the horizon, on clouds like dandelion fluff against the blue sky. She didn't glance toward the buckskin for fear the mare would sense it.

When Sam heard the rushing river and saw the soaring wood rectangle that marked the entrance to River

Bend Ranch, she knew they'd reached the final tests.

The mare would hear her hooves clack on the wooden bridge. She'd scent strange horses and humans.

And Sam had her own test to pass: Dad.

In the months since she'd been home, Sam had hinted, suggested, and implied that she wanted to adopt another mustang. Each time, Dad refused. Animals needed to earn their feed, he insisted.

Sam thought of Strawberry, Banjo, Ace, and Tank, River Bend's sensible, hardworking cow ponies. Then she thought of the buckskin. Even filled with expensive feed, she might remain skittish and nervy. But one thing weighed in the mare's favor: Dad wouldn't have been able to leave her behind either.

For nearly an hour now, the buckskin had followed Ace. He seemed to understand his responsibility. If the mare lagged behind, Ace shortened his stride. If she kept pace a quarter mile to the gelding's right, Ace's ears swiveled in her direction. Once, she'd come so close that her skeletal barrel had bumped Sam's stirrup.

Sympathy had welled up in Sam, but she stayed

quiet. Words wouldn't comfort a horse who'd received only pain from humans.

Almost there, she thought. *Little horse, you're almost safe.*

Gram must have glimpsed them from the kitchen window, because she was standing on the front porch as they rode up. A breeze blew Gram's denim skirt against her legs and picked at the gray hair pinned into a tidy bun. She wiped her hands on her blue apron, watching Sam, Ace, and the buckskin clatter over the bridge and into the ranch yard.

Gram smiled, and Sam knew that look on her face. Gram was wishing she could tell Mom all about it. Even though Sam's mom was dead, Gram said she talked to her daughter-in-law in prayers, every night.

The buckskin hesitated when a tide of horses gathered at the fence of the ten-acre pasture. The sound of those hooves, without being able to see if the other horses were welcoming or rejecting her, must have frightened the mare. But she stayed next to Ace until he stopped near the round corral.

Jake was inside gentling a horse for a neighbor, but the gate hinges squeaked. Any second now, Jake would appear, wondering what she'd done this time.

Jake was sixteen, older than Sam by three years. Right now, he looked even older. Obsidian hair tied back with a leather thong, fringed chinks buckled over his jeans, Jake took in all there was to know in a single glance.

Raising his brown eyes to Sam's, he nodded, assuring her that he wouldn't frighten the mare by speaking.

He didn't, until she'd ridden Ace to the barn, stripped him of saddle and bridle, and turned both horses into the barn corral with Gram's gentle paint, Sweetheart.

Exhausted and finally drinking from her canteen, Sam watched the buckskin. Clearly, she was familiar with corrals. She didn't fling herself against the rails as some wild ones did.

Still blindfolded, the mare stood sandwiched between Ace and Sweetheart. Heedless of the hot day, the buckskin let the two horses press against her. At last, she dozed in the security of her new herd.

As Sam walked back toward the house, Jake met

her halfway. She almost wished he hadn't. He wore the same lazy smile he'd taunted her with when she was a tagalong kid.

"What?" she demanded.

"Brat," Jake began.

"Stop calling me that. And stop laughing."

Sam tilted her canteen to take a long drink of water. Once her mouth was full, Jake continued.

"I just can't wait to hear what Wyatt says when he finds out his daughter is a for-real horse thief."

Chapter 3

"I'M NOT A HORSE THIEF!"

"Uh-huh," Jake said. "That freeze brand and bandanna probably don't mean a thing. Her owner just gave her to you."

"No," Sam admitted. "But I didn't steal her. Exactly. If you'd seen what they were doing to her—"

"The owner was right there?" Jake's brown eyes widened. "You mean we're not talking burglary but outright robbery?"

"Of course not," Sam said, but she wasn't sure. "I

just, well, there was nothing else I could do."

"Tell it to the judge." Jake turned back toward the round corral.

"Hey!" Frustrated, Sam gave Jake's retreating back a flat-handed push. "You can't just walk away."

"Bet me," Jake said, and kept walking.

"If you opened your eyes to look at her, you'd see that mare is starved, dehydrated, and—" Sam searched for words to explain the horse's terror. "And she's an emotional mess."

When he turned back around, Jake's face was shadowed by his black Stetson. "I'll help you get that rag off her head," he said, but Sam could tell his sympathies were for the horse, not her.

"I don't want your help," Sam blurted. "I want you to admit I didn't steal that mare. I rescued her."

"Whatever," Jake muttered. His spurs rang as he led the way back to the barn corral.

"You hate it when I'm right," Sam taunted, but Jake didn't reply. Sometimes she thought he had a daily quota of words, and when they were used up, he just quit talking.

DARK SUNSHINE

Jake approached the buckskin cautiously, coming through the shady barn to the corral. Sam blinked, letting her eyes adjust to the dimness, but Jake wasted no time. He set one boot on a fence rail, pushed himself up, and reached for the buckskin's head.

The mare exploded. Her piercing scream accompanied an attack. She went for Jake with such fury that one foreleg got hung by the knee over the top rail.

"It's okay, girl. It's okay," Sam heard herself babbling, but Jake stayed quiet, dodging the mare's teeth as he freed her leg, then jumped down.

Jake would only snap at her if she asked if he was okay, so Sam watched the horse instead.

The buckskin ricocheted around the corral. She slammed against the fence, banged into Ace, bumped Sweetheart, then collided with the fence again.

The mare had been calm and napping just minutes ago. Sam could see it wasn't captivity the buckskin feared; it was people.

Jake motioned Sam outside the barn, but he kept staring back toward the mare, trying to read her mind.

"I'm calling Brynna Olson," Sam said. Jake nodded, eyes still on the horse. "To see who adopted her and everything. And—"

Sam's heart sped up. How could she have put aside the safety of the other horses? "I'll ask her where someone would take mustangs to sell them for—" She couldn't swallow down the worry. "You know, to be made into dog food."

"They'd take them out to the auction yards in Mineral," Jake said. "But there's a brand inspector there. If he thinks the horses are mustangs, he won't let them go up for sale."

"Are you sure?" Sam thought of the two mares and the beautiful black yearling.

"Yeah." Jake sounded bored, but Sam could see he was just preoccupied, still staring at the buckskin. "When you get done, come back."

"Why?" She'd had every intention of doing just that, but Sam didn't like Jake bossing her around.

"She might let you take that blindfold off," he said.

Sam felt dizzy, remembering the mare's charge on the

mountain, remembering she'd almost fainted from fear. But Jake never suggested she do something dangerous.

"Piece of cake," Sam said, then hurried off to make that call from the land line inside.

"I'll dispatch two rangers the minute we hang up. One can check out the auction yards. The other can go up by Lost Canyon and determine who's responsible." Brynna Olson, director of Willow Springs Wild Horse Center, sounded crisp and businesslike.

She always did. Sam still had to look hard to see the kind woman inside that wrinkle-free government uniform.

Still, Brynna was awfully good at her work. With a few questions, she'd pried a lot of information from Sam's weary brain. Now Sam could clearly picture the three men: the freckle-faced one in camouflage, the white-haired one with the buggy eyes, and the cowboy who'd flicked the black whip with such easy cruelty.

The buckskin's screams invaded the kitchen. Gram, who'd been sipping coffee and listening to Sam's conversation, frowned.

"I'll read that location back to you," Brynna said. "Correct anything I might've taken down wrong."

Brynna read Sam's description of the trail into Lost Canyon. Of course, she'd copied it perfectly.

"You've got it," Sam said, trying to block out the commotion coming from the barn pen.

"When I drive out to talk with Wyatt," Brynna said, "I'll check the mare's freeze mark and start tracking her owner. What else should I know?"

Sam bit her lip. So far, she hadn't mentioned the Phantom or said it had been his herd driven toward the trap. The less folks thought about the stallion, the better. It couldn't possibly matter.

"They were using her as a Judas horse," Sam blurted. "They must have turned her loose farther down the mountain, then spooked the mustangs after her. She led them right into the trap, as if she knew there'd be food there. She's half-starved and dehydrated."

"I'll send a vet."

Suddenly there was a ringing thump outside, as if the mare were trying to kick her way out of the barn corral.

"Send a big one," Sam said. "She's a fighter."

It turned out Sam didn't have to remove the buckskin's blindfold. Sweetheart rubbed faces with her and accidentally peeled off the bandanna, and that was when the mare had gone crazy all over again.

"She's fine as long as she faces that way." Jake pointed. He'd been watching her the whole time Sam was on the phone.

"Looking into the dark barn, she's fine. She started coming unglued when I turned on the light to get a look at her."

Was something wrong with the buckskin's eyes? Sam had assumed the men had blindfolded the mare to make her helpless, but maybe she was extra sensitive to light. Sam knew nothing about horses' eyes, and she had no time to ask Jake before she heard riders approaching.

Dad and all three cowboys—Dallas, Pepper, and Ross—were crossing the bridge. They rode loose-jointed and tired, like men who'd already put in a full day's work.

Sam swallowed against the tension threatening to strangle her, but then she saw her calf, Buddy, frolic up to the gate to greet the riders. Ever since she'd been pulled from quicksand as an orphan, the calf had been peppy as a pup.

Dad stripped the saddle and bridle from Banjo and turned the horse into the big pasture. While he rinsed his hands and face at the pump, Sam remembered she hadn't brushed her hair since dawn, when she had pulled her ratty green sweatshirt over her head.

She forked fingers through her bangs and the tendrils at her temples, trying to fluff the hair flattened by her old brown cowboy hat.

Now, saddle and blanket in hand, Dad walked toward the tack room.

"Steady there." Jake's voice was so low only the horses heard, but he was talking to Sam. "The worst thing that can happen is we give the mare to BLM."

Jake was right, but Sam noticed he hadn't ridden home for dinner. Suspense had its claws in him, too. He wanted to hear what Dad and Brynna said about this frightened animal.

"What do we have here?" Dad asked.

Sam listened for judgment in his voice but heard only curiosity about the golden-tan mare who refused to look at him.

As Sam began to explain, Brynna arrived. So did the vet. Gram walked down from the house too, and all three cowboys put off dinner to see what was causing the excitement.

Sam supposed she did a fine job of explaining. After all, no one could contradict her except Ace or the rustlers, and one seemed as likely as the other. But Sam was distracted.

Not by Dad, who stood expressionless as a tree trunk. Not by Brynna, who took notes like a newspaper reporter. Sam wasn't distracted by the vet, who said he wouldn't sedate the mare for an exam now, since he'd have to tranquilize her again tomorrow when BLM moved her to Willow Springs.

Sam was distracted by a girl who'd arrived with Brynna. The BLM woman was so caught up in identifying the mare, she'd forgotten to introduce the girl who'd come in the white government truck along with her.

The girl had a pointy fox face and wispy blond hair, and though she couldn't be more than twelve years old, she was what Aunt Sue would call a "tough cookie." Hands on hips, eyelids slack with boredom, she looked at those around her—Sam included—as if they were barely smart enough to breathe.

The vet had to detour around the girl to leave. She wouldn't step out of his path. Only Sam seemed to notice.

Was the girl Brynna's daughter? Her niece? If so, Sam pitied Brynna. The girl looked mean. Her jaw jutted out as if she held a grudge against the world.

"I think they kept her in a dark stall, long-term," Jake suggested.

A flicker of fear lit the girl's face before she gave a forced and noisy yawn.

"It happens," Brynna said. She gave the girl a quick glance but gestured toward the horse. "Even a mustang gets to feeling safe when she's left undisturbed. Then, when they try to make her leave, she charges."

"Yes, she does." Sam could have kicked herself for saying it.

Dad and Gram turned frowns her way. Their expressions said that the hours they'd spent at her hospital bedside two years ago were still fresh in their memories.

"When I opened the gate up at the trap, she ran for it." Sam gestured toward Lost Canyon, then made things worse by brushing off the front of her jeans. "I fell getting out of her way."

Figuring the girl would be amused by her discomfort, Sam shot her a sidelong glance. She was wrong.

The girl wasn't listening to a word Sam said. She was watching the horses.

In the ten-acre pasture, Strawberry rolled the saddle stiffness from her back, launched to her feet, and ran, with the others galloping after. It happened every evening, but you couldn't guess that by the girl's expression.

For the first time, Sam thought she was seeing rapture. If the little creep loved horses, she couldn't be all bad.

Just then, Jake leaned forward to show Brynna the bandanna the buckskin had worn, and he accidentally bumped the girl.

"Sorry," he apologized.

Instead of shrugging off the encounter, the girl stepped closer, lifted her chin, and shot both hands out to her sides, fingers motioning him closer.

Sam blinked. The girl was clearly saying that if Jake wanted to fight, she was ready.

Jake looked stunned. Sam watched him calculate the huge difference in their heights and weights, but he only repeated, "Sorry."

Sam glanced at Dad to gauge his reaction to all this and caught him looking at Brynna. Something in the tilt of Dad's head said they'd already discussed this kid. Their eyes continued the conversation, and Sam felt left out.

"I forgot to introduce Mikki," Brynna said.

"Mikki," Gram repeated. "What a cute name."

Gram stepped forward to take the girl's hand in both of hers, but Mikki crossed her arms and cinched them close to her body.

Sam couldn't believe someone didn't tell the girl to straighten up and apologize.

"Mikki is from Sacramento, California," Brynna

went on. "She goes by Mikki, but her full name is Michelle Small."

The girl glared at Sam as if daring her to comment on the match between her name and her size.

"Mikki's agreed to be the first to try out the HARP program—that's the Horse and Rider Protection program—here in northern Nevada," Brynna said.

Sam felt her lips twist in sarcasm. With Mikki's attitude, people needed protection *from* her.

"Some people who adopt mustangs just aren't suited to the chore of training them. Sometimes, they make some pretty big mistakes," Brynna said. "When that happens, we take the horses back and match them with girls who gentle them and make them adoptable all over again."

Sam would have asked Brynna how they picked the girls if Jake hadn't chosen that moment to escape.

"'Scuse me," he mumbled. "I'm due home soon, and it'll take a while to finish up with Teddy and turn him out."

Dad glanced toward the round corral where Jake had

left the horse he was working, then nodded for Jake to go ahead.

"Bye, Jake," Sam said. She waved and watched Dallas, Pepper, and Ross go after him. Cowboys didn't willingly join in uncomfortable conversations. Sam was amazed Dad was still standing here.

"Teddy Bear is the nicest little horse," Gram explained. "He's a curly Bashkir. Maybe you've seen them in magazines."

When Gram added that, Sam realized why she'd gone off on this tangent. Once more, Mikki's face lit with that joyous look. Even though Mikki had been rude, Gram was entertaining her. Why?

"Jake's schooling Teddy for Mr. Martinez, a banker in town. He loves that horse, but he raised him from a baby and, well, spoiled him a bit. Some tricks that were cute when Teddy was a colt—like using his teeth to pull the wallet out of your back pocket—are downright dangerous now that he's an adult horse. And when he doesn't want to be ridden?" Gram raised her eyebrows. "He just sits down like a big old dog."

When Brynna noticed Mikki's smile, her own got bigger. "Mikki, why don't you go over and watch?"

Even Sam knew the girl wouldn't take the bait. Brynna had a lot to learn about kids.

"So you can talk behind my back? It's not like I can't guess what you're going to say." Mikki slung her thumbs in her jeans pockets before facing Sam's father. "Here's the deal, *sir*." She made the word an insult. "HARP can't place me in the California program because of my juvenile record, my *crimes*, got it?"

Mikki's head wagged a little as she talked. Her tone was sarcastic, as though trying to shock Wyatt Forster was fun.

"Shoplifting, fighting, runaway." Mikki ticked her offenses off on three fingers. "What Ms. Olson didn't say is that HARP matches *at-risk* girls with wild horses who've been messed up."

Sam almost nodded, and Mikki turned to her.

"Yeah, and I'm past 'at-risk.' Everyone in the state of California has given up on me. Even my mom. She's the one who sent me to this freaking desert—"

When Mikki stopped, Brynna took over without a hint of emotion.

"Mikki is living in a group home in Darton. Although she's just eleven, she's in a program for academically talented students, and she's going to middle school there," Brynna explained. "The situation's not as bleak as she says. HARP is a very popular program in California, and it's just getting started in Nevada."

"Look." Mikki's hands perched on her hips. She turned her back on Gram and Dad to face Brynna. "This perfect little family doesn't want me around. Can't you tell? And I really don't care. I only said I'd do this because I sort of like horses."

Mikki gave a snort. Then, carefully not glancing toward Teddy as Jake led him prancing to the pasture, Mikki walked to the white BLM truck, climbed in, and slammed the door.

As soon as the kid disappeared, Brynna started talking fast.

"River Bend Ranch is the perfect place to start HARP in Nevada. You've got the round corral for starting the mustangs and girls together. And once you get the rails up on that big pasture near the barn, it will work for an arena, when they start riding. As I've, uh, explained, before." Brynna hesitated.

The BLM woman looked from Gram, who looked excited by the idea, to Dad. His face was blank, not giving Brynna a flicker of encouragement. But she kept talking.

"And, of course, the big bunkhouse would be perfect."

For what? Sam wondered.

Brynna pointed to a weathered building with broken windowpanes and a roof buckled at the peak and stripped bare of shingles by the wind. Cowboys hadn't slept there for years. Sam had heard Dallas say it was home to spiders big as lions and he wouldn't go in there without a whip and a chair.

Gram must have been thinking the same thing. When Brynna saw Gram frown, she added, "It will take some fixing up, but HARP, as I've said before"—she glanced at Dad—"pays ranchers for hosting the program if the pilot program succeeds."

Brynna took a breath before she went on. "And the girls would do so much better here than at the Gold Dust. Mr. Slocum's volunteered, but Sam would be a far better influence than—" Brynna gestured in the general direction of Linc Slocum's ranch, and Sam mentally filled in the blank.

Rachel. The most popular girl at Darton High School, Rachel Slocum was beautiful, catty, and selfish. Her rich father gave her whatever she wanted. Rachel was bored by horses, and she'd scorn girls who had the bad luck not to be born wealthy and pretty.

Sam knew *that* from experience.

But wait. Sam reined in her dislike of Rachel and flashed Brynna a frown. Sam wouldn't let herself be bought out with flattery. Just because she wasn't as selfish as Rachel didn't mean she wanted the HARP program here.

Why should she share her family, horses, or Jake with strangers? And she didn't want sly kids spying on her friendship with the Phantom.

Just thinking of the silver stallion made Sam's pulse

race. He needed her help. She had to protect him from wild horse rustlers who'd kill him for dog food. She didn't have time to be a good influence on Mikki.

Get a grip, Sam told herself. She was overreacting. Dad would never go for this idea. A proud, hardworking man who spoke only when he had to, Dad was the next thing to a hermit. He wanted nothing to do with the federal government and its programs.

Sam was about to tell Brynna to save her breath, when Dad nodded.

"Ms. Olson," he said, "you've got yourself a deal."

Chapter 4

VOICES SWIRLED AROUND SAM, DISCUSSING and planning, but she just stood there, stunned.

"River Bend Ranch will help you out. We'll see how the pilot program goes," Dad cautioned. "No promises after that."

"Absolutely." Brynna nodded.

"We'd only have Mikki to begin with, is that right?" Gram asked. "For an hour or two after school?"

"Right," Brynna said.

"I'd like to cook for that poor little thing . . ."

Poor little thing? Hadn't Gram heard the part about shoplifting and fighting?

"... get some wholesome food into her." Gram clucked her tongue. "I suppose she'll go back to the foster home for meals, but I make nutritious after-school snacks. And then, if we get the program permanently..."

Sam's hands fisted so tightly, her fingernails bit into her palms. The longer she let these plans roll ahead, the harder it would be to stop them.

Sam glanced toward the white truck. Mikki still sat inside, where she couldn't hear a thing.

"Besides Rachel, Jennifer Kenworthy's over at the Gold Dust Ranch. She's the foreman's daughter," Sam explained to Brynna. "And she's as good an influence as I am. Maybe better."

Sam knew her desperate tone had given her away when both Gram and Dad looked disappointed. Brynna, on the other hand, seemed interested.

"If the work with Mikki turns out well, Jen could help next summer," Brynna said. "There's good funding for this program, enough to remodel the bunkhouse so you could host a whole group of girls. The program would pay for saddles, feed, and wages. You and Jen could be instructors."

Brynna stopped when Dad held out his hand in a move that clearly said *Halt*. But why was he smiling?

"When do we start?" Dad asked.

"I'll have Popcorn trailered out on Monday." Brynna looked as if she were making calculations. "If we start Mikki with him on Tuesday, that would give the horse time to settle in."

"Popcorn?" Gram asked.

Brynna's lips firmed into a straight line before she answered. "He's an albino gelding who's been 'shown who's boss' a few times too many. He's awfully shy, but he'll be a great match for Mikki."

Sam didn't see the logic in the woman's remark, but she kept quiet. She'd have time to work on Dad after Brynna left.

"Tuesday, then," Dad said, and stuck out his hand.

"Tuesday." Brynna shook Dad's hand. "Thanks so much, Wyatt. I hope it works out for all of us."

Not only had Brynna's brisk tone softened, but as she walked away, Dad watched her go with a small smile.

Frustrated down to her fingernails, Sam tackled her chores. She fed the dog, fed the chickens, topped off the water troughs, checked the hens' nests for eggs, then stood staring at Ace, Sweetheart, and the frightened buckskin.

She hadn't had a chance to groom Ace when she'd first ridden in. Now she wanted to do it. She'd made a habit of pouring her troubles into Ace's attentive ears while she curried dirt and sweat from his coat. But it would be cruel to disturb the horses now. And selfish.

Sam walked into the shady barn and hung her green sweatshirt back on its nail. Selfishness. That was the feeling boiling inside her. But wasn't she allowed to be a little stingy, when she'd just gotten her family back?

Sam sat on a hay bale. She tried not to look at the little buckskin. The mare was watching, waiting for Sam to do something scary.

Sam stared outside. The barn pasture was empty of animals because several fence rails were down and a few were broken. The pasture reminded her of one of her worst mistakes since she'd come home and tried to fit back into ranch life.

Sam hadn't noticed the missing rails a month ago, when she'd left Buddy in that pen. While Sam was gone, the orphan calf had wandered away. Now Dad was pacing along the fence line.

He was getting ready to fix it. Not for her, but for Brynna.

Accidentally, Sam glanced at the buckskin. The mare's ears flattened against her neck and her nostrils flared.

Sam pretended to ignore the horse. She leaned back and stared into the barn's dark rafters. Overhead, a pigeon moved in its straw nest, trying to get comfy.

Sam knew how the bird felt. She was still adapting to ranch life. Gram and Dad tried to help, but each time she got used to them treating her like a child, they expected her to act like an adult.

Now Gram wanted to cook special meals for a stranger and fuss over *her*. Sam knew she sounded like a pouty little kid.

Her mind understood that Gram and Dad meant to do something good and charitable, but Sam's heart wanted to know why.

Why, why, *why* should they help this smart-mouthed kid named Mikki?

Lost in her own thoughts, Sam stopped watching Dad until he was just a few yards away. She shot to her feet, looking for something to do, but she didn't think fast enough.

The buckskin sucked in deep breaths, testing the air for threats.

Dad stood silhouetted against the outside brightness.

"Gram wants us to come eat some sandwiches and potato salad."

"Okay," Sam said. Her stomach growled and she felt light-headed from eating nothing since last night's supper.

She knew she should politely follow her father inside and wait for her sulky mood to pass. But she didn't.

"Dad, we don't need more work around here. Especially with me at school all day."

"Outside work will lighten up as winter comes on. The girl will only be here five or six hours a week. I can spare Jake that much."

Jake? Sam muffled her screech of outrage, but it echoed in her mind.

Brynna had mentioned that Sam and Jen might be teaching the girls to ride. She'd said nothing about Jake. It must be Dad's idea, and that troubled Sam.

Sam tried to squash her jealousy. After all, Jake had taught *her* the patient Native ways of working with horses. She couldn't imagine a better technique for soothing the hurts of horses and humans. Still . . .

"Jake, huh? I guess you don't agree with Brynna that I could handle it?"

Dad said nothing. His silence hurt.

"Just when I think you have faith in me, you expect me to fail."

"I didn't expect it." Dad spoke slowly. "You surprised me, sayin' BLM should send a ruined mustang and that child over to Slocum's."

"But when BLM offered you the job tracking wild

horses, you didn't do it." Sam didn't add, *And we could have used the money.* "Why did you say yes this time?"

Dad nodded toward the buckskin mare, and even that faint movement sent her sidling away from the fence. But Dad didn't answer Sam's question. He asked one, instead.

"Why didn't you leave that mare up at Lost Canyon?"

Sam's spirits fell. She'd been so sure Dad would understand.

"She was—they had her blindfolded. She was standing in the dark, alone. I couldn't leave her there."

"Neither could I," Dad said.

"But, Dad—"

"That's my answer, Samantha. Chew on it."

Later that evening, Jen called to explain why she'd missed their early-morning ride.

Her cold had gotten worse.

"I didn't oversleep," Jen said, sniffing. "I was up getting dressed, but my mom heard me coughing and wouldn't let me go."

It took Sam a second to understand, but if she took

the word that sounded like "bomb" and substituted "mom," Jen's sentence made sense.

"That's what I figured," Sam said. "But I've got so much to tell you. And part of it involves the Phantom."

Jen gasped. "Talk fast. Mom only gave me ten minutes. Then I have to go back to bed."

"Okay, but—oops." Sam lost her grip on the phone she was juggling as she folded laundry. "Sorry I dropped you. I think Gram and Dad are giving me time to figure out how lucky I am," she told Jen.

"Lucky?"

"Lucky that I have a decent home and people who care enough about me to make me fold a mountain of laundry taller than I am," Sam said.

When Jen made a confused sound, Sam asked, "Have you heard of the HARP program?"

"Sure. They pair juvenile delinquents with problem horses, then step back and watch to see who kills who first."

"Jen, you're terrible." Sam shook her head at her friend's sarcasm.

Jen's laughter provoked more coughing. When she

finally stopped, she asked, "That's the program, though, right? They have it in California and New Mexico."

"Sort of," Sam said. "Except Brynna Olson and Dad have worked it out so that the Nevada program's first kid—"

"Just *one* delinquent in all of Nevada? I'm not buying that."

"—will meet the horse here. Then Jake and I will work with the kid and the horse. The mustang is an albino named Popcorn."

When Jen made a throat-clearing sound that sounded like envy, Sam told her Brynna's plan.

"It's a government program, and there's enough money set aside that if things work out with Popcorn and Mikki—that's the first girl's name—they might send more kids during the summer, and Brynna said they might need you as an instructor too."

"Wow." Jen sighed. "How cool is that?"

Would Jen like the idea so much if she were sharing her own parents?

"But wait," Jen said. "Do you really believe my mom,

who homeschooled me because she didn't want me corrupted by outside influences, is going to—"

Jen's voice faded as her hand muffled the telephone mouthpiece. "Yes, Mom, I know it's been . . . But I feel much—" Suddenly, Jen's voice was clear. "Sam, I have to get off now."

Disappointed that the conversation had ended so soon, Sam teased her friend.

"Oh, that's fine. I didn't really want to tell you about the wild horse rustlers."

"What?" Jen's squeak triggered her coughs all over again.

"And how the Phantom came to the rescue—" Sam stopped taunting Jen and bit her lip. She probably shouldn't mention the beautiful buckskin, either.

"Don't forget *anything*," Jen whispered. "I want details."

That night, Gram served up a lecture along with dinner.

"As soon as Brynna mentioned this program, I started reading up on it," Gram said.

And how long ago was that? Sam wondered. Gram had

seemed surprised, but apparently only Sam had been kept out of the loop.

"There's not a lot of data so far, but it's working. In most other programs, seven out of ten kids are back in trouble inside of a year. With HARP, it's three out of ten."

"If they get back in trouble," Sam mused, "can they come back to work with the mustangs?"

"Whatever do you mean?"

"I was just thinking," Sam said, remembering the joy on Mikki's face as she watched the horses gallop across their pasture. "If I were a bad kid, I might mess up again so that I could come back and work with the horses."

"Samantha Anne, I don't know why I try to treat you like an adult, when all you want to do is joke." Gram whacked the wooden tongs back into the salad bowl.

She *hadn't* been joking. Sam looked to her father for help. He balanced the lettuce on his fork for a minute, studying her.

"I think she's serious," he said.

"I am."

"Well, all right," Gram said. "Sometimes it's hard to tell."

"You know what else I was wondering?" Sam asked. "Why we couldn't use that buckskin mare instead of the albino Brynna was talking about." Sam looked from Gram to Dad.

Sam tried to imagine Mikki giving the buckskin the gentle handling she needed. She couldn't.

No, when she stared at the kitchen wall, imagining it was a movie screen, the girl she saw loving that frightened horse was herself.

Chapter 5

SAM DREAMED OF THE PHANTOM. IN HER dream, a giant swan floated down the river, gradually changing into the curve-necked, broad-chested stallion. But he didn't lose his wings. The mighty stallion launched into flight, and Sam woke to the rustling of feathers.

As she dressed in boots and jeans, Sam couldn't shake the feeling that the Phantom had actually been near. She'd fallen asleep yearning to see him, wishing she could go to the river, even though she'd known he wouldn't come to her.

The Phantom was the leader, the protector of his herd. After yesterday's near disaster, she knew he wouldn't leave the horses alone, even in their isolated valley in the Calico Mountains.

She couldn't read the stallion's mind, but Jake had tutored her in horse psychology. The Phantom wouldn't lead his band back up the narrow trail to Lost Canyon, even though the water seeping from the rock walls was sweet. The narrow trail, funneling into that tight trap, would have frightened the horses, so the Phantom would take the mares to an open area.

They'd be more visible, but that drawback worked to the animals' advantage. They'd see anything that could see them and have plenty of time to use their best weapon: speed.

War Drum Flats. That was where they'd go. The pond was scooped from the level sagebrush- and piñon-pine-dotted land that lay at the foot of the trail up to Lost Canyon. Best of all, a ridge overlooked the area, so the Phantom could keep watch and use his trumpeting neigh to warn his family of danger.

Dusk, Sam thought. She'd do all her chores and homework and ride Ace to War Drum Flats just as the sun went down.

Sam avoided the mirror and finger-combed her hair as she trotted downstairs.

The kitchen was already warm and filled with the smell of frying ham and eggs.

Sam kissed Gram and kept moving toward the door.

"Biscuits will be done in about five minutes," Gram said.

"I just want to check on the buckskin," Sam announced.

"Go on, then," Gram said, "But hurry back."

She had to make sure the buckskin hadn't escaped. Though the corral was too small to allow the running start needed to leap the fence, wings still fluttered in Sam's imagination.

Sam started to open the door, then let it close without leaving the kitchen.

"What's Brynna Olson doing here?" she asked.

Gram turned from the stove and stood just behind

Sam, looking over her shoulder through the window.

"My, my, I don't know. I wonder if she knows Wyatt's already ridden out?" Gram pushed her glasses farther up her nose, but the white truck parked in the ranch yard was still there. "Well, dear, run on out and ask her in for breakfast."

Sam might have protested if she hadn't disappointed Gram yesterday. It would be a waste of time, anyway. Gram always got her way, sooner or later.

Ace's nicker floated to Sam, but Brynna didn't turn to look at her. She watched the barn corral and stayed still to keep from startling the buckskin. The golden-brown mare shifted nervously, but she stood facing the barn.

Sam sighed. It was sad that the little mustang was happier staring into the darkness.

"Gram says—"

"I didn't come for breakfast, Sam. I came to talk with you." Brynna didn't look away from the horses, but Sam stood beside her now, and she saw the dark circles under the redhead's eyes. Brynna's tone made Sam wonder if she was to blame for the woman's sleepless night.

Brynna wasn't wearing her uniform. She wore gray cords and a teal pullover. Far from making her red hair and blue eyes more vivid, the teal emphasized the fact that Brynna's eyes looked faded and tired.

"I haven't been able to track down her owner yet," Brynna said. "But she was adopted by Mrs. Rose Bloom of Casper, Wyoming, who did enter a name for the mare." Brynna paused for effect. "Dark Sunshine."

Rose Bloom? Sam thought. "It's perfect," Sam said. "The mare's name, I mean. It's not just her color, but—everything."

"That may be all the woman did right," Brynna said. "Mrs. Bloom's phone is disconnected. There's nothing in BLM records saying she *didn't* gain title to her last May." Brynna sighed. "Which means, she might have sold the horse legally since then."

Brynna raised one eyebrow as she regarded Sam.

"So, one of those rustlers could own her?" Sam asked. "Maybe I really did steal her." She thought of the mare, thirsty and bewildered in that mountain trap. "But I'm not sorry."

"There are laws against mistreating animals, and they broke them. If they filed a complaint against you, I doubt a judge would take it seriously."

Sam felt a flush of warmth at Brynna's support, until the woman went on in her cold, official voice.

"The brand inspector at the auction yards in Mineral says no horses came in with fresh brands."

Anyone would have spotted a fresh brand. Sam remembered Buddy's. For days after her pet calf had been branded, Sam thought the mark looked exactly like what it was—a second-degree burn.

"That's good, I guess," Sam said. "But no rustler who was thinking straight would brand a wild horse and try to sell him the same day, would they?"

"True," Brynna said. "But I think the criminal genius is a myth."

Sam laughed.

"The brand inspector saw animals without brands," Brynna said, "but none appeared to be range horses. There were only three—two packhorses from Elko and a very old Shetland pony."

At that, Sam couldn't repress a frown.

Neither could Brynna, though she worked at being tough. Sam didn't know if she worked so hard at it because she had a responsible job, or because she was a woman in a mostly male profession, or because she was hiding a soft heart.

If Brynna hadn't hated the thought of people selling horses for pet food once they outlived their usefulness, she wouldn't have mentioned the Shetland pony.

Maybe I'm not in trouble after all, Sam thought. *Maybe thoughts of pitiful horses kept Brynna awake last night.* Suddenly, though, Brynna changed the subject.

"Mikki Small has had three stepfathers in the last four years. She's lived in eight different apartments and gone to seven schools between fourth grade and sixth grade."

Sam flinched at Brynna's accusing tone.

"That would be really hard," Sam said. She didn't say anything to fill the silence swelling between them. Instead, she touched a splinter on the fence. She'd have to get some sandpaper and smooth it down before a horse got hurt.

"I don't know why it happened, but Mikki was telling the truth when she said her mother sent her away."

Sam kept trying to smooth the splinter down as she remembered how she'd felt the few times Dad had given Brynna extra-long looks. She'd hated it. Even though her reaction made no sense, she felt like he was choosing Brynna over her. The feeling cut like a knife, then kept aching each time she thought of it.

How much worse must it be for Mikki, whose mom had married three different guys and then sent her away? And Mikki was only eleven.

All at once, Sam realized her hand had reached up to touch her breastbone. She didn't want to sympathize with Mikki, but her heart didn't know that. Deliberately, she put her hand back on the fence.

"Couldn't you get in trouble for telling me this?"

"Sure," Brynna said. "I could probably get fired."

Sam took a deep breath and glanced back toward the house. Gram would be waiting.

"But how about the way she refused to shake Gram's hand? And the way she squared off with Jake? And . . ."

Sam hesitated as a blush crawled up her cheeks. "I know it's no big deal, but she looks at me like I'm a . . . a hick."

"I'll tell you what you look like to her, Samantha. You look like the luckiest girl in the world. You have people who love you, and horses, and a future."

Sam didn't cry, but when Ace ambled to the fence and whuffled his soft lips over her fingers, she came close.

She didn't admit she felt like a spoiled brat. She didn't tell Brynna she'd make a great psychologist, either. But both were true.

After she'd finished her homework, Sam worked with Dallas.

One reason the River Bend foreman was well liked was his willingness to work. Although the gray-haired buckaroo let it be known his only talent was work done from horseback, he'd dirty his hands with most any chore.

The chore of the day was repairing the chicken coop.

For weeks, Gram had suspected her Rhode Island Red hens were laying more eggs than she was getting.

Something, she insisted, was slipping into the coop at night and stealing eggs.

By the time the hailstorm came and the hens resumed laying, Gram had also noticed the coop could use tightening up. Sam was awarded the job, but Dallas had offered to help.

Now he grunted as he settled his saddle-weary bones into a squat next to the coop.

"Snakes, weasels, ground squirrels could all get through something that size," Dallas said as he examined an opening in the wire. He measured it with his middle and index fingers. "There's no room for a raccoon, though they do like eggs."

Sam liked working with Dallas. As long as she did her share, he never criticized. And maybe because he'd known her since she was a toddler, Dallas never thought her questions were silly.

"Would any of those animals hurt the chickens?" Sam asked.

"Probably not," Dallas said. "If a critter ate one of these big fluffies"—he gestured at the fat hens, whose feathers puffed up at the disturbance caused by the two humans—"it likely couldn't get out again. Plus, they'd set up a ruckus that would wake us, or Blaze.

"Come spring, though, if we have any chicks, they'll gobble them down for sure."

Sam felt a little queasy, thinking of a chick-sized lump in the gliding length of a snake. She didn't say anything, but Dallas must have noticed her expression.

"What we need to do is take off this old chicken wire." Dallas gestured to the screening within the wooden frame of the enclosure. "Then we'll replace it with new. After that, we'll put out the word we need a rooster. A mean one. Anything comes sneaking along after that is in trouble. Let some weasel stick its head in, and the rooster will grab on and flog it till you can fold it up like your gram's hanky."

Sam worked quickly, lulled by the low clucking of the hens.

The chickens were set free daily to peck at table scraps and bugs. Dark Sunshine acted as if she'd never seen such creatures. The buckskin slung her head over the top rail of the fence. Ears pricked forward, eyes tracking every movement, the mare trembled with fascination as she watched the hens.

"Look." Sam nudged Dallas and nodded toward the mare.

"She's showing you that she can be smart and interested," Dallas said. "Now you just got to figure how to get her to look at you like she does those chickens."

"I wish I could." Sam sighed. "I'm worried about BLM returning her to her owner."

"Oh, I think she'll be sticking around River Bend for a good long time," Dallas said.

"I hope so. Whoever owns her doesn't deserve her," Sam grumbled. "I'd buy her from them if Dad hadn't forced me to put my reward money in savings."

Just a few weeks ago, Linc Slocum had offered a huge reward for the return of his Appaloosa filly, Apache Hotspot. Using horse sense and her talent with a camera, Sam earned the reward by unmasking the renegade stallion who'd stolen mares right out of their home pastures.

But Dad didn't believe in shopping sprees. He'd allowed her to buy a camera of her own, small gifts for

DARK SUNSHINE

him and Gram, a soft leather headstall for Jake's upcoming birthday, and a new well pump.

She'd had to fight him on that purchase. Sam and Dad had stood toe-to-toe, each with arms crossed. Sam figured Dad finally realized she was every bit as stubborn as he was and gave in.

If every other penny hadn't gone into her college savings account, Sam knew she could have convinced Dark Sunshine's owners to sell her.

An afternoon breeze blew over the sagebrush by the time Sam rode out on Ace. She'd had to display all her finished homework and promise to return in time for dinner, but at last she was riding.

Ace moved at a rocking-chair lope across the high desert, and Sam thought maybe Brynna had been right. With the wind in her face, a spirited horse carrying her across starkly beautiful land, and love waiting for her at home, she felt awfully lucky.

They'd almost reached War Drum Flats when Sam leaned forward to pat Ace's neck and saw the horse.

At first, peering through the frame of Ace's ears, Sam took the palomino for a lone mustang.

The mustang had wings.

Sam thought of her weird dream, then shook her head. Impossible. But something *was* flapping out from the horse's body. Ace's stride didn't change, but Sam felt him grow tense beneath her.

"What is it, boy?"

Sam squinted. She wished for a camera to bring the scene into focus. Then, all at once, she recognized the movement.

Stirrup leathers bounced out with each galloping step the palomino took, but the saddle above them was empty.

Sam urged Ace into a run, planning a path that would intersect with the palomino's. Out on the range, with darkness coming on, a riderless horse could only mean trouble.

Chapter 6

THE PALOMINO WAS READY TO STOP RUNNING. He slowed to a trot, a walk, and finally fell into step beside Ace. Sam snagged the palomino's reins.

Even if Sam hadn't recognized the horse, she might have guessed his owner by the horse's trappings. The silver conchos glittering on his noseband matched those decorating his black leather saddle. It was parade gear, and the only man in northern Nevada who'd tack up his horse this way for a Sunday afternoon ride was Linc Slocum.

"What are you doing, horse, running away from home?"

She wouldn't blame him. Champ belonged to Slocum, and the man compensated for his mediocre riding skill by using harsh bits and spurs. The palomino wasn't bleeding from spur gouges today, but his dark lips were smeared with foam.

Sam scanned the range. Slocum was nowhere in sight, and she was glad. For the first time, she'd have a chance to help this horse.

Crooning to keep the palomino calm, Sam dismounted and ground-tied Ace.

Today, Slocum rode with a spade bit. From outside, it was a thing of beauty, silver mounted with fine engraving, but inside a horse's mouth, it could be a torture device. The three-inch metal spade worked on the tenderest parts of the horse's mouth.

According to Dallas, the bit worked elegantly in the hands of an expert rider. But Slocum was no expert. Dallas said giving Slocum reins connected to a spade bit and expecting him to ride well was like giving a monkey a straight razor and expecting him to give you a nice, close shave.

She'd have to return Champ to Slocum, but she had time to adjust the bridle so that the bit moved with less severity.

Sam had just finished and remounted when Slocum appeared on the horizon, limping toward her in high-heeled cowboy boots.

She held Ace's reins in her left hand, Champ's in her right, and the palomino followed along nicely.

"You're a good horse, Champ," Sam said to the horse, "but it's just like your boss to get himself stranded when I'm in a hurry."

The good news was that she was nearly to War Drum Flats, and Slocum's Gold Dust Ranch was only a couple of miles away. Once she got Slocum back in the saddle, she should have the area to herself. She just hoped he hadn't created such a commotion that he'd frightened off all the wildlife in the area, from horses to jackrabbits.

"Well, now," Slocum bawled when he got within range, "aren't you a sight for sore eyes!"

Sam might have said the same, but she would've dropped the last three words. Slocum's plaid shirt and jeans weren't extraordinary, but Sam couldn't stop staring at his boots.

Working cowboys wore their jeans over their boot tops, but Slocum tucked his in to show off the red and yellow cutouts and fancy green stitching. The boots matched the silver-mounted tack for flashiness.

Though he had to have been walking for some time, balancing his barrel-shaped body atop his slant-heeled boots, Linc Slocum looked in good spirits. His slicked-back hair lay in place and the white grin on his flushed face made him look like an advertisement for quick-tanning lotion.

"Hello," Sam greeted him. "Going someplace special?"

Slocum didn't realize she was referring to his gaudy attire.

"Just to get my horse," he puffed, taking the reins from her hand. "Champ decided to give me an opportunity to see if the moon really is made of green cheese."

Sam managed a small laugh. Slocum loved using

expressions he thought were Western. If they'd come out of Dallas's mouth, they might have worked, but somehow Slocum didn't get the timing right.

"But seriously," Slocum amended, "what's goin' on over at your place these days?"

"Just the usual," Sam said.

Slocum loved gossip, but he rarely got stories even approximately straight. Sam couldn't mention the HARP program, wild horse rustlers, or the buckskin mare she'd sort of stolen unless she wanted to hear a twisted version of each item as she climbed onto the school bus tomorrow morning.

"Well, I've got some good news."

Sam braced herself. Slocum's "good news" almost never was.

"I'm going to start breeding Brahma bulls t'sell to rodeo contractors. Now, ain't that fine?"

Sam could force her lips to smile, but she couldn't erase the pictures of disaster playing in her mind. A man who'd accidentally hired a criminal to help him capture the Phantom, who gave his daughter thousands of dollars for clothes, makeup, and anything else she wanted, who couldn't stay on his own horse or dress for the rough country he lived in, should not get near two-ton animals and breed them for aggressive tempers. She might be only thirteen, but even she knew better.

Slocum didn't wait for her opinion. "Ought to have them delivered and in their new pens about two weeks from now. I wanted to invite Wyatt and Grace—and you, of course—to a special little Brahma-cue."

"You're going to eat them?"

"No, 'course not, honey. That's just a little play on words. I'll have my staff grill up lobster tails and T-bone steaks. Think you all would like to come?"

"Sure."

Sam knew Dad mourned the loss of every minute spent in Slocum's company, but he'd want to see the cattle. And Gram embraced any excuse for a party. She'd come carrying a chocolate layer cake or lemon meringue pie that would draw more compliments than Slocum's gourmet fare.

"Well, you saved me a trip," Slocum said. "And if you

would, tell Jake Ely's dad—what's his name? Luke?—that they're invited too."

Sam would have enjoyed seeing Slocum at Three Ponies Ranch. Jake's parents might have maintained straight faces at Slocum's getup, but Jake and his six older brothers would've had a good laugh.

Slocum sawed at his reins. Though trying to signal the palomino to wheel into a turn, Slocum only succeeded in pulling the animal's head from side to side. With role models like Linc Slocum at the Gold Dust Ranch, maybe it was better that Brynna had chosen the River Bend to host HARP.

Champ obeyed the reins, rolling his eyes and tossing his head. Sam thought the gelding's moves were done from habit rather than pain, and she was glad she'd made the adjustments. Slocum would never notice. Already, he was kicking the palomino into a run.

"Adios, muchacho!" Slocum yelled, then headed for home.

Sam waved.

Muchacho. Slocum's Spanish was even worse than his

English. He'd called her a boy. On the other hand, Sam didn't mind what he called her, as long as he left her alone to wait for the Phantom.

Five more minutes. Sam consulted her watch, knowing she shouldn't wait longer for her horse to appear. In only twenty-five minutes, she was supposed to be home. It would take her that long to ride to the River Bend bridge. Then she still had to cool Ace, strip off his tack, and brush him before releasing him into the corral. And who knew how long that would take if Dark Sunshine tried to escape?

It started to rain. Drops pattered on the brim of Sam's old brown Stetson. She couldn't sit here much longer.

Maybe because she wanted to see the Phantom so much, her eyes were fooled by a curtain of rain wafting down the hill. For a minute, she thought it was the silver stallion.

"C'mon, Ace. We're just going to get soaked if we stay." Sam lay the reins against the gelding's neck, but he didn't move. "Ace?"

Sam turned back and looked again. It *was* him! Pale

and silent as a wisp of cloud, the Phantom led his herd down the cleft in the hillside, toward water.

The stallion was so perfect; she didn't even feel disloyal to Ace. Ace was her friend. The Phantom existed as a king among horses. Tonight he moved with a deerlike caution she'd never seen before. With swift, head-swiveling movements, he tasted the wind and rain. He studied every bobbing bush to see if it hid a man. He sampled each scent for the stench of a human.

The Phantom paused, one foreleg lifted in midstride, when he noticed Sam. His nostrils distended; then a shudder ran through him as he decided she could be trusted.

Around him, mares moved in an uneasy swirl. Then he came on, bolder and faster than before. With hammering hooves, he bolted to the edge of the water hole and dipped up a quick sip. He answered the tiger dun's questioning nicker with a shake of his head. For a second, his eyes were veiled with white mane. Then he cleared the way for the others, racing toward the windswept ridge that was his lookout post.

Sam watched him go. Each of the mustangs at the water hole was beautiful. The tiger dun, the blood bay mares who must be twins, the chestnut colt who'd nearly been lost to the herd just yesterday, but Sam spared them only a glance.

The silver stallion, tail streaming like a waterfall as he navigated the path, was what she'd come for.

The stallion knew her, and since horses didn't forget, he must remember her mistakes. She didn't pretend to be nicer, more polite, or braver than she was, around horses. This one, least of all. And yet he'd given her his trust.

Before he reached the hill crest, the Phantom stopped. He pirouetted in a space that looked too narrow for his muscled quarters and looked down, watching.

The tiger dun turned away from the water's edge and stiffened. The others lifted their heads and followed the lead mare's gaze with their own eyes. Sam couldn't see a thing. What had frightened them? All Sam heard was buckbrush crackling under the big raindrops.

The mares moved away from the water at a trot and

DARK SUNSHINE

then ran. The stallion forced his way against the tide of fleeing mares, but they kept on, and Sam realized Ace jittered beneath her, grunting a troubled sound as his ears pricked toward the highway.

Sam heard tires hiss on wet pavement.

Ace had heard passing traffic hundreds of times, though, and so had the mustangs. And any vehicle would have to pull off the highway and navigate a bumpy dirt road to reach them.

But this wasn't just any vehicle. A mud-yellow truck left the highway. Its pinging engine labored and its tires spun as it roared onto the dirt road.

And then Sam knew why the Phantom had turned. Once more, he was protecting her, herding her with his mares to safety.

Before the stallion reached her, Sam clapped her heels to Ace's sides.

"Go!" Sam leaned low on the gelding's neck and called to his back-cast ears.

In a flurry of churning hooves, the Phantom and Ace sideswiped each other, pinning Sam's leg between them.

She gasped. It felt tight, but it didn't hurt. She kept Ace aimed after the wild mares. As the tiger dun led the band to safety, Sam followed.

By now the rustlers must know someone had rescued Dark Sunshine. They knew someone was onto their crime, and though there was little chance they knew it was her, Sam wasn't going to stick around to make sure.

Her Stetson blew off her head, and only the stampede string kept it from flying away. The braided horsehair string sawed against Sam's throat, and she blinked against the rain pelting her face. But running with the mustangs was glorious, uncontrolled. She grabbed handfuls of mane and clung low on Ace's neck, filling her lungs with the smell of wet rocks and hot horsehide.

The horses jostled, pressing together as they entered a gorge thick with brush. Stickers ripped Sam's jeans, scratched her hands. A dark horse built like a rhino jammed past, and Ace staggered.

Then the mustangs stopped. Their breath hung in the moist air. Sam hadn't been running, but her heart beat as if she had. Surrounded by the band of horses, Sam realized she was the only one making a sound. She tried to muffle her panting.

The Phantom stood nose-to-nose with Ace. Through strands of silvery forelock, he raised his eyes to watch Sam. His head bobbed silently, as if in greeting, and their eyes held.

The pinging of the truck engine echoed as it continued up the mountain, then braked to a stop.

Were the rustlers looking for horses or for her? It didn't matter. If the men found the mustangs, they'd find her. Sam stared into the Phantom's dark eyes. This moment, she was one of his band, in safety or danger.

A tremor ran through the horses as a truck door slammed and footsteps crunched on dirt. Sam closed her eyes, wishing the darkness behind her own lids could cover her.

On her first day back in Nevada, she and Dad had seen a helicopter herding mustangs toward a trap. In a blink, they'd scattered over the range, then vanished.

"Mustangs have secret getaway trails," Dad had told

her, trails humans couldn't find. That was where she was, hiding like a prey animal, waiting for the predators to lose patience and leave.

Finally, they did. The truck's door slammed and its engine started. The sounds of spinning tires and spattering mud grew fainter and fainter.

The Phantom backed out of the thicket. The mares followed, and Sam kept Ace reined in, making him wait for last.

As they emerged, Sam discovered that the rain had stopped, but dusk had turned into darkness.

She glanced at her watch. She was a full half hour late for dinner right now, and she still had to ride home.

The lead mare lurched up the steep hillside with her family close behind. A pale shadow against the darkness, the Phantom followed.

Good-bye, Zanzibar. Sam sent the message with her mind. Though she was probably the only human on this rain-slick hillside, she didn't call the stallion by his secret name.

Sam tried to look away; then she was glad she

couldn't. Halfway up the windswept ridge, the Phantom looked back. He stamped, stared, then left her.

They both started for home. But the stallion took the last shreds of magic with him. She had consequences to face.

This time, it wasn't her fault she was late. Gram and Dad would be worried, and she'd tell them the truth. All of it.

She'd felt scared hiding with the band of horses. Those rustlers were more trouble than she could handle on her own.

Chapter 7

THE RANCH YARD WAS FLOODED WITH LIGHT. Brightness glowed from inside the barn, and the kitchen door stood open. The headlights from the Elys' idling truck lit the path from the River Bend bridge to the two-story white house, which looked more welcoming than ever before.

Jake was there. Who else had Gram and Dad called?

From the bridge, Sam saw Dad, Gram, and Dallas talking on the front porch. Blaze barked at her approach, and they all looked up. Dallas gave a salute from the brim of his hat to Dad, then walked across the yard toward the bunkhouse.

"You okay?" Dallas asked as he passed through the beams of Jake's headlights. When Sam nodded, he added, "Horse okay?"

"He's fine. He's a great horse. We just ran into some trouble." Sam tried to keep her voice from shaking as she dismounted.

"Let me take him," Dallas said, moving to Ace's head. "You'd best tell the rest of it to the boss. Pronto. He hasn't called out the *whole* county yet, but he needs to know."

Sam had managed to keep her voice steady, but now, as Dallas led Ace away, her knees felt watery and weak.

Jake still sat inside the truck. She couldn't see his expression, but Sam knew he'd be mad. More like furious. He hated worrying about her, but whenever she told him to stop, he always went ballistic.

Gram had gone back into the kitchen, probably to get on the phone and call off the search. Arms folded, Dad leaned against a porch post, waiting.

This was a Western thing. Ranch life demanded she be self-sufficient and not cause trouble for anyone else.

All I have to do is walk across the yard and explain. Sam took a few steps. If she let her memory play the sound of the man who'd laughed and blindfolded Dark Sunshine, she'd cover her ears. If she imagined the man with the long black whip bursting out of the truck to come after her, she'd sit down right there in the dirt, pull her knees up, let her forehead rest on them, and wait for Dad to come to her. But Sam kept walking. Blaze licked her hand, whining as he bounced along beside her.

"You caught Slocum's horse for him, but that was more than an hour ago," Dad said.

"Yeah," Sam answered. If Slocum knew she'd been missing, Rachel would know. The drama would be all over school by the end of first period, but it didn't matter. She'd almost made it to the porch.

"You look a little pale." Dad uncrossed his arms as he studied her. "How 'bout sittin' down to tell me what went wrong."

Sam lowered herself to the top step and pulled her coat close against the wet wind.

Dad leaned down to rest a hand on her shoulder. "Want to go inside?"

Sam shook her head no.

"The rustlers came back. I don't know if they were looking for horses or for me—" Sam heard Dad suck in a breath as if he'd been punched in the stomach. "But I had to hide until they went away."

"It's all right, honey." Dad settled on the step beside her. Sam leaned into the circle of his arm and began to tell him everything.

It turned out Rachel Slocum didn't find Sam's adventure worth talking about at school. For that, Sam was grateful.

Jake knew, of course, and Dad had insisted that Sam describe the truck to Brynna, and Sam had told Jen.

Only one thing changed after that night of hiding. Sam wasn't allowed to go anywhere alone.

That was why, on Tuesday afternoon, Sam stood

talking with Jen instead of starting the mile-long walk home.

She'd felt totally fine hiding with the horses and had only been scared for a minute in the ranch yard. And, maybe, for a few seconds in a nightmare, when she'd had a stare-off with the bushy-haired rustler, but her family's caution seemed unnecessary.

"You don't have to wait with me," Sam told Jen. "Gram will be picking me up any minute."

"And miss all the excitement? Oh, no. I already missed part one of your adventure. You're not leaving me out of part two."

"There won't be a part two," Sam said. "Rangers are looking for the rustlers, and they're not making a secret of it. Brynna wants to scare them off, not catch them." Sam shrugged. "It wouldn't make sense for them to come back here. Besides, they want Dark Sunshine, not me."

"So you're really not scared?" Jen asked.

Sam drew a deep breath and took inventory of how she felt. "Not really," she said, and it was the truth, until Jen's emphatic nod.

"Good."

"Why 'good'?" Sam asked.

"Thursday we have a half day because of teacher meetings, right?" Jen drew the last word out.

"Just say it," Sam told her.

"So you can take me up to the rustlers' trap. In daylight."

Sam knew that if the situation had been reversed, she would want to ride up and see the site of all the excitement too. "There might not be much to see. The federal rangers have already been up there, you know."

Jen rubbed her hands together in anticipation. "Suppose they left yellow crime-scene tape or some of that dust they use to lift fingerprints?"

"I don't know, but what? Now you're practicing to be a detective instead of a vet?"

"I'm keeping my options open," Jen said. "So you'll do it?"

"I'll do it, but . . ." Sam lowered her voice as if she might be overheard. "If they'll let me, I want to start gentling Dark Sunshine."

"I hope you keep her," Jen said. "Then Silly won't be the only neurotic horse in the neighborhood."

Jen joked about Silk Stockings, her high-strung palomino, but she loved her as much as Sam loved Ace. Jen had come over after school yesterday to see Popcorn and Dark Sunshine, and she and Sam had been analyzing the mustangs' behavior ever since.

"You've got a lot to undo with the mare, and she's going to be unpredictable for a long time. Miss Olson's smart to use Popcorn with the HARP program. He looks like he has some draft blood."

"And soft eyes, so I think he'll be fine once he lets us get near him. And he doesn't have that haunted look."

Unlike Dark Sunshine. Sam didn't say the words, just pushed her bangs back and tried not to recall how the buckskin had wanted to follow the other horses into the trailer, up at the trap site. Dark Sunshine hadn't cared where the captive mustangs were going. She just hadn't wanted to be left behind.

"Besides," Sam said, "Popcorn wasn't abused on purpose. The people who adopted him told Brynna they tried to break him just like they'd seen in movies. The day after they got him, they snubbed him to a post, saddled him, and climbed on. He bucked. He ran through a fence. He was impossible to catch, so after a while they just ignored him."

"Hi, nice to meet you." Jen pretended to be Popcorn's owner. "I know you've lived free all your life, but let me tie your head at a weird angle, throw something heavy on your back, yank something tight around your middle, and oh, yeah, now I'm going to jump on you! What are people thinking?"

"Stick with being a vet," Sam told her friend. "You think like a horse. Brynna says Popcorn didn't hurt anyone, in spite of all that. In fact, BLM didn't take him away from the adopters—they returned him."

"Like shoes that didn't fit." Jen made a growling noise.

"Here comes Gram." Sam waved at the boatlike Buick coming toward them, but Jen wasn't finished grumbling.

"Some people don't understand that horses have feelings," Jen said.

"I guess not." But all at once Sam thought not of Dark Sunshine but of Mikki. Mikki's mother hadn't exactly returned her, but she *had* sent her away.

The seventh-grade troublemaker would arrive today for her first session with Popcorn and Jake. She deserved a little sympathy, so Sam would try to give it to her. After all, how hard could that be?

Mikki's hands were perched on her hips. She wore tight jeans and a pink nylon top that bared her tummy. Someone should tell her it was too short, and that her blond hair was sticking out like wet feathers.

But Jake had already told the girl something, and she didn't like it one bit.

"You want me to sit in the dirt inside that pen, just *sit* there, for an *hour*?" she demanded of Jake. "I hope you're not getting paid for this."

Jake didn't wear chaps today. He wore clean jeans and a short-sleeved white shirt. He'd even removed his hat to talk with the girl. Now he pulled it on, covering the shiny black hair he tied back with a leather string.

"You're not, are you?" Mikki asked. "Getting paid?"

Jake only walked into the round corral, leaving Mikki outside.

Mikki whirled on Sam. "Why isn't he saying anything?"

Mikki had just arrived, and already Sam was counting the minutes until the girl's counselor came back to collect her.

"Huh?" Mikki said. "What's his problem?"

"My guess is that he's treating you like he would a colt putting up a fuss. He's just waiting for you to finish, so he can go on with business."

"Like a horse?" Mikki asked.

"Yeah, and I'd say you're lucky. He almost never treats me that well. He really likes horses."

"Are you joking?"

"Not really," Sam admitted. "Jake and I grew up together, and he calls me Brat."

Mikki's lips twisted in a dubious expression. "So should I go in there?" She jerked her thumb toward the round pen.

"In a minute." Sam held up her finger. What she had to say next would be awkward, but if she kept quiet, the girl could get in big trouble. "My dad's pretty easygoing—"

"Yeah, they all start out that way," Mikki scoffed.

"Well, he's been like that for thirteen years I know of," Sam snapped, "but there's one thing he won't put up with: smoking around the barn."

"Why should I care? You don't see me smoking."

"No." Sam tried to keep her hands from closing into fists. "I don't see it, but you smell like cigarette smoke. If they don't care what you do at that place you're staying, fine, but the straw in our barn could go up like that." Sam snapped her fingers under the girl's nose. "If Dad catches you smoking, you'll be out of here so fast it'll make your head spin."

The sparkle in Mikki's eyes and her smirk said she'd tried to provoke Sam into losing control. And she'd won.

Get a grip, Sam told herself as she opened the gate to the round pen.

Popcorn's hooves snuffed the dirt floor of the round

pen. He sidestepped, eyes rolling. Mikki wasn't the only one who was supposed to get something from HARP. She might not even be the most deserving one.

Once captured and branded, wild horses couldn't be freed again. It was against the law. Since a home with other horses and kind people was the best Popcorn could hope for, Jake would make the transition as easy as he could.

Popcorn was tall for a mustang, about fifteen hands.

"Hey, boy," she whispered as he watched her with crystal-blue eyes.

Built like a heavy Quarter Horse, the gelding had already started growing a fuzzy winter coat that made Sam think of a stuffed toy. But when she leaned her head in to talk with Jake, who sat on the ground to her right, Popcorn backed off. The fearful steps accelerated, and the albino's body banged against the fence as if to escape.

"You comin' in?" Jake asked.

Sam felt Mikki crowd in behind her. The younger girl was the one appointed to help Popcorn, so Sam stepped aside.

"No," she answered, and then leaned down and whispered to Jake, "I'll watch from outside and leave you in here with the wild things."

Jake grunted and motioned Mikki in. As Mikki passed, she shot Sam an angry look. She didn't like being left out.

Sam smiled as she withdrew from the corral and closed the gate. One of Jake's horse strategies was built on the fact that they were herd animals.

Maybe the technique worked with kids, too.

Sam peered through the slats of the round pen and watched Jake, Mikki, and Popcorn. As usual, Jake didn't waste words.

"Sit there." He nodded to a place midway between Popcorn and himself. "Lean back. You're gonna be there a while."

"A whole hour?" Mikki didn't whine now that she was watching the mustang.

"How long ya got?" Jake asked. "He can't trust you if you're never around."

"Don't I know it," Mikki said, then plopped cross-legged in the dirt.

Sam glanced at her watch. She'd bet Mikki couldn't sit for five minutes without wiggling or talking.

Two minutes later, Mikki blurted, "What am I supposed to be doing?"

Popcorn bolted at her voice, and Mikki made a soft sound of regret. "I'm not doing it right, but I don't know how. Tell me."

"Not much you can do wrong," Jake said. "Just watch him. See what he does with his ears, eyes, feet, everything."

"Okay. I can do that."

This time, she did. Sam watched for about twenty minutes. She skipped the snack Gram offered and hurried through her chores. When she returned to the corral, Jake and Mikki were coming out.

Mikki stretched, then shoved her hands in her pockets and looked away from Jake.

"Okay, what did you see?" he asked.

Mikki shrugged.

"Don't interpret. Just say what you noticed."

"What's the point, if I don't know what it means?"

Mikki shrugged again. "He just stood there."

Sam wished she had a video camera so she could show Mikki herself "just standing there." Besides shrugging and jamming her hands in her pockets, the girl kept her gaze focused over Jake's shoulder. She looked worried, not sassy.

Maybe Mikki didn't venture a description because she didn't want to be wrong. She was acting just like the troubled horse inside the corral.

"What about his eyes?" Jake asked.

"Okay," Mikki almost shouted. "He had lines over his eyes, like he was worried, and he didn't like it when I looked right at him." She licked her lips. "He looked away if he caught me staring. Then, when I looked at something else and checked back, he'd be watching *me*. Then the whole thing started over again." Mikki rattled off the words, daring Jake to contradict her. "So what?"

"Anything else?"

"When I moved my hands or feet, just trying to keep them from getting all pins and needly, he scooted away."

Mikki looked down. "Why would he do that? He knows he can't get out of there."

"Maybe he doesn't," Sam said.

"What?" Mikki sneered.

"He broke down a fence at the place he used to live," Sam began. Then she told Mikki about the snubbing post, the bucking, and the weeks of being ignored.

Mikki listened intently until Sam finished. Then the girl looked frustrated. "So when can I ride him?"

"Not this year," Jake said.

"What?" Mikki's shrill words made Popcorn bolt around the corral. She glanced his way with regret, then plucked at her feathery blond hair. "I can't ride him? Are you afraid I'll screw him up worse?"

"No, we need him to trust someone."

"Like you," Mikki said to Sam. "You're the one reading his mind."

"I'm not reading his mind, just guessing."

"And what do you *guess* it means that he won't let me look into his eyes?" Mikki wagged her head mockingly.

"I think . . ." Sam swallowed and cast a nervous

glance at Jake. This was all his fault. When the Phantom was a foal, Jake had helped Sam think like a horse. She'd never expected to do it aloud.

"I think," Sam said, "that he got everything wrong with people the first time, right after he was captured. Actually, it was the people who got everything wrong, but he doesn't know that. Instead of trying to understand their new horse, they scared him, hurt him, and then shut him out. He wonders why he should try again."

For just an instant, Mikki looked sympathetic, but then she noticed Jake waiting for her response.

"The reason he should try it *again*"—Mikki pronounced each word slowly, as if Sam weren't very smart—"is because he's a horse. That's what horseys *do*. They give people rides."

"Not wild horses," Sam said.

"He could learn." Mikki flipped her hand toward the corral. "I bet he could learn in a week. You're just teasing me so I'll be a good girl. I've played this game before."

It was quiet for a minute, except for the faraway

drone of a small plane overhead. Sam noticed Jake watching it too.

"See that plane?" Jake nodded toward the cloudless sky and the white trail stretching behind the aircraft.

"Yeah. Why, are you sending me away on one?"

Jake almost smiled. "No," he answered. "Can you fly one?"

"Of course not."

"But there's a person flying that plane—"

"*A pilot,*" Mikki said in a singsong voice. "Duh."

"A pilot's a human and you're a human." Jake spread his hands out as if he'd explained something simple. "So, you could learn to fly the plane, right? People fly planes. How long do you think it would take you to learn? A week?"

"I'm only eleven years old—"

"Okay," Jake conceded, "so we could give you two weeks."

"I've never done anything like that. You have to learn about wind currents and flaps and—" Mikki stopped, breathless, then closed her eyes. "I get it."

"Three weeks?" Jake teased.

"I said I *get it*, so stop!" Mikki's face flushed.

Sam thought Jake had broken through the girl's cockiness, until Mikki squinted up at him and asked, "So, how long till I can ride him?"

"Jake," Sam muttered, "if I ever, *ever* criticize your patience, remind me of this."

"How long?" Mikki asked again, and Jake recognized the dare.

"When he trusts you," Jake said.

"How will you be able to tell?"

"When he eats out of your hand," Jake began, then shook his head. "No, when he comes to you instead of running away, but you're *not* carrying food." He numbered the first condition off on his index finger, then added, "And when he lets you pet him on the face and neck. Then we can try you on him. Bareback. In this corral."

The gray van that had delivered Mikki just over an hour ago rolled slowly over the River Bend bridge. Mikki's shoulders sagged. She knew it had come to pick her up.

DARK SUNSHINE

Before the van parked, though, Mikki started toward it as if she didn't mind leaving the ranch. She didn't say good-bye or thanks or anything, but just before she reached the van she turned back, pointed at Jake, and shouted, "You got yourself a deal, cowboy."

Chapter 8

"I'D LIKE MIKKI IF SHE WEREN'T SUCH A brat." Sam watched the gray county van's taillights brighten as it crossed the River Bend bridge.

"You would," Jake said, and it wasn't a question.

Sam thought of the way Mikki's shoulders had drooped when she saw the van. What was the place like, where the van took her? Probably halfway between school and the orphanage in *Annie*, Sam figured, where you didn't get to decide when to study, what to eat, or if you should go for a walk.

It would be a controlled, structured place. Sam wished she could creep inside with her camera and a roll of black-and-white film and show what the girls inside were really like.

"She's got a great vocabulary for a seventh grader," she said. "And sometimes she sounds really mature. Do you think that's because she's got a messed-up childhood?"

Jake shrugged.

"Well, *I* think she's intelligent."

"Probably is," Jake said. "But I'm going to tell Wyatt to watch her. She's dangerous."

"Just because she's a smart mouth?"

"I don't think *you're* dangerous," he said. "And you've never been anything but sassy."

Sam stuck out her tongue at Jake, then asked, "But really, what don't you like about her?"

Jake shook his head. "Hard to say. I guess 'cause she's trying to make us think this is no big deal to her." He gestured toward Popcorn. "When it's really the best thing that's happened to her for a long time. She might,

I don't know, sort of sabotage herself, and one of the horses might get hurt."

Sam brought Popcorn's food to the round pen while Jake retrieved Witch, his roach-maned black mare, from the barn.

Witch and Popcorn sniffed each other through the panels of the pen, and Witch gave a snorting whinny. Dark Sunshine answered from the barn corral. Sam longed to make the little horse happy.

"If Brynna says it's okay, I want to try everything you're doing with Popcorn on the buckskin."

"Well, that's a fool idea," Jake said.

"Why? I wouldn't do it in the round pen to begin," Sam said. "In fact, I'd leave her where she is, but isolate her from Ace and Sweetheart. What do you think? Maybe she'd start to see me as her herd."

"I won't be part of this," Jake said. "That animal is half-scared you're going to put her in the dark and half-scared you'll bring her into the light. You can't trust her to act like a normal horse."

Jake was always too protective, so Sam changed the

subject. "Are you going to tell Brynna what you think of Mikki?"

"Don't know. First impression could be wrong, but my gut says it's not."

"They'd probably pull her from the program." Sam heard herself almost defending Mikki, and she couldn't believe it.

"You don't know whether they would or not," Jake scolded. "They didn't send her to another state because she was an angel."

Jake tugged the front of his hat even lower, so Sam couldn't see his eyes. "Anyway, I want Wyatt watching her."

"Since when did you get to be northern Nevada's leading psychologist for humans, too?" Sam was sick of Jake acting superior. Why did he think he was so smart? she wondered. Because he was older, or because he was a guy?

Sam walked toward the barn corral. Dark Sunshine must have seen her, because the mare's high-pitched neigh split the late-afternoon quiet.

"It doesn't take an expert to diagnose that. Sam, look at her." Jake's voice softened.

As they watched, the tiny mare moved down the fence and back again. Her hip bones and ribs seemed to push against her skin. She kept her face turned away from them and toward the darkened barn.

"She's—" Jake searched for a word but came up empty.

"Tormented," Sam said. "I'm going to sit with her now."

Jake shook his head. "Do what you want."

"She'll get used to me. She'll see I won't hurt her."

Wordless, Jake gathered his reins, stabbed his boot toe into Witch's stirrup, and swung aboard. The black horse danced in place, eager to head for home, but Jake didn't go.

"Sam? Give this some thought. If no one claims that horse and she keeps acting loco, BLM's going to put her down. I just—" Jake set his jaw as he always did when he'd talked too much, then added, "I don't want you gettin' your heart broke over her."

DARK SUNSHINE

Sam sat in the shady barn and studied the mustang. It wasn't easy, with Ace and Sweetheart jostling for Sam's attention.

Sweetheart gave up as soon as she saw Sam's hands were empty, but Ace gave Sam a hooded look meant to make her feel guilty. It did.

Dark Sunshine stayed still. She gazed into the darkness. Beneath her shaggy forelock, the mare had a wide forehead and shining brown eyes that expected the worst. Her conformation reminded Sam of Kiger mustangs she'd seen online.

Those wild horses lived in the rugged country surrounding Kiger Creek in Oregon. Brynna said the woman who'd adopted the mare was from Wyoming, but the freeze brand on her neck could say she'd been captured in Oregon.

"You're far from home, aren't you, pretty girl?"

The mare flinched as if Sam had tossed a handful of gravel her way, but she didn't leave. One ear swiveled, listening for trouble, but the other black-edged ear cupped forward to catch Sam's words.

Amazed, Sam kept talking.

"I've got another horse friend who likes it when I talk. His name used to be Blackie. He was my horse." Sam took a breath, and the mare looked over her shoulder. "You saw him the other day, but you were busy having breakfast. You're eating well now, aren't you? And drinking, too. Except for all this sad stuff in your mind, you're doing good, Sunny."

She babbled on. Kigers were supposed to be friendly, but this mare had learned that humans meant windowless stalls, whips, blindfolds, and loneliness.

Those symbols tied Sunshine to men as surely as kindness and his secret name tied the Phantom to Sam.

Think. Sam knew she could turn this mare around. It was too late for a secret name. Nothing could make this horse her sister, but maybe they could be friends. Just as she'd won the Phantom's heart after he'd been roped and dragged back to captivity, just as she'd waited in the right place for Hammer, Sam knew she'd learn how to win Dark Sunshine's trust.

DARK SUNSHINE

"If only horses could give references," Sam said to Jen as they entered the crowded halls of Darton High School the next morning.

"References?" Jen pushed her glasses up her nose and regarded Sam as if she'd lost her mind. "Like when you apply for a job?"

"Sort of." Sam stopped outside her history class. Jen's classroom was right next door, so they could talk until the bell. "More like a personal reference. If I could get Ace or the Phantom to write Dark Sunshine a letter, she'd understand I'm not going to hurt her."

Jen pressed the back of her hand to Sam's brow. "I think you're coming down with something more serious than my cold, Samantha Anne."

"And I've got the cure," Mrs. Ely said, appearing at the classroom door.

"A healthy dose of history?" Jen asked.

Mrs. Ely laughed, and Sam envied Jen's easy way of balancing the fact that Mrs. Ely was not only a Darton High teacher but also Jake's mom.

Mrs. Ely had known both of them since they were

little kids. She was also Sam's history teacher and a talented photographer who encouraged Sam's work with a camera.

"Almost as good as history," Mrs. Ely said. "A photo contest. Jen, you'd better run." She shooed Jen away as the bell rang. "And, Sam, talk to me after class."

Sam moved toward her desk, but her way was blocked by Rachel Slocum. Darton High's reigning princess and student body treasurer, Rachel was duly qualified. As Linc Slocum's daughter, she was by far the richest girl in the school.

And the most stylish. Right now Rachel smoothed a wing of coffee-brown hair away from her eyes, negotiating a deal for last night's homework with a guy in orange-framed glasses. He didn't talk, just swallowed hard, as Rachel leaned toward him and said, "I'd be so grateful."

One of the advantages of really expensive clothes was that they flowed over you like liquid. At least they did on Rachel. She wore some kind of beige outfit that would have looked like a feed sack on Sam, but Rachel looked like she'd stepped out of a fashion magazine.

Sam sat and looked over her shoulder in time to see Rachel leave empty-handed. The guy hadn't given in, and Sam almost applauded.

Rachel caught her gloating expression, and Sam saw she was in for it. The last time Rachel had felt vengeful, she'd broken the expensive camera signed out to Sam from journalism class. What would she do this time?

Sam flipped open a notebook and looked toward Mrs. Ely. Before the teacher began talking, though, Sam wrote a note to herself. *Watch your back,* it said, and with everything else going on, she vowed to take her own advice.

After class, Sam approached Mrs. Ely's desk. The teacher was handing makeup work to one student and scolding another for gossiping in class, but she slipped Sam a flyer.

The first thing Sam noticed was that the contest wasn't limited to entrants under eighteen. It was open to professional photographers as well as amateurs.

She must have looked dubious, because as soon as the other students moved toward the door, Mrs. Ely said, "Samantha, that reward you won is as much as some photographers make in a year."

She didn't want to contradict Mrs. Ely, but she sort of had to. "But I earned it under pretty unusual circumstances."

"You did, but your work was fine, and look at the name of the contest. It's perfect for you."

"Night Magic," the contest was called. The subject could be anything shot at night, and Sam had once confided to Mrs. Ely that her dream was to photograph wild horses running at night.

"It is perfect," Sam agreed. "But with all the, uh, stuff that's going on—" She glanced over her shoulder.

Rachel picked up her things in slow motion, eavesdropping. Mrs. Ely nodded that she knew what Sam was talking about. After all, Gram had called Three Ponies Ranch first when she'd been looking for Sam that night.

"The deadline's near Christmas," Mrs. Ely said. "You've got plenty of time."

The warning bell rang in the hall, and Sam jumped like a racehorse leaving the starting gate.

"I can't be late," she blurted to Mrs. Ely. "If I don't earn all A's in citizenship, I can't ride."

"What a tragedy," Rachel murmured.

Even though Sam beat her to the door, she couldn't shake the feeling she'd given Rachel Slocum one more bit of ammunition to use against her.

Dad looked like he'd been to town on ranch business when he picked Sam up from the bus stop. By the time they reached home, Mikki was already working with Jake.

Sam went into the house. She let her backpack fall to the floor as Gram told her Mikki had not only decided to go along with the guidelines for the HARP program, which meant, among other things, keeping a journal about her experiences with the mustangs, but she'd finagled an extension to the time she could spend at River Bend each day.

"Why, she just gobbled up the chocolate chip

cookies I gave her, and as soon as Jake arrived, she followed him into the pen," Gram said. "She couldn't wait to see Popcorn."

Sam sat at the kitchen table to devour her own cookies and milk.

"That's great," Sam said, but she didn't exactly mean it. What was wrong with her? Just yesterday, she'd been telling Jake she liked Mikki.

Out of her school clothes and in riding gear, Sam peered through the slats of the round pen.

Whatever was "off" with Mikki, Popcorn felt it too.

Yesterday, though he'd stayed far away from Mikki, Popcorn had kept his side turned to her. Today he was showing her his tail.

You can't fool horses, Sam thought. Mikki would have to learn that.

Sam walked to the barn. She wanted to ride Ace. They both needed the exercise. But how could she get Ace out of the barn pen without giving Dark Sunshine a chance to bolt? She'd need to ask Dad for help.

That settled, she left the barn. Blaze met her with

a wagging tail. Even he was keeping his distance from Dark Sunshine.

"What's going on with Mikki, huh, Blaze?" Sam rumpled the dog's ears, and he whined with pleasure.

Had Mikki made gentling Popcorn a contest against Jake? Had she taken his standards as a challenge? Maybe she was trying to prove something to herself. Or maybe she thought that if she did a quick job of riding Popcorn, she could take on Dark Sunshine.

"That's not going to happen," Sam muttered to Blaze as the dog walked along with her. "No way."

Blaze wagged his tail and looked up at Sam with open-mouthed adoration, believing every word.

Chapter 9

IN SAN FRANCISCO, SAM HAD GONE RIDING twice on rented horses. After the second time, she hadn't wanted to go again. Aunt Sue had worried that Sam was afraid of horses after the accident. Aunt Sue always worried, but she wasn't pushy about it.

"Tell me what you don't like about it," Aunt Sue had said as they drove away from the San Francisco stable for the last time.

Sam had tried. Although she was still a little afraid of falling, Sam could push the fear aside, and she told

Aunt Sue so. The other part was harder to explain.

Her heart always sank at the end of a ride. Sam hated giving the horse back. She couldn't think of a word to describe the feeling.

"Selfishness? You want to sneak a horse home to my apartment?" Aunt Sue suggested, joking. "Disappointment?"

Together they'd tried, but couldn't come up with it.

Now Sam didn't have to worry about that feeling.

She rode at a rocking-chair lope across the range. With mustang sureness, Ace threaded between clumps of sagebrush. Over his hoofbeats, songbirds sang to the fading afternoon, and Sam rode with a joy she'd longed for during those two long years in San Francisco.

To her right lay War Drum Flats and Lost Canyon. To her left, three miles past the blackberry bushes hedging the river, she'd find Three Ponies Ranch, home to Jake's family. Dead ahead, but hours away, the Calico Mountains soared purple against the blue Nevada sky.

Sam knew just where she was, and it was exactly where she wanted to be. She'd do whatever it took to keep River Bend Ranch. If that meant working with Mikki and doing a good job so they'd win the contract for HARP, she'd cooperate.

Sam had drawn rein to watch a covey of quail rush for cover when she thought she heard someone call her name. She shaded her eyes and looked back toward River Bend.

Dad rode Banjo toward her at a walk. Worry swept Sam, until she saw why Dad rode so slowly. Beside him on Gram's pinto, Sweetheart, rode Mikki.

With both hands clamped to the saddle horn, Mikki leaned forward until her forehead almost brushed Sweetheart's mane. Mikki might love horses—the wide smile on her face said as much—but Sam guessed this was the first time she'd ridden one. Why wasn't Mikki in the round pen with Popcorn? Why wasn't Dad ponying Sweetheart on a lead line? Wasn't he risking a lawsuit or something by letting Mikki leave the ranch yard on horseback?

Oh well, Dad knew horses better than anyone. If he thought Mikki was safe, Sam wouldn't ask. All the same, she was relieved when Dad explained.

"Jake's been called in to observe the tracking of those rustlers."

"Wow," Sam said. The BLM had federal experts, so this must have been Brynna's idea.

"Kind of an honor for him," Dad said, "but it left Mikki here high and dry. I could've gone into the round pen and sat with her and the gelding, but introducin' a new human to Popcorn so soon isn't fair. I decided to let her try horses from a different angle."

Mikki glanced up. Her expression said she wanted to make a smart-mouthed remark, but she was just too happy to think of one. She sat on Sweetheart as if the pinto were made of eggshell. Was Mikki worried that Sweetheart would interpret any move as a command to gallop?

They rode together, three abreast, until Dad trotted off a short distance to check a water windmill. That was what he said, but Sam knew Dad hoped Mikki would like riding with another kid.

When Mikki didn't look at her, Sam wondered if the girl needed some reassurance that Jake wasn't the latest person to abandon her.

"This is a big deal for Jake; otherwise he wouldn't have left," Sam said.

"I don't care."

Sam's teeth gritted together. So, they were back to that.

"You don't care that he left?" Sam asked her. "Or that it's a big deal for him?"

"Whatever." Mikki stared down at the reins she'd wrapped around the saddle horn. "I don't care."

"He's a really good tracker. His grandfather—"

"Or he just thinks he is," Mikki said.

"No, he's good," Sam insisted. "And he doesn't just do it for pay. Once a local man tried to pay him to track a horse he'd hurt. He offered Jake a lot of money, but Jake wouldn't do it."

"You leave so many holes in your story, I can tell you're making it up. '*A* local man,' '*a* horse,' '*a* lot of money,'" Mikki said. "It's like a commercial on TV: 'many doctors recommend.' Yeah, so who are they?"

Sam didn't know whether to be amused or irritated. "Well, I'm not making it up, and I'm not going to tell you who the man is, though he deserves it, but the horse is the Phantom."

"Yeah, right." Mikki sat back with such emphasis, Sweetheart thought she meant "Whoa." The mare stopped. "Miss Olson told me that whopper too. I may not be from around here, but I don't believe in ghost horses."

"He's no ghost." Sam's legs asked Ace to move at a faster walk.

Sweetheart followed without Mikki's urging. When the pinto and her wobbly rider caught up, Sam glanced at the girl. Mikki bobbed in the saddle, blond hair blowing every which way, but it didn't cover her expression. Mikki's pointy fox face shone with curiosity. She wanted to know more about the Phantom.

Well, Sam decided, Mikki would just have to wait.

"Jake's tracking those rustlers because they're evil. They hurt Dark Sunshine and trapped other mustangs to sell for meat. Right now they probably have them hidden away, fattening them up so they'll bring more pennies per pound, but they'll kill them soon. And that trap"—Sam gestured toward Lost Canyon—"has been there a while. These are not the first horses they've slaughtered for money."

Mikki attempted to sit straighter in the saddle and hold the saddle horn with only one hand, but she didn't sway with Sweetheart's movements. She lurched.

Putting both hands back on the horn for balance, she asked, "And you don't think Jake's tracking them to get a big reputation?"

Clearly, Mikki had already made up her mind. Sam didn't want to defend Jake. She wanted Mikki to find out for herself, but Sam wasn't that patient.

"Look," she said, "Jake has his faults. For instance, he's obsessed with being my big brother. But he's shy, not a glory hound. He wants to lock up the bad guys. That's all."

Mikki's face turned red. Her hands fidgeted on the reins, and Sweetheart's gait turned choppy with confusion.

For the good of the horse, Sam tried to calm Mikki.

"You know, you're trying to teach Popcorn to trust you. Maybe you should learn a little something about it yourself, and admit Jake's a good guy."

"Men are scum!" Mikki shouted, drawing Dad's attention from where he rode ahead of them.

"Not all of them," Sam said. She was glad the entrance to River Bend had come into view.

"Well, my mom's married three and *they* were all scum. When Miss Olson told me HARP had men teachers, I almost didn't do it. Then your dad seemed sort of okay, and you weren't scared—" Mikki cut off the words. "So, isn't that enough *trust* for you?"

Sam swallowed. This conversation was too much for her to handle. Mikki didn't just think men were scum. She was afraid of them.

Sam felt a punch of warning, like she should shield Mikki from some threat. But she didn't know how. Mikki should be talking to a counselor. Or Brynna.

Still, Sam had no choice. She was here. Now. So she did what she'd do if Mikki were a horse. She rewarded this tiny bit of progress.

"You're right." Sam nodded toward Dad. "It's trust." Then, as they came up on River Bend bridge, she smiled and asked, "Speaking of trust, I think Sweetheart is starting to like you. Why don't you ride across first? The sound of their hooves on the wood spooks horses sometimes, but I think she'll do it for you."

Mikki crossed alone, not knowing she was more spooked by the sound than Sweetheart, who'd walked across the bridge hundreds of times.

Although Dad rode in behind them and offered to help, Mikki dismounted alone, then walked with wobbly knees to the round pen.

"Is it okay if I open the gate to check Popcorn?" she asked.

Sam glanced at Dad. He nodded.

"Go ahead," Sam said. "And watch him when he first sees you."

Dad stayed on Banjo and pretended to adjust the gelding's headstall. But Sam wasn't fooled. If Popcorn made a break past Mikki, Dad and Banjo would cut him off.

Mikki emerged from the corral and slid the bolt

closed on the gate, looking proud of herself for closing it the right way.

"His head went up and his ears went forward when he saw me," Mikki reported. "He took two steps backward, but he didn't run away. Is that good?"

"In just a couple of days? I think that's great!" Sam said.

Mikki turned and leaned against the gate she'd just closed. Sam couldn't see the girl's face. Was she proud? Happy?

But there was no time left to talk. Tires crunched on the desert floor as the gray van drew close, then rolled across the bridge.

Without a good-bye, Mikki trudged toward it.

Sam remembered the feeling of giving back horses at the end of a ride. She still didn't know what it was called, but it felt something like surrender.

Left alone to feed the horses, Sam saved Ace, Sweetheart, and the buckskin for last. All three were munching the hay she'd forked to them when Sam gave in to temptation.

Facing into the dark barn, the mare ate. The only sign she even knew Sam was there was the occasional shivering of her skin, as if she were scaring off flies.

Maybe she and Jake and Brynna were all wrong. Maybe the mare's first family had been kind to her, and she only needed to be reminded that the human hand could comfort as well as punish. It was worth a try.

Moving by millimeters, Sam placed one foot on the lowest fence rail, then matched the other beside it. She went up one more rail and leaned out over the top rail, arm extended toward Sunshine's golden hide.

The mustang ran. Ears flat, eyes narrowed, and mouth agape, the mare rushed the fence as if it were invisible. Kicking as she went, the mare collided with the fence. The vibration knocked Sam off the other side of the corral.

Before Sam could stand, before the cloud of dirt and straw could settle, the mare threw herself at the fence again.

Don't let her get out.

The rails held, but Sam blamed herself for being an

idiot. She'd moved too fast. The mare's trust must be won minute by minute. She needed more than a clumsy reminder that some people weren't monsters.

The mare trembled as if she wanted to batter the rails down with her chest, and her silence was scarier than any scream.

This was no warning. Dark Sunshine's attack wasn't a threat. The mustang's eyes blazed with fear. Sam knew she must be careful. The mare might not be hateful, but flying hooves could kill even if they were used in self-defense.

As Sam turned her back to the corral and walked away, the mare sighed with relief.

Sam rubbed the dust from her eyelashes and stood blinking. Her hands were dirty, and she'd only made it worse. Through blurry eyes, she glanced over her shoulder at the mare.

Dark Sunshine's head hung. She breathed short puffs into her hay, but she wasn't eating.

Poor girl, Sam thought. *We'll think of something.*

Tomorrow was Thursday. She'd promised to ride up

to the trap with Jen. Sam shivered. She didn't want to go back, but maybe Jen could help her find a clue to what those men had done to hurt Dark Sunshine so much.

That night, Sam tossed from her back to her front, tangling her legs in the sheets. She pulled her quilt up and pushed it off.

It was only eleven o'clock, but her brain had been spinning since she'd looked into the mare's eyes. Fear mixed with bravery was a dangerous thing.

Suddenly, Sam sat up.

She knew how to help Dark Sunshine. The Phantom had given her the answer.

How could she help a mustang who only felt safe in the dark? By moonlight.

Phantom had endured terrifying hours with people, and yet he came to her in the dark. The night he'd taken her to the valley that sheltered his herd, Sam had sat near dozens of wild horses. None had seemed afraid, though they could clearly see her in the brightness of the moon.

It could work. It *would* work!

Sam eased out of bed. Her nightgown swished

around her ankles as she crept down the hall to the door of Dad's room. One wooden board creaked under her toes.

"What's wrong?" Dad's voice cut across the sound of bedsprings and his feet hitting his bedroom carpet.

His outline showed in the hall before Sam reached his door.

"I'm sorry. I didn't mean to scare you," she managed. He'd sure scared her. Her pulse shook her whole body. "Nothing's wrong."

"You surprised me some. That's all." Dad's tone was calming. "Let's go into your room to talk. And keep your voice down. We don't want to wake Gram."

Dad followed her back down the hall and switched on the light.

"I wasn't going down to the river." Sam offered the truth as she climbed back into bed. More than once she'd been in trouble for leaving the house at midnight.

Dad nodded. Either he believed her or he was taking in her messy room. He hesitated near the chair piled with boots and jeans, then sat on the bed next to her.

For a minute he surveyed the room as if he'd never seen it before.

Dad's fingers brushed the white quilt with the patchwork star and then he stared at her shelf of horse statues: wooden, glass, and plastic. His gaze touched each prancing leg and backswept tail. He studied the unicorn wallpaper just visible inside her closet and the stack of schoolbooks and magazines about to avalanche off her bedside table.

"I don't blame you for going out there." Dad gestured toward the river. "If I were to blame anyone"—he chuckled—"I guess it would have to be Louise."

Sam held her breath. Louise was her mother, and Dad rarely talked about her. As a child, Sam had asked him about her mother all the time. But her questions so obviously hurt Dad, she'd finally stopped.

Now he'd just dropped Mom's name between them and laughed at some memory that pleased him.

"She named that river, you know."

"I didn't know!" Sam shook her head. The river had always been called La Charla. She knew it meant "chitchat" in Spanish, and she'd just assumed some lonely explorer had pretended the river's babbling was a voice from home.

"Sure." He nodded. "Before we got married, it was just River Bend's river. But she acted like it was a friend. When she was expecting you, she had a hard time sleeping." Dad gave Sam a sudden smile. "She swore you were doing somersaults inside her. So she'd slip out of bed and walk down to the river. I don't know how many times I found her there, sitting on a rock, watching the moon dance on the little waves."

Sam's arms wrapped around her ribs. She did the same thing.

"Louise said the sound of the river soothed you, and after she'd sat there awhile, you'd let her sleep. And then when you were born"—Dad shook his head, as if the rush of memories kept surprising him—"you were a colicky baby. But Louise and I would carry you out in the moonlight and stand by the river, yawning, and it always settled you down so we could grab a nap before you were hungry again."

"I didn't know any of that," Sam said.

"I haven't thought about it for years." Dad's voice changed as he left the past behind. "Just because I don't blame you doesn't mean I think it's safe. Especially now."

The rustlers, Sam thought, and she didn't mind the warning. It was nothing compared to the whole new picture of her mother.

Dad cleared his throat and picked up Jingles, the black plush horse that spent his days posed on Sam's pillow.

"What's had you tossing and turning ever since you came in here?" he asked. Dad's index finger touched the gold bells stitched to the toy's saddle. "I figured unless you had ants in your bed, you were stewing about something."

Dad looked up at her then, expecting her to explain.

"I figured out how to work with Dark Sunshine," she said. "You know how she keeps staring into the barn? I mean, it's natural, since the people who adopted her kept her in a windowless stall."

"Where'd you come by that information?"

"Brynna," Sam said. She hurried, hoping Dad

wouldn't point out that Dark Sunshine wasn't there to stay. "And I know how to start gentling her."

"How's that?"

"I could spend Friday night with her in the round corral. We'll put Ace and Sweetheart out in the barn pasture since the fence is fixed, and we'll put Popcorn, alone, in the little corral off the barn."

Dad didn't resist the idea. Not yet, at least, and he didn't say the mare had to go. He just gave Jingles a shake and listened.

"What I'd do is sit with her, then do that herd mirroring thing Jake had me do with Blackie after we'd first weaned him. Remember?"

It was hard to believe the small and scared colt had grown up to be the Phantom, but Sam knew her patient care and attention back then had knit the bond that connected them now.

Dad sighed. "Most days it seems a long time since you and that horse were little, but I can still see you in pigtails, following Blackie around when he walked away, then letting him follow you when he needed a leader."

"It worked pretty well, didn't it?" Sam whispered. She wondered if she had her mom to thank for Dad's unusual patience tonight.

"Yeah." Dad held up a hand before she could get too excited. "But Blackie was hand-raised, not born wild and abused. One more thing you don't want to forget: Blackie belonged to you."

"Yeah." Sam let the word stretch out.

"I suppose Brynna's mentioned the foster-care deal?"

Sam bit her lip. Brynna hadn't. Was Dad talking about Mikki or Dark Sunshine?

"No, huh?" Dad shook his head. "I suppose there's no harm in telling you. She's put through paperwork for us to foster the mare. They do it with orphan foals more often, but there's provisions for adult horses too. We get paid for helpin' her back to normal."

Sam didn't ask for details, and she didn't bounce on the bed and squeal with joy. She only said, "Oh, wow."

"Someone could still show up with a title to that horse," Dad cautioned. "A bill of sale would supersede BLM's agreement with us."

"No one will," Sam insisted. "You know it, Dad. Anyone who's treated her this way doesn't care."

Dad patted her back as if he were searching for words to explain. "Sometimes people want things just to own 'em. It's not fair and it's not right, but they don't know better than to abuse what's theirs. Look at Mikki." Dad shook his head. "That child's had hard use too."

To Sam, the buckskin was the more likable of the two, but she didn't say it. And the longer she kept her opinion inside, the more clearly she saw how both Mikki and the mare refused to show when they were afraid.

"I guess Mikki's no more to blame for her ugly attitude than Sunny," Sam admitted.

Dad put Jingles back on the pillow and gave Sam another pat on the back as he rose.

"Get to sleep now," he said. "You're going to need lots of energy if you plan to have a slumber party with a wild horse."

Chapter 10

"I'M NOT AFRAID OF RATS OR SNAKES," SAM said. "I just don't like being surprised."

Minutes ago, she'd stood in a shaft of sunlight that bathed the empty trap in autumn gold. Crowded with sagebrush and piñon pine, the old wood had looked picturesque. Only the feed-sack cover for the missing truck seemed creepy.

She and Jen weren't scared—the place was obviously deserted.

Feeling adventurous, they'd tied their horses at the

trap—which was disappointingly free of yellow crime-scene tape—and hiked in the direction Sam had seen the cowboy go to retrieve his whip. That was how they'd found an old bus wedged into a narrow chasm.

Now Sam hesitated outside the door of the old bus and rubbed her arms free of goose bumps. She couldn't hear anything moving in there, but it looked like a great hiding place for creatures she'd rather avoid.

"Well, I *am* afraid of rats and snakes," Jen admitted suddenly. "Nerve toxins and bubonic plague are things I'd rather enjoy through a microscope."

"The rangers have already been out here, and they probably disturbed whatever animals were living inside," Sam reasoned.

Jen gave Sam a lopsided smile. "Oh, good. Now they're ticked off and ready to protect their home."

Sam considered the bus again. Painted a pale blue that had faded almost to white, it was obviously not a school bus. Jen had suggested it was a prison bus for shuttling convicts between jail and work crew chores. Whatever its former purpose, someone had positioned it in this natural niche so that the windows on one side were smack against the hillside. The other side, the side she and Jen could see, was creased and rusty.

They'd thought it was long abandoned, until Jen noticed clothes tucked into windows in place of curtains and Sam saw the path worn to the door, which was folded halfway open.

"Okay, we don't have to go in," Sam said.

"Of course we do," Jen said. "The rustlers probably hole up here between horse trappings. We might find something the rangers overlooked."

"Not likely."

"But possible," Jen insisted. "It'd be great if we found something with a name on it."

"Oh, and how about an address, too?" Sam said. "A driver's license would be good. Then the rangers could just cruise over and pick them up."

"You're getting as sarcastic as me," Jen said, crossing her arms. "So knock it off. I just want the rustlers caught so that you don't have to keep looking over your shoulder all the time. Which reminds me . . ."

"Yes?" Sam couldn't help looking back down the canyon toward the trap.

"Does your dad know where you are?"

"He wasn't home. He doesn't get a half day off like we do. And I told Gram I was going riding with you." Sam smiled, but Jen's implication gave her chills.

"So. No one knows where we are. Two girls alone in the wilderness." Jen gave her voice a ghost story waver.

"Stop! Who did you expect me to tell—Jake?"

"No. Definitely no." Jen squared off, facing the bus door, then tugged Sam's shirtsleeve. "After you, Nancy Drew."

Sam pushed the door open the rest of the way and jogged up the stairs. Something *did* skitter inside, but Sam was more aware of the odor.

"Yuck, it smells like old sweaty socks." She grimaced.

"Mixed with a lingering aroma of canned chili." Jen moved ahead of Sam and nodded to tin cans scattered under a blanket-covered bus bench.

They both looked down the aisle. It was clear, almost as if it had been swept, but some seats leaned at weird angles, and several had come unbolted from the floor.

Sam was wondering if the bus had rolled down here from the highway, when Jen took a squeaky breath and pointed. "Behind you."

Sam whirled, gasping.

And saw nothing.

"Ow! You stomped on me!" Jen complained.

"Serves you right." Sam panted. "What are you looking at? I don't see anything." Sam scanned the driver's seat, the speedometer, a sun-cracked plastic frame where the bus driver's license was supposed to go.

"That," Jen said.

On the shallow shelf below the driver's mirror, Sam finally saw what Jen had spotted.

An empty cottage cheese carton held water with something floating on the top. It wasn't cottage cheese. Next to the carton sat a man's razor with gross bits of whisker still clinging to it.

Jen edged past Sam for a closer look.

She was welcome to it, Sam thought as she backed

away and started down the center aisle. This was ridiculous. What did they think they were going to find?

Sam looked to her right. A seat held two sleeping bags, one ripped with fluffy stuff poking out. She looked left. A coiled rope hung over a seat back and a glove lay on the bench part.

The floor slanted beneath her feet. The bus must have a flat tire on this side. Sam started to grab a seat back for balance, when Jen's voice startled her again.

"Don't touch anything," Jen said. "Just in case they haven't fingerprinted."

"You watch too much television," Sam grumbled.

That was when a shiny mouse ran over her left boot toe and ducked under the jean hem on her right leg.

"Oh no!" Sam bawled. She would *not* let it run up her leg!

She stamped. The mouse fell and scurried back the way he'd come. Sam shuffled and scooted her feet, trying not to crush him. Her foot slid out from under her, and she stumbled, landing facedown.

"Don't touch anything!" Jen yelled again.

"Tell that to the paramedics when they arrive," Sam mumbled.

Jen moaned, and Sam felt her friend's footsteps pound closer. She'd frightened Jen, and that wasn't very nice. But Sam wasn't feeling nice. She lay in the aisle of this convict bus, with the breath knocked from her chest. She needed to do a push-up to get upright, but she didn't like the idea of pressing her bare hands against this floor.

From her position, she saw the undersides of seats. No gum, just cobwebs and red-brown rust where a metal seat support had cracked, showing a corner of yellow paper.

Sam closed her eyes, then opened them.

"Are you okay? Sam, do you have a concussion or something?" Jen squatted nearby.

"Or something. I mean, I see something?"

Jen sat quietly for a minute. "Why are you asking me? Sam, you'd better be all right. I can't carry you down to—"

"You don't have to." Sam flipped into a seated position before she delicately removed a piece of paper that had been rolled and slipped inside the metal tube.

"Oh, wow." Jen sighed, and they read it together.

Sold for $125 and barter goods
1 bukskin mere,
3yrs old and tack
to Curtis Flickinger

"I can't read the signature," Jen said, "but this guy needs some help in English."

Sam read the words again.

"It's signed by Rose Bloom. See the *B* there? She's the lady who adopted Dark Sunshine and got title to her a few months ago. That's what Brynna said."

This bill of sale proved Dark Sunshine belonged to someone named Curtis Flickinger. He had to be one of the rustlers.

"What are you going to do?" Jen asked, and Sam wanted to hug her. This was what made Jen a best friend.

Jen wouldn't give advice until she was asked. They both knew they should turn the bill of sale over to someone in authority, and they both knew the horse would suffer even more if they did.

"What do you think?" Sam asked.

"I think that looks like a carbon copy," Jen said, "and Rose Bloom has the original, so you can't keep it a secret forever."

"I wouldn't do that." Sam folded the yellow paper into a square and tucked it inside her front pocket. "But I do want to think about it a little while."

Sam checked Jen's expression. Inside a frame of blond braids, her friend's face turned serious. Jen was a math whiz with a knack for logical, well-ordered thinking. If there was a flaw in waiting, her analytical mind would find it.

Outside, a breeze blew. A branch of sagebrush tapped against the bus. Finally, Jen shook her head.

"Other than the tiny chance we're being watched right now by federal rangers—and I think Ace and Silly would have let us know if they'd sensed them—I see no problem with waiting." Jen rubbed her hands together and stared at them, still thinking. "After all, we are juveniles . . ."

"And we can't be expected to know this is important?" Sam suggested.

"They're not going to buy that, Samantha Anne. Otherwise, why would we take it?"

"Right." Sam ignored Jen's gesture, which said *as usual*. "Let's get out of here. I'm supposed to be home in time to help Jake with Mikki."

Leading the way back to the door, Jen said, "Just don't tell Jake."

"Not in this lifetime," Sam promised. But by the time they'd made their way off the bus and back to the horses, she thought she might ask Jake what he'd overheard when he was hanging out with the official government trackers.

After all, it couldn't hurt.

The girls had parted and Sam had almost reached home when she had to rein Ace aside so that they could wait for the gray van to cross the River Bend bridge. Even from there, she heard Dark Sunshine's worried whinny.

As Sam rode into the ranch yard, she saw why.

Far back by the barn, Jake stood between Witch and Sweetheart. With Sam on Ace and Sweetheart outside the barn corral, Dark Sunshine felt abandoned by her new herd.

Right in front of Sam was another surprise. Mikki, who'd just arrived, was talking with Pepper.

Mikki wore jeans and a black T-shirt stenciled with the word MISFIT. Whether it was the name of a band or a description of the wearer, Mikki had better be nice to Pepper.

Sam shook her head at her own silliness. Why should she feel protective of a cowboy talking to an eleven-year-old girl?

Because she really liked him. Pepper, with his red hair and gangly legs, was only seventeen, but he wasn't quiet like Dallas or Ross, River Bend's other hands. He didn't offer Sam extra care because she was the boss's daughter or scoff because she'd been a city girl.

Pepper just accepted Sam. His winks, nods, and the stampede string he'd made for her hat kept Sam's spirits high while she was relearning her place at home.

As Sam rode close enough to eavesdrop, she heard Mikki ask why Pepper had become a cowboy.

"No choice," Pepper said with a slow smile.

"What does that mean?" Mikki demanded.

"I'm too lazy to work and too nervous to steal," Pepper answered.

Mikki laughed, but Sam winced with uneasiness. The bill of sale in her pocket and the technically stolen horse in a River Bend corral might make her a thief, but should Pepper be joking about stealing with Mikki?

Still, Mikki had been a runaway. Pepper had been too, when he'd first come to the ranch. Maybe he and Mikki could find things in common.

Before she dismounted to join them, Sam saw Jake hailing her from the barn.

She rode to him. Jake was already dusty, as if he'd been working. He'd loosened Witch's cinch, too, so the horse could relax.

Sweetheart was saddled. Had Jake used his half day off to work while she'd gone riding with Jen? Probably.

"I've been working with Popcorn," he said. "I've got him haltered."

"Jake, that's great."

He shrugged. "It's the horse, not me. He's sweet as pie." Then Jake's mouth twisted in irritation. "She probably *will* ride him before she leaves."

Looking embarrassed, Jake changed the subject. "Keep Ace tacked up so you can help me switch the buckskin and Popcorn after she's done working with him."

Sam noticed that Jake had avoided using Mikki's name.

"You still feel uneasy about her," Sam said.

"I arranged for the van driver to come back late so she could make some real progress today." He sounded a little defensive.

"But you still don't trust her, right?" Sam asked.

"I won't talk about it."

Sam took a breath, then let it go. "How about your tracking trip? Will you talk about that?"

Jake's face lit with a rare smile. "Later," he promised, and began walking toward the round pen.

"What, are you like a cop-in-training now?" she teased.

"Later." Jake shot Sam a look meant to silence her. It didn't work.

"Jake, was it really cool? Tell me."

"If I *were* training as a cop, the first thing I'd do is put you under house arrest."

"I haven't done anything!" Sam felt a zing of worry. There was no way Jake could know what was in her pocket.

"Unless your fool idea of spending the night with that mare counts." At her silence, Jake looked smug. "Your dad called and told me about it this morning while you were waiting at the bus stop."

Jake never missed a chance to gloat. While it took Sam over an hour to reach Darton High on the bus, he made it in half that time, driving in with his brother.

All of a sudden, that didn't matter. Sam had to know if she was rushing Dark Sunshine. If her idea was a mistake, Jake would tell her.

"Jake." She grabbed his forearm, tightening her grip when he tried to shake her off. "I'm only going to keep Sunny company in the dark and mirror her movements, like you taught me. That's all. What do you think? Really."

Sam released Jake's arm. He looked down, then rubbed the back of his neck in a thoughtful gesture.

"I think it's a good idea for the horse," he said. "I'm not so sure about you."

"You know I'm careful around horses."

"Bloody noses and black eyes. Shoot, now." Jake pretended to frown in confusion. "Who *was* that I saw all those times, if not you?"

Sam was sticking her tongue out at Jake when she felt Mikki's stare. Maybe it would be good for Mikki to see it was possible to disagree with a man and not fight.

Mikki turned on her heel, away from Pepper. She pretended she hadn't been watching Sam and Jake at all and started toward the round pen.

"Just a second," Jake called. "Before we go in, I want to tell ya what we're doing. It's different." He ignored the girl's loud sigh and tapping foot. "You're going to make a deal with Popcorn."

"A deal?"

"Yeah. If he doesn't run from you, you won't chase him. It's that simple. Sam, show her." Jake motioned her closer. "You be the horse."

"Oh, good." Sam tossed her hair, pretending it was a mane, then walked away. Jake followed. "If I were a mustang," Sam called back to Mikki, "this would make me nervous, especially when he speeds up like that."

Sam and Jake speed-walked in a circle. When Jake stopped, Sam slowed down to watch him. As soon as she faced him, Jake retreated a step.

"But you're letting the horse back you down," Mikki said.

"It looks like it at first, but pretty soon you'll have him coming to you—to eat, to get haltered—"

"To ride," Mikki interrupted. "Okay, I understand, but that'll take hours."

"If you're lucky," Jake agreed.

"Why not just rope him, pull him over, then hold him and pet him until he knows I'm not going to hurt him?" Mikki said.

"That wouldn't work for me," Sam said. "If some

creature tied me up and dragged me somewhere, then wanted to touch my head, I'd fight to get away, wouldn't you?"

"There she goes again, thinking like a horse," Jake said.

A blush heated Sam's cheeks from this best of all compliments, but the real warmth came from inside. Jake's praise meant a lot.

"That's not fair. It comes natural to her. She's been on a horse every day of her life. I just got here."

"Sam can think like a horse because she pays attention. And she cares about horses," Jake corrected. "If you're nice, Sam might tell you where she's really been these last two years."

Mikki didn't take the bait, only asked, "Okay, what are Sam Forster's rules for thinking like a horse?"

Why should I tell you? Sam squashed the thought. She'd act like an adult while Mikki played the bratty little kid.

"There are really only a few rules you'll need to be a horse today," Sam said. "One: The herd is where you're safe. Two: Run from anything that might hurt you."

"Don't I get to play?" Pepper joked as he moved closer, reminding them he was still there.

"That's it?" Mikki ignored him and moved toward the gate.

"That's it." Jake walked after her. "Now, you'd better get to work, because we're moving Popcorn to another corral today, and you"—he pointed at Mikki—"are going to lead him there."

Chapter 11

JAKE'S PLAN WORKED PERFECTLY. FOR A HALF hour, Mikki walked and talked with Popcorn as if she were one of his kind. During the second half hour, she did the same, except she held the end of a long rope attached to his halter. At last, Popcorn followed Mikki wherever she went.

"Just keep walking as long as you hear his hooves behind you," Jake told Mikki. "And don't look back."

"How far away is he?" Mikki asked as she walked past Jake.

"He's staying a good seven or eight feet back. That's his flight distance. He knows you can't grab him from there."

Peering into the corral, Sam noticed Mikki's smile. Right now, the girl wasn't trying to prove she was tough. She wasn't acting like she didn't care. She'd spoken Popcorn's language and told him he could trust her. She was proud of something that mattered.

"I wish my mom could see this," Mikki said as she passed Jake again.

"Maybe she can in a few weeks," he said casually. "I'm sure she'd be welcome."

Finally, it was time to take Popcorn outside the round pen and move Dark Sunshine into it.

Jake bolted the front gate, just in case something went wrong. Pepper walked out to the gate with Jake. Though he talked loudly enough for the girls to hear, Sam had the feeling something else was going on.

"I think Mikki can handle Popcorn, but I don't know what to expect from the mare," Jake said.

Mikki left the round pen with Popcorn. The albino's

head swung toward the ten-acre pasture, toward the barn, and though he picked his feet up high, showing he was nervous, he followed Mikki to an open spot near the house.

"Good," Jake said to Mikki. Then he nodded to Pepper as he settled on the front porch with Gram.

Everyone was watching.

"I'll put two loops on the buckskin," Jake told Sam. "You hold one and I'll take the other. We'll keep her kind of crosstied between Ace and Sweetheart. They're her herd now, so maybe she won't put up a fuss till we get to the round pen."

"She won't like that." Sam considered the pen as if she were Dark Sunshine. Would the mare remember the buzzing motorcycles, whooping men, and mustangs running into a trap?

"When we get her as far as the open gate, you'll ride Ace in and I'll release my rope. I think she'll follow."

Sam sized up the entrance to the pen. Blindfolded, the mare had followed Ace all the way to the River Bend. This might work.

"I talked it over with Wyatt," Jake said. "This is the best we could come up with."

"Let's go," Sam said.

Jake made a bow to Mikki, Pepper, and Gram. "This rodeo won't last too long," he promised.

Jake lassoed Dark Sunshine with such gentleness, she looked confused. Only when Sweetheart and Ace tugged her away from the dark barn did she snort in alarm.

Jake and Sam let the horses work the ropes as the buckskin tossed her head, trying to flip off the loops around her neck.

Sam found it hard to stay quiet, but her voice wouldn't soothe the mare. Maybe this time tomorrow, but not yet.

The mare rocked back, pawed in a half rear, then landed on four stiff legs. She trotted, black mane fanning on one side, then the other, as she looked from Ace to Sweetheart. Hopping and blinking against the sun, Dark Sunshine was nearly to the round pen when Mikki yelled.

"Popcorn, no! You're not going anywhere!"

After that, Sam only heard pounding hooves and Sunshine's screams. The mare reared so high, Sam feared she'd fall over backward. Ace and Sweetheart barely kept her earthbound.

Body thrashing, head slinging, the mare might have escaped, except that River Bend cow ponies were the best. Ace and Sweetheart had been schooled to sidestep charging steers and stay calm in the midst of stampedes. Tails swishing, they kept plodding toward the round pen.

"No! Oh, no, you don't!" Mikki's shrill voice rose loud enough for Sam to hear it, but she couldn't imagine what had gone wrong.

She didn't try. Her job was to get Dark Sunshine into the corral. Pepper and Gram would have to help Mikki.

Just ahead, the round pen gate stood open. Sam leaned low on her gelding's neck.

"C'mon, Ace, lead her in," she whispered.

Ace leaped forward, passed the mare, and entered the round pen. Ropes dropped loose, swarming around his legs, but Ace ignored them. Even when the gate slammed, Ace listened to Sam's hands and loped around the pen. Dark Sunshine followed him.

After several laps around the pen, Jake opened the gate so Sam could ride Ace through. But Jake had never seen the mare's need to stay with her band. She would not be left behind.

Head level, ears pinned so flat they were lost in the torrents of black mane, Dark Sunshine pressed close to Ace, joining his charge for the gate.

Before they got there, Jake slammed the gate. He stood in his stirrups to shout over the fence.

"Ditch Ace and climb over," Jake said. Then he vanished.

It wasn't that hard. If her hands hadn't been shaking, Sam could have stepped off Ace and grabbed the fence in one fluid movement.

But Sam was afraid to see what was happening outside the round pen. When she did, she wanted to give Mikki a shake.

Popcorn was trying to behave. He rushed toward Mikki as she stepped back, but the sight of five hundred pounds of horse coming at her made Mikki panic.

"No! No!" Mikki screamed at the gelding, jerking his head with the halter rope. She tried to make him stop, but he thought the pulls meant *come closer*.

At last, Jake signaled Pepper to move in. The young cowboy stepped between the girl and horse, slipped the rope from her hands, and gave her a gentle shove back.

Oh boy. Mikki didn't like that, Sam thought. But Pepper's concern was for the frightened albino.

At the end of the lead rope, Popcorn flailed with his front hooves, trying to break loose and run. Pepper hunkered down on his bootheels. He kept his weight low, so the horse couldn't jerk him off his feet and drag him.

Finally, sweat-darkened and breathless, the gelding stood still and waited.

Pepper straightened his knees. Gradually, crooning and talking, he stood all the way up and walked to the horse. Lazily, he coiled the rope, until he was just feet away.

"Hey, Jake," Pepper said, "what d'you say I walk this fella back to the barn corral?" With a calm stride, Pepper moved away and Popcorn followed.

The albino's willingness, after such a battle, made Sam so mad at Mikki, she didn't know what to say to her.

Gram was always sensible and straightforward—she should go over and lecture Mikki. But Jake snatched the job.

Without looking at Sam, he handed her Sweetheart's reins and then his hat.

What in the world? Sam looked down at the dusty Stetson and wondered what it signified.

Jake yanked the rawhide tie from his hair, then reknotted it tight. Even though Jake's breathing had slowed by the time he walked up to Mikki, Sam wished Gram would step between them.

Mikki looked around frantically, as if she were being bullied, but Gram stayed on the porch.

"Look, it's not my fault!" Mikki shouted. "Popcorn started being a jerk. He ran right at me. He tried to trample me. He just . . . well . . . I . . ."

Jake let her protests run down.

"Horses can be scared or pushy," he said. "They cannot be jerks."

"He was trying to act all tough—"

This time Jake interrupted. "He *is* tough. He's bigger and stronger than you are. Fighting won't work. It might've made other kids or your mom do what you wanted, but it won't work with a horse. A horse must trust you, and Popcorn was well on his way. He got scared and turned to you. He needed his leader—*you*—to be strong."

Jake waited for Mikki to meet his eyes. When she did, he wasn't easy on her.

"You let him down, girl. You panicked. What's he supposed to think if you've been saying 'Trust me and I'll take care of you,' then you yell at him, tug him around, and prove you're weak?"

Mikki looked small. Her defiance was gone. Both hands covered her mouth, as if that would somehow smother Jake's words.

Sam watched the two. Jake didn't trust Mikki, but he'd had enough confidence in her that her actions had disappointed him. Mikki didn't like Jake, and yet she was shrinking with shame.

DARK SUNSHINE

When the gray county van honked at the gate, Sam ran to open it. As it drove in, Pepper walked from the barn corral toward Mikki. At first, his head was cocked to one side, as if he were explaining something and trying to make the girl feel better.

Sam couldn't hear what Mikki said to him, but Pepper recoiled and his voice carried across the yard.

"I'll tell you one thing," Pepper snapped. "You're not gonna talk to me that way *and* get my help. You choose."

"Maybe I choose not to come back to this stupid ranch!" Mikki shouted. She ran toward the van, bumped into the side of it, and pounded on the door until it opened.

Pepper looked stunned. "I'm sorry, Jake," he said as the van rolled away. "It's not my job to scold her." He rubbed his palms on the front of his jeans. "Shoot, Sam, if I've wrecked this program for you all, after everyone's been so good to me, I just don't know what I'll do."

Jake clapped a hand on Pepper's shoulder.

"She deserved it, and she's tough enough to take

it," Jake said. "She'll be back. That kid has some major problems, but she's no quitter."

Friday night, Sam nearly fell asleep in the bathtub. Her head started off propped against the tile. Bit by bit, she slipped down until the water was lapping at her lips.

Warm water soothed muscles knotted by her fall in that creepy bus and from the buckskin throwing her weight against the rope.

The aromas of chicken soup and fresh-baked bread wafted up the stairs. Dinner would be ready when she went down.

Spending all night in the corral didn't seem like such a good idea anymore. Sam's eyelids drooped. She might have dozed if her gaze hadn't stopped on the jeans she'd tossed on the floor. One pocket held Dark Sunshine's bill of sale. Sam's eyes sprang wide open.

She pulled the plug from the bathtub, wrapped a towel around herself, ran shivering to her room, and hid the bill of sale inside a sock in her bottom drawer.

She knew she had to inform Brynna about the bill of sale. But she wouldn't do it tonight.

When she left the warm kitchen for the round pen, Sam hardly noticed the temperature difference. For her slumber party with Dark Sunshine, she wore thermal underwear, jeans, a long-sleeved shirt covered by a jacket, gloves, and a knit cap.

She also brought snacks. A can of sweet grain for the mare, a candy bar for herself.

The sun had set when she opened the gate, but dusk still lingered. Jake had managed to slip Ace out of the round pen. Now, disturbed by another human invasion, Dark Sunshine trotted away. She circled the pen until she neared Sam, then wheeled and ran in the opposite direction, shaking her head fiercely because, once again, Sam didn't retreat.

"I'm not scared of you, pretty girl."

To make herself smaller and less threatening, Sam sat in the dirt with her back against the fence.

The buckskin didn't know what to make of that. She kept shaking her mane, though her hooves moved in a regular beat. It didn't take Sam long to hear eight separate hoof falls, followed by hesitation, and then eight more steps.

Suddenly, Dark Sunshine changed her path. She galloped along the fence, until Sam's nearness made her veer through the middle of the pen. Instead of circles, she made ovals. Over and over again.

Dusk had turned to darkness when the mare stopped.

"That didn't take long," Sam said. Though she could see only the mare's outline, Sam heard her tail swish. "Ready to come over and have a little grain?"

Since it was too soon to ask the mare to take it from her hand, Sam used a scoop. She jiggled it to waft the scent toward the buckskin.

With a snort, Dark Sunshine began trotting ovals again.

"As if you'd fall for such a trick." Sam laughed. "Is that what you're telling me?"

Next, Sam tried the technique Mikki had used on Popcorn.

"Keep walking away and I'll follow you," Sam

explained to the mare. "Stop and I'll stop. Take one step toward me and I'll back up."

The mare uttered an insulted grunt, then resumed trotting around the corral with Sam right behind her.

After an hour, Sam yawned.

"Do what you want. I'm taking a break." Sam stopped and the buckskin stopped too, blowing a sigh through her lips.

Energy. I need energy.

Sam looked at her watch. It was 12:07. She felt hot and queasy, and it was hours until dawn. She took the candy bar from her pocket. The mare's ears twitched at the crinkling wrapper.

"I'll share," Sam coaxed. "C'mon, Sunny." She smooched at the mare. "No one can refuse chocolate."

The mare looked the other way, lifting her chin as if something far more interesting were happening outside the corral.

"We're making progress, even if you won't admit it," Sam told the mare.

Quietly, Sam mimicked a nicker. Clearly, the horse

didn't recognize it. Instead of pricking her ears forward, she let them fall to the sides.

"It wasn't so bad that you have to give me the mule look." Sam yawned again. "You know you're exhausted, so how 'bout just one step this way?"

As if she understood, the contrary mare backed a few steps.

"Show-off," Sam said. "I'm coming after you."

Sam's steps were sluggish. She glanced at her watch as she chased the mare: 12:12. Five minutes had passed like an hour. She had to do something to wake up.

She could stick her head in a horse trough. That would wake her, but it was a little gross, even for a girl who loved horses. If she went inside for a cold shower, she'd wake Dad and Gram. That left the river.

La Charla whispered to Sam. This time of year the river was low. After running over sun-warmed rocks all day, it shouldn't be too cold, even though the night air was chilly.

Sam slipped through the round pen gate and locked it behind her. Dark Sunshine gave a low whinny that probably meant *good riddance*.

"I'll be back," Sam called to her. "This party won't be over for hours."

The porch light and full moon lit the path to the river. Once she reached it, Sam sat on a rock and thought of her mother doing the same.

Then, before her thoughts turned dreamy, Sam tugged off her boots. She left them on the shore. Sucking in a breath, avoiding unsteady stones, Sam waded out.

An owl hooted nearby. Up to her knees, Sam stayed on one side of a big rock streaked with quartz. It blocked the river's rills and formed a tiny pond within the river. Its surface was satiny and smooth enough to reflect the moon.

Tonight's moon wore a halo of rose-gold mist, and it floated right there at her feet.

Hadn't she read about ancient people who stared into still pools to tell the future? Sam wished she knew how. What was the meaning of a haloed moon and a handful of stars?

Dizziness made her stumble forward. She caught herself before her knees hit the water, and she pushed herself up, planted her feet, and rubbed her eyes. The huge splash had silenced the owl. Sam was tempted to stand in the darkness, letting the murmuring waters lull her, but she was making progress with the buckskin and she needed to get back.

Drawing a deep breath, Sam tried one more time to tell her future. She looked into the pool. What she saw surprised her so much she didn't even gasp.

Another face was reflected next to hers.

Chapter 12

THE PHANTOM GLOWED ON THE RIVER'S SURface. As Sam looked up from the reflection, so did he, greeting her with a nicker so quiet only his nostrils quivered.

Sam wanted to hug him. Memory promised his neck would be warm and solid in the circle of her arms, but she stayed patient.

"Zanzibar," she whispered.

Three times the stallion bowed his head. With each nod, his forelock flipped up, sifted down. When the forelock parted the third time, his eyes shone with mischief.

A second later, he splashed closer. His head snapped down, then up. If she hadn't known the game, Sam might have thought the feathery touch was a whisper of wind over her hand.

It wasn't. Years ago, Sam and the stallion had played a game she called "nibbles." In it, the colt darted close, swung his muzzle her way, and gently lipped her hand before trotting off, pretending it had never happened.

"You're teaching that horse to bite," Dad had told her, but the colt never did.

Why had the Phantom remembered the game now? Why did this mighty stallion frolic around her like a dog? Flicking her hand through the air, Sam teased him, but she was also careful to dodge the stallion's rough moves. He couldn't know her skin was thinner than his hide.

As Dark Sunshine's neigh soared through the night, the stallion stopped. Head held high, he interpreted the mare's cry, then lowered his head and considered the girl

DARK SUNSHINE

before him. The Phantom had many mares, but Sam was the only human he loved.

She saw him decide to stay with her.

She hoped no one woke to investigate Dark Sunshine's neighs.

Moments with the Phantom were hers alone. Sam knew he'd run at the approach of another human. He could carry himself to safety, but she didn't want anyone else to see him vanish like a ghost up the hillside.

Face it, Sam thought, *you don't want anyone else to lay eyes on him.*

For two years, Sam and the colt had longed for each other. Once she returned, nothing could keep them apart.

She extended her arm, palm up. The Phantom buried his muzzle in the cup of her hand, but he didn't continue the game. He pressed down, then drew his chin toward his chest, urging Sam to move closer. She did.

Her other hand combed through his mane. Each time her fingers hit a snag, she untangled it.

Watchfulness vibrated through the stallion, but he

wanted the grooming and didn't mind the tugging of her fingers.

Since he hadn't been brushed in two and a half years, strands of mane pulled loose, and suddenly Sam had an idea.

Once before, she'd thought that what she really needed to tame Dark Sunshine was a recommendation from another wild horse. Maybe Zanzibar could give it to her.

Each time a long thread of hair worked free, Sam tucked it into her pocket. She'd braid a horsehair bracelet, a silver token to wear beside the black one she'd made from her colt's mane years ago. The untamed scent might tell Dark Sunshine that Sam could be trusted.

As she tucked more strands into her pocket, she looked down. The moon was still bouncing along the surface of the river when the image shattered.

They had company.

The click of the Border Collie's toenails on the bridge alerted the horse to Blaze's approach, and the stallion leaped, front feet tucked up like a carousel horse.

As the Phantom splashed to the distant shore, Sam ran for the ranch.

"Stay, Blaze, stay," she called. She could see his silhouette on the bridge: she had to keep him from barking.

Hours ago, Blaze had bedded down in the bunkhouse, so he must have scratched at the door long enough that someone had gotten up to let him out. That meant one of the cowboys could be up and walking around in the darkness.

Breathless, Sam paused on the bridge and looked around. The dog seemed to be alone. He growled and bristled, staring into the night, but the Phantom had vanished.

"You silly dog." Sam rubbed Blaze's ears.

At her touch, he shed his fierce stare and gazed up at her. Open-mouthed and happy, he seemed to figure that if she wasn't worried about the strange horse at the river, he shouldn't be either.

Blaze bounced along beside Sam until she reached the round pen. Then he sauntered to the house, climbed the front porch steps, and threw himself down to sleep.

Sam wanted to do the same. Instead, she entered the pen. Dark Sunshine moved away, but she didn't slam against the slats as she had before.

"You're not trying to ram your way out, are you, girl?" Sam leaned against the fence, then slid down until she was sitting in the dirt again.

The mare watched, waiting for Sam to get up and chase her. But Sam only yawned.

"You're gonna have to get used to me like this," she said.

Before another ten minutes passed, Sam was sound asleep.

Something told her not to open her eyes, not to gasp, not to jerk away from whatever was moving nearby.

Sam stayed still. It wasn't the early-morning chill that had wakened her. She heard snuffling and smelled the sweet, dusty scent of horse. Then she felt a bump against her denim-covered hip bone.

Dark Sunshine was nuzzling her pocket.

Sam lifted her eyelids just enough to see a stretch of

buckskin neck. The mare startled back a step. Her black-tinged ears tilted toward Sam, but when Sam didn't move, the mustang's muzzle returned. She was sniffing the pocket where Sam had stashed the Phantom's hair.

The nudging tickled, and finally Sam couldn't help laughing. When she did, Sunny trotted off a few steps, but she tilted her head, still looking curious.

"That's it." Sam stood and walked toward the gate.

As she glanced back, Sam saw that the mare wore the expression she'd been waiting for. If Dark Sunshine was curious, if she didn't want Sam to leave until she'd discovered what was in her pocket, that was good.

Outside the gate, Sam didn't stop to roll the stiffness from her shoulders. She hurried toward the house, thinking of bed.

In the entire history of River Bend Ranch, no one had been allowed to sleep until noon, and Sam was no exception. In fact, this was one of the busiest Saturdays Sam could remember. Ross, Pepper, and Dallas had gone over early to the Gold Dust Ranch to help unload Slocum's new Brahma breeding stock.

Sam had already put in a full day of work when Brynna arrived with Mikki at two o'clock.

At the sound of the white BLM truck, Sam pulled back the kitchen curtain and saw Mikki climb out. Arms crossed, she walked a few stiff steps, as if her legs were sticks.

"Look at her," Sam said to Gram. "She doesn't want to be here, and she sure doesn't look sorry."

Gram didn't look up from the cheese she was shredding for that night's taco dinner. "Who should she apologize to, the horse?"

"How can you feel sorry for her, Gram? After she jerked poor Popcorn around and just"—Sam swept her hand through the air—"threw away the trust he put in her?"

Gram flashed Sam a disappointed look. "I feel sorry for her because she was scared, and she failed at something she was about to get good at, something that matters to her very much."

"She sure doesn't act like it matters." Sam heard her childish tone even before Gram spoke.

"Samantha, for a girl who's so good at reading animals, you are downright dense when it comes to human beings."

"I probably am, but—" Sam stopped. She'd been about to point out Mikki's baggy jeans and frazzled blond hair, but she stopped just in time.

"You think that horse's trust has been betrayed?" Gram slammed the cheese grater on the counter. "Mikki's mother has married three men and—if Mikki's right—each time she's put the man before her child."

Sam stared at the whitewashed kitchen ceiling, trying to keep tears from overflowing. Her own mother had died and left her behind, but not because she wanted to go.

"Honey, can't you see why Mikki doesn't show her feelings? Can't you recognize a heart that's been broken one too many times?"

Sam swallowed hard, then cleared her throat. "If Popcorn will give her a second chance, so will I," she said. It was only for an hour. She could do it. "And if Popcorn is cranky, I'll help her make up with him."

Gram put her work aside and wrapped Sam in a hug. Sam shut her eyes, enjoying the closeness Mikki would envy.

"Used to be, I could kiss the top of your head when I hugged you," Gram said. "Now you're just getting too big." Gram gave her a loud kiss on the cheek. "You're a good girl, Samantha, just a little impatient. But you'll have a chance to practice: Mikki and Brynna are joining us for dinner tonight."

Popcorn gave Mikki a second chance, and Sam practiced patience. Since Jake was in Darton, helping his mom with the week's shopping, Sam took over.

The busy morning had become a quiet afternoon. After Dallas, Ross, and Pepper had helped Slocum with his Brahmas, they'd gone to town together. As they were backing Dallas's truck around to leave, even Blaze had jumped in the back and joined them.

Only the chickens' clucking and Dark Sunshine's lonely nickers broke the quiet.

Perfect, Sam thought. There'd be no noise, no interruptions. Since Popcorn was alone in the barn corral, she decided to let Mikki sit with him there.

The day's heat filled the barn, magnifying the smell of the hay packed in bales to the barn's rafters. Ribbons of light fell through the roof, turning the hay golden, then rippling down to stripe Mikki as she opened the gate into Popcorn's corral.

Sam held Mikki off a minute.

"Once you get inside, just sit," Sam said. "Remind him you're no one to be afraid of."

Mikki's condescending laugh said Sam was wrong.

"Mikki, you can't bully half a ton of horse."

"Yeah, I know."

"Why would you want to?" Sam let the question hang between them until Mikki blew out her cheeks and shook her head, then sat.

Sam stood outside the corral.

Dark Sunshine nickered from the round pen. The slats in the fence were set so close together, the mare could barely see out. She and Jake had thought that would give the mare the closed feeling she longed for. Now the buckskin seemed to want company. Sam would have gone to her if she hadn't been put in charge of Mikki.

Sam alternated between watching Mikki and Popcorn watch each other and trying to attract Brynna's attention. Sam had slipped the bill of sale into her pocket, but she was still deciding what to do about it. She itched to know if Brynna had more information about Dark Sunshine or the rustlers before she handed it over.

But Brynna was strolling around the ranch with Dad, pointing and gesturing. Although they never got within earshot, Sam knew Brynna was making plans for the HARP program.

The more Sam thought about it, the more she liked the idea of HARP.

What she didn't like was the way Dad was smiling. If he distrusted the government and blamed BLM for the high cost of grazing, why was he strolling around grinning at Brynna Olson?

Brynna might get the wrong idea.

When Gram called from the porch that dinner was

ready, Sam felt relieved. Dad would return to acting normal as soon as they sat around the kitchen table.

"Slip on out," Sam said to Mikki.

Popcorn followed the girl three steps toward the gate.

"I don't think he's mad at me," Mikki said, and her face said even more. Her blue eyes danced, her mouth wore a real little-kid smile, and her cheeks were flushed with satisfaction. She was actually happy.

Then something made both Mikki and Sam look across the ranch yard. Near the house, Brynna patted Dad on the back. That wouldn't have been so bad if Dad hadn't stopped and faced Brynna as if she'd meant something by it.

What's going on? Sam wondered. Whatever it was, it was *not* all business. Sam tried to make an excuse, but she couldn't say anything. If only Mikki hadn't noticed . . . but she had.

"Ha ha." Mikki gave a fake laugh like a donkey's bray. "You thought your dad was so perfect."

Too forcefully, Sam bolted the gate.

What did Dad's expression mean? Would Dad and

Brynna start dating? Aunt Sue had gone out occasionally. Hair upswept and formal, she'd attended the symphony with men in stuffy-looking suits. But Dad and Brynna were looking at each other as if something had changed.

What if they fell in love? Would they marry and expect her to make room for a stepmother? No. She'd only just come back home. Dad wouldn't shut her out of a decision that big.

Sam started back to the house without giving Mikki the satisfaction of a reply.

Still, Mikki kept talking. "Just watch. For the rest of the night, they'll have no time for either of us. First, they'll stare at each other with *goo-goo eyes*." Mikki made a sappy face to demonstrate. "Then, after dinner, they'll tell us to get lost."

Mikki sounded like a specialist on selfish adults. But the expert status didn't make her happy. Her lips drooped as if her satisfied smile had never been there.

"Thanks so much for inviting us, Grace," Brynna said as the five sat down for dinner.

It took Sam a second to realize Brynna was talking to Gram. Had Brynna ever called her Grace before? Was Gram part of this romantic conspiracy?

Without thinking, Sam glanced at Mikki. She turned away when Mikki flashed a told-you-so smirk.

Though she loved tacos, Sam chewed slowly, as if the tortillas were filled with sawdust.

Conversation bumped along. Gram and Brynna did most of the talking, and Brynna claimed she had no information about Dark Sunshine or the rustlers. What she *did* say was so boring, Sam nearly dug the bill of sale out of her pocket and flaunted it.

But then she'd get in trouble, and Mikki would be delighted. If there was ever a case of misery loves company, Mikki was it.

In fact, Sam did everything she could to avoid meeting Mikki's gloating eyes.

She even studied Brynna. This time yesterday, Sam would have assumed Brynna was telling the truth about not knowing anything. Or, at worst, that Brynna had official government reasons for not telling all she knew.

Now Sam figured Brynna just had a giddy crush on Dad and her high-powered brain had conked out.

Dinner ended and Sam couldn't wait for Brynna and Mikki to go, but Gram wasn't done playing hostess.

"Coffee will be ready in a few minutes," Gram said. "Sam, please set out cream and sugar."

Sam told herself she wasn't disappointed. She was simply tired. After all, she'd stayed up most of the night with Dark Sunshine. Still, she felt as if she moved in slow motion, carrying the creamer and sugar bowl with underwater slowness.

Mikki looked so fascinated by the sugar cubes, Sam thought the girl might snatch one and pop it into her mouth.

"Who wants fudge cake?" Gram asked.

Sam didn't moan. She resigned herself to believing this torture would never end.

Hands went up, including Mikki's. "I do, but please, can I run out to see if Popcorn will take a sugar cube from me? I'll be back before you serve dessert. I promise."

Since Gram always thought the best of everyone, Sam looked at Dad. He was watching Brynna smile at Mikki as if the girl hadn't smirked all through dinner.

"Hurry," Brynna said. "We'll wait for you."

Sam cleared dinner plates and wondered why she was the only one who heard phoniness in Mikki's voice. She rinsed the plates at the sink and looked toward the barn. She couldn't see Mikki.

Sam took a guilty glance toward Gram. Pleased at having company, Gram hummed as she sliced extra-thick slabs of cake.

Sam scolded herself. She'd promised to give Mikki another chance, but she wasn't doing a very good job of it. She carried the cake plates to the table before Gram could ask.

Mikki returned right away, and if anyone else noticed that the girl reeked of cigarette smoke, they didn't say anything.

Why not? Sam knew that if Dad thought she'd smoked anywhere, let alone near the barn and horses, she'd be grounded for life.

Gram invited Brynna and Mikki to stay and watch television, or play Scrabble, but Brynna was already standing.

Brynna looked uneasy. Her gaze follow Mikki as if she'd just noticed the girl's suspiciously sweet disposition. Brynna sounded strained as she said good-bye and herded Mikki toward the door.

Dad beat her to it. With a gentlemanly bow, he opened the door, then stood there, blocking it.

He froze, hands gripping the doorframe.

"Wyatt?" Gram said. "What is it?"

Even then, Sam knew she'd never forget the awful despair in her father's voice.

"Oh Lord, phone Luke Ely and have him call out the volunteers. The bunkhouse is on fire, and the flames are reaching for the barn."

Chapter 13

RIVER BEND RANCH WAS BURNING.

Dad ran and Sam followed.

Black smoke corkscrewed into the evening sky. There wasn't much smoke yet. In fact, the yard was bright as noon and popping filled the air.

Sam hesitated in the middle of the yard and stared around. On her left, the horses in the ten-acre pasture ran in a tight, nervous band. Ahead stood the barn, full of horses and winter's hay. No smoke. No fire.

She felt relieved, then even more relieved as she saw

that Dad had meant the black smoke came from the *old* bunkhouse.

Sam took off after Dad, and her relief ended the instant she came face-to-face with a sheet of orange flame three times taller than the ruined old building it consumed.

A wall of heat stopped her.

"Hose!" Dad shouted, and Sam jumped as he jerked the hose leading to the barn. It stretched behind him as he shot water on the fire.

At least the old bunkhouse is empty. That was what Sam thought, until an arm of flame reached toward the barn and sparks peppered the air overhead.

The other hose was by the ten-acre pasture. She usually used it to fill the troughs, but would it reach this far?

"What can I do?" Brynna demanded.

Sam had left her manners in the kitchen. "Nothing," she yelled, and brushed on past.

She felt an illogical rage toward the woman. Brynna had brought Mikki here. Brynna hadn't watched her. Worse than that, Brynna had distracted Dad so that even he, so careful and slow to trust, had missed the threat in Mikki.

Only Jake had noticed. Sam missed his solid common sense. She wished he were there. But Jake was in Darton. So were Dallas and Pepper and Ross.

Saving the barn was up to her and Dad.

Sam grabbed the hose, cranked the handle on, and ran. She hit the end of the hose so hard she was nearly jerked off her feet.

The hose was way short of the old bunkhouse. The arcing stream of water barely reached the new one.

"Wet it down," Brynna said, pointing.

"Good idea," Sam admitted. If she watered the new bunkhouse, it might not catch fire from the sparks swarming over the roof.

Even as Sam aimed for the bunkhouse roof, the water pressure lagged, and fear yanked at her heart.

Dad's complaints about the well had always sounded like background noise. Now his words made sense. Though they'd bought the new pump part, they hadn't dug the well deeper. That job cost thousands of dollars.

This wasn't like the city. Once these hoses used up all the water in the well, she and Dad would have to wait for the pump to suck up more.

They couldn't wait.

From the barn pen, Popcorn neighed nervously. Ace and Sweetheart answered from the adjoining pasture.

This smoke didn't smell like a fireplace; it was acrid and bitter. If it burned her eyes and nose, what was it doing to the animals? Sam wanted to comfort them, but she couldn't leave the hose.

Nearby, Dark Sunshine's hooves hammered in the round pen, trying to flee whatever lurked outside, frightening the other horses.

"You're all right, girl," Sam shouted, but the hooves ran on and on.

"The roof!" Suddenly Gram was beside Sam, pointing.

The old bunkhouse roof buckled into a V and quaked. There was a plastic smell as something inside burned hotter; then the roof collapsed and vanished.

That old bunkhouse roof had been built of wood. The barn roof was covered with tin. The house and new bunkhouse roofs wore some sort of shingles. Not wood. Would that make them safer?

One spark through the barn window into the hayloft could mean disaster, Sam thought, and that was when the water stopped. She shook the nozzle. She looked behind, but no kink in the hose had stopped the water flow.

She threw the hose aside, detoured around Brynna and Gram, who were dragging bunks, clothes, and cooking pots out of the new bunkhouse, and ran toward Dad.

He strode her way, his face so red it looked sunburned. The fire had outlasted his attempts to quench it. Now it rose behind him in a wavering red-orange tower. Instead of crackling, the flames roared like a huge truck speeding down on them.

"What are we going to do?" Sam shouted.

"Pray for Luke to hurry." Dad stared at the front gate as if he could will the red volunteer fire truck to appear.

Sam looked, too, but there was no truck with Luke Ely at the wheel and Jake's brothers piled in the back, and no sound of the siren that would bring neighbors to help.

Dark Sunshine began screaming. For days, the mare had pushed back her terror, trying to understand. Now the smoke and shouting and confinement freed her fear. The little buckskin whinnied for help, and Sam knew she'd lied to the horse. She'd told Dark Sunshine that she was all right, but nothing was all right.

"Make her stop!" Mikki stood on the front porch, hands pressed to her ears.

"You stupid little brat! Do you see what you did? My home is burning and it's your fault!" Sam lunged toward Mikki.

"Sam!" Dad's voice was like a slap. "Don't waste time."

Sam turned away from the crying girl. Dad was right. Nothing she did to Mikki would help.

Suddenly the siren wailed over the fire's roar. Nothing had ever sounded so good. The truck sped over the bridge and through the gate with mere inches on each side. The tires scuffed to a stop, and Jake's brothers, dressed in the yellow suspendered pants and coats called "turnouts," were everywhere.

They worked levers and unrolled hose, moving with an efficiency that said they'd need every second to beat this fire.

Gram and Brynna paused by the mound of stuff they'd hauled out of the bunkhouse to watch Luke Ely jump down from the fire truck.

Luke's long jaw looked as if his teeth were set together as he approached Dad. "Where do you want to start?"

"The barn and the bunkhouse." Dad pointed index fingers in two directions.

Luke gave a quick shake of his head. "Can't do that."

"We've *got* to do that," Dad snapped. "The bunkhouse is practically new, and the barn has the winter's hay and—"

Luke clamped a hand on Dad's shoulder. The two tall men stood eye to eye. Dad didn't shrug off Luke's hand. He would have if he'd been angry.

Dad was scared. The realization made Sam feel as if the earth had crumbled beneath her feet.

"Wyatt, this is just a five-hundred-gallon tanker." Luke pointed at the fire truck. "We can fight this fire for ten minutes. Fifteen, if there's a miracle."

"The Darton fire department should be here by then," Dad said.

"Maybe," Luke said. "But this is the deal right now. If you try to save them both, you're going to lose them both."

Sam's throat closed in panic, but Dad didn't falter for even a second.

"Let's get some water on that barn."

Every time the wind blew hard, Sam had heard a corner of the barn's tin roof creak, blowing up and down as the wind tried to peel it loose.

The fire found it right away. Despite the two fire hoses, a streamer of flame swirled on the barn roof. It started small, but in a single minute it became a red line of fire. So straight someone might have drawn it there with a marker, the flame licked down the corner of the barn.

Since they'd given the old bunkhouse up as a lost

cause, the fire thrived there, creating its own whirring wind. All at once, the wind shifted.

Sparks hit the ten-acre pasture, and Buddy cried. When Buddy bucked and bawled, Sam knew the calf had been singed. Luke and Dad shouted over the fire's roar. Sam ran closer so she could hear what they were saying. She was just in time to hear one of Jake's brothers curse at a dribbling hose.

Water from Luke Ely's hose kept coming, but it flowed in pulses. It wouldn't last.

Sam looked at her watch. The fire truck had been there for ten minutes, but there was no sign of the big tanker from Darton. Every horse on the ranch neighed as the ten-acre pasture began to burn. Dad shot one last, demanding look toward the gate, then turned to Sam.

"We've got to set the horses loose. Seth"—Dad pointed at the closest Ely brother—"unlatch these two corrals." Dad gestured toward the ten-acre pasture, but Gram was already waving her arm in the air, signaling she knew what to do.

Dad turned to Sam. "Sam, mount up on Ace and

make sure the horses get through the gate. When the truck comes from Darton, we don't want a bunch of crazed horses milling around, getting in the way. Forget the saddle," he shouted.

Sam shook her head. What had she been thinking? She'd actually started toward the threatened barn, headed for the tack room to get Ace's saddle and bridle. Instead, she unsnapped a lead rope draped over a fence. Out in the barn pasture, Ace wore a halter. That would have to be enough.

"Sam, can you do this?" Dad was already looking over the Ely boys, ready to choose one to take her place.

Sam took a deep breath, and it hurt.

"I can do it," she insisted, then scrambled over the fence before she could change her mind.

Ace trotted toward her, head tossing so that his black forelock flew away from his white star. He didn't care if she carried a halter rope. He wanted the reassurance a human could bring.

Grass brushed damp around her ankles, and Sam told herself she was foolish to worry. She had ridden bareback all during her childhood. One terrible accident hadn't robbed her of all her skills. She could do this.

Ace ducked his head. She snapped on the lead and flung herself toward his back. She scrambled up, closed her legs around Ace's warm body. As Seth Ely swung open the pasture gate, they galloped through.

Ace pulled left, then right. He didn't want to hang back to see that all the horses escaped the ranch yard. He snorted and grunted as Sweetheart bolted past, her pinto body bright in the firelight. Popcorn joined Sweetheart, and the ranch yard was filled with horses.

Slammed from behind by Strawberry, Ace staggered. Sam held on to his mane, but Ace uttered an angry squeal and lashed out his back legs. The high kick sent Sam forward against his neck and the halter rope went slack in her hands.

She needed to free Ace before the Darton pumper arrived, but not like this!

She planted her palms on the gelding's withers to press herself upright. Her balance returned and Ace's gait evened out.

Banjo took the lead. The bald-faced bay ran with his mouth open, body lean and lowered to the ground. He headed for open range. The others galloped after him.

Sam had just decided it was time to free Ace, too, when a pale shape separated from the bunch of saddle horses. Popcorn was doubling back.

The confused mustang ran a zigzag path, headed back to the barn pen. And the fire.

"No!" Sam shouted.

Ace cut Popcorn off as if he'd been a rebellious cow.

For a minute they were so close together that Sam felt Popcorn's confusion. First Mikki's panicky punishment, now the fire. Poor Popcorn. How could he trust when things kept going so wrong?

Even with Ace pushing against him, Popcorn tried to shove past, toward the fire.

"No!" Sam shouted again, but this time she spun the end of the halter rope, shooing him back.

It worked. In two long leaps, Popcorn joined the other horses. In another leap, he'd caught Banjo. Sam kept Ace at a lope, but as soon as all the horses were out of the ranch yard, running toward the open range, she pulled him to a stop.

Ace danced in place, head tossing, barely under control. Smoke and dust whirled around them as Sam slipped off and stood firm. She tugged on the halter rope, but Ace didn't settle down.

With short, fearful neighs, he bumped her. Sam fumbled with the snap on the halter rope. Her hands were shaking, and though affection kept Ace from knocking her flat on purpose, he would, sooner or later.

There. The gelding felt his freedom. He wheeled away from her, following the other horses.

Sam didn't watch them run away. She glanced down the dark and empty road, then turned toward the ranch yard, toward the fire. She jogged, though her smoke-tortured lungs protested.

Please don't let it take the barn. Please save the house. Sam didn't know if she muttered the words or just thought them, but her pleas were interrupted by shrill cries.

Dark Sunshine. No one had freed the mare. The

round pen shuddered from the impact of her body as she tried to batter her way out.

Panting, wondering where everyone else had gone, Sam slid the latch free. Before she could open the gate, the buckskin mare exploded through. Once in the open yard, she stood amazed and disoriented.

For an instant, the fire was reflected in her eyes.

"Go! That way!" Sam shouted, and ran at the mare. The horse jumped back, and Sam felt an instant's regret that last night's gentling had been wasted. Then her eyes fell on her own shadow, cast black and perfect by the fire behind her.

"Go!" she yelled, whirling the rope.

The mare ran, and Sam pursued her all the way to the gate.

Only then did she hear the sirens. The Darton fire department, all three trucks, huffed down the road toward the River Bend entrance.

The first truck had already turned, maneuvering its huge bulk through the gate, when Dark Sunshine reached it.

Horror and smoke snatched Sam's breath. She couldn't get even a sip of oxygen. They were going to collide. The delicate buckskin mare was no match for tons of steel and iron.

Dark Sunshine leaped over the cattle guard, inches ahead of the truck's bumper. She galloped on, turned golden by the next set of headlights, then swerved so quickly she seemed to have been brushed aside by a giant hand.

Even as the trucks passed her, Sam watched the mare. She was running wild now, catching Ross's big horse, Tank, at the back of the herd, passing Sweetheart, then Strawberry, Ace, and even Popcorn.

Dark Sunshine raced for the lead, and Sam knew she'd never come back.

Chapter 14

FIRE HOSES CRISSCROSSED THE RANCH YARD. A young woman wearing head-to-toe firefighter gear paused, flipped up the visor on her helmet, and smiled at Sam.

"We'll have this knocked down in a couple of minutes," she said, jerking a thumb toward the barn. "No problem."

"Thanks," Sam mumbled, but the woman had already jogged on to join the others.

They turned on floodlights and worked together as a

team. Sam didn't look away until Buddy's head butted into her palm and stayed there.

"Why didn't you go with the horses, Buddy?" Sam knelt in front of the calf and hugged her neck. "You silly baby."

As Sam's hands moved over the calf's body, she felt a few crispy places and smelled the acrid scent of burned hair, but Buddy didn't flinch.

The calf settled beside Sam on the front porch. Together, they watched the flames shrink and the smoke turn white. The firefighters kept watering the barn and old bunkhouse, but their movements had turned from urgent to leisurely. The volunteers were packing to go home.

The horses had escaped, and though they might be tough to regather, they were safe. Dad coughed as he helped the Elys roll up the hose, but he hadn't been burned. Gram looked fine too.

In fact, she moved like a teenager, lean and quick in her jeans as she walked Brynna and Mikki back to the BLM truck. The car door slammed, sealing Mikki safely inside. Before getting in herself, Brynna stood waving as Gram walked away.

This night could have been a lot worse, Sam mused.

Somehow she missed the arrival of Jake and his mom until Jake's shadow fell over her. Sam looked up at his broad shoulders and tipped-down Stetson, and she gave a tired smile.

"How ya doin', Brat?" His voice rumbled with something like concern, and Sam jumped up to hug him. "I wish—I *would've* been here, but I went to a movie with my mom." He talked over Sam's shoulder, since she refused to budge. "She likes that mother-son stuff 'cause I'm her baby, y'know?"

Sam nodded but didn't speak. Jake was no baby. He felt solid and dependable, and he was her best friend. She gave him one last squeeze, then stepped back.

She almost laughed when she noticed Jake rubbing the back of his neck. When Dad used that gesture, it meant he was thinking or embarrassed. Right now Sam would bet on the latter.

"Must've, uh, been a pretty bad night," Jake managed.

Sam sniffed, feeling a little sheepish.

"Don't let a little hug go to your head," she said. "I just hugged Buddy, too."

Jake's answer was half laugh, half groan, and Sam enjoyed his confusion until her eyes caught movement across the yard.

"I guess hugging is contagious." Sam's lips felt cold. She barely got the words out as she stared.

Jake looked over his shoulder. "Yeah, my mom's like that after a fire. She thinks Dad should stick to ranching. She says that's dangerous enough."

Sam glanced at Jake's parents, hugging beside the volunteer fire truck. She sighed. "I wasn't looking at them."

"Honest?" Jake looked around the yard.

Sam could tell when Jake saw what she did. He froze.

Dad was doing more than hugging Brynna Olson. He was kissing her.

Sam's hand went to her pocket. The bill of sale still crinkled inside. She knew how to get Brynna away from her father.

"Could you watch Buddy for a minute?" she asked Jake.

"I'll put her back in the pasture. She'll be lonely, but no fire truck will back over her."

"Thanks," she said. Sam felt like she was striding through a cold and narrow tunnel as she headed across the yard. She ignored Dad's embarrassment and faced Brynna.

The redhead's expression was so understanding, Sam wanted to scream. *Save your sympathy,* she wanted to say. *I can take care of myself.* But she only shoved the piece of yellow paper toward Brynna's hand.

"I think you'll want to look at this," she said.

"Sam, what is it?"

"Just look at it," Sam said.

She watched Brynna's expression turn professional, as if nothing had happened. Suddenly she couldn't stand watching them together for another second. She darted across the yard past Jake and into the house.

Once inside, she took the stairs two at a time, then growled with frustration when she cranked on the shower only to have water dribble out in teaspoons.

Sam returned to her room and buried her face in her

hands. She *really* needed a shower. She smelled awful. The odor was more like toxic waste than woodsmoke. She was polluting her own bedroom. She looked at Jingles, perched on her pillow, and nearly apologized.

"And I know they'll make me go to school tomorrow," she moaned to the plush horse. "Who cares if my house almost burned down, my horse is gone, Dark Sunshine belongs to a criminal, and my father has chosen this as a great time to get a crush on Brynna Olson?"

Gram had loved Louise, her mother. Maybe Gram could talk some sense into Dad.

Sam set her alarm clock for five thirty instead of six. It would take her that long to scrub the stink from her hair and skin.

She plopped into bed. She resolved to stay awake and talk to Gram when she came up, but she never heard a thing.

The next day turned out to be Sunday.

When Sam ran downstairs, freshly showered and hungry for breakfast, she was alone. It took her only a few minutes to realize her mistake, but she decided not to waste her early start.

Since she couldn't go ride, Sam made herself toast and jam and sat at the kitchen table reading a story she'd been assigned for English class.

It was really a pretty good story. Sam smiled and stretched as if she'd just wakened. She'd been so into that story that last night's disaster had fallen away. There were moments when she didn't mind homework. She could spend more time studying now that Mikki wouldn't be coming over. Certainly, HARP would get rid of a kid that destructive.

Sam was pouring herself more juice when she heard something hit the front porch. *Weird,* she thought as the heavy thing struck again.

When the sound continued and Blaze began barking, curiosity pulled Sam to the kitchen window. A horse stood with his front hooves on the porch. One of those hooves pawed at the porch for attention.

"Ace!" Sam burst through the door and let it slam.

Her horse was dusty. Clumps of burrs studded his

tail, and his deep neigh probably wasn't a greeting but a demand for breakfast. Still, he was home.

Sweetheart had come back with him. Across the yard, the pinto circled, tossing her head for attention. Near the ten-acre pasture, Dallas, Ross, and Pepper crawled out of sleeping bags.

Sam could imagine how smoky and unpleasant it had been inside the bunkhouse. They'd been smart to sleep outside.

She'd fed and brushed both horses, checked out the fire and water damage to the barn, and searched—unsuccessfully—for the hens when Jake and Jen rode into the yard.

Sam's heart swelled at the sight of her friends. Jake sat loose in the saddle on Witch. Jen rode her palomino and led a sorrel. Because Jen had brought a horse for Sam to ride, Sam knew they'd come to help search for the scattered horses.

"I didn't think your horses would be back," Jen started.

"They're not—just Ace and Sweetheart, and they look like they've been running half the night."

"It's a good thing I brought Kitty, then," Jen said. "She's not as skittish as she looks."

The sorrel's nostrils worked constantly as she took in the smells of smoke and charred wood, strange horses and an unfamiliar dog.

"You guys are great." Sam smiled at Jake and walked toward Jen. She stroked the shoulder of the wary sorrel. "And Kitty, pretty Kitty, can act however she likes, because she's my Blackie's mom."

"You make her behave once you mount up," Jake ordered.

Sam started to ask Jake who the heck he thought he was, but the worry lines around his eyes stopped her.

"Thanks, Jen," she said. "I'd like to give Ace a rest."

By midafternoon, all the horses except Dark Sunshine were headed for home.

Once the three friends got them past the road to the BLM corrals and the pond at War Drum Flats, the horses broke into a rolling lope toward River Bend Ranch.

All except Popcorn. River Bend hadn't been his home for long, and the albino was so jumpy they'd had to herd him most of the way. Now, within sight of the ranch, he seemed to remember the shelter and grain and trotted along without being pushed.

If only Dark Sunshine were trotting beside him, Sam thought. Jen must have understood her sigh.

"I bet the buckskin's joined up with a wild band," Jen said.

As their horses fell back to a walk, with Sam riding in the middle, she imagined the Phantom rounding the mare up and adding her to his harem. She'd be so much happier, knee-deep in grass in a wild horse canyon, with soaring red rock walls to hide her from cruel men.

Sam's mind wandered from that happy image, to the bill of sale, to Dad's announcement from just a few nights ago. River Bend Ranch would officially foster Dark Sunshine.

"Oh, my gosh," Sam gasped. "What does the government do to you if you lose a foster horse and it's a semi-stolen horse that maybe wasn't under BLM management in the first place?"

Jen cocked her head to one side, thinking, and a white-blond braid swung free. "Give me a minute to unravel that one," she said, frowning.

Jake wasn't half as sympathetic. "Why do I get the feeling," he said, eyes fixed forward as he trotted beside Sam, "that this is the start of something I don't want to hear?"

"Is this about the B.O.S.?" Jen asked cryptically.

Bill of sale. Sam nodded.

"It is," she said, ignoring Jake's irritation. "And it's not really a secret anymore."

"What do you mean?" Jen looked rather sickly. Sam couldn't blame her for not wanting to be implicated in a federal crime.

"The cat's out of the bag," Sam said. "I decided to give the bill of sale to Brynna."

"Bill of sale for what?" Jake demanded.

"I told you not to tell him." Jen's singsong voice made Jake shoot her a glare.

"For Dark Sunshine," Sam mumbled, but there was no doubt Jake heard.

"Where did you get a bill of sale for—" Jake broke off. "If you were tampering with a crime scene—" He stopped and glanced from Sam to Jen, then back to Sam. "I *know* you weren't doing that. Even you two would know better than—"

Jen leaned forward in her saddle, arguing past Sam.

"That's just where we found it, Jake Ely. Right where you and those federal officers couldn't." Jen gathered her reins and eased her palomino into a lope.

Sam turned toward Jake. A dozen sarcastic responses showed in his expression, but he didn't allow even one to escape. Good. Maybe if he was finished bickering with Jen, he could help figure things out.

Instead, Jake spoke very patiently.

"Are you saying," he began, "that you let Brynna award you foster care of that mare when you knew she belonged to someone else, and you even knew who?"

"Of course not," Sam said. "We didn't find the bill of sale until—"

"So, who does she belong to?"

"Curtis . . . ," Sam began, but she couldn't remember the rest.

"Flickinger," Jen supplied.

Jake's lower lip poked out a little as he considered the name. "Not from around here," he said. "But maybe Brynna can put him in some government database and see what she comes up with."

"Except he *didn't* adopt the horse," Sam said. "He bought her from Rose Bloom, the lady who adopted Dark Sunshine just over a year ago and got title to her." She paused for a breath. "So, she could legally sell Sunny to this guy."

"Curtis Flickinger," Jen repeated slowly. She wet her lips, glanced back toward the pond with a considering look, then shook her head. "Sam? I—wow, I almost know that name."

"Wishful thinking," Jake dismissed her. "Didn't Brynna say the horse was from out of state?"

"Captured in Oregon and taken to Idaho, then Wyoming," Sam admitted.

Jake leaned forward again and flashed Jen a satisfied look.

But Jen wouldn't be silenced. "Yeah, like cowboys don't move around a lot."

"Who said the guy was a cowboy?" Jake snapped back. "Because he's a rustler, he has to be a cowboy?"

Sam hated being in the middle. This had to stop.

"You know what's wrong with you two?" she interrupted. Jen and Jake glared at her. "You both have to be right."

Jen shrugged. They rode in silence for a minute.

"I'm headed for home," Jake said, as if Sam hadn't said a thing. "I need to get Witch rubbed down, then help my dad with some fool thing he said he'd do for Slocum's party."

"Brahma-cue," Jen corrected.

"Yeah, well, just hog-tie me and put a gag over my mouth if I ever say that in public," Jake answered. Then he reined his black mare away from them and jogged toward home.

"Give me a minute, Sam," Jen said. "I'll remember where I've heard that name."

Kitty saw the white BLM truck first.

Sam had been surprised at how well she and the sorrel had been getting on, but now Kitty shied and threatened to bolt. Clearly the truck had frightened the mare.

Sam leaned forward to pet Kitty's neck. "It's okay, girl. I'm getting pretty darn sick of seeing that truck myself."

"I don't know what you two are mumbling about, but Miss Olson's slowing down," Jen said.

Sam glanced back. If Brynna wanted to apologize for Mikki, she could save her breath. And if she wanted to talk about kissing Dad . . . she'd better keep driving.

Brynna stopped. As she lowered her truck window, Jen gasped.

"BLM," she said. "That's it." Wide-eyed, she looked at Sam. "Flickinger. Flick. Remember?"

Sam felt her brain trying to catch up. She was almost there when Jen blurted her conclusion to Brynna.

"It's him, isn't it?" Jen asked. "Curtis Flickinger is

Flick, that guy with the long droopy mustache who used to work for Slocum."

Brynna nodded. "I checked BLM's payroll records, and it is him. He worked for us while he was working for Slocum," she said.

Brynna stared at Sam. Then, just in case Sam had forgotten one of the worst days of her life, Brynna added, "Curtis Flickinger is the man who caught the Phantom."

Chapter 15

SAM GRABBED THE SADDLE HORN.

On the cattle drive, Flick had made her miserable. It had been her first week back in Nevada, and he'd mocked her horsemanship and called her a dude. He'd teased Jake, saying he'd better take care of his "little girlfriend."

Flick also made a point of calling mustangs "range rats."

She might have forgiven it as "joshing" if he hadn't captured the Phantom. Flick was an incredible roper, on horseback or afoot. Yards of lariat flew and tightened at his whim. That was why Slocum had hired him to rope the Phantom.

"It *was* Flick up there," Sam realized. "He'd shaved off his mustache, but . . ." She saw the scene at Lost Canyon replaying in her mind. "It was his lazy way of tossing his loop, and he used the whip the same way. It's him."

In Lost Canyon, Flick had missed his throw for the Phantom. Instead of feeling hopeful, despair weighed Sam down. Flick was too good to miss a second time.

"Law enforcement has done casts of the tire tread from the truck and trailer in Lost Canyon," Brynna said. "But they won't do us much good until we have a real tire to compare with them."

"So you'd have to impound a truck, then, see if they match, right?" Jen asked.

Brynna nodded. "I have a theory, which might hurry things up a little."

Jen leaned forward in her saddle, listening. Sam was interested, but she straightened an edge of saddle blanket instead of looking into Brynna's eyes.

"If they branded those horses the day they trapped them, the burns shouldn't look fresh by now. Add that to the fact that they've had time to fatten them up, and I think the rustlers will bring them to the Mineral auction yards this Tuesday."

"And you're going to be waiting for them," Jen said.

"Right, with a brand inspector and two rangers. But it would help if I had a witness to verify they're the right guys."

Sam couldn't help but look up then. She was the only witness.

"On Tuesday?" Sam asked.

"If I get Wyatt's permission for you to miss school, would you ride along with me?" Brynna's expression was hopeful.

Sam knew there was more at stake here than the rustlers. Brynna wanted Sam to like her, to approve of her affection for Dad.

Sam didn't want to go, but how could she refuse? The rustlers were a danger to all horses. The Phantom, his band, maybe Dark Sunshine, could be trapped and sold for meat.

"Okay," Sam said, but she looked away from Brynna's smile.

That night, Sam sat up late. She'd finished her homework and slipped it inside her backpack. She'd put out clothes for the morning and was about to throw her dirty jeans in with the laundry when she remembered the hair from the Phantom's mane, stuffed in her pocket.

Sam ran her fingers through the silky, silvery strands. She'd hoped they'd send a message to Dark Sunshine, and now it was too late. Just the same, she wove the hair into a tiny braid. *Let Zanzibar stay safe.* Sam lifted the right strands over the middle ones. *Let Dark Sunshine stop being terrified.* If the men who'd abused the buckskin caught her again, what would become of the mare?

Sam lifted the left strands and braided them in.

Hope was plaited with every strand, but hope wasn't enough. As Sam knotted the ends and slid the bracelet over her wrist, she vowed to be brave. She had not done enough to help catch those rustlers, but that was about to change.

Sam ambushed Jake in Darton High's rally court, a grassy rectangle in the center of the school and a busy place during lunch.

"I'll be right back," she told Jen.

"Don't take no for an answer," Jen said. "Next time it could be Silly or Ace."

Sam nodded and gave Jen a thumbs-up. Then, working like a cow pony, Sam cut Jake out from the rest of his friends.

A few of the guys made comments, and Darrell, with his baggy pants and lazy-lidded eyes, gave Sam an approving nod as she towed Jake away.

"What is it?" Jake crossed his arms and waited.

"If those rustlers don't show up at the auction tomorrow, you have to help me catch them. And you can just quit looking so skeptical, Jake Ely, because those rustlers *will* be hiding from the rangers. We could go up the canyon during Slocum's Brahma-cue, when no one else is out driving around. We can catch them, I know it. The rustlers won't suspect a couple of teenagers."

"There's a good reason for that, Sam."

Sam stared at him. Jen had convinced her silence could be an effective argument. She waited.

"Why me?" Jake complained. "Why don't you get Jen—"

Jake must have seen her satisfaction, because he shut his jaw and glanced over to where Jen waited.

"What am I saying? You and Jen riding alone in the canyon? They're criminals. There's no telling what they'd do. I won't be part of this."

"That's too bad." Sam shrugged. "I could've used your help."

"I'm telling Wyatt."

"Do you know how immature that sounds?" Sam wanted to wipe the smile from Jake's lips. He thought he had her now. "You were never a tattletale, Jake."

He stayed quiet. How could she have thought she'd win the silence game over Jake?

"What if they'd rounded up our horses while they were loose? What would you have told Mr. Martinez if they'd gotten Teddy Bear?"

Jake's eyes opened a millimeter wider, encouraging Sam to keep talking.

"I need you to do this with me," she insisted, "because you're really good at tracking, because you can drive"—Sam dashed her fingers through her auburn bangs—"and because I'm a little afraid to do it alone."

"You should be, Brat. It's dangerous."

Frustrated, Sam looked past Jake to where his friends stood waiting. Darrell was using the time to slick back his hair. Sam thought about saying, *I bet he'd help me*, but she didn't. Instead, she told Jake the one thing he didn't know about the rustlers.

"The rustler in the gray hat who acted like a cowboy, who tried to rope the Phantom? He's Flick."

Jake's face grew still. She'd heard Flick harass Jake and seen the unspoken scorn that had to do with Jake being Shoshone. What other grudges might Jake have against Flick?

The bell rang, ending the lunch hour.

"I'll think about it," he mumbled, and moved back toward his friends.

Gram and Sam drove into the ranch yard after school to find Mikki sitting on the front porch, alone.

"What is she doing here?"

"I'm rather surprised myself," Gram said.

"Jake's not here," Sam said. "What should I do?"

"Let her work with a horse, I'd say." Gram climbed from the car, and Sam had no chance to argue.

As Sam faced Mikki, she could smell the charred wood soaked by fire hoses. The stench still hung over the ranch yard, following Sam as she passed the blackened posts, all that remained of the old bunkhouse.

For once, Mikki looked her age. She wore a wrinkled yellow T-shirt and jeans. Her knees were tucked up against her chest with her arms wrapped around them. Instead of being moussed into spikes, her hair lay close to her head. She looked like a dejected baby duck.

Sam did not feel sorry for Mikki. The girl had

traumatized Popcorn. She'd set the ranch on fire. She'd gloated over Dad liking Brynna. Sam stood next to Mikki and looked down at her.

"If Brynna reports me, I'm out of the HARP program for good."

If? Sam couldn't believe there was any doubt.

"Do you think she will?" Sam asked.

"Why wouldn't she?" Mikki snapped, but then she seemed to melt. "I didn't do it on purpose, but I know that doesn't matter. Not really. It's just—after I did this pilot program, I was supposed to be able to come back here in the summer. And if I did really good, Brynna said I might be able to assist in one of the California programs. I'd be working with horses all the time if I didn't get in any trouble." Mikki's voice soared, then stopped.

Chin in her hands, Mikki stared out at the ten-acre pasture. Buddy was touching noses with Teddy Bear. Strawberry and Banjo stood head to tail, swishing the flies from each other's faces.

If Mikki didn't get in trouble with HARP, she would with Dad. Sam knew that for sure.

DARK SUNSHINE

"You'll know soon enough," Sam said. "So you'd better take advantage of today." She reached for Mikki's wrist and tugged the girl to her feet. "Popcorn was doing all right before." Sam didn't slow down when Mikki faltered.

"He was just watching me, is all."

"Watching, but then he followed you a few steps as you left, remember? We put him in the round pen since . . ." Sam swallowed. "Since Dark Sunshine is still gone."

"I'm sorry," Mikki said.

"You should be," Sam said. "If we do catch her, she could be hurt or traumatized." She stopped and reined in her anger.

Before she unlatched the gate to the round pen, Popcorn's nicker greeted them. "Go on in. I'll bring you a scoop of grain. He might be ready to eat from your hand."

"If he does, will you tell Brynna? Maybe, if she hasn't already reported me, she'll know I'm good at this." Mikki looked up at Sam. "I *am*, aren't I? I just messed it up, like I always do."

Like I always do. Sam knew there was something important in those words. For some weird reason, Mikki wouldn't let herself succeed. But telling her that might only make it worse.

"I'm going to let you borrow something," Sam said. With careful fingers, she lifted the horsehair bracelet at her wrist and slid it off her hand. "It's made from the Phantom's mane."

Mikki stared at the bracelet as if she expected jolts of magic powers to come crackling from it.

"I might break it," she said.

"You won't."

A dozen questions chased across Mikki's face as she looked at Sam, but she didn't ask even one, just extended her bony arm.

"I'll want it back when you come out," Sam said gruffly. Because Mikki's hand was shaking so hard, Sam had to steady it to slip the bracelet on.

"I'll give it right back." Mikki nodded furiously, squared her shoulders, and walked into the pen.

Twenty minutes later, Sam peered through the close-set fence rails. It was like watching a big-screen TV. Popcorn and Mikki were right in front of her, framed by wood.

Sam saw the minute Popcorn decided he'd been lonely long enough. She saw him walk across the pen, long mane sweeping forward at each step. She saw him stop, blow through his lips, and start lipping grain from Mikki's palm.

Mikki stood statue-still. Only her braceleted arm moved from the albino's questing nose. Soon, Mikki's cheeks were shiny from tears.

When the grain was gone, the horse still stayed close. Mikki's eyes slid toward the rails where Sam stood. She fixed Sam with a *what should I do next?* look.

The white gelding had chosen to trust Mikki, but his faith must keep building.

"Just stay there," Sam said.

Popcorn's ears pricked toward Sam's voice. His muscles rolled, ready to run if anything frightened him.

But nothing did, and Popcorn leaned forward, his muzzle thrusting at Mikki's empty hand. The girl's fingers opened. She turned her hand and gently touched the gelding's face.

Popcorn snorted. His head swung away, but his hooves stayed in place. He shifted his weight until his shoulder grazed Mikki's. Then he leaned against the girl as if she were another horse.

They'd stood together for several minutes before Sam saw Mikki's chest moving in gasps. She was trying not to scare the horse with sobs she could barely keep inside.

After a while, Mikki made for the gate, sobs breaking as she returned the bracelet.

"I don't deserve him," Mikki managed.

"No one does," Sam said. She kept her voice low, and Popcorn didn't seem to mind. His white eyelashes fluttered as his eyes closed. "All day long we go to school and forget about horses. Then we come home and expect them to do whatever we want. And usually they do."

"But I—" Mikki's voice caught, and Popcorn's eyes opened. The girl slowed her breathing before she went on. "I didn't just ignore him. I was mean to him because I was scared."

Sam felt almost dizzy with responsibility. She concentrated, trying to think of a way to respond to Mikki's confusion. Outside the ranch yard, across the bridge, La Charla rushed along. Sam heard no answers, but Mikki was waiting.

"That's how love is, I guess," Sam said. "Sometimes you get it even when you don't deserve it. All you can do is try."

Mikki's deep sigh said she was satisfied, and Sam had no idea where the words had come from.

She had the weirdest feeling that someone wise and understanding had stood beside her, telling her what to say. She'd never admit it to anyone, but Sam could almost imagine the silent voice had been her mother's.

Chapter 16

ON TUESDAY SAM GOT UP AT HER REGULAR time, had cereal and toast while Gram and Dad ate omelets, and reviewed what the three rustlers looked like. If she didn't recognize them, no one would.

"I don't have to worry about identifying Flick," she told Gram and Dad. "Even without a mustache, I'll know him."

"So will Brynna." Dad's eyes didn't lift from his newspaper. "You know, it's a darn shame that woman works for the government." Quickly, Dad forked another bite into his mouth, almost as if he wanted an excuse not to explain.

Sam stared across the table at Gram, who'd paused with a coffee cup halfway to her lips. Why didn't she say something?

Gram shrugged, then coaxed Sam to keep thinking. "What about the other rustlers?"

"The one wearing camouflage was stocky, with a broad face and freckles," Sam said. "The other one had bushy white hair and eyes like a scared rabbit."

"I don't think they're from around here," Gram said.

Neither did Sam. What if they'd taken the horses elsewhere? Brynna was probably dragging her off on a wild-goose chase.

Dad pushed his chair back from the table. He was frowning, and Sam crossed her fingers, hoping he'd come to his senses about Brynna.

"Don't plan on using Mikki with Popcorn," he said instead.

"What's going to happen?" Sam asked.

"When you get home this afternoon, there'll be a

dumpster sitting next to what's left of the bunkhouse. And Mikki will be shoveling every bit of burned wood and ash into it."

"Wyatt, that's a huge job," Gram said.

"You bet it is," he agreed. "And with every shovelful, she can look at our house and barn and the other bunkhouse and think what could've happened from her carelessness."

"What about Popcorn?" Sam asked.

"He'll keep," Dad said. "Mikki starts today. When she's finished, then we'll see about horses."

Frost clung to the edges of Brynna's windshield when she picked Sam up. She drove a tan sedan instead of her usual BLM truck, but she had on her khaki uniform and her hair was in a tight French braid. Although Brynna smiled as Sam climbed into the warm car, everything about her said, *On duty.*

Sam was glad. It probably meant Brynna wasn't planning on a heart-to-heart talk.

Sam and Brynna drove away from the bus stop, away from school, toward the Mineral auction yards.

DARK SUNSHINE

Red rock formations jutted from the land around them. The last time Sam had traveled this highway, she'd been coming from the airport in Reno. Dad had been driving her toward home when they saw a BLM helicopter pursuing wild horses.

Sam smiled, remembering how she'd thought her imagination conjured up a silver stallion standing under a stone overhang. Now she knew he'd been more than imagination.

"There he is." Brynna nodded down the road.

Sam caught her breath and stared, but Brynna wasn't pointing out the Phantom. She was looking a mile down the road as she lifted the handset of the car's police radio. Then she spoke into it.

"Hey, Jim," she said.

"Gotcha in my rearview mirror." A male voice came from the radio as a Jeep with a roof bar of amber, blue, and red lights pulled from the roadside and eased into the lane in front of them.

"That's the brand inspector, Jim McDonald," Brynna explained. "He'd be going out to Mineral anyway, but we're traveling together, just in case we spot the rustlers on the way out there."

"You have Wyatt's girl with you?" asked Jim McDonald.

"I do."

"Samantha, just speak up if you see something you don't like. Or if you recognize a driver, a car, a truck—anything—while we're on our way."

The radio voice clicked off before Sam could say she would. As they drove in silence, Brynna sipped from a Styrofoam cup of coffee.

Brynna and Jim McDonald stayed in the slow lane, so other traffic passed on the left, where Sam could peer past Brynna and take a good look.

Two cattle trucks chugged by, but Hereford steers were visible inside them both. A silver car towed a matching horse trailer past, but the dun horse inside was not one of the mustangs.

"Did Wyatt mention we were going to Slocum's Brahma-cue together?" Brynna sounded nervous.

"Like a date?" Sam asked, but Brynna didn't really answer.

"He was supposed to." Brynna hit the steering wheel with the flat of her hand, which probably meant it wasn't just a car pool.

Sam twisted toward the front so quickly, the shoulder harness of her seat belt tightened.

It was bad enough Dad wanted to go out with Brynna Olson. Why couldn't he have explained it himself? Had he been about to, this morning, when he'd said he wished Brynna didn't work for the government?

Sam would bet she was the last to know. It wasn't fair.

And then she heard pinging. The rustler's truck had a pinging engine. She stared past Brynna to the fast lane.

The Ford truck was black, not yellow-brown like the one from Lost Canyon, but it *was* towing a stock trailer. The trailer had been painted black to match the truck, but it had an orange reflective stripe. That and the pinging convinced Sam.

"Sam, what is it?" Brynna asked.

"I think . . ." Sam shook her head. It would be pretty awkward if Jim and Brynna pulled the vehicle over and it was filled with potted plants or something.

"Do you think they could have painted the truck?"

"Of course. That black Ford?" Brynna had already spotted it. She increased her speed and lifted the radio microphone. She turned to Sam once more before calling Jim McDonald. "Take a good look, Sam. Is that it?"

"Don't call," Sam fretted. "I'm not sure."

But then the truck drew ahead and she saw into the trailer. Three horses' rumps were visible: a bay, a roan, and a gleaming black.

"Do it," Sam said. "I'm almost positive it's them."

The instant Brynna spoke, the light bar on Jim McDonald's car flashed on. Red lights bounced from one side of the bar to the other, and a siren yipped.

The black truck and trailer swayed toward the roadside, then slowed with a crunch of gravel.

Jim McDonald's car nosed in behind the trailer. Brynna stopped just inches behind him. As the brand inspector climbed out of his truck, Sam noticed he wore a gun.

Brynna switched off the car. "Let's go."

She tugged on a khaki cap that matched her uniform. The pretty woman with a crush on Dad had disappeared. In her place stood a cold-eyed professional. Those rustlers had better watch out.

Sam slipped out of the car before Brynna could tell her to stay inside.

Jim McDonald approached on the driver's side, while Brynna strode toward the truck's passenger door.

"Sam, at least stay behind the trailer," Brynna said without looking at Sam. And she did.

Gunplay in the movies was exciting, but here on a lonely Nevada road, it sounded scary.

Sam felt safer back there with the horses. As the animals jostled against each other, she felt certain they were the mustangs. From what she could see, each horse wore a different brand, but even to her inexperienced eyes, the burns appeared to be at the same stage of healing.

The black mustang's coat was stiff with sweat. He was curious, trying to look at Sam, but each time he tried to sling his head around, he hit the side of the trailer.

Quietly, Sam smooched at him. "Okay, pretty horse. Things will get better real soon."

At the sound of Sam's voice, the roan tried to get away, but he could go nowhere. Sam stayed silent then, afraid the animals would hurt themselves.

"Out of the truck, gentlemen." Jim McDonald sounded casual.

"What's wrong?" a voice rasped.

From the rear of the trailer, Sam could hear everything. She thought the voice might belong to the white-haired rustler.

"Why'd you stop us?" said a second voice. "We ain't breakin' the speed limit."

That one sounded too young to belong to the rustlers she'd seen. What if she *had* made a mistake?

"I'm wondering if you've got some papers on these horses," Jim McDonald said, "and hoping you can show them to me."

"Why would we want to do that?" the rusty voice demanded.

"Because he's the state brand inspector," Brynna said cheerfully. "Not only can he impound this truck and trailer, but he can put you two in jail if he doesn't like the look of the brands on your horses. They are branded, I suppose?"

"'Course," said the young voice.

Sam heard Jim McDonald shuffle through papers. Dissatisfied, he asked the men to unload the horses.

Sam scuttled backward, away from the trailer, as truck doors creaked open, boots hit the pavement, and doors slammed. Sam saw the white-haired man first. The other one was a gangly guy with a long chin. He had a beard, sort of, but one side hadn't really grown in. He couldn't be over nineteen years old. Neither of the men was eager to unload the horses. They made aimless motions, each hoping the other would do it. Finally, White Hair stepped forward and glared at Sam.

"Out of the way, girly."

Girly? She wasn't in his way. Not even close.

Surprise kept Sam quiet until she thought of a good way to let White Hair know that she didn't like being called *girly*. She looked past the men to Brynna and gave a nod to confirm they had at least one of the right guys.

Jim McDonald saw, but he didn't say anything right away.

The roan launched a two-hooved kick at the trailer door, and the white-haired man jumped back.

"You sure this is necessary?" he asked.

"You mean to tell me you can't handle your own stock?" Jim McDonald looked startled.

"Shoot, these nags are wild as bobcats. They just came off the range."

"Which range would that be?" Brynna asked.

The rustlers looked at each other. Neither had an answer. If they named a local ranch, their story could be checked. If they said the horses had been free on BLM land, they'd be fined. They didn't know how to stay out of bigger trouble than they were already in.

"Gentlemen, I'll tell you what," said Jim McDonald. "Those documents are forged, and the way you're so afraid of 'em, I'm thinking those horses just don't belong to you."

Neither man spoke. To Sam, their silence proved the brand inspector was right.

"I'm impounding your whole rig," Jim McDonald continued. "A couple of rangers are on their way. One'll give you a ride back to the Darton jail. The other will drive these ponies to the Willow Springs holding pens until we determine who owns them."

The whole time Jim had been talking, the younger man had scratched at his sparsely bearded cheek. Finally, he shouted, "But they're not stolen!"

"You shut up," Rabbit Eyes grumbled.

Sam watched as Brynna and Jim zeroed in on the younger guy. Even Sam saw he wasn't as committed to the crime as the older man.

"Lucky it's not the old days," Jim said. "Horse thieves didn't used to get a fair trial in a court of law."

"I tell ya"—the younger guy lowered his voice—"they don't belong to nobody."

"Of course they belong to someone." Brynna laughed. "They're wearing brands, aren't they?"

"But they were wild just the other—"

Brynna grabbed White Hair's arm before he could slug the younger man. "He's not telling us anything we didn't already know," she said. "So simmer down."

"Things could go a little easier on you," said Jim, "if you tell us where to find the other two gentlemen." Rabbit Eyes's glare warned the younger man to keep quiet.

"I bet the other guys are worried sick that these two won't do what they were supposed to do," Brynna teased. "I bet they're waiting at the auction yards right this minute."

"Maybe they are, and maybe they're not," said White Hair.

"Here come the rangers to take these tough guys off our hands." Jim watched the approach of another car, but Sam noticed him give Brynna a wink. Without meaning to, White Hair had confirmed that there were two other rustlers.

After the rangers and rustlers left, Sam and Brynna drove on. They spent all morning at the auction yard. They strolled between corrals and trailers, looking everywhere for Flick and the freckled man.

They couldn't find them, and Sam's eyes burned by the time she and Brynna decided to start for home.

"One down and two to go," Brynna said.

Sam tried to smile, but she couldn't. It wasn't just about the rustlers. She wished the three mustangs could've been set free instead of taken back to the Willow Springs corrals. Brynna had explained the three horses would have been harassed—rounded up time and again—now that they were branded.

It still isn't fair. Sam stared out the car window, searching the range as she always did, watching for the Phantom and his band.

A swath of pale green grass covered a hillside, indicating there was water nearby. Water was life to the wild horses, but if she'd noticed it, so would Flick. No horses were safe while Flick was still out there, and Sam couldn't stop worrying.

"I hope you feel good about saving those three mustangs," Brynna said to Sam. "If you hadn't recognized the truck and trailer . . . Well, Jim probably would have sorted out those brands, but who knows?"

Sam nodded, but she kept gazing out the window. She should probably praise Brynna's smooth handling of the rustlers, but she didn't want to. She couldn't stop seeing Brynna in Dad's arms the night of the fire. There were plenty of unattached men in Nevada. Let Brynna date one of them.

Apparently, Brynna didn't get the message in Sam's silence.

"By now," Brynna said, "those horses are at Willow Springs with someone looking after them and tossing them flakes of hay."

Sam pictured the horses gobbling hay. Would the mustangs be given up for adoption? Would the Phantom miss the two mares and that fine black yearling?

Would the yearling grow up, black coat turning charcoal, then silver like his sire's? She'd probably never know, but at least she'd helped give him a chance to grow up.

The trail of grass swept down from the hillside and ended at a red rock wall that looked like crowded-together columns. Nearby, cottonwood trees shaded a dark spot that might be a brook.

Sam couldn't see the water, but the movement of a half-dozen mustangs slowly lifting their heads caught her eye.

After that first movement, the horses stood still as the tree trunks. A glint of sun sifted through the cottonwoods and dappled one horse with spots that shone like silver coins. Hidden in the shadows stood the Phantom.

"Stop! Oh, please, Brynna, stop."

Sam didn't want to share this moment, but she couldn't resist. The Phantom and his band were free, but were they unharmed?

Brynna pulled to the roadside. When Sam started to open the door, Brynna put a hand on her arm.

"Your dad will kill me if I let you approach that stallion."

"I've done it before." Sam heard her own impatience.

"But I didn't give you permission."

"So?" Sam's anger flared. Brynna had no right to give permission or withhold it.

"*I mean,*" Brynna corrected herself, "when you got into the Phantom's corral at Willow Springs, you sneaked."

"And we got along fine." Sam held her breath, hoping he wouldn't flee from the strange truck.

Brynna removed her hand from Sam's arm. "I'm not

saying go ahead. I'm just not watching," she said, but Sam knew she would.

Sam took nothing with her, and she didn't close the truck door. Slow and easy, she walked away from Brynna and the truck. The horses watched.

In the shade, only one horse moved. Her coat was the color of melted butter.

Dark Sunshine! The frightened horse had found a home with the Phantom.

The buckskin was the only horse spooked by Sam's approach. Trying to trot, she split off from the others, but something was terribly wrong.

The mare moved as if her legs were jointless. One leg was so stiff, the buckskin faltered sideways. When she did, Sam saw a red gash on the mare's chest.

Sam thought of the fire, of Dark Sunshine's screams as she flung herself against the round pen rails, trying to escape. The mare's spirit had been damaged by the rustlers. Now her body was injured too.

Dad's rules said that every person and animal on the ranch had to earn its keep. She hoped she could get close enough to help Dark Sunshine. If she were lamed beyond help, Dad would write her off as a lost cause.

The mare tried to escape, but the Phantom chased after her, charging from the shade into the sunlight. Metal-bright glints touched each muscle as he stormed past the buckskin, toward Sam. His legs moved like liquid silver, then blurred and thundered as he came. His head swung from side to side in savage warning.

Should she run back to the truck?

Sam took a step back, and the stallion slid to a stop. His neck lengthened until he stood taller than ever before. Head level, he drew a breath, and Sam saw his chest swell. His muzzle jerked upward.

He must know it's me, she thought. But he didn't show it.

Pacing like a lion, the stallion moved alongside Dark Sunshine. He shielded her, keeping his body between her and the humans.

It's me, Sam wanted to shout. Would anything relieve the ache beneath her breastbone? Only a sign of recognition. *You know I won't hurt her, don't you?*

The stallion caught Sam's scent. He faced her. His

nostrils quivered, but he didn't nicker in greeting or come to her.

"Then I'll come to you, you stubborn mule," Sam tried to joke, but she heard the quiver in her own voice. The Phantom wasn't acting like her horse.

Brynna sat within easy earshot, so Sam couldn't call out his secret name. Worse, she didn't think it would help. The stallion had bonded with Dark Sunshine.

Right now, he wasn't Zanzibar. He was a wild horse defending his territory. He was a stallion protecting his mate.

Suddenly, he turned. Galloping as if he'd been away too long, the stallion returned to his band in the cottonwoods. Sunny limped, but she followed.

In the shifting shade of leaves, the stallion looked back. Sam crossed her fingers so hard they hurt.

Now he'd come back to her. He must. Now.

But the Phantom only stood next to Dark Sunshine.

Chapter 17

BECAUSE GRAM AND DAD HAD ALREADY LEFT to pick up Brynna for Linc Slocum's Brahma-cue and Sam was waiting for a ride with Jake, Sam was alone at River Bend when Rachel called.

"Samantha, this is Rachel Slocum."

Sam's mouth opened, but no words came out. Rachel's put-on British accent was thick this afternoon, and unless she'd called to practice it, Sam couldn't imagine why she'd phoned.

They weren't friends, and it didn't sound like an

emergency. If Rachel hadn't said *Samantha*, Sam would have thought the rich girl had the wrong number.

"Samantha, did we get cut off?" Rachel sounded bored by the possibility.

"Uh, no. I'm here."

"Good, I'm in my bedroom spa, and sometimes the telephone reception is not what it should be."

"That's a shame," Sam said. Then another thought popped up. "Aren't you going to your father's party?"

"That's the thing." Rachel sighed. "My father requested that I ask your family to pick up ice on your way over. We've already run short. The caterers are busy serving and the regular hands are doing—cow things."

Sam might have laughed if she hadn't resented taking up the slack for the Slocums. Of course, there was a good way to view this. If she and Jake stopped in Alkali, they'd spend less time watching Linc Slocum act important.

And the longer the drive took, the better chance she had of watching the range for Dark Sunshine. The mare had been gone a full week.

Tires crunched in the ranch yard. Sam pulled back the kitchen curtain and saw Jake arrive.

"Samantha, can you do it or not?" Rachel asked. "Clara's Café thing is practically on your way, and we'll reimburse you for the expense, of course."

"Sure, Rachel, we can do it," Sam said. "I hope you'll forgive us if we're a little late." She hung up and went to answer Jake's knock.

When Sam opened the door for Jake, she was unprepared for his compliment.

"Hey, you look nice."

"I do?" Sam considered her orange sleeveless top, white shorts, and tennis shoes. She touched her hair, then changed the subject. "How much do you want to go to this Brahma-cue?"

Jake shuddered. "More than I want to pump out the septic tank. That was the choice my mom gave me."

"But if your hostess asked you to do a favor on your way to the party," Sam said, "how could you refuse?"

It turned out Jake couldn't refuse, nor could he resist buying two chocolate ice cream cones to pass the time while Clara bagged the ice and loaded it into insulated boxes.

Jake had gobbled his cone and lifted the boxes when Sam's ice cream dripped onto her shorts.

Sam gasped. It was a big blob, and there was no hiding it.

"It figures," Jake said.

"I'll run into Clara's restroom and mop it off. Just go on to the truck. I'll be out in a minute."

The diner's restroom was square and cramped. Because it smelled strongly of cleaning chemicals, a high window was open to the road running behind Clara's and the gas station.

Sam heard a car stop and the crunch of boots on gravel, but she didn't really listen. She didn't have time to go home and change, and getting rid of the chocolate wouldn't be easy.

Some people shouldn't wear white, Sam thought, blotting the spot with a wet paper towel. *And I'm one of them.*

She'd just decided it was looking better when she heard the voice.

"When d'ya think you'll be back?"

Sam stopped. The male voice was so near, it surprised her. It almost sounded familiar.

"Twenty minutes out to Arroyo Azul, maybe an extra five minutes driving back with a load . . ."

Sam recognized the second man. It was Flick.

"That stud's been bringing his herd in at dusk since we scared him out of Lost Canyon."

Flick's voice was low and secretive. She just knew he was talking about the Phantom.

"It doesn't look like I'll get my buckskin back from that kid, but that stallion? I've got a standing offer for him, and it'll earn me enough money to live out my days in a tropical paradise. Before I leave town, I'm gonna get that dude to make good on it."

Sam's hands were already shaking, but when he added "from that kid," the wet paper towel fell from her fingers to the bathroom floor with a splat.

Did Flick know she'd seen him, or only that she had his horse? No matter, she decided. Arroyo Azul sliced into the mountains next to Lost Canyon. If Flick could get there in twenty minutes, Jake could make it in ten. Nothing mattered except saving the Phantom.

"Go on into Clara's," Flick said, "and have yourself a steak dinner. Meet me here in an hour, and we'll swap the trailer onto the other truck, in case anybody sees me drive from the arroyo.

"And one more thing," Flick added. "She should be at Slocum's, but if that BLM woman shows up, tell her what you're supposed to."

How could Flick know where Brynna was right now? The fact that he did gave Sam chills.

"I'll tell her you've been out of the state for weeks, but I don't think she'll buy it."

"She'll have to," Flick said. "By the time she picks up my trail, it'll be true."

Flick's footsteps had started away when the other man called him back. "But if something else happens—"

"Lester, there's no trouble Dr. Winchester can't handle."

Lester and Dr. Winchester. Sam had more names to give Brynna. If the rangers matched the names with her descriptions, they'd come up with something. But not soon enough.

It was up to her and Jake to save the Phantom.

Sam listened as a truck door slammed, an engine started, tires grated on gravel, and then grew distant. Her patience almost snapped as she waited for the second set of boots to walk away. At last, they did.

Sam burst from the restroom and glanced around. She saw no one she knew, except Clara.

"Did you get that ice cream cleaned up, honey?" Clara asked.

Sam had almost forgotten, but her shorts looked pretty good. "Yes, thank you—"

"Big doin's out at the Gold Dust, I hear." Clara paused in wiping down the counter.

"Right," Sam said, shrugging. "Linc Slocum got some new cattle."

Clara chuckled, but Sam didn't stay to joke about Slocum, no matter how much fun she'd have.

"I'd better hurry and catch Jake before that ice melts."

Sam burst through the door and ran into Jake. He

staggered back a step, but she ignored his grunt of surprise.

"You'll never guess what I heard—" Sam stopped, gasping.

"And what might that be?" The man who spoke stood right behind Jake. He had a broad, freckled face she recognized.

It was Lester.

Jake gave him an irritated glance, but Sam thought fast. Giggling, she wrapped her arms around Jake's waist.

"Well, it's sort of private," she whispered, "but I heard you only have to be sixteen to get married in Reno. Isn't that great news, honey?"

Sam hugged Jake with what she hoped was a lovesick expression. Would Lester think she looked sixteen? Would Jake understand her eyes' message: *Don't blow it, Jake?*

"I don't know if that's true." Lester shook his head. "But good luck to you."

Jake nodded his thanks, then swept Sam toward the truck. Sam couldn't walk fast enough to keep up. If Lester had looked back to see what a cute couple they made, he would have seen Jake shoving her along until they reached the truck.

Once inside, Jake began roaring, "What in the—"

Sam clapped her hand over his mouth, in case Lester was still nearby, but Jake pushed her hand away and kept talking.

"Not funny, Sam! Do you want to start the kind of rumors that small town gossips live for?"

"Oh, Jake." Sam closed her eyes and shook her head. "I don't have time for this. That guy"—she stabbed her finger toward Clara's Café—"is one of the rustlers. I heard him talking to Flick."

Sam drew a deep breath as Jake settled down, frowning.

"Flick is on his way to Arroyo Azul to catch the Phantom. *That's* what I was trying to tell you."

"Why didn't you say so, Brat?" Jake nodded toward the road out of town. A feathery trail of dust was scattering on the wind. "That's gotta be him. Let's go."

Convincing Jake they should report Flick had been easy, but they didn't agree on when, so it took most of the drive to hammer out the ground rules of their ambush.

Jake wanted to drive to Slocum's, tell his dad, her dad, and Brynna, then return for a full-scale assault. Sam knew they didn't have time.

Jake wanted to go back to Alkali and phone the county sheriff. Sam knew the sheriff couldn't drive from Darton to Arroyo Azul before Flick escaped.

After twenty minutes of explaining and arguing, Jake declared that what he wanted most was to leave her at the roadside for vultures to peck at.

"Okay, Sam, now listen. This is the last time I'm going to say this," Jake began.

"Drive while you talk," Sam urged.

"I *am* driving!" Jake hit the steering wheel with his palm. "When did you get to be such an expert?"

"I may not be an expert, but I can read a speedometer," Sam insisted. "Every time you turn to yell at me, your speed drops about eight miles per hour."

Then they were back to playing the quiet game. Sam's patience frayed first.

"Let's try this," she said. "We'll go into Arroyo Azul and scare off the horses, then drive fast as you can to get help."

DARK SUNSHINE

As Jake thought about it, they didn't gain on the dust from Flick's truck and trailer, but they didn't fall behind, either.

"What's wrong with that plan?" Sam asked.

"Nothing," Jake said, finally. "But I still don't like it. I don't trust that guy. He hates me and my brothers."

"Oh, Jake," Sam said again.

"Don't 'oh, Jake' me until you've been referred to as 'you people.' You know, like 'your people never . . .' or 'your people always . . .'"

Racism. That was what Jake meant. And it didn't surprise her that Flick spouted that kind of garbage.

"That's Flick, but that's not how we—" Sam broke off.

She remembered when Rachel—rich, privileged, supposedly smart Rachel—had been assigned to interview Jake about the cross-country team. Jake had come into the journalism room.

Sam was working on a newspaper story of her own, only half listening, when she heard Rachel ask, "Why doesn't your family live on a reservation? Aren't you, like, supposed to?"

A bubble of silence seemed to expand around the classroom. Sam wasn't the only one watching when Jake shrugged and said, "I know you're enjoying most of our land, but we still own a few chunks and we kinda like it there, at Three Ponies Ranch."

Rachel had sputtered something about taxes and free stuff, and the memory of how Jake had set Rachel straight made Sam laugh.

"What's funny?" Jake sounded more astonished than angry.

"Not Flick. But remember what you said to Rachel, when—" Before she could finish, Jake was already nodding.

"Got that from my dad. Pretty good, yeah?"

And then Jake was driving so fast that Sam grabbed the door to stay upright.

They were nearing War Drum Flats when Jake pointed.

"When we turn off there, we're committed. He'll know we're after him, and I don't know any other way out." Jake looked at Sam with an expression that said he'd rather be stalking trouble with one of his brothers. "You still want to do it?"

"Of course."

The truck sped down the road after Flick. Even from this distance, Sam saw the rustler's outline inside the truck.

Was he watching them in his rearview mirror? If so, what was he planning to do next?

"What makes you think he has someone else with him?" Jake asked. "He sure looks alone."

"He's not, though," Sam said. "When Lester asked what Flick would do if there was trouble, Flick said there was no trouble Dr. Winchester couldn't handle."

Jake flinched.

"Gee, Sam," he said. "I sure wish you'd mentioned that earlier. Unless I'm mistaken, that means Flick has brought along a Winchester rifle."

The last climb into Arroyo Azul had to be done on foot. Flick had abandoned his truck at the roadside, but Jake wanted to hide his. He slowed the truck to a crawl and prepared to make a U-turn, so that he could park behind a stand of juniper.

This was taking way too long, and Flick had a head start. Before Jake could stop her, Sam jumped out.

"No, Sam!" Jake shouted.

Sam ran up the path Flick must have taken. With each step, she told herself this was a little foolhardy, but Jake would be right behind her.

The narrow path ran around the lip of the arroyo. Its steep sides had dozens of narrow rock shelves. She supposed you could reach the turquoise stream below by balancing on one shelf and stepping to another.

Sam looked over the edge. She caught her breath and then pushed away the thought of how far she could fall from here. The important thing was she could see Flick had set up a water trap. The small metal corral wasn't even camouflaged. All he had to do was get down there while the mustangs were drinking and slam the gate.

But she didn't see Flick anywhere. Had he taken a shortcut and climbed down to the stream already?

A quick movement across the arroyo caught her attention, but it wasn't Flick she saw; it was the Phantom.

Halfway down to the water, on a rock shelf opposite Sam, the stallion's silver body shone against tawny sandstone.

When she'd watched the mustangs come to drink from the pond at War Drum Flats, the stallion had run in and taken a quick sip of water before retreating to his lookout post. But she didn't see his band down below.

Was the Phantom still watching, unconvinced the stream was safe?

"Rachel said it was you."

The male voice made Sam whirl around. Flick stood on the narrow path beside her. This time she recognized him.

Tall and broad-shouldered, Flick wore a fine gray Stetson. He carried a set of piggin' strings for tying calves. They were tucked through a loop on his belt, and he had the attitude of a skilled buckaroo. He might have been handsome except for his cold, selfish eyes.

And he took up more than his share of space on this skinny path that verged on thin air.

"Rachel said *what* was me?" Sam wasn't sure how to act, but he wasn't carrying the rifle, and he'd sounded casual. Maybe she could keep him talking while Jake made his way up the path.

"When I ran into her at the mall in Darton, she remembered I'd worked for her dad. I bought her a cappuccino in a little espresso place with booths no man could fit in, and she couldn't wait to tell me the neighborhood news. Like how you'd adopted one of those range rats from BLM. She'd even heard it was a buckskin."

Flick smirked. "Then I started rememberin' how you talked the Olson woman out of letting Slocum have that gray stud. A girl your age shouldn't keep sticking her nose in where it doesn't belong."

He touched his upper lip, smoothing a mustache that was no longer there. Maybe because he was congratulating himself, Flick didn't hear the little scuff that made Sam think Jake was nearby.

"If you were a little more like Rachel," Flick said to Sam, "you wouldn't get into so much trouble."

"If I were like her," Sam snarled, "I'd want someone to put me out of my misery."

DARK SUNSHINE

No no no no no. Not a good thing to say. She couldn't see Flick's rifle, but they were standing on the edge of a cliff. Flick was one little push away from having no witness to his crimes.

Chapter 18

FLICK WAS A RUSTLER, NOT A KILLER, SAM told herself. He wasn't going to push her over the edge.

"I have the buckskin," she said calmly, "but I didn't identify you to the BLM. They saw a bill of sale with your name on it."

"From the bus." Flick's frown said he was kicking himself for not hiding the document better. Then he shrugged. "Don't matter, really, since we're gonna be doin' some horse trading. I know you consider that gray stud yours. So don't worry about the mare. If you ever catch her, we'll be even, horse for horse."

Across the arroyo, the Phantom picked his way down from the rock shelf. Nimble and wary, he found stepping-stones to take him lower.

Then, there they were. His band of mares was headed to the water trap.

"Not much of a deal for you." Flick chuckled and nodded to the horses, "That buckskin looks about used up."

Even through her fear, Sam could see that Dark Sunshine's condition hadn't improved. Stiff and awkward, she limped, still keeping up with the other mustangs.

Sam had to warn the horses away from the water. She picked up a rock and threw it, but the horses didn't even pause.

Flick laughed, then asked, "How'd you know I was comin' here?"

"Lucky guess," Sam said.

"Maybe," Flick said, but the way he watched her had changed. "This is just my lookout, t'see if the horses were in yet. Not my shortcut." He gestured toward the bottom of the arroyo.

As he moved closer, Sam backed up the trail, away from him. He didn't seem inclined to stop her, but he touched the leather piggin' strings in his belt.

"It'll take 'em a while to find you, all trussed up like a calf," Flick said, "but I don't think you'll die up here."

"She won't." Jake's voice sounded calm and confident, and Sam was very glad to hear it.

Flick lifted his chin in surprise. Because he'd faced Sam as she retreated uphill, his back was to Jake. Flick turned and saw what Sam did.

Jake held Flick's rifle.

"If it's not Jake Ely," Flick drawled. "You know, son, that rifle's not loaded."

Jake smiled.

Sam wished her brain would tell her what to do. She wanted to run over there and stand beside Jake. To do that, though, she'd have to pass within reach of Flick.

"You're just a kid," Flick added. "You're not going to shoot a man and ruin your life."

Jake's smile got a little harder. "You know what you always say, Flick. There's no telling what *my people* will do."

As Flick lunged for Jake, Sam tackled Flick's ankles. He was falling when Jake threw the rifle over the cliff.

In the arroyo below, mustangs called and galloped, but Sam barely heard them over Flick's cursing. The instant she let go of Flick's legs, he rolled onto his back, holding his ankle.

"Look what you done! Aw, look what you done to me!"

Sam didn't look. She pushed up from the ground and then, while Flick was distracted by pain, she darted past him to Jake.

The instant she was near enough, Jake grabbed her hand, and they started running.

"Hurry, Brat." Their feet flew along the path. "Don't fall and don't look back."

"If you'd quit pulling me—"

"No, wait," Flick howled after them. "How'm I supposed to get down? This ankle's already swole up inside my boot—"

Jake gave Flick the same poor sympathy the rustler had given Sam. "It'll take 'em a while to find you," Jake shouted, "but I don't think you'll die up there."

When they reached the foot of the trail, they rushed past Flick's truck and piled into Jake's.

Sam tried to talk around her panting. "What . . . what if . . . he can walk out before we get back?" Sam managed as Jake started the truck.

"Reach under your seat."

Sam did, and her shaking fingers closed over something metal. "Is this the key to Flick's truck?"

"Yep."

Sam clapped. She bounced up and down. They had him now. Flick couldn't escape before the rangers got here.

The wild horses were safe. Sam sighed, weak with relief. Then her sagging eyelids popped open.

"Jake, why did you throw that rifle over the cliff?"

She actually heard Jake swallow. He looked more serious than she'd ever seen him before.

"After he threatened to leave you there, I was afraid I might use it." Jake didn't say another word until they reached the Gold Dust Ranch.

For weeks, folks talked about the stir Jake and Sam created at the Brahma-cue. The story of Jake's pickup skidding to a stop just short of the life-sized ice sculpture of a Brahma bull was told along with a description of Brynna, in her lacy blue sundress, searching for her handcuffs before she'd leave her plate of lobster salad. Jen Kenworthy's favorite tale was how she'd piled into the back of a truck with five Ely boys and a dog, shouting, "I'll be all *right*, Mom" as the truck sped away.

Flick and Lester went to jail along with their white-haired partner, ending their rustling days for good. BLM awarded the Forsters full custody of Dark Sunshine for use in the HARP program, and Dad agreed to accept. Everything would have been wonderful—except that the mare was still lost.

Now the desert breeze smelled like autumn, and Sam walked from the bus stop toward home. She didn't hurry. It was the last day of the HARP pilot program, and Mikki's mom was coming to watch.

Sam guessed that meant the girl was forgiven. The

old bunkhouse had been the only thing lost to the fire, and Mikki had managed to load the black fire rubble into the dumpster. From the minute she'd finished, Jake had trained her and Popcorn.

Sam stared toward the Calico Mountains and touched the horsehair bracelet on her wrist. She turned it and turned it again.

She'd let Mikki wear it only that one day, but Sam knew she should never have taken it off. It had meant a lot to Mikki, but everything had fallen apart after that.

Not that she was superstitious. The Phantom had charged her because he'd bonded with Dark Sunshine, not because she'd loaned the bracelet to Mikki. That was easy to accept. It was harder not to blame Mikki for Dark Sunshine's escape. She hoped the mare survived her freedom.

Sam was almost home when the white BLM truck pulled up alongside her.

"Need a lift?" Brynna said through the truck window.

"No, I'm fine."

"Well, I need to give you one," Brynna said. "So hop in."

Sighing so loudly Brynna couldn't miss it, Sam crossed to the passenger side of the truck and threw her backpack in. As soon as she'd buckled her seat belt, Sam crossed her arms and stared out the side window.

As usual, Brynna didn't take the hint.

"You're still mad at Mikki, and at me for letting her continue in the program," Brynna said.

It was an obvious thing to say. And it wasn't even an apology. Sam tried not to answer, but she couldn't stop herself.

"It's all her fault—the barn, Dark Sunshine's injuries, Phantom hating me—and she barely got punished." Sam twisted away from the window to glare at Brynna. "Do you know what would happen to me if I was smoking? I'd be grounded for life. And if I burned something down and nearly cost us the barn?"

At a loss to imagine her punishment, Sam shook her head. She drew a breath to go on. "Not grounding, not restriction from television or talking to Jen. I can't even picture what Dad would do to me. And Mikki's off the hook completely."

"Do you think it would be better if I kicked her out of the program? Should I take her out to see Dark Sunshine and send her home brokenhearted over what she's done?" Brynna asked.

Sam nodded. "Yes, you should."

"I've thought about it," Brynna admitted, "and I don't blame you. But I think I know what would happen if I did."

"What?" Sam wished she hadn't asked, because Brynna braked to a stop just before the River Bend bridge.

"When she got back home, Mikki would paint bitterness over that painful memory, just like she has all the others. She'd forget the good things about working with Popcorn, and she'd keep getting tougher and meaner until it wasn't a cover-up anymore. It would be who she really is."

Sam tried to look away from Brynna's serious blue eyes, but her conscience wouldn't let her. Sam remembered her own mistakes. One of them had almost cost Buddy her life. And yet, she'd earned Dad's trust again.

Just as Sam couldn't dismiss Dark Sunshine and the Phantom as lost causes, Brynna wouldn't let her dismiss Mikki. Sam felt her heart open, to give Mikki just one more chance.

Mikki's mom had already arrived at the ranch. Her name was Kathy. Kathy's bleached-blond hair ballooned away from a thin, nervous face. She chewed gum, hard, as Mikki approached Popcorn in the ten-acre pasture.

Sam leaned against the fence with Dad and Gram while Brynna stood next to Mikki's mom.

"Why are they working here?" Sam asked her father.

"Sort of a test," he said. "It's harder with other horses and plenty of room to run off."

But Popcorn didn't run away. As Mikki walked toward him with the halter and rope, Popcorn quit grazing. Head on high, he trotted toward her.

Sam remembered the rules Jake had set out for Mikki at the very beginning.

Popcorn had to come to her without the lure of food. He had to let her touch his face and neck without flinching. He had to trust her. Only then would Jake let her ride the albino.

Popcorn not only tolerated Mikki's touch, but he loved it. Sam could tell from the way he pressed his face forward the instant Mikki lifted her hand.

"Yes, he really is a mustang." Brynna was answering a quiet question from Kathy. "He was very badly treated, and Mikki's brought him out of it."

Kathy clapped.

Mikki and Popcorn were startled by the sound.

The gelding sidestepped and his ears showed his discomfort, but he stayed with Mikki, even when she haltered him and Kathy shouted, "You go, honey."

And then the wind blew a message to all ten horses in the pasture. As one, they faced the mountains.

Mikki was leading Popcorn around the pasture when he stopped and nickered.

From the other side of the river, the Phantom trumpeted a challenge. The echo of his summons hung in the afternoon air.

Sam couldn't believe her eyes. The Phantom glowed

white and perfect as marble. His mane hung to his shoulder, until he reared, forelegs pawing.

"He's beautiful!"

"Oh, Sam, he's amazing!"

Sam didn't know who spoke. She only knew the Phantom had never before come to River Bend by daylight.

He reared again, neighing, and she hoped he was calling for her.

Sam broke into a jog, running to the bridge and trying not to cry.

Dark Sunshine was with him. He nudged the buckskin mare toward the river, but she hesitated in the shallows, afraid to cross without him.

"Come on, girl," Sam called. "You can do it."

The mare wouldn't leave him. She was thin and injured. She needed human help. The Phantom seemed to know that, but could he make Dark Sunshine understand?

With a deep, demanding neigh, the Phantom told the mare to stop her nonsense. With a nip, he drove her forward.

Dark Sunshine ran a few faltering steps, then stopped, and suddenly Sam knew what to do.

"Mikki, bring Popcorn." Sam glanced back over her shoulder.

Jake opened the pasture gate. Mikki walked out with Popcorn, but defeat showed on her face.

The last time she'd led Popcorn outside the pen, he'd panicked, and she'd failed him. This time she had to be strong. Everything depended on it.

"That's it," Sam encouraged. "Just lead him over the bridge, then down to the water. Sunny knows him. Maybe she'll come to him. Then we can help her."

Popcorn stopped at the clopping of his hooves on the wooden bridge. He gave a worried whinny and pranced at the end of the lead rope. Mikki stood still, waiting.

Sam couldn't hear her words, but Mikki spoke to the albino. Her face was nearly as pale as his. At last, Popcorn followed. He left the bridge and walked to the river's edge with Mikki.

Dark Sunshine greeted him with a wild neigh. In

a few splashing jumps, she reached the other side and nuzzled his face.

But then the mare turned back, looking at the Phantom, and Sam closed her eyes.

He let you go to help you. Don't leave. She turned the bracelet on her wrist, but when she opened her eyes, nothing had changed.

Dark Sunshine still trembled with indecision. The Phantom remained on the wild side of the river. For a full minute, he stood with arched neck and high-flung tail, motionless. Then, feeling all eyes on him, the stallion wheeled.

His muscled haunches propelled him away, tail streaming behind like hundreds of satin ribbons. And then he was gone.

"Lead them back into the pasture, Mikki." Sam's throat hurt, but she got the words out. "Go slowly."

Jake motioned everyone to give Mikki, Popcorn, and Dark Sunshine plenty of room. The small girl performed like a professional. Even after the pasture gate closed behind her, she stayed calm. With smooth movements, she stroked Popcorn's neck, slipped off his halter, and watched as he and the injured buckskin moved into a stiff but joyful run, side by side.

Sam's breath rushed out. She must have been holding it all this time. She heard Brynna's sigh and saw that Kathy was crying. As Sam walked past, Dad smiled and Jake gave her a thumbs-up.

The Phantom hadn't lost his trust in her! He'd proven it by bringing Dark Sunshine back.

When Mikki came back through the pasture gate, she leaned against it with her eyes closed. She'd been through a lot, and Sam knew she shared the credit for rescuing Dark Sunshine with Mikki.

Sam's fingers went to her bracelet. She slid it off, then held it so the setting sun struck the braid made of many shades of silver.

Sam closed her hand around it one last time, and then she extended it to Mikki.

"Why don't you take this home with you," Sam said.

Mikki tucked her hands behind her back. "I can't do that."

"Sure you can. It's not magical, of course, but—" Sam shrugged. "It stands for something."

Mikki nodded. With shaking fingers, she took the bracelet and eased it over her wrist.

A stiff wind blew the scent of grass and horses and leaves turning harvest gold. Popcorn finished his run with the buckskin. He nickered and walked back toward the fence, and Mikki.

"I'll take really good care of it," Mikki promised.

"That's good," Sam said. "Maybe you can wear it when you come back next summer."

"I will," Mikki promised. "If you're sure."

Sam smiled. Mikki was giving her one last chance to take the bracelet back.

"I'm sure," Sam said, but she wasn't looking at Mikki. She was watching the Phantom float ever higher up a trail to the Calico Mountains. "I think I can make another."

Read on for an excerpt from Sam's journal!

Dear Mom,

Why is it that no one's worried about the HARP girls having a bad influence on me? Jen said that her parents homeschooled her because they didn't want her corrupted by outside influences and would no way let her be part of HARP. I know that the girls who'll be in the Horse and Rider Protection program have had hard lives. I know, too, that I won't suddenly start smoking or stealing because I'm around girls who've done those things. I didn't start when I was in school in San Francisco, did I? I'm trying to believe it's because people trust me. And I should appreciate that.

    I won't purposely pick up bad habits just to show Gram and Dad they should worry about me.

They already do too much worrying because of the accident. Gram and Dad have both said that I'm jealous of the attention the girls will take away from me. That hurts my feelings, you know? I don't think I'm that petty. Am I? Was I that way when you were still here? Grr. Of course, I can tolerate anything if I get to work with at-risk horses. I think I'd be good at that.

Dear Mom,
I wish you could meet Dark Sunshine! She is the most beautiful little horse. She's tiny—bigger than a pony, but smaller than Ace. He's about fourteen hands high. Maybe she's not much shorter, but she

is so delicate and troubled. Since I've come home from San Francisco and really started watching wild horses, I've decided that there are three things that are really important to them: family, freedom, and food. From what I saw—from a safe distance, Mom!—the horse rustlers took all three of those things away from her, and then they pretended to give them back! No wonder she's troubled. Those men baited her into the trap with food. The way she was gobbling down every bit of grain in that bucket, I know they'd starved her. But then they gave her food. And when other wild horses followed her into the trap, she felt relieved, like finally she was surrounded by family again. And when the rustlers opened the gate to scare the horses into that big black trailer, maybe she thought—freedom! Her new family was escaping, and she was going with them! But no. The rustlers wouldn't let her go. Isn't that cruel? From what the rustlers said to each other, they've done that to her over and over again. And they laugh about it. So, I don't think it's really stealing that I'm hiding Dark Sunshine from them. And if it is, maybe I'll end up in the HARP program. 😃

Dear Mom,
Jen and I stumbled into a mystery today. We found this old battered blue bus crashed over on its side, wedged into a gully. We are 99 percent sure the rustlers were living in it, at least part-time. That's

not the mystery. But it looks like it was a prison bus. Why would a jail guard have been driving out by Lost Canyon when there are no real roads? Or did someone hijack it? Were there prisoners inside? And why would the state or county or whatever just abandon it? I'd ask the sheriff, except that I don't think Jen and I were supposed to be in there. You know, it had no seat belts—although neither does the school bus I ride in every day. What is that about? Do they think we're safe just because it's so big and yellow? This blue bus proves that's not true! One whole side of it is kind of crunched in, like if you'd stomped on a soda can. Anyway, Jen and I got out of there as fast as we could and when I got home, I washed my hands about a million times.

Dear Mom,

One thing I didn't tell you about the crashed blue bus is I almost screamed when a mouse started to RUN UP THE LEG OF MY JEANS! I'm not afraid of any animals. Not even snakes, if they don't surprise me. This was a cute mouse, all chocolate brown and shiny. It probably had a nice quiet nest in the bus (except for the rustlers) and Jen and I disturbed it. So, was it territorial? Was it charging me because I got too close to its secret nest and babies? Maybe it was just looking for a place to hide and ran into me. Instead of scampering right over my boot, it took a hard right turn and stuck its little whiskery nose under the hem of my jeans. I could hear its little claws scrabbling to get a grip on my boot. I stamped it off. I didn't hurt it, but I can't seem to stop thinking of this: What if it had made its way to the top of my boot, pulled itself up, and scurried up my shin? No thank you, mouse!

Dear Mom,

Horse meat. That's why the rustlers are catching wild horses. And they're not selling them for dog food. That's what I thought, but BLM Brynna—who I really don't like right now—says the horses are sold for "human consumption." My throat closed up and I feel sick just from writing that. In the old days people rounded up mustangs to sell for dog food (they even had pictures of horses on the cans!), but now horses are sold into Canada or Mexico, where they have horse slaughterhouses. Sometimes they're sent to Europe. Alive and scared or in packages? I don't want to know. Brynna said it's common for racehorses to die that way if they're not fast enough or if they're injured or if—and this really makes me mad!—they don't win. Instead of giving them away to a good home, they sell them for slaughter because they don't want a horse with their stable name on it out in the world! Some countries where they eat horses don't want racehorse meat because they've had vaccinations and painkiller injections. But mustangs aren't contaminated that way. So awful. Do you see why I don't feel a bit guilty about taking Dark Sunshine away from those guys???

Dear Mom,

It's weird how a few seconds of being terrified can open up such an amazing memory. During the fire, when Dad told me to jump on Ace bareback, I was afraid. I did fine, even though the horses around us were panicked from breathing smoke and seeing the flames. Even when they were practically stampeding around us and Strawberry slammed into Ace. I confess that I was worried about falling and afraid of a second concussion. After it was all over, though, I kind of congratulated myself for handling the challenges and sticking on Ace like a trick rider! But that's not the great part. Last night when I was falling asleep, I thought about riding the Phantom bareback.

He wasn't the Phantom then, and he wasn't silver. He was Blackie, my sleek, sweet two-year-old, the horse I'd touched before anyone else on earth even knew he'd been born.

Jake was helping me train Blackie, remember? And when it was time to ride Blackie for the first time, Jake and I led him out into La Charla. Jake wanted me to have a soft landing in the water if Blackie bucked me off. I wore my red bathing suit and slipped up on Blackie's back. He shifted from hoof to hoof, but he didn't even try to buck me off. We swam.

Blackie's soft sides and the water sliding past were like cold satin. Jake wanted us to just stay in one place, next to him, while Blackie got used to the weight of a rider on his back, but Blackie had other ideas. He turned away from Jake, took a few splashing steps, and then he neighed like he was excited by this giant surprise of water rushing around his legs. He walked toward deeper water and then, when we'd reached the deepest part of the river, he stopped walking on the river bottom and—lift-off!—we were floating.

I looked down and saw the surface of the river ruffled and foaming as his legs reached ahead, pulling and prancing, playing. When Jake yelled for us to come back, I looked over my shoulder and saw Blackie's tail spread out behind us like some kind of dark, exotic water plant or a mermaid's fan. Blackie surged on with gliding strokes until he decided to stop. Then Blackie, my big seahorse, swooshed around in an arc, making little river waves crash up to my waist, and went back to the River Bend side of La Charla. He ignored Jake, just sloshed past him. Once Blackie had all four hooves ashore, he shook like a big dog.

Sam's Dictionary

BRAHMA BULL: Jen says the real name of the cattle Linc's getting is Brahman, but she hasn't corrected Linc's pronunciation—Brahma—because her dad calls them something like Bray-mers. Jen thinks they were imported from India to Texas, because they tolerate heat and insects really well, but now they're all over the country. They have long, droopy ears that give them a sweet face, and a hump at the base of their necks. Linc's rodeo scheme might not work out, because these days bucking bulls aren't pure Brahmans. They're crossbred with longhorns or other breeds of cattle, and there's even a breed called an American Bucking Bull.

SEPTIC TANK: An underground tank that takes the place of a city sewage system. All the used liquid from the ranch house goes into it, and not just from the kitchen, but the bathroom, too.

Author's Note

Dear readers,

The Horse and Rider Protection (HARP) program in Dark Sunshine sounds like something many of us would want to join. We can't because it only lives in my imagination. HARP may be fictional, but the relationships and benefits of equine therapy are real!

Horses—some of them former wild horses—comfort and help heal people of all ages. Equine-assisted therapy is practiced worldwide, and it's very likely you can discover a center near you. "Hippotherapy" is another name for equine-assisted help. I hear the terms used interchangeably, but some people use "equine-assisted therapy" for emotional and mental treatment and "hippotherapy" for physical therapy.

Why does it work for the human body? On horseback, you move almost as if you're walking. Those motions help train the body to deal with many mobility issues. Not only can riding increase your balance, reflexes, and coordination, it can also grow your confidence and communication skills. Besides all that, it's fun!

In this book, Mikki is at-risk because of her behavior. Participants in equine-assisted therapy programs often find that horses are great teachers when it comes to trust, patience, and responsibility. Many such programs exist, including for incarcerated men.

Here are just a few of the diagnoses and challenges that horse therapy can help with:
- autism spectrum disorder
- PTSD
- cerebral palsy
- stroke recovery
- Down syndrome
- multiple sclerosis
- traumatic brain injuries
- spinal cord injuries
- depression
- grief
- anxiety

AUTHOR'S NOTE

Unlike Sam and Jake, real-life instructors often have college degrees in education, psychology, psychotherapy, or occupational, physical, or speech therapy. How can YOU get involved? The same way I did: volunteer.

As a volunteer, I've been a side walker and led horses while young riders learned from professionals how to work with the horse.

My favorite therapy horse at the Center for Adaptive Riding in Reno, Nevada, is Tang, a Belgian/Quarter Horse mare. I'll admit she has opinions of her own toward me (like Ace), but she is always gentle with her riders.

Just watching horse therapy can be exciting. I saw a tame black mustang named Cowboy cause laughter and tears in the same five minutes. A boy, who rarely smiles as a result of his condition, was startled when Cowboy nipped the boy's hat off his head and then trotted around the arena, flapping it. He stayed just steps ahead of the boy, teasing the boy into a giggling game of chase. Tears of joy came from the boy's parents, who promised they'd bring him back as often as possible.

Besides leading therapy horses, I've saddled, bridled, and groomed them, as well as cleaned hooves, filled water troughs, and shoveled up horse manure. If you wrinkled your nose at the image of cleanup, you don't know what you're missing. Off-duty therapy horses only rest with eyelids lowered for a little while. Soon, they come nudge the human helpers for a shoulder pat or neck rub.

If you're interested in learning more about equine therapy or volunteering, research is easy. Look into Professional Association of Therapeutic Horsemanship International (https://pathintl.org). The PATH Intl. homepage features a button tthat you can click on to find a center. Next, check with an adult before emailing or calling to see if they accept volunteers of your age with your abilities. If the answer isn't an instant YES, sign up for the organization's newsletter and follow their social media accounts. Within months, I bet you'll find a way to help with horses!

Happy trails,

Terri

AUTHOR'S NOTE

Publisher's note: This resource is provided for informational purposes only, and its inclusion is not intended to be an endorsement or promotion of any particular organization. It is also not intended to be a complete or exhaustive listing or a substitute for the advice of a qualified medical or mental health professional. The information was accurate at the time the first edition of this book went to press.

Read on for a sneak peek at the next book in the Phantom Stallion series:
The Renegade.

IN RIVER BEND'S BIG PASTURE, THE HORSES waited for rain. Cottonwood branches danced overhead, but instead of rustling, the dry leaves clacked. The horses stood with heads up and nostrils wide, searching for a trace of moisture on the breeze.

Across the dirt driveway, near the house, Sam did the same. She stood in the vegetable garden, where she was supposed to be turning over dirt to mix parched cornstalks and empty vines with the earth. Instead, she leaned on her shovel and wished she'd brought a water bottle outside with her.

Two sparrows dove for a worm her digging had uncovered. The birds cheeped and quarreled, then flew off in a flurry of feathers, leaving the lucky worm untouched.

Sam looked skyward. The sun was sealed down by a lid of gray clouds.

Irritated whinnies and the thud of hooves came from the big pasture. Banjo, Dad's roping horse, bolted across the sparse grass. Teeth bared, Strawberry sprinted after him.

Except for a few hammering rainstorms that ran off the drought-hardened land, it hadn't rained since spring. Now it was October. Every creature was edgy with waiting.

More hooves thudded inside the round pen, but these made a soothing sound, just like the voice that directed them.

"Other way," Jake said. "Good horse."

Friday after school, Jake had mounted Teddy Bear for the first time. Now it was Saturday morning, and the colt was already responding to the bit and reins.

The morning quiet didn't last for long. Blaze burst barking from the barn, and Sam noticed a plume of dust approaching the ranch. The roar of an overtaxed engine told her who was driving even before the beige Cadillac crossed the bridge too fast and skidded into the ranch yard.

Sam dropped the shovel. For their neighbor Linc Slocum, everything was a crisis. Still, it was always possible it was a real emergency.

The Cadillac's horn blared, even though Gram had already appeared, wiping her hands on her apron. Dallas, the ranch foreman, had emerged from the shady barn, blinking against the sunlight.

Jake slipped out of the round corral and beat everyone to Slocum's side.

"Rachel's missing," Linc said as Sam got close enough to hear.

Gram patted Linc's arm as the man removed his oversized cowboy hat and sighed.

"I don't know what to think," he explained. "I'd just got back from riding with Jed." Linc scanned faces, making sure they recognized the name of Jed Kenworthy, his foreman. "But he stayed out with the other hands and I came back. Otherwise I sure would've got him helping me."

"How long has she been gone?" Gram asked.

"Hard to say. Let's see." Linc squinted as he tried to recall. "When I got back home, Rachel was lazing around her suite, and then I had a snack and after that I sorta dozed off." He shook his head. "I'd say at least a coupla hours."

Sam's eyes slid toward Jake. Jake was only sixteen, but he spotted trouble better than anyone Sam knew. And he didn't look worried. In fact, when he crossed his arms over his belt buckle, he seemed to be telling Linc to get to the point.

"Thing is," Slocum said, sounding as if he were about to make a confession, "she was perturbed about something. In fact, she's been sort of put out—say, how long has it been since I had the rodeo stock contractor over to the house?" Slocum mused a minute. "All week. Yessir." Linc sounded amazed. "She's been perturbed all week long."

For an instant, Sam wondered how he could tell perturbation from Rachel's usual attitude, but then she understood his amazement. How could Rachel be dissatisfied for a full week? She wore the finest clothes and makeup. A driver took her to school in a baby-blue Mercedes-Benz, and her bedroom suite included a hot tub and state-of-the-art entertainment systems.

Rachel was her father's princess, and she pretty much ruled Darton High School as well. Her face, hair, and figure might have been composed by a computer designing the perfect girl.

Too bad no one had pushed the button marked PERSONALITY, Sam thought.

"Could the stock contractor have said something to upset her?" Gram asked.

"No, no way." Linc actually blushed. "We were cutting a deal for my Brahmas, that's all."

Did Linc redden because the stock contractor had rejected his bulls? City-bred Slocum really didn't know what he was doing when it came to animals, Sam thought. He just liked playing cowboy.

"Where do you think she's got off to?" Dallas asked. He sounded more sympathetic than Sam felt.

"Did she take a car?" Jake added. Though Rachel didn't have a driver's license, she wouldn't let such a formality stop her.

"No, she didn't, and no one came to pick her up or I would've heard tires." Linc wedged a thumb into the tooled leather belt that strained around his middle. "But my horse is missing too."

"Why would she take Champ? Rachel hates horses," Sam blurted.

"Well, now—" Slocum frowned.

"She does," Sam insisted. "She says they're dumb and dirty, and she can't understand why anyone likes them."

Gram made a cautioning sound, but Sam knew she was right.

"I don't mean to be rude, Mr. Slocum, but she told me all that herself."

"My ex-wife made the twins ride for three hours every day when they were little," Slocum said. "Ryan took to it and Rachel didn't. Maybe that's why he's in England.

Now that his mom's married that baron, or whatever he is, they have stables packed with horses."

Slocum sounded wistful. For about two seconds, Sam felt sorry for him. Then she remembered the spade bit he used on Champ, his gentle-natured palomino. In the hands of an excellent rider, the bit could work. Hauled on by an angry girl who didn't like horses, that bit could do terrible damage to Champ's tender mouth.

"Let's go find her," Sam said.

"I'll be glad to pay—" Slocum began.

"Land sakes, Linc, will you hush?" Gram snapped. One of her hands darted out as if she wanted to give Slocum a pinch. Instead, she shook her finger at him. "We'll help because we're neighbors, not because you have money."

Gram took Western neighborliness seriously. Her tirade made Linc look sheepish.

"Wyatt's checking the herd with Ross and Pepper," Gram said, "but the rest of us will saddle up. I don't imagine she's gone far. Have you called over to the Elys'?"

Gram gestured toward the Three Ponies Ranch, Jake's home.

"No," Linc said. "I think Rachel would be embarrassed. Mainly I came for Jake."

Jake shrugged modestly. Sam wished she had a skill she could be humble about. Jake was a first-rate tracker. Local ranchers, the Bureau of Land Management, and even the sheriff's department knew it.

"Sure," Jake said. His eyes darted skyward at a rumble of far-off thunder. "I'd want to start at your ranch, though."

"You do that," Gram said. "And, Linc, we'll go up the ridge trail, since it runs behind your place, ours, and Three Ponies." Gram removed her apron and started for the barn and her mare, Sweetheart.

"Hop in, Jake." Slocum gestured toward the Cadillac, but Jake glanced at the round corral, where Teddy Bear stood saddled and curious.

"I'll take care of the colt," Dallas said. "You go on."

Sam bit her lip. Jake had teased her forever, calling her a tagalong brat, but she couldn't help it. "I'd really like to watch you track," she said.